Pagan
Days

Michael Rumaker

SPUYTEN DUYVIL

New York City

Portions of *Pagan Days* first appeared in *3 x 3* published by North Carolina Wesleyan College Press and in *Oyster Boy Review.*

ISBN 978-1-933132-59-4

Library of Congress Cataloging-in-Publication Data

Rumaker, Michael, 1932-
  Pagan days / Michael Rumaker.
    pages cm
  ISBN 978-1-933132-59-4
  1. Childhood--Fiction. 2. Young men--Fiction. 3. Domestic fiction. I. Title.
  PS3568.U43P4 2013
  813'.54--dc23

                  2013005708

For Winifred Marvel

PAGAN DAYS

Part One

SOUTH PHILLY DAYS

...IN THE BEGINNING she was a drum in me ears and then it got all quiet and I dint hear nothing excepting the drum of me own heart in the beginning she told me I wasn't with her and whether she told me or I remembered it, don't matter it was all whiteness, like sugar, or snow white light overhead, white walls all around, white of diapers and nightgowns and sheets and people all in white leaning over the white iron sides of the crib that was cold as the sheets when you touched them sometimes, yes, she was a darkness standing at the railing, looking down, not saying nothing, with one of the white ones whispering to her, no, no, shaking its head other times in her darkness she was a blanket woolier and warmer'n any they covered me with and sometimes she would reach down and sometimes she wouldn't because there was always one of the white ones pulling her hand back and shaking its head, whispering no, no, no that was because in the beginning I wasn't with her she said, they kept me there in the whiteness where I couldn't hear her heart anymore and I couldn't eat and kept shrinking like I would disappear until one day when she come I made out it was her because she was again like a shadow, a dark warm blanket in all the whiteness, and that was all I could make out when she reached down to touch me the one in white pulled her hand away like it always done and shook its head no, no, but this time the darkness she was reached down again for the very first time and not only reached down but covered me, lifting me up so strange to be lifted up, even though she was easy it hurt like I was a bruise all over and she lifted me up and held me to her, the dark she was in all that white *He's* *dying*, the white one whispered, *dying* and out of her darkness, the voice echoing against me ear, *I don't care, I don't care* carrying me out, carrying me out of all that whiteness with white shapes scurrying all around us til I felt the blanket close loose around me head and all was a darkness like the darkness she was, like the dark inside her with her heart beating in me ears like a drum, I was inside her again, floating, floating hearing her drum beating in the little dark sea for the first time again in all that time is what she told and is what I remember

Mash up carrots and onions and potatoes, feed him that, the doctor with a funny name on 2nd Street told her, I throwed it up and she mashed up more and I throwed it up wanting so hard to keep it down so I wouldn't wake up in the white place again and dreamt in the dark when she wasn't there I was back in it anyhow and shook awake, me heart pounding, whenever she wasn't there me heart pounded I kept looking for her, afraid when she wasn't there the white lights would go on and I would be back there and dint feel safe til her shadow fell over me and I smellt her, she smellt of blood and heat, I fell back then, watching her, I could never get enough of watching her and little by little the mashed up carrots and onions stayed down and little by little I stopped dreaming of the white and dreamt red when I slept and felt weight and was laying there like I wouldn't fly away up into the white that was turning pinker and pinker when me eyes was open in time she begun to wheel me out in the street and Aunt Nell ast her how she had the nerve to wheel me out in the streets, she might get arrested for child-neglect, and after that when she wheeled me she stuck to the back alleys so's nobody'd see and smeared some of her rouge on my cheeks so's the neighbors wouldn't think she wasn't feeding me cold he smellt, and sweet, his clothes smelling sweet, like sugar, and sweat, the smell of his mouth like the way me mouth tasted

after I spitup "Beer," he called it, "You wanna zip? Huh? Huh?
You wanna zip?" He smellt like the ashtrays in the parlor smellt
when I pulled them down and she would yell at me for pulling
them down so high up he held me and rubbed me cheek again
and laughed, "Joe Louis," he was saying, "Joe Louis," and nodding at the radio, I looked, he wasn't on the radio, I dint see
nobody on the radio, they was inside, behind, where the dust
was, little people that lived there and talked when you turnt it
on and wasn't supposed to, she'd yell at me then too he rubbed
me chin again, grinning, his face all red smelling of beer and
sugar, smelling of like when I stuck me finger in the sugar bowl
when she wasn't looking because she said not to do it, she'd yell
and his teeth wasn't big and they wasn't no gaps between his
teeth *who was he?* I yanked me head back and stared at him "Joe
Louis," he was saying again, "the fight," and I looked around
again and dint see him on the radio, maybe he was inside of it,
and looked for me mother that was putting plates on the table,
put me down, put me down, but I dint say it outloud, stared at
him, he was holding a newspaper in front of me face, showing
me a picsture, a face all dark like the blanket she was, "Joe
Louis," he said, "Wanna fight? Wanna fight like Joe Louis?" and
rubbed his knuckles against me nose and rubbed his nose
against me nose, smelling of ashtrays and beer, his face all red
and pinched up, grinning, the face in the picsture that wasn't on
the radio, "Wanna fight?" and he nuzzled me again, smelling of
sugar—I looked to see if she knowed who he was, she was putting forks down now beside the plates, and I wriggled to be let
down *who was he?*

"You sit there til you go you hear?" I nodded, the rim of the
potty cold on me hiney She left the terlet I strained and strained
She kept looking in the door "You poop yet?" I shook me head,
biting me lower lip "Don't you move til you do," and she went

out again I strained and strained, afraid if I dint she'd send me back to the white ones leaning over "You done yet?" I shook me head "You holler when you're done, you hear?" I nodded I strained and strained the rim of the potty warmer now as I kept on straining then she took me out of the crib in our room where she slept in the bed with him and put me in a big bed in another room next to the one with hair standing up and he went "Heh? Heh?" and put his hand to his ear and her and the others called him Slap, the next bigger one with the dark hair called him Slaphappy! Slaphappy! because he went heh? heh? all the time That first night in the big bed I started to cry and he put his arms around me and kissed me and said don'tchou worry, don'tchou worry hugged me and kissed me like he was glad to see me, like he was afraid to sleep in the big bed too. Acrosst the room in a even bigger bed the other two slept, the one with bright eyes and bright hair she called Frank and the other, the dark-haired one she called Buster and they was always laughing and jumping up and down on their bed and wasn't supposed to and the one that smellt of sugar and beer that slept in the bed with her would peep in the door and holler at them On the wall over the bed was a cross with a man bleeding she said was Jesus, she bowed her head when she said his name and said I should too and on either side of the bleeding man was picstures of a man and a lady looking down at us Slap said they was grandmom and grandpop and when I ast him would we ever see them he said no we wouldn't see them because they was in heaven, I said where is that? and he pointed to the ceiling so I thought they was up on the roof

In my crib now was somebody even littler'n me, with a red face that cried all the time. She called him Danny and said ain't he cute? I said I wanted to get back into the crib and she laughed and laughed, showing all her teeth. "Gwan," she said, "You're too big for that. Gwan," she said, her hands busy pinning a diaper on Danny the way she done on me one time, "I ain't got no time now go play with yer brothers." At night Slap kissed me and hugged me and said don'tchou worry and when I tried to talk he went "Heh? Heh?" like he hardly ever heard anything and fell asleep.

The house was all brick on a street where all the houses looked alike when I looked out the front windows. I was glad when I went out with her she knowed which one to come back into because I would never have knowed, they all looked alike with brick fronts and with marble steps that was cool on your hiney when you set on them and had blue veins like in me arms running through them. Every Saturday morning she scrubbed them steps on her knees with Old Dutch cleanser and scrubbed the marble slab acrosst the front over the cellar windows and would holler at me brothers whenever they throwed their ball against the slab because it made pock marks in the marble. In the window sometimes horses pulling wagons went by and birds she said was sparrows et their poopy that I dint think I would like, and et it off the dirty ground besides, she said never to eat nothing off of the dirty ground, so I was glad I wasn't a sparrow. Sometimes trucks went by, and cars, and people hurrying by that looked important, I ast her where was they going and she said they're just going by, stop asking so many questions. When a yeller airplane with two wings flied in the sky between the houses I pointed up to ask her what it was and she said, "You point like that he'll drop a bomb on you," and I stopped me pointing after that. But I did ask her where was the airplanes going? where was the clouds going? and she said, "I ain't got no time for that."

When we went out Danny was in the buggy now and I held onto the side of the handle as she pushed it down the street. A trolley car turnt at the corner. I could hear it turning in the bed at night like somebody screaming. I thought only special people with important places to go was allowed to ride on it because we never did but walked everywhere we went. Sometimes they was people in the trolley windows with faces brown as grandmom and grandpop in the picstures over our bed and when I ast her why that was she said they was niggers God made them that way, poor things, they couldn't help it, then she told a story when Grandmom O'Rourke's grandmom first got off the boat from County Cork she seen her first nigger, she thought it was a devil and took a flying leap to jump off the dock but a sailor catched her just in time or she would've drowneded. I said Grandmom and Grandpop Lithwack in the pictures over our bed was brown was they niggers? She laughed right outloud in the street and said no, silly, that's the way they took picstures in them days, everybody come out all brown, your father's mother and father was as white as me or you. I was dying to know where County Cork was but knowed by now I mustn't ask too many questions.

We went up a alley and into a gate and a little backyard cemented just like ours, only flowers growed against one wall and they dint in ours, and another thing different was a terlet outside stead of inside the house. When I ast her why that was she said it ain't been used since she was a girl, they had one up on the second floor now like we did, and I wondered who "they" was. We come into a kitchen where somebody she called Nell lived, I whispered who is that? she said it was her big sister my Aunt Nell. She weared a cap even though she was in the house and said to me, "Whatsa matter, don'tcher mother feed ya?" I looked up at her and wanted to say yes she does but looked at me mother, not knowing what to say, and me mother laughed and said, "Yes, I feed him, you know he's always been skinny."

The lady she called Aunt Nell pinched my arm, saying, "You better git some meat on them bones," then she bent down and stared close in me face and turning to my mother said, "Whatzat, rouge on his cheeks, you still putting rouge on him? You'll make a girl outa him putting that rouge on him but maybe it's just as well you do, you won't get locked up for child-neglect." "Oh, Nell," my mother laughed. "You dint have the nerve to bring him out on 2nd Street, didja? You better still stick to the alleyways if you don't wanta git arrested for neglect," and my mother laughed again. "Oh, Nell!" she said, "I only done that in the beginning when you all made fun," her face turning as red as the rouge she put on me, and Aunt Nell said, "It's because you dint eat right, with him outa work filling up on candy and junk is why you almost lost him too proud for help!" And my mother looked away, her cheeks redder like Aunt Nell just slapped her, saying, "Now, Nell, less don't start in on that again." Then Aunt Nell looked at Danny in the buggy, saying, "Well, this one looks better fed now that old man of yours is workin at the sugar refinery, this one looks almost human." And my mother started giggling again, "Oh, Nell, can'tcha ever be serious?" I was dying to ask her why she weared a hat inside of the house but dint dare. Then a old lady come in from some-where else in the house and leaned down and kissed me, her face was whiskery too but softer'n his was and Aunt Nell called her Mom and my mother called her Mom too but how could she have a mother because she was my mother and was too old to have one anyway, if she was her mother why wasn't she living with her like I lived with her, and where was her father? The old lady reached into her apron pocket and unsnapped a little black pocketbook, she handed me a penny and kissed me again and my mother said, "Oh, look at him now, gwan, thank yer grand-mother." But I was too shy to and hung behind my mother's chair, peeping out, and the old lady she called me grandmother leaned in the buggy and looked at Danny and kissed him too but dint give him no penny and if she was grandmom she wasn't on the roof like Slap said, and her face wasn't the same as the grandmom in the picsture over our bed, the face in the picsture that was brown while hers was white as the bottle of milk Aunt Nell was taking out of the icebox. Then Aunt Nell poured a cup of tea in the biggest cup I ever seen like it was a bowl for Post Toasties and the old lady called me grandmother carried it in both hands and went out of the kitchen back to wherever she come from in the house. Aunt Nell poured tea then for my mother and her and give me a cookie that smellt sweet the way he smellt when he come home at night. I kept staring at her as she blowed on her saucer of tea, her whispering, like it was a secret, "Mom ain't feelin so good today," shaking her head and clicking her tongue, and the two of them got a look in their eyes like it was them not feeling so good stead of Grandmom, and I kept wondering why Aunt Nell weared a cap inside of the house when my mother never did and it wasn't even cold in there. On the way home I ast her why and she said it was a dustcap and I said what for? she said to keep dust off of your hair, silly, what else? now stop askin so many questions.

When she was washing me in the bathtub I ast her, "What're bellybuttons for?" She slapped me hand away and said, "To keep yer insides from falling out—Now you stop touchin yerself, God don't like it." I knowed who God was, he was up on the roof because Slap told me he was in heaven with grandmom and grandpop.

Alone with her in the parlor. My father at work at Franklin Sugar, my big brothers at school they called Sacred Heart,

Danny napping on the couch, his mouth hanging open. Alone with her while she ironed. Warm smell of bluing. Is what blue smells like? "Is what sky smells like?" I ast her and she laughed and I wondered why she laughed, if the sky was the same color wouldn't it smell like that? "Time for our stories," she said, and I run to turn on the big Scott radio my father bragged somebody named Mae West had one just like it and would show the picsture he cut out of a magazine to prove it, she was a lady with bright yeller hair even brighter'n Frank's and her hand on her hip. My mother had her ironing board set up in front of the radio and she used an electric iron, not the old-fashioned irons heated on the coalstove Aunt Molly that lived acrosst the alley from Aunt Nell still used. Me, I'd be sitting with me back against the loud-speaker, the brown cloth with orange specks getting warmer and warmer as I waited impatient for the tiny people inside to wake up, then the two of us would listen to Hilltop House and Big Sister and Aunt Jenny before we et lunch that was sometimes Campbell's tomato soup and Parkway bread with the cow on the wrapper. Or sometimes eggs fried in Spry because Aunt Jenny used Spry and my mother sent in so many Spry labels and a dime and got back in the mail a little lamp the color of cream with gold and orange flowers on the paper shade she put on the server in the dining room. While we et it was Helen Trent with the volume turned up loud so's we could hear it all the way out in the kitchen and in the afternoon it was Our Gal Sunday— "Can a Girl from a Little Mining Town in the West Find Happiness as the Wife of a Wealthy and Titled Englishman, Lord Henry Brinthrop?"—and the Goldbergs that always sound-ed like they was eating something good and Myrt and Marge and Portia Faces Life and Life Can Be Beautiful with a girl named CheeChee that always sounded like she was ready to cry. I knowed all the stations. Knowed where all her favorite stories was and could dial them in without nobody showing me, I could read the numbers through the light in the little red and green striped window so she wouldn't have to stop what she was doing. This made her smile like I done something funny. And sometimes when we was alone I'd swing out me arms and dance around and around in circles from the parlor to the dining room and back again, swirling the red velvet curtains hanging in the doorway as I went, singing to meself songs I learnt from her following her while she worked and sung around the house or that I learnt on the radio, I would sing her them ones I learnt on the radio, singing, "I Found a Million Dollar Baby at the Five and Ten Cent Store," because I knowed it was one of her favorites and she laughed and sung it right along with me like she often done, looking at me with a look like somebody tickling her, like it was a secret between us. When the stories was over she ast me to turn on the baseball game that I dint like because it wasn't no story you could follow or anything you could sing to but did what she wanted because she told Aunt Nell she was trying to get used to listening to baseball to see if she could get to know what it was about because my father and Frank and Buster listened to something called the Philadelphia Athaletics and the Philadelphia Phillies play baseball from a place called Shibe Park, listened to them so much all Saturday and Sunday afternoon while my father drunk beer in his chair, it was driving her crazy just the sound of it and not knowing what was going on. After I turnt it on a man said game called on account of rain and I was glad in secret and went and stood looking out the front window at the rain falling on the brick sidewalk in front of our house and on the cobblestones in the street, I couldn't take me eyes off of each drop that was a perfect circle I ain't ever noticed before. Sparrows was hopping in the gutter like they always was, picking through the soggy horse droppings. Seeing the birds all wet and bedraggled I turnt and ast her if I could go out and bring them inside and she laughed and laughed and that was another time I dint know why she was laughing, I wouldn't want to be out in the rain and pecking at horse poop, why was that so funny?

I talked all the time around her excepting when our ears was glued to the radio and excepting when he was there because if I did he would give me looks. At first he dint but then he did because she said you never knowed what "mood" he'd be in when he come in the door at night, sometimes he'd be laughing and tickling her, and sometimes he'd say mean things and she'd try to jolly him out of it. You couldn't ever tell how he'd be, excepting along with the sugar you could always smell beer on him. I learnt not to talk around him and not to talk at the table when he was reading the Philadelphia *Ledger*. He'd slap the other boys if they talked or cut up or got in a fight when he was reading, or Slap that never seemed to hear he wasn't supposed to be talking at the table, he'd get hit too. Me and Danny was too little to get hit yet but even so I kept me lip buttoned. When Danny could sit up all by hisself in a chair she ast me to watch him while she done the wash and hung the wash in the back- yard or run up to the terlet for a minute, I'd sit beside him in me father's armchair in the parlor and pretend to read him the Philadelphia *Ledger*, making it up as I went along. I could understand some words like bread and milk and ice because they was on the horse and wagons and motor trucks that went by our parlor windows. And more and more I was beginning to know the names of things so I dint have to pester her as much. The street was named Mifflin Street she said I lived at 126 Mifflin Street, if I ever got lost I was to tell a cop or a big person that.

She took me hand and touched me brow and moved it down and touched me chest, then swung it from one shoulder to the other and when I ast her what that was she said, "This is how you bless yourself, now you do it. No, no, dumbie, with yer right hand—the left hand's the devil." I was dying to know why the left hand was the devil, Slap used that hand all the time, but all she said was right was right and left ain't right and the nuns at Sacred Heart was trying to make Slap stop using that hand. I seen sometimes he come home from school the knuckles on that hand was all red and when I ast him why, he said Sister cracked them with a ruler.

Sometimes a man all in black with a black hat and a white collar come to the house, mostly during the day when me father was at work and me brothers was all at school. She called him Father even though he wasn't her father, her father was dead she said and I ast her was he in heaven and she said yes so I knowed he was up on the roof with the other grandmother and grandfather. Even though she ast him to sit down the priest would always stand up to talk to her and she was like somebody else then. She would talk different to him than she talked to me or any of us, not saying ain't or me this or me that, like she couldn't be the way she was in front of him but had to be somebody else, like us kids had to be on our best behavior when we went to one of our aunt's house but she wasn't anywheres but in her own house then. Before he left he always put his hand on me head and on Danny's head and said, "What two fine boys, are you good boys?" I'd look at me mother and she'd dip her head so's you could hardly see it and I nodded yes to the priest, and me mother'd say, holding her hand up to cover her mouth, "Oh, look at them now, if I'd of knowed you was coming, Father, I'd of combed their hair and put clean shirts on them. Oh, look at them," which only made me squirm inside the way I done when she talked the way she dint always talk, she'd be trying to hide her big teeth behind her hand like she was ashamed of them. I knowed she was ashamed of them because I heard her saying to Aunt Nell she wisht they wasn't such big buck teeth, maybe she should get them all yanked out and get false ones like Uncle Jake that could swally three tablespoons of horsereddish down without shedding a tear. Just before the priest'd go out the door she'd push me down to kneel on the parlor floor with her kneeling next to me holding Danny, the priest would make the sign of the cross over us and when she blessed herself she nudged me to do the same whilst he was muttering with his eyes shut in words I dint understand.

Another time he come to put his hand on me head and said to me mother, "Maybe this young man would like to come to school with Francis to see a movie?" I dint know who Francis was and only knowed a movie was something me brothers went to on Saturday afternoons and I was too little yet to go, I wanted to say no I dint want to go but when she nodded her head so fast, smiling all the while and holding her hand up to her mouth to hide her teeth, saying "Sure he would, Father," me heart sunk in me shoes. "Oh, look at the little bugger now! What do you say? Ain't...Isn't that nice of Father? Now thank Father Gallagher and show him how you bless yerself." Even though I dint want to I blessed myself, to please her, and he patted me head again, saying, "I can see he's a fine Catholic boy already," and me mother smiled and smiled, holding her hand over her mouth. I wanted to ask her who Francis was and what Catholic was but wouldn't ask while he was still there and after we knelt down and he give us his blessing and he went out the door I ast her what Catholic was, she said, "It means when you die you go to heaven where them that ain't don't." When I ast her where they went, she pointed to the floor, saying, "Down to hell." I said, "Will niggers go there?" She said, "If they ain't Catholics they'll go there, now stop asking so many questions."

So I dint get to know who Francis was but I knowed now heaven was on the roof and hell was in the cellar.

I forgot about going to see the movie because I dint want to go anywheres excepting where she was but one day she said, "Would you like to go to school with your brother Frank? Would you like to see a movie? You remember Father Gallagher said you could come see a movie at Sacred Heart?" I wasn't sure what a movie was but now I knowed who Francis was, she said that was his real name even though we called him Frank, I said was Mickey me real name? She said, "You was such a skinny little runt when you was born you looked like a mouse so that's why I named you after Mickey Mouse in the comic strips." But I dint think I wanted to go see no movie at Sacred Heart because I heard me older brothers saying how the nuns cracked their knuckles with the sharp edge of a ruler if they was bad, Slap got his knuckles cracked because he wouldn't stop using the devil's hand, and when Slap that was always forgetting things forgot his tie one morning the sister made him wear a big red crepe paper one all day long. My mother said, "See, maybe now you won't be so forgetful next time," but he was forgetful anyhow and would have to wear the crepe paper tie again, Buster said it was no wonder he was nicknamed Slap. So now I knowed that people had names and they had nicknames but what Buster's name was I dint know yet. But I did know she wanted me to go see the movie so I dint tell her I dint want to because I would've done anything to please her, I still had nightmares about white people bending over me like ghosts to kidnap me back.

The day I was to go she put me in the bathtub after lunch

even though it wasn't Saturday night and scrubbed me neck and ears til I hollered and put on me very best shirt and short pants and tied one of the ties Slap was always forgetting around me neck that I ain't never weared before so that it felt like a dog collar must feel. Then she combed me hair umpteen times til she was finally satisfied with it and told me to keep ahold of Frank's hand and do as he said and remember not to pick me nose and give me one of her crocheted hankies to put in me pocket that I never had in me pocket before.

Frank only held me hand til we was out of sight of me mother watching us go from the front steps holding Danny in her arms, I wisht I was Danny in her arms and I wisht Frank would've kept on holding me hand since I never been so far from home without her. I kept on looking back and looking back whilst she waved at me with a grin, I waved too but dint grin.

Now I was looking around at all the streets and the houses that some had porches and some had three stories but most looked just like our own street and house but I ain't ever seen before. The school was the biggest place I ever seen that went up and up and was made of brick like our house but bricks that was all dirty and old-looking. Boys all wearing ties like me and Frank was lined up in front of one door and girls all wearing the same black dresses was lined up in front of the other. Standing at the front and the back of the lines in long black veils and with bandages around their heads and with rosary beads big as Buster's marbles hanging down that Frank said was nuns when I ast him who they was, I wanted to ask him where their rulers was but they looked like big black birds with faces white as snow, like if they ever smiled their faces would break like ice in a zillion pieces. Just to look at them got my heart going.

Acrosst the street even higher'n the school was what Frank

said was Sacred Heart church, so now I knowed where I been baptised and where them and me mother and father went to Sunday morning. It was made of gray stones that looked even dirtier'n the bricks in the school and had high roofs with a cross on top like hung over our bed with the bleeding man called Jesus hanging off of it and the walls had streaks of white all down the sides that turnt out wasn't snow because when I ast him what it was Frank said, "Pigeon poop, ya dumbie."

Inside Frank's classroom was all big windows and smellt of dust and paper and had another cross on the front wall like over our bed, only bigger. When the nun with the glasses at the front of the room said I was Francis' little brother and come to see the movie and everybody turnt around and looked at me, I wanted to hide under the desk. Aunt Nell's Sonny was there sitting in a desk acrosst the aisle from us, he was making faces trying to make me laugh but I wouldn't look at him for fear the nun that looked like another big black bird would fly at me and crack me knuckles with a ruler like Frank said she would if I dint behave. She give me a piece of paper that was for real paper and wasn't a crackerbox, and give me a pencil that wasn't a stub to draw with while Frank and the other boys read outloud out of books without any picstures in them. I drawed the ice wagon pulled by a horse that come to our house every other day when me mother put the card in the front window that said 50-25-10, she turnt the corner of the card to how much ice she wanted so's the iceman could see. The sister was surprised when I printed ICE on the side of the wagon, she ast me how old I was. I said almost four so low she had to ask me again and Sonny was grinning and making faces behind her back, she spinned around and catched him at it and raised her hand to him and he cringed back in his seat and put on a serious face the way me mother done when she showed me how to draw cats. She ast Frank how old I really was like I was too dumb to know myself or would be telling a lie, and when he said I was borned in 1932, she raised her eyes all the way up to the bandage on her head that looked so tight I wondered did it give her a headache. Then she reached down, down, down into the folds of her dark blue gown and give me a piece of candy that was a orange cat with big eyes and ears like in the candy case at Willie's store and she told me I could eat it at the movies but not to eat it now and she dint give any to Frank or any to Sonny or to anybody else, Frank whispered, "Whaddaya say?" and give me a poke but I was too shy to say thank you and hoped she wouldn't smack me knuckles. Now her back was turnt Sonny was grinning again, sticking his tongue out at me, I wouldn't look at him, Aunt Nell told me mother he was such a bad little monkey he would end up in prison but she always said it with a grin like she was bragging.

I jumped when a bell went off, I lined up beside Frank with all the other boys and the sister led us down and down the stairs to a terlet in the cellar that was dark like our cellar but umpteen times bigger and smellt of something that stung me eyes where you peed into things that looked like big bathtubs turnt on their sides with statues of a lady with her hands stretching out on top of each and every one that was dressed in veils like the nuns only in a color like bluing that smellt of the sky and that was like the statue on top of the bureau in me mother and father's bedroom, only bigger, that me mother said the Virgin Mary was her name. I wanted to whisper to Frank if this was the movies yet and couldn't go with so many strange boys around me and Sonny gaping at me, teasing, and the statue of the Virgin Mary staring down at me with her hands out. I looked to see if the sister was watching outside the door to smack me with her ruler if I dint go and wouldn't let me go to the movies if I dint. Frank kept saying, "You done yet? You done? C'mon, c'mon. Hurry it up, will ya?" like me mother when she used to put me on the pot but I was big now and set on the terlet even though I was still afraid of getting flushed down with it when she pulled the handle. I said yes even though I ain't gone yet and hoped he wouldn't know and tell the sister. He said, "You need help to button up?" My face went hot and I said no I was big enough to do it meself now. He said, "You sure?" I whispered yes but he went and checked me buttons anyhow just to make sure and I felt meself turn even redder in front of all them boys watching and Sonny grinning and shaking his finger at me.

On the way to the movie that turnt out not to be in the terlet but in a big room with so many chairs I never seen so many chairs, I kept looking could I see Slap but they was so many kids crowding in I couldn't see him anywheres. But when I seen the nun was way up at the head of the line I tugged at Frank's sleeve and ast him in a whisper why the statues was in the terlet, we dint have any in the terlet at home, he said, "To stop bad thoughts." I started to ask him what bad thoughts? and he went shush with his finger and Sonny behind us that might end up in prison reached around and pinched me ear.

The movie was about Saint Theresa Frank said when I pulled on his sleeve in the dark to know, "Now shush! and gimme wacks," and I broke off the head of the candy cat and give it, then Sonny leaned over and whispered, "Wacks!" and I busted off the tail and give him that. Somewheres in the back some kind of machine started grinding and whirring, a big beam of light shot over our heads, whilst up front all of a sudden they was a big explosion of light, I just about jumped out of me seat, as the biggest picsture I ever seen in me life flashed on, with words coming and going that I couldn't spell out, they was so big and fast. Loud music started playing, sad and screechy music, and they was scratchy long lines running down the picsture like it was raining, it looked like it was raining the whole time the movie was showing they was so many long scratchy lines. I wanted to ask Frank why was it raining all the time, but then people come on and everybody was so big in the picsture I cringed back in me seat, they was coming out at me, I never seen people so big, and couldn't even eat what was left of me candy cat because Saint Theresa had blood coming out of the palms of her hands like she cut herself and she was sweating blood around the top of her head like she was wearing the crown of thorns Jesus had on the cross hanging between me grandmom and me grandpop that was over our beds at home even though they was up on the roof in heaven. And everytime Saint Theresa, with her eyes rolling up in her head and sweating blood, said Jesus, all the nuns and all the boys and girls bowed their heads in the dark when she said it, I bowed me head too like me mother said I should even though I dint know why you had to do it but everybody else done it so I did too so the sister wouldn't hit me.

When it was over it was as dark outside as it was in the movie, I ain't never been out in the dark before with the gaslamps all turnt up bright and took ahold of Slap's hand going home because I knowed neither Frank nor Buster would. When we got home she ast me did I enjoy the movie, I said I did because I dint think she wanted me to say I dint enjoy it, but more'n anything I was glad being home with her again. For the next couple nights after that I had nightmares, seeing the blood sweat out the top of Saint Theresa's head and would wake up hollering so loud even Slap heard me and he would grab ahold of me and hug me, saying, "Whatza matter, heh? Heh?" Me mother was standing in the doorway in her long white nightgown, whispering, "Gwan back to sleep now, it was jist a bad dream." And I said a prayer to the Virgin Mary I wouldn't have to go see no more movies no more and double-crosst me fingers like Slap showed me just to make double sure.

One night when me father come home he put a sign in one of the parlor windows wasn't like the sign me mother put in the window for the iceman, this one had a picsture on it of a man and words printed in red white and blue I dint know and when I ast her what it said she said, "Vote for Roosevelt," saying it like there was a rose in his name, and when I ast her who he was she said, "He's president, silly, who else?" I said why did me father put his picsture in the window and she said, "Because he's savin the country." I ast her was he a priest, she laughed and said no he was a proddisin but in spite of that was helping the poor people dint have no jobs. I said if he was a president and a proddisin and not a Catholic would he go down the cellar to hell when he died? She laughed again and said where did I get them ideas?

The next morning when I looked out the front window I seen all the parlor windows that I could see acrosst the street had signs just like the one in our window said VOTE FOR ROOSEVELT in red white and blue and the man in the picsture me mother said was the president wasn't smiling in any of them because me mother said they wasn't much to smile about these days.

The next time I went to the movies it was with her. He come home smelling of beer again after we was already done eating and he tried to tickle her and jolly her along but she pushed him away and he said, "Aw, to hell with you," and wouldn't eat his supper she had heating on the back of the stove. She said all right, all right for you, and grabbed me and took me upstairs and washed me face and combed me hair and put a clean shirt

on me that she never done at night and put powder on her face
that she hardly ever done and put on her brown beret Aunt Nell
give her and the old tan coat with the belt Aunt Bridget that was
married to the undertaker give her—handmedowns, she called
them, like all her clothes was—me going, "Where we goin,
Mom? where we goin?" She dint say anything but had a look in
her eye like she was fighting with him inside of her head. Then
she leaned down and lifted up her dress and unknotted the
lump in her stocking and took out money she always kept hid
there for when she needed it and put it in her pocketbook and
told me to go weewee before we left whether I needed to or not.

When we come downstairs into the dining room where the
boys was doing their homework around the table she told Frank
to mind the others, she was going out. Right away they all wanted to know where she was going, Aunt Nell's? and if I was going
why couldn't they go? She said shush and to mind Frank if our
father passed out and to warm up Danny's bottle that was in the
icebox if he woke up crying, and grabbing me hand again,
marched right past me father whilst he set in the parlor reading
the *Ledger*, he dint even look up when we went out the front
door.

At the corner she made like she dint know which way to go,
whether around the corner to Grandmom's like we usually done
in the day or up the other way and after a minute of first going
one way, then the other we went the other way up 2nd Street.

It was night and the gaslights all bright and a trolleycar
went grinding by with the lights all on inside so's you could see
the people and best of all she had ahold of me hand. I dint care
where we was going.

On the way, she stopped in the candy store called Finkel's
and bought two bags of candy, Mary Janes and licorish sticks
and nigger toes that was white inside and cinnamon outside

that was so sweet they hurt your teeth. When she was pointing to them in the glass case to old Mrs. Finkel her face dint have so mad a look now.

I felt so big going out so late at night, I felt lucky that it was just the two of us. I was even more excited by the yellow lights twinkling on and off outside of the movie that was called the Lyric at 2nd and Tasker where the three boys went with Sonny on Saturday afternoons and was a for real movie, not like the one at their school, and if they showed Saint Theresa with blood coming out of her head I wouldn't care since she was with me.

We followed all the people going in and when she give the man in a uniform our tickets at the door he give her a sugar bowl that I thought was nice of him and when I ast her why he did that as we went down the aisle so dark I hung onto her coat I could hardly see a thing, she said it was something called dish night, "And lucky for us, huh?"

When she found us seats that I would never been able to find not being able to see anything, she put the sugar bowl in her pocketbook real careful so it wouldn't bust. When what lights they was went down she handed me me own bag of candy, saying, "Eat it slow, don't make a pig of yerself. Can you see?" I said I could but I had to sit up real straight. The first thing that come on the screen was movies she said they was going to show, then there was something she said was a Our Gang comedy where a little pickaninny named Buckwheat, his mother dies and he sits on her grave and cries and cries, I stopped eating me nigger toe and leaned close to her in the dark knowing there couldn't ever be nothing worse'n to lose her, all the while thinking of the place that was all white and Buckwheat so dark and the heap of dirt he was sitting on so dark. She slipped me one of her crocheted hankies, saying, "Here, blow." I was ashamed she seen me sniffling because I dint think in the dark she seen but I should've knowed by now she seen everything. Then me heart give a jump because then come a cartoon like in the Sunday comics, only it was alive, and it was the mouse she said I was named after, she leaned over and whispered, "You know who that is?" I nodded but dint say nothing I was so afraid of missing something if I took me eyes off of the screen. Then something called "Poor Little Rich Girl" that I ast her to read out for me when it come on and had a little girl with blonde curls that could sing and tapdance that she told me later was named Shirley Temple but that wasn't her name in the movie, she was rich and weared pajamas to bed and got lost in a city and et spaghetti in a cellar with a old man and a old lady was Eyetalian, then her real mother and father found her and drove her home again in a big car, then Shirley Temple caught a cold and her mother was so worried. I talked about her so much after the movie, I was more excited about her than I was about being up so late and way past me bedtime. I pestered me mother so much for the next couple of days asking about Shirley Temple, where did she learn to tapdance and sing and why dint I wear pajamas in bed and when was we going to the movies to see her again, without me knowing it, she sent away a Ralston boxtop with a nickel, just like she done for Tom Mix bowls for me older brothers, and got me a blue cereal bowl with Shirley Temple's picsture on it as a surprise. And I et me Ralston out of it every morning the same as Frank and Buster and Slap et theirs out of the Tom Mix bowls, even though Buster sneered only girls et out of bowls like mine, but me mother said, "Never you mind." After that, whenever we was alone together in the parlor while she ironed and our stories on the radio was over for the day, I sung "When I'm With You" that Shirley Temple sung in "Poor Little Rich Girl" and when I danced for her now it was me trying to do the tapdancing I seen Shirley Temple do. She laughed and said if I only had enough hair she'd love to put it up in sausage curls like Shirley Temple's, why wasn't I a girl? I wisht I was, I would've done anything to please her. I ast her where did Shirley Temple live in South Philly because I thought like the little people living in the radio she must be alive on the screen and went home after the movie was over, or did she live in the Lyric? When she said, "She lives in Hollywood, silly," I said couldn't we go see her? thinking that was a street around the Lyric I ain't never heard of, she laughed and laughed, as much as when I said let's bring the sparrows in out of the rain.

My father never took me to the movies. He ain't took any of the others either, nor me mother. When Danny could walk he would offer to take me and him for walks on Saturday afternoons so's me mother could run around the alley to have her hair set in Aunt Nell's kitchen, but them walks usually went no farther'n the corner saloon that smellt like he smellt when he come home at night, only sourer and smokier. He set us up on stools on either side of him at the bar and ordered us orange sodas that tickled and burnt your nose when you drunk it, while he drunk beer and sometimes whiskey, but not whiskey too often because he couldn't handle whiskey, he got drunk too fast and passed out later on and me mother'd give him the silent treatment when we got back. The bartender me father called Hoolihan made a big fuss over me and Danny, and me Uncle Jake that was married to Aunt Molly was always there showing how he could eat three tablespoons of horsereddish in a row without crying, just like he done whenever he come to our house, and when he done it Hoolihan'd give him a beer. Uncle Ned with the sourpuss that Uncle Jake said if he was married to Aunt Maggie he'd have a sourpuss too, was there, and a man me father called Louie was there with eyeglasses thick as the bottom of the soda glass I was drinking out of and a dusty face the color of the cobblestones out in the street. Them and the other men sitting at the bar would buy us orange sodas too and feed us pretzels and give me nickels to play the jukebox for them when they found out I knowed the numbers, they'd say go play number so-and-so and I would go and stand on me tiptoes and reach up high as I could and drop in the nickel and play it. They couldn't get over I knowed me numbers and they'd slap me father on the back like it was him learnt me my numbers but it wasn't him learnt me. They'd be so tickled they'd buy him a beer and buy me'n Danny another orange soda and me father'd be all grins, getting bright-er eyed and brighter eyed the more the beers went down and the afternoon went on. I'd go back with me fresh glass of orange soda and stand and stare at the bright colors in the jukebox, not able to take me eyes away, and listened to "Who Stole Me Heart Away?" and "Me Buddy, Your Buddy Misses You," and wanted to dance and sing like I done for me mother but dint dare to do it there, I wondered how they got all them singers and bands all squeezed into them records, they must've been even tinier'n the people living inside of the radio, and was dying to ask him how they done that but he was laughing and joking and arguing or shooting darts and talking about the sugar refinery with Uncle Jake and Uncle Ned and the man he called Louie and all them other men as they all listened to the baseball game on the radio over the bar that I dint like to listen because there wasn't no stories or singing in it and that me mother tried to listen to when he wasn't home to get used to it but she never did.

Before we got to our door he would lean down to me and put a finger to his mouth, "Not a word," he said, "Say you had a nice walk like a good boy, huh?" I nodded I would and he give me a penny but he dint give Danny no penny because he was too little and dint know how to talk yet. Then he popped a couple peppermint Lifesavers into his mouth and give me one to put in my mouth too before we went in.

After all them pretzels and orange sodas me and Danny wouldn't want any supper, so me mother would know from that, besides the smell of his breath despite the Lifesavers, where he took us and be mad at him. He'd hug her and squeeze her and joke and tease, trying to jolly her out of it, saying, "Aw, c'mon, c'mon, Min," calling her Min stead of Nora whenever he teased her or was trying to get something out of her and she'd push him away, saying, "Oh, gwan witcha!" Most times she'd smile when she said it and you could see she wasn't mad anymore, but sometimes, specially if he drunk whiskey, she dint and wouldn't talk to him or even look at him the rest of the night, giving him the silent treatment. When that happened I kept hoping she'd grab me hand and we'd go up to the Lyric again to see Shirley Temple, only she never did. But the very next day her and me and Danny would go around the alley to Grandmom's and she would tell Grandmom and Aunt Nell he been drinking again, what should she do? Grandmom and Aunt Nell would shake their heads and click their tongues, Grandmom saying, "Make another novena to the Blessed Mother," and Aunt Nell saying, "He's jist like his brother," that I knowed by now from me mother was Uncle Stan that was Aunt Nell's first husband that fell off a ship in the dead of winter and got sick and died a long time ago.

I felt important walking with him, and shy with him too, but he dint hold me hand like she did, excepting when we was crossing the street, his hand was bigger and harder'n hers, and I dint pester him asking him anything because he looked a little green around the gills, as me mother called it, because of the morning after.

I never been in such a big place, it was even bigger'n me brothers' school, with so many people hurrying up the steps. All gray it was with bells clanging over our heads that hurt me ears and the pigeons flying up that made pigeon snow down the sides, only Frank called it that bad word. Inside was smoke that smellt sweet and so many candles and all the windows colored like hard candy. All the chairs was like benches and a ceiling went up and up, I couldn't get me head back far enough to see how high it went up, and the place at the front was like the server in our dining room, only bigger and was made of marble like our front steps with a little closet door in the middle. I wondered if that's where God lived. They was a picsture of a man with a beard in front of it and I was dying to know was it God but knowed I better keep me lip buttoned. All of a sudden the loudest music I ever heard bust out of big gold pipes behind the picsture that when they went off almost made me heart stop. They was sisters kneeling everywhere and I wondered did they carry their rulers and pieces of cat candy hid away in their gowns to church? I looked and looked to see could I see Frank's sister but dint see her, they all looked alike to me. I felt afraid to move or say anything like when I was in Frank's class that day, but when me father knelt down and folded his hands like he was praying, I knelt down and acted like I was praying too, and when he set down on the bench I set down. When a man come out it was like he come out of the picsture and he wasn't Father Gallagher that come to our house but another man that I thought must be God all dressed up like the Little King in the Sunday funnies, he was in a shiny gown the color of the apples outside Willie's store, he looked like he come out of that big picsture in front of the big server like happened in the Mickey Mouse cartoon at the Lyric, he goes in and he goes out, he comes out of anything—I couldn't help meself and tugged at me father's sleeve, even though you mustn't talk and he was green around the gills, to ask him how it happened, how did the man come out of the picsture, was it a movie and was he God? But he only leaned down and whispered, "Whatsa' matter, you gotta go to the terlet? You'll be able to go to the terlet soon," then he put his finger to his lips the same way he said don'tchou tell now and I wondered would the sisters line us all up and march us down the stairs to the cellar where the statues of the Blessed Mother was. I wanted to tell him I already went back at the house, what I wanted to know was, Who is it, is it God? and how did he come out of the picsture like Mickey Mouse? But just then the music boomed out of the pipes again like they was the biggest radio in the whole wide world, they made me jump and when me father knelt down I knelt down and when he stood up I stood up, we knelt down and stood up so much we was like we was Jumpin Jack in the Box, and when a man come and shoved a basket on a long pole at us me father slipped a penny in me hand and I put that in the basket like he done but kept the penny in me pocket me mother give me so I still had a penny.

Afterwards, as we was walking outside of the church and it wasn't bad to talk anymore, I was still afraid to ask him, his eyes looked so bloodshot and his face looked so frowning like his face always looked when he been drinking beer the night before at Hoolihan's, his face looked like the face in the picsture the man come out of that must've been God but I was too ascared to ask him if it was.

On the way home we seen Uncle Jake and Louie standing outside Hoolihan's that was closed today because it was Sunday and because of what I heard me father call the blankety-blank blue laws, only he called them a curseword me mother said it was a sin to say. Uncle Jake's face was all red like he just downed three tablespoons of horsereddish and his eyes was as bloodshot as me father's. "Got the kid witcha today, uh?" he said, jerking his head at me, and me father grinned, "Keeping on the good side of 'er—took 'im to church." Louie, that was wearing the same raggy suit he always weared that was all dusty the same color as the streets, cocked his head, giving them the high sign, and the three of them ducked up the alley, me father dragging me after him by the hand. Louie reached inside his coat and was looking around like he was ascared somebody might see them, then he pulled out a pint of whiskey and bit out the cork and Uncle Jake give a big grin showing all of his false teeth and made a grab for the bottle and wiped the neck with his thumb before he stuck it in his mouth and took a good long swally. Then smacking his lips and wiping his mouth with the back of his hand, that was as big as one of the shoulders of pork me mother roasted for Sunday dinner, he handed the pint to my father. My father wiped the neck too with his thumb and took a long swig, still grabbing ahold of me hand, and I stood staring up watching his adam's apple jumping up and down. When he was done he wiped his mouth like Uncle Jake and grinned and nodded and give the bottle back to Louie and Louie tipped it up and guzzled the rest of it in one long swally, me eyes was bugging, I ain't never seen nobody do that before without even coming up for air. We come out of the alley, Uncle Jake slapping me father on the back, hollering, "Back to me ball'n chain!" Me father laughed, and Louie was looking up and down the street like he was looking out somebody might catch them.

After that me and my father stopped at Heck's bakery near McKean Street that smellt of sugar more'n he smelt of sugar at night and the smell got me mouth watering so much I thought it was going to start dripping all over the place. He bought a big square cheesecake with cinnamon sprinkled on top and a dozen cinnamon buns like he always done after mass for our Sunday breakfast. His eyes wasn't bloodshot no more since he been up the alley and he grinned when the lady behind the counter with hair that was white as sugar said what a fine little man I was as she tied string around the box, then tied a knot that I watched her tie, all eyes, watching to see how she done it because I couldn't tie me own shoes yet and was dying to know how but her fingers went too fast, faster even than me mother's went.

Just before we got to the door of the house, he give me a peppermint Lifesaver, saying, "Remember now you don't say we seen Uncle Jake or Louie." He put his finger to his mouth like he always done and reached in his pocket and give me another penny, then popped two or three Lifesavers in his own mouth before we went up the steps.

When my mother said I was old enough now to go around Grandmom's with my brothers every Saturday morning I ast her what for? She said, "Grandmom wants to see you." I seen this was good chance to ask her where Grandmom's father was. She said she dint have no father, "You mean Grandmom's husband, dumbie, he was me father and he was your grandfather." She said he been something she called a cobbler, like the shoemaker up on 2nd Street, and sometimes he would disappear on what she called benders. I ast her what a bender was, she said it was when he drunk more'n was good for him and Grandmom dint have no money and had to go out scrubbing floors to put food on the table whilst her and me aunts and uncles went out and shoveled up the horse manure from between the trolley tracks to sell to people for their gardens back of the alley, some even bought it to burn in their stoves in the wintertime they was so poor. She said I wasn't supposed to tell anybody about Grandpop's benders, I wasn't ever to tell anybody our business, making me promise, like I promised me father I wouldn't tell on him, only she dint give me no penny but I promised anyhow, and when I ast her where her father was now she said, "Dead, God rest his soul, died in the Pennsylvania Hospital before you was born." When I ast her, "Is he up on the roof at Grandmom's house?" she give me a funny look and said, "No, goofy, he's buried in Holy Cross cemetery with your father's mother and father," which ever after that is where I thought they put you if you went on benders and wondered if they would put me father there too.

The first time I ever went around Grandmom's Saturday mornings with me brothers, Sonny was there and his two older brothers, Aloysius and Stosh, that was named after me father, was there, that all the rest of the time was in a place called Girard College that Sonny said was a orphanage for poor boys dint have no father and so they was only half a orphan. When I ast me mother why wasn't Sonny there, he dint have no father either, she said, "Because he's such a devil he will prolly end up in prison one day."

All me other cousins would be there too and Aunt Nell in her dustcap. She made Frank leave the bundle of old *Ledgers* he brung from home out in the backyard so's he could take them to a place called the ragshop afterwards, she dint want them messing up the house she said she just cleaned.

Grandmom was setting in a chair in the dining room that was all dark excepting for what little light come in from the kitchen from a tiny window up near the ceiling, and she had her big cup of tea setting at her elbow. Aunt Nell lined us up littlest to oldest and we was so many we stretched all the way into the parlor that was darker'n our parlor, the houses acrosst the street was so close. That was where the big upright piano was nobody was allowed to touch, when I first laid eyes on it I was just dying to touch it, to hear what it sounded like. When it come my turn,

Grandmom leaned into me face to see who I was, saying in a voice so low I could hardly hear it, "Ya look jist like your father," and sometimes she was wearing a dustcap and sometimes she wasn't. "Was you a good boy?" she whispered, and when she ast me that first time I got all rattled thinking about all the sugar I stole from the sugar bowl me mother got for nothing at the Lyric movies dish-night when we seen Shirley Temple, but I nodded me head anyways even though I knowed it was a lie because I knowed too if I dint lie I wouldn't get the penny like she give the others, like I knowed from me father if I dint say I wouldn't tell I wouldn't get no penny either. I was so anxious to get the penny because of the nigger toe I could buy at Willie's or at Finkel's but I was so shy in front of her I mumbled so she had to lean forward and clap a hand behind her ear like Slap done. She ast me to say again what I said and when I did she broke into a grin, saying, "That's a good boy," and reached into the little leather change purse in her lap that was all stuffed with pennies and took one out between her fingers that was all bent and shriveled up and pressed the penny in me hand. Then she put her hands on me shoulders and leaned over and kissed me, her lips thin and dry like paper and tickly from her mustache. "God bless you now," she whispered smelling like me mother, smelling like the lavender sachet me mother bought for herself and her from a blind lady stood out on 2nd Street even in the rain with the sparrows, yelling, "sweet lav-en-der! sweet lav-en-der!" Me mother kept it in her dresser drawers at home so her things'd smell nice she said.

After we come out of Grandmom's Frank hollered in Slap's ear for Slap to pick up the bundle of old *Ledgers* and carry them and Slap done it because he was so easygoing. Then they went up and down the streets looking in the gutters and in garbage cans, if they found a empty soda bottle or rags or a old piece of junk or a stack of old newspapers, they got all excited like they found money and grabbed them up, and that time Sonny was there and sometimes Aloysius and Stosh come along and sometimes they dint. But if only Sonny come along then him and me brothers looked in the gutters for cigarette butts and picked up any they spied and snuck in the alley to smoke them, just like me father and Uncle Jake and Louie snuck up the alley with the pint. They put the cigarette butts in their mouths even though me mother said not to put anything in me mouth was on the ground. Buster said if I told on them he'd cut me heart out and stuff me in a ragbag and sell me to the ragman and I said I wouldn't tell but he dint give me no penny like me father done not to tell.

They took the empty soda bottles to Willie's up at the corner even though he shouted at them so loud I was ready to run out the door, "Goniffs! Bloodsuckers! Are you trying to suck my life blood?" and waved his meat cleaver over his head, shouting "You never bought them sodas at my store!" But Sonny stood right up to him and said, "Yes we did, Willie, you must've forgot," and even though you could tell Willie dint believe him, he took the bottles anyhow, mumbling, "Goniffs! Bloodsuckers!" and give them the two cents deposit on every one of them. Later on outside Frank said Willie took the bottles because our mother and Aunt Nell was such good customers but Sonny said, "All them mockies think about is money." I wondered was I a mockie I hid away the pennies me father give me, and was me brothers and Sonny mockies, they was always looking for soda bottles in the gutters and the garbage to turn in for pennies?

Next they goed around 3rd Street to the ragshops but first they spied old newspapers blowing around acrosst the street in the schoolyard that was the school where Aunt Nell worked in the cafeteria slinging hash, as Sonny called it, and the kids was

proddisins and mockies he said and dint go to Sacred Heart but
went to that school that was a public school that was a whole
block big and was even bigger'n Sacred Heart school. And since
they wasn't Catholics and wouldn't go to heaven I thought public meant bad even though me mother said President Roosevelt
was a proddisin, he was saving the country putting poor people
back to work, so he couldn't be bad even though he wouldn't go
to heaven.

They rushed acrosst the trolley tracks, Slap grabbing me
hand, and they went in the schoolyard. I run around with them,
snatching up the papers that was like playing games with you,
they would fly away and come close and fly away again and then
fly flat against the iron fence. Me and Slap got to giggling, trying
to catch ahold of them and Buster growled, "Quitcher playin, we
ain't got all day."

The ragshops was lined up next to each other acrosst from
the school. They was like dark caves worse'n our cellar, they
smellt all moldy and greasy like no air ever got in and had bundles and bundles of rags and old newspapers stacked up to the
ceiling where there was only one lightbulb burning you hardly
could see by. The little old ragmen looked like bundles of rags
and smellt just like their shops smellt. When Sonny was there
he'd say "Lemme do the talkin," and if he wasn't there Buster
done the talking, even though Frank was the oldest, Buster and
Sonny was nervier and wouldn't let the ragman cheat them.

If they was only able to get enough old newspapers and junk
he could hold in his hand, the ragman would hang it from a
hook in a brass scale in his hand but if they was lucky and drug
in a whole lot, he would tell them to fling it on the scale in the
floor that was so black and covered with grease you could hardly tell it was there. He always weighed the newspapers first,
then the rags, then any old junk they found because they was a

different price on each one, and if Sonny was there he'd sneak
his toe on the scale and if the ragman catched him he'd scream,
"Goniff!" like Willie did, only then he'd holler, "Goyim!" and
spit over his shoulder. Later on outside Sonny'd say, "Them
mockies got eyes in their asses," that I knowed was a bad word
me mother said nice little boys dint say. And when the ragman
weighed up everything he said I give you such-and-such and
Sonny looked at Frank and Frank looked at Buster to see was it
enough money to pay their way into the matinee at the movies
and have extry money for candy for the show. If it was enough
they'd give each other the high sign but if Buster or Sonny dint
think it was enough they ast for more. If the ragman shouted,
"What ya trying to steal the bread from my mouth?" and spit on
the floor—it dint make no difference he spit on the floor, the
floor was so dirty already—they'd say forget it and would grab
the stuff off the scale and lug it to another ragman nextdoor or
up the street. But if they thought it was enough they nodded
secret so's you could hardly see, and the ragman'd reach in the
big dirty apron tied around his middle and fish out a fistful of
money that was black and greasy as his hands and count it out a
penny or a nickel at a time, Frank and Buster and Sonny watching him like a hawk. When he give the money to Buster or
Sonny they all got into a huddle and counted it just to be sure
he ain't cheated them, whilst the ragman muttered, "Goyim
goyim," under his breath and spit again everytime he said it. I
dint know what goyim meant but he said it like he was coughing up snot in his throat because next thing you knowed he
blowed his nose through his fingers and wiped it with the back
of his hand that I never seen nobody but the ragman do and it
always made me queasy in the belly.

When we come home me mother said what did I do fall in
the dustbin? Slap screeched, "No! we been to the radshop!"

talking like he talked because he never heard words right. Frank and Buster bragged to her how much money they made saying they made enough money to go to the movies that afternoon, and then some. Me mother said they made so much money in that case they could take me to the movies with them, "Snow White and the Seven Dwarves is playing at the Morris," she said, "Aunt Nell seen it and said it was a good picsture," and me heart give a kick in me chest when she said it. But Buster whined, "Aw geezo, Ma, do we gotta?" because they wanted to see "Rootin' Tootin' Rhythm" starring Gene Autry up at the Lyric with Sonny, but she said in no uncertain terms, "If he don't go and you don't go see Snow White, nobody's goin'," so that was the end of that, even though Buster had a puss on him a yard long, whining Snow White was a picsture for sissies and little girls, but me mother said, "Never you mind now."

After we et our Campbell soup and bread and butter me mother scrubbed me face and combed me hair and told me to stay with Frank and for Frank not to let me go into the terlet by meself, Buster growling they should take me into the terlet and flush me down and me mother said, "What did you say?" and Buster growled, "Nuthin."

The Morris wasn't too far down from the ragshops and oncet we got there Frank said, "Less us look at the stills before we go in." The stills turnt out to be picstures outside that showed what was playing inside and we looked at them and they was cartoon picstures of little men with pointy caps Buster sneered was nothing but runts and a pretty girl with black hair with birds was blue and wasn't sparrows flying around her and me eyes was gawking and gawking, I couldn't get enough of looking at them picstures, me heart was going a mile a minute I was so excited I was going to see a movie again.

Inside smellt like me brothers' sneakers under the bed on a

hot night. Frank, that was holding the money, bought us all pop-corn that Slap called potcorn and a whole box of Sno-Caps apiece at the little candy counter. They was nothing but kids inside like at the movie about Saint Theresa at Sacred Heart and some of them was hollering, "We want the movie! We want the movie!" and stamping their feet and whistling between their fingers. I grabbed ahold of Slap's hand.

When the movie come on they was something Frank said was the serial called "Mark of Zorro" about a man in a black hat and a black mask with a whip. I was dying to ask Frank why was the wagon wheels going backwards when the wagon was going frontwards but he was staring so hard at Zorro cracking his whip I knowed he would've never heard me. Then come the Our Gang comedy, Buckwheat wasn't crying no more about his mother, he was acting like she ain't ever died at all, he was talking like Slap talked. Then come Snow White that was a cartoon but not like the Mickey Mouse, they was people too, and when that come on, right from the very start, I was on the edge of me seat, me eyes glued to that screen so's I don't know where I was. All in color it was, the little house in the woods and the dwarves and all the little animals and the wicked stepmother with the poison apple said mirror mirror on the wall, I hollered "Look out! Look out!" to Snow White to warn her and Frank and Buster almost fell on the floor dying laughing at me, Slap going "Heh? heh?" in me face, "Whatsa' matter?"

We dint get home til way after dark and me mother was mad at Frank for staying to see the movie twicet, she said he should've had better sense, being the oldest, she thought we been kidnapped. And me father that you could tell already been to Hoolihan's he was so grinny and bright-eyed, said, "If only they was." She give him a look and told us to sit down at the table, "The baked beans is dry and the hot dogs all wrinkled up but that's your own fault, so shut up and eat." That was hard to do, all the popcorn and Sno-Caps we et, excepting for Slap that shoveled right in and would eat umpteen times a day if you let him. But I et anyway and so did Frank and Buster, not to make her any madder'n she already was.

I was just busting to tell her all about Snow White and all the songs they sung but seeing the mood she was in I knowed I better wait til we was alone together to sing them to her.

The next day when we was alone in the house and she was ironing away in the parlor and our stories on the radio was over for the afternoon and Danny was snoozing on the couch, she give me a look with a tease in her eye, knowing I was just dying to tell her all about Snow White. I seen a way when I ast her did she know why the wagon wheels went backwards in the movies whilst the wagon still went frontwards? She said, no she dint know why that was, but then it was like she knowed what I was getting at because she ast me in a way like she couldn't care less how I liked Snow White. I jumped up and told her the whole movie from the very beginning to The End, singing her the songs Snow White sung, "Wishing" and "Someday Me Prince'll Come," making up the words where I dint know them. When I was done she said, "Well now I won't' hafta spend a quarter seeing Snow White," and she ast me to sing "Wishing" again. I did and then the two of us sung it together while she ironed away, I felt so pleased and excited learning her to sing it, even though I dint have the words all right she sung them that way anyhow, and when we was done she sung it again and ever after that when she done her house-work or was washing the clothes or washing Danny in the dish-pan I could hear her singing it.

I thought about Snow White and dreamt about Snow White for as long as I thought and dreamt about Shirley Temple in

"Poor Little Rich Girl" and for a long time was thinking more about Snow White than I was about her even though the color of Snow White's skin turnt into nightmares. But during the day I thought of her and thought of the dwarves and their little house in the woods, I wisht I could go visit them sometimes behind the screen at the Morris the way I wanted to go see Shirley Temple at the Lyric even though she lived in the place me mother called Hollywood.

I wisht I could tie me shoes but at least I knowed how to spell our name now because I watched me mother when she wrote our name on envelopes to Aunt Jenny for the little lamp on the server in the dining room or sent away the Ralston box-tops for the Tom Mix bowls for me brothers. She wrote her name like she drawed cats, like she dint want to make no mistake, and I wrote it just like she done over and over on the backs of the cracker boxes I drawed on—so now I could write ice and bread and coal and milk and Lithwack and when I ast her why people was named what they was named she said, "Lithwack ain't our real name, when your father's father got off of the boat he couldn't speak no American or write no American and could hardly write in Litvak, so like they done in them days when you got off of the boat they wrote down what it sounded like to them and it come out Lithwack but in the old country was something else, they did that in them days, no matter if you was a litvak like Grandpop or a polak like Grandmom or a bohunk or a mockie like Willie owns the grocery story around the corner, they give you a new name and you was stuck with it and that was that." I ast her was that her Grandmom's name? and she said, "No, silly, they dint change that name when me mother's mother O'Rourke got off of the boat after the potatoes died in Ireland and she seen her first nigger she thought was the devil. Because if you was a mick or a limey they dint change your name." I said, "Why not?" and she said, "Because County Cork wasn't far away like Lithuania where your grandpop come from and everybody from County Cork could talk American even if they couldn't write it." I was about to ask her what a limey was when she said, "Now quit pesterin me and droor yer picstures," but what I done was practice writing our name over and over that Grandpop Lithwack couldn't write down but I could, watching her, even though she went too fast for me to tie me shoes yet.

"Measles" the doctor with the funny name on 2nd Street called it and during the day she put me up in her and me father's bed with the shades down because Doctor Smuckler, that told her to mash up the carrots and onions and potatoes after she took me out of the white place, told her the dark would help me get better and wouldn't be hurting my eyes. He give her some medicine to give me that tasted like cherries and just before he left he looked her up and down and said, "It's almost your time, isn't it?" She ducked her head like he said something out of the way but she nodded. I wondered what he meant, it's almost your time, but after he left I was too sick to ask her, I could hardly keep my eyes open and could barely talk, she said if I couldn't talk I really must be sick.

I felt like I was inside the oven and kept seeing movies even when I was awake and without me having to think about them, they just kept running in front of my eyes, and the sheets had the smell of her in them that was like a faint smell of peaches, so that it was like she was there with me all the time, and the smell of him there too, the smell of Chesterfield cigarettes and beer.

Slap snuck up to see me every day after school even though he wasn't supposed to because he ain't never had the measles yet, he would stand at the foot of the bed and stare at me. One time he brung me a nigger toe from Willie's but I couldn't finish it, that's how sick I was, so Slap et the rest of it, hoping for a penny inside but they wasn't one. Another time he ast if he could turn on the light so's he could take a gander at my spots and even though my mother said not to turn on the light I was too weak to raise me voice so's he'd hear not to, and he brung me the nigger toe besides, even if I couldn't eat it, so I nodded yes and he turnt on the overhead light and it stung my eyes and he leaned real close and stared at me face, his eyes bulging in my eyes so that I reared back on the pillow because of his eyes so close and the surprise of the light.

When he seen his fill, he turnt out the light and stood at the foot of the bed again and said, "You gonna croak?" I said I dint know, loud as I could that wasn't very loud, I never been this sick before, not since the white place. All of a sudden Slap bust out crying, blubbering I must be gonna croak I looked so terrible with more red spots on me kisser than they was polka dots on our mother's apron. He was bawling so hard I begun to think maybe I really was going to croak and a movie started going in my head of the little white caskets Aunt Bridget's Uncle Digby put little kids in when they died, or was bad, Frank said, so I better do like he said. I seen the white hearse Uncle Digby— that was called Digby me mother said because he put people in holes—the white hearse he drived them to the cemetery in that was used only for little kids, "Because they is pure as angels," my mother said when I ast her why everything was white for little kids and black for big people. "Some kids anyhow," she said with a dark look, and I wondered the way she said it did she mean Buster and Sonny, that if they croaked would Uncle Digby put them in a black box or a white one and would he drive them to the cemetery in the black hearse because neither of them wasn't no angel, not by a long shot.

Which is why Buster surprised me coming up one day after school—him and Frank already had the measles and could come up but Frank never come up and my eyes followed Buster suspicious, I was wondering did he come up to make fun of me or what? He tiptoed in and looked down at me. I was waiting for him to say something smart but instead he reached into the pocket of his knickers and brung out a yellow string bag of marbles. "Here," he said, shoving them at me, "I jist beat the pants off of Sonny."

I stared at the marbles and dint know what I was supposed to do with them and dint know what to say, it was so hard to say anything I dint say nothing, I only knowed he had bags and bags of marbles because he was the best marble shooter on the block and never had to buy but the one bag of marbles at the five'n tenny when he started playing—even in the poor light I seen his knees was dirty, my mother always complained on washdays because the knees of his knickers was always black as Slap's and he was always wearing a hole in one knee or the other that she had to patch, he knelt so much playing marbles she said if he would only kneel as much praying as he did playing marbles he would be a saint.

Without even asking if he could let in the light, he went and pulled up the shade to get a good look at me spots, same as Slap done, and when he seen enough he let out a whistle and said me kisser looked like a bottle of stuffed olives and he yanked down the shade and beat it out the door. I held the bag of marbles in my hand, wondering what I was supposed to do with them, then I knowed what I would do. I would put them in the bottom of my drawer along with the pennies from my father that I kept hid there under me underwear.

I wasn't allowed to sleep at night with Slap and Danny and had to sleep downstairs by myself on the couch so they wouldn't get the measles. I would wake up and sometimes I would see my mother standing in the parlor doorway in her nightgown, she was looking fatter now even in her nightgown, and whether she was there or wasn't there I felt safe seeing her there, I felt less by myself and could drift back to sleep.

The next night she let me come downstairs earlier and as I was laying on the couch falling in and out of sleep as I tried to listen to Jack Benny on the radio, Aunt Nell come in the back through the alley and brung me in one of her baked custards in a little green pot with cinnamon sprinkled on top. She put her hand on my head and shook her head and clicked her tongue in a way it looked like I was going to croak for sure. She told my mother she could send the custard pot back anytime, then ast her in a whisper, "How ya doin?" asking her in a way like she was asking her something else. My mother whispered back, rolling her eyes sideways at my brothers, that was all sitting around the old Scott laughing at something Rochester said, "It won't be long now," saying it like it was a secret she dint want my brothers to hear. Aunt Nell said, "You send around the minute you need me, hear?" and my mother nodded she would. Then I drifted off no matter how hard I tried to stay awake to hear Jack Benny crank up his old Maxwell and not caring at all about the pot of custard, that just showed how sick I still was.

I come up out of the doze when she leaned over me, smelling of perfume and powder, her lips red as blood with lipstick and her hair bright yellow—"bleached," my mother called it—and the radio was off and my brothers was gone upstairs. She was cooing nice things, her dress shiny red and her high heels pointy and black and shiny too. My father, setting in his chair by the radio, was giving her dark looks over the top of his paper, even though she was his baby sister and had the same name as Saint Theresa and was the only one of all his sisters and brothers, besides Aunt Magda that scrubbed people's floors, ever come to our house, her hair as bright as the halo around Saint Theresa's head in the movie, her mouth as dark as the blood on Saint Theresa's hands.

My mother was staring at her hair and her dress like she wasn't trying to stare and when she leaned close to kiss me her lips was so shiny and smellt like my father's when he had a few shots. Her hair was so bright, I felt like I was in a movie and it wasn't Saint Theresa anymore, it was Shirley Temple's mother leaning down worried did she have a cold, then that faded and with her hair so bright and blonde in my eyes she could be Shirley Temple's mother. I felt hot from the fever and my eyes kept rolling shut and when I opened them again she was gone, excepting for the smell of her perfume and powder, I could still smell it in the air like the smell of my mother like peaches in the sheets. My father still had that dark look in his eyes and was cracking his paper like he was mad at the news, he muttered, "Tramp," and my mother, looking even fatter now when she wasn't in her nightgown, was crocheting in the other armchair, she said, "You oughtn't to talk about your own flesh and blood that way, God forgive you." He snapped his paper again and when she said "flesh and blood" I seen her lips again coming down close to mine, coming down kissing me like her mouth was bleeding.

I only been back in the bed a little while after the measles when my father woke us up in the middle of the night and told us to get dressed and come downstairs. I wanted to ask him why we was getting up in the dark but he was gone before I could ask him, and when I ast Frank as he was buttoning up his knickers, he just shrugged and looked dopey from still being half asleep.

When we come down, my mother was sitting in the kitchen with her brown coat on that Aunt Bridget'd give her, like she was cold or was going out somewheres. She looked like she wasn't feeling so good, her face was the color of a cork, and she paid no attention to any of us. My heart started beating fast, wondering if she was sick or was going away. I wanted to go over and ask her what was the matter but Aunt Nell was there and Aunt Bridget was there, bending over her. My father was sitting at the kitchen table and Aunt Nell was handing my mother a bowl of tea. He told us to put on our coats and then took us out in the night before I even had a chance to go in the kitchen and see her again. He took us around the block to Grandmom's house and I knowed it was the latest I ever been out because there wasn't nobody out on the streets and all the lights was out in the houses. I wanted to ask him what was the matter, was she sick? but everytime I went to ask, he said to be quiet, I'd know all about it in the morning.

Grandmom met us at the door and Frank and Buster and Slap was sent upstairs to sleep with Sonny in the front room where there was room in the big bed because his two older brothers was in the place called Girard College for boys that dint have no fathers. My father left and my grandmother put me and Danny on either end of the couch in the parlor with a blanket over us. Danny ground his teeth the rest of the night and rolled around on his belly so I couldn't sleep, I couldn't get to sleep anyway in a strange place on a couch that smellt like the perfumey smell like moth balls in the terlet at the Morris moviehouse where I seen Snow White. More'n all that, I was thinking about my mother and what was the matter that we was all woke up in the middle of the night and sent to sleep at Grandmom's, and I worried what it was my father said I would know in the morning, thinking it might be something bad about my mother.

In the morning Grandmom made us corn fritters with Karo syrup and coffee she put egg shells in to cut the bitter taste that my mother never did. Danny ast for another fritter and Grandmom said, "A sufficiency is an abundancy," and even though neither of us knowed what that meant we could tell by the way she said it Danny wasn't going to get another fritter. Aunt Nell wasn't there and so Grandmom minded me and Danny all day while my brothers and Sonny went off to school. I wanted to ask her where my mother was but she put on a dustcap like Aunt Nell's and told us to behave ourselfs and went upstairs where I could hear her pushing a carpet sweeper around. There was the big upright piano in the parlor she told us not to touch and I was too afraid to ask if I could turn on the radio to hear the stories my mother and me listened to at home, I was almost as afraid to ask that as I was to ask her what was the matter with my mother. It was the morning and my father said I would know in the morning but I dint know yet.

She spent most of her time going between the kitchen and the upstairs with her big cup that said Killarney Tea on the side, the same was on the box of tea my mother drunk at home, so I knowed what it was. I set beside Danny on the couch and told him stories even when he nodded off, I just kept talking and talking and in between I kept getting up to peek between the rubber plants and out through the lace curtains in the front windows to see if my mother was coming to take us home.

I stood looking out the window all afternoon, they wasn't as much to watch on Hoffman Street as they was on Mifflin Street but I was only watching out for her anyway. My heart give a jump when I spied my father coming down the block after work with Aunt Nell beside him. When they come in the house he ast my grandmother if we been good boys and she said yes. I was all for running to get my coat but then Aunt Nell whispered something in Grandmom's ear and Grandmom bust out in a grin at my father, saying, "Well, she must be glad after all them boys." He grinned too but like he was embarrassed and pleased at the same time, and he thanked her for minding us. All the way home I wanted to bust out running so's to get there quicker and see was she there but he had ahold of my hand like he had ahold of Danny's, so I couldn't run even if I wanted to.

When we finally got there Frank and Buster and Slap was already there and he took us all upstairs where my mother lay in the bed even though it wasn't bedtime, and laying next to her was a little red face she said was "Kate." She smiled at it, then smiled at us but she smiled real weak like she still wasn't feeling so good but her face dint look like cork anymore, it was pale like Snow White's face. I wanted to ask her if Kate would be staying with us and where would she sleep if she did but then she ast in a way that sounded like she hardly had the strength to ask it, did we behave ourselfs at Grandmom's? We nodded yes and then my father got us all together again and shooed us back down the stairs and told us not to make any noise. In the kitchen he fed us Post Toasties and grape jelly and bread like it was breakfast stead of suppertime.

When you looked at the top of Kate's head you could see her heart beat. I would stare at it for a long time and knock the top of my head and wonder would hers ever get hard as mine, my mother laughed and said she hoped not. Kate smellt of baby oil and the sweet powder my mother used to sprinkle on me and used to sprinkle on Danny, and she had only blonde frizz for hair and eyes blue as the bluing my mother used that was the same color as my father's eyes and smellt like the sky must smell.

On the second floor landing between our bedroom and theirs was an electric socket in the survase that always caught my eye everytime I passed it, like it was talking to me. It had a little metal door covering it that when you pulled it open you could see the round dark hole of the socket like a mouth. "Don'tchou dare touch them sockets," she'd say, and when I ast her why she said, "Just don'tchou touch them, that's all." But it seemed like the mouth of that socket was calling to me and when she was busy downstairs, bathing Kate in the dishpan or hanging out the diapers, I'd tell Danny, that I was supposed to be minding, to go look out the parlor window and not to come up, I was going to the terlet. I'd sneak up and kneel in front of the socket and open the tiny door, then I'd bend down and listen and stare into it. It looked like a black hole that went right through our house and through all the houses on the block. I put a ear close and listened to see if I could hear like a radio through to the other houses, and it wasn't long after that I stuck out my tongue and touched it with the tip of it. I felt a shivery feeling run along my tongue and down my throat, the next time I done it tiny blue sparks shot out. I knowed it was alive then and talked in sparks and for a long time after that I couldn't wait to get up there and kneel down and put my tongue there to feel the shivering going through me, and one morning I looked and seen Danny staring at me through the railings of the bannister, he come up in spite of what I said to look out the parlor window. I quick put my finger to me lips, the way my father done when we come home from the saloon, and said not to tell because she said I shouldn't never touch it, and maybe that's why I done it. I liked the sparks and the cold waves shivering down me, touching the dark that spit blue like Tommy the cat spit at the other cats out in the alley, blue sparks that went through the wall and through the walls of all the houses talking blue like it was blue words from the sky like through the radio, and couldn't stop doing it, like the magnet big as a horseshoe my father had in the cellar that when it clamped onto something was metal I couldn't pull it off no matter how hard I tried, that socket drawed me to it again and again, like the sugar bowl up in the cupboard could whisper to me as far away as the parlor.

I couldn't tie my shoes yet but since I mostly wore mary-janes that was handmedowns from Aunt Patty's twin girls the way my mother's clothes was still all handmedowns from her other sisters, I could buckle them without her doing it for me. She dint have to dress me neither, I knowed how to button and unbutton myself by now and wash my own face and run the yellow comb on her bureau through my hair.

Mornings while she bathed and dressed the younger ones and boiled up formula for Kate she let me go out on my own— "Not too far," she warned at first, "Don't go crossin the street, be sure to stay on the block." The first time, I set on the top step looking up and down the street but the marble was so cold on me hiney I got up and went down and stood on the bricks and stayed mainly around the front steps, and dint go further'n that. But little by little the more she let me out the more I went further, first to the middle of the block, then as far as the corner, looking back all the while to see how far I come, our front steps looking a long ways away, I got a shiver in my belly being so far from the house all by myself.

At the corner a trolley was coming and I jumped back against the wall to watch it turn in a big screech of the wheels. I found out you could tell two ways if one was coming, you could hear the singing in the wire overhead or if you pressed your ear against the metal pole you could hear the roaring it made coming up the tracks even though you couldn't see it coming yet. And one day the man in the dark blue cap waved at me and reached up and rung his bell, I was so surprised I dint know what to do and wisht I'd waved back but the trolley, that had a big number 5 up in the window, already went around the turn up Mifflin Street. Everytime when the trolley made the turn and rolled past 3rd Street, when the long pole back on the roof with the little wheel on the end hit where the wires crossed overhead there was a big loud POCK! and a big blue spark shot out, blue as the sparks in the socket where I put my tongue. And if the long pole slipped off of the wire the trolleycar couldn't go no more and the man in the dark blue cap got out and went around back of the trolley and tugged on a rope there tied to the pole til the little wheel slipped onto the wire again. Blue sparks shot out that time too, blue as the sky, and a shiver went through me same as if I put my tongue there where the wires crossed. One day I was watching when the trolley turned and there was a big loud grinding noise and the back wheels went off of the track, the whole trolleycar was shaking and come to a stop. Two men in the dark blue caps run out of the trolley and they looked at the wheels off of the track and soon a big truck come with a lot of men and a crowbar umpteen times bigger'n the crowbar my father had in the cellar, they lifted the trolleycar back on the track and I couldn't wait to get home and tell my mother but when I told her she dint seem all that interested, all she said was, "You dint cross the street, didja?" I said no and wasn't lying because I ain't crossed the street, that time anyhow.

Another morning there was little girls with curls like Shirley Temple playing jacks on the top step of a house near the corner. I stopped and watched, I couldn't get over how they could throw up the little red rubber ball and scoop up the jacks all at once and was dying to ask them if I could try it and did they know where Shirley Temple lived? When one of them seen me looking she squinted at me, saying, "Whatter you lookin at, you ugly thing? Gwan, git outa here before I call a cop." I was so surprised I could hardly catch my breath the same as if she punched me in the belly. I run back to our steps because my mother said if you was bad the cop would put you in jail and I thought it must be bad to watch somebody playing jacks, when I seen them again out playing jacks I turned right around and come back to my own steps and set there despite the marble being so cold. When my mother called me inside for lunch I ast her was I ugly, she laughed and said, "You're as ugly as Mickey Mouse, now eat your soup."

After that, if I seen a red car coming I'd quick hide in the doorway or behind the steps because I knowed they was the cops that Sonny called "Two worms in a tomato." I was afraid they would take me away like my mother said they would if I done something bad and dint mind her, like going off the block or crossing the street by myself.

I kept my eyes peeled for red cars because it wasn't long after that one morning, my heart in my mouth, I crosst my fingers on both my hands and looked both ways umpteen times, even though all the cars and trolleys only come one way, before I finally dared race acrosst 2nd Street and was amazed I made it safe to the other side all by myself. And even though I knowed I shouldn't've, I went past the houses with the front porches on them we dint have on Mifflin Street and wished we did, and went down near Front Street that she told me never to go beyond because of the river where I might fall in like Aunt Nell's Uncle Stan and might get drowneded.

But since I went that far I went around 3rd Street because I was dying to look again at the picstures Frank called stills was out front of the Morris movie. When I got there I looked at everyone of them that was low enough for me to see and then looked at everyone of them again, my mouth hanging open and my heart starting to dance even though I dint see Shirley Temple in any one of them. Then I peeped in the lobby where we bought the popcorn and Sno-Caps to see if I could see Snow White but all I seen was a lady with a rag around her head pushing a vacuum cleaner like Aunt Bridget had that Aunt Nell said was the only one of her sisters could afford a vacuum cleaner, being married to a undertaker. The lady looked at me and I run away before she could holler anything, being sure to look umpteen times both ways again before I tore across 3rd Street where I stood outside the public school where Aunt Nell worked slinging hash in the cafeteria even though she was Catholic and where we picked up the trash paper on Saturday mornings to sell to the ragman after we got our penny at Grandmom's.

Looking both ways, I run across 3rd Street again, keeping close to the curb when I passed the ragshops for fear, being by myself, the ragman might grab me and stick me in a bag and sell me for rags like Buster said they would if I ratted. Then before I knowed it I'd gone as far as the icehouse where Aunt Maggie's Uncle Ned worked. That was down near Emily Street where Aunt Maggie and him lived, and Aunt Bridget and Uncle Digby the undertaker lived too, and Aunt Patty and Uncle Bill that give me the maryjanes I had on from their twin girls. I stood watching bug-eyed on the other side of the street as big slabs of ice we could never ever fit into our icebox come shooting all blue and steaming down the iron chutes into the backs of the ice wagons where the horses jumped every time one hit in a crash of light in the sunshine, and never once got broke. I was dying for a drink by now and wanted to cross over and sneak me a sliver of ice from the back of one of them wagons the way my older brothers done when the iceman come to our street. But I dint want to get caught by the men with the long hooks up at the top of the chutes or get crushed by a big cake of ice as it come sliding down, and what if one of the horses stepped on me? So I watched and watched till I couldn't watch no more, my belly was growling and I knowed it was time for me to get home to eat because she'd be looking out the front door wondering where I was if I dint.

Now she knowed I knowed my way to Aunt Nell's and Willie's she'd give me a note sometimes to take to Aunt Nell's, saying go up the alley, it's quicker, but most of the time, after I tried to spell out the words on the note, I went around by the street because there was more to see. If she give me a note to take around to Willie's for a loaf of Parkway's or a quart of Supplee's or a can of Campbell's, I could read it and remember it and dint need no note but she always give me one anyway with the money wrapped tight in it, saying, "Don'tchou dare lose this, hold onto it tight." All the way to Willie's I'd squeeze my hand so hard it hurt, if I lost the money I dint know what I'd do.

One time when I went around Willie give me a banana that I never et before that was all so brown and rotten he couldn't sell it anyway, so that was the taste of brown to me. And next time she give me a note to take around I smelled more rotten bananas and when he put the milk and bread in a bag and I give him the money I screwed up my nerve and said in a voice that was all squeaky like Mickey Mouse, did he have a rotten banana he was going to throw away? All of a sudden he grabbed up his meat cleaver, shouting he'd split my head open if I pestered him again for rotten bananas, did I want to steal the bread from his mouth? I couldn't breathe, I was so ascared I run out of that store and never ast him anymore about bananas because he got that same wild look in his eyes as when we brung him the empties we found on Saturday mornings for the deposit, he really looked like he would split my head open.

I was getting so nervy one morning I snuck all the way up to the Lyric movie at 2nd and Tasker that was the neighborhood where my father said he growed up in and was farther'n I ever been before on my own.

On the way home I stopped at the Jew butcher's with the funny writing in the window that looked like laundry hanging out and the chickens pecking corn in the window and wondered why they could have chickens in their window and my Grandmom Lithwack couldn't have chickens in her backyard, my mother said she dreamt of chickens and sometimes she dreamt of niggers chasing her but they was always chasing her down the street and not off the end of the dock like Grandmom O'Rourke's grandmom. My father said you dreamt of niggers I think I'll play such-and-such a number today because that was the number you played if you dreamt of niggers and you put it in a box.

I stopped and watched the chickens pecking and the men inside with long beards and curls and black felt hats on like Aunt Nell and Grandmom wearing dustcaps in the house. They had meat cleavers in their hands like Willie, I wondered did they wave them at you if they got mad at you? Buster said they liked to snatch little Catholic kids like me off of the street and take them in the back and suck the blood out of them, so I better watch my step. So my heart was always going a mile a minute whenever I stopped to look at the chickens or see what time it was, if the big hand and the little hand was close to twelve I'd scoot on home like she told me I should because that was time to eat.

But if it wasn't time to eat yet I ducked up Sigel Street to a place had a high wood gate in front that my father said was the slaughterhouse. I would peep between the slats in the gate and hear the cows mooing and the pigs squealing and sometimes there was sheep baaing in the back. You couldn't see any of them but you could hear them and you could smell them too, the smell was worse'n the smell of the horse droppings on the street or the terlets of the Morris movie and Sacred Heart school all put together.

If I waited long enough I heard screeching sharp as knives in my ears, the hair froze on my head as streams of blood come gushing down the gutters wore away in the cement floor like the gutter down the middle of our back alley. There was men in rubber boots and rubber aprons all smeared with blood. They was running around and there was old ladies in black shawls and a couple old men hunched over the drains in the floor, they had agate cups in their hands and was catching the blood that was as smoking as the slabs of ice shooting down the iron chutes at the icehouse, two pennies a cup my father said it cost them, bring your own cup. His mother, up on the roof, used to drink it he said, starting with chickens back in the old country, then in their backyard up at 2nd and Tasker until the cops come and said you can't keep chickens here, only the Jew butcher could keep chickens, right after she chopped off a chicken's head she had the cup right there he said, ready to catch the blood. Buster when he heard it rolled up his eyes and grabbed his throat, but my father said chicken blood and bull blood drunk hot give you strength and was good for the heart and whatever else ailed you. I thought that it must make you strong because the blood when it gushed out smelled like iron like the trolley-car pole I listened to smelled, like what I could feel in my mouth of the blue the electric socket left, like metal on my tongue, like the bottom of the metal ashtray in the parlor tasted that my father put his cigarettes out in, I wondered if I put my tongue on him would he taste like that too, dark and like iron?

When Kate had hair enough my mother brushed it up and tied a ribbon in it like she used to put in mine but didn't anymore now that Kate was there. She wet her finger in a glass of water and made little curls around it to make Kate look like Shirley Temple only she didn't because Shirley Temple had a lot more hair. She dressed her in a brandnew red and white check dress Aunt Kate that she was named for give her because Aunt Kate was her godmother that stood for her, and tied a pink ribbon in what curls there was and a man come with a camera and told her to set her in one corner of the couch while the man got under a black cloth and said, "Can you say 'cheese,' little girl?" Kate couldn't hardly say anything yet and just stared at him and my mother kept saying, "Oh, look at 'er now—ain'tcha, I mean, aren'tcha gonna smile for the nice man?" like she was ashamed of Kate in front of the man like she was ashamed of us and herself in front of the priest. If she'da put me on the couch stead of Kate I would've smiled and said cheese and even spelled it out for him, but she didn't, because it was like Kate was more important, even more important'n Danny'd been, she was always fussing with Kate and dressing her up and curling her hair with her finger so I never got to sing as much for her anymore and we never sung as much together either. When the picstures come back Kate's eyes was tinted a kind of blue they really wasn't, more like the painted eyes in the statue of the Virgin Mary on my mother's dresser, and her lips was painted like she had lipstick on bright as Aunt Theresa's lipstick, and her hair was painted yellow as the cheese she couldn't say and her dress and ribbon turned out pinker'n they was, like somebody'd gone and painted her with a water color set that made her not like Kate at all but like a color cartoon in the Sunday funnies and looking like she was ready to fall asleep. So I was surprised when my mother bought a glass frame at the five'n tenny up on Broad Street one day when we was out, going all the way up there special for it, and took out the picsture of Ginger Rogers that was in it and put Kate's picsture in and stuck it up on top of the radio for everybody to see.

One night not long after that my father brung home a big box after work. My brothers kept shouting what is it? what is it? but he only kept a secret grin, a merry one too, like he already been to Hoolihan's. My mother stood at the stove stirring her pots while keeping one eye on my father and the other eye on the box. Us kids all crowded around and when he opened it on the kitchen table for everybody to see Frank and Buster both made faces, Buster going, "Aw nerts, I thought it was something neat!" But my heart give a leap as I seen the bright blonde curls and shiny black tap shoes on a doll in a pink dress stood out all stiff and starched that looked like Shirley Temple.

He stood the box up in the palm of his hand, showing it to my mother, a bigger grin on his face like she was sure to be pleased. But she only stared at the doll and then at him so's you couldn't tell whether she was annoyed with him for buying it or because he had his bright-eyed look again. She give a sniff and turned back to stirring her pots.

He went on grinning, like he didn't see her look or was pretending not to, saying, "Some guy was sellin them outside the sugar works—for a song," saying it like that made it all right. All my mother muttered was, "She's too little for a doll that big," and shook salt in her pots like she wished she was shaking my father.

His mouth went down and he give her a look, growling,

"You'd pay twicet as much what I paid up at a department store, you'd pay three times as much any department store on Market Street, I betcha." She said, "How much did you pay?" He said, "A buck-and-a-half." She said, "That's a buck-and-a-half too much, that's a buck-and-a-half could've been spent to put food on the table," and she shook the shaker real hard again over the pots.

My father's mouth sunk even lower but he didn't say no more, he seen me gaping at the doll, I couldn't take my eyes off of it, and leaning down, he showed me the doll close up—My chest was beating, my hands was shaking, my hands shot out to lift it out of the box, thinking he was going to give it to me—didn't she say it was too big for Kate? But it wasn't too big for me, it wasn't too big for me to hold. Then he all of a sudden laughed like I done something funny, his eyes squinting and merry, he snatched the box away, saying, "Git outa here, this ain't for you." He tiptoed over to where Kate was sleeping like she always was sleeping in her bassinette by the stove and wasn't knowing anything, even when he took it over and peeked in to show it to her, she kept on snoozing away.

If he'da socked me in the face the way he sometimes done when Frank and Buster was acting up and he had a few in him, I couldn't've been more surprised—I thought at first he brung it home for me, didn't he know how much I liked Shirley Temple? Ain't she told him how much I talked about her and sung her songs to her? He must not have knowed because if he did he wouldn't be giving the doll to Kate that didn't even know she was alive yet. Frank and Buster thought that was the funniest, Buster jeering, "Neeyah, neeyah, the nitwit thought the dollbaby was for him—Boys don't play with dolls, ya dope, only sissies do." My mother said to him, "Never you mind now," and to my father she said, "It's a waste of money—and Slap needin new shoes for school," because Slap was always needing new shoes, he was hard on everything. My father said, "Aw c'mon, Min," calling her Min and not Nora like he done when he tried to jolly her out of something, "I got it for a song."

I would've sung for it, all the songs he wanted me to sing, all the Shirley Temple songs I knowed I would've sung, if he would only give me that doll. But my mother said again Kate was too little yet, saying it like that ain't what she was saying, like it was really his bright eyes she was talking at, and slammed down a lid on one of the pots like she wished she was slamming it down on top of my father's head, saying he'd done better if he bought grub for the table with that buck-fifty. My hope flared up, thinking he might give it to me after all, hearing her say again Kate was too small, but he tried to make her laugh, calling her Min and trying to tickle her so that Frank and Buster and Slap all got giggling and was egging him on, but she shoved him away, saying, "Gwan with ya." But he had the box up for her to see, grinning and calling her Min and saying, "Ain't she pretty? Ain't she pretty?" and I was saying yes! yes! but saying it inside of myself and not outloud, and you could see she was trying to stay mad at him but now she was staring at the doll and kept staring at it and staring. Finally, she laid down her mixing spoon and took the doll from him, saying in a quieter way, all the time not once taking her eyes off of her, "Well, there's no takin it back now, the damage is done"—she touched the dress that stood out so stiff and starched—"I better put it away til she's old enough to play with it, I'll put it away where it won't get dirty," and my heart sunk hearing it.

She told Frank to keep an eye on the cookpots and see that nothing boiled over and she went out of the kitchen and through the house. I heard her going up the stairs, and while my father was bending over Kate, going, "Wheresa bad girl? Wheresa bad girl?" talking to her even though she was dead to the world, I slid out the kitchen door and snuck up after my mother, hoping to see the doll again and see where she would put it.

I tiptoed down the hall and careful as I could peeped inside the doorway to their bedroom. I seen she was standing by the closet door holding the box open. What she was doing, she was looking into the face of that doll with that far off look she had sometimes where you couldn't tell where she was or what she was thinking, then she brung her hand up and patted one of the curls like she patted one of Kate's curls in place. Then all of a sudden she grinned, so tiny and quick I almost missed it, and putting the lid back on, she tucked the whole thing up on the very top shelf of their closet where I couldn't reach it even standing on a chair, as I found out later on when I tried. I run tearing back down the hall into the terlet, where I shut the door pretending to pee so's she wouldn't see me, and I didn't get to see that Shirley Temple doll again til Christmas time when she put it under the tree and wouldn't let nobody touch it, not even Aunt Patty's twin girls when they come to see our tree. And then I didn't see it anymore til a long while after that when Kate was big enough finally to hold it, she'd let her hold it but only for a little bit so's she wouldn't get it dirty, then back in the box and up in the closet it would go til the next Christmas. And by then when Kate could finally understand words and I begged her could I hold it, making sure first there wasn't nobody around to see, she pouted like she done whenever my mother brushed her curls and held onto that doll so tight and wouldn't let me hold it even though I could see she didn't care for Shirley Temple half as much as me.

In that first summer when I knew I was alive, an excitement would grab ahold me out of nowhere and make me sing or

dance in the parlor whether my mother was there or not. I'd get
so I could hardly stand myself—But if my father was there, no
matter I could hardly hold it in, I wouldn't sing or dance and
when he caught me at it he give me a look like he was mad I done
something bad. After supper them nights it was hot we'd sit out
on the steps on the cool marble. Sometimes my father would bring
the two little benches covered with carpet up from the cellar
that Grandpop Lithwack made for Frank and Buster when they
was born and now they was too big for them and Slap, they was
passed down like everything else to me and Danny and we set on
them at the side of the steps, my mother, with Kate in one arm,
fanning herself with a paper fan from Uncle Digby's funeral parlor, sighing over and over, "Mary Mother of God, if only there
was a breeze."

All up and down the block you could see the neighbors setting out on their steps, across the street was Colleen Browne
that was the same age as me and she come over sometimes
when I was setting on our frontsteps and she would stare at me.
She had curls even fatter than Shirley Temple, only hers was
brown like her name, and she had eyebrows that was all one
eyebrow like they was wings and her eyes was as brown as
Willie's bananas. She liked to sing and dance too and would
dance on the payment in front of her mother and father's house,
turning around and around and singing to herself, "Barney
Google with the goo-goo-googly eyes," like I sung for my mother, only I sung it in the parlor and not in the street. I'd watch her
and listen, sitting on my grandfather's little bench and my
mother'd see me watching and say, "Is she yer girlfriend, Mick?"
I'd turn all colors and wouldn't say nothing, *she* was my girlfriend, didn't she know that? But I wouldn't tell her that outloud with my father and brothers around.

One hot night when we was all out on the steps, Colleen

Browne was across on hers, staring at me, and her mother started nudging her with a tease in her eye like my own mother got
when she said is she your girlfriend? Colleen got down off of the
steps, her mother hollering, "You watch out for the cars now!"
She come across the street all by herself and started singing a
song she must've just learnt, she was singing it every other song
that week, "Jeepers Creepers Where'dja Get Them Peepers?" I
knew it too from the radio, and without even thinking I started
singing right along with her. She comes and takes my hands and
lifts me up from the bench and starts dancing me around and
around on the bricks. I got all excited like I felt when I danced
for my mother. Frank and Buster was holding their noses but
Slap was clapping his hands and grinning to beat the band
while my mother was grinning too but going, "Oh, look at 'im
now," and taking a gander up and down the block like she was
hoping nobody was watching, but they was. My father was grinning at first but when he seen the neighbors on either side of us
and Colleen's neighbors standing up on their steps grinning and
gawking, he started fingering his cigarette pocket like he done
whenever he got nervous or had the shakes in the morning. He
quit his grinning and part of me wanted to stop with everybody
looking and what with the look my father was giving, yet the
other part of me wanted to keep on dancing around and around,
singing, "Jeepers Creepers Where'dja Get Them Peepers?" in
spite of my father and in spite of Frank and Buster teasing and
holding their noses.

He grinned again like he was grinning for the neighbors and
not for himself, still grinning but muttering out the side of his
mouth, "In the house now, you," saying it in a way like I knew I
better get in the house. Colleen Browne looked at him all out of
breath from dancing, her cheeks all red like they was smeared
with rouge. My mother looked at him too, annoyed, even

though she ain't too happy about all the neighbors seeing, but seeing his face she said to me in a quieter way, "You better go in now, it's gettin dark."

I dropped Colleen's hands and picked up my bench and went up the steps and into the vestibule while Slap that never heard anything was screeching, "Ain'tcha gonna dance no more? Ain'tcha gonna dance no more?" My mother come in behind me saying, "It's time to get ready for bed anyhow," saying it like she was trying to make up for something. My father come in right after her still picking at his cigarette pocket, looking at me like he had a shame in his eyes. I felt myself shrinking inside and looked at him waiting for him to holler because it must be bad to dance and sing in the street with everybody watching, but my mother said, "They're only kids, Stosh," and he didn't holler even though I could see he was hollering at me in his eyes.

The front windows was all dark by this time and she called out the door for the others to come inside and then she said to me, "Gwan upstairs and get ready for bed," and I went up. For a couple days after that whenever my mother wasn't around Frank and Buster would dance around me, pretending they was holding skirts up, singing, "JEEPERS CREEPERS WHERE'DJA GET THEM PEEPERS?" shrieking it at the top of their lungs, then laughing and laughing like they thought that was the funniest thing.

Henry had yellow hair like Kate's in her picsture, only Henry's stood up worse'n Slap's. He always had crumbs of sleep in his eyes that was as blue as my father's, like looking into the sky, and he always smelled like milk the same way Kate always did even though he was big as me and wasn't a baby anymore.

On the mornings my mother left me out he'd be always setting on the steps of his house a few houses down from ours and he'd stare at me like Colleen Browne stared at me when I went by. I always looked away because I was too shy to look him right in the eye, even though I tried hard to since my mother said not being able to look somebody in the eye was a sign of a sneak and a liar, the same she said as when your ears was too close to your head or your eyes was too close together. I knew I snuck sugar and I knew I lied so I figured I better try to hide it and look somebody in the eye whenever I could and would look and look in the mirror over her dresser to see was my eyes and ears too close together.

Then one morning Henry got off of the steps and started following me, I kept looking back to see if he still was following me and hoping he wasn't. He followed me to the Morris movie to look at the stills of what was playing and the coming attractions, then he followed me to the public school where I always went next to open the door and look in to see if I could see Aunt Nell, and then to Willie's to look at the bananas outside. Then he followed me all the way up to the Lyric at 2nd and Tasker, then back down to the slaughterhouse on Sigel Street and didn't run away when the cattle and pigs started screeching and the blood gushed down the drains but instead he climbed right up the wooden gate to get a better look til one of the butchers come and chased him.

The next day when I passed him on his steps he slid down them one at a time and this time walked along right beside me. "Whatcher name?" I didn't want to tell him, I wanted to tell him it wasn't none of his business, like my mother said to tell people I didn't know, and he wasn't to follow me, but he kept asking me and finally I said, "Mickey Lithwack and I live at 126 Mifflin Street." "What kinda name is that?" he said. I didn't know what to say and said, "It's a name they give you when you don't talk

American," and he looked at me funny and said, "Me name is Henry and I live at 114." I asked him was he named for Henry in the funny papers that didn't have no hair since I knew I was named for Mickey Mouse and he said, "Naw, I was named after me fodder...You gone them places you gone before?" I clammed up, not knowing what to answer him. "Well?" he persisted. "Yes," I said finally, and he said, "C'mon, I know a better place." I didn't want to go but he grabbed my hand and pulled me over Front Street past where my mother's brother Uncle Aloysius and Aunt Veronica lived and where she told me never to go past you might get drowneded then you'll be sorry. I said, "Me mother said never to go past Front Street," but Henry went past Front Street and didn't seem afraid of the river, Henry didn't seem afraid of anything. He said, "Yer ole lady ain't here, is she? She can't see ya, can she? C'mon," and he kept ahold of me and pulled me along whether I wanted to go or not.

It seemed a long way away past houses people didn't live in but worked in Henry said and I wondered if I'd see my father in one of them because I heard my mother say the sugar works was down near the river. I hoped I wouldn't see him because then he'd see me past Front Street and tell my mother even though I never told her he stopped in the saloon when we was supposed to be out taking a walk. Finally we come to the biggest street I ever seen so far, Henry said it was called Delaware Avenue because it was on the Delaware River and it was umpteen times wider'n Mifflin Street and had trolley tracks that Henry said wasn't trolley tracks but was train tracks crisscrossing every which way over the cobblestones and even beside the water and run right into what he told me was called docks and warehouses when he seen me gaping, I ain't never seen houses so big, they was bigger even than Sacred Heart or the public school. Then a sound went off almost made me jump out of my skin, and a roar louder'n anything I ever heard was coming along the track that made me jump back far as I could, it was louder even than the trolley car turning on 2nd Street. I ain't never seen a steam engine for real. I stood with my eyes popping out as one come chugging along all black and grimy with steam hissing out its wheels and out its chimbley and making a terrible racket that shook me teeth up through the cobblestones. I was ready to run but seen Henry wasn't running so I stood far back as I could watching it go past but Henry went right up close and bent down and put his hands on his knees and took a good look at the iron arm shooting back and forth, so close I was afraid he'd get flattened by the wheels like when my brothers put a penny on the trolley track.

When the train went by he waved at me to come on and even though that was the last thing in the world I wanted to do, I took one look around me and I knew I didn't know where I was, so I scampered after him and crossed over all them railroad tracks, me all the while keeping an eye out for any more engines coming. We come to a space between a dock and a warehouse where the river was and I looked and looked, I ain't never seen so much water or none so wide and when I looked down below I was surprised to see it was all scummy and green with greasy bubbles floating on top and empty bottles and a smell like the dead fish in Willie's store. But further out there was a haze over it and a ship was going by moving as slow on the water as the steam engine moved slow coming down Delaware Avenue, and it had real smoke coming out its chimbley, like a house floating on the water. I got even more excited than when I seen the train because I never seen a real ship before neither, excepting in picstures in the *Ledger* or the *Bulletin* or in the newsreel at the Morris. I said to Henry, "Where is the sea?" and he pointed first one way, then he pointed another and I didn't see it nowhere so I thought he must not know where it was.

Far across I couldn't see anything but flat ground with nothing but trees stretching off in the haze in either direction and when I asked Henry where all the houses was he said, "That's Jersey," like that explained all I ever needed to know. When I asked him how did you get there he said he didn't know he never been there. I didn't know it then but I was going to be there sooner'n I knew and it's a good thing I didn't know it right then, it was enough for me just being past Front Street.

Then Henry climbed down on the rotting old pilings and squatted close to the water like he was looking for something, though what he could find there or want to find in a place that smelled of rotten fish I didn't know. I thought he'd fall in and drown like my mother warned me I would if I went there, so I set up on the broke wall of the dock far back from the edge, watching and watching, my heart was dancing in my chest, hoping he'd climb back up. But he found a stick and kept poking around in the water, then he found some stones and started throwing them at the bottles floating out in the river and it looked like he was never going to come back up.

"I think I better go back now," I called out to him, then looked around and realized I didn't know which way to go and would have to wait til Henry was good and ready since he didn't hear what I said, or pretended he didn't. When all of a sudden a man in a workcap like my father's hollered to Henry from the dock to get out of there my heart stopped and I was ready to beat it but Henry only laughed and stuck his tongue out at the man and didn't seem to be bothered and took his own sweet time climbing back up.

As we went back over the railroad tracks I kept saying to myself hurry up, hurry up but didn't say it outloud and kept looking back over my shoulder to see if the man in the workcap was chasing us and thanked Mary Mother of God he wasn't.

On the way home Henry got lost and wouldn't admit he was lost but kept pretending like he knew the way like he pretended he knew which way the sea was. All the streets was different even though all the houses looked the same as ours. I just knew I'd never see my mother or Mifflin Street again and felt like all the blood was draining out of me like the blood run down the drains in the slaughterhouse on Sigel Street, I wished I was there, I would know how to find my own way home from there.

Henry kept saying we turn here, we turn there, but it always turnt out to be the wrong turn and when Henry wasn't looking I blessed myself the way my mother showed me and kept my fingers crossed on both hands like Slap showed me and prayed to the Blessed Mother til after what seemed like hours we finally got back to Mifflin Street, more by accident it looked like than anything else, even though Henry bragged, "See, dint I tell you I knew the way?"

I didn't get in the door til it was nearly lunchtime and I was never so glad to see our door with 126 on it and see my mother, I wanted to hug and kiss her only she might've suspected something was up if I did, so I didn't. Even so, she said, "Where you bin, boy? I looked out the door and you wasn't around."

I said I was up watching the trolley cars turn, trying to look her in the eye so she wouldn't know I was a sneak and a liar but my eyes kept sliding away and even though I seen she seen them sliding away she didn't say nothing. Worse'n that was I couldn't tell her anything I seen, not the locomotive, not the ship, not the Delaware River where you could see across to a place called Jersey or tell her about Henry and being lost because I wasn't supposed to go there in the first place, and I wished I could tell her because I had so many questions to ask her, I was about to bust.

"You just make sure you stay on the block next time," was

all she said and I didn't say nothing, knowing it was a promise I couldn't keep.

I told myself I would't go with Henry anymore and when my mother let me go out in the mornings I went the other way up the block even though it was a longer way, just so's he wouldn't see me. But one time after that he must've caught on and run on ahead because there he was waiting for me at the corner by the trolley stop on 2nd Street.

"C'mon!" he whispered, waving at me, his eyes all bright like my father's eyes when he had a few. I pretended I ain't seen him but he whispered again, only louder this time, "Hey, Lithwack, c'mon!" I couldn't pretend he wasn't there so I stopped and stared at him. He jerked his head towards the alleyway where the gaslight was on even in the daytime, only lower and not as bright, and even though I didn't want to go with him he come and grabbed my hand like he grabbed it when we went past Front Street and he pulled me into the alley with him. "I got something to show you," he whispered, looking like he had a big secret, and pulled a box of matches out of his pocket and started lighting them one at a time, holding them til they almost burnt his fingers then dropping them into the gutter of dirty water that always run down the middle of the cement. He held the box out to me like he was offering me candy but my mother told me never ever to play with matches so I wouldn't light one, if I did maybe the cops might come and arrest us, so I kept an eye out for the two worms in a tomato in case they stopped at the entry to the alley. But Henry didn't seem at all bothered about no cops and stayed there til he lit every single match and with the last one he held up the empty box and set that on fire too, his eyes as bright as the flames in his hand.

I was ready to run, saying my mother was calling me, but before I could open my mouth he dropped what was left of the matchbox in the gutter and asked me if I would take down my pants and show him my hiney. But my mother told me it was a sin to show my hiney to anybody so I told him I couldn't and he said why not? I said me mother said. "Not even if I give you a penny?" he said— I caught my breath because I been dreaming all week what candy I could buy with the penny my Grandmom O'Rourke would give me on Saturday morning and almost said to him show me the penny but finally I heard my mother talking in my ear saying, "Don't you dare show your hiney," and I looked away, saying, "Me mother said." Then he said, "You ain't no fun—and neither's yer ole lady," and he pushed me against the fence and stomped out of the alley.

One time my father come home late in the morning, giving my mother a scare…"Whatsa matter? You ain't laid off, are ya?" she asked him right off the bat when he come in the door. He grinned and said no, the boss sent him on a errand in the boss's car and he had a few minutes before he had to go back to work and stopped by to take us all for a little ride. She said, "Oh, is that all?" She looked so relieved and then said she didn't have no time to go for no ride, she had too much to do, but he could take me and Danny but not Kate because Kate was too little.

I could hardly stand still while she washed me and Danny's face and combed our hair, my father growling, "C'mon, c'mon, I'm only gonna take them around the block, we ain't going to see the Pope." But my mother said she didn't want us going out looking like she never washed our faces or combed our hair.

The car was a shiny green new one I could spell out B-U-I-C-K on the hubcaps. Me and Danny set up front, stood up really, we leaned against the dashboard with our noses pressed against the glass, we was so anxious to see everything. My father was all grins like he was so pleased and proud to be driving a car he kept asking was we liking it and we both kept nodding our heads off, and when we went by Henry's house he was setting out on his steps and I waved to him, I was feeling so important I was riding in a car even though I wasn't sure I should wave to him, him wanting to see me hiney. Henry looked back, surprised, like as if to say what was I doing riding in a car? That only puffed me up even more like I really was important, like the people looked to me riding in the trolley car.

I was hoping we'd see Aunt Nell or somebody else we knew so I could wave again but Henry was the only one I seen that I knew, so I played a game of pretending my father owned the car. I could see just driving it made him all grins like I never seen him grin so much excepting when he was in a good mood when he had a few. He was so nice to me and Danny like he was somebody else, I wished he would be like that all the time and be it without having to have a few, and I felt so sorry when he pulled

up in front of our house again, saying he better get back to work or else he'd get fired. The ride was so quick I wanted the ride to go on and on and him go on being the way he was and have people think it was him owned the car, it made him look so pleased and proud to be behind the wheel, just grinning and grinning and him not even been to Hoolihan's neither.

Henry's mother invited me to his birthday party. My mother was surprised, she said she didn't know I knew Henry and Henry's mother said, "Oh yes, they're best boyfriends."

I didn't want to go but my mother said I should, it would be nice for me to meet other kids. I thought I knew enough kids as it was what with all my brothers and Sonny and Aunt Maggie's Neddy Jr. and Aunt Bridget's Tom, but she said she meant kids other than my brothers and my cousins—I wanted to, but I didn't have the nerve to tell her about Henry and the matches and his wanting to see me hiney, if I did I knew she wouldn't of let me go.

Since she knew I knew how to cross the street all by myself and that I wouldn't get lost, so's I'd look nice for Henry's party, she let me go alone to get a haircut at the Eyetalian barber across from the ragshops on 3rd Street, even though I would rather not. She squeezed fifteen cents in my hand and told me to hold it in my pocket and watched me go up the street.

The barber smelled of onions and cigars and he set me high up on a board he laid across the arms of the barberchair and if I so much as moved a hair, he slapped my head with the handles of his scissors.

Walking home, my head smelled as perfumey as my Aunt Theresa the time she leaned over me when I had the measles.

On the Saturday afternoon of the party she scrubbed me good in the tub and dressed me in a clean shirt and pants and put Slap's jacket on me that I wore to church the first time with my father and that was still way too big for me. She give me a present of hankies from the five'n tenny all wrapped nice that I didn't think Henry'd use, his nose was always running and he just wiped it on his sleeve the way Slap done sometimes and always got hollered at for it but it didn't do no good, Slap kept right on doing it like he kept right on using his left hand no matter how many times the sister wacked his knuckles.

My mother walked me down the street and rung the bell and I was wishing she'd come in with me but she told me to behave meself and not eat like a pig. Then Henry's mother, that had blue eyes and yellow hair just like Henry, let me in, my mother and her grinning at each other and bobbing their heads like they was going to bob them off, my mother thanking her for inviting me, then saying, "Oh look at 'eem now, look at his hair," and she smoothed down my hair even though I bet it didn't need it and she whispered to me, "Remember what I said," and left me there.

I never seen so many kids before jammed in one little parlor, as many as there was in Frank's class at Sacred Heart. I didn't know any of them, excepting for Henry, that when I give him his present and said happy birthday like my mother said to, he ripped it open and seen it was only hankies he made a face and throwed them on the table with the other presents like he was throwing away rags. His mother put a yellow paper hat on my head and give me some soda in a paper cup that wasn't orange like at Hoolihan's but turned out to be cream soda that was my favorite soda of all the sodas I drunk so far. She told me to have fun and I stood there like a dope not knowing what to do or say with all the other kids jumping around me like maniacs hollering and playing. My heart was bumping so hard against my shirt I was sure everybody could see it. I was wishing Colleen Browne at least was there but she wasn't and because she wasn't, there wasn't nobody else I knew excepting, as I said, for Henry that was running everywhere at once because it was his party and he wanted everybody to know it, I wondered if his mother knew about him playing with matches and wanting to see my hiney would she of give him a birthday party in the first place.

When I seen my chance I backed out into the hallway and looking towards the kitchen seen it was all clear and quiet out there and headed back that way. There was an old man sitting alone there bent over by the coal stove with the whitest hair I ever seen, whiter even than Grandmom's, and just as wrinkled as she was. I stood in the doorway watching him, ready to run if he hollered, but when he seen me he looked up and said, "Havin a good time?" I nodded even if it was a lie, and seeing he wasn't going to chase me I stepped into the kitchen and stood by the stove with him, drinking my soda. He asked me my name and where I lived and I told him, then he didn't say nothing and I was so nervous I didn't know what to do, so I asked him where the sea was. I was sorry I asked, he just looked at me like I was coocoo. Then to make up for it I started talking, saying anything that come into me head because I was so nervous I figured if I was talking to him I was doing something and wouldn't have to go back to the party. I kept talking even though the old man started dozing off the way Danny did when I was telling Slap and him a story at night in bed but I didn't care and kept on talking until Henry's mother come out to get the ice cream out of the icebox and the birthday cake out of the breadbox. She looked at me surprised and said, "Why, here you are, I was wonderin where you was, whatch'a doin out here, ain'tcha havin a good time?" I nodded I was because I was scared she'd holler if I wasn't. She said, "Well, you go back inside now, we're gonna eat now." At that, the old man jerked his head up awake and he give me a look like he ain't never seen me before. I went back into the parlor where somebody that looked like one of Henry's aunts grabbed ahold of me and stuck a blindfold on me and spun me around til I got so dizzy I almost fell over while everybody laughed and laughed. She told me to go pin the tail on the donkey which I couldn't do, not knowing where the wall was let alone the donkey and what with everything spinning around and around. What I done was I stuck the tail any old place just to get the thing over with and when the aunt took off the blindfold everybody was hooting and hollering because where I stuck it didn't even get nowhere near the donkey.

After that, we all set down at the dining room table for ice cream and cake. Trying to be polite, I tried to talk over all the screaming and gabbing to the boy on one side of me but he was too busy gobbling down all the ice cream and cake he could get his hands on and the only thing he said to me was was I going

to eat all mine? Then right in the middle of it he went and
threwed up all over the floor and Henry's mother and the aunt
run for mops and rags while the other kids all made awful faces
and held their noses and jumped away from the table, it smelled
so bad I couldn't even finish my ice cream and cake.

When I got home my mother said did you have a nice time?
and I said I did, I said it only because I knew she wanted me to
have a nice time. She asked me if Henry liked the hankies and I
lied again and said yes even though he threwed them on the
table like the ragmen on 3rd Street threwed rags on their rag
heaps and wiped his nose on his sleeve like them and like Slap
did too, but I didn't tell her none of that.

When I set down to supper I couldn't eat anything I was so
full of ice cream and cake and still smelling the throwup of the
boy next to me, and when I crossed myself and said my prayers
that night I prayed to Jesus I'd never get invited to another
birthday party ever again, even if they did serve cream soda.

The next Saturday we come home from Grandmom's and
the ragshops with our pennies, Sonny come back home with us
so's he could eat lunch with us before we all went to the matinee at the Morris. My brothers was all excited Sonny was there
to eat and my mother said they better run around Willie's for a
half a pound of baloney and a loaf of Parkway's, but before that
they all went down to the cellar, me and Danny trailing along
behind, so's they could practice their boxing. My father was
down there fixing something at his workbench in the corner
where he was always fixing something and when they come
down he asked them how many pennies they got altogether
from the ragmen. Buster and Sonny both yelled how much in
real loud voices like they was bragging and my father got a tease
in his eye and said, "You got so much money, how 'bout you

loanin me a nickel so's I can go get me a beer at Hoolihan's?" They all punched their bellies and laughed like that was the funniest.

When they got tired of watching him fixing what he was fixing they all started playing they was Joe Palooka in the funnies and started boxing with one another, then when they got tired of that they started tearing around the cellar playing they had guns and pretending they was cops'n robbers while me and Danny stood against the coal bin watching because whenever they played games they always said me and Danny was too little to play. So Danny climbed on the rocking horse Aunt Bridget give us when our cousin Tom got too big for it and he kept rocking and rocking til he got the same look in his eyes he had when he rolled on his belly in the bed at night and after he rocked umpteen times when I told him it was my turn he didn't hear me or pretended he didn't and when I told him again it was my turn, he said, "Jist one more time." I said you already had enough time and my father heard me and said, "You let Danny alone, you, yer gittin too big for that rockin horse anyhow, you let Danny ride it," saying it like he always done because he always took Danny's side. When I asked my mother why he done that she said, "Because yer older," but I thought it was because I wanted the Shirley Temple doll and I danced and sung with Colleen Browne in the street that night and he got a shame in his eyes looking at me.

The next minute my mother was hollering down the stairs, "Dint I tell you birds to go around Willie's for a half a pound of baloney and a loaf of Parkway's?" All of them, excepting Slap that ain't heard her, stopped their shooting at one another and put on a long puss, "Aw, geezoo, jist when we was havin fun." "...And your father needs a new pair of socks for church tomorrow. Frank, you run up and do that at Fischer's and, Buster, you run around to Willie's for the baloney." "...Somethin navy blue and nuthin too niggery," my father warned Frank. Frank and Buster said, "C'mon, Sonny," and Slap was going, "Ain'tcha gonna play no more? Ain'tcha gonna play no more?" and when Danny seen they was all going up the steps he hopped off of the rocking horse to follow them, saying, "Now it's yer turn," but by this time I didn't care if I rocked or not and I went up the stairs too.

Upstairs when they got the money from my mother to go on their errands, she said, "Remember, size eleven, Frank, and you all don't need to go, Sonny, you stay here or they'll never git back." Frank and Buster started their whining again, going, "Aw, geezoo, Ma," like they couldn't go nowheres without Sonny but my mother said, "That's enough out of you two, you better hit the road if you know what's good for you." They went out muttering geezoo and my mother said, "Upstairs with the rest of you blaggards and wash them filthy hands before you eat, what was you doin, cleanin up the gutters?" Sonny ups and says, "We was huggin nigger girls, Aunt Nor." She said, "I wouldn't be surprised, a blaggard like you," but I could see she was grinning in her eyes.

Me and Slap and Danny all followed Sonny up the stairs to the terlet where first he had to pee, then Slap had to pee with him. Slap got to giggling, the two of them was standing at the bowl and was peeing to see how high up they could pee without getting any on the floor, then Danny was giggling, watching them, he had to pee too and he went and stood on tiptoe at the bowl so's they was all peeing and seeing how high up they could pee while I stood up at the zink and washed my hands like my mother said to, I could see in the bottom of the mirror it was Sonny could pee the highest because he was the oldest.

He caught my eye in the mirror and he was saying to me in a whisper even though the door was shut, "Show us yer dunkey." I didn't know what he meant, show us your dunkey, until he pointed between his legs. Slap was grinning foolish and Danny was just looking and Sonny pointed to himself again and said, "See, this is yer dunkey, dumbie," then Slap screeched, "Heehaw! Heehaw!" grinning and grinning, and Sonny quick put a finger to his lips and cocked his head towards the door like a warning, so I knew it was bad.

Danny's had a cap on it that neither Slap's nor Sonny's had on that I wanted to ask Sonny why that was, but Sonny said, "Show us yer dunkey," and even though I knew it was bad, it wasn't my hiney like Henry wanted to see for a penny, she never said don't show nobody your dunkey, she said never to touch it, like you wasn't to touch yourself, you wasn't to touch your belly-button either or your insides'd fall out.

I could see Sonny was getting impatient, keeping one ear cocked to the terlet door like somebody might be outside, listening . . . "C'mon, c'mon, I betcha ain't got no dunkey." I said yes I do and just to prove it I unbuttoned myself and showed him. He looked and was grinning and Slap was looking and grinning too, and Danny he was grinning. Sonny said, "See, you ain't no girl like me mother said you was," saying it like being a girl was a bad thing, and excepting for Danny's all our dunkeys looked pretty much alike excepting Sonny's looked bigger and I knew what a girl looked like, like Kate when my mother was changing her, she didn't have nothing there at all and I was dying to ask my mother when would it grow in but knew better not to.

Then Slap screeched, so that Sonny had to put his finger to his mouth again, why didn't his have a cap on like Danny's, and Sonny went snip snip like his fingers was scissors and Slap giggled and bent over and showed us his hiney hole. We all stared at it, it was like an eye staring back at us, brown as Willie's banan-as—Our mother must've never told him not to show his hiney or if she did he never heard it, like he never heard a lot of things, she said he could always hear all right though whenever she yelled, "Soup's on!"—Or if she did tell him not to show his hiney he forgot about it like he was always forgetting his tie for school or forgetting not to use the devil's hand—But I would never show mine not even for a penny and I wondered what Sonny meant about the scissors going snip snip and decided I would ask Slap in bed that night if he had any idea why.

"What're you birds doing up there?" my mother was hollering up the stairs, and Sonny hollered back real quick, "Nuttin, Aunt Nor!" but in such a funny way she must've knew we was doing something. "You better git down here—I'm making up the sammidges."

I quick buttoned up my pants and helped Danny button his, you would think the house was on fire the way Sonny was acting, and Slap was going heh? heh? in Sonny's face because he ain't heard my mother. I hurried out of the terlet, afraid she'd come up or that my father'd come sneaking up the stairs the way he sometimes done when Frank and Buster was acting up in bed when they was supposed to be sleeping.

"Tell the rest of them to git down here and eat," she called up to me from the foot of the stairs, "If they wanna go to the movies on time they better shake a leg." I said I would tell them and raced back into the terlet. Sonny was combing his hair in the mirror and he bent down to me and put a finger to his lips again like my father done whenever I been with him and he been drinking, Sonny saying, "No squealin," and I promised no squealin, even though he didn't give me no penny.

Not long after that my father come home in the middle of the day when my mother was ironing and her and me was listening to our stories on the radio. She was so surprised to see him, her mouth opened up, and right away she got a worried look in her eyes like the day he come home with the boss's car to give us a ride.

"You sick? Whatsa matter? Anything the matter?" My father did look sick, his face was whiter'n it looked sometimes in the morning when you knew he had a hangover and you tried to keep quiet and keep out of his way. He give her the high sign, looking at me as much as to say little pitchers got big ears. They went out to the kitchen and I snuck after them and hid under the dining room table to listen. He was talking in a voice so low all I could hear him say was, "They laid me off, Nor'," and when he said it I heard her suck in her breath the same as if he slapped her in the face. Then he raised his voice, saying, "They fired me is what they done." I didn't know what fired was but that made me think of Henry lighting the matches. Then he used another word I ain't never heard before either, "This god-damned depression." I knew the other word was a curseword my mother said you must'nt ever ever say taking God's name in vain, but I didn't know what depression was. I wasn't sure what any of it meant excepting that it must be bad because my mother kept going, "Oh, no! Oh, no!" Through the lace tablecloth hanging down I could see she had a look in her eye like she had a bellyache and I wanted to run to her and throw my arms around her but I better not or else they would know I was listening.

When they come out of the kitchen I scooted out from under the dining room table and run back into the parlor and peeking out seen them standing in the hallway and could see her eyes was red. My father was saying, "Don't worry, Nor', I'll get something, don'tchou worry about that." He slapped his cap on and headed for the front door and her hand went up, she looked like she was about to say something like she was going to warn him, but instead she dropped her hand as he slammed the door. When she turned to come into the parlor she seen me peeping out, our eyes caught each other for a second and it was like she knew I knew and we both knew where he was heading.

"Life Can be Beautiful" with Chee-Chee was still on the radio and I leaned back down against the speaker but I could hardly pay any attention, seeing her turn off the iron and set down in the chair by the window. She made a fist and lay her chin on it and stared out in the street but her eyes wasn't seeing nothing, it was more like she was staring inside of herself thinking about what my father just told her and wasn't listening to "Life Can Be Beautiful" either, that was her favorite program. I was dying to ask her what fired was and what depression was but I seen the look in her eye, and I knew if I asked her she'd know I been listening in when she told me never ever to listen in when I wasn't supposed to.

But she did worry, even though he told her not to. When she went around the house now with the dustmop or the carpet sweeper she hardly sung at all and had a faraway look in her eye like she was busy thinking of other things. If I asked her questions she seemed not to hear or if she did she'd make a face like she didn't want to be bothered. Sometimes for no reason at all right in the middle of her washing or ironing, she'd bundle us all up and take us around to Hoffman Street to sit and talk with Grandmom while Aunt Nell was at work slinging hash at the public school. My grandmother would give her a cup of tea and feed us cookies to keep us quiet and drink her own tea from her big Killarney teacup and say to my mother just what my father said, "Don't worry now, Nora, don'tchou worry something'll turn up." Then she put in, "Pray harder and say your rosary, Nora... It'll be all right." Then she patted her apron pocket and said, touching my mother's arm, "If you need anything you're welcome to what little I got..." and my mother looked away quick, biting her lip.

He'd go out early every morning like he always done, only now he come home earlier too, sometimes in the middle of the afternoon, sometimes even at lunchtime, and when he come in the door I could see my mother stiffen, everytime watching him with a question in her eyes. Eventually when he kept coming home earlier and earlier she stopped asking him anything, she would only look at him and she could see without asking what she had to know, and would turn back to what she was doing with that faraway look, like she was thinking awful hard of other things.

Sometimes now when he come home, even in the middle of the day, he had that bright-eyed look, his face looked less worried and she was quick with him and wouldn't talk to him even though he tried to jolly her out of it, teasing her and tickling her ribs. She'd pull away and go scrub the stairs or do some other cleaning she didn't do that often, like sweeping behind the icebox or lining the bottom of the cupboard shelves with old newspaper. Times like that she would be quick with us too, more so now'n ever before, so that I tried to be quiet when he come home bright-eyed in the middle of the day and tried not to ask her anything or annoy her but would set Danny and Kate on either side of me on the couch in the parlor and pretend to read them stories from the Philadelphia *Evening Bulletin*, that we was getting now the *Ledger* went out of business. I would pretend to read to them stories that I was really making up so's they wouldn't bother her either while she worked off whatever it was going on inside of her at one of them jobs she didn't get the time to do very often.

Sometimes now he brung home heavy bundles on his back of long white mop strings from the mop factory on Delaware

Avenue. After supper when the dishes was done and the older boys finished their homework, we all set around the dining room table under the light from the lamp my mother got from Aunt Jenny for frying in Spry and with a grin like he was embarrassed and yet like he was trying to make a joke out of it at the same time, my father showed us what to do—You had to hold one end of the mop string and pull it tight through your other hand to straighten out all the kinks in it, and he kept a sharp eye on us, making sure we done it just right, the way he done everything, it had to be just so.

Kate just slept in my mother's lap while my mother pulled the mop strings over her head, and Danny's arms was too short to do a really good job, but because my arms was long for my age I set around the table with the rest of them, feeling grown-up and proud, pulling hundreds and hundreds of them mop strings hour after hour til my shoulders begun to ache and the palms of my hands got all burny from so much pulling, all of us pulling and pulling til the bundles was all done. Then my father would tie them all back up and take them away on his back early next morning and get half a buck a bundle for them, and if he was lucky he would bring home another bundle or two and that night we would all set around the dining room table after supper, pulling mop strings again. The mop strings smelled moldy and like they been dipped in some kind of disinfectant like what my mother used in the terlet and that got on your hands and into your skin, so that no matter how hard you washed your hands afterwards, the smell stayed in, the smell stayed in the dining room all the next day, the smell stayed in the whole house finally as my father brung home bundle after bundle, night after night—most nights anyhow.

At first it was like a game but then it got tiresome doing the same thing over and over with your shoulders aching and your hands all burny and when Frank and Buster complained once or twice my mother told them to keep still, what we was doing she said was putting food on the table and we shouldn't complain, I didn't complain because I didn't want to be laughed at for being a baby.

Some nights when it got late and there was still lots of mop strings to pull, my mother'd start singing. I wanted to sing along with her like I done when we was alone during the day but was too bashful in front of the others, knowing Buster'd say something smart. After she sung a few of her favorites, like "Pennies from Heaven" and "Wishing," that Snow White sung and I learnt her to sing, she got my father to sing along with her, songs she said they sung when they was going together before any of us was born. He didn't want to at first, saying, "Gwan witcha," but she teased him and coaxed him and started to sing and finally he joined in in a whispery way and all us kids was grinning like crazy, hearing them sing together because we never heard them do that before, the two of them singing, "Gimme a Little Kiss, Willya, Hon?" and "I Found a Million Dollar Baby in the Five and Ten Cent Store."

Listening, as the two of them was singing away and pulling at the mop strings, for the first time since I knew I was alive I had a feeling of us all being together, even more'n when we set around the parlor listening to the radio, all our hands and arms was pulling together to the beat in the song my mother and father was singing as we all pulled away, all of us busy and listening like we was all the same heartbeat under the golden light of the lamp that made me feel so quiet and happy and safe inside.

Not long after my father started bringing home the bundles from the mop factory, one morning I seen her rooting under the cushions and down the insides of my father's armchair. When I asked her what she was doing she said she was looking for loose change that might've fell out of his pockets. I thought it was a game and started poking my hands down the insides of the couch but all I found was a piece of hard candy from last Christmas that I popped into my mouth despite its being stale, and a tiny toy car with no wheels on it Danny lost a long time back. She rooted down the couch too in case I missed something and when she'd gone through all the chairs twice I asked her how much she found. With a look like I wasn't even there she opened up her hand and showed me two cents that I knew was enough to buy a sherbert ice cream cone down at the corner at Johnson's candy store on Front Street.

Right after that she bundled us up and got out the baby buggy from the hall and put Kate in it and around we went to Hoffman Street where she talked to Grandmom O'Rourke in low whispers I could hardly hear while the tea kettle hissed on the stove. When she was done, Grandmom nodded her head without saying a word and taking her little leather pocketbook out of her apron, she snapped it open and took out some coins and squeezed them into my mother's hand. My mother was biting her lip again and I felt a tightness in my chest as I seen her eyes had a shame in them, my grandmother seen it too and patted her hand and folded my mother's fingers over the money, just the way she done when she give us our pennies on Saturday morning.

She darned all our stockings now, so much so they was getting all lumpy in the heels, and the boys went to school with patches in the knees of their knickers that the two oldest didn't like but Slap didn't care, he always had the most holes in his knickers anyway. She done other little things she ain't done

before like instead of buying so many boxes of Rinso like Big
Sister used on the radio or Super Suds like Bess used on Hilltop
House, she saved the slivers of soap from the zinks and put
them in a little wire basket with a handle she got at the five'n
tenny and beat in the dish water to make suds. And another
thing was she didn't put meat on the table as much anymore at
supper, she said she didn't have it to cook because she didn't
have the money to buy it at Willie's or the Jew butcher's on 3rd
Street. Frank and Buster complained but my father didn't complain, he told them both to eat what was put in front of them, or
else. So most nights was like Friday when you couldn't eat no
meat, only there wasn't any fish either, only eggs and fried potatoes or Aunt Jemima pancakes or scrapple come from Willie's in
a tin pan with an inch of fat on top she sliced and fried up. I et
corn meal mush now out of my Shirley Temple bowl stead of
Ralston or Post Toasties because Ralston or Post Toasties cost too
much, and she fried up the leftover mush and sloshed Karo syrup
over it, when we had the Karo, and after the umpteenth time of
nothing but mush Buster'd whine, "Whut, mush again?" and my
mother'd say, "You're lucky to have that, you're lucky you ain't
livin in China where there ain't nuthin to eat and bombs fallin
all over, you're lucky you're breathin." But Buster'd only growl
some more, and if my father was there and in a bad mood from
too much beer the night before he might slap Buster in the head
and tell him to shutup and eat what was put in front of him.

We et lots of Campbell's pork'n beans in the big cans
because beans was cheaper, and Frank and Buster'd have farting
contests under the covers at night, Frank sniggering, "Ketch that
one and paint it green." We et corn fritters til they come out our
ears that even she admitted wasn't as good as Grandmom's.
After supper, if he was lucky to get a few bundles to bring home
that day, we set around the dining room table, once Frank and

Buster done the dishes, and we'd all pull the mop strings under the lamplight til it was bedtime, listening to the Lone Ranger and Amos 'n Andy and Charlie McCarthy on the radio that my father turned up loud enough so's we could hear it all the way from the parlor.

Sometimes there wasn't anything in the icebox until my father come home with money from our pulling the mop strings. When he come in the door my mother'd send Frank or Buster to run around Willie's for baloney to fry up or a can of corn to make fritters, not getting anything that cost any more'n that because she said she never knew how long what she had would have to last. Sometimes, though, as a treat for my father, she'd get a pound of cheap hamburger at the Jew butcher's and make gwoompkie like Grandmom Lithwack made, boiling up rice to mix with the meatballs she wrapped in boiled cabbage leaves.

Other times when she took us out walking to see her sisters or to go to Willie's, her pushing the buggy with Kate in it and me and Danny hanging on either side of the handle, we'd see my father setting on the second story window ledge of a house on our street, using his blowtorch to burn away paint in the windows, "Odd jobs," she said he was doing when I asked her what he was doing up there, "And not too many of them around with everybody so hardup and times so hard," she sighed. Another time we passed by we would see him staining the wood or running a metal comb down it, "To look like a grain, don't it look real?" she said when I asked her what was he doing combing the wood like it was hair.

If he seen us he would wave but most times he didn't see us, he was so busy doing what he was doing, and if he waved she would wave back but if he didn't see us she kept right on going because she said she was scared to death he might fall out of the window if she distracted him, then where would we be? But he never did fall out of a window, he wasn't ascared of heights like she was, when she set out on the ledge to wash the upstairs bedroom windows I could see how glad she was to get back inside, and I was glad too, I'd kept all my fingers crossed and shut my eyes and said a prayer to the Blessed Mother the whole time she was setting out there. She was afraid of a lot of things, she was afraid of falling in the river off of ferryboats and was afraid of gas explosions in the gas mains in the street that he never was afraid of, he would just give her a look and laugh at her whenever she told one of Aunt Maggie's stories she read in the Philadelphia *Daily News* about cars rolling off of ferryboats and whole famblies drowned and houses blowed up in gas explosions.

But that wasn't very often we seen him setting in windows with his blowtorch, my mother said it was because with people so hardup they couldn't afford to keep their houses looking nice anymore.

So sometimes if he found junk he'd take it around to the ragmen on 3rd Street, and he collected all the old newspapers— the *Bulletin* and Sunday funnies—collecting them both in our house and out in the street on trash day, the way we done in the garbage cans and in the public schoolyard on Saturdays so's we could get enough money to go to the matinee, Frank and Buster grumbling to theirselves our father's scrounging was cutting into their collecting so's they had to scrounge twice as hard. But with them it was mainly like a game but with him I watched him from the parlor window as he'd go up and down the street early in the morning on trash days like he had a stiff neck and looking like he hoped none of the neighbors was looking out their front windows to see him taking things from their garbage cans. He'd sell all that he could find for the little extra money it brung in so's to put food on the table, as my mother said.

Even though she said things was so bad one good thing was he didn't come home anymore as bright-eyed as many times as he used to but sometimes he would and she'd say it was like he was taking the food out of our mouths, just like Willie would say when we brung in the empties for deposit on Saturdays. And my father'd try to tickle her ribs and jolly her out of it but she'd say, "Gwan, git outa here, you're drunk," and be mad at him more times'n she wasn't for spending money over Hoolihan's bar instead of over Willie's grocery counter.

Now there was two tiny wrinkles like somebody pinching her between the eyes most of the time that I never seen there before, and it was a rare day when she sung as much around the house doing her work like she used to. Some-times I'd see her setting with her rosary in her hand by the parlor window, her lips moving as she stared out into the street like it wasn't the street she was staring at.

Early some mornings even though it wasn't a Saturday night she would scrub me and Danny harder'n usual in the bathtub and put clean clothes on us, then she would wash Kate extra good and wet her finger and make her sausage curls all around, then she put on Kate's best dress that Kate got her picsture took in, and after she checked us over umpteen times and decided we was ready she would wheel Kate in the buggy and tell me and Danny to take ahold either side of the handle and off we'd go to a place she called "the free clinic," that was a long walk up past Broad Street, farther even than the five'n tenny, farther'n ever me and Henry ever went.

Sometimes Slap come along and them mornings she told him he didn't have to go to school til in the afternoon, he was going with us to the free clinic, he'd jump up and down and screech so loud he was so happy. Buster'd mutter Slap was lucky being so deaf, he got to go to the free clinic and didn't have to go to school, and my mother give him a dirty look and said, "That's enough out of you, boy." But Buster went on muttering anyhow and you could see in his eyes it was only the green-eyed monster, as my mother called it. She'd throw Slap in the tub and big as he was she made sure to scour his ears extra special herself and that always made him hop around and kick up the water and screech his lungs out, singing a different tune now. And if Slap come along she let him push the carriage, but not across the street or up and down the curb, she always done that herself.

The free clinic was like a storefront, like Willie's grocery store, and it was always so crowded with so many other mothers and their kids there wasn't anyplace to set down sometimes. Some of the mothers had shawls wrapped around their heads and some of the kids had shawls wrapped around them up to their eyes and was all red like they was hot and was coughing their heads off and had little bags pinned to their chests that when I asked my mother on the way home the first time what they was she said they was little bags of garlic to keep away the germs. I asked her how come we didn't have them pinned on us and if they kept away the germs how come the little kids was sick? She said it was old-fashioned, it was from the old country, "like in yer father's mother's day, now quit askin so many questions."

There was a lady in a white cap and a white dress give me the shivers just to look at her, she was like the white light so long ago. And when she talked to the mothers wrapped in shawls she sounded like she had ice in her mouth, she sounded like she was mad all the time and always had a frown on her face, specially when she would say to the mothers, "Water and a cake of Ivory soap don't cost that much." When she went near their kids it was like she didn't want to get too near to them and kept lifting her head and sniffing the air like she was smelling something bad.

That first time we went the first thing I seen the minute we got in the door, like they was magnets pulling my peepers there like they was my father's horseshoe magnet down in the cellar, was books with colored picstures on them that they had on the little table you could reach up to near the chairs where you waited. We had to wait a long time and I just couldn't take my eyes off of them books, I looked at them and looked at them, then whispered to my mother could I go pick one up. She whispered back no at first but then she must've seen my face, she said, "Well, go ahead but you be careful and see you don't tear any of the pages or that nurse'll holler." That was a funny thing to say because when I snuck over to look at them books the pages already was all ripped and falling apart and had fingerprints smudged all over them.

The first book I picked up I spelled P-E-T-E-R R-A-B-B-I-T and it was the first book I read. I ain't seen anything like it since we didn't have any books in our house with colored picstures in them, all we had was my brothers' schoolbooks that didn't have no colored picstures, all they had was picstures from long ago that always looked like it was a rainy day in each and every one, and all we had was the funnies in the *Bulletin* that was a whole lot better, Toonerville Trolley and Little Orphan Annie and Mickey Mouse, that I was named after. But none of them was like Peter Rabbit that didn't have no balloons coming out of his mouth but had real words printed underneath, just like in the *Bulletin*, that I could spell out and read, just like I could spell out and read the balloons in the funnies—most of them anyhow— without asking my mother.

I read that book right through twice, I couldn't get enough of it, then I read it through again while the doctor in the long white coat come and looked first at Kate, thumping her chest then listening to it through a long nozzle I couldn't say the name of even after my mother said it for me twice. Then the nurse laid Kate in a scale and weighed her just like she was a chicken in the Jew butcher shop. Then if Slap was with us the doctor looked next inside of Slap's ears with a little flashlight. He talked louder and louder to him, asking did Slap hear him yet until Slap, grinning foolish, finally nodded his head he heard him, but by that time the doctor was yelling so loud like we had to yell to Slap at home everybody was staring at him. I could see my mother was wishing everybody wasn't staring like it was a bad thing Slap couldn't hear good as everybody else, she looked like she wanted to hide him under her coat and holler at all them others to mind their own business, all at the same time.

I didn't even know the lady all in white my mother called the nurse was standing there, holding herself back like she'd fall over backwards, I was so wrapped up in Peter Rabbit. My mother had to nudge me, going, "Oh, look at 'eem now, he's in another world." I didn't want to go and had to tear myself away when she come, she made me think of the white things that floated over me in the place that was all white before my mother took me out of it. My mother was still going, "Oh, look at 'eem, gwan with the nice nurse, she ain't—she isn't gonna hurt you," like she was ashamed in front of the nurse for me wanting to read Peter Rabbit. But the nurse, that was sniffing around us like she was sniffing for something, I thought she was going to say to my mother like she said to some of the other mothers, "Water and a cake of Ivory soap don't cost that much," but she didn't say it because I knew we used nothing but Ivory soap at home to wash in just like Our Gal Sunday on the radio washed in, but instead she told me I could finish looking at the book when I come back from seeing the doctor.

She stood me on the scale and first she measured me and she wrote that down. I was dying to ask her how high I was but she had such a froze look on her face I didn't dare open my mouth. Then she tried to weigh me and had to keep shifting the metal weight down and down, shaking her head and giving my mother a dirty look, I thought she was going to say, like Aunt Nell and her other sisters when they used to tease her, "Ain't you feedin him?" I seen my mother look away from the nurse with a look in her eyes the same as she had when Grandmom squeezed the money in her hand.

Then the doctor come that smelled of cigarettes like my father, and thumped me and listened to my chest and looked in me and Danny's eyes and ears and down our throats with his little flashlight, and the nurse wrote it all down. I was glad when he let us go but then he went and told my mother I was too skinny, he talked to her like he was mad at her and she talked to him like she talked to the priest, bowing her head and not saying ain't. He give her a paper with things wrote on it for me to eat and she promised him she'd feed me them but I knew she couldn't feed me them because it was hard times and no money coming in, what with my father laid off from the sugarworks, that was something the doctor didn't know, and I was so worried all I could think of was he might send me back to that other place he must've come from in his long white coat and where they kept you because you was too skinny and sick.

Then he went and stuck a needle in my arm and I didn't cry like Danny and Kate cried, like most of them kids cried when they got stuck, because I didn't want to be no baby. Soon's he let me go, I made a beeline back to the Peter Rabbit book, I couldn't get enough of it, I felt myself pulled to it just as if it was the electric socket up on our upstairs landing or the sugar bowl up in the cupboard. And when my mother was getting Kate all bundled up to go I whispered could I take the book home with me but she whispered no in no uncertain terms and told me to put it right back where I found it.

In the alleyway we was, though how or why...I know, it was after supper when my mother sent me around Aunt Nell's with a note because it was still lighty out, I could spell out the note on my way and it said could Aunt Nell mind me and Danny and Kate on Saturday while my mother went to Doctor Smuckler, and I got a scare in my belly, spelling it out, worried was she sick. I was so nervous, as I walked I started picking more'n usual at the scab where the doctor at the free clinic stuck the needle in my arm, it been itching me something terrible.

When I got there I give Aunt Nell the note and she scribbled an answer at the bottom and give it back, then handed me a cookie. Sonny was there and she said, "Walk Mickey home, it's gettin dark outside." Sonny grinned, "Let the boogieman kidnap him." Aunt Nell snapped, "I'll boogieman you," and went to punch him but he ducked out of the way.

On 2nd Street we met them, Colleen Browne from across the street and my cousin Patsy that was Aunt Molly's youngest girl. Her and Colleen was best girlfriends and was walking along and singing a song together with their arms around each other, they was singing, "Oh, Johnny, Oh, Johnny, How You Can Love," that I knew the words to from on the radio.

As we went by Sonny yanked Colleen's curls and she smacked him and called him fresh but you could see she was grinning in her eyes and wasn't mad. He grabbed her curls again and said, "I gotta present for ya." She said, "Where is it?" and he said, "Ya gotta come up the alley to see it." She said, "Fresh," and smacked him again, and it was like he wasn't even trying to get away from her like he tried to get away from Aunt Nell punching him. My cousin Patsy giggled and said to him, "I'm gonna tell Aunt Nell on you," and he said, "You tell her I'll tell Aunt Molly you been up the alleyway before." Patsy turned every color in the rainbow and give him a shove, saying, "Oh, you!"

I was squirming, knowing I was supposed to get home with Aunt Nell's answer to my mother folded in my pocket, but Colleen Browne turned to me and says, real nervy, "You wanna gimme a bite of your cookie?" with a look in her eyes like she was asking me something else. Then she falls into Patsy's shoulder, the two of them cackling like maniacs so that now it was my turn to feel my cheeks turn red as ketchup.

"C'mon, c'mon," Sonny went on, all impatient, "I wanna show ya me present," and Colleen said, all important, "Patsy's walkin me home on her way to Willie's for a quart of Supplee's before it gets dark." Sonny said, "C'mon, c'mon, it ain't too dark yet, I'll walk Patsy home." Patsy ups and says, "I don't need you to walk me anywheres," but then Colleen looked at Patsy and Patsy started giggling again and Colleen said to her, "I will if you will." Patsy shrugged but looked sideways at me saying out the corner of her mouth, "Li'l potatoes got big eyes," and Sonny leaned down to me and whispered, "You know how to keep your lip zipped, don'tcha, Mick?" I nodded I did even though I didn't know what I was to keep it zipped about, so that's how come we all went up the alley even though it was getting dark and my mother told me to come direct home, I tried to tell Sonny that but he only grinned and put his hand on my head, saying, "Keep yer pants on, I'll walk ya home in a minute."

It was in the alleyway near where the trolleycar turned and after Sonny looked both ways, like he was seeing if anybody was coming, we went up it and stood under one of the gaslamps that was lit all day but not as bright and wasn't as bright yet because it was still a little lighty outside. Sonny was saying,

"Show them yer dunkey." I knew I showed it that one time when me and Slap and Danny and him was up in our terlet but I didn't think I should show it again, specially in front of girls. But he said, "I'll show me dunkey and you show yours," and he unbuttoned his pants and showed his. My cousin Patsy and Colleen Browne bent down close to get a good look, then my cousin Patsy said, "Gwan, Mick, it's yer turn now," and even though I didn't want to I was afraid they would make me do it if I didn't, so even though I knew it was bad showing your dunkey on the outside in the alley I undone my pants and all the while I done it the tips of my ears was burning.

The three of them leaned down and looked. Sonny already seen it but he was looking again anyway, then my cousin Patsy lifted up her dress and pulled down her panties but just like Kate she didn't have no dunkey even though she was one whole year older'n me. Then Colleen Browne done the same, yanking up her dress and pulling down her panties and hers wasn't growed in yet either, I wondered how old a girl had to be, I wondered if Shirley Temple's was growed in yet, her dresses was so short all the way up to her hiney, you would see it easy if it was growed in but I ain't seen it yet.

All of a sudden a window flew up and I almost jumped out of my skin when a lady in a dustcap just like Aunt Nell's yelled down from a window at the back of a house, "Whadda you kids up to? Shame on you, I'm gonna tell yer mothers!"

Me and Sonny flipped our dunkeys away and quick buttoned ourselves up and my cousin Patsy and Colleen Browne dropped their dresses and we all went running out of that alley so fast our shoes was pounding on the cement like they was horses hooves. We didn't stop til we got to Mifflin Street and Sonny, all red-faced and grinning, kept looking back over his shoulder and Patsy and Colleen was leaning up against the bricks to catch their breath. Then Sonny bent down to me and put a finger to his mouth just like he done in the terlet that time, and he whispered just like then, "No squealin now." I shook my head I wouldn't but more'n anything I wanted to ask him if that lady seen us would tell my mother like she said she would, but he said, "C'mon, I'll walk you home now."

From the way my cousin Patsy and Colleen Browne was giggling together as they walked away with their arms around each other, I could see Sonny didn't have to tell them no squealing, they didn't look at all worried about the lady in the window. Colleen started singing, "Jeepers Creepers Where'dja Git Them Peepers?" and my cousin Patsy started singing along too, then the two of them bust out laughing and was falling all over each other like something was tickling them so much they just couldn't stand it.

I prayed in my bed that night the lady that seen us wouldn't tell my mother and I promised Our Lady I'd never go in the alley again, not with Henry, not with Sonny, not with nobody, if only she wouldn't. Everyday I kept waiting for that lady in the dustcap to come banging at our door but after a couple days went by and she didn't come, I begun to relax, knowing my prayers was answered.

Aunt Nell'd been minding us while my mother was to the doctor's. Even though she let us look at the lamp that when you turned it on made ocean waves and she even unlocked the piano to let me look at the keys but not touch them, I was so glad, like always, when my mother was back, it was so rare she ever left us, and when she did leave us I couldn't ever hardly wait for her to come home again.

She was back now and she set in Grandmom's parlor with her coat on that was the same brown coat with the belt Aunt

Bridget give her that she had on the night she set in our kitchen before Kate was born. That coat was looking as old and wore out as she looked today and I wondered was we going to have to stay overnight with Grandmom again and hoped more'n anything we wasn't.

Even though it was daytime Grandmom's parlor was dark. It was always dark anyhow because Hoffman Street was narrower'n Mifflin Street and the houses was more bunched together, blocking out the light. But it looked darker'n usual that day. Aunt Nell was setting by my mother but my mother was staring down at the floor like none of us was there and had a look in her eye like she didn't know where she was. I kept wanting to go up to her and look at her but was afraid to, the way she was staring down. Aunt Nell was saying, "We'll take care of the kids, don'tchou worry...You just go in and get it took care of...We'll take care of everything...." Then she shook my mother's shoulder, trying to make a joke, "You can use a vacation, can'tcha, Nor'? Can'tcha, huh?" only my mother didn't laugh and Grandmom that heard her come in and was standing in the doorway in her dustcap, said, "Nell's right, don'tchou worry, Nora, your sisters'll mind the kids while you're gone and we'll all be saying a rosary for you."

Hearing them words my heart turned to ice in my chest, the room seemed like it got even darker...*Where was she going?...What was the matter with her?...*Was she sick and going to have another baby like Kate?...If she was sick did she get sick because I went up the alleyway and showed my dunkey? I kept waiting for her to say what it was but it was like a secret only Aunt Nell and Grandmom already knew and I missed somehow—if she had wrote it in the note I might've known, I might've been able to spell it out and then I would know.

Then she was saying in a voice I could hardly hear, "Of all

the times for it to happen...when there's no money comin in...of all the times...." and Aunt Nell was saying, "What can't be helped can't be helped...Now don'tchou worry, it'll be all right... Mom and me'll make a novena to the Blessed Mother."

I was sent to Aunt Maggie's and Uncle Ned's down on Emily Street and I cried so much worrying where my mother was I was afraid Aunt Maggie would hit me in the head with the coffeepot the way she did Uncle Ned in the morning before he went out to work at the icehouse. He spit out her coffee in the zink, calling it "bilge water," and she got so red in her face she hit him in the head with the percolator and I set there quiet as a mouse, ascared she'd hit me next.

Even though they was nice things in Aunt Maggie's house, nicer'n what we had in ours, because Uncle Ned was working steady my mother said and they only had but Neddy Jr.—They had a new 1937 Zenith radio and a new fat sofa with new fat chairs covered with big round doilies so's the arms and backs wouldn't get dirty, they had a big picsture of birds and roses with a blue mirror frame all around it up on the parlor wall, they had a carpet so thick on the parlor floor your shoes sunk into it, they had a new 1937 Servel gas refrigerator in the kitchen, not an icebox, and the kitchen floor was all black and white tile that Uncle Ned put down himself and it shined like a trolley track, Aunt Maggie kept it so polished in a way my mother could never keep our old wore out linoleum polished with all of us kids tracking in and out, and Aunt Maggie only had but Neddy Jr. tracking in and out—but none of it didn't matter at all to me, I missed our house on Mifflin Street so much I could feel it every minute, I could feel it in every single one of my bones.

I wandered between the parlor and the dining room trying not to cry and upset Aunt Maggie that when she got mad she got all red in the face so that her chins begun to waddle and her hands flew up and she said over and over, "I don't know what to do with him, I just don't know what to do with him."

Every night right after supper Neddy Jr. would set at the kitchen table once the dishes was cleared away, doing his home-work, just like my brothers done at home, while my Uncle Ned would take a powder down into the cellar where I could hear him banging and sawing away at things like my father done some nights down in his workshop in our cellar where he had bottles of beer hid under the boards that me and Danny found one time. Aunt Maggie when she couldn't take any more of my sniffling and my long face would say to me, with her chin shaking, "Gwan down and see whatcher Uncle Ned's doin, gwan down and pester him for a change, I don't know what to do with you."

But much as Aunt Maggie's temper worried me, Uncle Ned's worried me even more. Even though he never hit her back with the coffeepot he looked like he would like to and would like to do worse'n that if he could, so I wouldn't go down, hearing the hammer banging like I seen in his eyes his hammering in the evening was what he might like to do to her for hitting him in the head with the coffeepot in the morning. I pretended I didn't hear her say go down to my Uncle Ned and hid out in the din-ing room where it was dark and nobody could see me, while she set in the parlor reading the rest of the pink edition of the Philadelphia *Daily News* that she sent me around the corner special to the candystore to buy every morning, for the num-bers. These days my mother been playing the numbers more'n more every time she got any extra pennies, "Times is so hard," she said and she would play numbers she dreamt all the time or if she dreamt of chickens or niggers she had numbers for them, but she never won nothing, only Aunt Bridget won that was married to the undertaker and didn't need a nickel of it, she won an awful lot, "Wouldn'tchou know it," Aunt Maggie said, pulling down the corners of her mouth.

"Be sure to get the pink edition," Aunt Maggie told me, "And you can buy yourself a penny candy for goin and then right back here." She wrapped the money in a note real tight that when I opened it outside I seen had numbers she wrote on it and some of the numbers was in a box that she said to make sure I only give to the man behind the counter and nobody else. When I got there I said to him, "There's a penny for candy," and he said, "Well, what do you want?" and I always picked a niggertoe and et it on the way back to Emily Street but it didn't seem the same as the niggertoes from Willie's, it didn't taste half as sweet, it was like nothing tasted the same or was the same since I been staying at Aunt Maggie's.

When I give her the pink edition she would turn right away to the back of the paper that was nothing but numbers and that I never looked at. She would shake her head and click her teeth, muttering to herself because she ain't hit a number she dreamt about and was so sure would come out, even when she put it in a box. At night she would set in one of them big new chairs cracking the pages like my father done reading the *Bulletin*, like they was both always mad at what they was reading.

I had to sleep in a narrow bed with Neddy Jr., the room was so little there couldn't be no big bed like we had. He was as old as Frank and didn't smell like Slap or Danny when I was in the bed with him, he had a funny soapy smell that was different from the Ivory soap we used at home, and when Aunt Maggie sent me in to take a bath I seen the orange soap in the dish and knew it was Lifebuoy because I heard it on the radio and I was glad when she didn't follow me in to wash me like my mother done and see my dunkey and my hiney.

I slept as close to the wall as I could so's I wouldn't be in his way, I kept my arms and legs squeezed in tight like I wasn't there because he never said anything to me the way Slap did in the bed, Slap would ask me to tell a story, and that was something Neddy Jr. never did, I could tell Neddy Jr. didn't want me there because he never said nothing. And when he went to sleep he would lay on his back and breathe through his mouth and would make gurgling noises like he was strangling to death and sometimes his arm would fall across my chest and I was afraid to move it off for fear of waking him up and have him holler at me the way his mother and father hollered at each other.

The second morning I waked up shivering and suddenly realized with a sick drop in my belly that I was wet all through and was hoping it was him done it, I was so afraid he'd really wallop me now if I done it, and what Aunt Maggie would do I didn't even want to think about. But I knew it was me and was so ashamed, I ain't never wet the bed before and here I was in a bed that wasn't mine with a cousin that didn't want me there to begin with, wetting the bed like I was a baby like Kate. I held myself tight and lay there shivering for a long time, watching the window over the alley go from gray to lighter and lighter gray, afraid to get up and go wash myself and not knowing where my clean things was anyway, worried to death what Neddy Jr. would do when he woke up.

When he did wake up he jumped up quick and turned over on his knees and stared down at the mattress. He felt himself between his legs, then he glared over at me like he didn't know who I was or where I come from. I snapped my eyes shut pretending to be asleep and at the same time was bracing myself for the punch I knew was coming. But instead of punching me he jumped out of bed and run out the door. I heard him at the top of the stairs yelling for his mother and pretty soon there was loud voices out in the hall and then there was water running in the bathtub, then Aunt Maggie come flying in the door, her teeth clicking. She pulled back the covers and took a look, then made a face, her lips going thin the same way my mother's done when my father come home bright-eyed.

I flinched against the wall, sure she'd hit me, but all she said in a real annoyed way was, "C'mon, c'mon, git outa that bed and when Neddy's done in the tub you git in," then she started ripping the bed apart like it was me she was wishing she was ripping apart.

I was glad when Neddy Jr. went off to school, but I was still so ashamed I tried to keep out of her way all the rest of that day and hid under the dining room table when I heard her coming and wouldn't answer her when she called, not even when she wanted me to go around the corner for the pink edition of the *Daily News* with the numbers for that day. At lunchtime when she found me under the table she yanked me out and hollered why was I hiding? her false teeth clicking, and I could barely eat the baloney sandwich she made me it was so hard to swallow. I stared down at my plate and wouldn't look at her because she kept staring at me with that miffed look in her eyes like she was wishing I wasn't there the same way Neddy Jr. wished I wasn't in his bed, I bet he was wishing it a hundred times now after what I done.

That night she wouldn't let me have anything to drink after supper and before bedtime she put a rubber sheet under me and said before I got in to go to the toilet again even though I already went, "Just to be sure," she said, and I went and stood over the toilet bowl even though nothing would come out, try as I might.

When I went back in she said, "Did you go?" and I said, "Yes," knowing it was a lie but knowing it would make her feel better when I said I did go even though I didn't.

When Neddy Jr. got in beside me and the light was out he

jerked himself over and away from me far as he could, taking most of the covers with him. But I didn't say nothing and forced myself to keep my eyes open so I wouldn't fall asleep, if I didn't fall asleep then I'd know if I had to go and would sneak out of bed quiet as I could and find my way to the toilet. When he drifted off, Neddy Jr.'s breathing like he was choking helped, but I still tried to think of everything I could to keep me awake. I thought of Slap and Danny and wondered how they was doing at Aunt Molly's and Uncle Jake's and did either of them wet the bed, and wished we was all sleeping together again in our own bed. I thought about Frank and Buster, they was staying at Aunt Nell's sleeping in the bed with Sonny. But I wouldn't think of my mother because if I did it was like when I had a sore throat, I could hardly swallow, I thought instead of Henry and the Delaware river and told myself stories and then when I caught myself drifting off, I tried to scare myself awake thinking of the time me and Henry got lost and when that didn't work no more I made myself think of the scary parts of Gangbusters.

But I kept dropping down and down and kept jerking myself awake, then dropping down and dropping down until I really was standing at the toilet, it was so real, and letting it go felt so wonderful, it was so good to go, like I was in a warm bath, I just went and went, it was so real, like the stories I told, I really believed them, like I really thought I was in the toilet at home, only now I was in our bathtub where the water was so nice and warm and I was waiting for my mother to come wash me.

It was then I woke up with a start and couldn't believe it—I done it again! My heart started racing as I felt all around me, and before I knew it I couldn't swallow no more and I turned to the wall, stuffing the blanket in my mouth so I wouldn't wake Neddy Jr. any sooner than was necessary.

That Sunday morning when Aunt Maggie and Uncle Ned went to mass, Neddy Jr. was left to mind me. He sprawled with a long puss on the couch reading the sports page of the Sunday *Daily News* while I kneeled on the floor as far away from him as possible, trying to look at Mickey Mouse in the funnies, and Maggie and Jiggs that I thought was Aunt Maggie and Uncle Ned, only Maggie hit Jiggs with a rolling pin and not a coffee-pot.

All at once I felt his eyes on me like they was my father's drills down in his toolchest drilling into me and when I looked up I seen he was glaring at me over the top of the newspaper. "Whatcha doin lookin at them funnies upsidedown for, pissant?"

I stared at him, not knowing what he meant, my belly shivering like Jello, then I looked down at the funny page but I couldn't see nothing the matter at first so I stared back up at him, thinking that since we was alone together he might smack me for peeing not once but two times in his bed. His eyes was like drills and I couldn't look at them so I looked down at Mickey Mouse again and seen he really was upsidedown the way I used to look at him when I was littler and still sometimes looked at him and all the other cartoons, it didn't make no difference, rightsideup or upsidedown, what was the difference? It didn't mean nothing, I was hardly looking at Mickey Mouse anyway, I was looking at my mother's face behind my eyes, that was all I could see them days.

All of a sudden there was a knock on the window that made me jump and when Neddy got up to cross the room to see who it was it looked like he went the long way around on purpose just so's he could walk right across the comic page I was looking at. He stooped down quick and swished the paper around, muttering, "What a dumbie piss-the-bed, can't tell rightsideup," and went to the window and looked out. "It's yer old man," he snarled over his shoulder as he unlocked the window. My heart give a jump and I jumped up with it. "I sure hope he's comin to take you home," Neddy growled. He flung up the window, then he says in a whole different voice, real friendly he says, "Hiya, Unca' Stosh, hiya doin? How's Aunt Nor'? Me mom and pop's at church. Whyn'tcha come on in?" I heard my father say something about how he just come from mass at Mount Carmel that was where Aunt Maggie and Uncle Ned went to church and he only stopped by for a minute on his way home to see if I was behaving myself.

I run to the window and leaned out over the sill, not thinking I'd ever be so glad to see him. He stood down on the payment grinning up at me in his navy blue Sunday suit that was all shiny in the seat and shiny in the elbows too because it was the only suit he had, his face was very red and smooth the way it looked when he just shaved it. The first thing I come out with was, "Is me mother home?" He kept on grinning and shaking his head, like he was embarrassed to say it but he said it anyhow, "She'll be home soon...don'tchou worry...In a couple days she'll be home." I lowered my voice so's Neddy Jr. wouldn't hear, "But can't I come home today? Can't I come home with you right now?" I wished Neddy Jr. wasn't standing right there I would've told my father how mean he was and how he didn't want me there and didn't want me to sleep in his bed and how Aunt Maggie hit Uncle Ned in the head almost every morning with the coffeepot like Maggie done to Jiggs with the rolling pin in the funnies, only it wasn't funny and she didn't want me being there neither. But Neddy Jr. was standing right there horning in with, "How 'bout them A's, Unc? How 'bout them Phillies?" and my father was nodding right back at him and talking about baseball players I didn't know because their names wasn't Aunt

Jenny or Big Sister or Our Gal Sunday, if they was I would've known who they was but since they wasn't I didn't care, but Neddy kept blabbing and blabbing about the Phillies and the A's and I couldn't say anything. I couldn't say anything anyhow about if my father would take me to see her and could I sleep under her bed because the knot in my throat got so tight I couldn't open my mouth if I wanted. I was trying hard not to cry in front of my father because I knew he wouldn't like it, like I knew Neddy Jr. didn't either, nor Aunt Maggie, and Neddy Jr. called me a crybaby and a wet-the-bed to his mother when he thought I couldn't hear him.

I could see my father get an impatient look on his face, he must've seen the look on mine, and I could see he didn't want to stand there talking to me because finally he said again not to worry, I'd be home before I knowed it, and reaching into his pocket he brung out a brandnew shiny penny and reached up and handed it to me over the sill, saying, "Now you be a good boy and do like yer Aunt Maggie says," and he says to Neddy Jr., "He been behavin hisself?" and Neddy Jr. turns up his mouth like he's smiling but I can see in his eyes he ain't. My father waved to him, and Neddy Jr. said, "See ya, Unc," and when my father started down the street I leaned as far out the window as I could, watching the back of his dark blue suit that was all shiny in the sun, watching it til he turned the corner at 2nd Street and I couldn't see him no more. I wondered was he heading for the saloon,—no, it was Sunday and he couldn't but he could go there now any other time he wanted and she couldn't say anything because she wasn't home anymore.

Once my father was out of sight, Neddy Jr. pushed me away from the window, saying, "It's gettin cold in here." I pulled my hands back just in the nick of time as he slammed the window shut like he was wishing he was slamming my fingers in it, then he went and flopped on the couch and snatched up the sports page again, putting his feet up on the cushions that I never seen him do when Aunt Maggie was around, she would've killed him putting his feet up on the new couch.

I stood squeezing the shiny new penny in my hand and staring out the window, thinking I might never get to go home, that I might never see her again. I could feel them drills in the back of my head again and knew without looking Neddy Jr. was watching me over the top of the paper.

"Whatcha doin, cryin again, crybaby? Whyn'tcha turn off them waterworks and give us a rest before I beltcha one?" And since we was alone in the house and I was afraid he might really belt me I bit my lip hard as I could and knelt down again to read Mickey Mouse but the page might just as well've been upside-down for all I could see through the blur in my eyes.

When my father finally come to take me home Aunt Maggie had me bundled up and my things thrown in a paperbag so fast my head was spinning. Going up 2nd Street I was walking faster'n him, I couldn't wait to get home and a couple times he had to say, "Whoa there, you, where's the fire?" But when we got to Mifflin Street I tore up the block and up the steps into the house. And there she was, setting in the armchair by the parlor window.

She was skinnier and whiter in her face like she was Snow White again and when I thought she wasn't looking I kept watching her, making sure she was there. She caught me at it and grinned, saying, "Was you a good boy at Aunt Maggie's?" I nodded, blushing, wondering if Aunt Maggie already told her I peed the bed not oncet but twice, but if she did tell her she didn't let on she knew. And I was glad because I didn't even want to think of it and didn't wet the bed at all once I come back home.

She got a tease in her eye and she said, "Did you learn any new songs to sing me while you was gone?" I had to say no and felt bad I ain't learned any new songs for her but couldn't tell her about how I couldn't listen to the radio at Aunt Maggie's, Aunt Maggie never listened to music on their brandnew Zenith like her and me done on our old Scott, Aunt Maggie listened to Gangbusters and anything else that scared you half to death and she never sung around the house like my mother done, I guess between Uncle Ned and me wetting the bed she didn't have much to sing about.

Because when she went away she looked the same as the night Kate showed up, I went looking around the house for the new baby but there wasn't any new baby, Frank said she went to Saint Agnes Hospital at Broad and Mifflin "fer her kidneys." I didn't know what kidneys was and when I asked him what they was he slapped me just over my hiney and said, "Them's yer kidneys, knucklehead."

For a couple of days afterwards I followed her from room to room and would even have gone into the toilet with her if she'd of let me, until one time she said, "Don't worry, I ain't goin nowheres." When she said it I all of a sudden felt so light all over, I started dancing around and around in circles from the parlor to the dining room to the kitchen and back, singing to myself all the while. "Silly," she said, "What's got into you? Whudja think, I wasn't comin back?" and the thought of it was still so hard I didn't dare even look her in the eye.

Now there wasn't no money coming in not only to buy something to eat at Willie's but for coal for the furnace, when it come winter, like a lot of the other kids in the neighborhood that didn't have fathers working, Frank and Buster took an old bushel basket they got from Willie's store down to the railroad tracks on

Delaware Avenue to pick up lumps of coal that fell off of the coal cars. I heard them telling Sonny they would even sometimes sneak up on top of the coal cars to steal it. Sometimes they had to fight off the other kids down there tried to steal their coal. Sometimes coming home I spied them from the parlor windows struggling as they lugged the heavy basket between them up Mifflin Street, their shirts ripped and their noses bleeding from fights they got in, keeping their coal from some of the bigger boys that stole from the coal cars too but was too lazy to pick it and so tried to beat up littler kids that already picked it and tried to steal theirs.

Now not only the knees of Buster's knickers was wore through from his kneeling playing marbles in the street but his clothes was ripped a lot because he got in so many fights after school, usually up in some alley or the alley that run beside the Sacred Heart church where the sisters couldn't see them fight. And excepting for when he was fighting for the coal, my mother threatened him every which way to make him quit his fighting but he wouldn't. He got so good at it, after the first couple bloody noses he got defending their baskets of coal at the railroad yards, he learned himself to box so good he never again come home with a bloody nose, and it was rare after that he ever come home from school with a ripped shirt either, bragging to Frank in bed at night that whoever it was he fought that day, "Never laid a hand on me." "A born boxer," my father'd say, with a pleased grin in his eyes, and my mother was pleased too because Buster wasn't coming home anymore with ripped clothes and bloody noses, she thought that meant he wasn't fighting no more.

He didn't get home til late Christmas eve, keeping us all on pins and needles, all excepting my mother that went about her work with that set look in her eye so that you could tell she was stewing inside. Frank and Buster already brung the boxes up from the cellar with the balls and strings of colored lights in them and the tinfoil star for the top of the tree and the tinsel my father made sure to save every year. They brung up the little cardboard houses and the church with their rooves all covered with sparkly grains that was supposed to be snow but looked like sugar. And ascared Buster might drop them, Frank brung up himself the set of electric trains he won a long time back in a Ralston cereal contest when he sent in so many boxtops and why he liked Ralston in twenty-five words or less.

I kept running to the window to see if he was coming, hoping I'd see him each time, hoping he wouldn't come too late and spoil everything, hoping he wouldn't be too drunk. When he finally did show up, dragging the tree up the front steps and in the front door, I was disappointed it was such a puny looking thing with a couple of its branches busted. I was even more disappointed to see how glassy-eyed he was, knowing that set look in my mother's eye would only harden all the more. And sure enough it did as she peeped in the doorway and she got a look at him as he held the tree up by its top in the middle of the parlor for all of us to see. It was so runty it barely reached to his shoulder.

Buster, acting the clown as always, shouted, "Hey, Pop, who'dja buy the tree from, the Seven Dwarves?" But my father give him a look and said it was awful the prices they was asking for trees this year in spite of the hard times, you think they would be practically giving them away. My mother give a toss of her head and said something about, "From the looks of a certain party he ain't deprived hisself of the price of a few beers." When he heard that, his face dropped for a second and I thought he was going to say something snotty but then he grinned at her, saying when he got the tree in the bucket and put it up on a table it'd almost reach to the ceiling, saying it like he was trying to jolly her. But she didn't say anything more, she shut her lips real tight and turnt on her heel and went back out to the kitchen to finish cooking supper.

Buster couldn't keep his mouth shut and shouts, "Hey, Pop, where're we gonna find a table that high?" My father give him another look, only darker this time, saying, "Awright, you, enough's enough—Gwan, you and Frank go git the scrub bucket from out in the shed and bring in the loose bricks." And Buster, knowing he overstepped himself and he better watch his step, scooted out into the hall with Frank double-quick to do as he was told.

He had to wrassle it around a bit and only had to smack Buster twicet for getting in his way, but when he finally got the tree in the bucket with the bricks to hold it and got it up on the old end table Grandpop Lithwack made so long ago and that he kept in the cellar, and after he strung the electric lights to suit him, he let my older brothers put the balls and other decorations on it whilst he let me and Danny hang some balls on the lowest branches, telling all of us just where to hang each one, Christmas balls and decorations Grandmom and Grandpop Lithwack used to have that was so old and tarnished they hardly had any shine on them anymore. But when it come time to put on the tinsel, he hung that himself, one string at a time, making it all even and exact, like he done everything else, not trusting any of us to do the job just the way he wanted it, even though I knew I could do it since I already pulled the mop strings. But he said a tree didn't look like no tree if the tinsel was throwed on any old way.

I was getting so excited I had to stand up, I was so squirmy, but the others set around watching him while Frank and Buster took turns saying, "You missed a spot there, Pop," and my father kept saying, getting annoyed, "I see it, I see it," and when the tinsel was finally all hung the tree at least looked fatter'n when my father brung it in the door. He grabbed ahold of Danny and lifted him up to put the star on the very top that Buster joked later he didn't have to lift him very high to do it.

Frank set up his trains underneath and soon they was whirring around the track, then my father let Buster turn on the lights and when they went on Slap started jumping and squealing. My father hollered for my mother to come see but she hollered back in a way you could tell she was still miffed at him she had supper to cook, and that night in bed where I couldn't shut my eyes, I heard Buster giggle to Frank, "Pop was lit up more'n the Christmas tree, wasn't he?" Frank said, "More'n three Christmas trees," and the two of them got to giggling.

We all got only one toy apiece because my mother said Kriss Kringle was poor that year. But Buster up in bed Christmas eve said there wasn't no Kriss Kringle, he made Danny cry when he said it and made him cry even more when he said Danny'd be lucky if he got a lump of coal in the morning. But what me and Danny got was a toy truck each, mine a blue and green oil truck with black wooden wheels and his a red firetruck that I'd much rather've had because of the color.

Soon as she got back from early mass, my mother brung Kate's Shirley Temple doll down from her bedroom closet and put it under the tree still in its box a safe way back from Frank's train tracks, and nobody was allowed to touch it, not even Kate that was still not much bigger'n the doll itself. I pretended like I wasn't all that interested but I set and watched it and once or twice when nobody was in the room I run over and knelt down and reached out and touched its hair, which surprised me, the curls was so stiff and dry. Even so, I would've gladly traded in my oil truck for Shirley Temple but knew enough by now not to say anything about that.

Aunt Molly sent around two plain brown boxes of broke candy that couldn't be sold that her two oldest girls that worked at Whitman's Candy up near the Benjamin Franklin bridge got for ten cents a box, one of chocolate, one of hard. My mother set them out on the server in the dining room for company but I kept snitching from one box then the other when nobody was looking.

Out in the kitchen a bottle of Schenley's from my Uncle Digby, that my mother said he must be looking for business, giving a fifth of whiskey to my father, set in the middle of the kitchen table for when my uncles and father's pals come by after church, he'd give them a shot and have one right along with them, which I knew didn't please my mother because he couldn't handle hard liquor, but I could see she was going along with it because it was Christmas. She was standing by the sink cleaning the chicken Aunt Bridget sent up with my cousin Tom for our Christmas dinner which if she ain't sent it we wouldn't have no chicken, what with no money coming in and Willie not putting anything on the eye anymore.

Even though I would've rather been playing with the Shirley Temple, I got down on my hands and knees and making brrr-rummm brrr-rummm noises like I was a motor, pushed my truck from one end of the house to the other, pretending I was making oil deliveries. It was one time while I was making a delivery out in the kitchen Louie from the corner saloon knocked on the kitchen door, so light a tap it was like he was afraid somebody might actually answer it. Most everybody else come in the front door because of the day but only Louie come in through the alley and wouldn't come in the kitchen when my father opened the door even though my mother told him not to be silly and come in out of the cold, but Louie wouldn't come in. So him and my father, that was already looking three sheets to the wind as my mother called it, even though it was only the middle of the morning, had their shots out in the backyard, Louie drinking out of an old jelly glass my mother quick handed my father to give him, the two of them, because it was Christmas, not nipping out of the bottle like they done up the alley that time, their breaths steaming up like clouds in the freezing cold air.

I watched them through the kitchen window and seen my father slap Louie on the back and Louie grinning sheepish behind his thick glasses like he always looked, his eyes squinting up like they was always shut so I wondered how he could see where he was going. His face was purple and the jelly glass was shaking in his hand when my father poured him another shot, his hand shaking from the cold I thought. But my mother said it wasn't from the cold and after Louie left, at a look from her, my father broke the jelly glass in the trashbin like Louie's mouth might be dirty with something not even Super Suds could wash off.

When I drove my oil truck back into the parlor to make another stop at the front door, I slipped my hand in the box of broke chocolates up on the server on the way and popped one in my mouth. Then when I seen nobody was in the parlor for the minute, I quick parked the truck by the front door and went over and leaned beneath the tree to reach out and touch Shirley Temple's face again. Just then the vestibule door slammed open and I jumped back like the doll'd all of a sudden become a redhot burner on the stove as big Uncle Jake, all red in the face like he just swallowed a couple of tablespoons of horsereddish, come in from the entry hall without seeing me at all and shoving the door shut headed right out for the kitchen, shouting as he went, "Where's everybody? Where's the man with the whiskey bottle?"

in a voice that shook my insides as much as I could feel his feet
shaking the floor.

In a second it hit me but I remembered too late I'd parked
my truck behind the door and I run over quick and knelt down
to look at it. The blue paint was all scratched on the side where
the door hit it, that was bad enough, but I didn't think there was
anything else wrong with it til I picked it up and one of the back
wheels fell off, split in two from the door slamming it against the
survase.

Seeing it, I felt my belly drop down into my shoes—I ain't
been playing with the truck hardly at all and here it was busted
already when Uncle Jake banged open the door, I could've busted
out crying, seeing it.

I carried the truck with the broke wheel out to the kitchen
and going to my father, tugged at his pants. But he was busy getting the horsereddish out of the icebox like he always done
whenever Uncle Jake come by. He unscrewed the lid for him
while Uncle Jake set up to the kitchen table and took the table-
spoon my mother got from the cupboard drawer for him. My
brothers was all hanging on their elbows around the table with
big grins on their faces like they couldn't wait. The kitchen was
so hot now and beginning to fill up with the smell of the chick-
en roasting. Uncle Jake dug the spoon into the jar and opening
his mouth so wide his false teeth slid out—Slap watching him so
hard his mouth was gaping open right along with Uncle Jake's—
Uncle Jake swallowed three tablespoons of horsereddish one
right after the other like he always done without shedding one
single, solitary tear.

My mother made an awful face with every spoonful, and my
brothers gawked like they always did, gawked even more today
as Uncle Jake washed down the horsereddish with the shot my
father poured for him. My mother started laughing and calling

him crazy as she leaned down and opened the oven door to baste the chicken. At the smell of it my guts begun squirming.

Uncle Jake offered her the bottle of horsereddish and the spoon and she went, "Git outa here," and slammed the oven door shut. Then he offered it to my brothers and they all turned away laughing with their hands over their mouths like they thought he was crazy too.

I tugged at my father's pants again and he looked down all bright-eyed, saying impatient, "Whaddaya want? Whaddaya want?" I held up the truck and broke wheel and tried to tell him what'd happened but I was afraid to say Uncle Jake done it and I got all tongue-tied and kept tripping over my words. He kept saying, "Wha? Wha? Whudja do, break it already? Not now, not now... I'll fix it fer ya later." Uncle Jake yelled, "Here, gimme it, I'll fix it!" He had a devilish look and he reached out for the truck with one of his hands that was bigger'n the chicken roasting in the oven, and my mother laughed and stepped in between us, saying, "Oh no you don't." She reached in one of the cupboard drawers and pulled out a roll of brown paper tape you seal packages with and she ripped off a piece and give it to me, saying, "Here, Mick, wet this and stick it on for now."

I took the paper tape and went into the parlor and wet the tape with my tongue and holding the two halves of the wheel on the axel stuck it on and let it dry. But when I tried to shove the truck over the carpet even a little the paper tape fell off and the wheel split in two again.

When I went back out in the kitchen carrying the truck Uncle Jake was gobbling more horsereddish and chasing it down with shots of whiskey, his face even redder, his forehead all covered with sweat. My mother was saying, good-natured with him like she wasn't with my father anymore when he was drinking, "Oh boy, Jake, wait'll our Moll sees you come in the door." Uncle

Jake snapped back, "Well, I sure'n hell won't see her!" and he roared with laughter like he'd break every window. Everybody was laughing so hard this time that when I pulled at my father's trouser leg it was like he didn't hear me, he brushed my hand away and kept on laughing and pouring himself and Uncle Jake another shot. Even my mother didn't see me, she was laughing so hard along with my brothers at Uncle Jake that was doing his trick of making his false teeth slide in and out now, he could always make her laugh, the first I seen her laugh so hard in a long time, she ain't had much to laugh about ever since that time my father come home in the middle of the day and they went into the kitchen and he said he was fired from the sugarworks—It was like my Uncle Jake was a couple of shots to her that she never had to drink and that I never seen her drink anyhow, and even though I was blue in my heart my truck was busted I was glad in my eyes to see her laughing so much.

Because it was New Year's eve we was all allowed to stay up, excepting for Kate. And because all the aunts and uncles took turns having the party at their house each year, this year it was at ours, and because my father was out of work everybody chipped in bringing pretzels and potato chips and potato salad and macaroni salad and all kinds of lunch meat for sandwiches, I ain't ever seen so much to eat in our house. And to top it off Uncle Digby had a case of ginger ale delivered that afternoon along with a keg of beer that my father tapped in the kitchen. The other uncles all brung bottles of whiskey in under their coats so's my aunts wouldn't see and set them in the middle of the table in the kitchen that was where the men all set like they always done—keeping close to the booze, Buster said—while my mother and her sisters, as always no matter whose house they was in, set in the parlor, keeping their ears cocked towards the kitchen. Aunt Molly's two oldest girls that worked at Whitman's Candy was setting with them, now they was working, but Grandmom O'Rourke wasn't there, she went to bed too early.

As the night wore on and the keg of beer went down and the bottles emptied, the noise and singing and laughing from the kitchen got louder and louder. My mother and my aunts listening in the parlor clicked their tongues and made disgusted faces, shaking their heads and sighing in a chorus while they et pretzels and sipped their little cheese glasses of ginger ale or a highball or the homemade Jew wine that tasted so sweet that Aunt Nell brung that was a Christmas gift from Willie the grocer, she was such a good customer.

My older brothers raced back and forth between the kitchen and the cellar with our cousins, Sonny and his brothers Aloysius and Stosh that was let out of Girard College for the holidays. But excepting for the littlest ones and the older girls, like Aunt Molly's Patsy and Aunt Patty's twins, the boys stayed mainly in the kitchen where we all could drink as much soda and eat as many pretzels and potato chips as we wanted and nobody said anything because it was New Year's.

I stayed mainly in the parlor, though, keeping out of the way as much as possible, because I liked to hear the stories my aunts would tell about gas leak explosions they read about in the Philadelphia *Daily News* where whole blocks of houses was blowed up in South Philly or Aunt Maggie's favorite story of cars toppling off the front ends of ferryboats and whole famalies drowning or who in the neighborhood had this or that disease and was dying or died of it or the manager of the American Store down on 3rd Street near where Aunt Maggie lived getting shot to death in a holdup. "Ain't it terrible, and him the father of five little ones?" she sighed, her eyes glittering with excitement, and my mother and my aunts all sighed along with her, "Ain't it terrible?" their eyes glittering too, while cocking their heads at the same time out to the kitchen now the laughing was getting louder, all of them sighing and clicking their teeth, Aunt Molly saying she'll stick to her old coalstove, thank you, all of them gas explosions, and Aunt Nell saying she always checks the gas jets on the stove twice before she goes upstairs at night, and the rest of them, including my mother, saying they done the same thing, my mother saying that's why she hates to ride on the ferryboats you never knew if the car you was in would roll over the edge, she said she always says her rosary inside of her pocketbook if she was going on the ferry or over the Benjamin Franklin bridge, and all of them was sighing and going, "Yezz, yezz, ain't it awful?" and stopping again to listen to the laughter of my uncles from the kitchen and all of them making a face and shaking their heads like they was all one head. Then Aunt Bridget that helped Uncle Digby wash the bodies to lay out for the wakes sometimes, she told about the lady died on Mercy Street her head was so crawling with lice they had to cut off all of her hair and put a wig on her before they could lay her out and bury her decent. My mother and all the other aunts all shook their heads and clicked their tongues like they was all one tongue, Aunt Bridget saying, "And the *nits*—you should've seen the nits!" and she clicked her tongue and they all clicked their tongues with her, Aunt Maggie saying how could any woman let herself go like that even if she was dying, and Aunt Nell said some women was just plain dirty like that and didn't care and let themselves go, and they all sighed together, clicking their tongues and shaking their heads. Then Aunt Patty leaned forward in her chair and started whispering about a lady on her block "running around," and when I leaned forward with all the others Aunt Molly that hardly ever come out of her house—even out of her kitchen Aunt Nell said—excepting to go to early mass on Sundays and celebrate New Year's eve and see the mummers parade, she give a cock of her head my way, saying through her teeth, "Li'l pitchers got big ears." My mother glanced over at me and said, "Whyn'tcha gwan out to the kitchen and have some soda and play witcher cousins? Gwan now."

From the sound of her voice I knew enough not to argue with her why all the girls was allowed to stay but why not me and went out of the room even though I was dying to know what running around was, Aunt Patty said it in such a sneaky whisper, so when I got into the dining room where there wasn't any lights on I ducked under the dining room table where everybody'd piled their coats on top and where I'd sometimes hide to play and make up stories and listen when I wasn't supposed to listen. I found out that by stretching myself far as I could towards the parlor and cupping my ears I could hear every single word Aunt Patty was saying, just as when I stretched the other way I could hear every word my father and my uncles was saying out in the kitchen, though I didn't have to put my hands to my ears to hear them, they was yacking so loud now, excepting when one of them told a joke and dropped his voice so low I had to strain all the harder to hear.

Now I could tell time I kept peeking out from under the tablecloth to watch the cuckoo clock up on the dining room wall that used to belong to Grandmom and Grandpop Lithwack that was either up on the roof or up in the Tree of Heaven out in the alley. When the big hand and the little hand got close to the twelve I slid out from under the table and went into the kitchen because I knew the next time the cuckoo sung something important was supposed to happen.

By now, my uncles was all red in the face, even my Uncle Digby that stood by the door in his black suit with the same highball in his hand like he was waiting for somebody to come in, "Or pass out," Uncle Jake teased. I could see my father's face was almost as red as Uncle Jake's as he kept hitting the spout and pouring glasses of beer from the keg all around. The kitchen was so blue with cigarette smoke and Uncle Digby's cigar I could barely see or breathe but I could see Danny falling asleep in Uncle Aloysius' lap at the kitchen table even though he was fighting hard to keep his eyes open—But I wasn't sleepy, I was so excited I could hardly stand it even though I wasn't sure what was going to happen, like maybe the night was going to turn into something important, something I ain't never seen before and didn't want to miss.

Then Uncle Jake ups and says he wished there was a piano there so he could hear Uncle Aloysius play. Uncle Aloysius was the only one Grandmom let touch her piano, he could play anything by ear, and Uncle Jake said he sure wished there was a piano there, and my father and all of my uncles nodded their heads, wishing there was a piano. Then Uncle Jake started singing so loud everybody, excepting Slap, give a jump, he sung "I'll Be Down to Getcha in a Taxi, Honey." Then Uncle Aloysius started singing along with him, then all my other uncles, even my father that looked so bashful and didn't sing as loud as the others, he said he never could sing, but he had enough in him and he joined in. My brothers and my cousins was grinning all goggle-eyed listening to them, and when my father and my uncles was done that song, Uncle Aloysius started them on, "Oh, Them Golden Slippers" and after that, "I'm Lookin Over a Fourleaf Clover" that they sung twice, then Uncle Jake started singing "Me Buddy Me Buddy Yer Buddy Misses You." The others started singing that too and Uncle Jake got a tear in his eye like the horsereddish never give him and after they sung it he had to blow his nose, he blew it so hard Sonny shouted he sounded like a foghorn out in the Delaware River and Uncle Jake grinned sheepish and give him a cuff on the ear.

My father poured more beers all around they all said they was so thirsty from their singing, then a few minutes before the cuckoo was to come out Uncle Jake gives Uncle Ned the high sign and the pair of them snuck out into the backyard with sly grins on their faces. Looking out the window and putting my hands either side my face to see in the dark I seen them take what looked like a shotgun like in the cowboy serial at the Morris from out of the old privy in the yard that was never used anymore excepting as a toolshed by my father, and then seen them hightail it out the back gate and up the alley with it. My father and my other uncles was all hopped up, Frank and Buster and Sonny and his brothers was all excited too like they knew already what was going to happen and was rubbing their hands like they couldn't stand it another minute. My father put his finger to his lips, going, *"Shhhh! Shhhh!"* at them, then they all went out and through the parlor, Uncle Aloysius leaving Danny sleeping in the chair. Aunt Nell give them all a suspicious look and right away yelled, "Now what're you goniffs up to?" And Aunt Molly and Aunt Maggie right away shouted in that piercing way of theirs that was like a nail through your skull, "Where's my Jake?" and "Where's my Ned?" My father said, "They're up seein a man about a horse," which I knew was a lie but he told it without batting an eye.

Right then the cuckoo went off in the dining room and him and my uncles made a rush for the door. They run out in the street, and before my mother or Aunt Nell or Aunt Bridget could stop them, Frank and Buster and my cousins run out too, my mother hollering through the open door, "Stick close to yer father now!" She grabbed ahold of Slap just as he was about to scoot out, she wouldn't let me or Slap go out even though Slap whined and complained, it didn't do him any good.

I run to the front window and pressed my nose against the glass, looking out, I couldn't believe it, Mifflin Street was crowded with more people'n I ever seen out there, they was laughing and shouting and whistles was blowing and horns and firecrackers was going off and there was my Uncle Jake with the shotgun on his shoulder pointing it up at the sky. All of a sudden I seen an explosion of blue light from the muzzle of the gun, the sound of the shot was so loud it echoed between the houses and made me jump, but Slap squeezed in beside me didn't jump like I done when the gun went off. Even so, he was so fired up watching everything his feet was going like he was dancing standing still.

Everybody in the street was clapping their hands and dancing and my mother and my aunts was crowded in the vestibule, clucking their tongues, Aunt Molly shouting, "You get in here, Jake, before you kill somebody!" When he didn't pay her any attention she yelled even louder, "Gwan, getcherself arrested, you old fool, see if I care!" Then farther down the block another shotgun went off and my mother and all of her sisters jumped back in the vestibule. Then Uncle Jake handed Uncle Ned the gun and Aunt Maggie let out a cry and put her hand to her mouth. Uncle Ned wasn't too steady on his pins but he pointed the gun at the sky anyway and pulled the trigger, his shoulder jumped and it spun him around but he stayed on his feet and all my other uncles clapped for him. Then another gun went off a few doors away, and my mother rushed to the door shouting for Frank and Buster to get right in here this minute. Aunt Nell was yelling for Sonny and his brothers and Aunt Bridget for her Tom, and my other aunts was trying to pull them back in, Aunt Molly hollering again for Uncle Jake to come in the house this instant like he was another one of the kids, and over all their screaming you could hear Aunt Maggie screeching the same to Uncle Ned but both of my uncles was laughing so hard and not minding them at all, like Frank and Buster and Sonny and the rest wasn't minding either, like they all of a sudden become deaf as Slap. Then Uncle Jake reloaded the gun and handed it to my father that looked like he never shot a gun before because when he squeezed the trigger the gun knocked him flat on his back on the cobblestones. This time my mother screamed louder'n Aunt Maggie even, and Uncle Jake and Uncle Ned couldn't stop laughing, they pulled my father up, and all my other uncles, excepting for Uncle Digby that was standing back by the wall with his hands folded behind him—"Like he was waitin for customers," Frank giggled to Buster later on in bed—they all slapped my father on the back and was laughing so hard they could hardly stand up, while my father looked embarrassed and tried to grin but his face was white as a bowl of Cream of Wheat, he looked so ascared.

More shotguns was being fired up the block and sireens and horns was blowing even louder. Everybody was shouting "Happy New Year!" and hugging and kissing each other, and Slap screeched, pointing out the window grinning like it just dawned on him, "New year's shooters shootin in the new year, that's what it is!" like he finally seen what it was more'n he ever heard it. Turning to me he says, "Do you know what year it is, Mick? Heh? Heh? Do you? Do you know?" and I said, "Yes, I do know, it's 1938." I knew it because I seen it in the *Bulletin* that day because that was what the sash said the little baby in the picsture on the front page was wearing across his chest and was one of the things I could read in the newspaper without nobody showing me. And Slap said, "What? What?" and I said "1938" again, only louder, so's he'd hear me.

We never went up to Broad Street to see the mummers parade on New Year's day but watched the tail-end of it, when it was the best my father and my uncles all said, as it come down 2nd Street later in the afternoon—or staggered down since most of the mummers was pretty drunk by then. Since most of my aunts lived just off of 2nd Street, like with the New Year's eve parties, each of them took a turn every year leaving their kitchen door open during the parade where anybody in the family could duck up the alley and let themselves in anytime to get warmed up and help themselves to a bowl of vegetable or pepper pot soup from the big pot they kept simmering on the stove. Or they could use the toilet, that was very important for us kids after standing out in the cold on the crowded payment for so long a time. This year it was at Aunt Molly's house that was on Dudley Street but was only across the alley from Aunt Nell's.

My father, maybe to make up for shooting off the shotgun the night before, was on his best behavior—even though, as Buster whispered to Frank before we started out, "The old man's eyes look like two hunks of raw meat, don't they?"

I didn't know where to look next there was so much to see I couldn't see it all and there was so much to hear, the stringbands going by right then and all the stringbands you could hear playing from blocks and blocks away, playing "Oh, Them Golden Slippers" and "I'm Lookin Over a Four-leaf Clover," all the music mixed up together and bouncing back and forth between the houses and sounding so loud in such a narrow street I thought my eardrums would bust.

I thought my eyes would bust too watching the mummers that was all men and big boys wearing rouge and lipstick, "Because it's New Year's," my father said when I asked him why. They had silky straps around their heads and over their shoulders so's they could carry the big round satin floats that was gold as the color of cream and was all decorated with sparkles and bright feathers. Even though the floats looked so heavy they still was able to dance with them, swaying and dipping and turning round and round. Their face powder and their paint was running from the sweat even in the cold as they bobbed and bowed to the music of their stringband that was strutting right behind them in their shiny costumes that was made out of the same satin as the floats and had long capes with high collars that had more bright feathers standing up even higher all around their heads and had little mirrors sewed in the capes that sparkled when they strutted.

Some of them was in blackface but most was painted like they was clowns or like ladies, and the feathers on some was all broke and bedraggled by now, and the hems of their costumes and the floats was stained all black from marching so long up Broad Street, then dragging them in all the dust and dirt and horse droppings as they strutted their way through the streets of South Philly. My cousin Patsy and Colleen Browne was dancing together to the music as best they could, the payment was so crowded, everybody could dance in the street because it was New Year's. I was dying to dance but even though I danced that time with Colleen Browne, there was so many people now and even though he was grinning and grinning like his face would break I wasn't sure if I did my father'd give me that look again.

Stringband after stringband was going by with their banjos and saxophones and xylophones playing loud as they could. "They're playin their best now," my father said, "They're back in the old neighborhood where people know their stringband music, not like up on Broad Street and at city hall with the stuffshirt mayor and the stuffshirt politicians and all the other bluenoses," saying mayor and politicians and bluenoses like he was cursing. They played even better he said now they was on their home

turf and was three sheets to the wind, and my Uncle Bill nodded saying, "Yezz yezz, bein half stewed makes them play all
the better," and the few other uncles that was left and ain't
snuck around to Hoolihan's yet, like the others been doing one
by one all afternoon when their wifes wasn't looking, was nodding their heads, agreeing with my father and Uncle Bill, all the
time keeping an eye open for a chance to sneak off.

There was clowns grabbing ladies squealing off of the pay-
ments and dancing with them over the cobblestones. My father
was grinning and grinning at them and waving to some of his
cronies he spotted in the parade that I remembered from
Hoolihan's. And me, I was squeezing his hand so tight and
keeping close to his leg, staring and staring like my eyes would
pop out of my head, I couldn't see enough of it.

Then all of a sudden one clown dressed in a skirt and a
lady's curly red wig come strutting by with the Quaker City
stringband. He was twirling a parasol and holding the hem of
his skirt up all dainty in his fingers like Aunt Patty and Aunt
Kate was holding up theirs doing the strut. Only the clown was
hiking up his a lot a lot higher and he was grinning at my father
that was grinning back at him and he was dancing in front of us
grinning like his face'd split in two. Then he stands right in
front of my father and gives his hips a shake and winks at my
father and before you knew it he lifts his skirt way way up so's
you could see his pair of panties with lace around the edges that
had a tiny little rag cherry swinging on a string sewed between
his legs.

I gawked and looked away then gawked again, not knowing
what to think, knowing as my mother said, it wasn't nice to
show your underwear on the street, her and her sisters was
always worried was their slips showing and looking behind
them and asking each other was they showing. I looked back over

my shoulder thinking her or one of my aunts or somebody else would holler at him, showing his panties in public. But my aunts that was standing behind us was only clicking their teeth and pulling their mouths down while my father and what was left of my uncles and the other men around us, even some of the ladies that looked like they had a snootful like some of the men, was opening their mouths wide and laughing and laughing like it was the funniest thing they ever seen.

But my mother, that'd been holding Kate up in her arms so's she could see everything, lowered her quick to the payment and turned her face away with her hand and looked away herself all flustered. Aunt Patty and Aunt Kate quit their strutting to stop and stare and then them and all of my aunts started shaking their heads at each other and looking the other way like they ain't seen nothing or was pretending they didn't.

Leaning down to me and Danny my mother grabbed both our hands in her one hand, whispering, "C'mon, you two, we're goin back to Aunt Moll's for some hot soup." When Danny started to complain and whine he didn't want no hot soup he wanted to stay and see the clown, my mother give him a shake, whispering again so's nobody else'd hear, "C'mon, c'mon, I wantcha to go to the terlet—I don't wantcha wettin them leggins."

Giving my father a dirty look, she told her sisters she'd be right back and dragged us off while my father, hardly noticing we was going, stood at the curb still grinning as the man dressed up as a lady kept switching his hips at him and twirling his parasol, at the same time he kept hiking his skirts up higher and higher to show him that thing that looked like a dunkey dangling between his legs yet didn't look like a dunkey, I was dying to ask my mother what it was but I knew from the way she went charging up the back alley to Aunt Molly's house with that look in her eye it was better not to ask.

After we gone to the toilet, which I did even though I didn't need to all that bad, and had some of Aunt Molly's pepper pot soup that she left steaming in the big pot on her old-fashioned coal stove, soup that I didn't want but slurped down fast as I could even if it was so hot it was like a fire in my belly because I couldn't wait to get back to the parade so's I wouldn't miss anything. I kept hopping from one foot to the other, my hat and coat and mittens on already, I was so impatient as my mother seemed to be taking her sweet old time bundling up Danny and Kate to go outside again.

By the time we got back to where we was standing my father wasn't there anymore, nor none of my uncles. My mother stood up on her tiptoes to look over the heads of the other people like she was trying to spot where he was, but like she knew it was a waste of time her looking, she knew already where he was. Then Aunt Molly leaned down to me and said, "Ja like me pepperpot soup, Mick?" and I nodded yes even though it was burning a hole in my gut, it wasn't never my favorite soup ever since Buster told me it was made out of a cow's belly.

After the sun went down 2nd Street was getting darker and the gaslamps begun to flicker up brighter and them that didn't, boys shimmied up the poles to pull the little wire loops and make them bright. There was fewer and fewer stringbands strutting by and the clowns by now was staggering and careening over the cobblestones, going up real brazen now and kissing all the girls and smearing their faces on purpose with their bootblack and their makeup, a couple of them tripping and falling over the trolley tracks. "Gettin fresher and fresher," my Aunt Maggie snapped with a toss of her head, "I think it's high time we went home now." But not a one of them made a move to go even though it was getting colder now the sun was gone and I was beginning to feel it in my feet, I could hardly feel my feet at all, but I didn't care I was so glad they didn't make a move to go, it was like they was like me and didn't want to miss a single bit of it.

All of a sudden my Aunt Kate was whispering, "Look! Look!" in a way like she didn't want nobody around us to hear it, and when I stood on my toes and craned my head out into the street in the direction she was staring, I was surprised as anything to see my father sitting up on the driver's seat of a horse and wagon pulling out of McKean Street. I didn't even know he could drive a horse but there he was with the reins in his hands and his hair parted in the middle like one of them hillbillies in the Sunday comics. His pal Louie set on one side of him and Uncle Jake set on the other, the three of them was lurching with the wagon as it bumped over the cobblestones onto 2nd—although as Aunt Molly said later, "It wasn't just the cobblestones they was swaying from."

They come in just at the tail-end of the parade, Uncle Jake shouting and waving to everybody, his face as red as Christmas morning when he swallowed all the horsereddish and whiskey, Louie grinning behind his thick glasses like he didn't want to be there, his face looking even more puffy and purple than when I seen him drinking shots with my father in our backyard. The big brown horse with its blinders on was snorting big clouds of steam from its nose as my father, looking as green with a horse as he was with a shotgun, pulled the reins first one way then the other, so's the horse, that despite how big it was you could still see its ribs sticking out, didn't know which to go and yanked its head up and back and bared its teeth and showed the metal bit along with it that was pulling hard against the corners of its mouth where strings of green spit was hanging down while my father was grinning his goofy grin and swinging back and forth on the seat, his hair hanging in his eyes like a Smoky Mountain Boy in the funnies.

Aunt Maggie was saying between her teeth, "Don't look, Nor', don't look," but my mother'd already looked, her mouth half hanging open, everybody on the sidewalk was looking, they was clapping and laughing and shouting out my father's name and Uncle Jake's name because they knew them, and there was boys running along either side of the wagon hitting the wheels with their hands and trying to climb up the sides and climb up on the tailgate, Frank and Buster and Sonny and his brothers was running right along with them. Uncle Jake was roaring at them and swatting them off with one of his hands that was the size of a ham and Louie was holding on for dear life with both of his hands that was so swoll and purple as his face, as the wagon went on jolting and rocking over the cobblestones, heading to where we was standing.

My aunts was all staring in the direction of the commotion, my Aunt Molly's mouth'd flied open once she seen Uncle Jake on the wagon and ain't shut since, her hand going up against her mouth like she couldn't say anything for once. But Aunt Maggie kept saying through her teeth, "It's him, oh, just look at 'im, wouldn't ya know it, don't look now, Nor', don't look," saying it like it was Uncle Ned up on the wagon instead of my father. Then she stopped saying anything because she seen the look on my mother's face, seen her with her lips shut tight and looking like she didn't know where to put her eyes. Because most everybody standing around us hooting and pointing at my father was neighbors of ours and knew him and knew who my mother was and was watching her as she looked at him making a fool of himself and she knew they was watching. She lowered her head and looked away, her mouth closing even tighter like it was closing against him.

Without looking up she turned around quick with Kate in one arm and grabbing Danny by the other hand, she jerked her head at me to follow and she headed right back up the alley again in the direction of Aunt Molly's house, Aunt Molly marching straight along behind us with a look in her eye like she wondered why she ever left her kitchen, while Danny whined and complained, "I wanna see Pop onna horse...I wanna see..." but my mother didn't want to hear another word and she give his arm such a shake, telling him he seen enough for one day and she said it in a tone that he knew he better shutup right away if he knew what was good for him.

It'd snowed all night and there was hardly any light in our bedroom window, only enough so's that I could see the fat icicles hanging down from the roof, the first thing I seen when the sound of the front doorbell ringing woke me up and I opened my eyes. Nobody ever rung our doorbell at that hour of the morning and I heard my father, cursing to himself, come out of their bedroom and go by in the hall and down the stairs. I leaned as easy as I could over Slap, leaned towards the doorway to hear what I could, keeping an eye on the window to see the icicles and watch the snow falling in the early light like thick gray dust, like when my mother shook the dustmop out our window because it was in the back where nobody could see. I was so excited that it snowed all night and wondered how deep it was, if we had a sled we could go out bellywhopping on it but we didn't have a sled.

From downstairs I heard my father open the vestibule door, then unlock the front door. There was voices, two men's voices, I couldn't make out what they was saying. Then I heard my father say, "Jesus Christ," which my mother said he wasn't supposed to say and I bowed my head like her and Slap told me I should when I heard his name. Then my mother was going by quick in the hall in her barefeet and stopped at the head of the stairs, whispering down, "What's the matter, Stosh?" She had to whisper it twice before my father heard her and said back up to her, "You better not come down," but she went down anyway, moving quick down the stairs.

Even though it was nice and warm under the featherbed with Slap and Danny still sleeping away, along with Frank and Buster that ain't heard anything either over in the other bed, I slid myself out from beneath the covers as quiet as I could, shivering as my barefeet hit the cold floor. I tiptoed out to the top of the stairs and peeped down through the railings. What I seen was my mother and my father standing huddled in the doorway, my mother in her old blue bathrobe bunched around her shoulders had her hand over her mouth, not like she was trying to hide her big teeth this time but like there was something was scaring her she didn't want to look at.

A cop was standing out on the top step looking to one side, and another man, on a step farther down, was looking in the same direction as the cop. Seeing the cop I started shivering more than I was shivering from the cold.

I knew I shouldn't've, but I creeped down the stairs quiet as I could and when I got halfway to the bottom I stopped and listened, trying to hear what they was saying, but what little I heard I didn't understand any of it.

"We found a piece of felt hat," the cop was saying, "...Sterno...He must've strained it through...tried to keep warm by the flame...Look at the soot mark in the corner a' yer steps... Out here all night it looks like."

I was wondering what Sterno was when I started shivering and shaking even more from the cold blowing in the open door and hurried down the rest of the steps and across the hall and into the parlor. Pressing my belly against the heat of the radiator under the window, I looked out.

There, curled up at the bottom of the front steps near the mudscraper, only you couldn't see the mudscraper anymore the snow'd buried it, was what looked like a bundle of rags at first. But when I looked closer I seen a purple hand flung out from under the snow that covered it, then a face turned sideways the same color as the hand, the eyes squinted shut like they always looked, a face I didn't know as Louie's at first because he didn't have his glasses on, and the snow besides'd drifted over his face so's you couldn't see it too good. He wouldn't have his glasses on to sleep I knew but I wondered why he was sleeping outside in the snow, and even though she didn't like him in the house, why didn't my father bring him inside, like I wanted to bring the sparrows in out of the rain that time and she laughed and laughed, why didn't he bring Louie inside and give him a shot of whiskey and warm him up?

I craned my head against the cold glass down in the far corner of the window to see where the cop said the steps was burnt, how could they burn if they was made of marble? And where was the felt hat? he should have a hat on it was so cold, my mother always made me wear one when it was this cold even when I didn't want to, but I couldn't see anything. Then the cop and the other man come into the vestibule, shaking the snow off of their feet, I figured they come to arrest Louie because he was drunk and sleeping in the street. Then my mother come into the hall and stood by the parlor door carrying the two bottles of milk with the froze cream sticking out the top, milk the milkman left whenever my mother could pay the bill, standing there with a scared look in her eyes. Spotting me leaning against the window she looked at me at first like she ain't seen me, like she was looking right through me like I was the glass in the window, then she put down the milk on the hall floor and come over and grabbed me by the arm. "You get back to bed," she said, "You get back this minute," and she yanked me over to the stairs, me going, "Why's he asleep outside? Ain'tcha gonna bring him in, Mom? Ain'tcha?" and she said, "You get back upstairs and back in bed and don'tchou dare come down til I call you."

She slapped my hiney and sent me up the stairs. At the top there was Frank and Buster peeping down through the bannister, Frank whispering, "What's goin on?" I said, "Louie's sleepin outside." Buster went, "What? Yer nuts," and Frank said, "Whaddaya mean, sleepin outside? It's zero outside." Then Frank and Buster both looks at each other like I really was nuts like they always said I was and Buster says to Frank with a grin, "Louie's got so much antifreeze in him he's prolly jist sleepin it off." I said, "Mom said not to come down, she said to stay in bed." But they didn't pay no attention to me just like they never paid no attention to me any other time, because Frank snuck halfways down the stairs anyhow and monkey see monkey do Buster followed right along after him.

I crouched down at the top looking over their heads to see better into the vestibule. The cop was standing there writing down on a pad of paper what my father was telling him, then I smelled coffee perking from out in the kitchen and even though the front door was closed I could hear a sireen coming down Mifflin Street. When the cop heard it he slapped his pad shut and stuck his pencil behind his ear and opened the front door and went out with the other man.

I could see it was still snowing because veils of it blowed in before my father was able to get the door shut. Then he craned his neck to see out the panes of glass in the door like I tried to look out the corner of the parlor window. I kept wondering why they left Louie laying out there in the cold and the snow, I knew my mother didn't like him in the house and always told my father to break the jelly glass he drunk out of after he left, but she always asked him in whether it was Christmas or not, even though he never would come in.

He seemed always to be bright-eyed now, when he was home, which wasn't very often. Most times at suppertime she would have to send Frank or Buster up to the corner saloon to tell him to come home and eat and sometimes he did but mostly he didn't. When he did come home, he was usually very quiet, we knew better'n to try to talk to him or bother him. I could see Frank and Buster looking at him out of the corner of their eye, watching him the way I watched my mother when she come home from Saint Agnes hospital that time, watching him like they was afraid he might go off somewheres and never come back. At the supper table or in the parlor afterwards he kept the newspaper up to his face like he was hiding behind it.

My mother went around the house, her lips tight, barely saying anything to us and nothing at all to him, that pinched look above her eyes that was there practically all the time now. Finally, when he kept on not coming home for supper, she stopped sending for him altogether and one night not long after that he didn't come home at all. During the night I could hear her getting out of bed and going down the hall and standing at the top of the stairs, listening a few minutes in the dark before going back into their room again. Once or twice after that, that same night I heard her footsteps padding across the floor of their bedroom like she was going towards the window to look out, then she come out in the hall again and went all the way down the stairs this time, even opened the vestibule door, like she was going to look out the front door window, maybe thinking he might be laying there at the foot of the steps by the mud-scraper like Louie was.

Just as I was drifting off, she come back up and I could sense she was standing in our doorway looking in at us like she sometimes done to check on us before going in to sleep herself. I felt a few drops of water hit my face and knew she was sprinkling holy water in on us that the priest give her the last time he come to bless us and say a prayer over us as her and me and Danny all knelt in the middle of the parlor floor. I couldn't get back to sleep, wondering where he was and when he would come back, if he didn't come back what would she do, what would all of us do then?

Then on top of that there was something called "court." I didn't know what it was when I heard my father telling my mother about it all serious and in a low voice out in the kitchen while I hid under the dining room table. Slap didn't know either when I asked him in bed that night, but Frank and Buster must've known because when they come up I heard Frank whisper to Buster about it, he run a finger across his throat and made a gutter noise so I knew court must be something bad like what public meant.

But from what I could make out that first time I heard my father say it from where I was hiding under the table, it was all about our house Grandmom Lithwack, that was up on the roof or up in the Tree of Heaven out in the alley, owned. She said my father could live in it as long as he wanted but now three of his sisters that I ain't ever remembered—not Aunt Magda, the one scrubbed floors and lived in Richmond where my father said a lot of polaks lived, or Aunt Theresa with the perfume and the pointy black shoes that leaned over me when I had the measles like Shirley Temple's mother in a dream—but the three of his sisters we never seen because Frank told us my father never got along with them, even the oldest one, Aunt Gert, that give us the old Scott radio like Mae West had when Aunt Gert bought herself a brandnew up-to-date Atwater-Kent. I always wondered why it was we never seen them because we always seen my mother's side of the family but not all of my father's side, so now I knew. Because what his three sisters wanted was for my father to move so's they could sell the house and split up the money themselves. And my father didn't want to move, specially now he didn't have no job. He said Aunt Gert wanted us to move because he wasn't able to pay rent to them no more, they said him not paying no rent he didn't deserve no money from the house. And that's why they was going to this place called the court because of it.

The night before my father was to go there I heard Frank whisper to Buster in their bed like he knew all about it, "Pop ain't got a leg to stand on, I betcha." When Buster asked him how come, he said, "'Cause Grandmom Lithwack didn't put it in writin, that's how come, she couldn't even write in polak let alone American—I betcha Aunt Gert wrote it all down herself and told her to sign it when she was so sick she didn't know what she was signin."

I was worried, hearing that, it give me the nerve to whisper across to Frank, "Will they put us out on the street?" like I seen some people with all their belongings out on the payment on Mifflin Street because my mother said they couldn't pay no rent. Frank sneers, "Listen to the big nose, he not only got a big nose he got big ears," and Buster butts in with, "Yeah, they're only gonna kick you out, big ears, they're gonna put you in Girard College with Aloysius and Stosh if they don't stick you in a garbage can first." And at that the two of them started snuffling together under the covers.

My heart started up because I didn't know if he was kidding or not, about Girard College, I mean, where they sent poor boys like Aunt Nell's Aloysius and Stosh didn't have no father. And since we never knew if our father was ever coming home again once he went out the door, I worried if we got put out on the street I might be sent there or sent back to Aunt Maggie's and Uncle Ned's, and thought maybe any place in all of South Philly would be better'n that, even Girard College, though to think it made my heart beat faster and started a lump in my throat.

But despite what Frank said, another time from under the dining room table I heard Aunt Nell tell my mother when they was setting out in the kitchen my father would be sure to lose the house, "You mark my words." She said he drunk too much like his brother Stan, "God rest his soul," and didn't keep his wits about him. But my mother said, my father's three oldest sisters was like their mother, sharp and with a nose for money and they was no way on God's green earth he could get around that. But all Aunt Nell said was, "You mark my words."

I only seen her once, standing in the doorway of our house, that was really her house, as I come down the street with my mother before there was Danny or Kate. She was standing in the front doorway in a long dress buttoned up the front like the priest wore, only it was brown, brown as the picture of her and Grandpop between our beds. Her hair was piled on top of her head just like in the picture, and she looked important-looking, like people riding on trolleys, and quiet, like she was in a dream looking down the street at me and my mother. I didn't know who she was and when I asked my mother she said, "That's yer Grandmom Lithwack."

That was the only time I seen her, and she had a nose like my father, long and thin and sharp, the same kind of nose everybody said I had and Buster did too. She come over in a steerage boat like Greatgrandmom O'Rourke, only she come from a chicken farm in a place my father called Galicia. He said she was so seasick coming over in the bottom of the ship they had to tie her to the mast to keep her from jumping overboard, like my mother's great grandmom tried to jump off of the dock when she seen her first nigger, and that's the way they come into America. And when Grandmom Lithwack got here my father said she kept chickens in their backyard up at 2nd and Tasker to eat them and to sell them just like she done "in the old country," until the cops come around with the Board of Health and said get rid of them chickens, or else. He said she stuck a knife up the beaks of everyone of the chickens and scalded them to loose their feathers, then she plucked them and what she couldn't keep herself she took up and down the alleys, giving every single one of them away to the neighbors, crying the whole time. Then she worked in a laundry after that while Grandpop was working in the sugar refinery where he got my father a job when he grew up, but they wasn't working there anymore with Grandpop up on the roof and my father fired. When she wasn't working in the laundry she made gwoompki and stuffed meat patties and made soup and sold it out her kitchen door, and all during that time she raised Aunt Magda and Aunt Theresa and Uncle Stan that died and another boy died little when he drunk the poison she was cleaning the bedsprings with for bedbugs, and the three other aunts I ain't never seen. She made homemade pear wine in a big crock in her cellar that my father had now down in our cellar and hid his bottles of beer in so's my mother wouldn't see. She scrimped and saved and done without and ended up owning their house up at 2nd and Tasker and our house at 126 Mifflin Street that she said my father could live in as long as he wanted after she died but now he had to go to court we might not live there anymore.

My mother said she died not long after I was born but I seen her that day in her long brown dress and couldn't remember if her face was brown like in her picture over our bed. That was the only time I seen her before she went up to the roof or up to the Tree of Heaven in the alley with Grandpop that come in the steerage boat from Lithuania and that died before I was born, like my Grandpop O'Rourke, so I never seen either one of them excepting Grandpop Lithwack in the other picture. He had a high starched collar and his eyes was as mild as her eyes was sharp, sharp as her nose. My mother always called him "a prince" even though he wasn't no prince, like in Snow White and the Seven Dwarves, he couldn't even write his name or talk in American. But whenever my mother was whispering to Aunt Nell or one of her other sisters about my father's mother, whispering even though my father was at work at the sugar refinery, when he used to work at the sugar refinery, and couldn't hear her at all, she called Grandmom Lithwack "tight with a nickel" and "a sharp one." I thought that was because of her nose and wondered if I would be a sharp one too because of my nose being like hers, I knew Buster was already, he could be sharp with me and sharp with the ragman we sold our old newspapers and junk to Saturdays to go to the matinee.

After she got Sonny off to school, Aunt Nell come around the day of the court with her Sunday hat on with the cherries, and her Sunday dress. She even had on face powder and rouge like Aunt Theresa that I never seen on her before, Aunt Theresa was like in the movies to me but Aunt Nell wasn't ever like that and never had the smell of whiskey on her breath either. She was going to be what my father called a witness.

My father and Uncle Jake both had on their Sunday suits, Uncle Jake, that was going to be a witness too, even had on a new salt and pepper cap he said he bought special at Fischer's that very morning and Aunt Nell razzed him about it looking so new.

Out in the kitchen when Uncle Jake asked my father for a shot before they left, my father give him one from the bottle left over from Christmas. I seen my mother watching while pretending that she ain't as her and Aunt Nell set having a cup of tea at the kitchen table before the time to go, seen her let out her breath when my father finally put the bottle away back under the sink and didn't have a shot himself.

My father and Aunt Nell and Uncle Jake been telling each other what they should say when they got to this place called court. My father looked so jumpy and kept fixing his tie, his fingers was fumbling over the pocket where he kept his Chesterfields, the way they always done when he was fidgety or hungover. And when Uncle Jake downed the shot my father's gullet jumped up and down like he wished it was him swallowing it.

After they went out the door, my mother, that wasn't going to the court, she said she couldn't stand to go and had us kids to mind besides, she set herself in the chair by the window in the parlor and started saying her rosary while I put Danny and Kate on either side of me on the couch and pretended to read them a story from the yesterday's *Evening Bulletin* so she didn't have to worry about keeping an eye on them, she could keep her mind on praying we wouldn't be put out on the street.

When my father come home through the back alley later that day his tie was off and his hair was mussed, he had that bright look in his eyes like he had a few. Danny and Kate was napping on the couch in the parlor and the older boys ain't come home from school yet. Out in the kitchen all he said to my mother while she stirred the pots over the stove and I listened from under the dark of the dining room table was, "Them son-sabitches! It was a lot of hooey, all they said...nuthin but a pack of lies...I'll never talk to them again...never!...never as long as I live." And stooping down under the sink he pulled out the whiskey bottle and poured himself a shot and gulped it down, then poured himself another, right in front of her like he didn't care anymore about her being right there seeing him.

She looked at him with that dark look she always had when he touched whiskey. There was a question in her eyes that it looked like she was about to ask but she turned her attention back to her pots and didn't say anything. But even through the lace of the tablecloth hanging down in front of my face I could see the worrying plain in her eyes.

He slumped down at the kitchen table, his head in his hands, staring down at the oilcloth. She set down across from him to peel the potatoes for supper, not looking at him, her face stiff. He started talking like he was carrying on a talk they already started another time, leaning across to her, saying, "...C'mon, Nor', won'tcha...Won'tcha do it for me?..." his arms laying along the table, his face red and twisted like he was ready to cry. I could just make out the two of them through the table-cloth. I was hardly breathing for fear I'd get caught or miss something, my arms wrapped around my knees to squeeze myself smaller. She kept her eyes down on the knife as it scraped quick over the potato in her hand, the skin curling away into the old chipped washbasin in front of her, that pinch between her eyes, her mouth set.

"If we moved, it'd be better," he went on, stretching over the table, moving his arms closer to her. "Better for the kids...They ain't no jobs here...I looked and looked... You know that... Maybe I can get me somethin down there...and have a little ground to grow things in...and chickens...If you grow things and have chickens you can always eat...like me mother and father...like me mother, in the old country...raisin chickens and growin things..."

Through the cloth, I could see her mouth tremble. My heart started up, seeing it. Move where? She dropped the peeled potato into the pot of water at her elbow. "I got me own mother here," she said, quiet, "I got me sisters... I wouldn't have nuthin down there..."

His arms scrabbled across the oilcloth, closer. "You would have yer old girlfriend Babes Beezley from the old neighborhood...and Sam...You could see yer mother and yer sisters anytime you wanted...You could come up any time...they got buses runnin..." His eyes lit up even brighter. "...Or I can maybe get us a ole car and come over on the ferry, easy...We could grow things, have chickens like me mother, only it'll be legal then... You could come back to visit anytime, Nor'..."

She snorted soft through her nose and looked at him for the first time, the first time she really looked at him in days it seemed like.

"And where would I get the time with all these kids? Where would I get the time to come all the way up on a bus? Where? You tell me that..."

But he broke right in with, "We'll work out somethin... You'll see...the kids'll like it, it'll be healthier for 'em... we'll..." But she held up a hand like she didn't want to hear it, like she didn't want to hear another word, like she heard it all too many times already now, and she went back to peeling another potato.

He shrugged his shoulders and looked away, down at the wore spots in the linoleum, like there wasn't anything else left for him to say, he said them same words to her so many times before. Then after a minute when all you could hear was her scraping at the potato he looked back up at her, his eyes all bloodshot so that they had a beat down look in them, like a dog I seen in the street one time. But there was something shrewd in them too like you'd see them get with her when he wanted something, like the witch's eyes got in the Snow White movie, his adam's apple working up and down like he was all of a sudden so excited. "I'll quit drinkin, Nor'…I'll quit…I swear…"

He waited a second like he was waiting to see how she'd take it, and her hand did fumble with the knife. Seeing it, he pushed on, all eager now, "I swear it…. If you'll only move to Jersey, Nor', I'll quit…"—*the trees far over the river flashed in my mind*— "…I'll take the pledge with Father Gallagher…I'll run up the rectory and take it right today…."

The knife stopped scraping over the new potato in her hand. She looked across at him in a way like she didn't dare look, afraid she might see a trick in his eyes, like she already heard him say this a hundred times before. "I got me mother…" she begun, like she was saying it to herself. He leaned closer, "I'll take the pledge…tonight…." He was saying it real fast, seeing her hold back, "I'll get up to the rectory right after supper…." She turned her head quick, like she wanted to get away from him, away from his arms that kept reaching across the table at her, away from his eyes that was all eager and grinning. "I got me sisters," she whispered, like she was whispering it to herself but softer and weaker'n when she said, "I got me mother…" "Let em have the house," he was saying, like he ain't heard her, half getting out of his chair and moving towards her, "Them sonsabitches, let em have it and ta' hell with them…. I'll quit…I'll take the pledge…I can write a penny postcard to Sam Beezley askin him if he knows of any houses for rent down in Lenape… Babes was yer best girlfriend…You won't be lonely…You'll see." And his eyes brightened even more, his eyes getting bolder the brighter they got. "Maybe ole Sam can even get me something at

the shipyard... And you and Babes... You won't be by yourself...
You and Babes can be girlfriends again like in the old days...and
me and Sam... Oh, Nor', we can make it, I know we can..." and
he stumbled around the table towards her, his arms out, and
when he got to her he done something I never seen him do
before excepting in church, he fell on his knees and then he put
his head in her lap the way one of us done when we was sick.
She stared at the brick wall of the kitchen, biting her lower lip,
her eyes pinching and unpinching, then, letting the potato knife
clatter out of her hand, she put her hand on his head. I heard
sounds coming out of him I never heard come out of him before,
his shoulders was shaking, and her hand was moving through his
hair the way it done with one of us when we was sick and hurting.

Not long after that a man come and hung a yellow metal
sign with big black letters spelled FOR SALE up on the front of
our house between the parlor windows. I felt as much ashamed
as I was ascared, everybody seeing we was going to have to
move because my father went to court and didn't have no job
and none of us knowing where it was we was going excepting it
was a place called Lenape that was across the Delaware River in
Jersey where, from what I could see of it the time me and Henry
went down to the river, there was nothing but trees.

Now my father took the pledge he was all excited about
moving to Jersey. The very next day he bought a penny postcard
and set down at the dining room table and wrote to the man
named Sam Beezley, while me and my brothers stood around
the table and watched him writing out the words as careful as
my mother drawed cats sitting on a fence, like he was afraid of
making a mistake and spoiling it.

He didn't talk about nothing but Sam Beezley for days after he mailed off the postcard and how wonderful it would be when we was living in Jersey growing corn and tomatoes and raising chickens and having our own eggs. When I asked my mother who Sam Beezley was she said my father and him grew up in the same neighborhood up at 2nd and Tasker near the Lyric movie, and that his wife, Babes, been her old girlfriend when she lived up there too, even though Babes didn't go to the same church, didn't even go to church at all, so that Grandmom O'Rourke didn't like my mother running around with her, and my mother frowned when she said it. I asked her if Babes Beezley would go to hell because she wasn't a Catholic and didn't go to church, and my mother laughed and shook her head, saying she didn't know, all she knew was, "Babes Beezley could always chase the blues," and she was grinning in her eyes when she said it.

When I asked her where they lived she said if you went down the river and looked straight across you could see where they lived and that was called Lenape. When she said it her eyes looked like they was in another place like she was seeing it in her head but didn't want to see it and didn't want to think about it. But all I could think of was maybe we was going to live in a town called Lenape and wondered what kind of a place it could be that had a bad word like pee in it. But since it was a bad word I couldn't ask her why that was and she still had that faraway look in her eyes anyhow so I knew she wouldn't've heard me.

Now my father took the pledge I felt easier. He come home nights now even after traipsing the streets all day with his blow-torch and sack of tools on his back looking for houses needed their front windows and doors burnt and scraped and stained. But times was hard, like my mother said, and people didn't have no money to fix their place up and he never found nobody wanted it done. If it wasn't for my mother's sisters, specially Aunt Bridget, some nights there wouldn't've been no food on the table.

Even so, my mother must've felt easier too the way she was singing more around the house, "If You Was The Only Girl in the World" and "Gimme a Little Kiss Will Ya, Huh?", songs she liked to sing. But it wasn't long after that I started running in front of cars.

She let me out on my own because she knew I knew to look both ways before crossing a street and wouldn't get lost because I learned all the streets as quick as I learned the stations on the radio or how to tell time so's I could know when our stories was on and know when to come home. But now when I was far enough away from our house I see a car coming, I don't know where it come from, the idea would grab ahold of me all of a sudden and I'd wait between the cars parked at the curb, then when the car that was coming got close I run out, hoping to get hit.

But all the cars I run in front of had good brakes, and loud horns, as loud as some of the drivers was when they shouted out their windows at me to watch where I was going, did I wanna get killed? I thought maybe I did, I thought maybe it would be better to get killed than to have to move to Jersey. Then I could stay up on the roof or in the Tree of Heaven with Grandmom and Grandpop Lithwack and never have to leave 126 Mifflin Street.

Because my father said there wouldn't be room enough for all of us in the Beezley's car he said the three older ones would have to stay home. Slap didn't like it one bit when he heard it because he been all excited about going and ain't talked about anything else for days ahead of time. I felt sorry for him, the

look on his face when my father told him. But when my father
said they could all go to the movies even though it was a Sunday
and give them the ten cents each plus a nickel for candy out of
his own pocket, Slap stopped his sniffling.

I could tell Frank and Buster was dying to go to Jersey with
us but them two wouldn't've showed it for anything, and you
could see they was looking down their nose at Slap for being
such a baby. But when my father said he'd treat them to the movies, their eyes lit up and they was all fired up about getting to go
to the picture show not only on Saturday but on Sunday too,
which none of us ever did before. And they didn't have to go
scrounge up papers and rags and bottles on the streets or in people's trash cans like we usually done, since it was my father's
treat. For a minute I was jealous I wasn't going with them
because Frank said it was a movie with the Dead End Kids.

My father and Danny set up front with Mr. Beezley that talked so loud like we all had to talk to Slap, I jumped everytime he
opened his mouth. He had curly black hair with streaks of gray
in it and a pointy nose all shiny like his ears from soap, he
smelled of Lifebuoy soap the way my cousin Neddy Jr. did. My
mother and me and Kate and Mrs. Beezley that my mother
called Babes and that had powder splattered all over her face
and had her hair all frizzed like she just crimped it, set in back
with Kate on my mother's lap but Kate would've been able to set
on the seat if Mrs. Beezley wasn't so big.

I kept my nose pressed to the glass, looking at everything, I
couldn't get enough of looking as we drove through parts of the
city, mostly along the waterfront, I ain't never seen before, not
even with Henry. My mother laughed and nudged Mrs. Beezley,
then leaned over to me saying, "Don't wear your eyeballs out." I
seen Mrs. Beezley, her mouth all red with lipstick, grinning at

what she said, her shoulders shaking, and still feeling shy with her and afraid she might be laughing at me, I quick looked back out the window.

The car Mr. Beezley showed up in was one I ain't never seen before but I spelled out L-A-S-A-L-L-E on the dashboard once we was inside it. It had big rusty dents in the fenders and the seats smelled like our back alley smelled sometimes. My father was full of questions, asking Mr. Beezley what year it was and how many cylinders and how many miles he got per gallon, you could see how worked up he was to know everything about that car.

"Lucky fer you it ain't up on the blocks, as usual," Mrs. Beezley snorted from the backseat, lighting up a cigarette which I ain't never seen a lady do before. I looked at my mother to see what she thought but she was acting like it wasn't anything to be surprised about, just to be polite, I figured, because her and her sisters always clicked their tongues about ladies that smoked, including my father's youngest sister, Aunt Theresa, that not only smoked but got her hair out of a peroxide bottle, my aunts all said.

Mr. Beezley, ignoring what his wife said, was going on in his loud way, like he was talking to the whole world, "There's a place for rent next door to the Mahoneys just a little ways through the woods on Lenape Road, not far from us. I picked up the key from the owner on the way down so's you can take a look at it."

Right away my mother wanted to know all about these Mahoneys, was they nice people and did they have any kids? Mr. Beezley, looking with a comic grin through the rearview mirror at Mrs. Beezley, piped up with, "Just a little girl." All of a sudden Mrs. Beezley, hard as it was for her, heaved herself forward and give him a punch on the shoulder, saying, "Oh, *you!*"

My mother looked at the both of them with a funny smile that said she didn't get it, like none of the rest of us did neither.

But my father was all ears to everything Mr. Beezley was saying. I could see he was wild about the trip the way he kept plucking the cigarette pocket of his good Sunday shirt in that nervous way of his. My mother and Mrs. Beezley, setting side by side so I could gape out the window, talked the whole time. Or rather Mrs. Beezley done all the talking, getting "reacquainted" she called it, as she kept saying remember this one, Nor', and remember that one? from when they was girlfriends in the old days in South Philly. I was so afraid of missing something outside of the window, even though I wanted to I scarcely heard a word she said, and when I seen we was coming to a redlight I grabbed ahold of the felt rope hanging across the back of the front seat and when Mr. Beezley put on the brakes I pulled on the rope, making out it was me stopping the car, all the while gawking and gawking.

When we drove up to a dark, gloomy place looked like a big shed, I leaned over the front seat and asked my father in a whisper what it was and when he said, "The ferry," then turned and grinned at me, "Yer gonna git a ride on the ferryboat," my heart almost stopped. I didn't know we was going over on any ferry! I wished for sure now I been able to stay behind and see the Dead End Kids and let Slap come in my place, picsturing clear as a movie how we'd all roll off of the edge of the ferry boat and into the river, just like the story Aunt Maggie read in the Philadelphia *Daily News* and liked to tell so much, that everytime I heard it I couldn't tear my ears away even though it always froze the hair on my head.

Mrs. Beezley wasn't bothered at all and just kept jabbering away as if it wasn't anything she might be drowned the very next minute as the old LaSalle jolted onto the boat behind the other cars. And wouldn't you know the man with the cap and a moneychanger waved us to the other side so we was first in line on that side of the boat!

I stiffened in the seat and stiffened even more, seeing my mother's hand slip into her pocketbook and knew she was holding onto her rosary beads but was pretending like she wasn't, nodding her head to everything Mrs. Beezley was batting the breeze about, but I could see a secret look rolling in her eyes that Mrs. Beezley couldn't see, she was so busy listening to herself.

I grabbed the felt rope in back and pulled on it like I wanted to pull it out of the back of the seat, I was trying so hard to hold the car back as Mr. Beezley, yacking the whole way to my father about the Philadelphia Athaletics, inched the car along to where I thought we was going right over the edge before he stopped it just in the nick of time in front of the skimpy little gate they had stretched across the front of the ferryboat that didn't look like it could hold back a fly let alone a big car like Mr. Beezley's LaSalle. It was only when he put on the emergency brake I let go of the rope.

The man with the moneychanger come around and my father reached across Mr. Beezley and paid him the money through the window even though Mrs. Beezley said he shouldn't've, "*He's* workin," she said jerking her head at Mr. Beezley. I couldn't understand why you had to pay twenty cents to be scared to death you might get drowned, it didn't make no sense to me.

When the ferry whistle went off I just about jumped out of my skin and jumped again when Mr. Beezley in his loud voice that my father said later on come from years of him having to talk so loud over all the noise in the shipyard, he said to my father, "How's about gettin out and givin our legs a stretch?" My father turned back to my mother with a teasing look, knowing how she felt about water, she was always dreaming she was in the water with a big black nigger trying to drown her, and he said did she want to stretch her legs too? But she pulled down the corners of her mouth and stuck out her chin, saying, "Me'n Babes'll just set here and talk, thank you," and when he ast me did I want to go, I found out I couldn't even open my mouth and so just shook my head.

He got out with Danny that was all big-eyed with excitement and too dumb to be ascared and they all walked up to the front of the boat while I shrunk back in the corner of the seat and tried to shut my eyes, wishing I could be like Kate right then and be asleep in my mother's lap and not know anything about going over on the ferry. The whole boat was shaking and shimmying so much I was expecting the car to roll forward any second and then us go crashing through the puny little gate into the river. Seeing my mother fingering her rosaries inside of her pocketbook didn't help any either. I wished I could be like Mrs. Beezley laying back so easy and gabbing and gabbing about the old days in South Philly, I don't think I breathed once til after what seemed like umpteen hours the boat finally bumped against the wharf on the other side and it was such a big bump I grabbed ahold tight of the rope, pulling back and pulling back, positive we was really going to roll for sure this time, and was so glad when my father and Danny and Mr. Beezley got back in and Mr. Beezley started up the engine and drove us off that boat. It wasn't til we was onto dry land I seen my mother slide her hand out of her pocketbook.

As we drove down the main streets of what Mrs. Beezley called Camden, I spelled out Kaighns Avenue and then Broadway on the street signs. Mrs. Beezley all the while was pointing out the window, saying to my mother, "Ya see, you got all the stores they got in Philly, you gotcher Hurley's Department Store, you gotcher five'n tennies, you gotcher movies." My eyes was bugging out reading the lightbulbs twinkling over the marquees, the PRINCESS, the STAR. "You gotcher buses run up this way from Lenape and acrosst the Benjamin Franklin bridge so's you can go visit yer mother and yer sisters anytime you want," talking like my father talked to her, like she was trying to persuade her, and I seen my mother was listening but she still had a big doubt in her eye.

I kept looking for the trees and when I didn't see any I thought maybe it wouldn't be so bad to live in South Jersey, it was almost the same as living in South Philly with as many stores and movies, even the row houses was made of brick the same—Only as we kept driving farther and farther away from Camden there got to be more and more trees and fewer and fewer houses until sometimes you didn't see any houses on the road and none of them even brick at all. Out the window, I caught glimpses now and again of the river that was gray and flat and dirty-looking, like it was on the Philly side, and once or twice I seen a boat. Everytime we passed where you could see the river my father leaned forward in his seat, gaping out the windshield as bug-eyed as me til he was practically leaning up against the dashboard, like he couldn't wait to get to where we was going and was pushing the car along, hunching forward that way more and more, pushing it as much as I was grabbing the rope across the rear seat, trying to hold it back.

When we got there finally I didn't know that that's where we was til Sam Beezley yelled in his loud voice like he thought he must still be at the shipyard, "Good ole Lenape! Back in God's country!" Mrs. Beezley sniggered and said, "Well, I wouldn't go that far," and seeing my mother looking around out either window with an uneasy look in her eyes, like her eyes was mirrors of what I been feeling inside, she caught herself and patting my mother's hand, said, "It ain't that bad, hon. You'll see."

I wasn't so sure, seeing as we drove through streets that was nothing but dust, lots and lots of trees now everywhere I looked, and weeds. There was some houses there after all but they was separated and not connected like the houses on Mifflin Street and they was all made of wood, not brick, and another peculiar thing was most of them was only one-story high. "Bungalows," Mr. Beezley called them, "From the camp meetin days when the bluenoses'd spend their summers here— But the house we're gonna look at's a two-story," and he cocked an eye back at my mother as if he seen on the ferry how scared she was of the river, "Which is a good thing," he said, in a way you knew he was a needler, "In case of floods." I could see my mother's eyes jump when he said it.

Mrs. Beezley leaned over and give Mr. Beezley another thump in the shoulder, saying, "Now don't tease, you!" Then she set back and brushed the ashes from her lap and said to my mother, "Don't you pay any attention to him, Nor'," and pulled her cigarettes out of her big black pocketbook which I seen was Raleighs on the pack when I spelled it out and wasn't Chesterfields like my father smoked. I was wondering what a bluenose was, seeing people in my head with noses blue from the cold like Louie's nose was blue, my father said bluenoses at the mummers parade, was that what it was? I was dying to know but knew it wasn't the time to ask and would ask my mother later.

It wasn't nothing but shacks even if they was called bungalows, and dirt and trees as far as I could see— "The sticks," my aunts all called it when my mother told them we might be moving here, "You're movin to the sticks and you'll be sorry..." and hearing that'd give her even a more worried look than she had before. A shiver went through me, remembering their words.

I started up when I heard Sam Beezley say in his loud way, nodding up ahead, "There she is—on the left there!" I thought my father's head was going to go through the windshield he was so eager to see. Standing up and looking between my father's and Mr. Beezley's heads I seen through the dust kicked up by the car a big gray wood house—"Clabberd," Sam Beezley called it—with a wide porch that run along the front and around the side, with a big tree by the road in front with branches so long and high they was like another roof over the house.

We drove up into a dirt driveway at the side. My father jumped out first and gaped around all bright-eyed like he was one of the sparrows hopping in the gutters in Mifflin Street. He held onto Danny's hand while Danny rubbed his eyes with the other, since Danny went dead to the world once we got off the ferry. My mother got out my side and stood holding onto Kate like she was afraid of dropping her and looked around with that pinched look like she had a headache or a pain somewheres, while Kate's eyes was rolling up in her head just waking up like Danny. Mrs. Beezley took her sweet old time getting out, we had to wait for her and when she got out she switched at the back of her dress and lit herself another Raleigh. I stood glancing around sideways at the house, glancing around sideways at everything, like I didn't have the nerve to look at it straight on. The air seemed to have a funny smell, like the gasworks near the river in South Philly, only it was a different smell, like beets cooking, and the smell seemed to come from somewhere behind the house. The path up to the place was dirt not brick, and instead of marble steps they was made of wood and was sagging and splintery and all wore looking, so I wondered if Mrs. Beezley would make it up them without their crashing through on her.

"You'll have to fix that," Sam Beezley said to my father, pointing to the steps as he went up them and onto the porch and unlocked the front door.

When we went in my mother warned us kids to stick close to her. The first thing I noticed was the parlor had a stale shut-up smell and was bigger'n the parlor we had on Mifflin Street and was shaped funny, like the front porch was. "L-shaped," Mr. Beezley called it. The wallpaper, like all the wallpaper in the house it turned out, had leak stains on it and looked old and crumbly. The dining room was bigger too, with higher ceilings and had windows that our dining room in Philly didn't have, like none of my aunt's houses had neither, so the dining rooms was always dark as night and a good place to hide but here it wasn't so dark. In the kitchen there wasn't no gas stove but something Mr. Beezley called a kerosene stove, that was all rusty and dirty and that I seen my mother glancing at with a leery look that Mrs. Beezley seen too. She give my mother's shoulder a squeeze, saying, "Don'tchou worry, a little cleanser and water and it'll look like new." Then there was a sink that instead of spigots had a pipe with a long handle on it that my father grinned at when he seen it and went right over and started yanking the handle up and down. It made a terrible squealing racket like something being choked to death, my mother looked like she was afraid he busted it and Mrs. Beezley bust out laughing. Mr. Beezley said, "Ya gotta prime it first."

Out back of the kitchen was a shed that was full of cobwebs and had a dusty smell, and that was the first floor. Upstairs was two bedrooms like we had on Mifflin Street, only here they was separated by a hall at the top of the stairs that wasn't as long, and there wasn't any radiators only "registers," Sam Beezley called them, stuck in the floors that you could see down through when you opened them and could hear through too, I bet. There was something called an attic you had to climb up into through the closet ceiling in the front bedroom and I was wondering where the toilet was, not only because I had to go but because I didn't see it where it was supposed to be, upstairs like at home. I hoped it wasn't up in the attic but I was too embarrassed in front of the Beezleys to ask where it was.

When we come downstairs again my father found the door to the cellar between the parlor and the dining room and with us all crowding around he opened it. There was a damp dark smell come up from it like the smell behind the house—not like the dry clean smell of our cellar in Mifflin Street—that made me queasy, "a mildewy smell," my mother said, wrinkling up her nose and stepping back. Since the electric wasn't turned on, my father struck a match and went half way down the steps with Mr. Beezley following while the rest of us stayed looking down after them, my father asking did the furnace work? "So the landlady says," Mr. Beezley said. "Looks damp," I heard my father say, waving the match around. "From the crick," Sam Beezley said, "You'll get water in a heavy rain, from the crick," saying it like it was nothing. Right away my mother called down, "Does that mean rats?" and Sam Beezley, with a mean twinkle in his eye, same as he had when he talked about floods, yelled back over his shoulder, "Only water rats, big as dogs!" My mother went, "Oh, my God!" and Mrs. Beezley shrieked down at him, "Quit yer teasin, you!" She looked like she would've socked him again if he only been close enough. I was wondering what a crick was and added that to the other umpteen questions I had to ask my mother later on.

When we went outside to look around the yard, I was standing almost to my waist in the high weeds—"Is there snakes?" my mother asked, looking around her feet, nervous in her voice the same as when she asked about the rats. "Only rattlers," Sam

Beezley answered and Mrs. Beezley told him to shut up again and for my mother not to pay him any mind, and this time she was close enough to give him a good thump. But I could see my mother was still looking down sharp in the grass anyway and I did too even though I couldn't see nothing for the weeds. The only snakes I ever seen in South Philly was in the serials at the Saturday matinee at the Morris movie.

At first when we was out there in the yard, I seen nothing but trees, their leaves all covered with the yellow dust, and a splintery little shack the same woreout gray as the house, that set way back near the woods. Mr. Beezley called it the privy even though it didn't look like the privy we had in our backyard on Mifflin Street and that we never used excepting as a toolshed. He slapped the privy door with a laugh when he said it, and when he did I heard my mother in a worried voice say, "I don't like the looks a' that." Mrs. Beezley said, as if to encourage her, "Oh, don'tchou worry, you get used to it, even on cold nights." My mother, still with a worried look, said, "I mean for the kids." Mr. Beezley laughed and said in that loud way of his that always made me jump, "It ain't so bad if they don't fall in!" and he cackled real loud like he said something funny. Mrs. Beezley, seeing my mother's face, give him a look and told him to shush, none of their kids ever fell in yet, she said, but he kept on cackling, "When you gotta go you gotta go!" I had to go so bad but I was still too shy to say anything in front of the Beezleys and since I never went in no toilet on the outside before and I sure didn't want to go in this one, I squeezed it back.

Off to one side through a patch of woods you could see shingles of a roof, the only sign of another house around. "The Mahoney's place," Mr. Beezley said, pointing it out, then jerking his thumb in the other direction, "The Snarps live up the other end of the road...Boy oh boy, there's a bunch for you...." He shook his head and I was all ears hoping he would say some more about who these Snarps was but at a sharp look from his wife he left it at that.

It was a pretty good-sized yard, a hundred times bigger'n our fenced in block of cement off of the alley in South Philly. I could see my father looking around and looking around like he was figuring and measuring things. Then the next minute he was down on one knee fingering the dirt, his eyes filled with excitement. Mr. Beezley nudged Mrs. Beezley and said out the corner of his mouth, "That must be the polak in him," and he laughed, then in a louder voice to my father, he said, "The serl's good, don'tchou worry." And sweeping his arm off towards the far back of the yard where the weeds and the trees was growing the thickest and where there was beyond that a lot of dead trees standing like gray skeletons against the sky with birds black as night setting in their branches—a chill run down me just seeing them—Mr. Beezley shouted, like we was all deaf as Slap, "The swamp's back there, so you got good rich serl for growin. Good Jersey dirt—You oughta see me tomatoes, huh, hon? Wait'll you see 'em, Stosh."

It was then I figured that's where that funny smell was coming from, like gas, like the smell of the gasworks down by the river in South Philly, only worser, and mixed with a smell like when my mother cooked beets. And as everybody was looking, my mother standing back a little, that worried look on her face—I could see, like me, she didn't want any part of it but wasn't saying anything—I thought I caught something bright out of the corner of my eye and looking, thought I was seeing things as, through the bushes in the woods where you could see the corner of the Mahoney's house, I thought I seen a head with blond curls just like Shirley Temple peeping out and watching us. But by the time I turned full around to look it was gone.

Then my father took my mother off a little to one side. I could see Mrs. Beezley watching her with an eager look, letting the smoke roll up her nose from her lower lip, her eyes looking like she was wishing my mother'd say yes, we'll take the house, we'll live here in Lenape, both her and Mr. Beezley bending their ear hard as they could in their direction but acting like they wasn't. I could hear my father say, even though his voice was real low, "Whaddaya say, hon?" saying "hon" the way he done when he wanted something out of her. I could see the doubting look on her face and could see she was pulled this way and that in her eyes because of his promise. He said, as if to push her, "Sam tole me on the ferry he looked for us everywheres and they ain't anything else around we can afford. And it's cheaper'n anything we could ever get in Philly, what could we ever get in Philly for ten bucks a month?"

She still looked doubtful, looking around with her hand to her mouth like she was looking at a horror movie, while she held onto Kate by the other hand real tight like Kate might get swallowed up in the high grass if she didn't. And Mrs. Beezley watching her every second, her eyes squinty, like she was afraid she'd say no. Then my father said, like he been saving it for the last, to clinch it, "Sam said he'd do his best to see can he get me somethin at the yard." She sucked in her breath and kept looking around and looking around like her eyes didn't know where to look next. I could see it was no use, and him, seeing it, quieted his voice down even more, saying to her, "Whaddabout it, hon?" After a long minute she turned to him with a wild look like she was trapped in her eyes and didn't know which way to go but all of a sudden she nodded her head anyway and my father bust out in a grin as his shoulders sunk down in relief. Mrs. Beezley was smiling at my mother as she took a last drag on her cigarette and ground it out under her heel in the weeds, and my heart sunk even lower. I felt like I might just as well've been the cigarette butt under her shoe because when my mother nodded yes it was as much as if she just told me I'd have to stay with Aunt Maggie and Uncle Ned for the rest of my life.

The house where the landlady lived was closer into town where the street was tarred and was called Hessian Soldiers Way Mr. Beezley said because it led to the battlefield at the end of it. The house was painted gray too like the house we just left but neat painted with white trim around the windows and lace curtains even in the round window in the attic, the hedge in front trimmed neat too, and I didn't see no privy in the backyard either.

Mr. Beezley went in with my father, my mother watching them go up the walk with an anxious look. I slumped in the corner in the backseat, half listening to Mrs. Beezley go on about the landlady, telling my mother how she was a widow and was called the Widow Scadder, how long she been a widow, and why she was a widow, secretly hoping whoever this Widow Scadder was owned the house she wouldn't rent it to us, or she'd already rented it, knowing I shouldn't hope that, but not able to help hoping it.

I set up quick when my father and Mr. Beezley come back to the car but I slumped right back down again soon's I seen my father was all smiles and heard Mr. Beezley yell out, "Well, that's done!" He told my father to get in behind the wheel, he could drive us back to their place, and you could tell my father was pleased to beat the band, he hardly ever had a chance to drive a car since he left the sugarworks, the only thing he drove since then was the horse and wagon in the mummers parade.

Mrs. Beezley squeezed my mother's hand, saying, "Looks like we're gonna be girlfriends again," and my mother smiled, a little faint smile like when she come back from Saint Agnes hospital that time. But at least she was smiling, the first time she did the whole entire trip.

I set hunched in the corner thinking everything was going too fast too fast and got to feeling bluer and bluer in all this green that was crowding around me like I couldn't hardly breathe.

The Beezleys didn't live too far from the house we looked at, just up Lenape Road and through some woods to another dirt road Mr. Beezley said the bluenoses named Saint Johns Walk years ago when they had their tent meetings near there in the woods and the road was just a dirt path then. Their house was bigger and even more ramshackle'n the one we'd be living in and was surrounded by trees too but was farther away from the swamp. It turned out they had two boys, Brother, that was about Frank's age that had black curly hair like his father, and Sparky that was closer to my age and had hair the color of straw and wore wire rim glasses like a grownup that I never seen a boy wear before. There was a girl named Sister that looked in-between and had a face pretty as Snow White only thinner and not as pale and her hair was longer and instead of being black was the color of the copper Buster always got a good price for at the junkshop on 3rd Street, when we was lucky enough to find any.

When the Beezley kids come running out of the house when they seen the car pull up, a dog Mrs. Beezley called Blackie come barking out at us and jumping all around like he was gone crazy. Me and Danny and Kate shrunk behind our mother, not being used to dogs, even though Mrs. Beezley swore up and down Blackie was too lazy to bite, we kept our distance. The Beezley kids all stood staring at us grinning, Sister wanting to know right away what Kate's name was but Kate hung behind my mother with her finger in her mouth, my mother going, "Oh, look at er now! Ain't she somethin? Say hello to Sister."

They had a privy in the backyard like at the house we just been to, only it was whitewashed on the outside and stead of holes drilled over the door there was a half-moon surrounded by stars cut in it, and the first thing she done, Mrs. Beezley took my mother and Kate out to it and they went inside and I wondered how they'd all fit in there together with the size of Mrs. Beezley and still be able to shut the door, but they done it.

When they come out my father took me and Danny in and the smell inside was something awful, worse'n the toilet at the Morris movie. I was glad I didn't have to do number two because there was nothing but two dark holes the stink was coming out of that if you had to sit you could fall down into just like Mr. Beezley said with no trouble at all. But because there was the two holes me and Danny could pee together and even though the whole place was spider webs up in the corners like in the horror movies and there was no handle to flush and fat green flies buzzing everywhere and my father was standing behind us and I never went in front of him before, I had to go so bad by this time I went with no trouble at all, peeing fast as I could the faster to get out of there, thinking to myself if that was the only toilet we had back at the other house I wouldn't like it at all.

When we was done my father said, "Now you two go on out," and we did because I knew he didn't want us to see him, even though I always wanted to see him but never did so far.

Inside their kitchen, Mrs. Beezley, with Sister giving her a hand, made us ham and swiss cheese sandwiches and potato salad and give us ginger ale like it was New Year's eve or a christening. My mother said she shouldn't've but Mrs. Beezley said, "Aw, gwan, *he's* workin," jerking her head again at Mr. Beezley. Mr. Beezley, saying his gullet was so dry it felt like the Sahara desert, went into their icebox and brung out a quart of Schmidt's beer.

I could see my mother stiffen a little in her chair when he offered my father a glass, but my father waved it away because he took the pledge, the first time I ever seen him do such a thing, but you could see his adam's apple bobbing nervous. Mr. Beezley's eyebrows shot up. "I ain't never knowed you to turn down a drink, Stosh Lithwack. What'er you, on the wagon?" My father said, like it was a joke but plucking at his cigarette pocket, "I give it up for Lent." Mr. Beezley shook his head and said he'd be turning into one of them bluenoses the next thing you knew and poured himself and Mrs. Beezley a beer, then tipped the bottle at my mother but she said no thank you she'd drink ginger ale just like my father and us kids even though she liked a glass of beer once in awhile. I could see the stiffness go out of her shoulders once we got past that.

After we all et, Mrs. Beezley said, "Gwan, you kids, gwan play outside." Right away she caught the worry in my mother's eye and said, "Oh, it'll be all right, Brother'll keep an eye on 'em," and turning to her daughter says, "Sister, you clear the table." Sister pulled down her face like she wanted to go outside too but done like she was told.

Brother was the bossy one, just like our Frank because he was the oldest, and the first thing he showed us was their chicken coop that smelled almost as terrible as the privy. Next he showed us their swing, an old rubber tire on a rope hanging from a tree. He lifted Danny up in it and swung him, he swung Danny so high and Danny's eyes was bugging out of his head and he was screaming because of being ascared and excited all at once. But I was too yellow to do it when it come my turn even though Brother sounded like Buster trying to shame me by calling me a big baby and Sparky called me a big baby too like he was his brother's echo, I still wouldn't do it. I kept staring around and staring around just as bugeyed as Danny like we was in a jungle in a Tarzan movie, only for real, and wished with all my might we was back in Philly so's I could feel the cobblestones under my feet again.

By now the sky was turning the color of turnips, and when they all went off to the other side of the yard so's Brother could show off his father's car like we ain't never seen it before let alone rode in it and he bragged was a 1928 LaSalle that I already knew, I seen my chance when they all climbed inside and Brother let Danny sit behind the steering wheel, I got down on my knees and started digging at the ground, looking for the bricks and the cobblestones I was sure must be there right under the dirt, wanting them to be there more'n anything, like they was in South Philly.

I was so busy digging away I didn't see the Beezley boys come sneaking up on me and Brother asks me in that bossy way of his, "What're you doin?" and his echo, Sparky, asked me, "What're you doin?" I turned red as the sky and said, "Nuthin," afraid to ask him where the bricks and cobblestones was and was there any trolley tracks, afraid he'd laugh at me. But even more'n that I was afraid he'd tell me there wasn't any bricks or cobblestones, suspecting it myself but not wanting to believe it, because no matter how deep I dug in the loose sand before they come sneaking up on me, I ain't hit anything but dirt and roots and was afraid it might be true there wasn't any bricks or cobblestones down there after all, nothing but dirt and more dirt, and trees and weeds, and everything scary as a jungle all closing in and choking you so's you couldn't hardly breathe.

Then Sparky, seeing the hole I dug, opened his pants. I jumped back just in time as he started peeing in it without going into the privy and his dunkey had a hat on it like Danny's that stood there gaping at him just as big-eyed as me. I looked around waiting to hear his big brother holler at him or somebody holler at him from the house for going to the toilet outside, but nobody did, the first time I seen anybody pee out in the open, he wasn't even ashamed of it and made it look like it was something he done all the time.

It felt funny being halfway there and halfway not. Most everything that could be was put in the cardboard boxes that Frank and Buster got from Willie's and was standing stacked in the middle of the rooms. My hiding place, the dining room table, already been took apart by my father, the round top leaning against the wall. The red velvet curtains hanging between the parlor and the dining room doorway come down, the pictures come down off the walls, the brown faces of my Grandmom and Grandpop Lithwack from where they always looked down at us never smiling while we was asleep, come down—All the rooms was starting to have an empty look, like the emptying out I was beginning to feel inside of myself and didn't like at all, like we was in-between, like we was all only halfway there but not anywhere else yet.

Excepting in my head as I lay in bed at night thinking of the new house across the river that wasn't new it was so old and falling down, and thinking of the privy and thinking of all them trees, thinking that we would have to take the ferry again to get to it—That worried me a lot, thinking about that ferry, that we might all get drowned this time and never get to the other side. But then I wondered if maybe that wouldn't be such a bad thing after all, drowning instead of getting hit by a car, and going up to heaven on the roof or in the tree, then we wouldn't have to move to Jersey after all.

Just then Frank and Buster come up, they was all atwitter

about moving and the promise my father made to learn them to doggie paddle in the river the way his father learned him to doggie paddle off the wharf off of Delaware Avenue when he was a kid. Slap was beside himself about that too but before Frank and Buster come up he whispered in my ear how he'd miss Mifflin Street and how he'd miss Sonny and miss Grandmom O'Rourke— And miss Aunt Bridget too because she was his god-mother that Buster said treated him like a pet and give him more'n she give the rest of us because she was his godmother and because he was deaf and she felt sorry for him. But you could tell that was only the green-eyed monster talking.

When Slap said, "Will you miss Mifflin Street, heh? heh? will you miss it, Mick?" I didn't tell him anything of all that I been thinking because a lump come up into my throat so's I couldn't even talk.

That's when Frank and Buster come in and started getting undressed and shoving their smelly socks in each other's faces like that was fun. They was in a pretty good mood because it was their last day of school at Sacred Heart and they all got their report cards ahead of time because we was moving—But not satisfied teasing each other shoving their socks in one another's face, they started teasing about Slap loud enough so's Slap could hear because Slap got leftdown again, Frank saying he was prolly gonna be in that same grade til he had a long gray beard and Buster saying he was prolly gonna be in that same grade til the whole school fell down, you could betcher bottom dollar Aunt Bridget ain't gonna give him one red cent for gettin leftdown again, no matter how much she sperlt him other times. All of a sudden Slap busted out crying because he knew they was making fun of him for getting leftdown and Buster whis-pered to him not to be such a crybaby, they was only teasing, and quick run to the bedroom door and looked out, ascared our father might be sneaking up the stairs, hearing the commotion. I petted Slap, don'tchou cry, don'tchou cry, I was so mad at them they was so mean.

As for the rest, Danny didn't seem to care one way or the other about us moving. He walked around like nothing was happening and after rolling around a few minutes on his belly, he always fell off to sleep real quick at night like he always done, even when I was telling a story to Slap and him before the other two come up. But I always laid awake longer now'n I ever done, thinking and thinking, and worrying there was nobody looking out for us now Grandmom and Grandpop's pictures was took down and put in a box.

Kate was still too little to know or care what was going on and mostly got in the way and falling all over herself now she was beginning to walk. My mother had us all pitch in to do what we could and I was give the job of wrapping all the dishes in old newspaper because my mother found out after my older brothers broke a few things, I was the only one could be trusted not to drop any of it. Which Buster right away out of jealousy I knew said was because I had sticky fingers from all the sugar he seen me sneaking. Not knowing he seen me, I pretended like I didn't hear what he said and hoped my mother ain't either, which she didn't I was glad to see, she was off and busy stacking pots and pans in one of the cardboard boxes from Willie's.

As she went around the house packing things up she was looking bluer and bluer with a faraway look in her eye and sometimes for no reason she'd drop everything and leave Frank in charge and untying her apron go running out the kitchen door and up the alley to go to see her mother. And if she sung at all, like she done when she

was first packing things up, it was some sad song like "Poor Butterfly" or "What'll I Do When You Are Far Away?" but as the day got closer to move, she stopped singing altogether.

But it looked like the sadder she got the merrier my father become, and the brightness in his eye now wasn't because he had a few either—as far as anybody knew he was keeping his pledge. He went around the house like he had more springs in his heels'n usual, unscrewing things, the tables and beds, and stacking them up, getting ready for the truck to come that he told my mother he managed to borrow from a man he used to work with in the sugarworks and said he would move us for the price of the gas and the ferry and a couple beers when the job was done.

In all the commotion that morning before the truck was to come move us, when I seen my chance I snuck out the back gate and made a beeline up the alley. I knew I had to be quick about it before I was missed and so's I could be back in time before the truck got there, but I couldn't bear going without saying good-bye to things, not knowing when or if I'd ever see any of it again.

Henry was sitting in his overalls on his front steps, his eyes as usual blue as the morning. "Where ya goin?" he asked me, that sleepy look on his face was always on his face. "Nowheres," I lied, not looking at him. "I'll comewitcha," he said, and started off of the step. "You better not, I'm goin to me Aunt Nell's, I got a note fer me Aunt Nell."

I was walking so fast he stopped at the bottom of his steps and stared after me with a funny look. "What're you lookin at?" I said, but he just kept looking and didn't say nothing. I felt bad lying to him and not telling him where I was going because I kept hoping in secret I wasn't going nowhere, I felt so bad about it I turned and waved at him, thinking goodbye, Henry, but didn't want to say anything outloud because saying it outloud would make it true and I wanted the feeling I wasn't going nowhere to last as long as I could the way I would a piece of candy I specially liked.

I run all the way without stopping up 2nd Street to the Lyric where I knew a new Shirley Temple started playing the last few days, a picture called "Heidi" that I was dying to see now it come down off Market Street, but never got to see. And because I didn't get to see it, I spent as much time as I could staring at the stills under the Lyric sign and as I was staring at her blond curls and her dress so short it showed way above her knees to where you could almost see her dunkey, I thought of the curly blond head I could've swore I seen peeping out of the woods watching us the day we went to see the house down in Jersey. And looking at them stills I started dreaming maybe she lived there, it would be something if she lived there, if she lived in the house that I could just make out the roof of through the trees where Mr. Beezley said somebody named the Mahoneys lived and had a daughter too, wouldn't it be something if it was, you never knew, it might be her, it might be her living there with her mother and father, only they called themselves Mahoney so's nobody'd know they was the Temples. And me and her'd play together everyday and we would sing together like I sung to my mother, and she would learn me to tapdance and she would take me with her back to South Philly when she went to work at the Lyric movie, then we'd come home together at night, her father would drive us in his car, and when the car come to the Delaware River it'd sprout wings by magic so's we could fly across the water and not ever have to take no ferry.... I snapped open my eyes as the number 5 trolleycar went grinding by just then clanging its bell. I seen myself grinning in the glass like I was waking up from the nicest dream, and past that I seen I was only staring at a shiny black and white picture of Shirley Temple riding in a horse and sleigh.

Even so, I stared and stared at her pictures like I would never see her again like I was never going to see Mifflin Street again. I felt my throat tighten up like somebody grabbing me around the neck, and turned away quick, not wanting to start blubbering right out in the street where everybody could see. I started running back down 2nd Street because I could see by the clock in the Jew butcher's window it was getting late and I knew my mother had enough to worry about without worrying about where I was. I was running so hard, even when I crosst over the street and cars was coming I run out like I done before, praying in secret one of them'd hit me, thinking maybe if one did run me over now and mashed me up maybe it wouldn't be so bad a thing if I didn't make it across the street, I wouldn't have to cross the river, it might be better then, it might be better to run back and let the Jew butcher grab ahold of me and suck out my blood after all.

At Moore Street I seen a car coming and was sorely tempted and looked around if a cop was there and not seeing no cop I run out in the street, not able to help myself. But the driver slammed on his brakes and there was a screech of the tires, the car rocking because it stopped so quick, and just before I scooted to the other curb and run off down the block I seen the driver's face all twisted and scared and he was shaking his fist at me in the windshield like all the other drivers done when I wanted them to run me over. But I didn't care and I run and run and fought hard not to blubber and didn't care anymore and told myself if I bawled it was only because I didn't get to say goodbye to everything, didn't get to see the schoolyard one last time or the public school where my Aunt Nell worked or the ragshops on 3rd Street or the icehouse where my Uncle Ned worked and the slaughterhouse on Sigel Street where the blood run down and I heard cattle and pigs screaming and bawling—There never would've been time enough to see it all even if I been given all the time in the world, it was like the butcher went and stuck me with a butcher knife and a part of me, like the time, was running out and down a dark drain to somewhere I didn't know and didn't want to know—where the blood that wasn't drunk went down the sewer and out to the river and across the water that was all greasy and scummy to the place where there was nothing but trees and dirt and a woreout old house by a swamp that didn't have no spigots or a toilet inside and smelled of gas like when my mother turned the gas burner on and it didn't light right away... I kept running and running and it felt like everything was running out of me and down like I was a drain and the time running out was a drain and I looked hard at everything as I run, trying to keep it in my eyes for as long as I could, not knowing when or if I would ever see any of it again....

Part Two

PAGAN DAYS

For the first couple of days, after the beds was set up and Kate's crib put in my mother and father's room and all the other furniture settled in the house, my mother was so ascared one of us would get drowned in the swamp behind the house she made us all stick close in the backyard where she could keep an eye on us through the kitchen window. I was more worried of falling down one of the holes in the outhouse than I was of drowning in the swamp because I had to go in the outhouse a couple times a day but didn't have to ever go back in the swamp for anything. Plants that smelled like the Life Savers my father used to suck on to kill the booze on his breath and that Sam Beezley said was wild peppermint, grew thick all around the outside of the privy, but I don't think all the wild peppermint in the world would've been enough to cut down the stink inside. Even though sunlight snuck through the cracks and through the holes drilled over the door to let out the smell, the place was still dark even in the daytime and was filled with spiders and cobwebs and them fat green flies always buzzing.

When I went in the privy I'd try to peep under the seat to see if there was a big brown snake curled there but it was always too dark to see. And if you left the door open somebody might see your hiney like my mother seen mine one day when I left it open, she shouted out the backdoor did I want the whole world to see? So I shut it, even though if she knew about the snakes she'd leave it open too. If it was getting dark after supper and too early for the bucket inside the house and I had to do number two, sometimes I'd coax Slap into coming and sitting beside me to keep me company by promising to tell him a story and I'd hold onto him to keep from falling down the hole.

Since the only plumbing in the house was the pump at the sink in the kitchen, that my mother or one of the older boys had to prime most mornings with one of the jars of water kept handy under the sink, I missed the spigots and flush toilet in our old house in South Philly. Specially now when we had to use the dented old scrub bucket my mother put up in the hall at night because she said it was too dark, and dangerous, even for the older boys, to go out in the privy, they might step on a snake or a water rat or being half asleep get lost in the dark and fall head over heels in the swamp.

So for the first couple days, what with my mother watching us like a hawk, none of us went no further'n the yard, which my older brothers, Frank and Buster specially, whined and complained about. But I couldn't've cared less, I was content to stick close to the house and shove my oil truck with the busted wheel through the dirt, because beyond the yard was all too big and open and green, I was missing everything all crowded together, all them streets and houses of South Philly with the backyards with their high green fences made of boards and where the only tree you ever seen was a Tree of Heaven pushing up through the cement in the alleyway—that was green enough for me.

Mrs. Beezley said she'd wait til we got settled before she'd come over but she sent Sister over sometimes with a bowl of eggs from their chickens or a pot of soup she made. And one time she sent a pan of macaroni and cheese which was a good thing she did because we didn't have nothing but a loaf of white bread to eat that night that my father told my mother he got "on the eye" at the store called Gottlieb's after he was done looking for work all day, he stopped there for a gallon of coal oil for the kitchen stove that he said he also got on the eye.

Then one time not long after that Sam Beezley showed up

after work with his boys, Brother carrying a box of peeps and Sparky a bag of feed for them. He said some of the peeps was from his setting hens and some he got from something he called the brooders at Gottlieb's store, Plymouth Rocks he called them, and Rhode Island Reds and a couple Leghorns. My father said he shouldn't've done it but Mr. Beezley said it was just to help him get started, he could pay him back when these peeps grew up and had peeps of their own. When he said it that way you could see my father felt easier about it, you could see he was pleased the way he held a chick in either hand and grinned at them like they was gold, they was so yellow. Then all my brothers had to hold one, and though I was skittish at first and didn't want to, my father handed me one too. I never felt anything so soft before, I could feel its heart beating quick in my hand the same way mine done when I was scared.

My mother come out the shed door, wiping her hands on her apron and looked surprised when she seen the chicks. When my father said Mr. Beezley brung them over she thanked Mr. Beezley and right away picked one up and held it in her lap as she set down on the back steps.

My father and Mr. Beezley sat there smoking, and Mr. Beezley said to my father, "I asked my boss just today if they was anything open at the yard and he told me they wasn't even hiring niggers to clean the heads." "Heads," he said, "is shipyard lingo for terlets," when Frank asked him what heads was. "But," he said, "I'll keep after him, maybe things'll change."

I looked over at my mother that was looking down at the chick in her hands like her hands was a nest, and I could see the disappointment in her eyes over what Sam Beezley just said but she was trying not to show it.

My father kept the peeps in the kitchen that night in the cardboard box and the next morning he found some old screens down in the cellar that wasn't too rusty from the water leaking in and nailed them around underneath the shed in back. Now it was warm enough outside he put the peeps in there, then built a little coop from some old boards was only a little warped he found under the shed. He made a runway up into it to get the chicks off of the damp ground. Then he showed Frank and Buster how to water and feed them like Mr. Beezley told him and them two right away felt like bigshots because they got to take care of the chicks and Slap was put out because he didn't, he asked them if he could take care of the chicks sometimes and they said they'd see but you could see from their eyes they wasn't ever going to let him.

Them first nights right after supper, my father took me and Danny out into the backyard to watch the sun go down. On the way he told us to make sure we didn't step on the cesspool that was like a hump of loose dirt at the back of the yard. When I asked him what would happen if we stepped on it he said, "You'd fall through and drowned in the muck, that's what would happen"—So I learned that that was one more thing you had to worry about and was always careful to walk around it, keeping a sharp eye out when I was minding Danny and Kate they didn't go near it neither, and watched when my mother was hanging out the clothes since the clothesline run close by it, if she got too close I'd holler out.

He had us each carry out our little bench covered with the little bit of carpet that Grandpop Lithwack made long ago. We set the benches down in the high grass right up at the edge of the swamp with our faces to the back of the sky while our father squatted down in the weeds between us and smoked a Marvel cigarette that he was smoking now because they was the cheapest, and looked around him like he was expecting something important to happen. He looked around the yard that same way, looking at the part of the ground he already dug up to grow the vegetables and then looking on under the house to where the peeps was and where Frank and Buster was kneeling pouring mash and water in the little pans and arguing over whose turn it was to clean out the coop—And even though he ain't found a job yet and there wasn't much to eat and sometimes there wouldn't've been nothing at all on the table if it wasn't for the Beezleys and for him putting things on the eye at Gottlieb's store, there was something in his face when he looked around as if none of that mattered at all. You could see he liked being here.

Sunsets the color of turnips was new to me, never having seen the sun go down in South Philly what with the houses being so high and crowded all around and blocking out the sky, but everything here was so open and flat as the palm of your hand and you could see everything, even a sunset. "Look now," he'd say, just the second before the sun dropped in a hole behind the old dead trees back in the swamp, their branches all shriveled against the red sky like my grandmother's hands. Then he'd point up at the sky because all the time we was setting there, at first in twos and threes, then in bigger and bigger bunches, birds was flying over our heads. He said they was going back to roost in the dead branches for the night, more birds than the sparrows in all of South Philly, more birds then I had names for, more'n I could ever count up to yet, all of them flying over our heads til the air was filled with the rush of their wings and you couldn't see the sky for all their dark beating wings.

Me and Danny set there goggle-eyed because soon the branches was black with birds as they flapped and squawked and pecked at one another, settling down for the night, the whole swamp was one big loud screaming as they jumped and flapped. But as the light went out they got quieter and quieter so's finally you could only hear little chirpings no louder'n the peeps under the shed, then everything was all still again. Excepting for the croak of the bullfrogs starting up and the whiny buzz of mosquitoes like fire sirens that took up where the birds left off. I wanted to ask my father could the water rats climb up the trees and eat the birds at night like they climbed up into the coop already and et two of the chicks, but before I got a chance to ask it, the mosquitoes was swarming up in such dark clouds from the slimy swamp water me and Danny was soon slapping right and left at our bare arms and legs. My father was laughing like that was the funniest but my mother seen us from the house and was calling out the backdoor for us to come inside and smear ourselves with citronella Mrs. Beezley'd sent over with Sister yesterday, before we got et alive.

Me and Danny picked up our benches and headed back to the house, our father walking between us, himself looking so much like one of the birds, all jerky and quick, as he looked up at the sky where some stars was starting to show through. He took a big breath with that grin of being pleased on his face, as if all the air was like a sweetness to him, like the perfume his sister Theresa wore, even though the air to me was nothing but the smell of mud and swamp gas, that funny smell like beets cooking.

In spite of everything, he seemed quieter just being where he was and I felt less jumpy around him now he took the pledge. And despite I was so homesick for Mifflin Street it set like a lead ball in my chest, I give a secret prayer as we crossed the yard that he would stay that way and that things'd go on like this for a long long time, and crossed my fingers on both my hands the way Slap showed me, to make double sure.

Before we went up to bed, we all set on the front porch listening to Amos 'n Andy through the parlor window, my father lighting the punks Sam Beezley sent over with Brother and Sparky to keep the mosquitoes away. Cattails they called them, that was already dried out from what they cut and had left over from the summer before, my father handing one to each of us, excepting for Kate even though she wanted one in the worst way, but he was scared she'd burn herself.

The lights was left off inside the house not only to save on the electric but to keep from attracting the moths and any more of the mosquitoes that was still screaming like fire engines out in the dark and that we all set there reeking of citronella to keep away. The smell of the smoke rising all around us made me think of the smell of the incense in the church, and I felt quieter with everything that worried me disappearing slow in the dark, it was only all of us setting together on the porch in the dark with Amos 'n Andy laughing and talking so soft and sweet as honey through the window and the tips of our punks burning so bright.

Knowing nobody else could see me, I set there grinning in the shadows and said my prayer again that it would always be like this forever and ever and crossed myself and crossed all my fingers just to make double sure.

We had to wait til my father come home looking for any jobs he could get before my mother'd let us go back into the swamp. Sam Beezley come over that same day with his boys and their dog Blackie to tell my father he put in another word for him at the shipyard. Brother was carrying another bag of the chicken mash for the peeps, that was a good thing since there wasn't any left from the other bag they brung. My brothers been pestering my father so much to take them back in the swamp when they begun pestering him again that day he said all right and Mr.

Beezley said he'd come too to show us what was back there before he went home to wash up and eat. Danny, and Kate of course, my mother wouldn't let go and I was wishing she would've said the same for me but she told my father I could go seeing's he was there and Mr. Beezley was taking us. I went even though I should've known better and stayed behind with Blackie, "The laziest dog in the world," Mrs. Beezley called him, like she was bragging about it, that flopped in the long tall weeds and started scratching his fleas as hard as I scratched my mosquito bites.

After that first time I didn't ever like going back there in the swamp, it was so hot and mucky with things I ain't never seen before in my life nor ever dreamt of, slithering away from us faster'n you could see them as we crept around the edges where the ground wasn't so muddy, Mr. Beezley and then my father up ahead in the lead. Mr. Beezley kept pointing out things in his loud voice like, "Looka the skunk cabbage, up already!" sticking his finger at heads of cabbage off in the black mud bigger'n any my mother ever cooked, and saying things like, "Watch out you don't step in the quicksand," turning back to wink at my father, then looking at me and my brothers with a teasing twinkle in his eye, while my brothers snuck along bugeyed and practically walking up my father's heels they was sticking so close, their faces all white and their mouths hanging open, but like me trying to hide how scared they was. I was thinking of one of them Saturday matinee serials we seen at the Morris movie where the man in the jungle stepped in quicksand, he sunk down so slow and couldn't get out no matter how much a stick was shoved at him, the more he struggled to get out the more he sunk down so that all you seen at the Continued Next Week was fingers fluttering at the top of the muck like he was waving goodbye.

And the mosquitoes! "Jersey mosquitoes," Sam Beezley called them, like he was proud of them, and kept swatting at them along with the rest of us, they was so big and fierce and so many, Sam Beezley said he'd need a blood transfusion by the time we got out of there. I was beginning to think Blackie the dog had better sense'n we did to come back in here.

Weeds three times taller'n me that Mr. Beezley said was punkweed grew to either side of us, thick and high it was, high as the green fences closing in the backyards of South Philly. All of a sudden he stopped and took out his jackknife and started cutting off the tops of some of the dead plants that was the punks he was cutting that was already dry and brown and looked like the big cigars my Uncle Digby, the undertaker, smoked. He handed them back to Frank and Buster to put in their pockets so's we could burn them at night.

I ain't never seen frogs before excepting in the movies and they was hopping every which way, splashing into the muddy water when they heard us coming, some as big as Uncle Jake's fists, with eyes as big as his was too whenever he swallowed the horsereddish, the bullfrogs we heard croaking when the sun went down. All of a sudden Sam Beezley lunged into the mud and caught one all dripping with slime, its big fat legs flapping, and before you knew it he had his jackknife open again, he stuck the blade of that knife right into the bullfrog's head til them big legs was only twitching and blood gushed out that was red and not green like you'd think it might be. What he done was he started hacking off its legs, and threw the head and gizzard in the swamp.

Brother and Sparky was clapping like mad and yelling, "Nice grab, Pop!" while Frank and Buster screwed up their faces and forced themselves to grin too to show it ain't bothered them any but you could tell it did, their grins was only skin-deep.

Mr. Beezley, with another wink at my father, that was grinning too, Mr. Beezley handed them legs all bleeding back to

Frank with a teasing snigger. Frank cringed away and wouldn't take them at first but Brother and Sparky razzed him so he finally took them, holding them out from himself so's none of the blood would spatter on him, whining, "Whaddaya want these for?" "Them's good eatin," Mr. Beezley said, and both Frank and Buster looked at him like he was nuts while Brother and Sparky was laughing so hard seeing Frank and Buster's faces as green as the frogskin, they was falling all over each other so's they almost went headfirst in the mud.

I must've looked just as green because I was afraid I was going to puke right then and there and was all for going back to the house right away. But when I looked around me I couldn't see nothing but skunk cabbage and punkweed so high that made everything look the same and couldn't even see the sky and didn't know which way the house was.

Then my father got into it, lunging after them slimy green things like they was dollar bills instead of bullfrogs— "Only the big suckers!" Mr. Beezley yelled out, just about breaking my eardrums—and soon they was all lunging and grabbing at frogs for Mr. Beezley to stab in the brain, Frank and Buster grabbing them too, so that soon they was clutching frog legs in their fists thick as bunches of flowers all dripping and red.

With everybody else's hands full, Mr. Beezley started handing legs back to me and Slap at the end of the line. Slap took the pair he give him and wrinkled up his nose, holding them by the toes, but I stuck my hands in my pockets and wouldn't touch them for anything. Mr. Beezley give one of his cackles that sent the birds flying up out of the trees and my father give a sneery laughing look. Buster razzed me along with the others and shook the bloody stumps he was holding in my face, forgetting how ascared he was not a minute before. I quick swung my head away the same as if he'd slapped me but wouldn't cry just to spite them. My father finally said to Buster, "That's enough now," because he was easier now he took the pledge, and we went back to the house because nobody could carry any more of the frog legs in their hands, and I didn't care, I wasn't going to touch them frog legs.

Like me, she made a face like she didn't even want to be near them let alone cook them, but Sam Beezley before he left to go home told her how to fry them, "In a little egg and flour and lard, just like chicken," he told her. After she got used to the idea she pumped water on them and scrubbed them good and fixed them up the way he said. Then she opened the valve on one of the burners on the oil stove, the fuel jug at one end burping up like it always done as the oil run in. She lifted the burner that was big as a big tin can all burnt in the trash, and leaning back far as she could like she always done like it might blow up in her face, she struck a wood match and lit the wick that was all sopped now with oil, and all charred and burnt to a nub too, she said she couldn't get no new wicks because my father put so much on the eye at Gottlieb's already.

After the first orange flames spit up above the burner she quick turned it down and when it got to burn a cone of steady blue flame she slapped a hunk of lard in the frying pan, lard so used and old it was brown as dirt, and when the grease was spitting in the pan, she dropped in the first of the frog legs and started frying them up, wrinkling her nose and standing way back from the stove even farther back'n when she lit it.

I didn't want to eat them at first but because there wasn't anything else to eat and I was so hungry, I peeled off the skin because I couldn't stand the look of it and was surprised when I seen the meat underneath was white as Snow White's skin. I was even more surprised when, after shutting my eyes, I bit into it, it tasted just like Sam Beezley said it would. I et every bit of it right down to the bone, giving the skins to Kate because Kate liked to chew fried skin, my mother said she was going to turn into a chicken someday, and now maybe she'd turn into a frog, but it didn't stop Kate from eating fried skin, she liked it so much.

After supper now there was no more of me and Danny setting on our little benches watching the sun go down with our father. He took the coal shovel he brung with us from the cellar on Mifflin Street and went on digging up the driest part of the yard not far from the backdoor that he already had a good-sized part of dug up for the vegetable garden he was going to plant with Sam Beezley's help. Sam Beezley already give him packages of seeds that he bought at Gottlieb's and give to my father as a present to get him started, and when my mother seen them, she complained, saying him and Mrs. Beezley'd done so much for us already. But he said, "You can give me some a' yer peppers when they come in, I ain't never had no luck with peppers." When he said it that way she seemed to feel easier about it.

The seeds was setting on the shelf over the kitchen sink for when the ground was all dug up and the weather got a little warmer, which wouldn't be long now, my father said. When nobody was around I got up on a chair and since the seeds was on the same shelf as the sugar I first wet my finger and quick stuck it in the sugar bowl and licked it, then I took down the seeds and looked at them for the pictures on the packages: tomatoes and corn and radishes and lettuce and peppers and some plants I ain't never even seen before, spelling out the names the way I done the names on the sides of the trucks and wagons in South Philly. I shook the packets, wondering how the vegetables in the pictures could be inside such tiny little seeds like my father said they was. I asked Slap about it in bed that night and he said he didn't know how that was, so I thought they must be like the tiny people inside of the radio to be so tiny to live in there.

The next afternoon while Danny and Kate was playing up on
the porch and my older brothers was off with the Beezley boys
somewheres in the woods, I didn't know what to do with myself. I
walked around the house three times and on the fourth time
around on the side of the house where the woods was that separated our house from the Mahoney's, I seen something flash in
the sun from the bushes.

I stood still and looked, I couldn't believe my eyes seeing it
looked like the same head of blond curls I seen the first time we
was here. Just to make sure I wasn't seeing things, I blinked my
eyes and turned my head away and stared again—There it was,
as real as real, the same curls that looked like Shirley Temple's
curls and a pair of blue eyes staring out of the weeds like they
was spying on me and maybe been spying on me all the time I
was wandering around the outside of the house with nothing to
do. I stood and stared back, but whoever it was when they seen
me staring ducked down and then run off in the direction of the
Mahoney's house.

I stood there a minute longer gaping at the empty bushes,
then I went around back to ask my mother why we never seen
the Mahoneys, did she know if their little girl looked like
Shirley Temple? She was carrying the empty wicker basket back
into the house to get more wash to hang out and she held the
basket against her hip and pushed a strand of her sweaty hair
back from her forehead. All she knew she said was what Babes
Beezley told her, "The Mahoneys keep pretty much to theirselfs
and they have a little boy has girlish ways but ain't a little girl,
Mr. Beezley is such a needler." When I asked her did their little
boy have blond curls like Shirley Temple she laughed and said,
"I don't know, I ain't never laid eyes on him yet like I ain't never
laid eyes on his mother or father for that matter, if he is a boy

your age he's too old to have Shirley Temple curls."

I was still restless and went and stood out by the road looking both ways. As usual, there wasn't nothing coming, like there would've been on Mifflin Street if we was there, there was hardly anything ever come by here excepting Bill the breadman once a day or Mr. Carey the iceman, if my mother had the money for ice, or the junkman from Camden every two weeks, and if something did go by the dust in the road was so thick you couldn't hardly see it anyway. I glanced back at the house to make sure my mother wasn't watching, then I crossed over the road to the path that went through the woods that the Beezleys always come out on everytime they come from their house over on Saint John's Walk. I listened at the break in the trees—All you could hear was bugs and things buzzing and the birds making a terrible racket and things going like the crickets at night that I was getting used to by now. I took a few more steps in along the path, peeping all around like any minute something was going to jump out and grab me, then stopped again and listened. There was nothing but trees and weeds, I didn't see nothing else, no snakes or nothing, so I took a few more steps in. I could hear my brothers and the Beezley boys a little ways off and a dog barking that must've been Blackie and knew they must be coming back through the woods.

I was just about to turn and go back to the house before they come, when all of a sudden the hairs froze on my head because right there in the middle of the path I seen the ugliest thing of all I ever seen so far around here, even uglier'n the bullfrogs. It was something with four claws all shriveled up and a wrinkled old head like a dunkey with eyes peeping out from under a thick hard-looking shell that looked like a rusty old wash basin turned upsidedown. I freezed where I stood, my eyes bulging, my throat so tight I couldn't make a sound, like in a nightmare when you want to yell and you can't.

Finally, when I could let out a yell I let out such a loud one it wasn't long before my brothers and the Beezley boys come running out of the trees all out of breath, with Blackie waddling after them. Right away, Brother and Sparky seen me staring at this awful thing and seen I was starting to cry, so they begun hooting and hollering and calling me a sissy, sneering, "What're you? Scare't of a little turtle?" Only it wasn't so little, anybody could see that. Blackie was trying to stick his snout under the shell and started barking loud so that the turtle quick snapped in its head and legs. They all laughed when it did, laughing at Blackie with his head cocked to one side, wondering as much as me where the turtle went.

Then they all grabbed up sticks and poked it, and nudged at it with the toes of their sneakers, Blackie barking his head off again, and when the turtle wouldn't come out no matter how much they poked it, they got bored with it and went on their way back to our house, laughing about what a scaredy cat I was.

Along with frogs and snakes, that was bad enough, now turtles was one more thing to watch out for and because of that I didn't dare go into the woods alone again for a long, long time. For a couple days after that, every chance he got Buster'd yell at me out of nowhere, *"Is zat a turtle behind you?"* and him and Frank'd bust out laughing when I'd jump and look, and if the Beezley boys was there they'd hoot and holler too, til I caught on to it and quit jumping and looking behind me and after that they got tired of their teasing, seeing I wasn't jumping no more.

Most every afternoon now Mrs. Beezley'd come swaying through the woods to see my mother—"Now the dust's settled," she laughed, the first time she come over, and for somebody laughed as much as she done, she still had sad, wore-looking eyes like half-moons turned upsidedown. She brung the day-old newspapers that old Seamus O'Reilly delivered in his banged up old truck that my mother didn't have the money to get delivered, the Philadelphia morning *Inquirer* and the *Evening Bulletin* and something called the *County Seat Weekly*. We got them after all the Beezleys was done reading them so's the comics and the news was always the day after. My mother turned first thing to what she said was the "obits" to see if anybody she knew died from the old neighborhood, then after that she read every single word for any news about South Philly, she was as homesick for it as me.

Sister come with her mother sometimes, walking behind her on the path because Mrs. Beezley was too big for the two of them to walk side by side on it. Sister'd always be carrying something for my mother since Mrs. Beezley never come to our house emptyhanded, a dish of macaroni and cheese or a bowl of eggs from their hens and sometimes, as a treat, a plate of cupcakes covered by a teatowel that she baked herself. My mother'd always say, "Oh, Babes, you shouldn't've," but I knew most times she was glad to get it and Mrs. Beezley'd wave her away like she always done, saying, "Don't worry, hon, *he's* workin."

While Sister played with Kate out on the porch, holding her and hugging and kissing her like she was a dollbaby and sometimes making curls on her head like my mother done with a comb dipped in a glass of water, Mrs. Beezley and my mother sat and talked in the parlor while my mother peeled the potatoes for supper. Mrs. Beezley sat there with her legs spread in a faded old housedress, her stockings all runs and knotted at the knee like my mother's, and if she was on her way to Gottlieb's afterwards for hamburger or something for supper, you could see the dollar bills tied in the knot the same way my mother kept money tied there she didn't want my father to see when he was drinking, like their stockings was their pocketbooks.

The first time I tried to sit in there with them my mother give me a look, saying, "Ain'tchou got something better to do, boy?" I quick took the hint and went out through the dining room like I was going out the backdoor but instead I dived under the dining room table just like I done in South Philly when there was something I wanted to hear. Even though this dining room wasn't as dark as the one on Mifflin Street, the lace tablecloth hung down so far it hid me pretty well, I could hear just about every word was said in the parlor, even if Mrs. Beezley was whispering something secret and I had to strain forward far as I could and cup my hands behind my ears, I could hear it okay.

It seemed like there wasn't nobody she didn't know in town and what their business was. She filled my mother in on just about everything was going on in Lenape, "All the dirt," she called it, about who was having a baby and who was having a baby wasn't married and who wasn't talking to who and who was "running around" with who, while my mother scraped away with her potato knife and I could hear the splash as one spud after another hit the pot of water at her feet. Mrs. Beezley talked as good as the stories on the radio and at night in bed I tried to remember what she said and how she said it, then I'd tell it in a story to Slap and Danny before the other two come up. What I specially liked was when she told my mother the latest movies she seen at the Rialto that was a movie-house in this place called the county seat, not only telling the whole story from the beginning to The End but acting out all the parts like she was the whole movie all in one, her knees fanning a mile a minute when she really got going. My mother always said Babes Beezley telling a movie was the same if not better'n being right in the moviehouse itself, and that was no lie.

Because Mr. Beezley had a job at the shipyard and depending on if he had their old LaSalle running, Mrs. Beezley got to go to the movies over in the county seat every Saturday night, more'n my mother ever went, which was never, since the twenty cents for adults to get in she said could buy a pound of hamburger at Gottlieb's or two loaves of bread from the Bond breadman that come every morning now, my father said he was spreading out what he was "puttin on the cuff," he put so much on the eye already at Gottlieb's.

Us kids never got to go to the movies either since there wasn't much scrap paper and junk to collect in the streets of a town like Lenape like there was in South Philly, and even if there was there wasn't no ragshops like on 3rd Street neither. There was just the old "guinea," my father called him, driving down from Camden in a beatup junk truck that was even more beat up'n Seamus O'Reilly's, and that had cowbells strung over the tailgate. He come around once every two weeks hollering, "Any rags, any bones, any bottles today?" If my father had any junk he found to sell him, he'd go running out to the road and wave him down. One day he found a little radio was busted and thrown in somebody's trash. He didn't sell that to the junkman he fixed it and put it up on the shelf over the sink in the kitchen so's my mother could listen to her stories while she cooked or done the wash, and I'd set out there with her and listen and help her wring out the sheets in the sink when it come time.

Me and my brothers was over at the Beezleys one Saturday night before they went to the movies, the two oldest sucking around hoping Mrs. Beezley'd feel sorry for all of us and take us too. Before she went out to the car, I seen her sitting at the kitchen table crimping her hair with the electric curling iron she got from smoking so many Raleigh cigarettes and trading in the coupons come on each pack, her hair was so thin it was a wonder she didn't burn it to a crisp. She had on a nice dress with big yellow flowers like she was going to church, only, like my mother said, she nor none of the Beezleys ever set foot inside of a church. She slapped powder on her face and smeared on lipstick and put on her tinted glasses she only wore when she went to the movies, she told my mother she wanted to be sure she seen everything.

All the Beezley kids was so scrubbed they was shiny with Lifebuoy soap, Brother and Sparky both had clean shirts on and Sister had a clean dress and her hair was crimped too with the curling iron like her mother's. After they all piled into the car Mr. Beezley, the pointy tip of his nose smudged with grease because he had to lean under the hood to get the old LaSalle started because it been acting up again, he leaned out the window and put his hand to one ear, saying to us, "Ain't that yer mother callin you all to come home?"

Even though we didn't hear nothing we knew what he meant and took the hint and turned around and started trudging through the woods back over to Lenape Road, while the big LaSalle roared off down Saint John's Walk in a cloud of blue smoke and dust yellow as the flowers on Mrs. Beezley's dress.

Frank and Buster was both pulling a long puss as we went because they didn't get asked to the movies but I knew Mrs. Beezley would've took us all if it was up to her, like she said she would've liked to take my mother sometimes just to get her out of the house. Only my mother said she couldn't go because of the kids and besides Mrs. Beezley already done too much for us, she didn't want her wasting no twenty cents taking her to no movie, she'd just as soon hear Mrs. Beezley tell her about it a day or two after, like she didn't mind reading the newspapers the day after.

The very next Monday afternoon (she never come over on a Sunday) Mrs. Beezley was in our parlor telling my mother all about this movie "Jezebel" that starred Bette Davis and George Brent. She told it all the way from the beginning to The End like she always done while my mother sat peeling her potatoes or darning our stockings or patching and mending all our pants and knickers and shirts, she always had a pile, with Slap's clothes the worse, he was always ripping holes in everything.

Mrs. Beezley sat smoking like a chimney, she smoked Raleighs like I said because of the coupons and was always bragging to my mother how she just about furnished her entire parlor and her bedroom with knickknacks from the Raleigh coupons and got the electric curling iron her and Sister used on movie nights and how, "Just now I got my heart set so much on a porcelain shepherd girl with an electric clock in her belly, the cutest thing." She said she was smoking more'n usual so's she could accumulate coupons that much faster so's she'd have that clock by Christmastime.

I was straining my ears out under the dining room table, as hungry for the movies as I was for sugary things, and at certain parts in telling the movie when Mrs. Beezley's voice dropped down low and I knew she was talking about secret things, I had to lean all the way out from under the tablecloth and cup my hands harder behind my ears and risk getting caught if any of my brothers happened by, so's not to miss a word.

"...and then Bette comes sailing in in her hoopskirts, her curls all bouncing, and jist fer spite..." *whisper whisper whisper* "... then George puts his arm around her and jist then Henry..." *whisper whisper whisper*—and my mother would get laughing sly and quick in that merry way she had, laughing like she wouldn't laugh at the dirty jokes Mr. Beezley told my father or things my father'd say sometimes, trying to be funny, that she thought was off color and wasn't right to say in front of ladies like her and Mrs. Beezley, or in front of us kids.

When Mrs. Beezley picked up in her regular voice once more I could lean back and hide behind the tablecloth again, listening as she told about the plague hit town, it was so real it froze every hair on my head and even made Bette Davis stop being so mean and spiteful at The End.

When the cuckoo popped four times out of the clock on the dining room wall I heard Mrs. Beezley give a sigh, then start hauling herself up out of the chair, saying, "Listen to the time, I better git goin, *he'll* be comin home any minute and I ain't got a thing ready for supper," saying "he" like it was some nuisance she was talking about.

Usually after supper Sam Beezley'd come through the woods with Brother and Sparky tagging along and Blackie waddling behind them. Mr. Beezley's ears and hawk nose was shiny from his washup after work, and even though his face had a soft babyish look, like Brother's did too, and there was a puffiness around his eyes, them eyes that was black as tar was sharp as his nose and let you know he didn't miss a thing. Them eyes made me nervous like he was seeing right inside of me, and he had that voice could still make me jump and a laugh to match that could get not only Blackie but all of the other dogs in the neighborhood barking.

He'd always sit on the top step of our porch with my father and tell him about his day's work at the yard. My father'd lean forward, his hands gripped between his knees, his lips half open like he was expecting something good, his face so bright and eager as he listened you could see everything Sam Beezley was saying about the shipyard plain in my father's eyes. And when Sam Beezley brung my father up-to-date on what bigshot he used his pull on that day to try to get my father a job, from the way my father's adam's apple bobbed up and down you could see he was almost tasting that job.

My mother started dreaming each of us kids was drowning one by one, a different one of us every night, and so she told us never to go down to the river without our father, the same as she told me not to go past Front Street in South Philly, even though I did. My father said her dreaming was nothing but wishful thinking and she give him a look and said that was an awful thing to say and he better tell it in his next confession but he just grinned back at her.

Scared as her and me was of water, I was having dreams the two of us was sailing across the river on nothing but a raft, her sitting up front steering it, me kneeling behind her holding on with both hands. I was afraid of drowning but was just about dying with excitement because we was going back to the city. I always woke up before we got to the other side but, even so, the thrill of going back lasted long after I begun to feel blue knowing it was only a dream.

When I told her about it as we was wringing out the sheets in the washtub by the kitchen pump she laughed at first and shook her head but then she turned her face away and got that far off look in her eyes as she bent back over the tub, so that I could see that going back was still her dream too as much as it was mine and always would be.

Sometimes she'd stop in the middle of her work and that distant look come into her eyes, if you spoke to her she didn't hear you no matter what, and times like that I knew she was with her mother and sisters.

One Saturday afternoon my father and Mr. Beezley sat smoking and talking on our backsteps, Mr. Beezley saying there wasn't no news to tell him about a job at the yard yet. His two boys was flopped down on the ground as usual beside Blackie, just like they was dogs themselves. I was still too skittish to sit on the bare ground like they done all the time and so sat myself on the bottom step like always. But my brothers that was learning to do everything the way the Beezley boys done it, flopped down in the dirt like the ground was a chair to them by now instead of something damp and dirty and hard as a rock.

When Mr. Beezley went on and on talking about the shipyard my brothers started getting restless and got to slapping and picking at each other. Then they started pestering my father to take them down to the river since none of us seen it yet since we come over on the ferry. They was dying to see it and Mr. Beezley said to my father, "I know some good places I can show you where to ketch minniegudgeons and eels for bait and catfish fer fryin, I betcher sick 'a frog legs." When he said it my father got a look in his eyes like he didn't want to admit he was still sneaking back catching frogs when there wasn't nothing else to put on the table.

My brothers started dancing up and down wanting to know right away if they could go fishing. My mother heard them through the kitchen door and she came out carrying Kate on her hip. She said, "Don't let them go in, you know all the dreams I been havin." My father huffed at her saying he wouldn't do that since he ain't learned any of us to doggie paddle yet. At first she said the others could go but I couldn't go, then after my father said, "Oh, let him, do you want to make a girl out of him?" she started to argue, and when he gave her a sharp, impatient look and threw up his hands, she said, "Well, it's your lookout."

I was dying to see the river just as much as my brothers but was thinking about her dreams, and asked her in a whisper what if I fell in the water and her dreams come true? But she said I better not go anywheres near it and in a louder voice to all my brothers she hollered, "Stick close to yer father, you birds, and no goin near the water. Slap, you hear?"

We started off down the road, staying on Lenape Road and not going onto the path through the woods towards the Beezley's house like I thought we would, my father and Mr. Beezley in the lead, and the rest of us following behind them, oldest to youngest, so I was last and taking in everything, I ain't been so far from the house since we first moved in.

Not far down the road we passed another house that looked even more fallen down'n ours did and there was an old-fashioned green car in the front yard up on cinder-blocks like Mr. Beezley's old LaSalle was most of the time. A man needing a shave and in his undershirt with his arms all greasy was banging away with a hammer at something under the hood, and since his back was to us he didn't see us as we went by. The side yard was crammed with rusty old washing machines and motors and all kinds of junk, including stacks of bald car tires. There was a couple chickens pecking around, scrawny looking things, not plump like the Beezley's chickens was, or like ours was getting to be. On the porch that looked like it was ready to collapse any minute was a girl about Kate's age sitting on the floor playing with a dirty rubber dollbaby and a little boy about as old as Danny. Another boy that looked a little older'n me and that had teeth hung out big as my mother's, come to lean on the porch rail and stare out at us. Mr. Beezley nodded his head to the skinny lady leaning against one post of the porch, she had long straggly hair and skin the color of the clay out back in the swamp. She nodded her head in return and when she opened her mouth to grin you could see she only had one tooth in front—"*The Snarps*," Mr. Beezley muttered under his breath to my father but still saying it so loud I was sure the lady on the porch heard him. "Boy, there's a bunch for you," saying just what he said the first time he mentioned them the day we looked at the house.

I been wondering ever since who they was, like I been wondering about the Mahoneys, and I could see my father was too, he was watching the Snarps out of the corner of his eye and taking in everything but acting like he wasn't. My head was turned and I was staring too, not caring about hiding it because I was with the others, and I was looking so hard I didn't see the others'd gone on ahead, leaving me behind. All of a sudden the boy on the porch with the buck-teeth leaned over the rail and stuck his tongue out at me. I stared at him and not knowing what to do I run on quick ahead to catch up with Slap.

Once we got closer into town the first thing you could see everywhere through the trees was the big silver water tower that when we finally passed it I seen was up on a yellow hill of sand which was why you could see it everywhere you looked. We left the dirt road and come out on a road that was cement that Mr. Beezley said was called Hessian Soldiers Way after some soldiers he said marched down it once in the battlefield at the river. Right away Frank and Buster got all worked up, wanting to know was we going to see the battlefield. Mr. Beezley said we would and you could see my brothers could hardly stand it they was so excited.

Then we passed what Mr. Beezley called the volunteer firehouse that was two stories high and made of cement blocks yellow as the dust in the roads. Through glass in the doors you could see part of a firetruck that looked older'n any of the fire trucks in South Philly. Standing out front was a stooped over skinny man or maybe it was a boy, it was hard to tell which, he looked like a crippled bird and had his red hair that was red as the fire engine slicked straight back like my father combed his and that my father called a teddybear. Mr. Beezley shouted out, "Sireen ain't blowed yet, Charley?" The crippled man he called Charley looked embarrassed and grinned and shook his head and Brother and Sparky fell all over each other in a fit of giggles like they'd heard their father tease the man like this lots of times before. Mr. Beezley was muttering to my father, "When he ain't snoopin for gossip for the *County Seat Weekly*, Charley stands there all day waitin for the first whistle to blow." He shook his head then said in a lower voice that with him was like anybody else's normal talking so's you could hear every word, "Watcher boys around him, tell 'em not to go back into the woods with him, if you get my meanin." Brother and Sparky started giggling again when they heard this, Frank and Buster looking at them like as if they just told a joke that neither of them got.

My father took a quick look back at the man named Charley like he didn't want to get caught looking but was taking a good gander all the same, while I stared open at him, wondering what Mr. Beezley meant about not going in the woods with him.

Beyond the firehouse, across a flat field of yellow dust where not even weeds grew, and past where the hill begun that the water tower sat on, was a building made of clabboard painted gray that Brother pointed to and said was the schoolhouse that he called state prison that him and Sparky and Sister went to and that my brothers'd be going to too when it opened, which he said could be never, so far as he was concerned. I figured it couldn't be like the Sacred Heart school my brothers went to in South Philly since there wasn't a cross on the roof so it wouldn't have statues of the Blessed Virgin in the toilet either. Beyond the school you could see the swamp stretching off as far as you could see in either direction so it looked like the town was surrounded by nothing but swamp.

At the firehouse we turned down a tar road Mr. Beezley called Camp Meeting Walk where he said the bluenoses used to go to shout and pray under tents in the grove. We come to a store where there was a big washed out sign over the front door that when I spelled out the letters that was all peeling off said GOTTLIEB'S, then in littler letters underneath, "Dry Goods & General Notions," and under that, "U.S. Post Office, Lenape, N.J." I right away knew from the sign that was where the chicks and mash and seeds came from, and the coal oil and hamburger and other things my father got on the eye there.

It was a big yellow, dusty looking place with a big falling down porch off to one side with a rusty table and rusty wire-back chairs two boys was sitting in drinking sodas out of the bottles. There was an old-fashioned gas pump out front with a glass tank up top and right next to it was a black greasy red pump with a handle said KEROSENE painted on it so I knew now where Frank and Buster got the coal oil for the stove when my mother sent them with the empty javellie water jug. There was more things stacked out front than Willie ever had out in front of his store—there was fruits and vegetables and cartons of eggs 25¢ "Fresh from the Henhouse" and shoes and hats—and what wasn't out front looked like it was jammed in the windows, rolls of chickenwire and rakes and bags of feed and seed and oil cans and oil stoves and I don't know what else, all crowded in behind the big panes of glass that was so dirty and full of old fly paper hanging down and spider webs as thick as in our privy where moths and bugs and flies was caught that looked like they been dead since long before I was born.

Mr. Beezley opened the screendoor and took us inside to treat us to candy while my father waited outside because he whispered to Mr. Beezley he ain't been able to pay yet what he put on the eye and would rather wait outside. Inside was as big and dark and like a cave as one of the ragshops on 3rd Street, only instead of smelling mildewy like a cellar it smelled of Jew pickles in a barrel like Willie had in his store one cent apiece, and smelled of rubber and leather from the boots and smelled of salt pork and smoked hams and slabs of bacon hanging from the fly-specked ceiling along with fly-specked lightbulbs that didn't have no shades on them. There was a big rack with all kinds of comic books and magazines, I seen *True Romance* that Mrs. Beezley brung my mother when she was through with it, and movie magazines that Mrs. Beezley must've got here too that I looked at the covers for Shirley Temple but didn't see her picture anywhere.

Like in the window, flypaper hung down everywhere from the ceiling that was so thick with flies stuck on them there wasn't no room for anymore flies. Like he was standing in shadows the place was so dark, a man with long arms and long legs and a mouth that looked all greasy like he just et pork, was putting cans of things on shelves that was sagging like they was going to fall down. Later Mr. Beezley told us he was called Lenny and was something called a Lenilenape Indian that used to live around here "before most all of them got killt off," and that's how the town got its name. I wondered if they was killed off by the soldiers marched down Hessian Soldiers Way and was this Lenny the only Indian got away? I wondered how come he didn't look like the Indians in the cowboy pictures with pigtails and feathers and nothing on but a rag around their middles?

"How's it goin, Mr. Gottlieb?" Mr. Beezley hollered over to the other side of the store to another man in a baseball cap jammed down over his ears that Mr. Beezley said, once we was outside, was so's he wouldn't have to listen to Mrs. Gottlieb. He was wearing a bloody apron like the butchers in the slaughterhouse on Sigel Street and he was standing at a butcher block slicing pork chops with a cleaver just like the way Willie done, fast and quick you wondered why he didn't chop his fingers off. But Mr. Gottlieb didn't look up from what he was doing and I wondered if he was hard of hearing like Slap, you'd have to be not to hear Mr. Beezley, but when he stopped chopping he looked across the store at Mr. Beezley with eyes like a fish through his glasses that was thick as fishbowls and nodded once real quick without saying anything. He threw the pork-chops up on the scale, his thumbs fluttering around the wax paper while he read the scale through the bottom of his glasses, the lower plate of his false teeth slipping out he was breathing so heavy because, Mr. Beezley said again outside, Mr. Gottlieb been gassed in the First World War.

The candy display was up near the front of the store and instead of being in a glass case like at Finkel's on 2nd Street the candy was in open boxes and jars behind chicken wire that was all poked and bent out of shape. My eyes went to it like two magnets right off and my mouth started watering since I ain't had any candy since we left South Philly, only sugar I snitched from the sugar bowl. The biggest lady I ever seen in my life, even bigger'n Mrs. Beezley, with so much fat hanging down her arms you couldn't see her elbows, she put down her knitting and heaved herself up off of a wood packing crate behind a window with bars said "U.S. Post Office" over it at the end of the counter. She come waddling up to wait on us and Mr. Beezley nodded and called her Mrs. Gottlieb and told her who we was and she grinned and said in a voice that was almost as shrill and loud as Mr. Beezley's what nice looking boys we was. That made Frank and Buster look down at their sneakers but Slap just grinned back at her with his sweet and goofy grin.

Frank and Brother picked out sourballs that Mrs. Gottlieb poked out to them through the chicken wire and Buster and

Slap picked niggertoes while Sparky took a maryjane. I couldn't make up my mind between a niggertoe, a maryjane or a candy I ain't never seen before that was shaped like a banana, and when Mr. Beezley said in his loud voice, "C'mon, c'mon, we ain't got all day," I pointed to the banana. Mrs. Gottlieb shoved it through the wire at me, saying with that big grin of hers, "Where'djou git them pretty eyelashes? I wisht I had me them pretty eyelashes, they're just wasted on a boy." I got all flustered, I thought she was making fun of me because Frank and Buster was always saying I had eyes sneaky like a mouse and my mother was always saying my eyes was bigger'n me belly but none of them ever said my eyes was pretty.

She wouldn't take no money from Mr. Beezley for the candy and he thanked her and she said to him, eyeing us, "I seen their daddy a whole lot of times now but I ain't never seen the missus, why don't your missus bring her in next time she comes shopping?" Mr. Beezley said he'd tell Mrs. Beezley to do that and told her he was much obliged and thanked her again for the candy.

Once we was outside, my father right away asked me and my brothers did we thank Mr. Beezley for the candy. Buster piped up and said we didn't have to thank him because Mrs. Gottlieb treated us, but my father give him a look and he said well did we thank Mrs. Gottlieb? and when Frank said we didn't but Mr. Beezley did he made us thank Mr. Beezley for thanking her.

Me, I couldn't wait the minute we was out the door I took a bite out of my candy banana that turned out to be even sweeter'n the rotten bananas Willie used to give me. It made my teeth ache even more'n a niggertoe ever did so I only et little nibbles out of it to make it last as long as possible, as long as til we got to the river anyhow.

We come on a road Mr. Beezley said was called "the boulevard" and I thought maybe they called it that because it was wider'n all the other roads and was tarred like the one Gottlieb's was on, but Mr. Beezley said years back the bluenoses named it Blood o' the Lamb Boulevard but everybody just called it the boulevard now for short.

On the boulevard we passed a place that said Borough Hall over its door that was another big clabboard two-story that looked like our house. There was men lined up on the rickety old steps and men coming out of the front door with sacks of potatoes on their shoulders, watching us like they wasn't watching us.

Mr. Beezley said that was where home relief was and my father could go there for it if something didn't open up for him at the yard pretty soon.

As we turned onto the boulevard we passed a saloon. I was hoping my father wouldn't see it so's he wouldn't be tempted. But wouldn't you know there was a man with thick wire glasses and flat gray hair and an apron on standing in the window behind the bar. He was looking out and when Mr. Beezley seen him he waved and the man waved back, his face stiff and serious. I seen my father look at the man in the window and sneak a glance sideways at the beer signs said Schmidt's of Philadelphia and Valley Forge Beer and Lord Camden Ale nailed either side of the door, then he looked away quick, his adam's apple going a mile a minute like he was tasting the beer in every one of them beer signs.

Over the door I spelled out the sign swinging there said TARKIE'S SALOON and under it FRIED OYSTERS. I held my breath til we was pretty well past the place and didn't let it out til I was sure my father and Mr. Beezley wasn't going to go in.

Sometimes we passed other people on the side of the road, ladies in raggedy housedresses, more raggedy even than my mother's, with their hair cut short in what my mother said was a bob, some of them holding onto the hands of kids no bigger'n Kate and carrying an empty gallon jug in the other like they was heading to Gottlieb's for coal oil. When Mr. Beezley nodded to the ladies and they smiled back you could see most everyone of them had teeth missing like Mrs. Snarp and I wondered why that was, my mother had big teeth with gaps in between that she hated and was always holding her hand up to hide but there wasn't any missing that I could see.

Then two boys in barefeet slunk by watching us sneaky-eyed. They had a dog following them was so skinny you could count its ribs. One boy had dirty-looking yellow hair and snaggle teeth and the other had a squint eye and pimples that both the Beezley boys must've known because they waved to them. I heard Brother whisper to Frank and Buster like he didn't want his father to hear, "Them two's in the Swamp Rats," saying it like it was something awful to be in but his eyes was glittering when he said it.

I never seen boys walking around with no shoes on before, you never done it in South Philly what with all the horse droppings and dog turds, I wondered if that was what being in the Swamp Rats meant, you walked around in your barefeet and lived back in the swamp.

The boulevard made a sharper turn and near where it did was a big white place, bigger even than Gottlieb's store, its walls made of clabboard too but the boards wider'n any I seen up to now. There was four big glass windows like at Gottlieb's only they looked all dark from the outside and they was nothing in them except twisted crepe paper that was so faded from the sun you could hardly see what color it been to begin with. Through the screendoor we could hear "A Tisket a Tasket I Lost Me Yellow Basket" that I heard on our radio and knew all the words to by heart. Mr. Beezley muttered to my father, throwing the place a dirty look, *"Jitterbuggers,"* which I didn't know what jitterbuggers meant but that sounded like he was spitting something out of his mouth that didn't taste good. Over the screen door was a sign that spelled DIXIE JAZZ DANCE PALACE ABBOTT'S ICE CREAM, and even before my mouth started watering over the word ice cream, when I seen the word dance I was dying to know if people danced in there, if they danced and sung like I done for my mother in the parlor on Mifflin Street but ain't done anymore since we moved to Jersey.

Across the road from the Dixie Jazz Dance Palace was a lot full of cinders and in it sat a big bus painted red on the bottom and cream on top. What made my heart start up was seeing the sign in the little window over the windshield said PHILADELPHIA, so I knew it went to where I wanted to get back to more'n anything in the world and that it was the bus Mrs. Beezley mentioned coming through Camden that first time we came over.

I right away had the idea that my mother and me could run away and go back to Philly on the bus instead of on the raft that never got there in any of my dreams. I kept it to myself and day-dreamed about the bus for days and ever after that when I heard its motor that was so loud you could hear it all the way through the trees from the boulevard to our house, and heard the driver shift gears on the hill, the sound of it meant Philadelphia in my ears and it got me so excited I'd listen to that motor for as long as I could hear it, wishing with all my heart everytime I heard it that I was on it and on my way back to the city.

The boulevard, that Slap called "the billavar" in his own way of hearing things, kept curving around and around. We passed a woods that was nothing but tall and skinny trees with white trunks and leaves all shiny in the sun like sparks when the wind shook them. I kept wondering where the river was when after that we came to a place Mr. Beezley said was the fort where the Revolutionary battlefield was, and hearing that, Frank and Buster's eyes grew big as saucers.

The fort was full of nothing but long holes in the ground where grass grew at the bottom that Mr. Beezley said was called trenches where soldiers hid one time. Behind the trenches was a big flat field where he said the soldiers that marched down Hessian Soldiers Way was all buried. There was nothing there but grass that a man in a straw hat was mowing and I wondered, if people was buried there, where was all the tombstones? I wanted to ask Slap where they was but I was too busy gaping around looking for the river.

You could see cannons everywhere like I seen in the movies. They was all painted shiny black and was up on blocks of white cement and all of them was pointing in the same direction toward some hedges that when we got to them, my heart started pounding, I thought I was going to jump right out of my skin because I seen for the first time we was high up on a hill and far down below was the river and across the river as plain as anything was Philadelphia. I stared and stared at it as if my eyes would break.

Even if we couldn't go back to Philadelphia, I wished at least we lived here on the river and not back by the swamp, I wished we lived high up here so's I could look across the water anytime I wanted and see the city, and at night in bed see all the lights go on and the ships going by in the dark....

Frank and Buster was jumping up and down like jack in the box, they couldn't wait to get down to the water and see where the fishes was. As we started off toward one of the long flights of steps cut in the side of the hill, that Mr. Beezley called a bluff and not a hill, we passed a big tree with a heavy gray branch hanging far out over the bluff that Brother and Sparky was just busting to tell us about, Brother telling us, "Two limey spies was hung on that branch!"—"Look, you can still see the rope marks!" Sparky butts in and Brother give him a rabbit punch for butting in. You could see two deep grooves ground in side by side all around the branch that was all grown over with bark now and my brothers was gaping and gaping at them rope marks.

They was the longest steps I ever seen, all made out of cement. I counted them as we went down and down and counted up as far I could go, to fifty, and there was still plenty more steps.

Mr. Beezley took us to where the bluff ducked down under some trees he called willows. It was there he said, "Here's where the minniegudgeons and catfish bite, and eels for bait." Brother and Sparky right off got themselves all big-eyed telling us about all the big catfish they caught and Mr. Beezley said to my father, "They're good eatin, if you don't mind the bones." He told him he'd lend him one of his fishing poles and my father was nodding his head like he couldn't wait to go fishing. Frank and Buster was hopping up and down hollering could they fish too? and my father said, "We'll see," like big people always say when they don't want to right out say yes or no.

I couldn't take my eyes off of the city. I kept sneaking looks that way every chance I got, trying not to gape too much for fear Buster or one of the others'd catch me at it and guess what I was thinking and needle me. So when Mr. Beezley pointed up the river from where we was and across to the shipyard where he worked and pointed out the boat he was working on to my father, a boat that looked like nothing but a big rusty thing up out of the water he called a tanker, my eyes followed his finger like a magnet, just like my father's done, only for me it was because it was part of the place I was so homesick for, whereas I knew by the way he grinned and the way his eyes got so all of a sudden bright, it was because the shipyard was a place he was hoping he might be working someday.

Most of the boats was under high high roofs made of steel beams that crisscrossed every which way like an erector set that Mr. Beezley called the ways. He was going on telling my father all about the shipyard and pointing out things, he pointed to an old rusty boat with a white flag with an orange in the middle of it flying at the back he said was a Jap boat tied up there to take on scrap iron from the yard. Then he pointed down our side of the shore and said the ferry that took him to the yard docked right around the bend. My father was nodding his head like crazy, his eyes galloping like horses as they chased after Mr. Beezley's finger, you could tell by his eyes he was all eager to get on that ferry and go across to work in the shipyard with Mr. Beezley in the worst way.

The boys started getting restless and monkeying around and Frank said, "Hey, Pop, kin we take off our sneaks and stockins and go in a water?" My father looked at Mr. Beezley and Mr. Beezley said to us, "You better watch out the crabs don't bitecha." "Aw, the crabs won't bite us," Brother said, and Sparky put his two cents in, saying, "I'll tret on any ole crab and crush it to death if it tries to bite me."

My father started rubbing his cigarette pocket like he was remembering what my mother said and didn't want to get in no hot water but Mr. Beezley, like he was reading his mind, said, "Aw gwan, Stosh, let 'em go in," so my father said we could go in, "But not out too far since I ain't learnt any of you how to doggie paddle yet." Sparky bragged he knew how to doggie paddle already and Brother, sticking his chest out, said that was nothing, he could do the breast stroke, and you could see when he said it Frank and Buster was green with envy the look in their eye.

I was scared at first to go in, not knowing how deep it was and remembering what my mother said about drowning in the river, but I didn't want to ask my father how deep it was for fear of showing everybody all over again what a scaredy cat I was. So what I did was, when the others sat down on the rocks and started taking off their sneakers and stockings I hung back and took my sweet old time, letting the older boys go in first, and when I seen none of them dropped out of sight after sticking their feet in, I unhooked my maryjanes and rolled down my socks and with my heart pounding, I walked across the wet sand that felt so cool and gritty under my bare feet. I stuck my toes in the water then jerked them back real quick and could see why the boys was jumping up and down hugging themselves and hollering how cold it was, it was like ice.

"Gwan, Mick," my father said, settling down on a rock with Mr. Beezley while the two of them lit up a cigarette, "Gwan gitcher feet wet."

I knew there was no way out of it and so shutting my eyes and holding my breath I wriggled my toes in the water again. By this time the Beezley boys'd waded far out and monkey see monkey do my brothers soon got bolder and was wading right out after them so that my father hollered at them to come back in closer and when they did they started razzing me because I was only barely in the water since I was still only going in little by little.

With every step my feet sunk in the sand it scratched my soles like little ticklings so that when I wriggled my toes it tickled between them even more. I could feel the shivers going up my legs and up my spine and liked it so much I got almost as bold as my brothers and waded out almost up to my knees. The water was so clean on this side, not like it was on the Philly side the day me and Henry seen it when it was all greasy and bubbly with dead fish floating on top—The water was so clean here because it wasn't the war yet and the polio ain't come yet and I could see my toes clear to the bottom it was so clean.

Slap came wading near me, stooping and running his fingers through the water like they was boats and making speedboat noises with his mouth, *Brrrutt! Brrrutt!* He grinned and swerved his boats around me.

"Where is the sea?" I asked him and he looked at me and creased up one side of his mouth and went, "Heh? Heh?" I asked him again and he shrugged his shoulders like he couldn't care less where the sea was and went on scooping his hands on top the water. *Brrrutt! Brrrutt!* I was so busy wondering where was the sea I give a start, my eyes just about popping out, seeing the fish, that I found out later was the minniegudgeons, and the catfish too, that had whiskers and the ugliest eyes, even uglier'n Mr. Gottlieb's fish eyes behind his glasses. They come nibbling around my toes and being so ugly I thought they must have ugly sharp teeth and would eat my toes, so I jerked up my feet and let out a howl and come splashing out of that river faster'n I ever moved in my entire life. And when Mr. Beezley shouted out with a grin, "A crab gitcha?" and I screamed back, "No, the fishes!" him and my father bust out laughing and all the boys did too, thinking that was the funniest.

I sat on a rock on the beach, my heart going a mile a minute, trying to count all my toes. When I seen they was all there, I quieted down a little and stuck them out and let them dry off. Then I peeked across the river to where I figured Mifflin Street was and where I wished I was that very minute where there wasn't no catfish or no frogs or no snakes and there wasn't a swamp, dreaming in my head I had wings like an angel in one of them picture cards my brothers brung home from Sunday school, I dreamt I was flying over the water back to Philly, I dreamt my mother was flying along with me, flying so high over the river where no catfish or minniegudgeons could bite your toes....

I got to dreaming so hard I thought I was really back there again and give a start when I heard my father shout for my brothers to come out of the water, we was going home now... *home* to me was still so much 126 Mifflin Street my heart gave a little leap when he said it, but then it sunk back down again when I knew he only meant we was going back to the house by the swamp, which was only what my mother ever called it, the house, home to her still being on Hoffman Street where her mother was.

They went out so far my brothers' knickers was all wet, I just knew my mother would yell when she seen they got their clothes all wet. Mr. Beezley let Brother and Sparky go barefoot but my father made Frank and Buster and Slap put their sneakers back on even though the two oldest pulled long pusses about it, Buster grumbling why couldn't they go barefoot if Brother and Sparky could, they never got to do anything. My father give him a look and said we was still city boys and didn't know how to walk without no shoes yet and said it in a way Buster knew he better shutup and put his sneakers on right away.

As we went up the beach, the two Beezley boys held back and when I looked around I seen they was both peeing in the river, their mouths hanging open like they was dreaming and like what they was doing out where anybody could see them was nothing at all to them. I was waiting for their father to look back and catch them and holler but he was so busy gabbing to my father and sticking his arm out to point across the water at this and at that, he didn't see nothing else. I got the feeling he wouldn't've said anything even if he did see it, but I knew if my father seen me or any of my brothers do it we would've got hollered at and probably even got a licking.

We came to a place Mr. Beezley said was called Snake Hill and you could see why it was called that, it was so long and so twisty. Near the bottom was a place that looked like a long low shack made out of nothing but tarpaper with beer signs plastered out front like was out in front of Tarkie's saloon and another sign nailed over the door spelled out YE OLD SHIP BOTTOM. There was music coming out the open windows sounded just like the music did on the jukebox in Hoolihan's that my father used to take me and Danny to on 2nd Street.

I curled up inside tight as a spring and held my breath when I seen Mr. Beezley elbow my father and nod towards the place, saying something in his ear. I could see my father looking and looking, his gullet going a mile a minute like it done when we passed Tarkies, his hand scratching at his cigarette pocket. But then I felt the spring in me snap and run down when I seen him grin sheepish and shake his head, and even though Mr. Beezley asked him again, louder this time, saying, "Aw c'mon, Stosh, just one to wet our whistles, I got a couple of bucks on me," my father said, "Naw naw, you go on, I'm still on 'a wagon." Mr. Beezley said he didn't like to drink alone, then got his needle out, saying, "She," meaning my mother, "won't smell one little beer on yer breath and who is it wears the pants in yer house anyhow?" But my father still just grinned and shook his head and when he shook it that second time I let out my breath and felt my shoulders drop like an awful danger just passed.

When we got back to the house again, Slap, that didn't know any better and hated to take a bath more'n anything, shrieked out to my mother like it was a good joke, "You won' hafta heat up no water fer us ternight!" and when she said, "Why not?" he said, "'Cause we went wadin in 'a ribber and our feets is all clean!" My mother said, "I can see that, look atcher clothes!" She gave my father a dirty look but all he said was, "They wanted to go in with Sam's boys, I kep' a eye on 'em."

In spite of Slap thinking the river was his bathtub he was sorely disappointed when it turned out we all had to take a bath anyhow that night, my mother scrubbing me harder'n usual when it came my turn in the tub, like she was trying to scrub the river off me hard as she could.

Now that we didn't have no bathtub upstairs nor no spigots where the hot water run out whenever you turned them on, on Saturday nights after Frank and Buster done the supper dishes, my mother had to heat pots of water on the stove, then pour them into the washtub she dragged out into the middle of the kitchen floor and that's where she scrubbed us, starting with the youngest first, meaning Kate. She wouldn't let any of us boys in the kitchen while Kate was bare in the tub, which meant even though I was dying to I never got the chance to see if Kate's dunkey grew in yet.

The water got grayer and grayer as she worked her way on up through Danny, then me, then Slap—She still had to wash Slap, he hated a bath so much he never cleaned himself good enough to suit her when he done it himself, especially his ears. When she went behind Slap's ears with the washrag wrapped around her finger, you could hear him yowling loud as Kate done when my mother brushed her hair in the morning.

Frank and Buster was old enough now to heat up their own water and to wash themselves. They was even allowed to have a clean towel of their own to share instead of having to use the one was all wet and soggy from her drying the rest of us, and they would scream bloody murder if one of us come in the kitchen when they was in the tub or drying themselves off, which meant I ain't yet got to see their dunkeys or see if they had hats on them or not.

When she was drying me off I told her what we seen that day going to the river and first told her about looking to see if I could see our old house on Mifflin Street across the river and about seeing the Philadelphia bus in case she forgot Mrs. Beezley told her there was a bus went there through Camden and over the Benjamin Franklin bridge. I said, crossing all my fingers under the towel, would we ever go there on the bus, then take the number 5 trolley down to see Grandmom and Aunt Nell? She all of a sudden quit drying me and looked dreamy a minute, then said in a quiet way, "We'll see." Then she began rubbing me even harder'n when I was in the tub.

Next I told her about the crippled man that looked like a boy we seen in front of the firehouse had hair red as a fire engine and asked her why he was crippled the way he was. She said, "He was prolly born that way or maybe he done something bad in another life." I said like what? She said, "Maybe murdering somebody or not going to church on Sunday. If he had hair red as a fire truck he prolly been singed by the fires of hell already in another life because everybody knows red hair comes from being born too close to the fire."

I figured that must've been why Mr. Beezley warned my father not to let us go back in the woods with the crippled man named Charley because he must've murdered somebody or not ever gone to church. But if that was so I asked her why didn't Mr. Beezley and all the Beezleys have red hair since none of them ever set foot inside of a church? She said, "Yer jist full of questions, ain't'cha?" and jabbed the towel in my ear til I thought she was going to bore right through my skull. "Speakin of church, you want to go to the children's mass some Sunday with your brothers?" she said, rubbing away. I wasn't sure I did but I nodded I did anyway because I knew she wanted me to and I didn't want to come back in another life to have red hair and be all humped over like the man named Charley if I didn't go to church.

I didn't get to go to church that Sunday because the next morning when the little hand was near the nine my older brothers left for the children's mass at Saint Theresa's, leaving me alone to play with my oil truck in the front yard, pushing it through dirt roads I was making in the sand.

All of a sudden I felt something bright behind my shoulder. I swung around and looked. There, staring at me from the edge of the woods was a face with the same blond head of curls I seen the first day we come here to look at the house. Wondering again if I was seeing things, I blinked my eyes and looked again. It was real all right, hair so bright in the sun it hurt my eyes to look at it. Then, before I knew it, whoever it was—he or she, I couldn't be sure—slipped out of the bushes and first looking towards our house like afraid of being seen, he or she came and stood where I could see them in plain view. We stared at each other. Mr. Beezley said the Mahoneys had a girl even though my mother said she was a boy, and if this was her I was wondering why was she wearing boy's pants? Girl or boy, whoever it was looked at our house again, then peered into the backyard and not seeing anybody, came a couple steps closer. Out in the sun that blond hair really shined. With them gold curls and pug nose whoever it was, except for the short pants, looked just like the picture of Shirley Temple stamped on my blue Ralston cereal bowl.

A little at a time he or she come over until they were standing right over me, staring down at me like I might be a hoptoad or a snake.

"What're you doing?"

My tongue got tangled in my teeth but finally I managed to say, "Nuthin."

"You must be doing something sitting in the dirt with that truck. How come its wheel's missing?"

The way it was said made me feel I was doing something I should be ashamed of. It sounded like a boy. I was pretty certain that's what it was.

"My Uncle Jake done it."

He looked at me like he didn't believe me.

"I have lots of trucks and they all have wheels."

I didn't know what to say to that so I just looked down in the dirt. He ran the sole of his shoe over one of the roads my oil truck'd dug, making one of its deliveries. The shoe was like the maryjanes I was wearing only it was black and shiny and looked brand-new like it hardly ever been wore. A clean white sock was folded neat down at the ankle.

"You want to come over to my house and play?"

I looked at him like he really was Shirley Temple the way I daydreamed about her living next-door. I wanted to ask him if that was his name even though he was wearing boy's pants like I was, except his had a crease in them like they was brand-new too and didn't have no patches. Seeing I was holding back, he said, "I have lots of toys."

I wanted to know had it been him in "Poor Little Rich Girl," but instead I said, "I have to ask me mother." I got the idea he knew I wasn't sure if I should go or not, so he came up close this time, his lips curling in the sweetest smile.

"I got coloring books, I got stuffed animals, I got a tricycle from my Grandmother Mahoney, I got a hobbyhorse from my Grandmother O'Shea, I got Scarlett O'Hara paperdolls from *Gone With the Wind...*"

That done it. It was like my dream come true and I jumped up and ran quick as I could into the house to ask my mother could I go play with the boy next-door looked just like Shirley Temple.

My cheeks was still stinging and must've been red as Kate's eyes after her hairbrushing from the quick rub my mother gave them with the washrag before she let me go off to the neighbors.

"Now behave yourself, don't pick your nose and watch what you say," she said, running the comb through my hair, "Don't go tellin them all our business."

I promised I wouldn't and, even though she just about scrubbed them raw the night before, after she gave a squint in both my ears to make double sure they was clean, I ran out the back-door, the smell strong in my nose of the puny shoulder of pork she was roasting for our Sunday dinner that my father got on the eye at Gottlieb's the night before.

As I raced across the yard, afraid if I didn't hurry the boy with the Shirley Temple curls might be gone and then I'd know I only imagined it after all, I knew she was watching me from the kitchen window, craning her neck to get a good look at the boy nobody'd seen up til now.

His name turned out to be Ronnie and not Shirley. He said he was named after his father, Joe John Mahoney, but that his mother thought it was too common, so later on she started calling him Ronald Tyrone Mahoney after Ronald Colman in "If I Was King" and Tyrone Power in "Suez," that was her favorite movie stars. Her name was Ginger that wasn't her real name either he said, which was really Agatha Mary O'Shea, but was a name she gave herself after Ginger Rogers that was her favorite lady movie star of all the movie stars.

He told me all that in a fast-talking way as I followed him through the woods, like he ain't talked to anybody in umpteen years, and the only other thing he said was to ask me what my name was. When I told him he said, "Are you named after the mouse?" When I said how did he know he gave me a look over his shoulder and laughed like I was a silly. "That means we're both named after movie stars," and he gave another laugh that was like a little bark from a dog.

I felt the tips of my ears burning, thinking he might be laughing at me, and stared down at the path and didn't say nothing the rest of the way, only looked at him from behind, seeing that even though he didn't seem much older'n me he was a lot pudgier, his hiney filling out his short pants and bouncing up and down in time with his Shirley Temple curls as he stepped along real careful like he was afraid he might get his new patent leather maryjanes dirty.

Their house wasn't exactly a two-story house like ours but had a long roof that slanted down with a row of little windows sticking up out of it in front and in back. Their porch was wider'n ours, the ceiling painted blue like the sky, and only went across the front and not around the side too. The whole house looked like it just been painted in fresh cream it was so clean and bright, you could see right away everything about it looked newer and neater'n ours did even though it might've been as old or older. Even the porch steps was painted and didn't look like they'd sag under you when you went up them. They even had a garage in back. The doors was flung open and there inside was a man laying under a Chevy with his legs sticking out. His undershirt hanging out of his pants was smeared with grease and looked like it shrunk in the wash so that you could see his round belly sticking out with hair on it as blond as Ronnie's curls, so I figured that must be his father, Joe John Mahoney.

He was so busy poking around under the car with a bare lightbulb in a cage that was connected to a long wire running out the kitchen window and fixing whatever it was he was fixing, he didn't see us when we came around the corner. Ronnie seen him but acted like he ain't seen him laying there as we went up the backsteps and never did say who he was. If it wasn't for the hair on his belly I wouldn't've never known.

I followed Ronnie in through the kitchen door that was cut in half so only the top part was open, I never seen a door like it. I could see right away everything was shiny and new, with a real electric frigidaire in one corner instead of an icebox like we had. Over by the windows that had bright white curtains in them was an electric stove that I only seen pictures of in ads in the Sunday newspaper. The black and white tile floor shined as bright as my Aunt Maggie's ever did.

After the kitchen was a hall and on either side was bedrooms I never seen on a first floor before. In one was a big bed with a doll in a hat and long dress propped up on the pillows. In the other was a smaller bed that had to be Ronnie's it was piled high with teddy bears and monkeys and so many other stuffed animals I didn't even know the names of. My eyes popped even bigger because next to that room a door was part open and I could see a bathtub and a real flush toilet like we used to have on Mifflin Street. Right off the bat I went green with envy, wishing we had one like it again instead of the smelly old two-holer.

The dining room had chairs around the table that all matched and a bowl of paper flowers in the middle and even had drapes that tied back at the windows instead of only plain paper shades all tore and rain-stained like we had in ours. Through the doorway I could see a lady was sitting in the parlor in a chair fat as the chairs in Aunt Maggie's parlor. Next to her was a shiny new floor model radio that was playing dance music real low. She was smoking a cigarette, only the second lady besides Mrs. Beezley I ever seen do that, and she was reading a movie magazine like I seen in the racks at Gottlieb's.

She was as plump as the chair she was sitting in and didn't look much taller'n Ronnie and had bobbed black hair that had streaks of gray in it. She looked up surprised when I came walking in the door with him but I come to know she done that no matter how many times she seen you come walking in the door, like everything she seen was always a surprise to her. When Ronnie told her who I was and we was going to play together "upstairs," she smiled real sweet just like Ronnie done, only she showed a tooth missing right in front. He told me later she was scared to death of the dentist and so was he and that was why her teeth was all rotting out of her head. But then as quick as a blink her eyes that was as green as grass and as round as Betty Boop's in the cartoons, got an annoyed look like I said or done something wrong, and that I found out later was her main two looks, looking surprised and looking annoyed.

Them eyes was climbing all over me like I was something she might want to buy. I got all shy and flustered and looked away, staring at the dial of the radio that I could see now was a brand new RCA Victor where "Who Stole Me Heart Away" was playing that I knew all the words to, having learned them from my mother.

She went from my hair to my shirt to my maryjanes and back up again, all the time asking me what was my name and how old was I and how many brothers and sisters did I have?

Her eyebrows shot up when I told her, four brothers and one sister, then she smiled real sweet again and asked me, "Do you like living next-door?" I lied and nodded and then she asked me, "What does your father do?" I said I didn't know, answering her like I answered each and everyone of her questions as little as possible, remembering what my mother said about telling too much of our business. She looked at me funny like I must be an awful dumb cluck not knowing what my own father done, but even if he did have a job I probably wouldn't've been able to tell her I was so tongue-tied in front of her.

I could see Ronnie was getting the fidgets with all her questions and finally he made a face and grabbed my arm and pulled me into the hall toward the stairs, saying to her, "We're going up to the playroom now." He said it in a way, all bossy and snippy, that surprised me since neither me nor any of my brothers would ever be allowed to talk to our mother that way without getting walloped. But all Mrs. Mahoney done was smile sweet as sugar and say, "You and your new little friend have a nice time, dear, and not too much noise, I don't want to get one of my you-know-whats."

"You and your you-know-whats," Ronnie muttered under his breath but if his mother heard him she acted like she didn't because she lit up another cigarette and went back to her movie magazine.

The playroom was all there was upstairs under that slanty roof and my eyes almost popped out of my head when I seen the size of it and all that was crammed in up there. Ronnie wasn't lying when he told me all he had, and there was lots more he never mentioned, nor ever could, it would take a year to name everything. I never seen so many toys in my life, it was like a whole toyshop, it was like ten toy counters in the five and tenny jammed with every toy you could ever dream of: stuffed animals and dolls galore, electric trains and the rocking horse and the tricycle from his two grandmoms and a yellow car with a real steering wheel you sat in and pushed with pedals, and a red locomotive you sat on the roof of and skipped along with your feet and not one but two scooters and a Flexible Flyer sled leaning in one corner and a blackboard on legs with the ABC's and numbers and bright pictures of birds and flowers and cities that changed when you turned the knobs, and stacks of paint sets and coloring books and loads of toy cars and trucks without one busted wheel, just like he said—There was more things'n you could ever get to play with in a million years, and I looked around and I looked around and then I looked around some more but Ronnie went strutting through it like it was nothing at all to him and started rummaging in some boxes in the corner, he said he couldn't wait to show me what he called his newest paperdolls of all the movie stars that was going to be in "Gone With the Wind."

He brought out one box from the big stack and opened it and then began hooking paper clothes on paper shoulders and walking the dolls across the floor that was tile shiny as the kitchen floor downstairs. I was sure he must have Shirley Temple paperdolls and was about to ask him if he did when all of a sudden something caught my eye more'n anything else done so far and that was a whole bookcase under the row of back windows that was filled with nothing but picture books like the Peter Rabbit at the free clinic in South Philly. When I went over to them and stared at the covers facing out, not daring to touch them, my eyes dancing from one book to the other, Ronnie came over, all snippy and impatient, and pulled me away, saying we'd play with the paperdolls now and sat me down on the floor like I was a paperdoll myself. He dressed up one he called Scarlett O'Hara in a long wide paper gown came down to her ankles that I thought was a nightgown but was hoopskirts he said. He told me him and his mother and father was going to see "Gone With the Wind" when it came to the movies in Camden because it would come to the Savar or the Stanley long before it ever came to the Rialto in the county seat, did I see "Suez"? did I see "If I Was King"? But before I could say anything he started bragging how his mother read *Gone With the Wind* all the way through twice and the third time he sat in her lap and she read it to him, did my mother read it to me?

He made me feel there was something the matter with me when I said she didn't, she never even had time to read the *True Romances* Mrs. Beezley brung over let alone a whole big book. "But I seen 'Poor Little Rich Girl,' I seen 'Snow White and the Seven Dwarves,'" I said, trying to make up for it. But Ronnie said, "Oh them, they're old hat everybody's seen already, did you see 'Angels With Dirty Faces' starring Jimmy Cagney and Pat O'Brien? did you see 'Jezebel' starring Bette Davis and George Brent? me and my mother and father saw 'Jezebel' twice it was so good"—I wanted to say I almost seen it, hearing Mrs. Beezley tell it to my mother while I was hid under the dining room table but he wouldn't let me get a word in edgewise, "Gone With the Wind" he said was going to be just about the best movie ever made, it said so right in the latest issue of *Silver Screen*, and that was that and no more to be said and he grabbed up a man paperdoll and started dressing him up in what he called a Rhett Butler suit and had him and the lady he said was Scarlett O'Hara act out all the scenes he knew from the book and finally, when there was others come into it, he let me dress up some of them paperdolls myself, a big black lady like on the Aunt Jemima pancake box and a little pickaninny he said was Missy—He told me to walk and jiggle them while he walked and jiggled Rhett Butler and Scarlett O'Hara and talked out all the parts, even talking out the parts to the dolls I was jiggling and wouldn't let me say nothing.

So while he talked, I kept sneaking looks back over my shoulder at the picture books in the bookcase, wondering if Peter Rabbit was there and if Ronnie would let me read it if it was, but he seen me looking and he slapped my hand, saying, "You're not paying attention, jiggle Mammy," and I jiggled her, seeing right off you had to play what he wanted to play or you didn't get to play at all.

After we gone through all of his favorite scenes in *Gone with the Wind*, ending up with Rhett Butler carrying Scarlett O'Hara up the make-believe stairs, his mother came up the real stairs carrying a tray that had two glasses of milk on it and two pieces of cake. "What time's your dinner?" she asked me with that real sweet smile, and I said, "Sundays when the little hand's on the one." She said, "This nice coconut cake won't spoil your dinner, will it?" Naturally I said no, it wouldn't, not able to take my eyes off of the coconut icing that I never tasted before.

She sat us down at a little play table that had dolls with eyes that open and shut propped up in two of the little play chairs. The table was set with toy teacups and a toy teapot made out of metal that Ronnie shoved aside with his elbow. His mother said, "Careful, dear, you'll dent them," as she put down the tray. He got a pouty look on his face and said, "I'll dent them if I want." I almost jumped out of my skin when she screamed at him, "You want to give me one of my you-know-whats? You know how you give me a you-know-what!" and he screamed back, "Get a headache! See if I care—I hope you get twenty million trillion headaches!"

Hearing that, she ran her fingers through her bobbed hair, her green eyes bulging big at him, her mouth opening and shutting so you could see all her bad teeth. She snapped her head around and shrieked at me, "You see how he is? You see?" and of course I ain't seen anything like it and didn't know what to do or say, my heart was running so fast in my chest. Then all of a sudden, like she turned into a total different person, she smiled at me sweet as pie and says, "Are you having a good time?" and puts the plate with the piece of cake in front of me and a napkin and a fork. I mumbled I was, hardly able to open my mouth.

Ronnie picked up his fork and started digging into his cake without another word. I didn't know you et cake with a fork, we never done it at our house, you just et it with your hands. But monkey see monkey do I picked up the fork and et it like Ronnie even though I had a hard time swallowing I felt so funny about eating it that way and about the way they hollered at each other just like I wasn't there. But Ronnie went on shoveling it in with crumbs falling out of his mouth and grinning at me like he ain't just been screaming his head off at his mother, like he was another person too, and never said what he said that me nor none of my brothers would ever dare say to our mother if we didn't want to get murdered. Then Mrs. Mahoney was standing over me, saying, "You seem like a nice little boy and maybe sometime you'll come over and play with my Ronald again?"

I looked up at her like there was another lady in the room, like she was two persons, one person one time and another another, I didn't know which one she was. She really looked like she wanted me to come again, there was something in her big eyes like she was afraid I mightn't want to. Then I looked at Ronnie, not sure what to say, and he mumbled through a mouthful of cake, "He can come over if he wants to."

Mrs. Mahoney, all of a sudden annoyed, said, "Don't talk with your mouth full, dear." I tensed up right away, thinking he was going to scream at her again but all he said was, "Can we have another piece of cake?" and even though it was hard to eat it, I was hoping she'd say yes, I liked the taste of the coconut so much. But she said no, Ronnie'd be having his dinner soon too even though I didn't smell nothing cooking down in their kitchen, and I breathed a sigh of relief inside when Ronnie didn't holler about getting no more cake but just swallowed his glass of milk all in one big swallow.

When we was finished, Mrs. Mahoney flashed her sweet smile at me one more time and said that I better go home now it was close to my dinnertime. Ronnie started whining why couldn't I go with them to his grandmother's to eat? Then just as quick as she smiled she gave him an irritated look and said, "Maybe another time, dear, we'd have to ask his mother first anyway." He said, "Well, let him go run ask her." She shrieked, "Now don't you start with me, Ronald Tyrone Mahoney, you're giving me one of my you-know-whats!" But he shouted right back, "If he can't come I hope you get a triple of your old you-know-what!" Then it was like right out of nowhere the other lady was in the room, her eyes got all wild and bulging and she ran her fingers through her hair and swinging around to me she shrieked, "You see how he is? You see?" But Ronnie only stuck out his lower lip and stared at her like if looks could kill she'd be dead in a minute.

Then just as quick she smiled at me sweet again so that I didn't know which way I was going. She started cooing to me to be sure and come again as she put her hand behind my head, steering me towards the stairs. Ronnie followed, clunking down the steps behind us, whining, "Why can't he stay? Why can't he go to Grandmother O'Shea's with us?" And even though I liked all the toys and the books and the coconut cake and being in the house, I was glad to be going, feeling like it was because of me they was fighting, not knowing, like I would know later on, they was just fighting each other, and anything or anybody was handy would set them off.

At the kitchen door she told me to tell my mother she was glad to have me over and I could come again sometime, and someday my mother would have to come over and see her, "You be sure to tell her that, hear?" Then she shoved open the bottom half of the door and eased me out by the back of my neck.

I ain't barely reached the bottom step before I heard Ronnie yelling, "He didn't have to go right then! He didn't have to!" and Mrs. Mahoney screaming, "Where's my aspirin? Where's my aspirin? See the headache you're giving me?" But Ronnie went right on shouting back at her like I ain't never heard anybody shout at their mother before, big or little.

As I rounded the corner of the house I peeked over toward the garage where Mr. Mahoney's legs and fuzzy belly was still sticking out from under the car, his legs twitching as he seemed to be tightening something up under the motor, so busy at what he was doing he never did see me and didn't seem to hear any of the shouting going on in his own house.

Glad as I was to get out of there, when I came out the other side of the woods and seen our house, I began to feel blue, and the closer I got as I crossed the yard, the bluer I got. It looked so rundown and shabby compared to where I just been, even my brothers, back now from church and sprawled out on the front porch waiting for Sunday dinner, looked like they was a part of the house too in their wore out and patched up clothes that they changed into after mass, clothes that wasn't much different than their Sunday best. I looked at the house and at them, then at the privy in the backyard that I couldn't stand the sight of and that Danny was just then coming out of, buttoning up his pants. I felt a secret shame rising up in me and felt ashamed for being ashamed, a feeling I ain't never felt so strong before.

As I went up on the porch Slap asked where I been and all I said was next-door. He screeched, "What was you doin there, what was it like? did you git to see the Mahoneys?" all eager to know, while Frank and Buster pretended they wasn't at all interested but you could tell they was. I suddenly didn't feel like telling Slap about it let alone having to talk as loud as I would have to for him to hear me. I felt ashamed about that too and promised myself I'd tell him that night in bed before Frank and Buster came up. I went by him into the house that looked even shabbier to me than the outside looked after what I just seen inside at the Mahoney's. I felt so blue even the smell of the roast pork filling the rooms didn't make my guts squirm like it usually did whenever I smelled it, coconut cake or no.

When I came in the kitchen door my mother was mashing the potatoes at the table and she asked me did I have a nice time? I nodded I did and she stopped mashing long enough to ask me what the Mahoney's house was like. I told her it was like Aunt Maggie's and Aunt Bridget's house all rolled into one. Her eyes got a wondering look but I barely seen it, I still felt so blue. But she went on about what was Mrs. Mahoney like and what was her boy like and did I see Mr. Mahoney? asking me this question and that question and kept at it til gradually my cheeks got all hot as I started telling all I seen up in Ronnie's playroom, my tongue was going as fast as she was pounding the potatoes again as I told her about all the toys he had and about their inside toilet like we used to have and the electric stove and frigidaire and the kitchen door that opened in half. But I didn't mention the piece of coco-nut cake knowing I wasn't supposed to eat nothing sweet before dinner, and didn't say nothing about playing with the paperdolls either, knowing that was bad for a boy to do.

The more I talked the harder and louder she pounded the

masher in the pot of potatoes, like finally she didn't want to hear it after all, like she was trying to pound out not only what I was saying but something going on in her own mind too.

Like the Beezleys, it turned out the Mahoneys never went to church either, even though Ronnie said his mother was born a Catholic. But Mr. Mahoney was baptised proddisin which meant he was orange Irish and not green Irish my mother said, like we was, and would've gone to the red brick church where the bluenoses went if he went to church at all but he never did.

As I got to go over Ronnie's house more and more I found out Mr. Mahoney worked on the assembly line at RCA Victor in Camden, which was where Ronnie bragged they got the new radio that was in their parlor—only he called it the living room because he said his mother said parlor was old-fashioned and he laughed at me everytime I said parlor. His father got the radio "at a discount" Ronnie said because his father worked there. I wondered if Mr. Mahoney could get my father a job on the assembly line since it didn't seem like Mr. Beezley was ever going to get him one at the shipyard.

Mrs. Mahoney treated Mr. Mahoney like a big kid so that she seemed as much his mother as she was Ronnie's. He never seemed to mind the way she dressed Ronnie sometimes in lacy things like Little Lord Flauntleroy, that looked more like clothes for a girl 'n a boy, or that she curled Ronnie's hair or that he played with paperdolls—He didn't seem to know, or care if he did, that Sam Beezley sniggered behind his back about his "daughter."

Mr. Beezley may've called Ronnie that, and Frank and Buster when they seen him calling me from the edge of the woods called him a sissy, but he was pretty strong for his age, as strong or stronger'n Frank or Buster was, because when nobody was around, which was most of the time up in the playroom, Ronnie would sit on my chest and twist my arm til I did what he wanted. He was used to getting his own way in everything and if he didn't he went into hysterics because he didn't have no brothers or sisters to rub up against.

Most every Sunday afternoon the Mahoneys drove up to Camden to have dinner with Mrs. Mahoney's mother and father. Ronnie would always come back with his arms full of more stuffed animals and toys so that soon there wouldn't be no more room in the playroom for anymore of anything, including Ronnie. But they kept on giving him things just like his Grandmom and Grandpop Mahoney done that lived the other side of the county seat but that they didn't go to see too often because Mrs. Mahoney didn't get along good with Grandmom Mahoney.

Mrs. Mahoney sat up late at night reading mysteries and movie magazines and books like *Gone With the Wind*. I never seen my mother read a book, the only thing I seen her read when she had the time was the *Catholic Messenger* she got at church on Sunday, and the day-old Philadelphia *Bulletin* from Mrs. Beezley.

All the newspapers when everybody was done reading them, except for the *Catholic Messenger* that my mother said wasn't right to use that way, ended up in the outhouse for toilet paper.

Like my brothers with the Beezleys, I was praying for the Mahoneys to ask me to go with them to the Rialto and pay my way since we never had no money to go to the movies now. But they never did, even though Ronnie whined and carried on about it like he done about me going to his Grandmother O'Shea's that first time for Sunday dinner—But Mrs. Mahoney told Ronnie if they took me they'd have to take Kate and all my brothers and there wasn't room in the Chevy for all of us, so that was that.

But I was the only one of my brothers to ever get to play in the playroom, or even get to set foot in the house, because Ronnie's mother said she got the headaches so easy, and she also let it be known in so many ways she thought my oldest brothers was too old and too rough for her Ronnie. And at the mere mention of the Snarp boys she just rolled her eyes in her head like she was about to have another big headache. But she never seen her Ronnie sitting on my chest and twisting my arm like he would break it off if I didn't do like he said. "He's makin a girl outa you," Buster would sneer and I wondered if that meant Kate would grow up to sit on people's chests and twist their arms because if that's what a girl done Ronnie was doing it. Mainly though I think Buster said that because he was never invited up to the playroom and was only being bit by the green-eyed monster.

Meantime, my father was out everyday looking for work. Sometimes he got two bits or if he was lucky even four bits cutting somebody's grass or cleaning up their yard or clearing out a cellar, like he sometimes done for the landlady against the rent he owed her. But he said with plenty of boys around to do them jobs, most days he couldn't find anything and would come back home with a look of shame and resentment in his eyes.

Everyday after the sun went down he'd pump water from the kitchen sink into the old watering can Sam Beezley gave him and carry it out to the backyard to water his plants. He'd make seven, eleven trips a night carrying water, his garden was so big. Frank and Buster wanted to help so he let them carry the watering can between them, but like everything else he didn't like the way they done things, wouldn't let them hoe or even weed, saying they mainly got in his way anyhow and with their big feet they kept tretting on his little corn and tomato plants, especially Slap when he tried to help, so he told them to leave the watering can at the edge of the garden and he'd take it from there, as usual ending up doing it all himself, happier doing everything his own way.

When he wasn't working in the garden he was working on the chicken coop he was building out back now, making it out of the old lumber he found here and there as he went around town, and down a place he called the dump, and carried home on his shoulders, making a coop because the chickens was getting bigger now, a couple of them so big he had to clip their wings to keep them from flying over the wire.

He found lots of things that way, in other people's trash or down the dump, like he found the old radio up on the shelf over the sink in the kitchen that he fixed himself so my mother could hear her stories while she worked out there that when she turned it on that morning after he went out to look for something to do wouldn't turn on. She turned on the kitchen light and that wouldn't turn on either. He came home late that day with no money but a pile of old boards on his back for the coop, and when my mother told him the electric been shut off, he dropped the wood in a cloud of dust and just stood staring down at it like all he could see was the rot and holes the bugs et in them old boards. She looked at him and pulled back her mouth like she was going to say something but it was like she didn't know what to say anymore and looked away from him and turned and went back into the house.

In the daytime we didn't miss the electric being off it being lighty, and since my brothers never cared for soap operas anyhow they didn't care. It was only after supper that night, that was only catfish my brothers caught down at the river, and what bread was left, when Buck Rogers and Flash Gordon and Jack Armstrong All-American Boy was on the radio, that they missed it the most. Frank and Buster whined and complained they couldn't hear their serials and my father gave them a look and told them to go out and see if the chickens needed water, and they went.

The worst was not having no lights because my mother made us younger ones go up to bed earlier'n usual so we could see our way before it got dark, and she made sure we all peed in the bucket in the hall before we got in bed. I told Slap and Danny longer and longer stories every night under the covers to try to make up for what we couldn't hear anymore. I tried to keep the stories close to what we'd been hearing everyday on the old Scott instead of the gossip I heard Mrs. Beezley telling my mother from under the dining room table, because sometimes when I told one of Mrs. Beezley's stories to them because it was so good and juicy, next day Slap or Danny would let slip something about it in front of my mother. She'd give them a sharp look like she was wondering how on earth they heard about that, and I'd look away pretending I ain't heard either of them say nothing.

That first night my mother burnt citronella candles for light, then the next day my father went to Gottlieb's and got an oil lamp on the eye and brought it home and filled it with coal oil from the stove and put it in the middle of the dining room table. So that night there was a little more light at least. But you couldn't see much by it. My father hunched close trying to read the help wanted ads in the *County Seat Weekly* that Mrs. Beezley brought over that day, and my mother sat close as she could trying to patch a pair of Slap's knickers.

When my mother lit the stump of what was left of a citronella candle from the night before and put it in a saucer and told us younger ones to follow her upstairs, it was time for bed, I wanted to ask her how long it'd be before we had the electric back on, but she had such a worried look in her eye, that seemed to be in her eyes most of the time now, the words died away in my throat.

The next morning after the electric was turned off and we woke up and came down into the kitchen my mother told us we wouldn't be having any breakfast because there wasn't no food in the house, not even so much as a speck of coffee or even a teaball. When Danny started to whine and complain she told him to shush, and when Buster put on a long puss and asked her why there wasn't nothing to eat, she said we would have to wait til Bill the breadman came later that morning. Buster started grumbling, "Aw geezoo, Ma," but my mother, not looking any of us in the eye, said there was nothing she could do about it and told us all to go outside.

We went out on the porch, Slap screeching in his high way if the blackberries was ripe we could pick them, if the wild apples and pears out in the woods was ripe we could pick them too, but Buster gave him a shove and yelled in his ear, "But they ain't ripe are they, dumbie? So whyn'tcha quitcher hollerin!" Then Frank and him started balancing along the railing, then they shimmied up the porch posts to pass the time. When they got tired of that they did one of their shows for us that was mostly things they seen the Three Stooges do like banging their fists on each other's head and shoving their knuckles in each other's eyes and cracking jokes and giving each other lots of rabbit punches til Frank, being the oldest, finally knocked out Buster and hauled him off the stage by the heels while the rest of us, no matter how many times we seen it before, clapped and clapped and begged them to do it again. They did it one more time but after that they wouldn't do it no more no matter how much Slap and Danny begged and instead they slumped down against the clabboard, starting to tell each other tall stories, trying to see which of them could tell the biggest whopper. But after awhile you could see they didn't have much enthusiasm for it and they soon got tired of their lies and grew quiet.

Not long after that my mother came out and sat with us and you could see she had that look in her face she had whenever she was bothered by something, like she was somewhere else in her eyes, and only answered half-hearted, "Be patient," when Danny started his whining again about when was the breadman going to get there. Frank started rubbing his knuckles in Danny's head and told him not to be such a baby, did he see Kate whining? but Danny jerked away from him and said he didn't care, he was hungry. "Hungry enough to eat catfish?" Frank teased and Danny got a look in his eye he didn't have to say nothing, you could see he wasn't that hungry.

But in my mother's eyes we could all see the worry. The older ones kept sneaking looks at her now and again as much as I was. I suspected by now she was too proud to tell even Mrs. Beezley we didn't have nothing to eat because if she did I knew Mrs. Beezley would've been there with something to put on the table, even if she had to bring it over herself. But I overheard my mother telling my father a few nights before after they got in their bed she felt the Beezleys already done too much for us and she didn't want to ask them for help anymore, they had to do it on their own if they was going to do anything. Then I heard my father say he put so much on the eye at Gottlieb's he couldn't get anything else there til he paid something on it. My mother didn't say nothing after that and I heard the bed creak as my father turned over and I laid there awake for a long time afterwards worrying what was going to happen to us all.

The very next morning I caught her alone in the parlor saying her rosary and I knew she must be praying my father'd get a job soon. And I couldn't help but think she was praying he wouldn't start drinking again either, which is what I prayed for too more'n his getting a job, though I prayed for that too before I shut my eyes at night.

Frank asked her where our father was and she said, "Down at the burr hall," and when he asked her why was he there, she said, "Seein about gettin us something to eat til he finds work."

I remember when we went to the river Sam Beezley said the borough hall was where you went for relief and where we seen the men coming out with sacks of potatoes over their shoulders with shifty looks in their faces like they was stealing them.

Frank jumped up, shouting, "Hey, Ma! me and Buster can go back in the swamp to catch frogs or down the river and catch catfish for our breakfast!" Slap, hearing him, yelped out he was sick of frog legs, "I et so many frog legs I'm gonna turn into a frog," and he started hopping around the porch like one. My mother let out a sigh and said, "You know I don't like you goin back in the swamp or down to the river without your father, the breadman'll be here soon," and Danny whined he wanted Post Toasties for breakfast and no more catfish.

Frank started to argue they wouldn't go in the water either way and double-crossed his heart, but she put up her hand like she didn't want to hear another word, she said she didn't have even a speck of old lard to fry them in even if they did catch any, and as she was saying it just then a brand new car drove up in front of the house in a big cloud of yellow dust.

Frank and Buster forgot all about going to the river, they got so wide-eyed leaning on their bellies far out over the railing to get a better look. My mother gave a start, staring hard at the car, then gave her hair a quick swipe and smoothed down the front of her dress like there was crumbs on it, which there wasn't, as a big man with a white collar and black suit like Father Gallagher's got out and started up the path to the porch. He had a round belly and was wearing a hat so light it was the color of the cream at the top of the milk bottle. He gave us a big smile as he came up the steps, beaming at us through his glasses that didn't have no rims, and spreading his arms out, his red face sweating even though it wasn't all that warm yet. I held my breath, seeing the woreout steps bend under him.

"Ah, look at them all, such a fine, big family!" he boomed out in a voice so deep it sent shivers up my spine. "I hope you'll forgive my dropping in like this, Mother Lithwack, but I was just passing by and thought it was time to officially welcome you all to the parish."

The two youngest stared at him with shy eyes as he took off his hat, my sister sticking her finger in her mouth. You could see he had a head of thick hair the color of iron with more gray in it even than Ginger Mahoney's. He patted his forehead with a hanky and looked around at all of us. My mother, as always in front of company, held her hand up to hide her teeth, and looked all flustered that he caught her in her oldest housedress that was all faded, with rips under the arms. She looked wild-eyed around at us and seemed even more flustered that none of us was washed or had our hair combed yet or had on clean clothes. Grabbing Kate to her she snatched Kate's hand out of her mouth as Kate went on staring bug-eyed at the priest. Then, trying to do it so's nobody'd see, she tried to brush at my sister's tangled hair with one hand while smiling and still bobbing her head at the priest.

She called him Father Mack even though he wasn't her father and said it was no trouble him dropping in, even though you could see it was. Then she went on apologizing umpteen times for the way we all looked.

But Father Mack waved her aside and started rubbing his palms along the sides of his belly as he looked us over, then stroked the tops of the heads of Buster and Slap since they was the nearest to him.

"What fine looking boys...fine looking boys you have, mother," he grinned, calling her mother when she wasn't his mother and not saying one word about Kate.

I could see Buster squirm like a blood worm and turn just as red but he stood where he was as the priest went on stroking him and didn't run away like he looked like he wanted to more'n anything, while Slap grinned up at the priest happy as a pup.

"If I'd'a knowed you was coming, Father, I'd'a got them cleaned up a little..." my mother began again in a shaky way, her hand flying to her mouth. Then she looked around quick like she wanted somebody to smack. "Oh, look at them—You there, Slap, tie your laces and put in your shirttail..." And turning to Father Mack she said, "I was just about to brush my daughter's hair when you come, Father..." She grinned like she hoped he'd grin back and when he didn't the grin melted from her lips, her voice trailed off and she looked around at us with a frantic look like she wished we wasn't there.

"A fine, *fine* family," he repeated, ignoring her, and beamed again at Frank and Buster, then leaning over and having a hard time doing it because of his belly, he rubbed Slap's hair again as Slap was bending down tying the laces of his sneakers, sneakers I seen now the priest was there, looked more raggedy'n I ever noticed them before. My mother must've seen it too, the look in her face was like she was wishing maybe she'd never asked Slap to tie his sneakers and call attention to them. After he petted

Slap's hair Father Mack laid a hand on one of my cheeks and stared down at me, smiling. I ducked my head and felt myself blushing so much to the roots I was sure my hair must be on fire.

My mother, just like she done with Father Gallagher, was careful not to say ain't and made sure she put all the ings on the ends of her words, talking like she never talked, being one way with us and another way with a priest, or the doctor and the nurse at the free clinic, or even with her own sisters sometimes, like somehow we was never clean enough or dressed good enough, like she had to be always pointing out to others there was something the matter with us.

"You there, Frank, go in and put some... " I knew she started to say, "Put some water on to berl," but caught herself in time, her face reddening as she remembered there wasn't any tea or coffee left in the house to offer the priest a cup of. She threw Frank a quick look that said never mind and don't you ask any questions, saying instead, all in a hurry, like to get attention away from her mistake the same way she done to get attention away from herself, "Oh, look at them now, the little buggers! Buster, stand up straight and, you, Slap!" she hollered so's he'd hear her, "Haven't you tucked in your shirttail yet?" And Slap, looking down like he was seeing a shirttail for the first time in his life, grinned up at the priest and started tucking it in.

Father Mack petted him on the head again and wanted to know who of us'd made their first holy communion and who ain't. Frank and Buster looked like they all of a sudden got lockjaw and my mother rolled her eyes and threw up her hands, saying, "Look at them now! Where's your manners? Don't stand there like dumbies, tell the Father!"

Frank and Buster nodded and said they made their first holy communion at Sacred Heart church, and Slap seeing them nodding nodded his head too even though he didn't look too sure what the question was. When Father Mack stared down at me I mumbled, "I ain't made it yet," even though I didn't know what first holy communion was, my mother saying, "Mustn't say 'ain't' now, Mick." Danny and Kate just stared back at Father Mack with their big round eyes, too little to ask.

Then my mother ran down the list for him just to make sure he knew, telling him I'd be the next one to make my communion and Father Mack wagged his head, looking all pleased, and rubbed my hair again and said to my mother, "Well, you've got a fine bunch of prospective altar boys here," and glanced at the three oldest with a teasing gleam in his eye. I seen my mother's eye dart worried again to Slap's sneakers, then at the raggedy sneaks of the other two that you could see plain as anything not even one of them long dresses they would have to wear on the altar would hide. But in spite of that she told Father Mack she'd make sure they came to see him after the children's mass next Sunday and the priest said, "For a boy to serve on the altar is the same as serving God," and my mother said she couldn't agree with him more.

Then Father Mack said he hoped to go on seeing them all each and every Sunday at church, "*And* on holy days," he tacked on, smiling and lifting a finger like a warning. My mother swore up and down he'd be seeing us regular, "And me husband too, Father, you can be sure of that."

Before he left he went inside and blessed the house with holy water, my mother scurrying ahead picking up a newspaper here or straightening a rug there, apologizing left and right for the way the place looked even though it didn't look no different'n usual. He even went upstairs and blessed my mother and father's bedroom, my mother telling Mrs. Beezley afterwards she was so glad she had the brains to make the bed before she came down that morning and stuffed the dirty clothes out of the way in the hamper. When Father Mack came down the steps he got us together on the porch and my mother made us kneel as he gave us all his blessing, mumbling a prayer in latin and making the sign of the cross over us as we knelt with our heads bowed around him in a circle.

When he went down the steps, this time my mother as well looking like she was holding her breath for fear, with the size of him, he'd go crashing through the rotted boards, he waved his hat at us with a big sweep of his arm before clapping it back on. Slap grinned and waved at him, and my mother, with Kate hanging behind her skirts, leaned against the porch post watching him go, plucking nervous at the top of her faded housedress.

Even though she shouted at them not to, Frank and Buster, once the priest squeezed himself in behind the wheel and started up the engine in a roar of blue smoke, ran out anyways to get a closer look at the car. Father Mack gave them a big grin through the windshield and one more wave and after he drove off in another cloud of dust they talked about nothing but what that car must've cost and how many cylinders did it have and how a Chrysler compared to a Cadillac and which was the more streamlined. Frank said only bishops drove Cadillacs because they was bigshots and Slap wanted to know what did the Pope drive then? Buster said he didn't drive anything he was carried around all the time on an armchair with poles.

Bill the breadman came late that day wouldn't you know. It was almost lunchtime before he got there and by that time most of us was laying on the shady side of the porch, the day'd gotten so warm, all of us except for Danny that was snoozing away in the sun. When the bread truck pulled up out front Buster went and hollered his favorite cowboy movie line, "Ahm so hongry me belly thinks me throat's bin cut!" My mother gave him a look, warning him and the rest of us not to breathe a word to the breadman we been waiting all morning for him.

The next afternoon my father came home with a sack of corn meal and a pound of lard from the relief that was all stamped NOT TO BE SOLD and we had fried mush and bread for supper, and for breakfast next morning my mother boiled corn meal mush we et like it was cereal. When we came downstairs and Frank asked her where our father was she said he already gone down to the relief to work on the dump truck that day. That night when he came home he had a sack of potatoes over one shoulder that also said NOT TO BE SOLD and that when he dumped them out in the shed you could smell the ones near the bottom was all rotten but he said my mother could peel around the rotten parts. She didn't say nothing, just stared at the sack the same way she stared at Louie laying in the snow that morning outside our front door on Mifflin Street, and the more she kept staring at them potatoes the more it was like she was remembering what she told me why her Great-grandmom O'Rourke and her sisters and brothers left Ireland in the first place when there wasn't no more potatoes to eat except what was rotting in the fields, like looking at that sack she seen it all come back around again.

A couple afternoons later Mrs. Beezley came walking through the woods a little faster'n usual and hurried up our porch steps waving a copy of the *County Seat Weekly*. By the time we got out to the kitchen she was already settling herself down at the table with the newspaper opened in her lap while my mother stared at her holding her scissors open in her hand from cutting off catfishtails, not knowing what. Us kids shoved in, leaning our elbows all around the table. Even before she caught her breath, Mrs. Beezley was starting to read from what was called "Social Notes" under Lenape that I knew was page after page of news about who went where and who visited who from all the towns all over the county. What she read was: "'Mr. & Mrs. Stosh Lithwack just moved from the City of Brotherly Love to the Widow Scadder's old place on Lenape Road with their six children, five of them fine-looking boys named, from oldest Master Lithwack to youngest, Frank, Buster, Slap, Mickey and Danny, and last but not least, little daughter Kate.

"'Newly joined members of St. Theresa's R.C. church, Father Gregory Mack officially welcomed the family to his parish on a morning visit a short time after the Lithwack's moved into our fair town. This reporter welcomes them too and wishes them a happy stay. He plans to keep all of our readers abreast of their social doings—and misdoings. (Ha, ha, just kidding, Mr. & Mrs. Lithwack.)'" Mrs. Beezley came up for air, ending with, "And it's signed, 'Your Gadabout Lenape Reporter, Charley.'"

She grinned over at my mother, then all around at us, saying, "Ain't that cute? Ain't that nice? All your names in the paper!"

Right away Danny had to see where his name was and Mrs. Beezley pointed it out to him even though he couldn't even read it yet, then Slap had to see his and started shrieking like you wouldn't believe, he was so excited his name was in the paper.

My mother, looking embarrassed, went back to snipping her fish, asking Mrs. Beezley who this Gadabout Charley was and how did he know to get our names? Mrs. Beezley lit up a Raleigh, saying, "Why, he's Charley the cripple lives with his mother near the burr hall, you see him hangin out in front of the firehouse—or if you can't find him there, he'll be more'n likely standin out front of either Tarkie's saloon or the Dixie Jazz Dance Palace. He's whatcha call a stringer for the *Weekly*." And Frank busts in with, "Oh, we seen him all right, drives around town on that big tricycle like a kid's tricycle only it's drove by a chain, he's so lame he couldn't never balance on a two-wheeler, Brother says he drives around on it gittin all the gossip—" Mrs. Beezley gave him a look like she didn't appreciate being interrupted and went right on talking over him, saying, "I met him in front of Gottlieb's, Nor', right after you told me the priest come by that mornin—Lemme tell you, they ain't nuthin Charley don't know, and I could give you a earful about him—I hear—"

She sounded like she was just getting warmed up to spill something nice and juicy and my ears shot up so quick she must've heard it because all of a sudden she stared at me, then stared around the table at the rest of us, catching herself in time. Taking a long drag on her cigarette, all she said to my mother was, rolling her eyes in our direction and putting a hand to the side of her mouth, "I'll give you the lowdown later on."

The very next Sunday after Father Mack came to see us, my mother said, "Remember you said you wanted to go to church with your brothers? Well, it's high time you went."

She put a clean shirt and pants on me and combed my hair with water and showed me how to genuflect, making me practice it a couple times til I got it right. Then she untied the knot in her stocking and gave the three oldest a penny each she got from somewheres, I don't know where, but that was all the pennies in the knot. So she went rooting down the chairs in the parlor like she done in South Philly when she didn't have no money and she found two buttons and a penny and handed me the penny. My heart jumped up thinking it was to buy candy but she said you make sure you put this in the collection.

Once we started up the road I could see Buster didn't like me going to church with them because I was the littlest of the three and was still a baby to him, that's why he made me walk behind with Slap while him and Frank walked on ahead like they wasn't with us. Slap kept running off to look at something he spied. One of his old shoes that even though they was his Sunday shoes still had one sole half flopping off, the lace came untied so he kept tripping over it. But none of that seemed to bother him, he was as happy as if nothing in the world ever bothered him.

Up ahead Frank and Buster kept darting down in the gutters every now and then, picking up things and jamming them in their pockets. Soon I seen it was cigarette butts they was collecting.

The closer we got into town the more we seen other kids coming out of the houses and out of the woods, heading in the same direction as we was. Some of the kids, girls mainly, was carrying thick black books Slap said was called bibles, and they turned off at the road called Tabernacle Trail going to the red brick church where the bell now was clanging and clanging. I looked real close but not one of them kids, boy or girl, had blue noses, I figured it must only be the grownups did.

Most of the kids, though, was going like us in the other direction, up the road toward Saint Theresa's. Out in the fields surrounding the church I seen ladies and little girls bending and picking armloads of the wild flowers that was all up now everywhere like the wild roses all around our house. The air was so sweet with them it made me dizzy. As we climbed the hill, my heart began to beat the closer we got to the church and I seen all the kids going in. I stuck close as glue to Slap.

Just as we was about to go up the steps Frank and Buster came walking back to us, their pockets bulging with cigarette butts. Frank stooped down and told me not to put my penny in the collection if I wanted candy afterwards, just to watch him when the basket came around, did I get that? I started to say, "But Mom said..." but Buster butts right in with, "If you tell, we'll cutcher gizzard out and throw the rest of your carcass down the outhouse."

The way he said it made me shake inside and I promised I wouldn't tell, didn't my mother tell me to do like Frank done? why would anybody want to tell if they was going to get candy out of it?

Inside the church was shaped just like a cross, the plaster walls inside was just as white as they was on the outside. The window frames was stained dark like my father done the window frames in the houses on Mifflin Street, and was tall but not as tall as the windows in Sacred Heart church and had yellow glass in them you couldn't see through, instead of stained glass pictures. With the sun shining through it made everything even yellower inside'n it was out in the daylight. The slanty ceiling was all dark with dark beams of wood so heavy running across, with hoops of light bulbs hanging from long black chains from the ceiling that even though it was high up wasn't near as high as the stone ceiling in Sacred Heart. Everything looked like black and white lit up by all the yellow light, even the altar that was carved all white had a big round sun at the top with rays of sun painted gold streaming out all around.

Slap's shoe was slapping all the way down the aisle of brown linoleum as we went way down to the front of the church where the boys all sat together in one arm of the cross. All the girls sat across the aisle in the other arm of the cross with one nun apiece sitting in back of all of us on either side, the first sisters I seen since that day in Frank's school. They was dressed just the same like big black birds with their veils like long black wings and I wondered did they live in the rectory with Father Mack. But when I asked my mother later on she said no, they came down on the bus every Sunday from the Cathedral of the Immaculate Conception in Camden.

All the girls had hats or bandanas on and I wondered why it was girls had to wear hats but boys didn't. Hanging on the white-washed wall over the little girls' heads was a big black crucifix like the one hung over our bed at home only it was umpteen times bigger and Jesus Christ hanging on it in nothing but his underwear that looked like a diaper was umpteen times bigger too. His skin was as white as the wall of the church, with a crown of thorns on his head with blood gushing out where the thorns stuck in him and blood gushing out of his hands and feet from the nails and out of his chest where somebody must've stabbed him.

Over Slap's shoe you could hear my brothers corduroy knickers whistling all the way down, and when Frank genuflected in the direction of the altar he grabbed my shoulders and made me genuflect at the altar too before he shoved me into the pew ahead of him. Remembering what my mother said, when he knelt down with my brothers and blessed himself and folded his hands and bowed his head, his lips moving as he said a prayer to himself, I did the same, except I kept my eyes peeled looking around to see what I could see, trying to see as much as I could without turning my head around and have the sister see me.

Down near the altar railing was the statue of a lady in a robe that looked as long as my mother's bathrobe only this one was black and brown and it came up over the lady's head like a shawl. Her eyes was half shut and her hands was lifted so's you could see blood was coming out of the palms of her hands like she cut herself peeling potatoes. When I whispered to Frank who was it? he whispered back it was Saint Theresa the church was named after and when I whispered in his ear again why was she bleeding? he said, "That's her stigmata, dopey," and when I went to ask him what that was and how'd she get it? he snuck a look back at the nun and went *shhh!* in a way I knew I'd better shutup, so I didn't get the chance to ask him if that was the same lady we seen in the movie at Sacred Heart with blood streaming out of her head that I had nightmares over.

On the other side of the rail was a statue of a man I thought must be Saint Theresa's husband with a bald spot on top of his head and a bird sitting on his shoulder. He was holding a lily in his hand but his hands wasn't bleeding like hers was. Next to him in front of trays of little red candles like what my mother called the votive light on her bureau was a statue of a little baby with a crown on its head and what looked like a ball in its hand. You could see its heart sticking out of its chest like you could see Kate's heart beating in her head when she was a baby but its heart was all on fire and bleeding drops of blood, it gave me the shivers just to look at it.

On the side of the cross we was sitting in was another altar that wasn't as big as the main one. It had a statue on it as high as the one of Saint Theresa, only this lady wasn't bleeding anywhere I could see and had a blue robe on that was the color of my mother's bathrobe, only it went up over her head too like Saint Theresa's, so I seen even the statues of ladies had to have hats on in church. She looked just like the statue my mother said was the mother of the son of God in her and my father's bedroom so now I knew the statue of the baby was her baby, Jesus, except here she was a hundred times bigger'n my mother's statue and had more of the trays of the little votive lights in little blue jars burning in front of her.

Through the open windows you could hear the bell from the red brick church still banging away and when it finally stopped, like that was a signal, we all stood up as two altar boys came out through a dark doorway onto the altar, followed by Father Mack in a funny black hat with a puffy black rabbit's tail on top, the only man in the church with a hat on. I didn't recognize him at first, all dressed in a long satin bib purple as the Jew wine Willie gave Aunt Nell each Christmas, with a long white dress under it. Father Mack took the hat off and gave it to one of the altar boys, that looked just like Freddie Bartholomew in "Captains Courageous," that took it and put it on a table off to one side.

As Father Mack stood up at the altar with his back to us, mumbling in latin, I just about jumped out of my skin when all of a sudden the loudest music, louder even than the bell from the red brick church, broke out. Forgetting I wasn't supposed to, I spun my head around and seen up in the back on a balcony stretching over the front door of the church was a lady with hair whiter'n Grandmom O'Rourke's and bobbed shorter even than Ginger Mahoney's. Under the balcony I caught a squint of Charley kneeling all humped over on one knee and looking around all bright-eyed like a bird like he was looking for more names to write in the newspaper.

The lady with white hair was pumping away at an organ and when she opened her mouth her throat started shivering like a bowl of Jello as she started to sing so warbly and shrill, "*Immaculate Mary, our hearts are on fire!...*" Even Slap heard her and even though he must've heard her before, he swung around to look like he still couldn't believe it. Frank and Buster stuck their heads together giggling amongst themselves at the lady singing. The nun behind us went *shhhh!* and they both looked around at her with a sneaky look then looked back at the altar, trying hard to put on serious faces but you could see they was still laughing in their eyes.

Everybody sung along with the lady screaming at the organ

"Immaculate Mary, our hearts are on fire!..." but even that wasn't loud enough to drown her out. Even though I was supposed to do what Frank done I didn't know all the words since my mother never sung hymns at home, she said hymns you sung in church not home, so I just moved my lips, pretending I knew them, afraid the nun back of us had her eye on everything, including me, and that if I didn't act like I knew the words, she would come swooping down on me, her veils flying out like big black wings and peck me in the head.

When the hymn was over, Father Mack turned around and stood facing us on the top step of the altar while the altar boys went scurrying for the chairs against the wall. He folded his big red hands under his bib and looking first at the boys and then at the girls, he gave us all his big smile. Then he cleared his throat and started giving us a speech that began quiet enough, calling us "my children," even though we wasn't, and "dear ones" and "beloved lambs of God," reminding us today was Mary's day and we should all come to the May procession that afternoon to honor Mary the mother of God. The more he got cranked up the more his voice boomed louder in the church, even louder'n it done on our front porch, so that all he said boomed around high up in the ceiling like an echo as he started shouting about going to heaven, saying how being Catholics was like being Cadillacs compared to them others that wasn't Catholics, they was like tin lizzies in the race to heaven and it wasn't hard to see who would get there the fastest, the Cadillac or the jalopy, and hearing that Buster grinned and gave Frank a poke with his elbow, nodding his head as much as to say that was a good one.

Just then, wouldn't you know it, the bell from the red brick church started ringing again like they sent a spy over to peep in the window to see when Father Mack started talking and then ran back fast as they could to ring the bell just so's we'd have a hard time hearing him. Slap had to lean farther forward in the pew, clapping a hand behind his ear so's he could hear over the racket. Father Mack stopped dead in the middle of what he was saying and threw a dirty look out the windows in the direction of the bell before he started talking again in an even louder voice, his face getting red as the bricks in the red brick church the louder he had to talk like if he got any redder his glasses would steam up.

The louder he shouted the more he kept throwing looks out the window where you could hear the bell still banging and clanging, he wasn't calling us "my children" and "dear ones" anymore, his eyes looked like two roosters fighting each other in the Beezley's chicken run, so that everytime when he said "Jesus Christ" and the whole church bowed their heads, it sounded like he was cursing.

The other boys was grinning at each other and Frank and Buster got to giggling again, putting their hands over their mouths to keep from laughing outloud like this was something they seen happen every single Sunday. All of a sudden my heart jumped up like a fish in my throat as the sister behind us came swooshing down the aisle, her veils flying behind her like a sailboat in a wind as she leaned into the pew with a look as annoyed as Father Mack's was. She put a finger to her mouth and gave my brothers and the other boys a look that if looks could kill they'd all be dead on the spot. She was so mad she looked like she really would reach under her veils and pull out her ruler and give us all a wack but instead she went *shush!* like she really meant business this time before she went sailing back to her seat.

All of a sudden the bell stopped ringing, catching Father Mack bellowing so loud we all gave a jump when it did. He stopped and cleared his throat and tossed another dirty look out the window, then like he was shifting gears right in the middle of what he been saying he started complaining about how if all us kids would only be sure to give all the pennies and nickels we could to his Saint Theresa's Church Bell Fund, if he could just get enough money in the collections from us kids and from our mothers and fathers, he could make the belltower strong enough to hold a bell. Then if we all gave more money he could buy a bell and stick it up in the belltower, if only all of us kids would go without a piece of candy or a popsicle or an ice cream cone and put that money in the collection basket. Or if all us kids would even go around town collecting empty soda water bottles in the gutters and in the trash for the two-cent or nickel deposit at Gottlieb's, and put that money in the basket God would be grateful and he would be grateful. He said it like if it wasn't for us kids not collecting soda bottles and putting the money in the basket he would've had a bell in that shaky old belltower a long time ago and said he wouldn't be so ashamed everytime the bishop came down from Camden every confirmation time and looked up at the belltower and said, "I see you don't have a bell in the belltower yet, Father Mack," he would've had a bell if everybody gave more'n they been giving, and to be sure and tell our mothers and fathers he said so.

Then like he was still in a huff because of it, Father Mack boomed out, like the proddisin bell was still ringing, that because today was Mary's day, while the basket was being passed, everybody should sing "Bring Flowers of the Rarest," and he didn't want to hear nothing out there but the jingle of money dropping in the basket, though how he expected to hear anything over the white-haired lady singing I didn't know.

He blessed us with a quick sign of the cross, first the boys, then a quicker one to the girls like he almost forgot it, then he spun around on his heel and turned back to the altar while the altar boys, like there was tacks on their chairs, jumped up and rushed over to stand in their places down below him at the bottom.

As the organ started up again, Frank and Buster gave each other sly looks, like Father Mack just reminded them how they used to collect soda bottles in South Philly so we could buy penny candy and go to the Saturday matinees, their eyes lighting up like there was imps playing with matches in them reminding them what a good idea it was.

I gave another jump as the lady up at the organ began to sing again, *"Bring flow'rs of the fairest, bring flow'rs of the rarest, from garden and woodland and hillside and vale; our full hearts are swelling, our glad voices telling the praise of the loveliest Rose of the vale..."* And as she sang and everybody joined in, a skinny man my mother told me later was married to the white-haired lady at the organ, came down the aisle with a basket on a long pole, his face was red, his eyes looked like two hunks of raw hamburger like my father's did when he used to have hangovers. His hands was shaking so much the basket was shaking right along with them as he slid it into our pew, you could hear the pennies jingling inside like the basket was a tambourine, but not loud enough I bet so Father Mack could hear it over the singing. Frank gave me a pinch on the sneak and shook his head so you could hardly see it, giving me a look saying no with his eyes, and I remembered what he said about keeping the penny my mother gave me in my pocket, despite what Father Mack said about getting the bell, so I did since my mother said to do what Frank done.

When the basket went shaking under their noses, him and Buster and Slap made like they was putting pennies in but didn't. I was afraid the sister watching behind us would see none of us didn't put our pennies in and come tearing down on us again with her veils flying, but she didn't, she must've been too busy singing along with everybody else, *"O Mary! we crown thee with blossoms today, Queen of the Angels, Queen of the May…"*

After mass there was Sunday school. I sat with my brothers on the boy's side with the nun sat behind us standing up in front now, while the other nun stood up in front on the girls' side. The whole time, the ladies and little girls I saw out in the fields around the church was coming in the side entrance with their arms full of the wild flowers and was putting them in vases all around the feet of the statue of Our Lady up on her altar to the side, so many flowers there was hardly any room for anymore, the whole church was soon smelling so sweet like the fields outside.

Just like when I was in Frank's class at Sacred Heart school I sat with my hands folded in my lap and tried to keep still as possible so the sister wouldn't crack my knuckles with her ruler. This sister had round glasses with metal rims and a round face to go with them that was white as the candles up on the altar, that the altar boy who looked like Freddie Bartholomew was snuffing with a long pole had a metal cap on top. She asked all the boys questions out of a little blue book was called a catechism.

"Who made the world?"

"God made the world."

"Who is God…?"

When it came Frank's turn he knowed the answer to the question she asked and she gave him a card, and when it came Buster's turn he knowed the answer too and he got a card. But when it came Slap's turn he ducked his head and grinned his goofy grin and gave some answer that mustn't've been the answer but was more like a answer he was making up in his head because the sister shook her finger at him and didn't give him no card.

When she went all around the pew she asked them all one last question, what day it was, and they all hollered, "Saint Mary's day!" She said that was right and she hoped they'd all come to the May procession that afternoon. One of the big boys in the back sneered, "That's for the grrr-rulls," but the sister shook her finger at him and said it was for the boys too, that Mary was the mother of us all, even boys, and him and all the others should come. But I seen Buster sneak Frank a look as much as to say not on your life if he could help it.

Then we all said the "Hail Mary" and when it was over the nun leaned into the pew and gave my cheek a pinch, saying her name was Sister Joseph Mary even though she didn't look like a boy. She asked me what my name was and when I told her, even though she didn't ask me no question from the catechism, she gave me a card anyway, saying she hoped I came back next week with my brothers.

The first chance I got I peeked a look at the card and seen it had a picture on it the same as the statue of the lady on the altar with her hands bleeding that Frank said was Saint Theresa. Only in the picture her head was bleeding too like somebody stuck needles in it, her eyes rolling up just like in the movie I seen at Sacred Heart school, so it must've been the same lady.

The sacristy was off to one side of the church in the other arm of the cross where the girls sat. Despite I was dying to know what it looked like inside, before my brothers went in Frank told me to wait outside and not move, then he poked his head inside the curtain that was the color of red wine hanging in the door and I heard Father Mack's voice boom out telling them to come on in. They was in there an awful long time and when they came out they was each carrying over their arm one of the long black dresses and the white blouses the altar boys wore.

On the way home along Hessian Soldiers Way there was a big apple tree growing by the side of the road with the blossoms all out, that the three of them stopped at and gave me their dresses and blouses to hold and even though they was in their Sunday-best, they started climbing up in it, like it was something they done every Sunday after mass. I didn't know how to climb a tree yet, it looked awful high, I was afraid if I went up in it I'd fall down on my head.

When we came to Gottlieb's store we went in and it was like going from day to night. Some ladies was across the store by the butcher block buying bacon Mr. Gottlieb was slicing with a butcher knife from a big slab of it, his baseball cap yanked down over his ears. I didn't see the Indian they called Lenny even though I looked all around for him. But Mrs. Gottlieb was there, sitting on her wood crate behind the counter of the store since the window of the post office had a big CLOSED sign hanging on it, it being Sunday. She was whispering something to a lady standing on the other side of the counter but her whispering, like Mr. Beezley's, was the same as other people talking normal so you heard every word she said which was something about somebody called Charley that must've been the cripple wrote our names in the *County Seat Weekly* telling her about a girl in town being "in a fambly way—and she ain't hitched, poor thing, my heart just goes out..."

When she saw us poking our eyes through the chicken wire where the candy was she cut herself short and pushed herself up off of the crate with a grunt and came up pulling her dress out behind her. She asked us how was our mother and was our father working yet and was we coming from church, she cocked an eyebrow up, saying she hoped the pennies we was spending for candy wasn't pennies we was supposed to put in the collection basket. Both Frank and Buster shook their heads so hard I thought they'd unscrew them right off of their necks, Buster shouting, "Not us, no siree, no, *sir!*" as if the louder he said it the truer it was. But Mrs. Gottlieb had a grin behind her eyes and gave each of them a look that you could see she didn't believe a word they said.

While the others picked out what they wanted, my eyes bounced all over them jars and boxes of candy, my mouth watering so's I could taste each and every kind there was, wishing I could have one of everything, and like last time wasn't able to make up my mind. Frank and Buster both picked out chocolate fudge this time and Slap took a niggertoe like he most always did, each of them pushing their penny through the wire at her when she handed them the candy. Now it was my turn, I had to hurry up and decide and since I remembered it tasted so good from the last time I pointed to the candy shaped like a banana. She shoved it through the wire at me and I stood up on tiptoe to push my penny through when all of a sudden she poked her finger that was so fat it hardly fit through the chicken wire and stabs my cheek with it, saying, "I *sure* wisht I had me them perty eyelashes!" and shoves me back my penny, saying in that shrill voice of hers, that was almost as loud as the white-haired lady singing in church, "Next time you put that in the collection, you hear?" and rolling her eyes at my brothers, she said, "And don'tchou listen to these goniffs."

Outside, Frank stood grinning at me like he was proud I done something bad and got away with it. But Buster got a sneer on and started shrilling out just like Mrs. Gottlieb, "I wisht I had *me* them perty eyelashes! I wisht I was as perty as a grrr-rull, I'd git *me* some free candy too!"

The two of them slapped each other on the back and bust

out laughing, Slap going, "Heh? Heh? What's so funny?" and everytime he said it they'd laugh all the harder and punch each other again.

All the way home Buster kept singing at me, "Jeepers Creepers Where'dja Git Them Peepers?" but I didn't care and held on tight to the penny in my pocket.

Like the last time on our way to the river I et the candy banana slow as I could to make it last and by the time we started through the woods by the Beezley's house, where Frank and Buster emptied all the butts in their pockets into a hole up in a tree just off of the path, the three of them long since finished their candy and Frank turned to me and said, "You better finish that before we get to the house."

I gobbled the rest of it down and rolled my tongue slow around my teeth to get the last flavor of banana out of it, wanting to have it last til we got through the woods. After Frank and Slap went up the front steps Buster grabbed me by the arm and leaning over made slits out of his eyes, muttering, "You better let me hold that penny for you so's you won't lose it," and when I guessed he saw in my eyes I didn't want to, he said, "How'djou like me to slitcher throat and throw you down the outhouse?" I reached in my pocket and gave him the penny.

When we came in the kitchen she was frying up catfish my father caught down the river after he came back from church that morning. She'd breaded them with what was left of the cornmeal and was frying them in the last of the old lard that was sizzling and spitting so hard in the frying pan she was rearing back so she wouldn't get splattered. When she saw the cassocks, which is what she called them and not dresses, she said, them being so long, they would hide the patches in the seats of my brothers' knickers even though the skirts wasn't long enough to hide their wore-out sneakers. But Frank joked, "It's awright, Mom, our sneaks're so holey anyway, git it, Mom, git it?" Him and Buster bust out laughing like that was the funniest and even my mother had to grin despite her not liking anybody joking about anything about the church, not even my father. Then she asked me did I like church? I said yes and started asking her all the questions I had stored up but she broke in, saying did I behave myself? I nodded but didn't tell how we spent the penny for the collection, I was feeling funny about it especially since I was already thinking about next Sunday when me and my brothers'd go to Gottlieb's and I could spend the penny Buster was holding for me for more candy. I was wondering, out of all the questions I had to ask her, was that a sin but didn't dare ask her that one.

Then she asked me if I would like to go back to the church with her that same afternoon for the May procession. It would be the first time I ever been to church with her, and ain't Sister Joseph Mary said we all should come? I danced around the kitchen when she asked me.

This time I wasn't near as jumpy, the closer we got to the church. Now it was mostly mothers coming out of the woods holding the hands of kids that was mainly little girls, so it wasn't only all kids heading for Saint Theresa's like this morning. After she parked the buggy around the side of the church, my mother reached in her pocketbook, bringing out one of her clean hankies with the crocheted edges she crocheted herself and laid that on top of her head and pinned it in place with bobby pins, not wearing the faded old black hat she usually wore to mass. Then she tied a tighter bow in Kate's bonnet that Kate tried to yank off so that my mother smacked her hand, saying, "Don'tchou start now, girl," so I saw now even baby girls had to wear hats in church. She picked up Kate and warning me and

Danny to behave ourselves we went around the front.

The smell of the flowers seemed even stronger now the day'd wore on. As we got farther down the aisle and into that part of the church that formed the arm of the cross where I sat that morning, I saw the altar on that side where the Virgin Mary was was now so jammed with flowers all up and down and around her statue that all you could see was her face sticking out.

While my mother said her prayers I kept sneaking looks up at the statue of the Virgin, thinking there mustn't be not one single flower left outside in the fields anymore, the ladies picked them and brung them all in here.

When my mother was done praying and sat back in the pew, I sat back too, watching as she reached in her pocketbook and brought out her rosary, then snuck glances at her as her fingers went from one bead to the next, her lips moving saying the Hail Marys as she stared up at the face of Our Lady peeping out of the flowers. I bet she was praying my father'd get a job at the shipyard soon.

Just then the organ music started and I snuck another look back to see if it was the same lady with the whitest hair I ever seen was playing and it was and her name was Agnes O'Hara my mother told me that morning when I was pestering her with all my questions in the kitchen. Agnes O'Hara started singing and both Danny and Kate swung around like I done that morning, their eyes so big with a look of fright. Then my mother and all the other people in the church started singing along with Mrs. O'Hara:

Mother dearest, Mother fairest,

Help of all who call on thee...and I could see my mother was singing the whole time right up into the face of that statue of the mother of Jesus that was staring so quiet and calm out of all of them flowers, singing as hard as she was praying when she was saying her rosary beads. *Virgin purest, brightest, rarest, Help us, help, we cry to thee...*

When the hymn ended the organ kept playing, only lower this time, then there was a flurry in the back and everybody stood up and people's heads started to turn around to look back towards the open doors.

Coming down the aisle was little girls dressed all in white, even their socks and shoes was white, and instead of hats and hankies they was wearing wreaths of flowers in their hair that looked just like the wild flowers up around the statue of the Virgin that came from the fields around, and they was carrying more baskets of flowers in the crook of their arms while their hands was together like they was praying. As they came down the aisle, there was the sisters walking behind them with their arms folded underneath their robes, so they ain't gone back to Camden after all. We all kneeled and as we did Mrs. O'Hara let out a blast that made Danny and Kate both jump at the same time as everybody started singing again:

Lady, help in pain and sorrow,
Soothe those racked on beds of pain;
May the golden light of morrow
Bring them health and joy again.

Mary, help us, help, we pray,
Help us in all care and sorrow;
Mary, help us, help, we pray

Then there was a bustle at the doorway leading to the altar and Father Mack came out with two altar boys, only this time he was dressed just in his long black dress and had on a surplice like the altar boys, only his looked like the lace tablecloth

on our dining room table, except it didn't have no rips or holes
wore in it. One of the altar boys was the same one was serving
mass that morning had eyes as pretty as Freddie Bartholemew
and skin white as milk and the blackest hair I ever saw that was
cut short like a hairbrush.

Everybody sat down and my mother held her rosary in her
hand as she listened to Father Mack talk about the Virgin Mary,
how this was her special day and how she was the mother of
everybody and looked after us all. It wasn't long after he begun
talking that Kate nodded off first, then Danny, his head falling
on my shoulder. I hoped he wasn't going to start grinding his
teeth.

I began wondering if the bell from the red brick church was
going to start up again like it did this morning in the middle of
Father Mack's speech, but it didn't.

To keep myself awake I looked at my mother and saw that
instead of listening to the priest her lips was moving again, she
was saying her rosary one more time, pinching each bead so
tight between her thumb and forefinger like she would break it if
she pinched any harder, her eyes all the time trained steady on
the blue eyes in the statue of the Virgin Mary that looked to me
like they was looking right back at her—I wished with all my
heart they was, and crossed all my fingers again hoping Mary'd
hear and help with what I knew my mother was praying to her
for.

It was the time of the wild roses and they was the first wild
roses I ever saw, growing everywhere you looked in our front
yard and in all the fields around, even back near the swamp.
Seeing them along the road on the way home it gave me an idea
after being at the May procession. I thought of the statue of the
Virgin Mary at church just about smothered in flowers and

thought of the little statue of her up on the bureau in my mother and father's bedroom, so as we came up to the front of the house I asked my mother if I could pick some of the wild roses in our yard and put them around the statue like I saw in church.

She gave me a funny smile but when we got inside she gave me a pair of her scissors, not her good ones but her old ones my father cut our hair with and she cut off the heads and tails of the catfish with. She told me to watch out for the thorns and not to step on a snake and to only cut the roses close to the house. I wished she ain't reminded me of the snakes, it didn't seem like such a good idea when she reminded me of that, but I went out anyhow to the rose bushes in front and checked the ground first to see if there was any snakes before I leaned in and started snipping, right off the bat sticking myself anyhow on the thorns so the blood came out of my fingers like the stigmater on Saint Theresa's hands, but I didn't care. I felt like I was going to pass out again, the smell of the roses was so sweet in my nose it made me dizzy all over again so that I staggered closer into the bush, wanting to go in and in to the roses that was all like a pink fire, and shut my eyes, not caring about snakes for the minute as I sniffed and sniffed like I couldn't get enough of sniffing them roses, thinking if she didn't have a penny for a candle then all the flowers I was picking being pink like fire, each and every one of them could be a candle on her bureau, as many as the candles was burning in front of Our Lady's statue in the church.

When I got my hands so full of roses and couldn't carry anymore and was going around the back to the kitchen door, wouldn't you know it, my father and Frank and Buster was coming around the side of the house, all of them carrying bunches of dead frogs in their fists that they caught back in the swamp for our Sunday night supper, their hands all muddy and frog blood dripping through their fingers like mine was dripping from the thorns of the wild roses. Buster seeing me elbowed Frank, sniggering, "Looka the flower girl, will ya?" and Frank of course laughs like Buster said something funny, going, "What's yer name, honey?" and Buster goes, "I wisht I had *me* them perty eyelashes!"

I felt my cheeks go pink as the roses while at the same time a chill went shivering up my spine, seeing the dark look my father gave me that was louder'n anything Frank or Buster could say. As he yanked his hatchet out of the backstep where he always stuck it and started chopping off the legs of the frogs, every chop my father took he snuck a look at me as I walked right by them up the backsteps, not saying nothing, the smell of the roses all around me like perfume, the look in his eyes that was usually blue as the sky looking like rainclouds came into them all of a sudden.

My mother raised her eyebrows when she saw how many flowers I cut and got that funny grin on her face again, but all she said was, "Scratched yerself, eh? I told you to be careful."

Buster brought the frog legs in, braggin to her how many they caught while through the window I could see my father and Frank going to fling what was left of the heads and gizzards into the vegetable garden. She told me to wait a minute while she washed off the frog meat and wouldn't you know that darned Buster had to start teasing me again about the flowers until she told him to shutup and wash his hands and go outside to help his father.

When she was done at the sink she gave me two empty milk bottles she said to pump water into and when I did that I stuck the roses in them and she wiped her bloody hands on her apron and plumped the flowers all around to make them look nicer before I took them upstairs.

In their bedroom I climbed up on the chair and put one milk bottle of roses on either side the statue of the Virgin standing on top of their bureau. I climbed down and stood back, leaning against Kate's crib and looked up at the roses, then went and moved one of the bottles a little closer to the statue, climbed down and stood back again and looked, then got up and moved it just a little closer still before I was satisfied it looked right.

All the time the hymn we heard at the May procession was going though my head and I looked into the eyes of the statue the way my mother looked into them in the church and sang real low so's nobody'd hear me, crossing my fingers and squeezing them so tight I started them bleeding again from where the thorns'd scratched them, singing, "*Mary, help us, help, we pray...*"

That night I woke up to hear my father complaining of the smell of the roses, so many, the air was heavy and thick with them. I could smell them even clear through to our bedroom.

I lay in the dark, thinking of how funny she thought it was, me wanting to pick the flowers, but how pleased she been by all the armloads I brought. I lay there breathing in the smell of the roses, their sweetness helping to take away the stink of my brothers' sneakers tossed under the beds, my brothers breathing soft all around me, asleep.

All of a sudden from the other room I heard their bed creaking, then my mother whispering like she was mad or was arguing with my father. "C'mon, c'mon," he was whispering, "Whatsa matter with you?" She whispered something back I couldn't hear, then that was followed by his muttering, "Jesus Christ!" only like it was a curse like the way Father Mack said it that morning when the bell was ringing. But even though it sounded like a curse I bowed my head anyway when he said it.

Now my mother was whispering to him to stop his fussing and go back to sleep but he still sounded annoyed and said how did she expect him to go back to sleep? "Goddamn roses," he said and she went, "Shhh! You'll wake up Katie! You'll wake up the kids!" And he said, talking right outloud now, he didn't care, let Kate hear, let us kids hear, "Goddamn roses!" and I cringed, like he was cursing me for bringing them in their bedroom.

Then I heard him get out of the bed and heard the scratch of a match, saw the sudden little light from it filling the hallway outside our room, and that followed by the smell of cigarette smoke.

I lay there awake listening if they was going to say anything more but it got all quiet and in a few minutes I heard him come out and heard the sizzle of his cigarette as he chucked it into the pissbucket, then his barefeet slapping against the floor as he went back to their room and got back into their bed. The bedsprings groaned again as he turned over on the mattress. After a couple more minutes I finally heard his breath catch and soon he was snoring.

The spring night was blowing in through the mosquito netting at the windows, blowing in the smells of the swamp mud and green things, the green plants growing up in his garden, the night in the window as blue as the barrel of his father's gun asleep in the bottom of his drawer, the smell of the night mingling with the roses on their bureau and the last of the smoke from his cigarette hanging in the air, all of it making me so excited and restless I couldn't go to sleep—I leaned close and smelled Slap's ear as he slept, touching it with my tongue, tasting what deaf tasted like, like what rose tasted all curling in the petals of his ear, then turned my head on the pillow and stared up in the dark, breathing in the roses like I was breathing in Mary, Queen of the Angels, Queen of the May, and now Mary, Queen of the Night. It was like her scent was on the air where everything smelled like it was ripening out in the night, her scent light in my nostrils as her veils was light, light as the breeze blowing over my face and bare arms between my sleeping brothers, so that I pictured her veils was the breeze fluttering everywhere in the night as dainty as the petals of the sleeping wild roses, as dainty as the mother in the buds curling out of the dark trees, Slap's ear asleep in the dark on the pillow beside me, was he deaf in his dreams?.... *Mother dearest, Mother fairest... Help of all who call on thee*...the mother in her eyes looking into my mother's eyes, looking into my own, all of it mixed with the night and the wild roses mixing with the ground outside the windows where everything all of a sudden was rising and rising, springing up in the roses *the wild roses...*

Slap didn't last long as an altar boy—he wasn't quick enough and couldn't seem to pay attention or know what to do next, and since he couldn't hear most of it, naturally he couldn't remember the latin. So it wasn't too long before Father Mack asked him to turn in his cassock and surplice and on the way home that Sunday that he did, Slap bust out crying he felt so bad. But Buster said, "What're you cryin about? You should consider yourself lucky." But I could see to Slap it was like getting leftdown again and even though I felt sorry for him there wasn't nothing anybody could do about it.

Buster didn't last much longer either, he was quick enough but he just plain hated it and wouldn't go no more to learn how to do it no matter how much my mother threatened him. Frank lasted the longest of the three of them, he got so he was even talking about being a priest, then all of a sudden he quit, my mother said he probably just grew out of it—Being the oldest, she was always making excuses for him like she never would for any of the rest of us.

Frank never did say a word why all of a sudden he quit being an altar boy and he stopped talking about wanting to be a priest around about that same time too. I wouldn't know why it was maybe he quit until I got to be an altar boy myself after I made my first holy communion and Father Mack got me in a corner and stared into my eyes.

I didn't have to wait so long to learn about Charley, though. I was hiding under the dining room table not long after Charley wrote our names in the *County Seat Weekly*, listening to Mrs. Beezley. She started telling my mother gossip she said Charley told her about the girl in town going to have a baby didn't have a husband. My mother clicked her tongue but then said the same thing Mrs. Gottlieb said, "Poor thing..." but said it in a way like having a baby was the worst thing could happen to a woman whether she was married or not. She said, "I see this Charley kneeling in the back in church a lot," and Mrs. Beezley said, "Oh, he gets a lot of his news for the *County Seat Weekly* going to church. He's good at that and he's good to his mother and crippled as he is he's good at carvin all kinds of things out of cakes of Ivory soap, angel heads and dog heads and flowers, he can carve just about anything out of a plain bar of soap, he's good with his hands that way despite them bein all shriveled and he's the best stringer the *County Seat Weekly* has, but..." and here she dropped her voice to a whisper so's I had to crane my neck way out from under the tablecloth, since she was whispering like what she was going to say was a deep dark secret, *"It's too bad he has a likin for the boys..."*

When I guess my mother didn't catch on to what she meant,

she said, "Ya know, he likes to…" then in an even hissier whisper, *"kiss their peepees…"*

I could hear my mother suck in her breath the same as if what Mrs. Beezley said was a slap in her face.

"I'd keep an eye on your boys, specially your Mickey…" It seemed like she was letting that sink in before she let out a big sigh, saying, "Your Mick's a strange one, ain't he?" saying it just the way Aunt Nell said it. My ears perked up even higher than they was, waiting to hear what my mother would say but all she said, and I was glad to hear it, was, "But he's good around the house, he minds the littler ones, he helps me rinsh out the sheets—

He'll outgrow it."

Mrs. Beezley let out another sigh, saying, "Let's hope so."

Being on relief meant my father worked on the town dump truck a couple days a week, emptying the trash and garbage cans. Other times he worked with a gang of other men that was on relief, fixing the roads, throwing dirt into holes and gullies from the rains and smoothing them out with shovels, or else steering the yellow grader that was pulled by the dump truck on the days there wasn't no garbage pickup.

When he wasn't doing that he worked on building the road they was hacking out through the thick swampy woods off where they dumped all the garbage and that would someday— "Prolly doomsday," my father said, "It's such slow work"—connect one part of the town to the other. In return for all his work they gave him whatever they had in the bins at the relief in the borough hall, mainly the burlap bags of rotting potatoes my mother plenty times had to peel down to the nub to get anything to throw in the pot. And butter that was rancid more often than not and bags of sugar hard as cement and sometimes full of ants and sacks of flour and corn meal sometimes so wormy my father had to bury them, along with most of the potatoes and butter, out back in the swamp because he said, "If you don't act like you're usin it all they'll think you don't need it and mightn't give you any more."

When my mother sifted the flour it was as much to strain out the bugs as the lumps.

Every once in awhile they gave us big cans of things with black and white labels on them spelled out U.S. GOVERNMENT NOT TO BE SOLD, stringbeans and corn but mainly grapefruit slices that nobody liked much, they had such a bitter taste, but that we et anyway, if you heaped sugar on it it didn't taste half bad.

The clothes relief gave us was old-fashioned underwear that buttoned all the way up the front and had trapdoors in back that Frank and Buster would pull down at night trying to see who could pinch the other's behind—white cotton for summer, itchy wool longjohns for winter, that no matter how much my mother scrubbed them still had a smell like the disinfectant she used to scrub the outhouse.

Then there was bulky dark blue leggings for winter for me and Danny that was so big and all pinned up by my mother so they'd fit, they was such a struggle to pull down I sometimes wet my pants before I could make it to the privy.

Most of the clothes was made out of pillow ticking, including the suit with short pants had red piping that my father brought home one day and that my mother put away for me to wear for when I went to school. The shoes they gave us was all shiny black patent shoes that looked fancy when you first saw them but turned out to have cardboard soles painted to look like leather that fell apart if the ground got even a little wet. Slap's pair lasted barely a day, he was so hard on shoes anyway, like he was on everything else he wore. Since my father had to take what the people at relief gave him, the pair of shoes he got for me was too tight and pinched like anything when I walked in them, so I was relieved when my mother put them away in the closet, along with the pillow ticking suit, for when I went to school and I didn't have to wear them right then.

Once when they got a lot of flour in at relief, despite our having so much of it and most of that useless, he took what they offered him anyway, getting my older brothers to help carry the sacks home between them from the borough hall. My mother, lucky to sift one good sack out of all of it for all the bugs and worms, still had so much flour she baked biscuits and bread so we never had to wait for the breadman again, baking the way Mrs. Beezley showed her, and sometimes if there was enough eggs and sugar and vanilla extract she'd bake a cake. When it came the time of the wild cherries when the cherries came out black as drops of blood on the trees, and it was the time of the wild blackberries, us kids'd all take empty cans and milk bottles to pick them, I still couldn't believe they was for free, you didn't have to go to Gottlieb's to buy them or put them on the eye. What we didn't eat raw or with milk and sugar, my mother cooked and put up as jelly in jars that she sealed on top with wax like Mrs. Beezley showed her to do. And if there was any of it left over she made pies and cobbler, sweetening the cherries extra heavy to kill the bitter taste of them. But when it came the time of the mulberries down in the yard and out in the woods, them you couldn't pick for canning they was so squishy you had to eat them right away, and they had a milky-sweet taste, especially the white ones, like the smell of the river was in them.

We had so much flour that one time even my father tried his hand at baking biscuits one Sunday after mass. They turned out so thin and hard and salty not even Slap would eat them, and even my father had to laugh they was so awful. Since the birds wouldn't eat them either, he buried the whole batch back in the swamp with the sacks of wormy flour and corn meal.

Another time relief didn't have no flour but had plenty sacks of corn meal, so for two weeks straight my mother made nothing but corn meal mush and fried corn meal mush with Karo slopped on top and baked corn bread til corn meal came out our ears. After all that time the only one wasn't sick of the sight of corn meal was Slap that et it right down like it was something new everyday.

When he worked on the dump truck sometimes when the truck passed our house my father'd fling off broke toys and dolls he found in the trash cans and we'd all run out to pick them up from the gutter, Frank and Buster divvying up who got what. In no time at all my sister had a pretty big family of dolls, some bald and without eyes, some with only one arm or a leg missing, some with both arms and legs gone, so that she was playing nurse with them more'n she was playing mother. When I asked my mother why she didn't let Kate play with the Shirley Temple doll she still kept wrapped in tissue paper up in its box in her closet, she said because it was too good for Kate to play with, she wanted to keep it clean to only bring out to show under the tree at Christmastime.

One time he flung down an old boxing glove, the leather all moldy and rotting away, that Buster grabbed and him and Frank took turns putting it on and practiced boxing with each other with one arm behind their back. Another time my father found a box of books in somebody's garbage. They was spotted with green mildew but he brought them home and spread them out in the backyard to dry in the sun. A lot of the pages was ripped like somebody tried to tear up the books but even so, after he read the day-old Philadelphia *Bulletin*, he would read them books in the evening, sitting close up to the oil lamp at the dining room table, books he said he ain't read since he was a boy, *Luck and Pluck* and *Cash* and *Tattered Tom* and *Ragged Dick*. The last one Frank and Buster made jokes over when they thought they was alone and nobody could hear but they was always joking over things I never could see was funny.

The more he read them the more them books seemed to cheer my father up and gave him a bigger hope about things getting better and him maybe getting a job at the yard one of these days. And when he said it I saw my mother look up from her sewing with a look in her eyes like she wanted to believe it too, but I saw another look behind it said it was getting harder for her to believe. Still and all when she ducked her head over her needle again her lips fluttered a prayer.

My father talked about them books so much he done everything to encourage my two older brothers to read them, saying this man Horatio Alger understood boys better'n any man he knew and what he wrote was about how poor boys could make something of themselves if they wanted to, "If they ain't lazy bums," and he gave them a look.

They didn't want to read them at first, all they wanted to read was comic books, but finally they gave in, he nagged them so much. You'd see them slumped on the porch all the afternoons that was getting longer and longer now summer was coming, they'd be so wrapped up in reading them they didn't go down the river or off in the woods to smoke with the Beezley boys til they read each and every one of them books, both of them so lost to the world the house could've caved in on top of them, they wouldn't've known it.

I was out in our front yard playing cemetery, the game my mother learned me, where you dig holes in the ground and you bury burnt matches in little empty matchboxes, then you make little crosses on top with some more of the burnt matches, then you say a prayer over them like they was dead.

Danny and Kate was snoozing up on the porch and my brothers'd gone off with the Beezley boys after lunch with their homemade fishing poles to try and catch whatever they could for supper. The days was really getting warmer now and I could hear my mother singing through the open windows as she was sweeping the floors downstairs, sweeping them for the second time that day. "All this sand," she complained, like the sand we dragged in on our feet was an enemy always invading the house she could hardly keep up with.

In spite of everything, it was good to hear her beginning to sing again.

I'd just started patting down the dirt over the umpteenth grave I dug when I caught something moving out of the corner of my eye. Glancing up, I saw a boy a little older'n me going by in the road. I did a double take seeing it was the exact same boy on the Snarp's porch the first time we all went down to the river that day, the one with the big teeth that stuck his tongue out at me. He went by in nothing but barefeet and an old pair of raggedy overalls like he wasn't looking at anything, but I could tell he wasn't missing a trick. I saw the overalls was made of pillow ticking same as the ones my brothers wore and figured the Snarps must be on relief too.

I went back to start digging another hole and in a little while I looked up to see him come by on the road again from the other direction and this time take a gander in the yard. When he saw me looking he swung his eyes away real quick, trying to look like he ain't been looking at all. He had mousy hair the same color as me but his stuck up in the back like a rooster's comb. He had a shuffly walk with his head tilted to one side and his shoulders shoved back with one arm swinging loose and easy.

He went on by and I went back to my digging, thinking good riddance, I wouldn't want to know somebody stuck their tongue out at you, when the next thing I knew there he was standing over me, his face creased up, his hands plunked on his hips, looking me up and down with a squint-eyed sneer. My heart began to beat.

Close up, it looked like his teeth was so big he couldn't get them inside and shut his mouth all at the same time. All of a sudden without no warning, he spit between my legs and I stared down at the glob of spit, my heart going faster. Then with a hitch of his foot he screwed his bare heel into the dirt, squashing the little mounds of the graves I dug with their crosses on them. I saw his toes and ankles was freckled with old dirt, the edges of his feet all tough like an elephant's skin I saw in the movies once. He had rings of dusty sweat in the creases of his neck too, his wet hair plastered to his forehead like he been running.

"I'm Earl Snarp Jr.," he said.

I stared at him. The smell of him reminded me something of our outhouse.

"Whatcher name?" he said, "Pissant?"

I looked up at him quick, I wondered how did he know about my wetting the bed at Aunt Maggie's?

Never once taking his eyes off of me, he squatted down beside me. I stared around, looking if I could see my mother but all I could hear was her singing in the parlor as she swept. Danny and Kate was still dead to the world up on the porch.

"What're you doin?"

My tongue felt like a sack of relief potatoes in my mouth.

Can'tcha talk? What're ya, a dumbie?"

I shook my head.

"So, whatcha doin?"

"Playin cemetery," I whispered and looked down at the ground.

"What kinda dumb game is that? Where'd you learn a dumb game like that, pissant?"

I looked towards the house again. I could hear my mother singing, "Some one of these days yer gonna miss me, honey…"

"Me mother learnt me…" I whispered, wishing I was in the parlor singing with her right that very minute.

He stuck a hand behind his ear, squinting like Slap, only you could tell he wasn't deaf. "Hah? Hah? Speak up, can't hear ya."

I repeated what I said, trying to talk louder, my voice croaking like a frog.

"Looks like a dumb game to me, buryin matchboxes." He pointed to the fresh grave I just dug and said, "If this hole's yer ass, tell me where your ass is."

I shrunk inside, knowing he said a bad word and didn't know if I should answer him or not.

"C'mon, c'mon—If this hole's yer ass, where's yer ass?"

But I was more scared not to answer him, so finally I pointed to the hole I dug.

He let out a yelp that made me almost jump in the air and reaching back, he gave me a hard smack right on the hiney, hooting, "This is yer ass, dumbie! You don't even know yer ass from a hole in the ground!" Then he jumped up and ran across the yard, whooping and laughing and ran down the road towards his house.

I stared after him, my mouth hanging open til I couldn't see him anymore.

When I looked back at the house Danny, hearing all the

noise, was blinking awake and staring out at me, and Kate was beginning to stir. My mother was standing in the screendoor with the broom in her hand, looking out.

"Who was that just out here?"

I shrugged my shoulders, my hiney still stinging.

"Dint I hear somebody laughin?"

Kate, hearing her voice, started to whine and my mother came out and picked her up off the floor. I stared at all the smashed graves he dug his heel in.

"It was a boy," I said finally.

"What boy?"

"He said his name was Earl."

"What Earl?"

"He's one of them Snarps live down the road."

"What was he laughin at?"

I didn't dare tell her.

"He was jist laughin."

"Was he nice?" She was bouncing Kate up and down and looking at her just to look at her.

"Ummm," I said, that was the same as not saying nothing.

She was nuzzling her face in Katie's hair now. "Well, if he's nice maybe he'll come back again and play with you another time."

When she said that I quick crossed all my fingers on both my hands praying I hoped not.

The very next Sunday when we got home from church my father was already done working in his garden and seeing to the chickens, so he asked my older brothers did they want to go down the river. Buster yelled out, all excited, "You gonna learn us to doggie paddle, Pop?" My father said, "We'll see."

You could see my mother wasn't too crazy about the idea but

since she knew they was sneaking off to the river anyway, I guessed she figured they might just as well learn to swim. She went through her ragbag out in the shed and pulled out enough old pants of theirs was so patched up there wasn't another place to put one more patch on anywhere. Taking her old scissors she cut up fish with, she cut off the legs high up and gave each of the three older ones a pair, then she cut off the legs of an old pair of work pants of my father's and gave them to him, saying, "Now don'tchou let them go out too far."

At first she didn't want me to go but my father said did she want to turn me into a girl like a certain party nextdoor that I knew he meant Ronnie Mahoney. She looked troubled in her eyes for a minute then said, "No, I don't want to make no girl out of him," saying it like to be a girl was the worst thing a boy, or even a girl, could be, and he said, "Well, it's better he drowneded'n he turnt into a girl." She still looked doubtful but finally heaved a big sigh and said I could go but I could only get my feet wet and I was to stick close to my father. So she didn't reach into her ragbag for a pair of my old short pants for me to wear in the water since I was only going to take my socks and maryjanes off and I was awful glad of that.

When Danny heard her say I could go he started screaming bloody murder he wanted to go too and even though she gave him a cuff on the ear, saying he was too little, he still kept screaming. My father said, "Oh let 'im go, he can wade with Mickey."

My mother gave him a dirty look for going against her another time and pressed her lips together with another doubtful look, but she turned to me and said, "Well, Mick, you be sure to hold onto his hand when you're in the water," and shook her finger in my face, saying, "and don't go out too far, you hear me?" I nodded my head I did.

My oldest brothers right away rolled up their swimming pants and ran out of the house and out to the road, hollering, "C'mon, Dad, c'mon!" Slap hollering the loudest. But my father, calm as you please, stood on the porch and lit up one of his Bugler cigarettes, gave one last look over his tomato plants, then tucked his sawed-off workpants under his arm before he came down the steps and we set off for the river.

You knew you was getting close to the water when you came to the pine trees and the loose white sand so hard to walk in that Frank said Mr. Beezley said once been the ocean bottom. Slap asked him when that was and Frank said long, long before they fought the battle at the fort but Slap couldn't see how that was because if it was, where had all the water gone? I saw my chance and I asked Frank where was the sea now? He pointed down the river and I looked but all I saw was more of the river fanned out all flat against the sky.

Because we was going to the river my father slipped into one of his good moods. Despite being on relief, he seemed to have a lot of good moods lately. Like my older brothers, he seemed to take to living in Jersey right off the bat. He seemed more at home in Lenape'n ever he did in South Philly, like this was where he belonged. Because he wasn't drinking I wasn't as ascared of him.

Already through the pine trees I could smell the river, that milky odor when it wasn't the war yet and the river still smelled so clean and sweet like the smell of the morning was coming up out of the water. I was walking a little ahead, feeling like it was a treat us being taken for a walk by our father. I kept glancing back to catch a glimpse of him, like I wanted to make sure he was still there, seeing his face and neck burnt black as berry juice from working out in the sun on the roads or up on the dumptruck all day.

It was in turning my head to look back at him for the umpteenth time that I first saw the man, then the lady. It just about took the wind out of me when I saw them. Off to the side of the sand trail in an opening in the trees the branches was so knotted and thick they was like a big umbrella made of shadows and under the umbrella stood a big-eared man with thick lips and a belly fatter'n Ronnie's father even, and a big round head that was almost all bald. The thing that took my breath away was he didn't have any clothes on.

He was standing next to the lady that didn't look as old as him. Her hair was damp and it was so black it looked like she dyed it.

She was sitting beside a picnic basket on a rumpled tablecloth spread on the ground that had chicken bones and scraps of food scattered all over it. An empty wine bottle was knocked on its side in the grass. She was just putting on the top of a swimming suit and I was surprised at how big and purple her nipples was, the first time I ever saw them on a lady. But it was the man I spotted first, seeing dangling between his legs what looked at first like a slippery red snake in a tangle of dark weeds.

I looked and looked away quick, pretending I ain't seen anything, not daring now to glance over my shoulder at my father, or my older brothers that was walking behind him, because I ain't never seen a grown person bare before, not even my father or my mother because I knew from them that that was bad and the only time you could be bare was on Saturday night in the washtub in the kitchen.

When I got up the nerve to sneak a peek back again, I saw Buster's eyes was big as saucers and a big grin stretched over his face that he tried to hide from my father as he gave Frank a poke. When he spied them, Frank's eyebrows lifted up so high they was practically disappearing into the curls of his hair.

If my father saw any of it he didn't make like he did but I had a feeling he had as I peeked back real careful this time out of the corner of my eye, wanting to look again at the man and lady but knowing I shouldn't and afraid if I did my father'd catch me at it. But Slap and Danny that was walking either side my father had their heads turned completely around so that they was practically walking backwards, staring back at the two people in the woods with their mouths hanging open. My father, without saying a word or missing a step or doing anything but stare straight ahead of him, put his hand on top of both their heads and screwed them front-ways, so I knew he saw the man and the lady. But Frank and Buster being behind my father, everytime I snuck a look back they was just about falling all over each other trying to get a good look, and looking and looking like their eyes'd pop out, big grins on their faces.

At first the man and the lady didn't see us, the man spied us first and when he did, he watched us through eyes that was like little slits as we passed and he was swaying on his pins like my father done when he used to have one too many. When he saw us he just looked away so casual, like he wasn't in any hurry to cover himself up, like it wasn't nothing to him being caught bare in the woods and people seeing you.

The lady had her top on now and was pulling herself up off the ground, the skin on her heavy legs was shivering like my mother's homemade jelly as she stood up. She started raking her fingers through her hair, brushing out bits of weeds and straw and when she saw us, she gave a little cry and turned her back to us real quick, then stepped deeper into the bushes so's we couldn't see her. The big-eared man gave a snort, grinning so's you couldn't see his eyes, and followed in after her, staggering a little before he caught himself and tried to straighten up.

We marched on by, none of us saying anything, walking now under pine branches that was dark and heavy like a roof. The only sound you heard was the sand whispering under our shoes as we headed for the steep path cut in the bluff through the trees ahead, the shortcut the Beezley boys showed us that Buster, running to catch up with my father, was just busting to show him before Frank did.

We came down the cut in the bluff that was so steep the pebbles and stones rolled under your feet like they was trying to knock you down, so I took Danny's hand so's he wouldn't fall. But he stuck out his lower lip and knocked my hand away, wanting to go down by himself, so naturally he falls smack on his hiney first thing. I picked him up and dusted him off and he took my hand this time and we started on down again, my father and them way ahead of us now calling for us to hurry up as we came out on the beach.

When we caught up to them, my father was looking around like he was looking for somebody but there wasn't anybody around except for far down near where Mr. Beezley said the ferry was you could see some boys throwing stones at a bottle floating in the water. Far out a tugboat was going by pulling a string of barges behind it. When he saw nobody was around my father told the three oldest to go change in the woods while me and him and Danny walked across the beach to the water. At the edge he squatted down and scooped his hand in and Danny, looking all bugeyed since he ain't never seen the river so close up before, asked him was it cold? For an answer, my father grinned, sprinkling some in his face, and Danny twisted up his face and jumped back.

When my brothers came down in their sawed-off pants,

stepping careful over the sharp stones in their barefeet and rubbing their arms against their sides like they was chilly even though it was a warm day, my father told Frank to keep an eye on me and Danny while he went back in the woods to change, and gave strict orders for none of us to look while he was changing.

Frank and Buster went right in the water up to their hips and Slap went in after them but only a little at a time, hugging himself and shivering and screeching how cold it was. The older ones laughed at him and told him, "Quit actin like a grrr-rull."

While they was all splashing water at each other I sat Danny down on a rock beside me and even though he told us not to look I looked back anyhow, never having seen my father before and wondering was he like the man with the big ears in the woods or was he like Uncle Jake when I dreamt he was a cop without no clothes on? But all I was able to see because of the shade under the trees was my father stooping and hopping around on one leg as he kicked off his pants like the cripple named Charley hopped when he walked. Once he had them off, his face and arms that was so dark from the sun you couldn't hardly see them they was like part of the shadow, he pulled on the old work pants my mother cut off at the knees for him, pulling them on so quick while his head darted around like somebody might be watching him from the woods. Even though the rest of him was white as milk, even so, all I saw was a shadow between his legs that was as dark as the light in the shade of the trees.

He came out of the woods, stepping as careful over the stones as my brothers done, so brown in his face he looked brown as the faces of his mother and father in their pictures over our bed. But except for where the black hair curled on his skinny chest, the rest of him was white as Snow White now, out in the sunshine.

That monkey Buster yelled out from the water, "Hey, Pop! You look just like a bathin beauty!" and my father, still in his good mood, grinned sheepish and said, "I'll bathin beauty you." He went and stuck his foot in the water, shivering just like my brothers, Frank hollering, "Come on, Pop, getcher tootsies wet!" All of a sudden my father bent over, stuck out his arms and pointing his hands together like he was praying dived headfirst smack into the water, making such a big explosion in the river, the others jumped back, their eyes so wide they couldn't believe it. All you could see was his arms shooting up out of the water like he was going to swim clear over to Philly. He was soon so far out I thought we'd never see him again.

I jumped up, pulling Danny along with me, the two of us staring far out where my father's head was bobbing up and down and spitting water out of his mouth. He ducked under and disappeared and my heart started up, afraid he drowned like my mother said you did if you went under, but after what seemed a long while he popped up again and swum back in, slower this time. When he was in close Buster yelled out, so's you could hear the surprise in his voice, "Geez, Pop, I dint know you could swim like Johnny Weismuller!" As my father swum up, tossing his head to toss off the water, he said, "Oh, I ain't near as good as him, but I don't do bad for a kid learnt to swim off of the South Philly docks." He pointed across the water in the direction of where that was and I saw it was up from Fort Mifflin, near where Tasker Street and the Lyric movies must be, the old neighborhood where he grew up.

Then he was yelling at me to take off Danny's shoes and socks and to keep ahold of his hand when the two of us came in the water to wade. Danny wanted to take off his shoes himself of course, an old pair of maryjanes I outgrowed but was still good enough for him to wear, no holes or nothing in them, since I was good on shoes. Once we had our shoes and socks off, I walked with him to the edge of the water, looking first to see if I saw any catfish or minniegudgeons or eels, and when I didn't, I stuck my toes in and shivered like the others all done, it was so cold even though the air wasn't cold at all, and I wondered how that could be. Danny made a face but little by little he came in and when we was over our ankles he started grinning and reached down with his free hand and started smacking the water while I kept a sharp eye out for anything nibbling around us.

When I was sure there wasn't, I looked around down the beach both ways. The boys we saw earlier throwing stones down near the ferry were gone now and there was nobody on the beach that I could see. But just as I was turning back to look across the river at Philly again I thought I spied a pair of eyes staring at me from behind some bushes in the woods far back off the shore near where my father and brothers took off their clothes. I blinked and looked again and it was like whoever it was saw me looking because all of a sudden I saw a flash of red hair and the branches started whipping back and forth. It looked like whoever it was was hurrying away in a hoppy kind of run like I saw the way Charley the cripple moved. I wondered could it be him. I remembered again what Mr. Beezley said, not to go in the woods with him, but if it was Charley, I wondered why he was spying on us and figured maybe it was because he was getting more things to tell about us so's he could write it in the *County Seat Weekly*. That must be it, he'd write that my father was learning my brothers how to doggie paddle.

Meanwhile, my father'd started showing my older brothers what the doggie paddle was and got them down in the water and kept hollering, "Kick your legs like yer runnin! Kick yer legs!" Frank and Buster kicked their legs in big splashes while Slap, with all the water in his ears I guess, he didn't hear my father so good even though my father was yelling, so he didn't kick as hard and kept sinking and spluttering even though he was beating his hands like mad in front of him and spitting out water like he was the pump in our kitchen. The three of them paddled up and down a little ways out in the water from where me and Danny was wading and it wasn't long before Frank and Buster was doing it without sinking or swallowing water but it took Slap a little longer because he wasn't as quick or easy at it as the other two was.

Danny started whining he wanted to doggie paddle too and my father waded in and held him under the belly and slid him through the water while Danny kicked his legs and squealed and batted his fists like a maniac til he got a noseful of water and started choking and coughing. Seeing the look of surprise on his face, my father couldn't help but laugh but Danny, still hacking away, didn't see nothing funny in it and so my father picked him up and held him against his chest, grinning at him, saying, "Swallyed some water, dintcha? Swallyed water, huh?"

For days afterwards, Frank and Buster did nothing but snigger about seeing the man and the lady in the woods. I could hear them under the covers up in bed that same night sniggering about it. After the two of them finally quieted down for the night and was breathing deep asleep, I got to thinking myself of what we saw that day, not so much of the lady, though I ain't seen tiddies before, as Slap called them—When I asked him what they were for, he said they were pillows for the baby to lay their head on—What I was thinking of was the man and his dunkey that was bigger'n any I dreamed ever could be, like a bloody snake all shiny between his legs. I wondered if my father's or Sam Beezley's or Joe John Mahoney's looked the same.

The Beezleys were over visiting that night like they did every Sunday night so my father and Mr. Beezley could hear Walter Winchell on the radio, but now there wasn't no radio because the electric was turned off they talked even more'n they ever did. So as not to wake him, I leaned as careful as I could over Slap to hear what I could. My father was telling about the man and the lady we saw in the woods that morning, then his voice dropped down so low I couldn't hear what he was saying but whatever it was his voice was all excited. Mr. Beezley was cackling and kept going, "Yer kiddin...Gwan, git outa here..." but my father swore up and down every word he was saying was true. Then my mother cut in saying to my father, "That's enough, I don't want to hear anymore about it," and my father said to her, "Aw gwan, go flap yer ears," but said it good-natured like he wasn't mad at her for telling him enough was enough. Sam Beezley said, "They musta been down here from Philly for the Sunday with the saloons closed over there, they don't sound like anybody I know, they musta come down here to do their Sunday drinkin...and their diddlin...." And he sniggered just like Frank and Buster did when he said it. Mrs. Beezley butted in saying, "I don't care where they was from, the least they coulda done was go back in the weeds so's none of the kids woulda seen 'em." My mother said, "Yes, they could of done that the very least and I blame the lady more'n the man, the shameless huzzy." But Mr. Beezley let out one of his cackles again, hooting in his loud way, "Kids gotta learn sometime," and my mother said so quiet I almost didn't hear it, "But not so soon...."

Once the Beezleys left I lay back down again and it wasn't long after that I heard my father pulling the chains of the cuckoo clock down in the dining room like he always did at bedtime.

Then I saw the light of the oil lamp coming up the stairs, then the light of it shining in our room for a minute as my mother stopped to look in at our door like she always did before she went into their bedroom. I snapped my eyes shut, pretending to be asleep and when the doorway went dark again, I opened them. Through the netting my father'd tacked at the windows came the smell of the night again and I breathed it in, so restless from all the talk downstairs I couldn't get settled. Slap in his sleep was beating his fists up and down, like he must've been dreaming he was still doggie paddling. I listened to my mother and father undressing and just as I was drifting off I heard a noise in their room and heard the bedsprings creak followed by my father talking real low, talking in that excited way like he been talking downstairs when he was telling Mr. Beezley about the man and the lady in the woods. I heard my mother give a sigh and tell him, "Go on to sleep, it's been a long day." When she said that, he sounded like he was trying to jolly her like he did when he was drinking and wanted something. And like the last time I heard them on the night he was complaining of the roses they were too many, she whispered something back I couldn't hear, something quick and impatient like the way she talked to us kids when she didn't want to be bothered. Then my father said something sharp sounded nasty, the way things he said sounded when he used to be drunk. I heard the springs twang again, only louder this time, like they were groaning and he was turning over in the bed. Then everything was quiet.

The next afternoon when I was up on the porch minding Danny and Kate, I overheard Frank and Buster tell the Beezley boys about the man and the lady. They were all smoking cigarette butts under the porch while my mother was making the beds upstairs. Brother kept asking them to tell him what the lady's nipples looked like, only he called them tits and not tiddies like Slap, and when Frank and Buster kept butting in on each other telling him they were big and purple as plums, he begged them to tell it again, cackling all the time to himself when they did, cackling just like his father did the night before.

I dreamt of the naked man for a couple nights running but I didn't dream of the naked lady, she wasn't never in the dream somehow.

...Cool in the dark under the dining room table, the buzz of flies around my head like the buzz of the heat outside the windows...Buzz of talk in the parlor.... Mustn't slap at the flies, mustn't be heard, get caught... Scrape of my mother's peeler peeling potatoes for our supper...Smell of Mrs. Beezley's Raleigh drifting in under the table.... "He gets that way," my mother is saying,..." well, you know how they are...and he knows well and good we just can't have another mouth to feed...." Her voice low in a sigh...the scrape of her peeler..."Not right now anyway...with him not workin...He knows that...." She really does sigh now and Mrs. Beezley clicks her tongue, "They're all alike, they're always at you..." and she sighs too...."I don't know what to do, Babes, if I only knowed what to do...." The scraping on the potato stops, then there's a loud creak of the chair like Mrs. Beezley's heaving herself up out of it, then the sound of her slippers heavy on the linoleum as she crosses the parlor floor..."There, there, honey, it's gonna be all right now, just don'tchou worry...." saying it like she was trying to quiet my mother as if my mother was crying.... "Come on now, honey, it ain't no crime to say no to them oncet in awhile..." and I heard my mother say barely in a whisper, "I ain't so sure, Babes, I wisht I was...."

Hearts was the card game my brothers played all that first summer up on the front porch. Brother Beezley learnt it to them, and in the beginning it got so bad some days they didn't even bother sneaking down the river to practice their doggie paddle and would only go fishing whenever my mother needed some fish for supper— If they weren't playing hearts or reading Horatio Alger Jr. they were looking at the comic books the Beezley boys brought over when they were done with them, Nickel Comics and the Amazing Mystery Funnies and Action Comics with Superman, and one of their favorites after Superman, Sheena, Queen of the Jungle, in Jumbo Comics, that was a lady with long blonde hair swinging from vine to vine in nothing but a skimpy little leopard skin her tiddies was just about popping out of that all the niggers with next to nothing on themselves were always bowing down to and that Frank and Buster read and reread over and over so many times out on the porch that summer the pages were all curled up and smudged and smeared from their hands so sweaty. You could hear them and the Beezley boys putting their heads together and giggling so much over Sheena, Queen of the Jungle, my mother heard them one day and came out and snatched it out of their hands. She took one look at it, her eyes getting big as the spots on Sheena's leopard skin. Then she told them in no uncertain terms they shouldn't be looking at such dirty trash, she didn't want nothing like that around the house. So when the Beezley boys brought over the next issue of Jumbo Comics with Sheena, Queen of the Jungle, that they got at Gottlieb's, they all hid under the porch and read it together and after that my brothers kept it hid under there up under the steps that was another one of their hiding places for the cigarette butts they smoked under the porch when they knew my mother was somewhere else in the house.

They wouldn't let me play hearts with them even though I knew the numbers on the cards, they said I was too little even though they let Sparky Beezley play and he wasn't much older'n me and wore glasses besides. So lots of times I just sat watching them play or listened to them giggling under the porch while the smoke from their cigarette butts drifted up through the cracks in the floorboards. I breathed it in wanting to know what smoking tasted like, it tasted like what I bet my father tasted like, he smoked cigarettes all the time, he smelled like walking smoke.

It was one of them afternoons they were up on the porch playing hearts when I caught a bright yellow glint in the woods beside our house, yellow as Sheena, Queen of the Jungle's hair, and looking saw it was Ronnie squatting in the bushes giving me the high sign.

I slid down the porch steps and made a run for the woods.

Ronnie's cheeks were red as two tomatoes he looked so excited when he popped up out of the bushes and grabbed me by the hand, whispering all in a rush like my brothers might hear him, "Come on! I got a good game for us to play!"

He jerked me after him as he ran away so fast towards his house, I figured it must've been one of them days his mother didn't have a headache for once for him to bring me over. But the way he had me tiptoe up the steps to his playroom I was wondering if I was wrong, maybe his mother did have one of her headaches after all the way he was sneaking me upstairs and putting a finger to his lips to be quiet as I could. Looking over my shoulder I saw Mrs. Mahoney sitting reading one of her books and puffing away on a Camel in her armchair in the parlor, I mean the living room, them being more up-to-date'n us.

She was so caught up in what she was reading, she didn't even look up or seem to hear us over the radio as we snuck up the stairs. Once we were up there Ronnie, still all excited, asked me did I ever play dressup? I said I didn't know, I didn't know what dressup was. He rubs his hands together and looking all sneaky and sly he put a finger to his lips one more time and tells me to wait right there as he goes creeping back down the stairs.

I saw my chance and quick ran to the bookcase to look at the picture books while he was gone, spelling out the words in a book called *The Wizard of Oz*, when Ronnie came creeping back up the stairs his arms loaded up with old dresses and hats and high heels he said he got from his mother's closet. He dumped them all on the little play tea table, then pulled out of one pocket of his short pants a string of pearls he whispered was really only fake, and out of the other pocket a necklace of cutglass beads he whispered all came from his mother's jewelry box. In amongst the dresses was a fox furpiece that looked awful moth-eaten he said once belonged to his Grandmother O'Shea. His eyes were as glassy bright as the eyes in the fox, brighter'n I ever saw them, as he rummaged through the clothes trying to decide who should wear what, like it was Halloween even though it was only in the summer. Whether I liked it or not, he handed me a bright yellow dress with big white flowers to put on and since I never wore a dress before I didn't know front from back or which end was up and got to giggling, I couldn't help myself. Ronnie made a face as much as to say what a dumbie I was not knowing how to put on a dress, so he helped me into it and buttoned me up, pulling it in here and tucking it up there, as if he did it lots of times before.

When it came to his own dress he had a hard time making up his mind which one he was going to pick. Holding up one after another in front of him he finally threw over his head a purple dress covered with tiny rosebuds, and because his mother was so short the hems came down to our ankles so we didn't have to roll them up at all. He got to wear the furpiece and pearls but he let me wear the glass beads, which I liked anyway, they sparkled so. His hat was a pink one to match the roses in his dress he said, and had a white feather and white veil stuck on it, whilst mine was a little straw hat with a narrow brim that had a bunch of cherries on the side like my Aunt Nell's best Sunday hat. Because his mother's feet were so tiny, the high heels just about fit us but Ronnie walked in them a lot better'n I did, like he already had some practice.

He said they were his mother's old clothes but I saw right away they looked a whole lot newer and better'n anything my mother had in her whole closet.

Once we were all dressed up, he hoisted his skirt and slid a tube of his mother's lipstick out of his pants pocket, telling me to quit my laughing and hold still as he smeared a blob of it over my mouth. "Cherries in the Snow," he called it, "It's Ginger Rogers' and my mother's favorite." Then he smeared a streak of it over his own mouth, rubbing his lips together like I saw Babes Beezley do when she put hers on for the Saturday night movie, and between the lipstick and the dress and the blond curls sticking out from under his pink hat, he really looked like a girl more'n he normally did.

Holding the hem of his skirt up high, he wobbled around the playroom, his nose in the air, acting snooty. I followed right behind him, doing like he did, starting to laugh again, I couldn't help laughing, like it was all play, all a big show like at the mummers parade. Then the two of us got to giggling so hard we couldn't stop and he quick put a finger to his lips like he didn't want his mother to hear us. He went to the top of the stairs and cocked an ear down, listening, but all you could hear was the dance music still playing low on the radio down in the parlor. That light of the imp in his eye got even more glittery and sly, he was so excited he bit down on his lower lip getting the Cherries in the Snow lipstick all over his front teeth as he crooked a finger at me to come follow him.

It was still all play, all the same as that, so I clumped down the stairs after him, thinking we were going to surprise his mother showing her our getup because Ronnie kept looking quick over his shoulder with a finger to his mouth again not to make any noise, which was hard to do with high heels on, not to mention my being afraid of falling head over heels down the stairs, they were so hard to walk in.

When we got to the bottom I could see through the dining room into the parlor. Mrs. Mahoney was still so caught up in whatever she was reading she didn't even look up or seem to hear us as, instead of going into the parlor to show her our dressup, Ronnie surprised me by jerking his head at me to sneak instead through the kitchen with him and out the back door.

Outside, we hobbled around the side of the house and I thought that was going to be it, but then he started off through the woods heading towards our house, still acting the highfalooting lady, me behind him, having a hard time walking in the sand in heels. I felt funny in my getup in broad daylight and it not really being Halloween but I pretended it was and laughed along with Ronnie to cover up how nervous and silly I was feeling.

I didn't want to go no farther'n the woods, because my brothers and the Beezley boys were still up on our porch, but Ronnie kept waving me on, throwing me back a look like he might wrassle me to the ground right then and there and sit on my chest if I didn't do what he said. Which surprised me no end he was always so shy about showing himself, he always hid in the bushes in the woods and would never come in our yard if he knew my father or my brothers were around. I figured maybe in his getup he thought nobody'd recognize him, like the hat and dress and heels were hiding him and he could go anywhere he pleased and not be seen for who he was, like putting on the dress made him somebody else who was bold as brass, like I felt I was somebody else, like I was my mother and like I was my Aunt Nell and Mrs. Mahoney all together, and my mouth tasting like Cherries in the Snow was Babes Beezley and Ginger Rogers.

When we got out on the road all I could do was hope when we passed our house nobody'd be out front. But wouldn't you know my three older brothers and the Beezley boys were still sprawled out on the floor of the porch playing hearts, with Danny and Kate asleep in the corner.

Slap saw us first and his eyes bulged out, he started his screeching and pointing, and of course the others looked too, their mouths flapping open. I could feel my ears burning bright as the lipstick smeared on my mouth and was wishing even more than ever we hadn't come this way, thinking maybe this wasn't such a good game after all and that I never should've let Ronnie put a dress on me in the first place. All of them were staring at us without saying anything as Ronnie sashayed on by with me hobbling like Charley after him in the sand, wishing for once the sand was the quicksand back in the swamp so's I could be swallowed up. Ronnie was holding up the skirt of his dress so dainty the way the men dressed as ladies did in the mummers parade. I tried to tell myself if boys could dress up like ladies in the mummers parade with cherries hanging down from their panties, what could be wrong with us two doing it even if it wasn't New Years? But then that Ronnie couldn't keep a straight face and got to laughing so much he fell against me, almost knocking me off my pins when he did. Slap saw him laughing and was grinning and waving at us but he was the only one on the porch that did.

What the others did when they got over their surprise was Brother Beezley stuck his little fingers either side of his mouth and let out a whistle so loud it scared the birds out of the trees, and monkey see monkey do Sparky of course went and did the same though it wasn't half as loud, while Buster, like my father did sometimes, scowled dark as a raincloud in his eyes like he wanted to smack somebody, mainly me, I was thinking.

I wanted to say in the worst way let's go back now, cut through the woods and go back to his house, but Ronnie was flouncing along, one hand on his hip and the other one still holding his skirt up, enjoying himself like all the trees on either side of the road were people watching him.

When we came to the Snarp's house some of their kids were out front playing in the dirt with the chickens pecking around them, and there was Earl Snarp Jr. out front swinging in the old car tire hanging from a rope in a tree. He stopped swinging long enough to gawk at us and kept on gawking before he pinched his fingers to his nose like something was stinking all around him that wasn't just himself so then it must be us. Ronnie, seeing him do it, stuck his own nose up even farther in the air and swung his head away like he didn't want to insult his eyes looking at Earl Snarp Jr., while for a different reason at the same time it was all I could do to keep from looking at him either, I felt a tingling in the seat of my pants, remembering how he smacked me in the hiney that time when I didn't know my you-know-what from a hole in the ground.

After we gone by the house all of a sudden I heard a rock or something like a rock go whistling over our heads and crash into the trees across the road. I was all for running away right then and there, high heels or no, but Ronnie just snapped his head around with a look of daggers that would've stabbed Earl Jr.

dead on the spot if they really were, but Earl Jr. was swinging in the tire hard as he could, whistling like he ain't done nothing at all.

After we got past the Snarp's I told Ronnie I couldn't walk anymore, his mother's shoes were killing me, and what with the sand and my feet hurting, what fun there been it was long since gone by that time anyhow. He made a face and gave a sigh, "Oh well," he said, "since there aren't any more houses close by to parade past to show ourselves off to anyway, we might just as well go back." So we turned around and took the shortcut through the woods to his house that I was as glad we did, I sure didn't want to pass Earl Snarp Jr. or my brothers and the Beezley boys a second time.

Before we tiptoed in the Mahoney's backdoor again, Ronnie slipped off his high heels and made a motion for me to do the same, and I did, I was glad to get out of them as I was to get out of the shoes that pinched me from relief. When we got inside I saw his mother's nose was still buried in her book with the radio playing, so we got upstairs without her knowing we been gone at all. Up in the playroom we took off all our dressup and Ronnie managed to get it all back down in his mother's closet without her ever finding out. When he came back up he brought with him a jar of her cold cream and some toilet paper and we wiped the lipstick off of our mouths.

I tried to keep on telling myself it didn't mean anything, it was just for fun, playing dressup, but a part of me knew different. I knew by now a boy could only dress up like a girl on Halloween or in the mummers parade or up on the altar at church but not no other times unless he wanted to be jeered at or hollered at, and that's all there was to it. And there wasn't no time ever a boy could play with a babydoll, and that was that, no ands ifs or buts about it, no matter it didn't make no sense.

So, having stayed as long as I could so I wouldn't have to face the music any sooner'n I had to, after I left Ronnie's house later on that afternoon and started back through the woods, my heart began to beat the closer I got to my house because I knew I was in for it and was hoping with all my might none of my brothers or the Beezley boys'd still be there. But of course they were, they were always around when you didn't want them around, and as I came up on the porch where they were all still playing hearts, my older brothers gave me a queer look, then looked back down at their hands and didn't say nothing, they didn't have to, their eyes was saying it all. But the Beezley boys mocked at me over their cards, Brother curling up one side of his mouth in a snigger that said everything he had to say without him having to say anything either.

I was trying to slide past them into the house but Buster looked up and said, like I wasn't even there, "He's makin a grrr-rull outa him more'n he already is," then he snapped down a card like he wished it was something in me he was snapping.

"I don't think Mom should let him go over there anymore," Frank said. I acted like I was as invisible as they were making me out to be. I had a hand on the screendoor, ready to jump in. "I don't think she knows the half of it, him dressin up like a grrr-rull."

"Does yer old man know?" Brother put in, not looking up from his cards, his voice as oily as kerosene.

"Not yet," Buster said, slapping down another card then giving me a look like maybe my father would know soon enough, and at the thought of it my heart froze like a chunk of ice in my chest, even if he wasn't drinking anymore.

"We was only playin," I said, begging-like, but thinking they were probably all just jealous because Ronnie had so many things they never had and would've give their eyeteeth to have when they were his age. "We was only playin like it was Halloween."

"He's making a grrr-rull outa you," Buster muttered again, as if that was that and was all there was to it.

I began to shake inside, not knowing why it was I was shaking or what it was I did was so terrible except dressup when it wasn't Halloween or New Years or anything in the church.

"We was only playin," I begged again, saying it so low I don't think either one of them heard me, and hoped they wouldn't tell our father, he been acting more and more nervous lately, more'n he ever been since we came to Jersey, you couldn't tell what he might do.

Slap piped up with, "Where'd you git them high heels? How'd you walk in them high heels shoes? Dint they hurtchou?" I yanked open the screendoor real quick and jumped into the house before Slap asked me another question and so I could get away from the eyes of the others drilling into me.

I stopped halfway through the house, not knowing which way to go. I could hear Kate out in the kitchen talking her babytalk to my mother while my mother was getting supper ready. I wondered if she saw me in the dressup too, and not wanting to face her in case she did, or if either Frank or Buster already ratted on me, I dived under the dining room table where it was always so cool and dark and where I felt so safe like I was in a cave and nobody could see me or find me. I hugged my knees to my chest and started thinking that although I knew what my older brothers meant, finally learning it was bad for boys to be girls, my head began to whirl thinking about it. I was too fast and too slow, like I was fast in some things like knowing to read without nobody showing me and slow in other things, like trying to get the hang of what a boy was that all my brothers seemed to know right off, and that was so hard and slow for me to see, like I still couldn't see what was so wrong about being like a girl, except when a sister got born and everything got changed around so you didn't know what you were supposed to do or what was expected of you anymore because it was her got her hair curled now and it was her got a Shirley Temple doll and her got her picture took and even hand-tinted and you didn't, if you were a boy you were to behave one way and if you were a girl you was to behave another, and I never got the hang of which way was which, if I could only get the hang of it I knew everything'd be all right, but I just couldn't seem to get the hang of it no matter how hard I tried.

I hugged my knees tighter and thought about it and thought about it, and it only went around in my head like a pinwheel in the wind, I never got nowhere with it, I just wasn't quick enough.

Just like I figured, my two older brothers razzed me for days after that, making a big show of holding the screendoor open for me and calling me madam, calling me sissy and mama's boy and two new names I never heard before but when they said them I knew meant bad, fairy, that I saw pictures of flying around in Ronnie's picture books, and pansy, that I thought was only a flower. So they were teasing me every chance they got, saying it was too bad Kate's dresses were too small for me to get into, maybe I would like to wear Kate's dresses too, then they could have two sisters, and Buster sneers, "Maybe they got piller ticking dresses for him down at relief Pop can bring home!" And Frank and him bust up laughing like that was the funniest ever. But after a week it soon died down when they got bored with it and I don't have to tell you how glad I was of that, being made to feel like something under a rock back in the swamp.

None of us saw Charley come hobbling over the beach, least of all myself as I sat pretending to dig away in the sand, wishing, foolish as I knew it to be by now, I'd find cobblestones underneath and suddenly everything'd be Mifflin Street again.

He probably came onto the beach from the woods at the foot of the bluff directly behind us, and with our backs turned we ain't spotted him at first.

Close up he was taller and you could see how skinny and bony he was, with a sharp nose and face like my father, his hair slicked back the same as him, his red hair looking almost pink in the bright sun. I saw he had freckles too and that his skin was the color of the wax candles in church. I knew now he wasn't no boy because you could see he shaved, but I still couldn't tell if he was old or not. From under the dining table one time I heard Mrs. Beezley tell my mother Charley'd been "born that way," and I looked sideways at him trying not to stare at his one arm bent up at the elbow and hugging his side, with the hand pointing straight out, the fingers curling down and back like a hook. The lame leg he dragged along after him in the sand gave him a stooped, stumbly kind of walk making the crooked arm he held up in front of him look just like a broke wing. He looked like the stork brung babies I seen in the comic strips.

Despite the heat, he had his shirt buttoned all the way up to his neck and even the long sleeves buttoned to his wrists. He came and stood about a yard from where we were sprawled in a little circle and my brothers grew quiet, watching him as he came up like they weren't paying too much attention but I knew they were watching everything about him. They kept looking down at themselves like they were annoyed he caught them in their underwear.

Slap was the only one grinning at him like he always did with everybody, like the whole world was his friend, as my mother said. But the two oldest were watching him curious but careful because he was a grownup in a place and at a time of day where grownups, even our father, hardly ever showed up.

Because I was with my brothers, I wasn't very scared and since we weren't in the woods but out in the open on the beach I knew we didn't have to worry about what Mr. Beezley said about being in the woods with Charley. He nodded first to Frank and Frank nodded back. He nodded to Buster but Buster just glared at him. I could feel his eyes going over us one by one without them seeming to, and although I didn't know what it was about the way he looked at us, it made me feel funny. Yet, he knew our names. I wanted to know how he knew our names to write them down in the newspaper and hoped one of my older brothers'd ask him.

When he finally opened his mouth, his lips that were thin as a hair barely parted.

"You boys havin a good time?"

Slap and me looked to the oldest and when Frank cocked his head to one side and nodded, then Slap did too, grinning even more'n before. But I could see Frank was as squirmy all of a sudden as Buster and me was, digging his bare toes in the sand to hide it yet stealing peeks like Buster was at Charley's twisted arm and leg but pretending like they weren't. Then wouldn't you know that Slap piped up with, "Does it hurt you when you walk?" saying it like Charley had on Ginger Mahoney's high heels like I had on that day when Slap asked me the very same thing.

Charley looked at him, then looked away and didn't say nothing. He kept swallowing like it hurt him to swallow, his adam's apple jumping up and down just like my father's when my father got jumpy. Looking at him, there was something buried about him, his voice was flat as the ground, there was some-

thing like a funeral about him, like our Uncle Digby the undertaker, his eyes were just like Uncle Digby's, serious and digni-
fied, like he was there and wasn't there all at the same time.

Them eyes was climbing all over us again.

"Any you boys got any problems? I can help you, you got
any problems."

He was looking direct at Frank and Buster. Them two stiffened their spines like they did when we were company at somebody else's house. They stared at Charley like he was talking
Chinee, then stared out over the river. You could see they were
still feeling funny Charley seeing them in their underwear. But
Slap didn't care, he was looking from them to Charley and back
at them again, his mouth half turned up in that way of his when
he didn't hear what was going on. I looked at Charley and wondered what he meant, asking did we have any problems? Did he
mean my father not having no job and being on relief? Did he
mean not having no money to go to the movies? Something
about what he said, the way he said it, despite the day, made my
belly go cold.

He swallowed, his adam's apple going again. He cleared his
throat. "Didjou see I wrote about you in the paper?"

Buster squinted, even more suspicious-looking than he been
before. "How'djou know our names?"

I was all ears. Charley swallowed hard this time. "I got
some from Father Mack, I got the rest what he dint know from
Mrs. Beezley…." He stopped and cleared his throat again. " I
know she's best girlfriends with your mom…." His voice trailed
off like his words were going down in the ground again, they
were so gravelly and low.

Buster snapped, "We know she knows our mom!" saying it
like he was real mad Charley wrote our names in the paper. He
stared out at the river again, that mad look darkening his face.

Charley saw it too and looked down at his shoes like Buster'd accused him of something terrible. I wondered was Buster mad because Charley might write our names in the *County Seat Weekly* that we been down the river when we wasn't supposed to be and them swimming in their underwear and Mrs. Beezley see it and tell our mother.

Then all of a sudden Frank, that been getting more and more fidgety, jumped up like he couldn't sit still another minute, and blue as he was from being so long in the water before, raced across the beach and dove into the water. Buster, looking relieved somebody made a move, chased after him, yelping, then Slap shot up like a spring and he ran too, jumping in the water feet first. Soon the river was filled with their shouting and splashing, Frank right away slicing off, doing his sidestroke Brother Beezley learnt them, and Buster cutting out right along after him.

I stared down at where I been digging for cobblestones, afraid to look up, even more aware now my brothers were gone of Charley standing there. Like Slap, I was dying to know did his leg hurt him when he walked, and how did he tie his shoes or button himself with just one hand, did his mother do it for him? And was it him peeking out of the bushes that day we saw the naked man and lady in the woods and my father learnt my brothers to doggie paddle? But I dared not ask him.

"You got any problems?"

At first I didn't think he was talking to me, grownups didn't always talk to me, even a grownup that's cripple, when you are so little and close to the ground it's like big people don't see you and you don't count.

"Someday you got any problems you tell me."

His voice coming again, real quiet, quiet as if he was talking somewhere underneath himself. He was standing right over me, putting me in a shadow, his eyes as washed out as the sky. His mouth'd move but them eyes of his was speaking more'n his words and I wasn't sure of what they were saying. I didn't answer him, not understanding the question, or the one he wasn't saying. I thought of what Mrs. Beezley told my mother, she better keep an eye on me with Charley. I would've loved to ask him did he know what she meant, here he was standing right there, looking down at me in the sand…My heart began to beat…

"You get in here!"

It was Frank yelling to me from the water far out near the sandbar that he'd swum to first, beating Buster that was still walloping the water, trying to catch up. I jumped like a trained dog, hearing my older brother's voice, bossy, just like our mother's could be sometimes, and my father's most always.

"You git in here or you're gonna git it, boy!" He was shaking his fist now standing up on the sandbar, the flying drops of water hitting the sun.

Charley's eyes were still watching me. They had a look in them said, Don't pay him any attention. There was something damp and gray in his eyes, like something buried and hid, something you might see back in the swamp or like the strange things we had no names for we'd sometimes find under the rocks here at the beach. They had a look the way I felt when my brothers razzed me for playing dressup. The cold feeling came back in my belly.

"Hey! Are you comin or do I have to come and drag you away?"

He sounded like he meant business this time so I scrambled up and hurried down to the water where, what was nervy for me, I waded right in up over my knees. The others were batting around and hollering out by the long sandbar you could hardly see, now it was near high tide.

I turned and shaded my eyes and watched the shore.

Charley wasn't where he was when I left him and I wondered how he'd managed to get away so quick with his leg and all when finally I spotted him, dark as a shadow limping against the glare of the sand back in the direction of the woods. I watched until he disappeared into the leafiest shade, the exact same place where I saw my father changing that day, his pale red hair, out of the sun now, gleaming like it was all icy fire in the shadows.

When we got back into the woods where my brothers had their clothes stashed, they found they were all knotted up so tight it took them a long time to untie them. Frank said, "It must of been them guys call theirselfs the Swamp Rats playing us a trick," but Buster, furious as he picked the knots out of his undershirt, said, "No, I know for sure who done it and I'd like to kill the sonuvabitch if I could jist git me hands on 'im!"

Slap wanted to know who was he talking about, but even though I knew right away who he meant, I wasn't so sure. Charley ain't looked strong or mean enough to tie knots that tight, what with his lame arm that couldn't even button his own buttons I bet. I saw boys anyhow other times we were down here were always prowling through the woods. In fact, I saw two older ones sneaking through the trees earlier, before Charley ever showed up, that looked like the same boys we saw when we were coming that first time to the river that Brother whispered were Swamp Rats, the one with snag teeth and dirty yellow hair and the other one squint-eyed with pimples and a dog with ribs sticking out sharp as razors—So maybe Frank was right.

But that was nothing unusual, seeing boys in the woods, and since I didn't know for sure who might've done it I kept my mouth shut, just like we all did about Charley when we got home, once their hair and their underwear dried out so they could lie to my mother and say they ain't been swimming if it turned out to be one of them times they had to lie—Figuring, without ever having to say it, there are things there is no use telling older people, specially mothers and fathers, things I was beginning to learn we all knew in some deep place between ourselves but didn't have no words for, some place that was dark and deep where there wasn't any words anymore.

Now with the electric off and no radio for my mother and me to hear our stories on I played more and more outside. I was all alone in the yard playing with my oil truck the next time Earl Snarp Jr. came by, walking that funny way of his, lifting one leg higher'n the other, his one arm swinging wide while the other one he held stock still at his side. Like Ronnie, it was like he waited til he saw nobody was around and before I could get up and run in the house he jumps over the hedge bold as brass, snarling at me right off, "Whatchou doin, dressin up in girl's clothes for?" He had that sneery grin on his face and a look like he knew already why I did it, no matter what I said.

I wasn't going to say nothing but he kept glaring me down.

"We was just playin dressup," I said in a voice so low he went, "What? What? I can't hear you!"

"Like it was Halloween," I said, only a little louder. And he went "What? What?" like no matter how loud I talked he'd say what? what? so because of that I wouldn't answer him again. When he squatted down next to me I wanted to leap away for fear he'd smack my hiney like he did last time.

He still had on them raggedy overalls made of pillow ticking but this time he had on sneakers that were as wore as Slap's and smelled just about the same too.

"Whatchou doin playin with that girl nextdoor?"

I didn't answer him.

"I seen you go by dresst like a girl with that girl nextdoor."

I said, "He ain't no girl, I thought at first he was Shirley Temple but he ain't no girl, he's a boy, so there!"

He hooted, then yelled, "*Shirley Temple!* That's a hot one! How you know he ain't Shirley Temple, you see he got a pecker?"

I felt my cheeks turning red as a Philadelphia cop car, not knowing exactly what a pecker was but suspecting it must be something like a dunkey.

"Well, *didja?*"

But this time I wouldn't answer him at all, the nasty thing, and he reached over and with a look daring me to say something, started pushing my oil truck through the dirt without even asking if he could, but soon gave up on it, saying it wasn't much fun pushing something around with a busted wheel. He said it wasn't much fun just sitting around with a dumbie like me either and even though I did dress up in girl's clothes and played with "that sissy with the Shirley Temple curls," still and all maybe he could learn me something, maybe if I came down his house he could show me a thing or two but said he didn't have any high hopes, seeing's what a dumb pissant I was. He said it like he was doing me a big favor but ducked his head and wouldn't look me in the eye when he said it, like I just might say no.

I couldn't think of anything I wanted to do less in the whole wide world than go to his house, but I was so surprised he asked me and he looked so funny when he asked me, almost like he was ashamed to ask, even though I didn't want to, I said I'd have to ask my mother first, hoping from the earful she got about the Snarps from the Beezleys that she wouldn't let me go.

He got a nasty look in his eye and said, "Well, gwan mama's boy if you gotta go ask her." Then like he was reading what I was thinking, he snarled, "I don't care one way or the other—

who wants to hang around a dumb pissant like you anyhow?" But I could see, like with Charley on the beach, his eyes wasn't matching what his mouth was saying.

So I was stuck and couldn't get out of it and when I went in the kitchen to ask her, she was ironing with the old rusty irons she was heating on the stove that my father found working on the garbage truck and brought home to her now there wasn't no electric. Now there was no radio either I knew how much she missed not only our stories but the music too, so she was humming to herself as if to make up for it, while Kate was taking a nap on the couch in the parlor and Danny was playing in the middle of the kitchen floor with his fire engine and all the busted toy cars my father threw off the dump truck for us.

When I asked her could I go play with Earl Jr., she raised her eyebrows, saying, "Them Snarps down the road?" I nodded and she said, "What's he like?" I was too ashamed to say how he smacked my hiney so I didn't say nothing. She set down her iron and went to the window to take a squint at him. He was standing with his hands on his hips in the side yard where I left him and when he saw her looking he looked away real quick like she caught him standing there just waiting his chance to steal something.

"He's got a sneaky look," she said, crinkling up her eyebrows. "And they ain't Catholic neither." Neither was the Beezleys but I held my tongue. Seeing his overalls she said, "They're on relief like us," and when she said that her eyes got a softer look.

Turning back to her ironing board by the stove she picked up the iron heating on the metal plate on the burner and replaced it with the cooled down one, saying, "Well, I know you ain't got nobody to play with, so you go play with him if you want. But Babes says he has a awful mouth so if he starts cursin or if he gets too fresh you come on home, you hear?" Then she held up a finger at me. "And don'tchou eat nuthin in their house, Babes Beezley says Mrs. Snarp ain't none too clean."

I promised I wouldn't, wishing with all my heart she'd said I couldn't go so's I'd have an excuse. And as I went out the front door instead of the back to stall for time, as I was crossing the porch I made up my mind to lie and tell him she said I couldn't go, even though God might strike me dead for it. But as I was coming down the steps I saw he was looking off in the woods towards the Mahoney house and he had such a hangdog look like people do sometimes when they don't know somebody's watching them, I didn't have the heart.

Earl Jr.'s two sisters and two brothers, all younger'n him were sitting in holes in the front yard the chickens'd dug from scratching themselves, the littlest girl, about Kate's age, squeezing a rag of a doll with its stuffing falling out. Being on relief too, I wondered did Mr. Snarp get it for her on the dump truck like my father got Kate's. Their faces was the color of oatmeal and they stared at me with their mouths hanging open as we crossed the yard, like I was somebody just fell off of the moon. Chickens were jumping in and out of the windows of the old 1929 Dodge that was up on cinder blocks like the car was their chicken coop.

The man I saw out in their yard banging with a hammer under the hood of the Dodge the first time on our way to the river turned out to be Earl Snarp Sr. that was sitting up on the porch now in an old broken down easy chair with the springs poking out the bottom. He was reading a comic book and drinking beer out of a jelly glass that was so greasy the beer was flat as your feet, as my father used to say when he drunk and there wasn't no head on his beer, he would sprinkle salt in it to put a head on it but maybe Mr. Snarp didn't know that or else didn't care if he had a head on it or not. He had a red face, either from the sun or from the beer or from both, and was barefoot, his feet looking about the same shade as Earl Jr.'s that first day I saw him, like you could grow potatoes between his toes. He was wearing a pair of pants all bunched up at the middle and so stiff with grease they looked like they could've stood up all by themselves. On his head was an old captain's hat so greasy the crown of it just shined. His lips were moving slow, he was concentrating so hard on his comic book, which I saw as we passed him going into the house was an old Action comics with Superman, he didn't even see us going in. I saw their porch floor was in worse shape'n ours and had boards missing you could fall right through if you weren't careful where you were stepping.

Inside, the floors were all congoleum wore blacker even than ours was, with wicker furniture in the front room where all the wicker was busted and nothing matched anything, not only there but everywhere else in the house, like they picked up whatever they had wherever they found it and stuck it in the house whether it went with anything else or not. Pictures of movie stars and President Roosevelt cut out from calendars and magazines were tacked and pasted all over the walls like they tried to make everything pretty whilst at the same time trying to hide the old peeling wallpaper and all the holes in the walls. In one corner of the parlor was an old-fashioned radio with the speaker on top like a big horn but it wasn't playing and even though there was a floor lamp with a battered paper shade there was an oil lamp on the table beside it, so I figured their juice must be turned off too. There wasn't no screendoor or no screens anywhere in the windows so the house was as buzzing and full of flies as Gottlieb's store and had a soury milky smell everywhere you sniffed.

Mrs. Snarp was out in the kitchen leaning over the sink

pumping water from a pump just like ours. "Any Kool-Aid, Floss?" Earl Jr. hollered at her, calling her Floss and not Mom, like he was making fun of her. I thought she must be going to holler at him like I knew my mother would've if any of us was that fresh and called her Nor', but instead Mrs. Snarp turned from the sink and when she saw me she stopped what she was just about to say and stared at me. I saw now besides the one tooth hanging down in front one of her eyes was crossed like some people have a cast eye my mother called it. She asked me what my name was and when I told her, I was so tongue-tied I had to tell her twice before she understood me and when she did she bust out laughing, showing all of her long tooth, cackling, "Mickey Mouse, Mickey Mouse," over and over, laughing like I didn't know if she was laughing at me or what. Then right away she started in asking me all about my mother and my father and all of us kids and did I have any dead brothers or sisters, squinting up her eyes like that was what she wanted to know more'n anything else. Nobody ever asked me a question like that before, I was so surprised all I could do was mumble, "Not that I know of," though sometimes when he teased and made fun of me I sure wished that Buster was dead, but I knew that was a sin to wish for that so I didn't mention it.

All the while Earl Jr. was going into the icebox and bringing out a big old mayonnaise jar of red Kool-Aid and slopping it into two jelly glasses on the kitchen table, each one as greasy as the glass his father was drinking his beer out of. There was an open can of evaporated milk on the table the two holes in the lid covered with flies like black scabs, and the wore-through oilcloth that was stacked with dirty dishes wasn't much better, it was more black with flies'n white with oilcloth.

I thought of what my mother told me and wondered how I could get out of drinking the Kool-Aid. But before I could say yes or no Earl Jr. slapped one of the glasses in my hand, saying, "C'mon out back." I followed him out through the shed where we sat ourselves down on the backsteps that swayed under me and was just as rickety as the front ones. I looked around and saw their backyard was filled with as many old washing machines and junk as the front yard was, and there were more chickens running around loose in the back there that ran up to us soon as we came out the door, thinking when they saw us we had something to feed them. But Earl Jr. kicked his feet out at them, and they all went squawking and flapping off, their feathers flying. I saw their outhouse looked in worse shape'n ours and was leaning to one side so much I'd've been scared to death to go in for fear it'd topple over once you had your pants down.

The Kool-Aid felt as warm as the day so I figured there mustn't've been no ice in the icebox, and the jelly glass was so dirty I was afraid to drink out of it, but I saw Earl Jr. that'd already gulped his down without even once coming up for air was looking at me kind of funny. "Ain'tchou gonna drink it?" Just to be polite I took a sip. It was strawberry, my favorite, and so loaded with sugar, more even than we ever put in our Kool-Aid at home, it didn't matter to me anymore the glass looked like it'd never been washed, I just shut my eyes and swigged it down as fast as Earl Jr. swigged his.

Just then out the backdoor comes Mrs. Snarp with a big grin on her face, saying to me, "I wantcha to see my baby." I saw Earl Jr. make a face. I looked up at her as she stood over us on the top step, looking for the baby and when she saw me looking she grins even wider, showing her tooth, then pulls out from behind her a picture in a cardboard frame and flashes it in front of my eyes and like to scare the daylights out of me when I saw what I first thought was a picture of a little monkey with its head turned to its side turned out to be a photograph of a baby laying in a little white coffin. Its head was resting on a white satin pillow with satin ruffles all around and it was wearing what looked like a long white nightgown like it was ready for bed, its little hands were folded over its chest on a frilly white blanket like it was praying and there was a tiny sign at the head of the casket I could spell out, read, "ASLEEP WITH THE ANGELS IN HEAVEN."

"Little Edward, one month old," she sighed, staring down at the picture with her one cross eye like the baby in it was still alive. "We took him in the car in his last little crib all the way up to the photog'pher on Broadway in Camden just to have it took special."

I didn't know what to say but like I tasted the Kool-Aid just to be polite, I looked at the picture again even though it gave me the creeps, the baby looked like such a little shrunk thing.

"Little Edward," she said. "Gone but not forgotten."

I see her mouth quiver and I looked away, not knowing what to do, and all of a sudden spied four pairs of eyes peeking at me around the corner of the house and looking saw it was Earl Jr.'s sisters and brothers trying to get a gander at me. When Earl Jr. spotted them he flapped his arms and kicked his legs out at them just like they were so many more chickens and all them eyes disappeared around the side of the house so fast you wouldn't believe it. Earl Jr. growled out, "C'mon, you," and grabbing me by the arm he all but dragged me across the yard, kicking chickens out of the way as he went, hustling me off back in the direction of the swamp so quick I hardly knew what was happening.

Even though I didn't want to I followed him partly to get away from the picture of little Edward and partly because of the way he did it, like there wasn't any question but I would follow him. Another thing was, by this time he wasn't acting like he was going to haul off and slap me in the hiney again so I wasn't half as leery of him. I told him, though, I didn't like going back in no swamp but he said don't be such a scaredy cat, "You bin playin with Shirley Temple too much," and even though hearing that got my goat, I didn't say nothing. Even more'n my two older brothers, he had a way of saying things like he was positively absolutely sure of it, no ands, ifs or buts about it, no matter what you said he'd be sure to top it, so I knew I might just as well save my breath and go along.

Now it was warmer the swamp had a terribler smell, the punk'd shot up at least ten times taller'n me so that the place seemed a lot darker'n it was the time I came back here with my father and Mr. Beezley. I kept a sharp eye out for snakes and things, keeping close behind Earl Jr. that seemed to know pretty much where he was going, like he been back here hundreds of times. He was moving along at a pretty fast clip so I had a hard time keeping up with him. He looked like he wasn't at all worried about stepping in any quicksand and didn't seem one bit bothered by the slithery things that were slipping and sliding off on either side of the muddy path as we came up on them. He didn't seem bothered either by the zillions of birds all of a sudden batting up in front of us with shrieks that just about made my heart stop. I still didn't like the place one bit but I was feeling less nervous being with him, he looked so much like he knew where he was going and didn't seem afraid of nothing, like he was right at home here.

Finally we came up out into daylight and climbed up a bank onto the road I saw was the same road called Camp Meeting Walk that went past the school farther back in town. It was all gray with dust with the tar shimmying up in the heat and not a car or a soul on it as far as you could see—And there on either side of it was the swamp water, full of mud banks looking like sand bars and stretching off as far as to the river. Over my shoulder I could see the silver water tower up over the tops of the trees and it looked so far away I started getting worried again. I thought we were going to go along the road, which I would've been glad of, it would've been easier walking and less scary and smelly, but instead Earl Jr. made a beeline across it, then down the bank on the other side where there was nothing but more swamp and more punkweed but it wasn't as dark.

I was getting jumpy now we were in the swamp again not knowing which way to turn if I had to find my way home on my own. I finally screwed up the nerve to ask him where were we going and all he said was, "Keep yer pants on, you'll see." I hoped I'd see pretty soon, my belly was beginning to squirm like minnies was jumping in there.

I heard splattering up ahead and gave a start wondering where it was coming from and saw it was coming from Earl Jr. that was peeing in the mud while he was walking, as if it was the most natural thing. I was surprised you could pee and walk at the same time, I never saw nobody could do that before, not even the Beezley boys, but I would come to see Earl Jr. could do it anytime, anywhere he wanted. "Stroorberry Kool-Aid runs right through me," he said, "Weak kidneys. Weak kidneys runs in our fambly," saying it like he was bragging and half turning on purpose like he wanted me to get a peep at it before he stuffed it back in his overalls. I saw it was a big floppy thing, bigger'n mine, with a hat on it like Danny's and almost as fat as Sparky Beezley's, excepting it didn't have no birthmark on it like Sparky's did.

He grinned at me over his shoulder, "Don't a pissant like you ever have to pee?" I mumbled yes but I didn't have to pee right then because the way he said it I knew it wasn't that he was asking.

Not long after that we came out of the punkweed into the open again where there was a place by the edge of the water that was nothing but heaps of garbage all steamy and stinking in the sun. A couple of men and boys pulling homemade wagons made of orange crates or pushing old rusty baby buggies were going up and down over the hills of trash, poking through it with sticks, most of them dressed in shirts and pants made from the pillow ticking relief gave away.

Having heard my father say this was where they took and emptied the garbage from the dump truck, I looked around quick to see if I could see him, knowing he wouldn't want to see me so far from home without my older brothers. But I didn't spot hide nor hair of him or the truck and began to breathe a little easier, as easy as I could considering the place stunk to high heavens, a million times worse'n our outhouse ever did on such a hot day.

Earl Jr. started walking close to the edge of the swamp, keeping a distance between him and the others, keeping a sharp eye down at his feet at the piles of garbage we were squishing over. I didn't know what he was looking for but I kept a sharp eye out too, watching for snakes or rats, I heard my father say many a time he saw rats down here big as cats. All of a sudden Earl Jr. stoops down so quick I bumped into him as he stuck his face close in the muck and pulls out an empty soda bottle covered with slime. He shoved it at me like he was handing me a million dollars, telling me to hold onto it, as he bent over and went searching through the garbage again. I didn't even want to touch it let alone hold onto it but he had that way about him there was no question I would do as he said, so I pinched the mouth of the bottle between my thumb and my finger, holding it away from me as far as I could for fear of getting any mud on me and have my mother hollering and asking where I been.

One of the men picking through the garbage was the Indian they called Lenny I saw working at Gottlieb's. Mr. Beezley said Lenny worked there whenever he felt like it, the Gottlieb's must've fired him umpteen times but they always got to feeling sorry for him because he was an Indian and hired him back.

Out in the daylight I could see he had eyes all sunk in and deep lines on either side of his mouth, his mouth still looked shiny with lard or bacon fat like it was medicine he smeared on it because his lips were chapped. His skin was dark as shoe leather and since he was the biggest man there he was standing tallest against the sky as he poked around with a stick like the others on top of one of the hills of garbage, flipping the rubbish over to see if there was anything he could find underneath. He was pushing an old wicker baby buggy like Kate's, only his was older and more broken down'n hers was. When he found something he'd toss it into the buggy that was already weighted down about as far as it could go with all kinds of empty bottles and junk.

Right away I saw this was a place me and my brothers could come hunt for rags and junk and cardboard to sell the junkman from Camden when he came around in his truck so we could get some money to go the movies in the county seat just like we did in South Philly.

Besides needing shaves so they all looked like gangsters in the movies, most of the men were short and dumpy with big beer bellies sticking out of their relief shirts. Most of them, and the boys that were with them, kept to themselves, nobody talked to anybody else, all of them, like Earl Jr. and Lenny, keeping their eyes steady on the ground like the chickens in the run in our backyard.

Earl Jr. pawed through everything with his bare hands, not caring what might be under it or worrying about broke glass.

Looking around sharp at the others to see if they saw him, he pulled another empty out of the muck, a quart size one this time, five cents deposit. He grabbed the two-center out of my hand and took both bottles down to the edge of the swamp where he rinshed them out in water wasn't any cleaner'n the bottles were. He stuck the bigger one down in his overalls and handed me back the smaller bottle to carry, saying we'd turn them in for candy at Gottlieb's. I quick felt my mouth starting to water, I could taste the candy banana I already picked out in my mind.

Looking around he saw Lenny was pushing his baby buggy, that was so loaded he couldn't've got another thing in it, up over the garbage heaps. Earl Jr. gave me a poke in the ribs, whispering, "Less go."

Once we got out on the road what I saw he was doing was following Lenny. Ahead, through the dust and the heat, I saw over the tops of the trees the top of the water tower getting nearer and nearer the closer we got to town and was glad we were heading back, hardly able to wait to get to Gottlieb's and the candy behind the chicken wire.

But just before we got to the schoolhouse Lenny, that we been following at a safe distance, all of a sudden scooted his baby buggy down into a gully and onto a path it was hard to see was there from the road unless you knew it was there. Earl Jr. put an arm across my belly, holding me back, then when he seemed to think Lenny was far enough ahead, he jerked his head for me to follow. With my heart in my mouth we went down the gully and along a skinny little path into the woods where there were so many trees it was as dark as back on the other side of the swamp but nowhere near as hot or as smelly.

Just ahead, I could just make out Lenny loping along on his long legs and bumping his loaded baby carriage over the tree roots. My own heart was really bumping now too. But Earl Jr. was creeping along ahead of me, his head stuck out like a turtle, just the tip of his tongue showing, like he was in the movies and was an Indian himself stalking another Indian, only this one was a for real one.

Pretty soon this part of the woods began to look familiar and not long after that when we crossed a path where the dirt was the color of silver dust, I knew it was the one we took to go through the woods near our house over to the Beezleys, so I figured I must be close to home. I wanted to tell Earl Jr. I was going back, candy or no candy, but suddenly like he was reading my mind he was hissing at me and putting a finger to his lips again, motioning me to come on. I had that same feeling I had before that there wasn't any question I would do as he said, like as if he was one of my older brothers.

After what seemed like we'd gone a long distance, Lenny disappeared off the path up ahead. Earl Jr. all of a sudden dropped down on his hands and knees and signaled for me to do the same. I was scared I'd put my hands on a snake but he turned and gave me sharp look and I got down and started crawling behind him, dragging the empty bottle along.

We came to a clearing that was surrounded by nothing but the dirt looked the same as the silver dust in the path and had little low bushes with tiny leaves I learned later from Earl Jr. were called huckleberries. It was thick there with trees I already knew were called sassafras. He dropped on his belly and motioned for me to do the same and I did it even though I knew my mother'd holler at me for getting my clothes dirty.

My heart was really beating loud in my ears now as up in the middle of the clearing I saw a shack made of packing crates and rusty Pepsi-Cola signs. Out of the slanty tarpaper roof smoke was curling out of a tin chimney poking through it. An axe was stuck in a stump off the side and a big heap of split wood was stacked up against one wall. There were empty javellie water jugs and all other kinds of empty bottles sitting on a rickety old kitchen table. Tires and other junk was stacked behind the shack, most of the tires so wore through you could see the threads. The baby buggy sat out front but Lenny was nowhere in sight.

All of a sudden the door of the shack, that was really only the lid off the top of a big packing crate, swung open and Lenny, stooping because he was too tall to get through any other way, came out. Right behind him was another man a lot smaller, so he never had to stoop at all. This second man was in a raggedy blue workshirt and pants as dirty and bunched up at his waist as Earl Snarp Sr.'s was. He was wearing a pair of oxfords like my father's Sunday shoes only these were old and broke shoes without no laces, and he wasn't wearing no socks either, so you could see his scabby ankles. He was scratching his head and yawning and Lenny was pawing through the things he brought back in the baby buggy, saying, "Looka this, Eddie," and "Looka that, Eddie," like they were buried treasure he brought back instead of just the plain old junk they was. The man he called Eddie just kept nodding his head and yawning, going, "Yup, yup," like he couldn't care less.

Despite the heat, through the open door of the shack a tongue of flame now and again lit up the insides. I could see it came from under what looked like a rusty old oil barrel made into a stove and set in the middle of the dirt floor with all kinds of pipes looping in and out of it. When the light flared up again I saw a pair of bare feet sticking out on a mattress near the door that looked like little more'n a bundle of rags on the ground like it was somebody sleeping.

Then the man called Eddie stumbled inside the door and

brought out a javellie water jug half full and to my surprise he started gulping down whatever it was inside, so it mustn't've been no bleach. Then he handed the gallon jug to Lenny and Lenny took a sniff and made a face, muttering, "Still smells green as rotgut." But he took a big drink anyway.

"Good ole white lightnin," Earl Jr. whispered in my ear with a gleeful grin in his eyes. "Good ole firewater."

I stiffened, wishing he wouldn't whisper anything for fear they'd hear, and then wouldn't you know, suddenly I saw Lenny the Indian stop with the jug of firewater hooked on his thumb right up to his nose and cock his head to the side like he was a rooster listening. Every hair on my head froze as he turned real slow and looked in our direction. Seeing him, Eddie looked too, going, "Whut? Whut?"

Earl Jr. hissed, "C'mon!" and I didn't need a second invitation as the two of us squirmed backwards on our bellies under the huckleberry bushes. Then Earl Jr. whispers, *Run for it!* and the two of us jumps up and starts crashing through the brush. I run even faster when I heard Lenny's voice booming out through the sassafras trees, "Goddamn kids! I ketch you here again I'll skin you alive! You goddamn kids, you hear?"

I could hear it, even my brother Slap would've heard it, but I didn't dare look back, running faster'n I ever remember running in my whole entire life, even faster'n I ran down 2nd Street the day we moved from South Philly, and only hoped Lenny didn't see my face so that if ever he saw me in Gottlieb's again or out on the road he wouldn't skin me alive or scalp me.

We saw Charley peddling down Camp Meeting Walk past Gottlieb's on his big tricycle and I found I was wishing I had me one like it, I thought it would be worth being crippled just to have a bike like that.

All of a sudden Earl Jr. picked up a rock from the side of the road and to my amazement he hauled back his arm far as it could go and sent the rock flying just over Charley's head, just like I suspected he did at me and Ronnie in our dressup. Then, before Charley had a chance to turn around and see where it came from, Earl Jr. snatched me by the hand and dragged me into the front door of Gottlieb's faster'n I could blink an eye.

Even though there were customers in the store, Mrs. Gottlieb would holler at Mr. Gottlieb, it didn't bother her none if the customers heard her, and this time when me and Earl Jr. came in she was hollering across the store at him, "You buy more of these hipboots, we got hipboots you bought back in 1927 and ain't sold yet, you got so many things we can't get rid of you don't know what you got!" But Mr. Gottlieb with his baseball cap jammed over his ears went right on grinding up hamburger in the machine like he ain't heard her, so she picked up one of the brandnew boots out of the crate and she flung it with all her might clear across the store at him, screeching, *"I'm talking to you!"* Mr. Gottlieb ducked without even looking, like he had to duck any number of times and knew just when to duck, and went on stuffing meat in the grinder with a look in his eye like he wished it was Mrs. Gottlieb he was grinding, whilst the ladies standing around the butcher block looked from one to the other but didn't look at all surprised, like they saw this happen so many times before, they didn't think nothing of it.

I hung behind Earl Jr. as he handed the bottles over the counter to her, afraid not only of her being mad but afraid she'd start teasing me again about my eyes, but she was so upset with Mr. Gottlieb and the hipboots she didn't even see me.

"You never bought this soda here!" she shrilled right off in the same high voice she hollered at Mr. Gottlieb, shrilling at him even before Earl Jr. ever got the chance to open his mouth and tell the lie she looked like she already knew was coming. I was

ready to turn and hightail it out of there, afraid she'd throw the
bottles at us like she threw the boot at Mr. Gottlieb, but Earl Jr.
stood right up to her and insisted he *had* bought that soda there
but so long back she must've forgot. She cocked an eyebrow at
him, her mouth going again so that her lips disappeared into her
jowls like dough as, just like I did, she held the slimy bottles
away from her in her pinched fingers, "Like they was dog turds,"
Earl Jr. laughed once we were outside.

Earl Jr. picked three orange slices and I picked three banana
candies and since there was one penny left over he picked one of
them little wax people filled with red-colored water sweetened
with sugar you bit the head off and sucked the juice out, then
chewed the wax, he said we would wack up outside.

"Was he nice?" my mother asked.

"Yes," I lied.

"Is their house clean?"

"Yes," I lied.

It was like she was Sister Joseph Mary in the catechism class
at Sunday school.

"You dint eat nuthin in their house didjou?"

"No," I said, which I knew wasn't a for real lie since *drinking*
strawberry Kool-Aid wasn't the same as *eating* something.

"Did he curse and use bad words?"

"No," I lied again, lying because a part of me was scared if I
told her the truth she wouldn't let me see him anymore.

He came around almost everyday after that, either hollering
out my back door or, if he seen my brothers around, whistling for
me through the hedge. I always told my mother I was just going
up his house to play, even though we never hung around his
house for long, he always had someplace to go or some new

place to show me, despite he kept saying he didn't know why he was wasting his time on a pissant like me. Ronnie spied me from the woods the very next Saturday afternoon and called me over and says, "Where have you been? Don't you ever want to come over and play with me anymore?" I got all confused like maybe I did something wrong, and he said, a mean look in his eye, "I know where you've been, you've been with that awful bucktooth Earl Snarp that looks like you could plant potatoes in his ears!"

It was the first time I felt I ever had to choose between one person and another, I didn't know which way to go. Then Ronnie melts a little, getting a sly look in his eye as he says, "I just bought me a new Judy Garland paperdoll book from the five and dime," and when he saw I wasn't all that thrilled about that he says, "You come to my house I'll let you read my picture books all you want." He must've seen me weakening because he looks even slyer, saying almost in a whisper, "My mother just got a fresh coconut cake from the County Seat Bakery ...."

That did it. My mouth started watering like our pump when it just been primed, so naturally there wasn't no question, that day anyhow, who I'd go play with.

But he didn't let me read his picture books. That was only a trick to get me up to the playroom. Soon as he saw me heading for the bookshelf he grabbed me by the shoulders and pushed me down on the floor saying we were playing paperdoll movies with his new paperdolls of Judy Garland that was going to be in "The Wizard of Oz," and that was that. He allowed me to dress up and jiggle the Scarecrow and the little dog Toto and The Wicked Witch of the West whilst he dressed up and took all the other parts, like The Good Fairy and Dorothy that was Judy Garland, the star.

Mainly me and Earl Jr. stuck to places in the woods or down along the river my brothers or the Beezley boys didn't know of or never went to. But where he took me one day not long after we went to the dump was down to the ferry Mr. Beezley took to get to the shipyard every day. On the way we saw the road crew from the WPA with their picks and shovels digging the road out through the swamp to the other side of the town, both our fathers among them. My father was swinging a pickaxe to beat the band while Earl Snarp Sr. was leaning on his shovel with his captain's cap shoved back and with a cigarette butt plastered to his mouth, looking around and hitching up his pants with one hand. My heart started going even though I knew my father probably wouldn't see me, they were so far away, and he was swinging his pick with his back to us anyhow and wouldn't've seen us even if he was closer, but it still gave me a start, knowing him or my mother didn't want me so far from home. Earl Jr. just went on by in that lopy kind of walk of his, loose and easy, his hips stuck out and his shoulders back, his head tilted to one side in that way of his that gave him a look like he was miles away thinking of something. So if he ever saw his father he didn't make no sign he did, they never seemed to have too much to say to each other anyhow anytime.

We went through a clearing that was surrounded by thick trees and deeper in the woods'n I ever been. "O-nay-od-bay-ee-ay ows-knay is-thay ace-play," he said in pig latin, something he been trying to learn me so's we could talk if others was around and they wouldn't know what we were saying. Most of it I could catch if only he didn't go so fast, which he always did, mainly to show off, I thought.

"Ott-way?" I said, not catching it. He looked annoyed, saying, "Listen careful, dumbie," and repeated it, and I could see it was as he said, so far off in the woods with no clear path to it and all so heavy with trees and vines, anybody'd have a hard time finding it. As we crossed the clearing, he unbuttoned himself and without missing a step he started peeing, aiming it at the trunks of the wild cherries we passed, like I saw the Beezley's dog Blackie'd do as if it was lifting a leg to mark a place as its own.

"This is my hideout," he said in pig latin, buttoning himself up again, "and don'tchou ever breathe a word about it to your brothers or them scurvy Beezleys."

I promised I wouldn't.

The road to the ferry was a tar road ran the other side of a pond Earl Jr. called Goldie's pond where he said you could catch the biggest bullfrogs and where kids came in the winter to ice skate, "If you got the skates." There weren't many houses along the way, fields and woods mostly, and an occasional stretch of swamp—Such a long walk I thought we were never going to get there. But I didn't complain—I was feeling a lot easier now being with him, despite my being scared silly of some of the places he took me, but I'd still follow along, even in the places I was afraid to go, more afraid of his making fun of me than of the thing I was afraid of. I decided it was better being scared than having to play all by myself. My only worry was coming across my older brothers somewhere along in our travels because they were always prowling through the woods with the Beezley boys, and them telling my mother or father they saw me so far from home and that I might get a licking and not be allowed out of the yard anymore, which is why my heart started up when I saw my father awhile back swinging his pickaxe on the road gang and was so relieved he didn't see us.

I could smell the river before I saw it, that funny sweet milky smell that, leery as I was of the water, always lifted me up in my heart. We went down a deep dip in the road and when we came up we were walking all of a sudden on a dam made of dirt, the water backed right up to the lip of it, the water so dark and so high it surprised me when we came up on it so quick, I backed away. Earl Jr. seeing me, jeered and said that was a good place to skinny-dip but I couldn't imagine it, it looked so dark and deep, and there stretching beyond it was the river off in the distance with the ship's ways and the cranes across the water that you could see a whole lot clearer here than down near the fort and hear clearer too with the whistles and the sounds like jackhammers and the steady boom like a piledriver over the river. I could feel that excitement going again in me, seeing Philly—and seeing the ferry, I thought it was another good thing to know and tell my mother that besides the bus, there was another way to go to Philly. I asked Earl Jr., "Can anybody go on it?" but he made me ask it in pig latin, which took longer, and then he answered in pig latin, "Don't be such a dumbie, it's only for them that works in the shipyard," so I knew the ferry was out as far as a way for my mother and me to get back to the city.

Past the cars was a little shack with a smokepipe sticking out the roof like out of Lenny's shack in the woods, where a fat old man sat with a captain's hat on his head like Earl Snarp Sr.'s, only it wasn't so greasy. He was sitting on a bench inside with the cap tipped over his eyes and with his hands folded over his belly, dozing. Past the shack I saw the entrance to the ferry that was a walkway stretching far out into the river with pilings in the water at the end of it, just like the ferry we came over on from Philly. Except I didn't see how no cars got on this one and when I asked Earl Jr. all he said was, "Ou-yay ust-jay alk-way on-ay, opie-day," and I thought that made a lot more sense and was a lot less scary'n driving a car on where you could topple over the edge of the ferryboat and get drowned.

We were still a safe distance away from where the watch-man's shack was, up beyond where the cars were parked, when all of a sudden, not even looking back to see if the watchman woke up and was watching, with a quick sharp jab with the side of his hand Earl Jr. snapped off at the base the radio aerials on every single car we passed that had one.

"C'mon!" he whispered, when we got to the end of the lot, his eyes glittery as we left behind us a trail of aerials like so many broke matchsticks, "Less head on up to the fort."

He ducked into some thick bushes at the side of the road and onto a path through the trees I would've never known was there if he ain't showed me, and that wound up along the bluff.

Even though I figured I'd had enough excitement for one day, I chased after him like he was my father's horseshoe mag-net pulling me on.

My main worry was that somehow my mother and father'd find out I was with Earl Jr. when he busted the aerials and I'd catch the dickens, or worse. This is what I worried about, like there was suddenly a rain cloud in my eyes as I followed Earl Jr. through the woods along the path high up on the bluff that led to the fort. It always surprised me how we'd come out from a place I never been to before to a place I been, like somehow them two places couldn't ever come together, but that's what happened when I saw we were on a trail, only coming from the opposite direction leading down to the cut in the bluff, where me and my father and my brothers saw the man and lady with no clothes on.

Earl Jr. was telling me he knew of some crab apple trees right around there near the river he'd show me when they got close to ripe, "We'll eat them apples til they come out our ears, they is always so hard and sweet." We were just starting down

the steep cut in the bluff, me grabbing on to some bare roots so's
not to slide down too quick, when all of a sudden out of nowhere
off one of the slopes a gang of boys came charging down out of
the trees after us, whooping and hollering in bloodcurdling
shrieks that froze the hair right on my head. They were followed
by a pack of their dogs that were barking as loud as the boys
were hollering, the dogs leaping around us and showing their
teeth. I didn't know what I was more ascared of, the dogs or the
boys, particularly a big brown dog that the tallest boy with
wavy black hair kept yelling at to "Sic 'em, Butch! Sic 'em!" and
he grinned as the dog yelped and leapt around us, baring its
fangs that was all dripping with spit, "Sic 'em!" he yelled.

The gang surrounded us, looking us up and down, squint-
eyed and squinching their mouths up tough. I recognized a few
of them, like the wavy-haired one, as boys I saw at a distance on
the streets of the town or else in church. I was breathing as fast
as my heart was beating, thinking we'd never get out of this one,
and stole a glance at Earl Jr., that was trying to look as squinch-
eyed and hard-mouth as they were but I could see he was nervous, not scared nervous but watching like a cat his main
chance to somehow get away.

One of them, with a pimply face and a cast in one eye like
Earl Jr.'s mother, only worse, like his eye was stuck to one side of
his nose, the same boy we saw walking barefoot the day Mr.
Beezley first took us all to the river and Brother Beezley whispered
was a Swamp Rat, he ups and snarls, his one cross eye squinting,
"Where you two think yer goin?"

My throat was so paralyzed I could barely breathe let alone
speak and I looked at Earl Jr. to say something but he didn't say
anything at first, just stared back real defiant. But when the boy
with the cast eye and pimples demanded to know again, Earl Jr.
snapped out, "What's it to you, Squint, you don't own these here

woods," my heart began to beat faster, wishing he ain't said nothing.

The dogs were still yapping around us, the hair rising stiff on the spine of the big brown one called Butch. I was wishing they would at least call their dogs off and clinched my hands behind me so they wouldn't bite them and crossed all my fingers, swearing again to myself if I got out of this one this was the very last time I ever left home again with Earl Snarp Jr.

The pimply-faced one lifted a fist and stepped up close to him.

"Nobody goes through these woods 'less we say so. These're our woods. No trespassin."

But Earl Jr. stood up to him, knuckling his hands just as tight and banging them against his own legs. "Oh yeah? You and who else says so, Squint?"

"The Swamp Rats say so and *we* are the Swamp Rats, all us here." The pimply boy he called Squint, like he must've known him from school, gave a sneer and swept his arm around at the others, then shoved out at Earl Jr. "Got that?" Earl Jr. started to shove back, saying, "I know who all you are and you don't look like Swamp Rats you look like *drowneded* rats to me," and when he said that the tall, thin boy with black wavy hair shining with hair oil that I saw in church, all of a sudden snuck around and pinned Earl Jr.'s arms from behind. Earl Jr. fought and kicked like a maniac, calling him all the bad words you weren't supposed to say and a few more I ain't never heard before, but the other boy, being taller, held him so tight in his long stringy arms he couldn't move at all.

The boy called Squint stood right in Earl Jr.'s face, saying, "And we know who you are, Earl Snarp Jr. We seen you sneakin through our woods before. You got a sneaky look," and Earl Jr. shot back, "Not half as sneaky as you, you squint-eyed sonuvabitch!" Hearing that, Squint's face turned redder'n his pimples, he was doubling up his fists when all of a sudden a buck-toothed boy with skin like clay and yellow hair slicked up in a pompadour, that I saw was the other barefoot boy with Squint that day, and that one of the dogs barking around us was the same dog with ribs like razors, he piped up with, "We look like drowneded rats, huh? Well, let's just pole the bastids out to the middle of the river and chuck 'em in the drink and see who's drowneded rats then," talking high through his nose like somebody needed his adenoids out. The others laughed like he said something was real funny and started punching him on the back, one of them hollering out, "We can use them for poles, eh, Snag? Specially that one looks like a toothpick!" They laughed all the harder and I looked around at them wild-eyed, wondering who they were talking about, my heart turning to ice when I realized they were talking about me. I was wishing I could disappear right that instant and wake up safe in my own frontyard.

"Who's this rabbit wearin girl's shoes?" the boy named Snag asked stepping up to me, and the tall one said, "He's one of them Lithwack kids just moved to town, the ones we see swimmin in their underwear," saying it in a sneery kind of way like swimming in your underwear was the worst possible thing you could do.

"Well, he's awful skinny for a rabbit but less us cut his throat and roast him on a spit," and they all chuckled and rubbed their hands and smacked their lips as my heart dropped down to my maryjanes. I promised Jesus, Mary and Joseph and all the saints in heaven if I ever got out of this one I'd never go against or disobey my mother ever again, I'd stay right in my own yard where I belonged.

Hearing all this, I looked around quick at Earl Jr., my guts twisting, knowing he was the only one could save us. But he was just looking at the boy named Snag in that slit-eyed way as the tall one kept ahold of him, only now I was surprised to see a smile curling on his lips, like he was double-daring them to pole us out and chuck us in the drink. He had no worries, he already told me how he could swim like an otter and he said it like it wasn't no bragging neither, but I could see the flat light of the river over the tips of the trees where out in the middle I bet must be over a hundred feet deep and knowing I couldn't even doggie paddle a lick, I all of a sudden felt what little heart I had left go fizzling out of me.

"Why don't you guys leave them alone? They're not hurting anybody."

A boy been hanging back a little from the others like he been enjoying it at first, particularly the way Earl Jr. was standing up to them, but wasn't enjoying it anymore, he was the one'd spoke up. He had a pale face like milk and a jet black crewcut with a widow's peak and looked stronger built'n any of the others. He seemed older'n they did too though he probably wasn't. He looked a little embarrassed as he caught my eye and looked away quick. I knew I saw him somewhere before, then it hit me he was the altar boy looked like Freddie Bartholomew in "Little Lord Fauntleroy" served at the children's mass I went to with my brothers on Sundays, I just didn't recognize him without his dress on.

Seeing him, I got my hopes up, knowing if I had to I would tell him I was a Catholic too, that I saw him serving mass at Saint Theresa's, even tell him how much he looked like Freddie Bartholomew, tell him I just knew he'd never let them hurt another Catholic boy, and would maybe let Earl Jr. go too even though Earl Jr. wasn't a Catholic, Earl Jr. wasn't anything.

The one called Squint started up in a whiny kind of way, "But we gotta keep out intruders, Rev. This is *our* territory."

The boy he called Rev lifted one eyebrow at him, saying, "Show me your deed, Squint. Only God owns anything and you sure don't look like God to me."

The others sniggered at this, and Squint made a face and rubbed his toe in the dust.

"Let go that kid's arms, Horse, you trying to break them? You've all had your fun." Rev spoke like he was used to being listened to. And when he made a threatening gesture at the dogs, they right away quieted down and slunk off behind the legs of the others, their eyes rolling up sideways like they were scared they might get a whipping.

The tall boy named Horse loosened his hold on Earl Jr. but didn't let go of him altogether. A teasing smile creased up his mouth as he glanced first at the one they called Rev and then at Squint. His oiled hair was shining in the sun and I could see by his looks he looked just like one of them pretty boys in the movies Buster was always sneering at, but he wasn't near as nice-looking as the boy called Rev.

You could see Squint was doing a slow burn the way he stared furious at Rev, clinching and unclinching his fists before he swung around at me and Earl Jr. and snapped even tougher like he had to save his face, "Anytime you wanna go through these woods you gotta get our okay, see?"

My heart stopped when, for an answer, Earl Jr. hacked up a lunger and flupped it in the dust between Squint's bare feet. A couple of the others started sniggering again, including the tall one, Horse, that looked like he was getting a kick out of it even more'n the others. Squint turned so red now you couldn't even see his pimples as he glared first at Earl Jr. then snapped his head around and glared at the others, his eye with the cast so squinting and fierce you could see how he got his name.

"Well, okay this time," he muttered, backing off, "But next

time youse won't git off so easy." He made a big show of saying it but I could see the real boss was Rev, you could hear it in the way Rev said real quiet but like he meant business too, "Let him go, Horse."

Horse shrugged and gave a goofy grin and let go of Earl Jr.'s arms and Earl Jr. stumbled a step or two down the gully where he stood rubbing at his wrists and scowling back at all of them.

Rev waved an arm at me and Earl Jr. "Go on, you guys, beat it."

I didn't need to hear it a second time and the two of us started down the steep path at a trot, I didn't care if I slid and fell and skinned myself on the stones or not, I was so glad to get out of there. I swung my head back once, just to make sure they weren't following us and was relieved to see they were all heading back up the slope into the trees above where they came from when they first came roaring down on us. They were sneaking back looks at us as they went.

I kept hoping he wouldn't but I could see Earl Jr. was just itching to shout something back, the way he kept turning his head around as if to see how far away they were. It was like when he was sure there was a safe distance between us and them, he cupped his hands to his mouth and shouted, "OU-YAY IG-PAY UCKERS-FAY!" and just in case they didn't understand pig latin he shouted it again in plain English.

Not waiting to see how they took it, he grabbed me by the arm and tore off like a bat out of you-know-where down the path going out to the beach. I didn't need to be asked twice even though if I ain't been in such a rush I would've stuck my fingers in my ears knowing that was a word you mustn't never never say but I had brains enough to know I better tear off right after him. Maybe his laughing like a maniac slowed him down some, since I knew he wasn't no slouch on his feet, but I was amazed to find myself not only catching up to him but outrunning him by a good couple yards.

I saw him pass the house, making sure nobody was out front, like he usually did if he came down for me. At first I pretended not to see him. Thinking of all he got me into the last couple times I went off with him, I was determined I would stay in my own front yard from now on. But the next time he makes a pass in front of the house, I look at him and see his loose lopy walk and see him jerk his head at me, grinning and showing all of his teeth, he became like a magnet again to me, pulling me out to the hedge, where I could smell among the leaves the tiny blossoms that were all so milky sweet.

"C'mon, pissant," he whispers, "I got something real good to show you."

I don't know how it happened, I knew I should have my head examined, but suddenly seeing that look on his face, all of my determination of only a second ago went right up in smoke. I ran around back and told my mother I was going up his house and she gave me a look but let me go, reminding me again if Mrs. Snarp offered me something to eat not to eat it, and not to be late for supper. I ran out front again and as usual never asked him where we were going, I just fell into step beside him, following wherever he took me like I always did.

Instead of heading for the river or the swamp he lit out for the part of the woods led off to the ferry, which I wasn't too crazy about, afraid he might be going to bust more car aerials. We weren't very far along before I heard somebody coming up ahead on the path and my heart stopped, thinking it might be them Swamp Rats but it turned out to be somebody just as bad. It was Lenny the Lenilenape pushing his baby carriage through the trees, heading for the dump probably. I was all ready to duck into the bushes to hide, thinking Earl Jr. would want to hide too, but instead he just kept right on going, looking at Lenny bold as brass when we got up close, like he was daring him to recognize us or say something about us sneaking up on his shack. When he rattled right on by us with his black eyes flat on the ground like he wasn't seeing anything let alone us two, I was as surprised as I was relieved.

Where we were going it turned out wasn't the ferry but the clearing with long-haired Indian grass over it like a carpet, and honeysuckle and huckleberry bushes, and all the trees so thick around it the sunlight came down through the leaves hardly at all. The minute we got there Earl Jr. flung himself on the ground and stuck his nose in the dirt, sniffing like a dog'll do. I gaped at him like he'd gone crazy, particularly when he started rolling over and over, his eyes shut tight, his face split up the middle in a goofy grin like he been waiting all winter just for this minute as he rolled one way then another, then rolled all around in a circle like he couldn't get enough of it, getting himself so covered in mud and dead leaves and dry grass sticking to him it was like all that was another pair of overalls covering him.

"Don'tchou jist love it! C'mon, rabbit," he hollered, "Git down here and gitcher bottom dirty."

I guess from my eyes he could see I didn't love it as much as him, not enough to roll around in it like a dog scratching its back or a chicken taking a dust bath. He gave a whoop and jumped up and did a hoppy little dance from one foot to the other before he flung himself down on the ground again and started rolling and rolling all over again, rolling his shoulders and letting the dry pine needles scratch his back for him.

Finally when he had enough of it he sprawled on his back with his arms and legs flung out and stared up at the branches that were all black with new leaves, his chest heaving up and down. I could see the blood running in his face and down his skin was the same color as the wild roses I picked in May and stuck in milk bottles in front of the statue of the Virgin Mary in my mother and father's bedroom. Not wanting to get my bottom dirty, I stood watching him, peeping around me sometimes like I was a bird watching out for eyes, but what I was doing was watching him mainly, wondering what it was he brought me back here to show me. He saw me watching and turned his head and looked at me with a tease in his eyes like he could see how jumpy I was. "Will them Swamp Rats come back here?" I asked him, peeping around and peeping around.

"Nobody comes back here, nobody knows where this place is, it's so far off the beaten path I betcha even Lenny the Lenape don't know where it is, don'tchou worry, rabbit." He gave me a wink and like he can't wait another second he reaches in the pocket of his overalls and pulls out one of them little square books like what I saw in the five and tenny with cowboy stories of The Lone Ranger or stories of Buck Rogers, only not as thick, where if you flipped the corner edge of the pages you'd see The Lone Ranger riding Silver or Buck Rogers whizzing through space in a rocketship. With a sly grin, he pats the grass, motioning for me to sit down beside him, so I stopped my peeking around, worrying was the Swamp Rats sneaking up on us, but I only squatted down, I wouldn't sit. What I saw was the cover of the book said ALLEY OOP with a cartoon of Alley Oop in his leopard skin holding his big club in front of his cave just like I saw him in the Sunday comics and wondered why Earl Jr. was so excited about that since Alley Oop wasn't never one of my favorites like Mickey Mouse or Blondie and Dagwood.

"Me ole man's got a stack of these hid under the mattress and in the bottom of his bureau," he said, saying it like he was real proud of his father, and real proud of himself for having snitched it, and when he said it I all of a sudden saw my father's bureau drawer with my Grandpop Lithwack's gun hid under his underwear.

When Earl Jr. opened the book my eyes popped, seeing Alley Oop's girlfriend with a bone in her hair saying in the balloon over her head was that his club under his leopard skin and Alley Oop saying in his balloon yes, it was, only it wasn't, it was his dunkey that was big and fat as the man's with the big ears in the woods that time. The more he turned the pages the more excited Earl Jr. got, his lips moving quicker and quicker reading the balloons, like I saw his father's lips moving when he was reading the Superman comic book on their porch that time, Earl Jr. grinning and turning every so often to say to me now, "Looka that, jist looka that, will ya?"

I ain't never seen anything like it. I looked and what I saw was Alley Oop doing things with his club he never did in the Sunday funnies, I never saw no books like that in my father's bureau drawer, I only saw the pistol hid under his underwear. It was all drawn so big and loud. Alley Oop's girlfriend didn't have no dunkey, it wasn't grown in yet like Kate's wasn't grown in yet, and Alley Oop's was like his club, if it was me I knew I would be hollering, only she wasn't hollering, she had a big grin on her face and where her dunkey should of been it was like the electric socket I stuck my tongue in up on the second floor on Mifflin Street and the blue sparks shot out like the big drops shooting out the top of Alley Oop's dunkey was sparks...dark hers was, dark as the dark between my father's legs when I peeked that time and wasn't supposed to, like when Slap bent over and showed us it up in the toilet, a brown eye staring out at us, only she had straggly hairs like spider's legs crawling all around where her dunkey should've been and his dunkey was a pole big as his club in the big thick lips with long whiskers all around, it was shiny and greasy as Lenny the Lenilenape's mouth, and thick like the big-eared man's in the woods, a greasy club there were big drops of sweat coming out of, like in the Sunday funnies when Alley Oop got mad or ascared big drops of sweat shot out of his head, like he would never stop, like he was a volcano, spouting and spouting in big drops like his sweat, like the blue sparks from the socket, like the blue from the muzzles of the shotguns the New Year's shooters were shooting, like my father knocked flat on his back after shooting it, the barrel of it blue as my Grandpop Lithwack's pistol, like Alley Oop's big drops were bullets shooting into her....

I looked and looked but didn't know what it meant in words but knew, in that deep dark place where there weren't no words, just what it was, like Charley on the beach asking did we have any problems and like the big-eared man all bare in the woods, it both scared and excited me all at the same time.

Then Earl Jr. flipped the corner edge of the pages with his thumb to show me, "See?" he said, and I saw Alley Oop moving like a cartoon in the movies and saw his club that wasn't his club slamming up and down with the big drops of sweat popping out the side of his head and his girlfriend grinning like her face would break.

Earl Jr. went through the whole book one more time, teasing me every other page, saying, "Do you know what this is, do you?" and I had to admit I didn't. I saw now the pages were smeared with thumbprints bigger'n his, and where you flipped the edges of the pages it was all grubby and wore. Finally when he had his fill of it he slid the book back in his overalls and lay down on his back in the grass, propping his hands behind his head, grinning and looking up at the trees like the Alley Oop book was up there in the leaves with its cartoons still crossing in front of his eyes.

Even though I was beginning to imitate him in little ways, in the way he walked or the way he said things, most things he did I wouldn't do, even so easy a thing as laying back on the ground, afraid of snakes or frogs or bugs, not to mention turtles. But the grass here looked so soft and quiet, it was all so dark and quiet here, except for the birds you could hear but couldn't see off in the dark branches, everything was dark but just light enough with the sun coming through the leaves in spikes of light skinny as the trunks of the sassafras scattered in amongst the bigger pines around the edge of the clearing...I was just about to slide down when all of a sudden Earl Jr. was up like a shot unbuttoning his bib as he darted into the bushes where he shoved down his overalls and squatted behind the huckleberry bushes.

I gaped at him, surprised he didn't care if I was there or not and even though I knew there was nobody around but us and the birds, I still peeped over my shoulder to see if anybody'd snuck up in the meantime and was spying on us, like Charley maybe, looking to find some news to write about in the *County Seat Weekly*. Then I heard Earl Jr. tearing off leaves from the bushes, and when he stood up he just let his overalls drop to his ankles and stepped out of them and came back dragging them behind him by one strap, grinning and saying, "Them prunes from relief run right through me."

Since he wasn't wearing no underwear, I looked and saw his face and neck and arms were all brown, but where the overalls was his skin was white as the whitest cream, like my father in his sawed-off workpants that day at the river when he told us not to look but I looked anyway. Earl Jr. saw me looking and I looked away real quick but he grinned a bigger grin, saying, "You can look, if you want." He gave his hips a little shake and it shake his dunkey like a floppy bell, then he started prancing around over the grass in his hoppy little dance. I turned my head a little towards him, watching him slantways like he was a light too bright to look at, watching him shaking himself and prancing around. Every place he put his barefeet down he left dark prints of them in the Indian grass.

When he had enough of dancing he flopped down again beside me and rolled over on his back, lacing his hands behind his head and staring up again at the branches that were so thick they were like a roof of leaves and pine needles over us. I could see the little pimple marks next to each of his little fingers, he already told me how him and his brother Walter were born with an extra little finger on each hand, twelve fingers in all so that the midwife had to cut off the extra ones, leaving the little pimples. "Six fingers runs in our fambly," he said, like it was something to brag about, like Ronnie was always bragging he was named after two famous movie stars.

"Grass feels so good," he whispered, shutting his eyes and wriggling his whole self up and down against it, like the grass was fingers scratching his back. "Ummm..." he sighed, like my Aunt Nell sighed whenever she asked one of us to scratch her back, "You oughta take yer things off'n try it...ummmm..." he went, humming like bees in his mouth, and rolling over on his belly he started wriggling himself from head to toe in the grass, like Danny rolled on his belly in the bed at night before he went to sleep.

But I was shy about taking my clothes off, like I always felt funny to pee in front of him, like I always felt with anybody, and never did, except with Slap when he sat with me in the outhouse. I would never dream of dropping my pants in front of him like he did in the bushes just then, doing it as if it was nothing, as if it was the easiest thing, just like the Beezley boys did, but my brothers would never do it neither—I looked around me and even though a part of me still knew there wasn't nobody there but me and him and the birds and the trees, it was like my mother was standing right there, it was like my father was standing right there too, watching and shaking their finger, saying, *Don'tchou dare.*

By this time it was like he could read my mind, though. "Whatsa matter, you scare't?" saying it quiet enough, saying it like he knew it'd get my goat. I looked away from his eyes and rubbed my fingers in the grass that was silky as hair and softer'n anything I ever touched. "Scare't?" he said again, quiet and sly, and got me so worked up, which is just what he wanted, I didn't know where to turn because I knew he was right. But like everything else, I wouldn't do nothing that first time, if he was a magnet pulling me, there was an even stronger magnet inside of me pulling me back.

But seeing he liked to dance so much I jumped up and starting to hum "Jeepers Creepers," I did a little dance for him like I used to do for my mother in the parlor on Mifflin Street, swirling myself around and around. He pitched his head up on his hands, his eyes bright and grinning with a look of surprise. I didn't care if he gaped at me and wasn't sure if he was laughing at me or not, I didn't care, I was just so happy to dance for him, I was just so happy to have somebody to dance for again.

Other times we went back to the clearing he brought Maggie and Jiggs and Blondie and Dagwood and Mickey Mouse and Minnie Mouse that he snitched one by one from under his father's mattress or out of his father's bureau drawer and kept hid in his overall pockets til we got to the clearing. So that after that I never saw them comic strips the same way again in the Sunday papers.

We'd look at the books a couple times, sitting side by side in the grass, our heads so close together they'd bump sometimes, our heads so close together I could smell the sweat of his hair. After he flipped the edge of the pages at least a dozen times to see Mickey Mouse's hiney bouncing up and down on top of Minnie Mouse that still had her flowerpot hat on with the daisy sticking up out of it, I'd do a dance for him. And sometimes if he didn't have them off already so's he could lay in the grass and feel the grass under him, he'd drop his overalls and do a goofy dance for me like he did that first time. He would shimmy his hips like a hootchie-kootchie dancer I saw in a Mae West movie me and my brothers saw by mistake once at the Lyric that my mother said we shouldn't've seen, she said Mae West was a tramp because she bleached her hair, like my father said my Aunt Theresa was a tramp because she did the same, and hollered at Frank for letting us see it. Earl Jr. would be rolling his eyes like Mae West and shaking his hips, his dunkey growing like mine did when I woke up in the morning and had to pee real bad, shaking and shaking himself, that got us both to laughing before he flopped on his belly in the grass to catch his breath—And no matter how dirty he was he had that smell of the salt in the air when a storm blew up that Sam Beezley said was the smell of the sea blowing up from the bay that reminded me I must ask Earl Jr. where was the sea—And now that I let myself get closer to it, he had the smell too of the Indian grass that was all mixed up with the smell of his skin and the smell of his hair all sweaty from dancing and plastered in dark curls around the back of his neck.

Dancing for him more and more, little by little I took things off, first my blouse, then my undershirt, him egging me on all the time. Even so, safe as I knew the clearing to be it was so far back in the woods and hid, there was still that fear in me the Swamp

Rats'd come crashing through the trees or Lenny the Lenilenape would come sneaking through the grass on his belly to take our scalps, or my brothers or the Beezley boys'd sneak up and be peeking at us and run home and rat on me to my mother and father—or just as bad, Charley hiding there so's he'd maybe have something to tell everybody in the *County Seat Weekly*— Afraid even more'n that that Earl Jr.'d laugh at me because even though he always had a grin in his eyes as he watched me dance, I wasn't never sure was he jeering. But finally I came to see it wasn't a grin to make fun of me, I saw he was watching me the way he watched Mickey Mouse or Minnie Mouse or Blondie and Dagwood in his father's comic books, his mouth hanging open showing his big teeth, and breathing through his mouth, his eyes as round as Little Orphan Annie's, I saw it was an enjoying himself grin, so that soon I was able to dance around over the Indian grass with nothing on, not even my maryjanes, and felt the grass underneath my feet all soft and springy, it lifted up my feet and helped me dance and made my dunkey grow without my having to pee. And if I closed my eyes as I twirled around and around, singing "Jeepers Creepers" or "A-Tisket, A-Tasket, I Lost Me Yellow Basket," singing to him as much as to myself, singing like I used to sing to my mother, I imagined the grass was hair I was dancing in, like I was dancing in long green hair, like the Indian grass was the long green hair not only in the clearing but over all of the ground everywheres all over the world.

That first time I danced bare in the woods I was worried that when I got home my mother'd see in my eyes what I did because I still believed she could see right through my head like Slap said God could. I found myself watching her on the sly to see if she knew and one time she caught me at it and said, "What's the matter with you? What're you lookin at me for?"

I blushed and mumbled, "Nuthin," and still wasn't sure she didn't know even though she wasn't saying anything.

That night in my dreams I was dancing and dancing and Earl Jr. was dancing with me without no clothes on, then Mr. Mahoney came out of the trees with nothing on and he was dancing, then Sam Beezley and Lenny the Lenilenape danced out, and all except for Earl Jr. there were big red snakes twisting between their legs like the big-eared man, that were twisting and shaking, like Earl Jr.'s shook like a bell, as we all danced and danced over the Indian grass in the clearing in the woods, til I woke up with my legs kicking the covers off and my heart beating more from excitement than fear.

When it came the time of the blackberries again we picked them, and then the huckleberries and bitter wild cherries the same as last summer, me and my brothers going out in the mornings with empty milk bottles and buckets into the fields and woods around our house to pick them, me and Danny picking the cherries closest to the ground while my older brothers climbed up in the trees, our fingers and mouths black with juice at the end of the day. And like with the frogs in the swamp and the fish in the river, it was still hard for me to believe, being from the city where everything I knew of came from Willie's store, that all them berries that grew wild in the woods and fields not only around our house but all over town was ours for the picking—Except for them times, without our knowing it, we trespassed on somebody's property, like our landlady's, the widow Scadder up on Hessian Soldiers Way, and was chased. Earl Jr., besides learning me to spot Lenilenape arrowheads in the sand up on the bluff and down along the beach so that finally I had a whole collection of them hidden away in the bottom of my bureau drawer, showed me places where to spot berries that neither my brothers nor the Beezley boys ever found, especially the huckleberries that grew thick around the clearing deep in the woods where we looked at his father's cartoon books and danced for each other and that only he seemed to know about.

We brought home so many berries, what we couldn't eat with milk and sugar or in our cereal, like Mrs. Beezley showed her last summer to do, my mother cooked up to make jam and jelly out of, sealing up the jars with wax she bought at Gottlieb's so they'd keep for winter. And now it was high summer, as Mr. Beezley called it, when the leaf lettuce in my father's garden was red at the tips like it been scorched by the sun, and when it got to be time for the tomatoes to be ripe, and along with my brothers I took my first bite into a warm juicy tomato I picked myself fresh off of the vine, it was like the taste of the August afternoon was all jammed inside of that tomato. I et the rest of it with a palmful of salt my father gave me to sprinkle on it because he told us a tomato wasn't a tomato without no salt sprinkled on it. And what we had left over from what we didn't eat from the garden, which wasn't all that much, beans and tomatoes mostly, my mother canned them for the winter too. And what tomatoes didn't ripen, I was good at spotting the ones hid under the heavy vines, as good as I was spotting cigarette butts on the way to church for my brothers, or spotting arrowheads or huckleberries, and picked the green ones for my mother to can for sour tomatoes or grind up in piccalilli relish from a recipe Mrs. Beezley gave her.

We had a little peach tree grew by the kitchen door but when it came the time of the peaches they were small and hard and not very many, but when it came fall and it came the time of the wild apples and the wild pears, Earl Jr. showed me all the secret places where they were too. And they were so many, he'd climb up like my brothers did in the apple tree they always climbed in on the way home from church, and he threw them apples down to me from up in the branches that looked higher'n our house. And some of them were still green but we gorged ourselves on them anyhow and got the skitters so bad I thought my insides were coming out everytime I had to run out to the outhouse. One afternoon we et so many of them green apples Earl Jr. got caught short up the tree where he was throwing the apples down to me, so he just dropped his overalls and squatted over the branch he been standing on, shouting, "Look out below!" laughing up among the branches, his laughs so loud they were ringing through the woods and up in all the other trees, I was afraid the Swamp Rats might hear him, or Lenny the Indian, and they'd come running to chase us out of their woods.

After we et our fill, we'd always carry home as many of the apples or pears as we could stuff down our shirts and in our pockets, and my brothers did the same in the trees they found, and my mother canned them pears and apples too. And when it came the time of the little purple fox grapes that always looked like they had a dew on them, Earl Jr. knew the best places to find them too and there were so many, I showed my brothers where they were even though Earl Jr. chewed me out for telling. Me and them brought them home by the bushel basket and my mother made grape jelly out of them that was so good smeared on her cornbread it didn't look like any of it was going to last us til winter.

In the fall we shook down hickory nuts and chestnuts from the trees in the woods across from our house, lugging them home in gunnysacks. And out in our clearing Earl Jr. heaped stones together and built a fire from the dead cherry branches and roasted chestnuts, that I et just to be polite, never being fond of nuts, Earl Jr.'s eyes watching the flames, while the chestnuts roasted, with the same glittery grin he wore when he was looking at Alley Oop or Maggie and Jiggs. And far down in the corner of our yard we had a wild persimmon tree that was like the ones Earl Jr. knew of deep in the woods on the way to our clearing. He told me you didn't eat the persimmons til the first frost came and they fell on the ground, if you didn't wait til then they puckered up your mouth something awful, no matter how ripe they looked on the tree. They tasted to me like the bite in the air now said that winter was coming.

But before the first frost came me and my father and my brothers picked the garden clean of the last of the turnips and parsnips, my father not wanting to let anything go to waste. Then as the chickens got fat there were the eggs from the chicken coop that was all built now with help my father got from Mr. Beezley. Me and Danny and sometimes Kate collected eggs everyday, I liked the hot chickeny smell of the place, and sometimes on a Saturday night my father would yank his hatchet out of the back step and go in the run and grab a rooster and bring it out in the yard and lay its head on a rock and chop off its head for our Sunday dinner—Or later, as they got older and tougher and didn't lay as much, he'd chop off the head of one of the hens. That first time when I saw the hatchet in my father's hand and the blood spurting out the rooster's neck, gushing like the blood down the drains at the slaughterhouse on Sigel Street, and the rooster's wings flapping and its head on the ground with the eyes and the beak still opening and shutting and all the red draining out of its comb, I had nightmares for weeks, dreaming it was my neck stretched out on the rock with my father standing over me with his hatchet, a look in his eye fierce as a rooster, the look he used to have when he was drunk.

And Buster, rough and tough as he was, he wouldn't never eat any of the chicken meat, he been feeding and watering them chickens since they were peeps they was like pets to him, so everytime he saw my father go to pull his hatchet out of the back step he'd run and hide in the woods and wouldn't come out til my mother finished scalding and plucking and cleaning that chicken and stuck it on the ice in the icebox til morning, and neither Frank nor Slap ever dared tease him about it if they didn't want to get a sock in the eye.

But it didn't matter if my father killed one of the chickens once in a while, the chicken coop was always getting more chicks because there was always a brood hen setting down in the cellar on a nest of straw in a box my father put her in, putting it high up on another box in case the swamp water came in again. And sometimes he'd slip a couple wood eggs Sam Beezley gave him under her to get her started.

He built shelfs high up in the cellar too, to store the jars of things my mother canned that couldn't fit on the shelfs out in the shed, building them out of lumber he found drifted up on the beach at the river that was so old and water-logged it was rickety and warped.

These days my mother looked a little easier in her eyes, what with all the wild berries and fruits and nuts we were bringing in from the woods and fields, and the vegetables from out in my father's garden and the eggs from the hen house, and then too whatever my father could get now and then from relief—It wasn't really all that much with all the mouths to feed and the way my older brothers et—"*They're at that age*," I heard my mother whisper to Mrs. Beezley one time when I was under the dining room table, her saying it like they had an incurable disease—a tapeworm my father said they had—and so whatever we had all went pretty fast. But it was better'n it was when sometimes there wasn't anything in the house to eat and we were depending on Bill the breadman to come or were depending on the frog legs in the swamp or the catfish or occasional crab from the river or Mrs. Beezley sending Sister over with something extra from their table. Somedays now I'd even hear my mother singing loud and strong when she was doing the wash, like she sang when we lived in South Philly, and I felt glad in my heart, hearing her singing again.

"Walk like they don't hurtcha," she said with a look in her eyes that said there was nothing else she could do. Even though we were all alone in the kitchen, she said it in a low voice like she was ashamed somebody might hear her.

"Show me how you walk now."

I walked around the kitchen table again, putting my feet down careful as I could, trying not to make a face with every step I took.

She sighed.

"Try to walk like that," she said. "Don'tchou worry, they'll be broke in in no time."

But I been walking in them off and on like she told me to do ever since my father brought them home from relief, and they still weren't broke in. I knew if there was something she could've done she would've done it, but it was either that or going to school barefoot and she said they wouldn't let you go to school without no shoes, that was the rule. I asked her why couldn't I wear my old maryjanes or even my old sneakers and she said, "They're too falling apart and sad looking and the teacher won't like it and the other kids'll laugh." Then she told me to wear the new shoes as much as I could that day so as to get used to them by tomorrow but not to get them dirty. And even though I did like she told me, feeling funny walking around in such fancy shoes that shiny as they were still only had cardboard soles, they still pinched my feet something awful. I was so glad when I couldn't take the pinching anymore to get into my old sneakers that were so ragged and wore my toes showed through but never once hurt me to walk in them.

Later that same day in the kitchen, Buster started razzing me, knowing I was going to start school next day, telling me the teacher'd hit me with the ruler I was so dumb, and my heart started up, worrying about it.

Slap busts in with, "Oh, she won't hit 'im, he kin read! And he kin spell! Gwan, ask 'im to spell somethin!"

I turned every color of the rainbow and could've killed Slap, blabbing my secret.

"Spell cat," Buster said, teasing, and though I was all flustered and didn't want to, I spelled it.

"Well, that's easy," he said with a sneer.

"Spell red," my father said, because of my face I guess, and I spelled that too. My father gave me a look. "Spell dog," he said. I spelled it and he gave me another look, even more peculiar this time.

"See!" Slap hollered in his loud way, and I could've killed him all over again.

"You can see he takes after my side of the fambly," my mother sang out from the sink, taking a dig at my father, as she swished bleach around in the bottom of her tea bowls to get out the stains.

I stared down at the floor like it was something to be ashamed of for them to find out I could spell, like it was a secret was all mine til Slap went'n spilled the beans, like hiding under the dining room table was a secret, or leaning over Slap in bed and listening down the stairs at night when my mother and father and the Beezleys were talking in the parlor, or Earl Jr.'s clearing in the woods was secret and all that we did there.

That night my mother scrubbed me in the tub like I thought she would take the skin off of me, and put me in new wool underwear my father got from relief that itched like the dickens, she even cleaned under my finger and toenails which she hardly ever did before.

It felt like my heart was right inside my ears, I could hardly say a word that first day my mother walked me and my brothers up the road and into town to the schoolhouse. On the way we saw Mr. Mahoney go by driving the Chevy with Ronnie and his mother in the backseat, and even though Slap waved they went on by in a cloud of dust like they never saw us. "Afraid they'd have to give us a ride," Buster sneered, and my mother said, "Now don'tchou talk like that—All of us couldn't fit in the car anyhow."

Danny was whining was he going to school too? and my mother said for him to shush, he'd be going soon enough, and Kate, dragging along one of her dolls from the dump truck that only had one arm, was looking mad as a hornet, her eyes still red from the combing my mother gave her to get all the knots out of her hair just before we left the house.

My brothers were wearing their new clothes from relief that looked as stiff as my pillow ticking suit, but they weren't wearing no neckties, that was another thing different about public school, you didn't have to wear no necktie and that made Slap awful glad. Besides my suit that had a funny smell of disinfectant and been in the closet so long it smelled of mothballs, I was wearing a blouse with a sailor collar that was also from relief that was so big on me I wished it was my shoes instead, that was pinching already, but my mother said not to worry, my jacket would hide how big the sailor blouse was.

Underneath my blouse she'd hung a medal of the Virgin Mary before we left the house, she said so the Mother of God'd watch over me among a bunch of proddisins and said to keep it under my undershirt and not let the teacher or the other kids see it in case they didn't like Catholics.

I was carrying a brown paper bag with two blackberry jelly sandwiches on bread that my mother baked just like she made the jelly, and when I asked her why my other brothers didn't have no lunchbags, she said in first grade you had to stay for lunch it was such a long walk home. I didn't like hearing that at all and would rather've come home with my brothers but didn't say nothing, knowing the good it would do me.

Brother and Sparky and Sister Beezley came out behind us on the path through the woods coming from their house. My brothers and the Beezley boys walked together, talking and laughing and not looking worried at all, like they were going to the movies stead of to school, "Goin to jail," as Brother called it, wrinkling up his nose like he smelled doggie dirt or something just as bad. Sister, that had her hair all frizzed and was wearing her Easter hat and cape, walked beside my mother and Kate and took Kate's hand, making a big fuss over her like she always did, saying to Kate, "Do you want to be my little girl, huh, do you?" And Kate, still in a bad mood from her hair pulling, yanked her hand away, pouting, "No, I don't!" My mother gave her a shake, saying, "Ain't you ashamed, talking that way to Sister that's been so sweet to you." But you could see Kate didn't care a hoot, she wasn't never cheerful this early in the morning anyhow.

When we passed the Snarp house I saw Earl Jr. sitting on

their porch rail. He had on the same ripped overalls he always wore and a shirt that I never saw him wear before that looked washed but wasn't ironed. He had his hair plastered down with water and instead of being barefoot he had on his raggedy sneakers. I was wondering how come he could go to school in his sneakers and I couldn't but I was so tongue-tied about going to school I couldn't open my mouth to ask my mother.

I looked at him and he looked at me. He looked like he was waiting for us to go by and after we went on by I kept looking back over my shoulder to watch for him and after a little while I saw him coming along far behind us with his little brother Walter that was wearing a pillow ticking suit and carrying a lunchbag just like me.

As we went up the front steps of the school with all the rest of the kids, a beefy big lady with big arms and big shoulders and a face that was red as if her hair was pulled back too tight in her bun, was standing on the top step. She smiled at my mother like smiling hurt her face and said her name was Miss Jickers and she was the principal. Then her eyes that was black and tiny as beebees shot around at the rest of us and she wasn't smiling anymore as she looked like she was sizing us up from head to toe and ain't too pleased with what she saw. My mother was bowing and scraping left and right and trying to hide her teeth, like Miss Jickers was the priest the way she was talking all of a sudden real different like she never talked at home as she told Miss Jickers who we were, all the time fussing with my hair and my too big collar like she was trying to hide it but was only drawing attention to it with all her fussing—as if she ain't fussed a hundred times with me already before we left the house. While at the same time she was trying to smooth down the back of Slap's hair that never would stay down, saying, "Oh, look at them now—not two minutes out of the house and his shirttail hanging out already!" She told Slap to fix his shirt and looked around at us with that frantic look like she always had in front of strangers, looking like she wished we would all disappear like she wished my collar that was too big would disappear the way she kept grabbing at it.

Miss Jickers said my two older brothers'd be in her class, that was seventh and eighth grades, and when she said it her mouth was smiling but her little eyes weren't, and the way she was staring at the two of them I saw them duck their heads like they did something bad already just by standing there. She said Slap'd be in Miss Prouty's class, third grade, because he been left down again, and I would be in Mrs. Feek's first grade, like Ronnie said, and a shiver went up and down my back, remembering all the terrible things he said about Mrs. Feek.

As she led us in and down the dark hall and showed the others what rooms to go into, I sniffed how the place had a smell of dust and burnt rubber and disinfectant like the school Aunt Nell worked in, and a smell a little bit like our cellar from being shut up. I was looking around so wild-eyed I even forgot for the minute my shoes were pinching. I kept looking around to see could I see Earl Jr. and there he was going into the classroom Slap'd just gone into and before he went in he saw me and sliced his finger across his neck like he was cutting his throat.

Mrs. Feek's room was at the very back and she was standing outside the door greeting all the other kids my age were with their mothers. She was wrinkled and had a face like the principal like she never smiled and had glasses with metal rims and crimped gray curls. When we came up Miss Jickers told her who we were and my mother went into her bowing again and looking ashamed and putting her hand to her mouth. My heart was really thumping now as Mrs. Feek looked down at me through her glasses and without a trace of a smile, said to my mother,

"I'll take over now, Mrs. Lithwack."

The first thing Mrs. Feek did was steer me to a green chair at a long green table next to a gawky girl with long frizzy Shirley Temple curls and what my mother always called pink eye. The girl gave me a pop-eyed look as I sat down next to her, like I was somebody just landed from another planet. All the other kids were turning around to gape at us, the only two sitting at the back table, so the first thing I learned in school was there must be something the matter with being tall because you were made to sit in the back of the room like it was a punishment for being different.

Mrs. Feek'd gone up to the front of the room and stood behind a big desk and the first thing she did was open a book and begin to read from it. My mother warned me and my brothers the night before not to listen to when the teacher read the bible because it was a proddisin bible, so I figured that must be it and I snuck my hands up over my ears not to listen. When Mrs. Feek snapped the bible shut she said we were to bow our heads and say the Our Father after her, but I remembered just in time the other thing my mother warned us about was not to say the end of the Our Father that was a proddisin ending and was a sin for a Catholic to say, so I shut my mouth when it came to "For Thine is the power and the glory…" Then Mrs. Feek had us stand up and put our hands over our hearts and look at the flag hanging over her desk and had us repeat after her the pledge of allegiance. After that we sat down and she started calling names out of a book and everybody was to say "Present!" real loud. When she came to a little blond blue-eyed boy named Gerald at the first table right in front of her desk, he hollers out *"Present!"* louder'n anybody else and Mrs. Feek gave him a big smile, the first she give so far, and says, "How's your mother and father, Gerald?" and Gerald said, "Just fine, thank you, Mrs.

Feek." "Give them my regards," Mrs. Feek says, and Gerald grins like his face would break, saying he'd be sure to do that. Mrs. Feek turns to the rest of us and says, "I hope you will all learn from Gerald to be so happy and smiling," and Gerald looked even more bright-eyed and grinny when she said it. I see right off he's one of the few kids in the room has on new store-bought clothes like I saw Ronnie had on too when he went whizzing by us in his father's car.

The next thing I learned was my name because Mrs. Feek kept calling out somebody named Stanislaus and when nobody answered Present, everybody including me started gawking around wondering who that could be. But Mrs. Feek was looking straight at me, her eyes hard as Lenilenape arrowheads through her glasses as she hollers, "You! You, young man, back there, don't you even know your own name?" I said, "That ain't my name, my name is Mickey," and she said, "No, your name is Stanislaus." I said, "No, that's me father's name, and me cousin Stan's name me father was godfather to," and she rolls her eyes up to the ceiling like I'm the dumbest thing on the face of the earth don't even know my own name, whilst the other kids put their hands over their mouths and started giggling. Mrs. Feek said, "Well, that's your name too. You're Stanislaus Jr., and don't say ain't and don't say me father say *my* father."

That was news to me, Mickey is all I ever knew my name was and all they ever called me at home—except for some of the things Frank and Buster called me. My mother said I was named after Mickey Mouse and that Mickey Mouse was my godfather and Aunt Maggie was my godmother. "You're Stanislaus from now on," Mrs. Feek said, puckering up her mouth, and ever after that that's what I was in school even though I was Mickey at home and my father was Stosh, like his father was given the name Lithwack when he got off the boat even though that wasn't his name, and that was that and nothing you could do about it.

Everybody laughed because I didn't know my own name, Margaret whispering out the side of her mouth, *"Dumbbell!"* like she was mad at me anyhow for being tall like she was and stuck in the back of the room. "Stanis*laus!*" she hissed, "What kinda name is that? Sounds like a name for a cootie." But if that was my name how come nobody called me it before and if I was named after my father how come I wasn't called junior like Earl Jr. was? I ain't been in school five minutes and here I was already so full of questions I could hardly even think straight and couldn't wait til I got home to ask my mother all about it.

The next thing Mrs. Feek did was write down orders for milk, three cents for white milk, four cents for chocolate. Even though I only tasted it once or twice in my whole life, my mouth started watering thinking of chocolate milk Buster said came from brown cows. But it was only for them brought money from home, like blond-haired Gerald and the other kids in new clothes, like the girl sitting next to Gerald named Virginia had Shirley Temple curls like Margaret but was a lot shorter. So I couldn't order any milk because I didn't bring no pennies and knew I wasn't ever likely to neither, there wasn't no more pennies down any of the chairs in our parlor after the last time my mother and me looked, no matter how deep we dug down in the cushions.

Along the wall under the windows was a long shelf with little boxes in it that already had our names printed on each one. Mrs. Feek said for us to put our lunches and anything else we wanted in that place where our name was, we would keep our crayons and our paste jars and our scissors there too, and hearing her say crayons I got excited, hoping she'd give me a box of my very own crayons to draw with.

I saw most of the kids dressed in new clothes bought from a store had new lunch kettles while the rest of us that was wearing clothes made out of the pillow ticking had paperbags, Walter Snarp's lunchbag looking the greasiest and wrinkliest of the bunch. Mrs. Feek was helping the ones find their box didn't know how to spell their names, which was just about everybody, except for Margaret and Virginia and little Gerald that never stopped smiling. I was hunting and hunting for Mickey, then I remembered that wasn't my name anymore and hunted for the name the way my father spelled his and when I found it down near the floor with the S's I wondered why if you were tall you were given a box you practically had to get down on your knees but if you were Gerald you were given a box you had to stand on tippy-toe, it didn't make no sense.

When I put my lunchbag in the box marked Stanislaus, Mrs. Feek gave me a funny look when she saw me do it, like my father gave me a funny look when I spelled red for him, and when I sat down in the back again with Margaret, she swung her Shirley Temple curls in my face when she leaned over to whisper, "Yer on relief, ain'tcha?" I didn't know what to say to that, my mother warned me not to tell nobody our business in school, but I could see Margaret wasn't blind, she was swinging her curls at this one and at that one, whispering, "He's on relief and she's on relief and that one over there," pointing to Earl Jr.'s little brother Walter, that I already knew was on relief. All the ones she was pointing at I saw all had clothes on made out of pillow ticking like me but I still kept quiet because of what my mother said and because I thought school was like church where you weren't allowed to talk and folded my hands in front of me on the table like my mother told me to do and kept quiet. But Margaret, seeing Mrs. Feek was still helping the last of the kids find their boxes, swung her curls at me again, whispering,

"You a mackerel-eater?" I knew from the Beezley boys mackerel-eater meant Catholic because of eating fish on Friday that we et most of the rest of the week anyhow because there wasn't no money to buy meat at Gottlieb's, we et so much catfish she should've asked me was I a catfish-eater.

I didn't say nothing but that didn't stop her, she whispered, "I seen you clamup at the end of the Our Father, so I knew you was a mackerel-eater, I go to the baptist tabernacle myself." When I looked like I didn't know what she was talking about, she said, "The church down near Gottlieb's on Tabernacle Trail," and I remembered seeing a church was in a store didn't look like no church that Mr. Beezley said a bunch of holy-rollers went there, but I didn't say anything about that.

"Sometimes we go to the methodist church," she said, lifting her brows up and saying it snippy, like it was something to be proud of instead of ashamed of because I knew that was the red brick church where you went to heaven in a tin lizzie and not a Cadillac, if you got to go to heaven at all, which Father Mack said was doubtful.

I was dying to ask her did she see Shirley Temple in "Poor Little Rich Girl" to curl her hair that way but I was too shy to ask and more'n that I was afraid Mrs. Feek'd holler at me like she already did over my name if I so much as opened my mouth again.

Then Mrs. Feek gave out the crayons and give each of us a piece of paper with balls and blocks and triangles already drawn on it in blue. "Color the ball red," she said, and held up a red crayon. "Color the square orange," and she held up an orange one. "And color the triangle green," holding up the different crayons to show us which color to use. But I knew the colors already and under each little drawing the color was spelled out in letters anyhow so you couldn't help but know what crayons to use, so I didn't see why she was telling us all that but she did.

The only crayons I ever had were the stubbly ones Ronnie gave me that weren't all of the colors and were so wore down they were about ready to be thrown out, so I was all excited having brand-new crayons. They were so brand-new they still had a point on them and had a brand-new waxy smell even better'n the wax my mother poured on top the jars of her home-made jelly and jam to keep them for winter. When I colored in the ball and I saw that red I got even more excited, staring at it and staring at it. I quick filled in the other colors, pressing down harder and harder to make the green more greener and the orange more oranger, my eyes so excited, and my nose too, seeing and tasting in the red my father's tomatoes, smelling oranges in the orange, and seeing the green in the green like the green of the long-haired Indian grass in the clearing only me and Earl Jr. knew about, all of it there between my fingers in a crayon.

When it came time for recess I found out that meant we all go out and play in the schoolyard, only we were kept in the back of the school separated from the bigger kids that I could hear whooping and hollering out front.

The first thing Mrs. Feek did once we were outside was line us up, boys in one line, girls in another, and take us all to the toilets that were like a great big outhouse out in the schoolyard back near the swamp, only this one was made out of the same yellow cement blocks as the firehouse was, with doorways that didn't have no doors on them, only a wood wall in front so you couldn't see in. She took the girls in their side first and then when she was done that she came around and hollered in the boys' door was there anybody in there and you could hear quick flushing inside and then some big boys came hurrying out tucking in their shirts and buttoning themselves. She came right into the toilet with us. Inside, smelled like the disinfectant in the school, only terribler, and the cement walls and floor were painted all the same gray as the school was. Even though it was still warm outside the place was chilly and damp and had a feeling like frogs sticking on you that gave me the shivers. Mrs. Feek showed us how to push down the handles behind the commodes and then shook her finger at us, warning us not to dawdle, and we all looked relieved when she went marching out, I know I was.

We stood around staring at each other. Then one of them flushed a toilet after he peed and the water rushed down into the dark hole with a roar so loud he jumped back like he ain't seen nothing like it, and that made the others laugh but made me think I'd never be able to sit down on one of them hoppers, the water might suck me down. Even though now I had to go so bad I decided I'd hold it in til I got home because, scary as our outhouse was, at least when you shut the door you knew you were by yourself without a lot of boys looking, and the hole, dark as it was, didn't have a roar of water in it that might suck you down, not even our flush toilet on Mifflin Street sounded like that.

After we learned how to use the toilets, Mrs. Feek got us all in a line again and marched us across the playground, me and Margaret at the tail-end like we were still sitting at the last table in the classroom. I was trying hard not to limp so nobody'd see my shoes didn't fit and I wondered if the other boys and girls had on relief shoes were doing the same. The playground was scattered with ashes and cinders that I found out later came from the furnace in the cellar that Mr. Floud the janitor spread over the ground so that when you fell down in the games at recess you could really skin your knees and elbows and sometimes even get cinders stuck in your kneecap your mother had to pick out with a needle she heated the tip of first with a match so you wouldn't get no germs. Mrs. Feek took us to the edge of the swamp that stretched all along back of the school like it did in back of our house. I saw it was even a whole lot darker back here'n it was where we lived, the mud was different too, black as a tar road. I wondered why she brought us back here like we never saw the swamp before, I hoped she wasn't going to march us right through it, this part of the swamp smelled and looked even smellier and scarier'n our swamp was at home. Some of the boys went right up to the edge of it and others, like Walter Snarp, started walking right into it, Mrs. Feek shouting at him so loud I gave a start, *"Where're you going, boy! Get back in here! That's why I've brought you all here to tell you never to go back in the marsh—It's dangerous. You understand?"*

I couldn't of agreed with her more, and nodded my head harder'n the others when they all nodded theirs, but that Margaret pipes up asking was there quicksand back there? her pink eyes all excited like she was hoping there might be. Mrs. Feek said, real cranky, "Never you mind—There're snakes and the water is deep, if you don't want to get bitten or drown, you just do as I say, you hear?" and everybody nodded their heads again.

Mrs. Feek walked us back all in a line to the middle of the playground, then had us all stand in a circle and told us a game of walking around in the circle, stopping when she said stop and going when she said go, like we were horses. When we started walking around, I was trying so hard to listen to what she was telling us to do, I forgot not to limp because the next thing I knew she was shrilling out, "Stanislaus! Why are you walking like that?"

At first I was looking around trying to see who she meant, and she hollers, "You! You! I'm talking to you, Stanislaus!" Then

I remembered that was my name now and she says, "Walk right. Put your feet on the ground. And stand up straight. Why are you all bent over like a hunchback?"

Everything came to a halt and all the others were looking at me, specially them with relief clothes on and with shoes with cardboard soles like mine, most of them looking like they knew what was wrong but letting on like they didn't and looking away when they saw me looking, looking like they knew they were lucky not to get caught, like their mothers told them too not to let on if their shoes pinched them.

But I didn't say anything about the shoes, like my mother told me not to say anything, and as for the other, I should've known that all my stooping wasn't going to make me look shorter, like Gerald with the blond hair or any of the others, and get me moved up any closer to the front of the room. Even though I tried to straighten up because of the way she was glaring at me, later on I started stooping again without my knowing it and she scolded me any number of times after that before she finally gave up on it. And as for the tight shoes, I tried extra hard after that to watch how I walked, especially when she was around so she wouldn't be hollering at me to stop walking like I was a cripple, like Charley.

But I could spell Lithwack, and I could spell ice and I could spell bread and I could spell coal from seeing the letters on the trucks and wagons stopped at our house when we lived in Philly, and I could read most of the words in the balloons over the people's heads in the Sunday comics, and in the comic books Earl Jr. snitched from his father and we read in the woods together. And when we came back in from recess Mrs. Feek asked if we knew who the president was, and a couple kids called out his name, Gerald calling it out the loudest. But when she asked, as a joke, so that everybody giggled, did anybody know how to spell it, without even thinking my hand shot up. Mrs. Feek's eyebrows shot up too and she gave a smirk and looked around at the class, saying, "Well, Stanislaus, you think you can spell our President's name you go right on ahead," and she gave a wink around at the others.

I ain't never said nothing outloud in front of so many people before, or spelled anything outloud until Slap trapped me into it yesterday in the kitchen, but I went ahead and spelled R-o-o-s-e-v-e-l-t because my father'd stuck the red white and blue VOTE FOR ROOSEVELT poster in our parlor window when we lived on Mifflin Street, and I thought now that I was in school that was the place you could spell things outloud, not home where your brothers'd razz and tease you and look at you funny like my father did too, spelling it so low Mrs. Feek told me to speak up so I had to spell it twice and I wished now I had the brains not to go putting my hand up, I was shaking so.

When I was done spelling it Mrs. Feek's eyebrows shot up even higher and now she gave me a still funnier look. But even though I could spell Roosevelt she still didn't move me out of the back of the room, and I wished now I'd've kept my big mouth shut because of the way the others were swinging their heads around looking back at me with their mouths hanging open like I said a curseword or was some kind of freak just landed from the moon, Margaret shaking her Shirley Temple curls in my face, hissing, "*Showoff!*"

In the next couple weeks, after we learned the names of colors, that I knew already, and started to learn the alphabet, that I already knew too, all of us singing the letters over and over like a singsong, then Mrs. Feek learned us how to print them, giving us each a nice yellow pencil she showed us how to sharpen at the pencil sharpener, and we wrote them letters over and over.

Then after a few days of that she went and put cards with words printed on them on a stand at the front of the room and when it come my turn I read them right off—I, Me, Boy, Girl, Cat, Dog. When I finished she give me that same suspicious look she give me the first day of school when I spelled Roosevelt. After I did the same with the cards had sentences on them—I am a boy, I have a dog—it looked like I was getting on her nerves and so she let me read the books in the bookcase against the wall in back while the others went on learning the rest of the cards.

But no matter how much I could read and knew my colors and could spell Roosevelt I still stayed in the back of the room with Margaret and thought it was all because I was tall even though I stooped to look shorter. And when I heard my mother say none us should smoke, it'd stunt our growth, I took to sneaking butts out of the hole in the tree where my brothers hid them, and even though I should've seen it ain't been stunting their growth none, I started smoking on my own, stealing the wood matches from the metal box in the kitchen when nobody was around, despite my mother warning us never to touch no matches, she'd kill us if she caught us playing with matches, she was so scared of fire.

What I was scared of was inhaling like my brothers done, and the Beezley boys—and Earl Jr. too, he bragged he been smoking since before the first grade. Sometimes I'd lay in the Indian grass with him in our clearing and smoke the home-made cigarettes he stole from out of his father's cigarette pocket when his father was snoozing in his chair after too much beer, cigarettes that was rolled out of Bugler tobacco just like my father rolled his because that was the cheapest tobacco you could buy at Gottlieb's.

Earl Jr. said I smoked like a girl and since I wanted to do everything the way he done it I let him learn me how to hold the cigarette. Then fool that I was I let him learn me how to inhale and the first time I did the trees overhead started spinning around and around, I got to coughing so hard my eyes was watering like they sprung leaks, I never felt so sick not even when I had the measles—And do you know what that Earl Jr. was doing? why, he was rolling around in the grass holding his sides and laughing like a maniac! I couldn't believe it, I couldn't see what was so funny about me just about dying inhaling my first puff of cigarette smoke. But that's the way he was, he could be so mean sometimes, as mean or meaner even than our Buster, if that was possible.

But since I wanted to be like him in every way, little by little I learned to inhale without getting so dizzy or feeling like I was going to vomit up my guts, and when I did learn it I was so proud because after that Earl Jr.'d treat me sometimes like we were almost the same age.

Everytime after smoking with him in our clearing back in the woods, he gave me one of the little balls of chewing gum he snitched with his finger through the chickenwire at Gottlieb's, and when the weather got nice and it came the time for the wild peppermint growing again around our outhouse, he told me to rip up a handful and chew it before I went in the house so my mother or nobody couldn't smell my breath, just like my father when he was drinking chewed peppermint Life-Savers before he came in the house so she couldn't smell his breath either.

One day Mrs. Feek took her grown up scissors like my mother's best scissors, that were pointy and not blunt on the ends like ours. She took a sheet of yellow construction paper and cut a school bus out of it, then she cut faces for each of us out of the clothes for kids part of the Sears Roebuck catalog and printing our names under each window of the bus, she put our pictures in the window with little brass clips so you could move them up and down. Then she hung the school bus up above the blackboard where everybody could see it.

The picture of me was a little boy didn't look nothing like me, he had red hair, but he was so pretty, as pretty as blond-haired Gerald, and smiling like Gerald was always smiling, I wished he was me, maybe then Mrs. Feek'd ask me how my mother and father was and let me sit up at the front table beside Gerald and Virginia.

After she tacked the bus up, Mrs. Feek'd go around the tables and have us hold out our hands and show her our teeth. If you had dirty hands or fingernails or hadn't brushed your teeth, she'd go up and turn the picture of your face down, saying, "Well, so-and-so's not riding with us on the bus today, is he, boys and girls?" And the class would shout, "NO, Mrs. Feek!" while whoever it was, usually Walter Snarp or one of the other kids in relief clothes, would stare down at their hands. If their hands and teeth passed the next morning when she came around, their face was turned up again and they were allowed to ride that day on the school bus.

In the beginning she was turning down lots of faces but as time went on she didn't have to turn down as many.

Every morning after that I stood leaning over the sink after breakfast making sure to rub my teeth real good with salt on the end of the washrag, and before I went out the door for school I'd check to see if my fingernails were clean and if they weren't I'd scrub them with my mother's Fels Naptha soap. She give me a funny look the second morning I did it, saying, "Why're you bein so clean all of a sudden?" I blushed and said, "So's I can ride on the school bus." She looked at me even funnier as I dried my hands on the towel hanging there that was practically nothing but threads from all of us drying our faces and hands on it for so long a time, then I ran out the door to catch up with my brothers because if you were so much as one minute late you heard it from Mrs. Feek.

Even so, my heart always got going whenever Mrs. Feek came around the tables and told us to hold out our hands and show her our teeth, the rest of them tittering whenever she said, "Walter Snarp, your teeth are green as grass—You better tell your mother to buy you a toothbrush and a tube of Ipana toothpaste, you tell her that, you hear?" And Walter Snarp'd snuffle in his hands saying yes he would but I knew he never would because the Snarps were as broke as we were and toothbrushes and toothpaste, even Arm & Hammer baking soda my mother said was best to wash teeth with over the salt my father said was best, was so dear at Gottlieb's. But Mrs. Feek mustn't've known that because she was always at Walter about his dirty teeth til finally she gave up on it, Walter being just like his brother Earl Jr., dirt and green teeth didn't bother him at all, or Mrs. Feek trying to shame him.

But I always heaved a big sigh of relief when after looking me over Mrs. Feek went on to Margaret without saying nothing to me. But for all my worrying, it turned out it wasn't my nails or my teeth finally got me turned down in the school bus.

Not long after she made the bus, Mrs. Feek stuck a chart up in front of the room. On the chart were pictures of all kinds of things to eat printed in shiny bright colors. She was telling us how important it was to eat what she called a balanced diet— "Particularly a well-balanced breakfast, children," saying, "That's the most important meal of the day." Then she pointed with her rubber-tipped pointer to the things we should eat when we woke up: orange juice, hot Wheatena cereal with fresh milk, buttered whole wheat toast, two fried eggs and four strips of bacon, all of it topped off with a big glass of milk.

Our breakfasts at home were mainly oatmeal or cornmeal mush, sweetened with Karo or corn syrup, and white Bond bread, if there was any, my older brothers fighting over who got the heel, that was like a great big prize to them, or fighting over who was putting more sugar in their coffee'n they was supposed to, until my mother had to settle it with a thump on their heads.

The pictures on the colored chart were so real, just looking at them my mouth started watering.

The very next morning after she went over our hands and gaped in our mouths, she went around the room asking each one of us what did we have for breakfast. When she got to me, just like a dumbbell—as Margaret hissed at me later on at recess—I told the truth, saying I et corn meal mush and coffee with canned milk, the only kid in the class so far to admit eating such a breakfast. Even them was in the class in pillow ticking clothes like mine didn't admit it, not even Walter Snarp, though I knew that's probably what him and them had to eat too since bags of corn meal full of bugs was all relief gave out for breakfast that week.

Mrs. Feek clicked her tongue and shook her head, turning to the class, asking them, "Now, boys and girls, is corn meal *mush* and *coffee* a proper balanced breakfast?" And the class let out all in one loud shout, *"No, Mrs. Feek!"* Walter Snarp shouting louder even than blond-haired Gerald, and turning with her pointer, Mrs. Feek ran down her bright-colored pictures of food again for my benefit, while I squirmed in my seat and liked to die.

When she was done she twisted up her face in a look of surprise, "I don't see corn meal *mush* here, I don't see *coffee* here—or *canned* milk either. You'll have to tell your mother to do better than that, young man. Now I want to hear a different story tomorrow morning, do you hear me, Stanislaus?" looking at me through her glasses with those eyes were hard as my Lenilenape arrowheads.

With everybody looking around to stare at me, I mumbled that I did, ducking my head in my hands so they wouldn't see my face which I knew was burning something awful. I felt it burn even more when Mrs. Feek marched over to the yellow school bus hanging on the wall and turned my picture down in the window so you couldn't see me anymore.

When I got home and my mother asked me like she usually did what I learned in school that day, I didn't mention a word to her about eating a balanced diet everyday, knowing the good it would do and knowing she had enough troubles as it was. But I worried all of that night what I would say next morning when it came my turn, and when I finally drifted off to sleep I dreamed all night of all the colored pictures of things to eat on Mrs. Feek's chart so that when I woke up my guts were churning, my dreaming made me so hungry I could hardly wait to get down to the table even though it wasn't no balanced diet I could smell my mother was cooking, nothing but another pot of corn meal mush.

I walked slow behind my brothers to school and it wasn't just from my relief shoes hurting but because I was still worrying what was I going to say when Mrs. Feek asked me what I et that morning. The more I chewed it over and chewed it over and the closer we got to Camp Meeting Walk, the more the answer came to me, and even though I knew I might get struck dead, still and all when it came my turn and Mrs. Feek asked me what I et I crossed all my fingers and clinched my hands between my legs and with my heart pounding up in my throat so I could barely talk, I rattled off to her all that was up on the chart, "Ora ngejuiceWheatenaandmilkwholewheat-toastandeggsandbacon-andaglassamilk," talking real fast before I lost my nerve.

Mrs. Feek gave a little froze smile and turning to the others shrilled out, "Now, class, isn't that a much more *wholesome* breakfast than what Stanislaus ate yesterday?" And the class answered, *"Yes, Mrs. Feek!"* like they were all one voice. Then Mrs. Feek gave her tiny smile again like it hurt her face and marched over to the yellow school bus hanging on the wall and turned my picture, that was really the red-haired little boy and not me at all, back up in the window. When she did I even felt myself grinning like the red-haired boy I felt so relieved I was back on the bus and felt even more relieved I'd gotten away with it and was able to hold my head up when the others, along with the teacher, turned and smiled at me like they were giving me some kind of reward for having learned my first school lesson in lying.

Lucky days were when Miss Jickers let salesmen come to the school to give away their free samples. One day a man all dressed up in a business suit and soft hat and wearing rimless glasses like Father Mack came during recess to give out free samples of little boxes of Wheatena like was on the chart Mrs. Feek said was a balanced diet. No matter how much Miss Jickers tried to shoulder her way in and bust it up, the bigger boys and girls in the front playground crowded around him so eager, especially those in pillow ticking clothes, their arms clawing out like they were afraid they weren't going to get any, the salesman looked scared and instead of handing them out one at a time like he did already with us littler kids in back, he started throwing them up in the air. The big kids just about trampled all over each other trying to snatch up as many of the little blue and orange boxes as they could, while Miss Jickers went shoving her shoulders around, her face red as an inner tube, trying to make them behave. And the salesman, now he'd thrown away all his samples out of his bag, grabbed the back of his hat and made a beeline for his car.

Frank and Buster got so many boxes, and between them and what me and Slap got, it made up almost what would be a couple big boxes of Wheatena that my mother cooked up the next morning. It was a nice change from all the wormy oatmeal and corn meal mush, and I only had to tell half a lie when Mrs. Feek asked me that day what I had for breakfast, I could say Wheatena. She gave her little smile, all pleased, saying, like she was talking on the radio, "That's a good, nutritious whole wheat cereal—You should eat Wheatena every morning, Stanislaus, all of you should." But I knew as soon as the free samples were gone that would be the end of it, since relief never yet gave out no boxes of Wheatena.

The next salesman came around was giving out little itty-bitty red and yellow tubes of Ipana toothpaste but this time Miss Jickers passed them out herself, saying she wasn't going to have the carryings on happened last time with the Wheatena, and you can be sure not even the biggest Swamp Rat would try anything with her. But since it wasn't nothing to eat and since like at our house most of the kids didn't own a toothbrush, hardly anybody was too excited about the Ipana toothpaste, even though they took their free sample like they took anything was given out for free.

I was glad my brothers all took theirs even though they never washed their teeth half the time, and I didn't care if my mother and father said salt or baking soda was better'n toothpaste to wash your teeth with, I was sorry when our little sample tubes of Ipana ran out and I had to go back to rubbing salt on my teeth, the Ipana was so sweet like candy in my mouth, I squeezed and squeezed the last of the tubes to get the very last speck out of it, that toothpaste tasted so sweet to me.

The county nurse came to the school once a month. The first time she showed up, dressed in her dark blue uniform and carrying a big black leather bag Margaret whispered to me was full of needles to stick me with, she lined us up against the windows to catch the better light and like Mrs. Feek did every morning, she inspected our fingernails and took a gander inside of our mouths. Only she did more'n that. She checked our ears and checked our scalps and pushed our necks back to see if they were dirty. Her face, with eyebrows thick and black as her bag, looked like it didn't have no blood in it, and like Mrs. Feek and Miss Jickers she was another one looked like her face'd break if she so much as smiled even ever so little. Like all the teachers in the school, she didn't have on no makeup and her hair that was the color of her eyebrows was pulled back tighter even than Miss Jickers' was.

Me and Margaret was, as usual, at the end of the line and me and her and the rest of us all stood peeping over each other's shoulder, trying to see what the county nurse was doing while we waited for our turn. Mrs. Feek, hugging a clipboard to her chest, was standing beside the nurse. Those with dirty fingernails, mostly boys like Walter Snarp that the nurse said had the dirtiest ears she ever saw, which meant I guess she ain't seen Earl Jr.'s yet, were sent to the sink in the closet with a brush to scrub them. There was one of the girls in a pillow ticking dress named Eleanor the nurse told everybody right outloud she had a ring around her neck, like she wanted to shame her so she'd never have a ring around her neck again.

Sometimes after running her fingers through somebody's head the nurse would mutter something out the side of her mouth to Mrs. Feek and Mrs. Feek would click her tongue and scribble it down on her clipboard. I was the last in line and when it came my turn my heart was drumming to beat the band, and when the nurse lifted my hands to look at my nails then dropped them without a word I figured they were all right and when she pulled my head around and grabbed my ears and took a peep in them and still didn't say nothing I figured they were all right too. But when she told me to open my mouth and she gaped inside it, she shook her head, saying in her loud high voice, "Just look at all these cavities, Mrs. Feek, he sure must have some sweet tooth!" talking over my head like I wasn't even there. Mrs. Feek clucked her tongue again and scratched something down on her clipboard, the nurse saying to the rest of them already sitting at their tables, "I've never seen so many cavities, you boys and girls shouldn't eat so much candy if you want to keep your teeth," and Mrs. Feek says to us, "Do you all hear what the nurse says?" and me and everybody went, "Yes, Mrs. Feek!" even though I couldn't imagine never wanting something sweet to eat. But the nurse went on and on about how bad candy was for our teeth, ending up saying, "I'm sure, Mrs. Feek, you've told them to use their toothbrush twice a day and to use a good toothpaste like Ipana?" Mrs. Feek said, "Indeed I have." And the nurse said, "Well, let us hope they listen to their teacher," then she closed her lips tight across her face and twisted my head around again to the light and while the whole class watched, her fingers that were like icicles went slithering through my hair, stopped once, twice, then stopped again as I heard her click her tongue like Mrs. Feek and give a deep sigh, saying, "Another one." I looked up from under my eyebrows in time to catch Mrs. Feek's eyes as she nodded sharp and scratched another mark on her clipboard, her jaw jutting out like the nurse just blamed her for something wasn't her fault. The nurse pushed me away and Mrs. Feek told me to take my seat. I slunk to my chair and didn't dare look around, seeing that everybody probably knew now what a sneak I was always sneaking sugar and eating candy every chance I got that the nurse said made my teeth so rotten. I couldn't look especially at Margaret that I knew was staring at me, just waiting her chance to hiss something mean, and when she saw Mrs. Feek and the nurse with their heads together going over Mrs. Feek's clipboard, she leaned her curls in my face, whispering, "You eat so much sugar but it ain't done nuthin to make you sweet," I just pretended like I was deaf'n dumb.

When the schoolbell rang for dismissal, Mrs. Feek was handing out envelopes at the door to a couple of us to take home to our mothers, mainly those in relief clothes, so I got one. Margaret did too, even though she wasn't in relief clothes, her cheeks turning pinker than her eyes as Mrs. Feek handed it to her. She stuck it quick in her lunch kettle like she didn't want anybody to see it even though everybody did.

All the way home I was wishing I could open the envelope to see what Mrs. Feek wrote inside, wondering was it about my rotten teeth, I even held it up in the sun but that didn't do no good. When my mother, with a look of worry, tore open the envelope and read the paper inside, her jaw dropped, then she got an irritated look in her eyes and asked me, "Who do you set next to in school?" When I told her, she said, "Does she have long hair?" I said she had curls like Shirley Temple and she said, "Well, don't you be letting her get them curls near you again," which I knew would be hard to do with Margaret, her curls were so long and she was always swinging them at me when I was least expecting it.

"Don't get too close to Earl Snarp's head neither," she warned me, and I said I wouldn't, even though I knew our heads bumped sometimes when we were sitting side by side in the clearing reading the comic books he stole from under his father's mattress.

Kneeling between her knees on the kitchen floor, my head lay in her lap as she sat by the window, like the nurse at school, to catch the better light—But her fingers running over my skull were warm and careful, not icy and jabby like the nurse's were. When she found something she'd go, "Ha!" then she'd give a sharp tug at one of my hairs as she slid a nit all the way up it and caught it between her fingernails. Or she hollered out, "Gotcha!" as she dug her fingernail into my scalp and pried another louse loose, showing it to me with a big grin like she'd just found a dollar.

The nits were like itty-bitty seeds that shined I could hardly see on the tip of her nail when she showed me one, and a cootie was like a tiny smudge of brown scab that wriggled. Her grin and her eyes'd get bigger when she cracked a nit or louse between her thumb nails, sometimes holding it close to my ear so I could hear the pop. "Ja hear that?" she'd say, "Ja hear it?" And if it was a cootie and squirted a speck of blood she'd show me that too, saying, "It must've just et—Well, that was its last supper...."

Then her fingers'd move through my hair again like she couldn't wait to find another, and my eyes were half closed as I laid against her knees, I was so dreamy and content, wondering did all girls with long curls have cooties? wondering did Shirley Temple have them? breathing in the smell of my mother that was like the peaches when they were ripening in the tree outside the kitchen door....

All of us that had notes sent home had our faces turned down in the school bus windows next morning, which was just about all us kids on relief, except for one or two others, like

Margaret, that was madder'n a hornet because her picture never been turned down in the school bus before. It got her to stop swinging her curls in my face, though, because while Mrs. Feek was busy turning her picture down Margaret hissed at me, keeping her distance across the table, "It was you I got the cooties from in the first place!" I wanted to say if that was so how come my brothers Slap and Danny that I slept with every single night and was always bumping heads with didn't have them, if it was me gave her her cooties? But I knew it'd be just a waste of breath trying to tell that Margaret anything, she'd never believe me and would just be ready with another one of her smart-alecky answers, so I just kept my mouth shut.

Whenever me or anybody else in the class said "me pencil" or "me crayon," Mrs. Feek corrected us, saying, "Say *my* pencil, *my* crayon," even though I couldn't see what was the difference, it all meant the same. If you said "et" she said "ate." If you said "ain't" she said, "Ain't ain't in the dictionary." If you said "erl" she said "oil," if you said "keller" she said "color," and on and on. She was always correcting us and it was hard to remember what was the right way and what was the wrong way to talk because by the time I got to school next day I'd already forgotten all she said the day before about how to say things because of talking the way we always talked at home, and she'd start correcting me all over again—The same as when she caught me picking my nose she'd say, like my mother always said, if I didn't stop picking my nose I'd have a nose bigger'n I already had, then I'd be sorry. But no matter how many times both my mother and Mrs. Feek told me to stop it, I couldn't and would sneak picking my nose on the sly, it was such a bad habit with me, the same as eating the paste in my paste pot that was so sweet and tasted like cream of wheat, me and Walter Snarp and a couple others sneaking it even after Mrs. Feek hollered at us not to eat it, our insides would stick together, I couldn't help myself, it tasted so good.

Some days at school I don't know what came over me, I couldn't stop myself from telling stories, just talking and talking, I'd get on Mrs. Feek's nerves. And one day at afternoon recess when she was trying to explain how we were going to play Crack-the-Whip where if you were on the tail-end you could take a fall and really get some of Mr. Floud's cinders stuck in your kneecaps, she told me in no uncertain terms to stop my whispering to Walter Snarp, she said I was only filling his head with a lot of nonsense that was nothing but lies anyway. I don't know what made me say it or where I got the nerve to, but before I knew what was happening I heard myself answering back, "They're not lies!" because I didn't think I was lying, my stories were all so true, they really were true to me.

There was an awful silence as everybody stopped and gaped at me because nobody ever sassed Mrs. Feek back before. I wasn't meaning to sass her back but I guess that's what it sounded like because the next thing I knew, Mrs. Feek was gaping at me with her mouth opening and shutting like a minniegudgeon out of water, and started hollering, "Who do you think you're talking to, young man? Just who do you think?"

She looked at me so hard and long with her hard dark eyes, and with everybody else staring at me, it got me so rattled it made me bust out crying right in front of them all. I don't know why but all of a sudden I started blubbering, "I'm sorry! I'm sorry!" over and over like I did something awful bad, something even worse'n sassing her back, like I was crying for a whole lot of things I wasn't to blame for, like being on relief and wearing a pillow ticking suit and wearing shoes that pinched and being too tall and not having blond curls and not smiling all the time, like that was all something to say I was sorry for even if they weren't my fault, she was always giving me looks like they were.

"Well, from here on out you just better watch your tongue, my boy," she warned, "Because if you don't Miss Jickers'll watch it for you!" Then with a flick of her eyes she turned her back on me and went on telling the others what Crack-the-Whip was. I got a shiver in my belly at the mere mention of Miss Jickers' name while all the other kids kept on staring at me like I did something worse'n murder, including Margaret that had a grin on her kisser like she was glad I got hollered at and made a fool of myself blubbering like a big baby.

I hung my head and didn't dare look up at anybody for the rest of the afternoon, and didn't dare tell anybody any stories or nothing in school, not even Walter Snarp, for a long time after that.

The days were getting really colder now, so cold my big brothers and the Beezley boys went less and less down the river or back in the woods after school. But I still followed Earl Jr. back to the clearing where he taught me how to bird whistle. I practiced my bird whistling so much around the house once I knew how to do it real good, like when I first learned to whistle, I was driving everybody nuts, including my mother who said I could only whistle outside from now on.

On the way to the clearing we'd stop at certain trees and Earl Jr.'d shimmy up them for the last of the wild apples or pears, and now the persimmons were ripe and starting to fall on the ground after the first frost, we stuffed ourselves on them too, and they had in them the taste to me of what the autumn was.

The Indian grass was beginning to turn yellow and the ground was too cold for me to sit on, so I just squatted and practiced my whistling while Earl Jr., that the ground was never too cold for, laid down on his back and slipped out of his pocket another of the comic books he stole from out of his father's drawer, Joe Palooka with Little Orphan Annie and her dog Sandy this time, doing things, like the Alley Oop and Blondie and Dagwood, you never ever saw them do in their Sunday comic strip.

We smoked the Bugler cigarettes he snitched from his father while we read the book and after we looked at it a couple times and after Earl Jr. flipped the edges of the pages so he could see Joe Palooka and Little Orphan Annie doing that word Earl Jr. said all the time but I knew I must never never say, not even to spell out, he asked me did I want to dance for him?

I didn't want to take off my clothes at first because it was so chilly but he gave me one of those looks I couldn't say no to, so I took everything off, including my medal of the Virgin Mary that my mother put around my neck my first day of school so the Mother of God would watch over me in a proddisin school, that Earl Jr. jeered at, saying I might just as well be wearing a chicken's a-s-s around my neck for all the good it would do. But I didn't say anything, knowing he was a heathen that was never baptised and never went to church and was sure to go to hell, specially saying the things he said and making fun of God and making fun of me for going to church and going to Sunday school.

Even though I was shivering at first, when I really started getting into it, shaking my hips the way I saw him do and whistling instead of singing to show off to him how good I was getting at it, but mostly just swirling and swirling around whistling "The Dipsy Doodle" while he watched me, sitting up now with his head cocked to one side and that lopsided grin on his face, I got warmer and warmer and soon wasn't bothered at all by the chill in the air. I was so glad to be dancing, and dancing for him, and danced around the edges of the trees and danced back, then danced all around the edges again—All of a sudden I gave a start, thinking I saw two eyes way back in the bushes that weren't as thick now as they used to be in the summer. I wanted to jump for my clothes but I kept right on dancing, wondering could it be Charley, he must've found out our hiding place like he found out everything else, and I got in even more of a panic thinking he might write about me dancing bare in the woods in the *County Seat Weekly*. Even so, if it had to be anybody, I was hoping it was him and not one of those Swamp Rats, and so long as he didn't try to come any closer I decided not to say anything to Earl Jr., knowing how much he liked to make fun of Charley, aping his being crippled and the way he walked and throwing rocks at him on the sneak every chance he got.

So what I did was I turned my back so whoever it was would only see my hiney and I danced faster and faster, whistling my brains out whistling "The Dipsy Doodle" to keep Earl Jr.'s attention so he wouldn't spot those eyes that might be Charley's—But he must've known something was up from the look on my face, or could smell there was somebody close by because his head shot up like the Beezley's Blackie sniffing the air. Whoever it was watching must've seen him do it and must've ducked out of sight because Earl Jr., like Lenny the Indian back at his shack that time, after sniffing and sniffing and looking and looking, looked like he didn't see anything and turned around to watch me dancing again.

I would've wanted to dance all the harder to keep him watching til whoever it was got away, and would've wanted to dance all the harder too knowing there wasn't much longer when we would be able to come back here in the woods, it'd really be too cold, and like Earl Jr. said, with all the leaves gone it wouldn't be so hid anymore, it wasn't even so hid right now. But I made a run for my clothes and when he gave me a look of surprise, I said, "It's too chilly," pulling my pants on fast. Next he gave me a suspicious look since he would have to be blind not to see I was all hot and sweaty I been dancing so hard.

My father found out the old furnace in the cellar was so rusted from years of the swamp water seeping in, it was pretty much shot and wouldn't be any good to heat the place. Mrs. Scadder the landlady told him he'd have to fix it himself or do without, the rent he paid—Or more often than not, the rent he couldn't pay. He told my mother it was just as well, they could never buy even the quarter ton of coal to keep it going anyhow, a quarter ton being the least amount you could buy from Mr. Carey the iceman who sold coal in the winter. When my mother asked what was we going to do for heat, that worried look coming full into her eyes that always seemed to be lurking somewhere not far behind them, my father said they still had time yet, something'd turn up. When he said that, I could see that other look come into her eyes, like she wished she was anywhere but here, wishing probably more'n anything she was across the river with her mother.

But just like my father said, not long after that Mr. Beezley heard of an old coal stove somebody was trying to get rid of and told my father it was his for the hauling away. So one day when he was working on the dump truck for relief he had the others on the truck help him haul the stove back to our house where over the next couple days he fixed it and cleaned it, brushing off all the rust inside and out with a wire brush. Then, as luck would have it, he found some old stove pipe here and there and cleaned it and patched it too and set the stove up in the dining room so it could throw heat in the kitchen and parlor and some of it could go up the stairs into the bedrooms. He got some stove black from Gottlieb's must've been on the shelf he said since before the Revolutionary War, the bottle was so dusty. He painted the stove til it was all shiny and black and when he was done my mother looked easier in her eyes, with one less thing to worry about.

Him and my older brothers went and cut down dead trees in the woods and out in the swamp back of the house and dragged them into the yard and sawed them up, stacking them under the shed where the peeps used to be. Soon they cut so much of it there wasn't any room left under the house, so they started stacking it by the back door, Sam Beezley lending my father an old tarpaulin to throw over it against the weather. Gottlieb's sold pea coal by the bag and whenever my father had an extra thirty-five cents, which was hardly ever, he'd bring home a bag over his shoulder to save on the wood that he said the stove et as fast as us kids et everything in sight.

Now with nothing from the garden and what my mother canned over the summer all going pretty quick, and the hens hardly laying and the frogs and catfish that Earl Jr. said were all froze asleep down in the bottom of the swamp and the river, my father depended more and more on relief. Only there wasn't all that much work for him to do on it, except for the dump truck once in a while, since the ground was so froze now they couldn't work no more on the WPA making the road through the swamp. And since what you got depended on how much you worked and how much they had to give out, which wasn't a lot most of the time anyhow, there wasn't all that much to eat coming into the house. Some nights we'd go to bed with our bellies growling. Mrs. Beezley sent over what she could, sending pans and pots of things with Sister, telling her to say she just happened to make extra and thought we'd like it, saying it that way so my mother'd feel better about taking it. We owed so much to Bill the breadman and to the Supplee milkman they stopped coming around long ago. And when he really had to, my father went to talk to the Gottliebs and because, as my mother said, despite Sadie Gottlieb's sharp tongue and temper she had a heart as big as she was, my father got things on the eye again, especially coal oil for the cookstove and oil lamps, that I knew I better say oil now since Mrs. Feek didn't like me saying erl no more and shamed me in front of everybody when I slipped and did.

I was glad when she quit asking us what we et, I mean, ate for breakfast, it was getting so I was just about throwing up the corn meal mush or the gluey oatmeal I had that morning, it was making me so nervous to keep on lying.

Christmas Eve afternoon my father yanked his hatchet out of the backsteps for the second time that day and we went off into the woods with him to cut down a pine tree because there wasn't no money to buy one of the trees the Gottliebs were selling out front of their store. Since he said he didn't like killing anything on Christmas day, he'd killed two of the roosters a little earlier so my mother'd have them to roast next day for our Christmas dinner.

We went off to a sandy place Frank and Buster knew of not far from Goldies pond and the other side of Earl Jr.'s clearing where there were a lot of big and little pine trees growing. My father picked one out he said had a nice shape and as usual insisting on doing everything himself, started chopping. After he been chopping away for awhile Frank began begging so hard to let him have a few whacks my father, despite you could see in his eye he didn't think Frank could do a good a job as him, handed him the hatchet anyway and when he saw Frank was doing all

MICHAEL RUMAKER

right he let him cut it down the rest of the way.

Instead of using bricks like he did in South Philly where there wasn't no dirt, my father shoveled dirt from the backyard into one of my mother's old scrub buckets and stuck the tree in that and put it in a corner of the parlor where it didn't even reach to the ceiling. He draped an old torn sheet my mother gave him to drape around the bucket and spread it out underneath so Frank, despite the juice was still off, could set up the electric train he won in the Ralston contest a way, way back. Then he let us all help put on the balls, telling us to be real careful since there weren't too many left, letting Danny and Kate hang them on the lowest branches, then letting them put under the branches inside the railroad tracks the little cardboard houses and the church with snow sparkling like sugar on the rooves. But like before, he hung most of the tinsel himself, saying the rest of us hung it too sloppy to suit him. Buster, for a joke, said, "We gonna hang the lights, Pop?" My father gave him a look and said, "I'll lights you," looking at him like he was crazy, the juice was still turned off and been turned off so long I was forgetting what it was like to have it on, I was even forgetting what listening to the radio was like. Frank and Buster busted out laughing, seeing my father's face, because they knew it was Christmas and he wasn't drinking and they could get away with it. Slap wanted to know why couldn't we put candles on the tree like in olden times if we didn't have no electric lights and my mother hearing him as she stood in the doorway taking a minute from cooking supper to watch, gave a shudder, saying, "Not on yer life, that's all we need fer Christmas is fer the house to ketch on fire."

Then, despite Danny whining, he was so jealous he didn't get to do it again this year, my father handed Kate the tinfoil star that was Grandmom and Grandpop Lithwack's and lifted her up squealing, her legs kicking, to stick it on top of the tree, my mother watching from the doorway with her hands folded under her apron saying, "Despite it don't have no lights, it's still a pretty tree and makes the house smell so nice."

The two older ones were left to mind us that night, my mother warning them to be careful of the oil lamps, while her and my father went off with the Beezleys in Mr. Beezley's old LaSalle, that for a change was running that week. When Slap asked where was they going? they made a big secret of it and after they were out the door Buster spilled the beans they were going to the county seat to bring us home toys from charity. I asked what charity was and he called me a dumbie and said charity was when you don't have no money they give you things for nothing. I said, like relief? and he said, no, not like relief, dumbie, you don't have to work your a-s-s off for it, and Kate said wasn't Kriss Kringle bringing the toys? Buster said there ain't no Kriss Kringle and Kate started to cry til Slap goes and starts petting her.

Then Frank and Buster did a slapstick for us like the Three Stooges, like they always did when they had to mind us, and we all laughed so hard they did it three times before Frank took us younger ones out to the kitchen and washed our necks and ears at the pump and took us up to bed.

When we came down in the morning under the tree was a rag doll for Kate looked like somebody made it by hand, it was so lumpy—I was thinking, that's all Kate needs is one more doll, but at least this one had all its arms and legs and eyes. Then there was a play car you sat in and pushed the pedals you could see was old and been painted two-tone brown and tan to look like new, but the rubber on the wheels was all so worn it wobbled. There was a wagon too, all rusty and wasn't painted and I could just barely read RADIO EXPRESS on its sides.

My mother said that the wagon, as soon as our father painted it, was for us three younger ones and the play car was for me and Danny to share. But my legs were so long now I couldn't fit in behind the wheel so Danny got to ride it all by himself, saying he was glad to have it all to himself anyway, and drove it around the parlor so fast he drove everybody nuts and my mother told him to stop it and go play with it outside before he wrecked the whole house. By the end of the day one of the pedals was busted and no matter how hard he tried, my father couldn't fix it and Danny cried and cried but there was nothing nobody could say or do to quiet him, not even my mother nor Slap, so that was the end of that.

There was a football you could see was old and nicked my father said the three oldest were to share and play catch with, but they only got to throw it around a few times out in the yard before it began to leak air. My father said, "Don'tchou worry, I'll put a patch on it and it'll be like new," but it never was, it was always springing a new leak somewhere else.

The rest of the presents were more of the long brown stockings and clothes made out of pillow ticking from relief that Frank and Buster groaned at when they saw them, and I did too, only I groaned inside so nobody could hear me. And sitting there under the tree like last Christmas and looking out of place, she was so new and shiny and clean, was Kate's Shirley Temple doll my mother still kept wrapped in the tissue in its box all year long and on this day only let Kate hold once, warning her not to wrinkle the dress or get it dirty, before she took it from her and put it back in the box, no matter how much Kate rolled up her lower lip in a pout because she wanted to keep on holding it. This year I never even got a chance to sneak a touch of it before my mother whisked it back upstairs and put it back in her closet where she said it would be safe, like it was her doll,

my father kidded her, instead of Kate's. But all she said was
never you mind and got that same look in her eye I saw her have
when she first put the doll away in their bedroom closet on
Mifflin Street, as if it was somehow a part of herself she wanted
to keep, as if she was thinking she wanted to keep something
nice and clean and new despite everything else.

Later that morning after church, that was all decorated in
ropes of laurel and pine boughs hanging from the beams and the
altar boys and father Mack all in red cassocks, Ronnie came
over to take me back to his house to show me his tree. No matter how much my mother asked him to, he wouldn't come in but
stood out on the front porch in a new velvet suit the color of
plums he must've got for Christmas because I never saw it on
him before. As we went down the steps I caught Buster standing
in the window screwing up his face and wiggling his fingers in
his ears at us behind our backs, which I knew was only the
green-eyed monster and didn't pay no attention to it.

The Mahoney's tree looked like they bought it at Gottlieb's it
was six times bigger'n ours and all covered with angel hair and
nothing but red lights and made ours look the way our house
looked that first time when I came back from Ronnie's playroom, so shabby and poor. You could hardly get in their parlor—I mean the living room—it was so stuffed with new toys
for Ronnie—I wondered where they was going to put all those
new toys, the playroom upstairs was so jammed already. He
gave me a present turned out to be one of those new-style coloring books from the five and tenny all you had to do was brush
water on the picture and the color comes out, but only in pink or
green no matter what the picture was, any moron could do it. I
felt funny not having no present for him, especially since his
Grandmom and Grandpop O'Shea were down from Camden and
looking at me with big grins because Mrs. Mahoney told them I

was her Ronnie's best boyfriend. Even though it was still only morning his grandpop's face was red and his eyes were shining just the way my father's did when he was drinking last Christmas in South Philly and I was so glad he wasn't today.

Mr. Mahoney looked a little merry himself and everytime he looked at me with a grin, I looked away, like I was afraid he might see in my eyes the dreams I been having about him.

The rest of the day I went around with my brothers to see people's Christmas trees. We went to the Beezleys first where Brother and Sparky bragged they bought theirs, the biggest one there, they said, from Gottlieb's, although I saw the Mahoney's was even bigger. They couldn't wait to show my brothers what they called the electric football game they got that was really run by batteries not electric. My brothers eyes bugged out, seeing it, I could see the way they were gaping at all the other things the Beezley boys got their mouths were practically watering.

Blackie, the only day of the year he was allowed in the house, was snoozing under the tree with a big red bow Sister'd tied around his neck. Sister herself was wearing her main Christmas present to show it off to us, that was a new plaid winter coat with one of the new Sonja Henie ice skating caps tied under the chin, wearing the whole getup even though it was so hot in the house you could hardly breathe.

She handed around a box of chocolates but said for us to take only one apiece, so's not to spoil our dinner. Then Mrs. Beezley gave us all something, more long stockings, for my brothers to wear with their knickers and me and Danny to wear with our short pants. But at least they were store-bought stockings and not from relief, they had colors and a design on them and weren't just plain brown. And for Kate there was a little blue dress with bows Sister made all by herself, "To match 'er eyes," that she was going to take over our house later on when they all came to see our tree, that I could see wouldn't be much to see compared to theirs.

Frank said thank you to Mrs. Beezley for the stockings and gave us a sidelong look that told us to do the same. I thanked her along with the rest, even though I would've rather had a picture book or a set of water colors than the stockings.

We went to other houses to see the trees, other kids Frank and Buster knew from school, some of them on relief with made over toys like we got. And every place we went, except those were on relief, they gave us chocolates or hard candy and I was in seventh heaven.

We went right on past the Snarp's house, though. Frank and Buster started joking the Snarps must have nothing but an old corn stalk for a tree with nothing under it but Earl Snarp Sr., dead drunk. Then Frank said Buster shouldn't talk like that, seeing's Earl Jr.'s best pal was here, rolling his eyes my way. Buster said in a big exaggerated way, "Oh, *excuse me!* Maybe we should *dump* him off here so's he can spend the rest of the day with his boyfriend—This is the dump, ain't it?" and that set them both off again, grabbing each other they were laughing so hard.

The streets by this time were full of other kids going from door to door to see people's trees, and Buster, always the nerviest, except when it came to eating the chickens my father killed, even marched us right up to houses of people we didn't even know, mainly houses the people didn't look like they were on relief, doing it more I think to get the chocolates than to see their trees. We went to so many houses that soon I was so full of candy I was afraid I was going to throw up and when we came home for dinner we were all so full of chocolates and hard candy and Christmas cakes and cookies and egg nog, hardly any of us ate anything, except Slap that could eat for three anytime, anywhere, my mother always said. And even though she complained we shouldn't've ate so many sweets, it was a good thing we weren't hungry, seeing the scrawny little roosters she put on the table that seemed to've shrunk even more in the oven. But since it was Christmas she didn't holler at us like she would've done any other time, she didn't even holler at my father like she always did when he was cutting up the chicken and he snipped off the tail, grinning and holding it up, saying, "Anybody hungry for the Pope's nose?" Because it was Christmas and I suspect too because he still wasn't drinking, and her cheeks were so red from the heat in the kitchen, in spite of everything, she looked almost happy, I crossed all my fingers, hoping she was.

The morning Mrs. Feek announced there'd be tapdancing lessons after school for the first and second grades, I didn't remember her saying it was for the girls only. Or if she did say it I was so excited at the word "tapdancing" I didn't hear anything else. I could hardly sit still for the rest of the day and couldn't wait for Miss Jickers to ring the bell to send everybody home. When she did, and after the others left, Mrs. Feek, and Miss Riggs, that'd come in from the second grade, began shoving tables and chairs against the wall to make a space at the front of the room, and I stayed behind along with just about every girl in both classes. I was hoping Ronnie would stay too but he wasn't there, I guess because, like he told me umpteen times already, he was taking private tapdance lessons at Ruby Estelle LaPorte's Tapdancing Academy over at the county seat on Saturday mornings at fifty cents per lesson. He said Ruby Estelle LaPorte, that just that minute came sailing in the door, wasn't her real name, her real name was Esther Joops, but she called herself Ruby Estelle LaPorte because it sounded more like a movie star's name, Ruby for Ruby Keeler and Estelle that meant star in

Eyetalian and LaPorte that was French and sounded more fancy'n Joops.

The girls, all shy and nervous, stood around in the cleared out front of the room or along the walls gawking at Ruby Estelle LaPorte, a few of them, like Virginia that sat next to Gerald at the first table, had tap shoes on they brought from home, but most of them were wearing just their regular school shoes, and not one of the girls was any of the ones on relief that I knew of. They stared at me, giggling behind their hands, and in their eyes I saw they were wondering what was I doing there. Practically all of them, whether they were blonde or not, had curls like Shirley Temple's, including of course Margaret that stood gawky and looking even taller at the tail-end of where the girls were standing like she was still at our table in the back, staring at me with her usual sneer like I was about to make a fool of myself again.

Mrs. Feek and Miss Riggs were busy making a big fuss over Ruby Estelle LaPorte but when Mrs. Feek spotted me, her eyebrows shot up and she marched right over and asked me why I was hanging around, why hadn't I gone home with the other boys? My heart started banging but I told her I wanted to learn to tapdance and a funny look came over her face followed by that little froze smile should've told me something was up. She went right off to Miss Riggs that had a face smooth as Sister Joseph Mary's, only she had hair you could see that was tied in a bun and she drove a brand-new Ford V-8. She was sitting at the piano that was an upright piano like at Grandmom O'Rourke's on Hoffman Street but was a lot more battered and not at all as shiny polished as Grandmom kept hers. She was going through books of music like she was getting ready to play for the tap-dancers, when Mrs. Feek leaned down and talked close to her ear in whispers, and when Miss Riggs heard what she said, she looked back over her shoulder at me. They both stared at me, then back at each other, the corners of Mrs. Feek's mouth pulled down now in a frown, Miss Riggs giving me a sorry little smile like she didn't know what to do. Then the two of them went over to Ruby Estelle LaPorte that was wearing enough makeup for a dozen movie stars, and that Ronnie said put on a show of all her dancing pupils from Lenape on the second floor of the Lenape Volunteer Firehouse once a year and was sure he would get a tapdance to do all by himself this year. Ruby Estelle LaPorte was sitting in Mrs. Feek's desk chair leaning down to tie on her tap shoes that had laces that was the brightest of red ribbons, as Mrs. Feek bent down and whispered in her ear like she did in Miss Riggs', while all the girls watched them bug-eyed.

My excitement that been building all day at learning to tap-dance like Shirley Temple was starting to take a nosedive as I began to see it looked like I made a mistake and that nobody wanted me there. At first I thought maybe it was because we were on relief and they didn't want nobody there was on relief, that maybe it cost money. Only I never heard Mrs. Feek say anything about that—But then I never heard her say it was for girls only either.

Ruby Estelle LaPorte had her shoes tied now and stood up brisk and quick, smoothing out the pleats of her tapdancing shorts that were like the ones I saw Ruby Keeler wearing in "Ready Willing and Able" that I saw with my brothers at the Lyric when we lived in South Philly. She took one look at me and gave her head a fast shake. Both teachers nodded just as quick like they would do anything to please her and Mrs. Feek came over with her smile like ice and said to me, "Why, this is only for girls, Stanislaus. Miss LaPorte said this isn't for boys. Didn't you hear me say distinctly this morning it was only for girls? Do you see any other boys here? Now you get on home before your mother begins to wonder where you are."

I stared down at the floor, wanting to ask her couldn't I stay just to watch, but when I looked up in her face to ask I saw her eyes were hard as ever and knew it was no use. The last thing I heard as Mrs. Feek prodded me out the door were the giggles of the girls.

Even though I didn't get to learn to tapdance, I did get to be a bluebird, all dressed up in crepe paper feathers and a head with a yellow cardboard beak. Margaret said I only got the part because I was the only one in the class could whistle, because I certainly couldn't sing, "Not," she said, "as good as I can."

It was a play about spring, for Parents Night. Most everybody was birds or flowers. Margaret was a hollyhock because she was so tall and could stand behind the shorter flowers. Walter Snarp said she was a hollyhock because the color of a hollyhock matched her eyes and she said if that was the case he should've been a skunk cabbage instead of the daffodil he was. Gerald, of course, was the sun, because of his bright blond hair Mrs. Feek said, "And his sunny smile that I wished you all had." She made him a big paper circle of gold to wear around his face that gave him a look like Sister Joseph Mary in church on Sunday. I sang "The Bluebird's Song" that went, "Hope you have a happy time in all your work and play," while Miss Riggs played it on the upright piano. Then I was supposed to flap my wings and whistle it.

We practiced for days and days and even though I was scared to death to sing in front of people I was so excited about it, despite Frank and Buster, when they heard me practicing my bluebird song to my mother in the kitchen, kept saying I was for the birds, and when my mother wasn't around would rub my hair real hard with their knuckles, asking me if I was molting yet, like our chickens did when they lost their feathers once a year.

The night of the show, I could hardly eat any supper I was so nervous and even though it was only a Wednesday and not a Saturday night, my mother scrubbed me extra hard in the washtub before we left the house. And even though it said Parents Night on the note I brought home, only my mother went with me, my father saying with a grin he'd stay home and mind the kids, even though it meant he'd have to suffer missing seeing me in the show. My mother shut the kitchen door and gave herself a wash and put on her Sunday best dress and shoes and made sure, weak as it was, to bring along the flashlight to help us see our way in the dark.

It was so funny being in the school at night with all the lights on and seeing grownups sitting in our little chairs, and seeing my mother there too—I was so jittery I was afraid I'd forget the words to my song. But when it came my turn and Mrs. Feek shoved me out in my paper feathers on the little stage Mr. Floud the janitor built special for the show, I sang the song all right, all the while watching Miss Riggs pounding away at the piano and keeping time with her head, and I flapped the crepe paper wings when I was supposed to. But wouldn't you know, I was so amazed I got through the whole song without a mistake, I forgot to whistle! I thought Miss Riggs'd gone crazy the way she kept trying to remind me by puckering her lips up at me with her eyes so big and thumping the piano so hard the hair in her bun came loose and fell down her neck. It was only when she played the song a second time, that she wasn't supposed to do because we never rehearsed it her playing it twice, that I caught on I was supposed to whistle. But by the time I puckered up, my lips were so dry from being ascared I couldn't've whistled if my life depended on it, which pleased Margaret no end, as she never let me forget for days afterwards. Besides, by that time Virginia'd already knocked me aside busting into her tapdance number, singing "I'm Li'l Robin Redbreast," even though she was so chubby Margaret said they should of had her sing "I'm a Big Fat Goose," and Mrs. Feek was hissing at me to get off of the stage.

On the way home I was wishing to myself I could go back and do my whole song all over again, putting in the whistling this time, but I knew that wasn't possible. I was hoping nobody, especially my mother, noticed my mistake but once we were past the houses in town and starting down Lenape Road she all of a sudden says, "Forgot to whistle, huh?"

I felt myself blush and was glad it was dark so she couldn't see. Ducking my head I stared down at the feeble beam of the flashlight that she was letting me carry and that made me feel so grownup, she was letting me carry it to shine what light there was.

"It ain't the end of the world," she said, and smoothed my hair like it was mussed. Then she said, "Gwan, whistle it for me."

And because it was just the two of us in the dark I was able to whistle the bluebird's song and for a minute it was like it used to be, when we were still living on Mifflin Street and I'd sing to her in the parlor while she was ironing.

When I was done she said, "You whistle now pretty good, did the teacher learn you that?" I said, "No, Earl Jr. did," and she said, "Well, you whistle real nice."

And all of a sudden I got tight in my throat and wanted to turn around and grab her, begging, *Let's go back! Let's go back and make it like it was before!* But she was saying, "Feel better now?" and I nodded because my throat was so tight I couldn't say anything but knew she could see I was nodding even if it was in the dark because it was like she saw everything.

At night now I could hear their voices again, like they were arguing in bed, like the night the roses I'd put in front of the statue of the Blessed Virgin in their room kept him awake. Their voices now, like they were then, whispery at first like they didn't want none of us to hear, my father coaxing at first, then my mother sounding like she was pleading with him, then my father complaining, his voice like last time growing so loud she begged him to shush, *"The kids'll hear!"* It always ended with him cursing and the springs groaning as he heaved himself over on the mattress.

The quiet that followed felt so dangerous, like the upstairs was all of a sudden so dangerous with something I didn't understand, as I lay there between Slap and Danny listening in the darkness for a long time after, not able to sleep no matter how hard I tried—Wondering what it was, was it him not having a job yet and not enough to eat in the house? Was it she wanted to go back to South Philly and he didn't?—At the thought of going back my heart gave a leap. Whatever it was, I doublecrossed my fingers and prayed to the Blessed Mother he wouldn't go back to his drinking, no matter what.

But she began to get moodier, her lips getting tighter again like they were in South Philly with him drinking and no money coming in. And just like then she began to sing less and less often around the house and had that across the river look in her eyes, like she was more and more with her mother. He became more sharp-tempered so you could never know which way he'd go, a look like he resented everything always on his face. And now whenever he killed a chicken for Sunday dinner, he hit it so hard in the neck with his hatchet it looked like he was trying to kill more'n just killing the chicken, so that after that when I saw him go for the hatchet stuck in the backstep and head out for the chicken run, like Buster, I beat it somewhere else, I wouldn't watch anymore.

Hidden under the dining room table one afternoon not long after they started arguing in bed again, I heard her tell Mrs. Beezley in a whisper from the parlor while she peeled the potatoes for supper, she was afraid of another mouth to feed, things as bad as they were. She dropped her voice even lower, so I really had to strain my ears to hear her say, "*He* wants to use them *things*," saying "he" in that way when either of them said it you knew exactly who they were talking about.

What "them *things*" were I didn't know but figured they must've been something pretty awful the way she said it. All of a sudden the comic books Earl Jr. snitched from under his father's bed for us to read in the clearing jumped up in front of my eyes and I wondered if "them *things*" was like what Dagwood caught Baby Dumpling blowing up like they were balloons but what was what he put on his dunkey when him and Blondie were in bed at night?

Mrs. Beezley kept clicking her tongue, saying how terrible it was, she knew what she meant. "But I ain't goin through that again, I make my Sam wear 'em." My mother with a catch in her throat said like she didn't hear what Mrs. Beezley been saying, "If I don't he gets mad at me and if I do as he wants, the priest'll get mad at me. I'm damned if I do and damned if I don't—And I'm so ascare't he'll start hittin the bottle again if I don't do like he wants."

Her voice trailed off and another peeled potato dropped in the pot of water with a plop while Mrs. Beezley kept on going tch, tch, like Joe Palooka in the funnies. Then I heard my mother sniffling, then I heard Mrs. Beezley's chair give a loud squeak as she pulled herself up out of it and come across the parlor floor in her heavy step, saying in a soft way, "Gwan, Nor', and cry—it's all right—Bette Davis always does in everyone of 'er pictures, she cries and it always makes her feel better—Gwan now, you jist go ahead and cry."

I could hear my mother sniffling louder now and I wanted in the worst way to rush right in and throw my arms around her and beg her not to cry, but that would've given me away and she'd of known I been listening in, which was the trouble with listening in. But there was no sense me thinking about it because I knew I never would've had the nerve to rush in anyway. Besides, from the quietening sounds Mrs. Beezley was making, it sounded like she had her arms around her already, and there wasn't no need for me or anybody else to be there, except maybe her mother, or her sister Nell, that Mrs. Beezley seemed right then to be both of them rolled into one.

Since Aunt Bridget was the only one in the family had a telephone because of Uncle Digby being in the funeral business, it was her called on the pay phone at Gottliebs. Mrs. Gottlieb sent Lenny the Lenilenape, that was working there that day, to tell my mother Aunt Bridget said Grandmom O'Rourke was sick and for her to come right away. When I saw him coming in our yard, I ran and hid under the porch, thinking he was finally coming after me for spying on his shack with Earl Jr., since everybody knows an Indian never forgets. But I could hear him through the floorboards talking to my mother and even though she was so upset when she heard the news, you could hear she was still embarrassed she didn't have a nickel to give Lenny for his walking all the way down to our house. She told him she'd make it up to him later but he just walked off the porch without saying nothing.

I was hoping and hoping she'd ask me to go to Philly with

her but she packed some extra things in a shopping bag and went up on the bus alone with the twenty-five cents she borrowed from Mrs. Beezley and was gone for three days.

I missed her so much it was like a stone was sitting right in my chest, and at school Mrs. Feek had to rap her pointer any number of times on her desk to get my attention. On the third morning she came home on the early bus and as I was rushing to get dressed to go downstairs to see her, I heard Slap, that'd run down ahead of me in only his underwear, bawling his eyes out from down in the parlor. By the time I got there, Slap was all red-eyed, and Frank and Buster were there, and my father, standing by the door, looking serious. My mother was sitting on the couch looking so tired and Slap was kneeling in front of her sniffling and she was holding his head in her hands. When she saw me come in she said, "Grandmom died," and that started Slap crying again. I didn't know what I should do, it didn't mean anything at first I was so glad she was home. "She died with the priest," she said, "And we was all around her bed."

I wanted to go and touch her, I wanted to be sure it was her and that she really was back.

Mr. Beezley lent my father his old LaSalle and even filled it up with gas from Gottlieb's pump and that night we all piled into it and went up to Camden and caught the Kaighns Avenue ferry to Philly. Going over on the ferry I was scared all over again just like my mother was, her lips were moving as she told her rosary inside of her pocketbook, the water was so choppy in the wintery wind. But I was so excited about going to Philly I wasn't half as afraid of drowning as I thought I'd be and said a prayer if we had to drown let it be on the way back, just so's I'd get a chance to see Philadelphia one last time. And when I was done praying I tried my hardest not to feel glad my grandmother'd died just so's I could walk down Mifflin Street again.

The wake lasted three days and three nights. There were long clay pipes and jars of Irish whiskey on the kitchen table for the men, while all the women crowded in the tiny parlor, that was lit by nothing but candles, saying the rosary around the casket and gossiping in low voices. Most of the furniture, except for the piano, been moved out of the parlor, and up where the couch used to be was nothing but wreaths and flowers and Grandmom O'Rourke laid out in a dark wooden coffin with white satin ruffles all around, just like in the photo Mrs. Snarp showed me of little Edward. The first thing my mother had us do when we got there was take off our caps and line us up and have us kneel two at a time on the little step beside the coffin to say a prayer. Kate got so terrified, right away she started bawling, and that got Danny going, so my mother had to pull the both of them away and squeeze them and tell them to shush, it was only their grandmother. Then me and Slap knelt down, Slap gaping and gaping with his mouth hitched up to one side like Grandmom said something to him he ain't quite heard. And even though his face was white as the satin ruffles in the lid of the casket, he wasn't crying, and when he blessed himself and started moving his lips saying a prayer like my mother said to, I did the same, craning my neck up to see inside.

What I saw was what looked like Grandmom only with her hair dyed red and with lipstick and face powder on her, "To make her look nice," my mother said when I asked her why in a whisper later on because she never dyed her hair or wore makeup before that I could remember. She looked like she was all painted up like my father's sister, Aunt Theresa, that he called a tramp, or like the tapdancing teacher, Ruby Estelle LaPorte, so I hardly recognized her at first. I guess Slap didn't neither the way he kept gaping and gaping, which is maybe why he didn't bust out crying like I thought he would. She looked like she was taking a nap, her head was resting on a satin pillow that was the same color as the gown she had on that was the same blue as the veils of the Virgin Mary. And my mother, to quiet down Danny and Kate, whispered to them that Grandmom was in heaven now, and Aunt Nell standing behind her whispered, yes, she was in heaven now, and all my other aunts jammed into the parlor for the rosary hummed yes, she was in heaven.

I still had my coat and leggings on and could hardly breathe, the air in the little parlor was so hot and heavy from all the candles and the pipe smoke from the kitchen and the too-sweet smell of all the flowers—There were so many flowers around her, even more'n was around the statue of the Virgin Mary on May day at Saint Theresa's church, and there was a candle in a glass burning over Grandmom's head, like the one hanging from the long gold chain over the altar at Saint Theresa's to show God was at home in his tabernacle, Sister Joseph Mary said, only this one was in a gold glass not a red one.

When it came time to decide who was going to sleep where, even though I wasn't nearly as scared coming over on the ferry this time because of knowing I was coming to Philly, I was shivering in my boots now, I was so afraid I might have to sleep at Aunt Maggie's and Uncle Ned's with my cousin Neddy Jr. I soon saw Neddy Jr. hadn't forgot how I wet his bed not once but twice because he turned and whispered to his mother so I could hear it real plain, he'd rather sleep with Ole Faithful'n sleep with me one more time. He begged Aunt Maggie to ask my mother to let Buster sleep with him since Buster and him were about the same age and would have more things like the Philadelphia Athaletics to talk about'n Neddy Jr. would have to talk about with me, that he never ever talked to anyhow that whole time I was there when my mother was in Saint Agnes hospital. Lucky for me, my mother said yes because Aunt Bridget piped up saying, "We got a extry bed in my Tom's room and he can sleep there." Neddy Jr. wisecracked out the corner of his mouth, "If she's smart she better have umpteen rubber sheets to put under him," and Aunt Maggie told him to shush, "That ain't no way to talk at your grandmother's wake." Hearing him say that, I'd liked to of died and was glad it was so dark in the parlor, my face must've been as red as the bunch of roses hanging over the lid of Grandmom's casket.

Now that Uncle Digby laid out Grandmom—for only half price Aunt Bridget bragged because Grandmom was family—she said he was off on another job somewhere up on Dickinson Street, he was just so busy that winter with more jobs'n he could handle with so many people dying left and right, so it was just me and her and Tom walking back to their place, while my mother and Aunt Nell and Aunt Molly took turns sitting up with Grandmom through the first night.

Because Uncle Digby was an undertaker, their house was even nicer'n Aunt Maggie's and since it was on the corner of 2nd and Daly it had a lot more windows and turned out to be a lot more lighty'n all my aunts' and uncles' houses that were dark as a cellar, being more towards the middle of their blocks. Like every one of their houses seemed to have its own particular smell, like Grandmom's house always with a smell of mothballs and sweet lavender, Aunt Bridget's smelled like tea leaves.

With Aunt Bridget's help I got my leggings off just in the nick of time and only wet my pants a teensy bit before I made it upstairs to their bathroom. It was so nice to pee in a real toilet again, so white and clean and lighty and not a green fly or a cobweb anywhere in sight, and sweetest of all, not none of that terrible smell. Another nice thing was, except for my crib, it was the first time I ever remembered sleeping in a separate bed all by myself. The only trouble was by now I was so used to sleeping between Slap and Danny, I couldn't get to sleep for a long time, and for another thing, even though I liked hearing the trolley cars rumbling by all night out on 2nd Street, I wasn't used to loud city noises no more—And worse'n that I kept seeing Grandmom's face that wasn't her face all painted in the coffin and her hair so red that wasn't her hair, her hair was like it was on fire behind my eyes, so what I did was I prayed to Our Mother in heaven I wouldn't wet the bed, saying so many Hail Marys over and over til finally I drifted off to sleep.

Because of all the whiskey around it put a scare in me, I was so afraid my father might get tempted, like I knew my mother was worried he might get tempted too because I saw her when she was kneeling in the parlor saying the rosary with her sisters, in the middle of a Hail Mary she'd look up all of a sudden and cock her head towards the kitchen, listening and looking like she wished she had X-ray eyes could see like Superman right through the kitchen wall to see if my father was drinking or not. So what I did was, I decided I would be her eyes for her, I wormed my way in between the legs of my uncles til I found a good spot under the kitchen sink where I could keep an eye on him. By this time, Uncle Jake, that was smoking one of the long claypipes more for a joke, was stuffing his handkerchief back in his hip pocket and, turning off the waterworks like he was turning off a spigot, he all of a sudden grinned at the others, saying, "Ja ever hear the one about the Jew at the Irishman's wake?"

Even though they all groaned like they heard it umpteen times before they said go on ahead tell it, Jake, you'll only tell it anyhow, and at the punchline they all laughed just as if they ain't never heard it before, but was trying not to laugh too loud, out of respect, my father grinning along with them but not with as big a grin as theirs. He wasn't as talkative or lively as he used to be around them and he wasn't glassy-eyed like they were, which I was so glad to see everytime I stared out at him from under the sink, keeping an eye on him.

But wouldn't you know that Uncle Jake, when he was pouring another round of shots, got to teasing him, and Uncle Ned did too, Uncle Jake saying, "One little one can't hurtcha, Stosh, one little one to toast a grand ole lady goodbye." Then the others started in, saying, "C'mon, Stosh, don't be such a ole stick in the mud."

I held my breath, double crossing all my fingers as I stuck my head out from under the sink, watching my father like a hawk, watching him grin sheepish and duck his head, mumbling, "What, d'ya want to git me in trouble with me old lady?" But I could see his adam's apple going a mile a minute and his thumb plucking nervous at his cigarette pocket.

"C'mon, Stosh, jist one li'l snort...." they persisted, and the more they persisted the more I wanted to jump out from under the sink and squeeze through all my uncles' legs and beg my father not to listen to them. And if he wouldn't, I knew what I would do, I would push through back to the parlor and get ahold of my mother and make her come out and stop him from drinking the whiskey. But I stayed right where I was because at the same time I knew I was too yellow and too scared of what my father would say or do if I did, he was getting so you could never tell what he was going to say or do, now him and my mother'd started arguing again in their bed at night.

I let out my breath and uncrossed all my fingers, I was so relieved when he just kept on grinning his sheepish grin and shook his head, like no matter how much they teased he wouldn't touch a drink. Even when Uncle Jake got his needle out, saying he was getting to be just like an old farmer he was living in the sticks too long, my father just went right on grinning. But I saw his gullet was still snapping up and down like he been thirsty so long he could just taste that whiskey so bad he was tasting it in his imagination going down his throat.

I don't know what happened between that time and the third night, I should've known it was too good to last. Because that last night of the wake when I squeezed my way out to the kitchen and hid myself under the kitchen sink again to be my mother's eyes, I felt like somebody booted me in the belly when I looked and saw his face was as red and his eyes as bright as my uncles' was.

I knew, even if I wasn't so yellow and crawled over to him and grabbed him by the pantleg and begged him to stop, it was too late now once he was started. My uncles' razzing must've worn him down, that's all there was to it. He was swapping stories with them and was just as lively and talky, I couldn't stand to watch it and wormed my way back into the dining room where I got in under the dining room table and hid myself behind the lace tablecloth hanging down all around, squeezing my legs up and pressing my head on my knees, glad at last to find a place to be by myself that was dark and nobody squeezing around you and stepping on you because when you are little big people don't see you and step on you. I shut my eyes, listening to my mother and my aunts droning soft and quiet from the parlor, "Hail Mary, full of grace, the Lord is with thee, Blessed art thou amongst women..." And when the prayer was done I lifted up my head and just before they started the next Hail Mary, I saw through the lace in the tablecloth my father making his way through the dining room, heading upstairs to go to the toilet, and saw that my mother, that was kneeling with her sisters in front of the coffin, saw him too because, like I said, these last three days her head been like a bird's, watching and listening.

Her lips stopped moving and she bit her underlip, her eyes going darker'n they already were from thinking about her mother laying dead in the casket—But seeing my father, there came a look in her eyes like she knew she couldn't do anything, knowing like I knew, once he started it was too late to stop him. And there was nothing she could do about it, she couldn't say nothing to him with all the people around and her being with her sisters in the middle of the rosary, she couldn't remind him that even though he took the pledge he'd gone back on his word, she didn't have to say anything anyway her eyes said it all.

Those whole three days I kept thinking what I wanted to see as much as seeing a movie again and walking in the streets of South Philly seeing the houses all made of brick and seeing trolley cars and horse and wagons—crazy as it sounds, I was even glad to see and even smell the horse manure on the cobblestones—was to see our old house on Mifflin Street. I kept looking and looking for a chance to sneak away but there was hardly a time when there wasn't somebody watching. Still and all, early next morning on the day of the funeral, it was easy because so many people were coming and going to take one last look at Grandmom and there were so many relatives crowded in the house, I looked to see if my mother or my father or any of my big brothers were looking and when I saw nobody was watching me, especially my father that was so red-eyed that morning from a hangover it looked like he wasn't seeing nothing, I snuck out the kitchen door and high-tailed it up the back alley and ran around as fast as I could to Mifflin Street so I could get a quick look at our old house and be back before anybody missed me.

My heart was racing as fast as my legs as I came tearing around the corner where the number 5 trolley turned, thinking at first I was on the wrong block, surprised that Mifflin Street and all the houses, like Grandmom O'Rourke's house, looked smaller'n I remembered. When I got to 126 I stood on the worn-down brick sidewalk in front, scrunching and wriggling my toes in my shoes, I was just so glad to feel that red brick under my feet again. And I stared and stared like the house was made of something sweet I couldn't get enough of as I tried to see into the windows, wondering who was living there now.

I stood there staring at every brick in the wall and at every step in the marble steps with the hollows worn in them from so many years of people tramping up and down them, that my mother used to scrub with Old Dutch cleanser every Saturday morning along with all the other mothers on the block scrubbing theirs, and saw the steps weren't near as high as I remembered them, nor the house as high. I wanted at the very least to go put my foot on the mudscraper at the bottom of the steps where they found Louie sleeping in the snow but I didn't dare because just then I saw a lady moving in the parlor windows and after a time a boy about my age came out the front door, eyeing me suspicious as he came down the steps and walked off towards the corner of 2nd Street like he might be going to Willie's store for something for their breakfast. He looked back at me once or twice over his shoulder as he went and when he turned the corner, I looked down the block in the other direction to see if Henry was sitting on his step but he wasn't.

All of a sudden I wanted to go up the front steps and ring the bell and ask the lady I saw in the parlor windows if I could come in and just walk through and see the house again, I'd promise her I wouldn't touch nothing and I wouldn't stay but a minute, if I could only just see it again.

All at once, like she heard inside my head, the lady pulled aside the lace curtains and looked out, peeking out at me between the leaves of her aspidisters like Aunt Nell and all my aunts peeked from behind theirs through the lace curtains so they could spy on their neighbors. I didn't know what to do so I looked down at my feet right away and in looking down I saw a broke brick in the pavement by the curb. Bending down I pretended I was tying my shoelace but what I did was I pried a piece of that brick loose and stuck it in my pocket on the sneak. Then as I was straightening up, my heart just about stopped, hearing a window being flung up and looking I saw it was the lady in our old house leaning out the parlor window, hollering, "Whaddaya want, little boy? Why're you hangin around here? You better gwan home to yer mother right now!"

I didn't need to be told twice. I turned and ducked my head and ran down Mifflin Street so fast towards 2nd, squeezing the piece of red brick tight in my pocket so I wouldn't lose it, I didn't stop til I got around to Grandmom's house on Hoffman Street, surprised to see the street filled now with a shiny black hearse with big shiny black cars behind it that had little gray flags stuck on each fender said FUNERAL— And when I saw the crape that was the wreath of flowers tied to the door with a black ribbon I all of a sudden came to see it wasn't Grandmom's house no more just like our house on Mifflin Street wasn't our house no more either.

Now there were more people packed into the house'n ever before so it was easy for me to sneak in the back gate like I never been gone. By the time I crawled and wormed my way through all the legs into the parlor, Father Gallagher was already there standing at one end of the coffin muttering in latin from a little black book. Uncle Digby, in a black suit just like the priest and a collar just as starched and stiff but with a pitch-black tie, was standing at the other end, while my mother and all her sisters and brothers were going up one by one to take a last look and kneel and say a last quick prayer over

Grandmom. My Aunt Kate that was the youngest and was our Kate's godmother, was the last to kneel on the step and as she was getting up and Father Gallagher was standing up on his tiptoes to blow out the gold candle over Grandmom's head and Uncle Digby was turning and reaching up to close the lid of the coffin like he was in a big hurry, like he might have another job to rush off to, Aunt Kate all of a sudden flung her face into the casket and started crying louder'n ever she did at the wake, shouting, *"Please take me with you, Mom! Please take me!"*

Uncle Digby, with his hand still on the lid, gave her an annoyed look like all this carrying on was only holding things up, but Aunt Kate kept holding on so tight to her mother the hair that wasn't Grandmom's hair began to shake like Aunt Kate was trying to shake Grandmom awake. And as she began to shout louder and hold on tighter, the whole casket began to shake too like she would shake it right off of whatever it was sitting on. So that Aunt Nell and Aunt Molly, being the oldest, when they rushed forward to pull her away they had a hard time of it, Aunt Kate had such a hold on their mother and hollering the whole time like I never heard anybody holler before, not even in the movies, *"Oh, Mom, I wanna go with you! Please take me with you, Mom!"* At the meal back at the house afterwards all her sisters praised Aunt Kate among themselves for flinging herself in the coffin and hollering what she hollered, saying it was hardest for her because she was "the baby," and as Aunt Maggie said with a pout was always their mother's favorite.

Grandmom got to ride all by herself in the hearse that Aunt Nell said later on back at the house was the fanciest car she ever got to ride in in her whole entire life, while we got to ride in one of the shiny black cars parked out front that all looked like the big black cars in the gangster movies and that was bigger'n any I ever rode in before, even bigger'n Sam Beezley's LaSalle, that I wondered why we didn't ride in that, Buster said, "It looks like a old wreck, that's why." Another thing was, my father didn't drive the shiny black car, there was a man in a black suit and cap driving it that Frank said later on Uncle Digby rented all the cars and drivers to the family at a discount because of him being the undertaker. But Aunt Bridget made him pay for the car we rode in and even made Uncle Digby give my father the dollar tip for the driver because my father was so broke he couldn't even put gas in Sam Beezley's car to come over here.

Big as it was there was still so many of us, me and Danny had to sit on our bigger brothers' laps on what they called jump seats. I had to sit on Buster's lap that annoyed him no end because I kept swinging my head from one window to the other, afraid to miss anything, until he gave me a punch and told me to quit my jiggling. My father, his eyes like pieces of raw hamburger from the night before, told us both to behave ourselves or we'd get it when we got home. I was so ashamed because the man driving the car heard my father hollering at us like we didn't know how to behave ourselves in such a big fancy car and with our grandmother not even buried yet. But my mother, in the black hat with the veil Aunt Maggie lent her and the black dress and black coat Aunt Bridget lent her, was staring straight ahead like she wasn't hearing anything.

The hearse and flower car and all the big black cars pulled up in front of Sacred Heart church where my father took me to my first mass. I saw now how all of Saint Theresa's could fit inside of it at least a half a dozen times, it was so big, but like everything else I saw so far it wasn't near as big as I remembered it.

We all sat together in the church. Danny didn't take his cap off so I took it off for him and Kate when she saw that, she didn't want to have her bonnet on but my mother made her keep it on

because girls weren't supposed to take their hats off in church—
But then Grandmom wasn't wearing a hat either, unless Uncle
Digby snuck her dustcap on her head before he closed the lid, I
figured maybe when a girl or a lady died she didn't have to wear
a hat no more in church, they called a hat a lid, so maybe the lid
of Grandmom's coffin counted as a hat now.

Behind the altar the organ pipes were booming ten times
louder'n the little organ at Saint Theresa's, but all the choir put
together didn't sound near as loud as Agnes O'Hara singing all by
herself. The priests were all in black because it was the Mass for
the Dead Frank said, more priests and altar boys'n I ever saw on
the altar at our church. Father Gallagher was one of them, stepping down into the aisle and sprinkling holy water on
Grandmom's coffin.

When the mass was over and we were coming down the
aisle with everybody looking as sad as the organ music sounded, even Uncle Jake's face was red with tears running down I
never saw on his face when he ate the horsereddish. I kept
twisting my purple knit cap from relief in my hands and when
Slap that was just in front of me started sniffling and bawling
into his knuckles, that set me off. I was surprised I started blubbering for the very first time ever since my mother first said
Grandmom was dead, and I was so glad I did, it made me feel not
as guilty I was secretly glad she'd died so I could get to go to
Philly, which I never would admit, even to myself. But I right then
really did feel so bad she had to die just so I could see it all again,
the tears were raining down my cheeks in as heavy a downpour
as my Uncle Jake's, it made me feel so good.

I saw now why they had windows in the back of the hearse
where Grandmom was riding because after church they drove
the funeral procession back past 138 Hoffman Street so
Grandmom could have one last look and say one last goodbye

to the house she lived in all those years and where my mother and all of her sisters and brothers were born—just like I wanted to see 126 Mifflin Street one last time. It cost extra Uncle Digby said later back at the house, when we were all eating the cold cuts and potato salad the neighbor ladies laid out, while all the men, including my father, that made me so nervous to see it, was finishing off the Irish whiskey, but everybody agreed it was worth it.

We drove and drove, we drove through the city and we drove outside of the city where I never been, we drove even farther it seemed than it was to Lenape, til finally we came to a place said Holy Cross Cemetery over the gate and drove inside.

By the time we got out of the car they already had Grandmom's casket sitting on the straps on top of her grave and the heaps of dirt around it were covered with green carpet made to look like grass that was greener'n any for real grass, that was dead now anyway all around in among the gravestones. When we were all gathered together, Father Gallagher began droning on and on reading from his little black book like bees were buzzing in latin in his mouth, and while he did that I looked around me and tried to read the names and dates on as many of the tombstones as I could. As they were lowering Grandmom's casket in the grave all of a sudden I spied Lithwack on two of the gravestones nearby that had little pale green plants growing around them my father called wax plants that none of the others had—I was so amazed to see our name, I forgot for the minute where I was and right outloud said to my father, "There's our name!"

He went *"Shhhhh!"* at me, his adam's apple galloping a mile a minute like he wished he was anywhere but here, like he wished he had him a nice big cold beer right then to help put out the fire in his eye.

Then wouldn't you know, Slap saw me staring at the grave-stones said Lithwack and he said to me in a voice he always thought was whispering but was really louder'n anybody else, "Them's our grandmom and grandpop, Mick!" so that when every-body turned around I could've sunk in the ground, and my father bent down and this time went *shhhh!* right in Slap's ear so he'd be sure to hear him.

So they were here all the time and never up on the roof on Mifflin Street or in the Tree of Heaven out in the alley like I used to think, though I wasn't sure how they could be here in Holy Cross cemetery and up in the sky in heaven all at the same time.

After Father Gallagher snapped his black book shut and said his say, saying what a fine Catholic mother Grandmom was rais-ing her sons and daughters to be good Catholics and them rais-ing us grandchildren to be good Catholics too, and had us bow our heads a minute in silence then say the Our Father and after that sprinkled more holy water on top of the casket, Uncle Digby stepped forward and handed us each a lump of dirt from under the green carpet and a flower apiece from all the wreaths and baskets of flowers stacked around the grave now. I didn't know what I was supposed to do with them til I saw when I filed past the grave behind my mother and father and older brothers that they were flinging first the dirt then the flower in. When I threw mine in, I looked down into the hole and saw the lid of the coffin that was once as shiny as Grandmom's piano was now all spattered with dirt and covered in the flowers each of us was tossing in, and that the flowers were all shriveling in the cold and spattered with dirt too—I thanked my lucky stars I wasn't down in there, how would you breathe? how could you talk? could you holler out? Where did you go to the toilet and when you were hungry, what would you eat? What would

Grandmom eat now?

As the casket creaked down Aunt Kate was crying the worst of anybody again and had to be held up by Uncle Tom, even Uncle Digby had to lend a hand which didn't seem to please him, he looked annoyed all over again and kept sneaking peeks at his wristwatch from under his cuff that was as white and starched stiff as his collar.

But my mother wasn't crying—I could see her eyes were as dark behind her veil as the veil was itself and she was staring down into the hole as the coffin creaked down and down like something in herself was going down with it, and when I saw that I all of a sudden began to hope with all my might that for her sake it was all somehow a joke or a trick, that the lid would fly open like Jack-in-the-Box and Grandmom'd spring up out of it and ask if somebody'd be good enough to get her a nice hot cup of Killarney tea....

Her eyes after that, when they had that faraway look, I knew she wasn't thinking of being in South Philly with her mother anymore—like that was all gone now—but as if she was maybe thinking of where her mother was in heaven. And after awhile when my father still didn't have a job in the shipyard and he started in his drinking again, another look came into her eyes that I could barely stand to see because I knew it was as true for me now as much as it was for her, that there never would be any going back now, that this is where she was stuck and would have to stay and would never get out of it.

I carried the piece of brick from our old brick pavement on Mifflin Street for weeks and weeks in my pocket, I even put it under my pillow at night, and when I touched it it was like touching a part of South Philly and a part of our old house, and if Mrs. Feek hollered at me or my father gave me one of his dirty looks once he started his drinking again, or I couldn't sleep at night hearing them arguing in their bed, I touched the piece of brick and it was like a magic stone that took me back to the way things were before any of this and quieted me down.

Spring came early that year and my father was right out there in the backyard with his shovel turning the ground over. Pretty soon there were a whole bunch of new peeps running around the chicken coop and two hens setting at the same time down in the cellar. I stayed after Sunday school now with those were going to make our first holy communion that Sister Joseph Mary was getting us boys ready for, while the girls sat separate in the pews across the aisle with Sister Veronica Rose, the two of them teaching us what sin was and what we were to say to Father Mack in the confession box, "Getting our hearts ready," Sister said, "to receive the body and blood of Jesus Christ."

When Ronnie heard about it and heard me say the boys got to wear white suits with white satin armbands and the girls got to wear white dresses with wreaths in their hair, that's all he had to hear, he right away went running downstairs and begged his mother to let him make his first holy communion too.

Even though we were pretty well along in the class, when Mrs. Mahoney, all decked out like she was going to the movies on Saturday night, brung Ronnie to mass the very next Sunday, Sister Joseph Mary went into the sacristy afterwards and asked Father Mack if he would let Ronnie come in, and when Father Mack came out he looked Ronnie up and down, all the while grinning and playing with Ronnie's blonde curls, and turning to Mrs. Mahoney said, "What a pretty little lamb he is—yes, yes, it's best to get him into the flock before he gets much older."

With the weather turning so nice it wasn't long before Earl Jr. came hollering out my backdoor when he saw there wasn't anybody around, and by the way I jumped up when I heard him holler that first time that spring, I saw my mother wasn't too pleased. Ever since Mrs. Beezley put a bug in her ear, she been asking me lots of questions about Earl Jr., especially did he use bad language and did he smoke and play hooky. I knew you weren't supposed to curse or use God's name in vain, Sister Joseph Mary told us that in our first holy communion class. But Earl Jr. did it all the time, he was always saying, "I spit in yer God's eye!" and would hack up a huge lunger and let it go at the sky. But I knew that was only to see could he shock me, which he did, even though I tried not to show it, and because he wasn't even a proddisin.

"Yo, Mick!" Earl Jr. was hollering out the backdoor, "Yo, Mickey!"

One thing I knew for certain was that if I told my mother the truth about Earl Jr. she'd never let me see him again, and despite his cursing God he was like such a powerful horseshoe magnet to me I lied to her and said no he didn't use bad language nor smoked and as for him playing hooky I said I never got the chance to see him in school, so I didn't know about that, which was only half a lie. She gave me that look, her eyes boring right into mine so that I had to look away like looking into her eyes was like staring into headlights that were too bright, like she might've seen, if I didn't look away, that Earl Jr. already taught me how to smoke and take off my clothes in the woods and look at the comic books he stole from under his father's mattress. She said, "Are you sure? Don'tchou lie to me, boy." I crossed all my fingers behind my back so I wouldn't be struck down dead just in case lying counted before you made your first holy communion, and said, "I'm sure."

She looked at me awful suspicious, saying, "Whyn'tchou go nextdoor and play with yer boyfriend Ronnie, he's more yer own age anyway?"

Without batting an eye and because I wasn't struck down dead the first time, I lied again, saying, "Because Miz Mahoney been havin her headaches all week."

She looked at me like she didn't believe that one either but she sighed and said I could go out and play with Earl Jr. if I stayed in our yard. But I knew Earl Jr. wouldn't have any of that, so I begged and whined could I go up to his house with him and play. She looked doubtful again but I begged and whined so much she finally gave another deep sigh like I was getting on her nerves along with Earl Jr.'s hollering, and said I could go but not to go no further'n the Snarp's yard either.

I promised I wouldn't even though I knew that was a lie too and one more thing I would have to tell Father Mack when I made my first confession.

It was Earl Jr. started it. I would never of had the brains, or the nerve, to think it up on my own. It was just the two of us at first. That first nice day he came hollering for me when my mother finally said I could go play with him, I just followed along behind, just like we were picking up where we left off in October, like the winter never happened. I didn't even have to ask him where we were going, knowing without asking he was making tracks first thing for the clearing deep in the woods, walking like he couldn't wait to get there. He was in such a hurry I wondered did he have another picture book he stole from his father to show me.

Despite it being chillier, now we were so far back in the woods out of the sunlight, no sooner did we get there than Earl Jr. unhitched the straps of his overalls and let them drop, kicking them out of the way, then he dropped right onto the ground without a stitch. Just like he did last spring when he brought me here, he started rolling over and over and rubbing and wriggling his spine like a dog in the new grass, shutting his eyes and grinning and grinning and sniffing the ground like he'd been waiting all these months just to be able to take off all of his clothes and get down bare and roll in the dirt.

When he had enough, he sat up, patches of dirt all over his skin and twigs and pine needles stuck in his hair, gaping at me with his big bucktooth grin, saying, "You gonna do yer dance fer me, Rabbit?"

I blushed and wouldn't say anything, seeing the tease in his eye, and when he asked me again I looked away, but he kept persisting. I said, "Ain't it too cold?" He slapped his head like I was the biggest fool, saying, "Looka me, I ain't cold." Then he got that sly grinny look I could never say no to, saying, "I thunk up a good game for us," then he stuck all his teeth back in his mouth and clammed right up which of course got me dying to know all about it. Still and all, I looked at him suspicious, seeing those eyes, teasing me and daring me.

"What good game?" I said. He said, "You'll see," and before I knew it, he jumped up and was gone into the cherry trees growing wild at the edge of the clearing and started combing through the branches.

I stared after him, wondering what could he be up to but had enough sense not to ask, and when I heard a snap I saw he was breaking off one of the skinniest branches down near the bottom of one of the trees, then he went and snapped off another and came back across the clearing, peeling each one down til they looked like switches. Grinning again, he handed me one of them. "Gwan," he said, when he saw me holding back, "Take it. I'll show you what to do with it." Then that foxy look came into his face. "Oh, you'll like this game, Rabbit, but the first rule is you gotta take off all of yer clothes."

Even though I didn't want to right then, it being so chilly and the trees so bare and it being the first time I would be bare in the woods for so long, I felt a shyness all over again like I did the first time he asked me to do it.

"C'mon, c'mon," he said, all impatient, cracking one of the cherry switches in the air as if to see how quick it bent. Then when he saw I wasn't making a move he turned to me and gave me another one of those looks of his, his eyes steady on me like I was the only one in the whole wide world right then, like I was the most important, and when he hitched the corner of his mouth up in a grin, saying in an awful soft way, "C'mon now, Mick, you'll like it, I swear you will," I knew I was a goner, I knew I would do, like always, anything he asked me to do.

I took off my things and spread them over the branches of the huckleberry bushes so they wouldn't get dirt on them. Right away I started shivering and hugging myself and was surprised when I looked down at myself and saw beneath all the goose pimples how white I was out in the daylight, whiter even than Earl Jr. was, white as the snow we had that winter. I was sure I was going to catch pneumonia, my mother said if you caught so much as a chill you could catch it.

What we did was play a game he called Slaves and Masters where he said he'd be the master first off to show me how to do it. What he did was, he had me dance around him in a circle while he shouted at me and spit at my feet and swished his cherry switch at me if I didn't cringe and bow fast enough in front of him. After I danced around him a few times, he shouted I wasn't bowing and cringing fast enough and flicked out at me with his switch, catching me in the shoulder, just a little sharp flick like a mosquito bite. But I must've looked so startled the next time he brought the lash down he shouted, "I won't make a mark! I won't cutcha! Nobody'll see nuthin! Them's the rules."

So I bowed faster and he said bow lower and when I didn't bow low enough to suit him he flicked out at my other shoulder, a glancing little bitey flick I hardly felt at all, but I could feel the color rising up my throat and in my cheeks and felt resentful and excited all at once, but didn't feel the chill at all anymore and liked the game and didn't like it, all at the same time too, like it was for real and not for real, like a movie.

When it came my turn to be master, he said I didn't shout loud enough to suit him, I thought he was going to hit out at me with his switch again even though he was the slave this time. So I tried to shout louder but was nowhere near as loud as he was. Even though I knew we were so deep in the woods I was still afraid somebody might hear me and those eyes that looked like Charley's eyes might show up again, peeking through the branches. Another thing was, I was so nervous about hitting out at him with my switch, afraid I'd hurt him. He saw that and shouted, "Wack me! Wack me! C'mon now! Make me dance! Spit on me! Make me bow and kiss your feet! I told ja, them's the rules!"

So I swung out at him but not too hard and he was bending and bowing before me as he danced around and around me and got down and kissed my feet that nobody ever did except my mother when I was little, she sang, "This little piggy went to market...this little piggy stayed home...." And while he was crouching in front of me he had to remind me to use the switch and I brought it down across his back but only light and easy, not wanting to do it, yet all of a sudden wanting to do it, seeing, light as I hit him, a long pink stripe light up across his shoulder blades. Seeing it, I felt a terrific rush of excitement, so much so when I tried to spit on him like he shouted at me to do, I couldn't, my mouth was so dry, and I blushed something awful when I looked down and saw my dunkey was all swollen up just like it was when I woke up in the morning and had to pee real bad. And when Earl Jr. stood up and started dancing around me again I saw his dunkey was standing up too and he looked at me with that sly and secret grin, like this was our secret together, shaking it and shaking it, hollering, "Hit me! Hit me! Where's yer spit? Make me be yer slave! C'mon, Rabbit, dammit, don't jist stand there like a dumbie!"

I hit out at him again and again, playful and light, missing him mainly and glad I did, not wanting to cut or make a mark. But I still couldn't manage to work up any spit as he dodged and bowed and cringed away from me, wriggling his belly, his belly-button looking like the mouth of a minniegudgeon opening and shutting underwater. I lashed away all right but try as I could I still couldn't spit, but by this time the switch was spitting. It was sticking to my palm with sap as sticky as the black buds looked all over in the trees up above us, sticky as the speck like dew on the tip of my dunkey looked, wondering what that was, the same, now its cap slid off, was shining out of the eye of Earl Jr.'s too as he pranced around and pranced around, his face and all his skin dark now like all his blood gone dark, but the drop of dew there in the eye of it flashing.

"Saint Theresa," she was saying, "saw Jesus as a little person inside her heart."

As Sister Joseph Mary was talking I looked past her dark blue veil at the statue of Saint Theresa near the communion rail. When she said we should all do like Saint Theresa did and put Jesus in our hearts, I stared at Christ hanging on the big black crucifix against the white wall opposite, then at the little statue of the Infant of Prague with the bleeding heart and the red votive light in front of him not far down from where Saint

Theresa was standing, and couldn't decide which Jesus Christ I wanted to put in my heart, the grown up one or the baby one. I wanted to ask Sister Joseph Mary if I could put the both of them in at the same time or did I have to make a choice, but I was too shy to ask.

Sister Joseph Mary's face was white as the skin of Christ on the cross, like all the blood was drained out of her like his was drained out because of all the cuts and slashes and wounds in him. I wondered did she have cuts and slashes in her like Saint Theresa only we couldn't see them with all the veils. In our game, Earl Jr. said not to make a mark, not to make a cut, those were the rules.

Her eyes were bulging bigger behind her glasses and her breath was coming faster as she told us all to put Saint Theresa in our hearts along with Jesus, I knew if I tried to do that I really would need a heart as big as our radio.

"See her suffering, see her rapture—All for the love of Jesus Christ," she whispered, holding up her trembling hand and swooping in close over the pew so that those of us in the front row reared back from her like she was going to smother us in her big black veils, her voice so out of breath like she was running standing still, bowing her head when she said Jesus and we all bowed our heads with her.

I was so glad I got promoted into the second grade and wouldn't have Mrs. Feek anymore but would have Miss Riggs that was a whole lot nicer. And I was glad for Slap Miss Prouty promoted him even if it was only by the skin of his teeth. That Buster of course had to go and say she only promoted Slap so she wouldn't have to smell his feet no more, and kept it up and kept it up til he got Slap crying, which is just what he wanted in the first place. But I was so glad for Slap all the same.

Now school was out I had to spend more and more time minding Danny and Kate, my mother was so busy with everything else. I didn't mind except it cut into my going over to Ronnie's or more especially, now the weather was good, going off with Earl Jr. Now that both Danny and Kate were getting bigger, my mother let me take them for walks into town—or rides, really, in the secondhand wagon we got from charity for Christmas that my father oiled and painted and fixed up better'n when we got it. I'd put Danny and Kate in it and pull them as far as Gottlieb's so I could take a look at the Rialto poster in Gottlieb's window to see what movies were playing that week. But on the way back I'd be so tired by then I made Danny get out and walk, it was so hard pulling the two of them through the sand.

One day we were just starting up Lenape Road when I saw Earl Jr. coming down from their house with his brother Walter. When they met up with us he says, "What er you, uck-stay ith-way uh-thay ats-bray again?" saying it with an annoyed look like he was wishing the two of us could go off somewhere together. When I shrugged, he rolled his eyes at Walter like he was stuck with him, and Walter, seeing it, grinned and jeered, *"Brat brat brat,"* showing he understood pig latin talk and saying it real fast that so irritated Earl Jr. he gave him a rabbit punch in the arm. "Shutcher hole, Walter," he snarled, and Walter clamped his mouth shut but in that jeery kind of way you could see he wasn't at all afraid of his big brother the way I was of my two big brothers, he looked just as sassy as Earl Jr. did.

Earl Jr. says, "Where you goin?" I shrugged my shoulders again. "Gottlieb's probably." "You got money to buy anything?" I shook my head. "Then why the hell er you goin to Gottlieb's?" I shrugged one more time. "To look at the movie poster, I guess." "That's a dumb thing, haulin two brats in a wagon all the way up there just to see a movie poster," and he stuck his hands on his hips and spit in the bushes. Kate pipes up with, "He said a *curse* word!" Danny giggled and put his hand over her mouth and she gave it such a bite he yanked it away real quick shaking it and yowling. Earl Jr. looked at the two in the wagon, then at Walter, then looked at all three of them. "C'mon," he said, jerking his head at me. I stared at him. "C'mon," he said, "I'll earn-lay em-thay uh-thay ame-gay I showed you." *"Game game game,"* Walter went, like a poll parrot. I stared at Earl Jr. again, thinking I didn't hear him right the first time and if I did he had to be kidding. "C'mon, c'mon," he persisted, "I ain't got all day," and I could hear by the tone of his voice he wasn't kidding. *"C'mon c'mon c'mon,"* Walter screeched like a parrot and didn't duck fast enough to miss getting a smack on the ear. "I tole you to shutch-er yer hole dint I?" Earl Jr. muttered and must've given him such a thump Walter really did shutup this time.

I gave a worried look, first at Kate, then at Danny, Danny by now all excited, going, "What game? What game?" while Kate, bored already, was grabbing both sides of the wagon and rocking herself forward, whining it was time for us to get going.

Of course Earl Jr. saw right away I was holding back and got that sneery look in his eye he always got when he saw I was hemming and hawing.

"Goddammit, c'mon," he said. "And if it'll make you feel any better, nobody'll have to ake-tay eir-thay othes-clay off-ay, we'll just have us some fun." He jerked his head again at me and started off towards the path through the woods.

"He said a *curse* word," Kate said again, like a broke record, and even though h-e-l-l and G-o-d-d-a-m-m-i-t were nothing compared to some things he said, I was already worried she'd tell my mother and prove Mrs. Beezley right about Earl Jr.'s bad mouth—Worse'n that, I didn't even want to begin to think about Danny and Kate finding out, let alone spilling the beans, about the games we played in the woods, just thinking about it put me in such a sweat.

"Geez, maybe we...maybe we better not..." I began again, "Maybe we jist better go on our way to Gottlieb's..." and hated the way I sounded, so wishy-washy. Earl Jr. swung around sharp and hacking up a lunger, spit it in the dust. "You comin or not?" he said, that look in his eye. "I toleja, it-ay ill-way ee-bay un-fay. Nobody'll have to get down to their irth-bay-ay-day oots-say. Ou-yay ared-skay?" Danny and Kate stared at his talking pig latin, Kate saying, "Is them curse words, Mick?" "Shhh!" I said

I guessed he knew by now all he had to do was shame me to get me to do whatever he wanted, he didn't have to sit on my chest like Ronnie or twist my arm. Even though I wasn't so sure I better, knew I'd oughtn't to as a matter of fact, when I saw that look that I saw so many times before I felt all of a sudden like I was the hoptoad and he was the snake, I couldn't resist jumping into his trap, much as I wanted to. And besides didn't he say nobody'd have to get into their birthday suits?—Maybe we would just dance around a couple times and that would be that.

So, hoping for the best, I picked up the handle of the wagon and started pulling Danny and Kate off of the road and into the woods, following behind Earl Jr. and Walter on the path back to the clearing, Earl Jr. throwing a look back at me with his face half hitched up in a grin as much as to say "I knowed I'd win," Danny, even more excited now, saying at the same time, "Where're we goin? Are we gonna play the game now?" I was so nervous about where we really were going I didn't know what to tell him, so didn't say anything, acting deaf and dumb like I ain't heard anything at all.

Once we got back there, Earl Jr. told them all about Slaves and Masters and when he said one of the rules of the game we were going to play was we had to take our clothes off I saw Danny and Kate look at me. My jaw dropped as I looked at Earl Jr. like I couldn't believe my ears because didn't he just say not a minute ago none of us'd have to take our clothes off? But I could see now that was just a trick to get me to come back here with Danny and Kate, I could see it plain now the way Earl Jr. just stood there with a smirk on his face like he was double-daring me to say something.

But Walter Snarp when he heard what his brother said bust out in a big grin and without another word just unhitched the strap of his overalls and let them drop at his feet simple as that and kicked them aside as neat and easy as ever I saw his older brother do. Kate was staring at him from the wagon bug-eyed at first like he was some kind of peculiar insect she ain't never seen before, saying, "I see his peepee."

Danny started giggling, hearing that, but he was looking too, looking at Walter's dunkey, then looking away and looking back again, and got the giggles all over again like Kate said something real funny. Then when Earl Jr. unhitched his overalls the two of them swung their eyes over at him and stared, Kate with her mouth hanging open as wide as her eyes and pointing at Earl Jr. from the wagon but for once not saying anything. I wanted to pick up the handle of that wagon and pull Danny and Kate out of there so fast, I was wishing we were anywhere but here, even back in the deepest part of the swamp. I dug my toe in the grass and stared down, feeling the blood coming into my face, a fear coming up in me even stronger this time Danny and Kate might tell, the scare stronger even than that somebody might see us, even though I knew, despite those eyes once looked like Charley's eyes in the bushes, we were so deep in the woods nobody could see us.

When I raised my eyes again I saw Earl Jr. looking straight

at me without a stitch like I'd seen him so many times, only now with Danny and Kate there he somehow looked more bare'n he ever did before. In his eyes was another I-double-dare-you look I winced away from the same as if he'd raised his hand to me.

Like the frog staring at a snake I couldn't lift a muscle and stood there staring in those eyes like his eyes were forked fangs that bit me so I couldn't move at all. I was surprised Kate wasn't at all bashful about it, pulled her dress right over her head as quick as she always tried to pull her bonnet off in church, her skin white as all the milk she drank. Danny giggled at first, but when he saw Earl Jr. and Walter with their overalls off and saw it was a game, he hopped right out of the wagon and took his off too. I saw all the boys had caps on theirs, I was the only one didn't and had it in my head like to have the cap still on was old-fashioned, like having a Scott radio or a LaSalle car wasn't having an up-to-date model, wasn't streamlined like Father Mack's new Chrysler was. And like Blondie and like Alley Oop's girlfriend or like Little Orphan Annie in Earl Snarp Sr.'s comic books, Kate didn't have any dunkey at all, I wondered how she peed.

Even though we saw each other without no clothes on plenty of times in the washtub Saturday nights, somehow I felt more bashful out there in the woods in front of either Danny or Kate, and felt even funnier, being older and supposed to be minding them and all. My big worry, like I said, was that one or the both of them would blab once we got home, and I saw Earl Jr. looking at me again with that mocking look like he was reading what was in my eyes and sneering at it.

The truth was, I couldn't never bear to have Earl Jr. mocking me or thinking I was ascared. I didn't know why but I always wanted him to think high of me, I seemed to need it as much as I needed to eat or breathe. So when I saw that sneery look, it right away pushed out the fear of anybody at home finding out, or Charley spying, and so I gulped down a deep breath and quick as I could before I changed my mind, I unbuttoned my shirt and slid down my pants and underdrawers and picking up Danny's and Kate's clothes on the way, I went and spread them over the new shoots of the huckleberry bushes at the edge of the clearing so they'd be out of the way and not get trampled on and dirtied so my mother wouldn't have a chance to ask us how it happened.

Another surprise was how quick Danny and Kate took to it. Walter was so quick I wondered did him and Earl Jr. play it before by themselves. Like when he first showed me the game, Earl Jr. went off into the wild cherry trees and broke off a handful of switches, smaller ones for the two littler ones and bigger ones for me and him and Walter. After he peeled them down he handed them around, keeping the longest one for himself. Then he got us all around him in a circle and told everybody what to do, how we were to dance and whoop and holler as slaves, and how each of us would get a turn being master and bossing the others around. Walter when he heard that rubbed his hands all excited, and Earl Jr., looking sharp at him, warned us how when it came our turn to be the master we weren't to hit so hard so's to leave a mark, that we could hit light enough to sting but not hard enough to draw blood. And when Walter, looking disappointed the minute he heard that, wanted to know, "Why can't I draw blood if'n I'm the master?" Earl Jr. told him the same thing he told me, "So's there won't be no telltale marks when we get home, that's why, dumbie."

He said he'd go first being the boss to show them that didn't know how to do it what to do, and they were to follow what I did dancing as the slave since I been the slave once already. When he cracked his switch in the air, shouting, "Dance now! Dance!" he shouted it so loud Kate gave a start, but when he cracked the switch again and I started bending and bowing and shaking my hips as I began dancing around, she laughed and followed behind me in the circle, dipping and bending like I was, doing as best she could, and Danny and Walter did the same. It wasn't long before we were all whooping and hollering and dancing around in the circle like a bunch of Indians in the movies with Earl Jr. in the middle lashing out at us with his cherry switch, shouting, "You call that dancin? Dance, you slaves, dance!" not hitting anybody at first but just letting the switch whistle over our heads as we stamped around, him shouting, "Bow down, you dogs! Bow down!"

When I bowed down Danny and Kate bowed down too like we did in church when we genuflected, the two of them giggling now like it was a real good game and acting like they weren't scared at all of the way Earl Jr. shouted or the way his whip cracked over our heads, it was all a game.

I was the first one he started to really hit out at and I was glad of that, afraid of what Danny and Kate might do if he'd hit out at them first thing, scratchy little flicks around my shoulders and arms I hardly felt in the beginning. Then the more we danced and hollered and the more he called us his slaves the harder he brought the switch down on me, mosquito bites at first like the last time, but then he landed a few of them where I could really feel the sting. He got us moving all right. I pretended to dodge the whip and cringe and cry and beg for mercy, but not really meaning it, and got more and more excited everytime the switch came down, my blood rushing up and down so fast I all of a sudden felt my dunkey waking up and once it did I started to dance in a livelier way, seeing Earl Jr.'s dunkey'd woke up too, he was swinging and swiping at us with his mouth wide open, his teeth looking bigger'n they ever looked.

He flicked out at Walter next and Walter just grinned and hippity-hopped away quick as Peter Rabbit, but Earl Jr. was quicker and kept right on his tail, catching him a few times, light and easy. Then he flicked it out at Danny and he dodged away too, laughing, but Earl Jr. caught him like he caught Walter, light and easy, and the way Danny and Walter were laughing and dodging as they danced and whooped, Kate, not to be left out, started hollering, "Me too! Me too!" Earl Jr. flicked his switch out at her and she shrieked and ran out of the circle like he was tickling her and next he gave a long reach of his arm and flicked her hiney real light and she squealed and came running back into the circle, still shrieking with laughter and got us all laughing she was enjoying herself so much.

Beads of sweat were popping out on Earl Jr.'s upper lip, even his hair was beginning to sweat, as he sent his switch whistling through the air. Walter started whining when was he going to get his turn being master, why should Earl Jr. have all the fun, and got his nose out of joint when Earl Jr. dropped his arm and taking a minute to catch his breath, told Kate she could be master next. Walter wanted so bad to go next his face dropped but Earl Jr. said, "Ladies first, Walter, your turn'll come."

Kate was shy at first and kept putting her hands to her mouth and giggling so much Earl Jr. started hollering at her, "C'mon, girl, be the boss! Hit us! Hit us! Ya gotta play right!" Even though she couldn't stop her giggling, she at least started taking swipes at us with her switch. At first her aim wasn't so hot and her hitting, when she managed to land one, wasn't too strong, being's she was so little, coming no higher'n our belly-buttons. But she got right into it as best she could and as we danced around her she got her nerve up and because her arms were so short she didn't wait in the middle of the circle to swing out but ran after who she wanted and chased after Danny the most and landed a few good ones on his backside but not enough to hurt, the two of them laughing and squealing as Danny tried to get away from her, he could of got away only he was pretending like he couldn't. Then she came after me and gave me a few smart cracks around my legs where it was easier for her to reach and I cupped my hands between my legs she was swinging so wild. Even Earl Jr. got to laughing she was getting so into it, she forgot to holler things at us even when Earl Jr. shouted reminders at her, her cheeks red as cooked beets and her blonde curls that my mother'd just brushed before we left the house that morning, all in a frazzle and a tangle now. Then Earl Jr. gave Walter his turn, he been pestering so, and he right off wacked Earl Jr. between the shoulder blades a few times til red stripes showed, shouting, "Dance, you niggerboy! Dance!" then he hit Danny so hard Danny started to cry. Everything came to a sudden halt and we all stared at Danny, then stared at Earl Jr., you could see his throat going as he glared at Walter. I went over and bent down and petted Danny, and Kate petted him too, her making cooing sounds, telling Danny, "Don'tchou cry, he dint mean it." "Yes he did!" Danny hollered out, so that Earl Jr. yelled at Walter to stop hitting so hard or else he'd be out of the game. Walter got all pouty and Earl Jr. said, "I ain't kiddin you, boy." After that when Walter hit at me it wasn't as hard but still plenty hard enough I knew for sure I was getting switched.

When Danny had his turn, he was as excited as Kate was and ran around big-eyed slashing out right and left. Walter started yapping he was hitting him too hard but we knew he said that only because his big brother'd spoke to him in no uncertain terms to quit hitting Danny so hard, so he might just as well of saved his breath.

When it came my turn, Earl Jr. kept them cringing and

bowing and bending and I still had that rushing excitement, my dunkey straining and lifting its ears like it wanted to run away with me. Earl Jr.'s was still standing and straining too, flip-flopping from side to side as he danced, and Danny's and Walter's too, the caps pushed back on theirs and bareheaded like mine now, their dunkey heads hard and shiny and streamlined in the light like they were the little pink buds up in the trees wet with dew in the morning. And as they danced by I brought my switch down, but playful and light, singing out, "Dance now! Dance!" all of a sudden feeling like I was in a movie and we were all niggers in darkest Africa or redskins out in the wild West. And Kate was grinning and rolling her head from side to side, shaking her curls, and Danny was rushing around like a maniac, ducking and holding both hands over his hiney whenever he scooted by me, but Walter would stick out his backside when he strutted past, daring me to hit it, which I did, quick and light, and he'd scoot away quicker, shrieking. And Earl Jr. when he came by kept hollering, "Make me dance harder! Make this nigger dance his ass off!" his eyes rolling up in his head like Saint Theresa's, his breath coming hard, it was like he was drunk, it was like we were all drunk and like we were in a Tarzan movie or a cowboy movie with Indians on the warpath—I felt that rushing in me like all my blood was trying to beat out of my skin and the sap again sparking in the eye of my dunkey.

We danced and danced until we couldn't dance no more, until all of us just fell down in the grass laughing and breathing hard, our faces red as the wild roses blooming everywhere again, we lay sprawled on the ground, our arms and legs stretched out and could see up into the branches above, I saw the birds all black against the sky flying down again and disappearing into the leaves like we were birds like them and they came down to watch us, watch our secret in the woods away from the eyes of mothers and fathers and older brothers, like we were kids with secrets like trees, like the birds themselves hidden in among their leaves....

After Earl Jr. and Walter started up the road to their house and just before we got to our own, I dropped the handle of the wagon and had Danny and Kate each cross their heart and hope to die if they told about our game. Kate crossed her heart right off but Danny got smart-alecky, saying, "Make me, I don't have to cross me heart if I don't want to."

I bent down in his ear and whispered if he promised not to tell I wouldn't tell about him rolling around on his belly at night riding his dunkey and he quit looking so smart when he heard that, turning all colors of the rainbow, and crossed his heart and promised.

Before I picked up the wagon handle again I crossed all my fingers on both of my hands just to make sure the both of them would keep their word.

Just before we got to the house I ran my fingers through Kate's curls trying to make them look a little less tangled and picked out the bits of weeds and grass, then tore off leaves from the trees were already out and rubbed at the palms of hers and Danny's hands to try to get the sticky sap off of them as much as I could.

My mother said, with an annoyed look, "Where you been? I was beginnin to git worried." Danny and Kate looked at me and I said with my eyes not to say nothing. To my mother I said, lying coming easier now, "We went as far as the church, that's why it took us so long."

Lifting her out of the wagon, she said to Kate, "Didjou have a nice ride?" Kate looked at me and I gave a nod with my eyes. She looked at my mother and nodded. Then my mother said, even more annoyed, "Looka them hands, what was you doin, did somebody give you candy?" I said real quick, "She was playin with sticks." She said, "Well, you be more careful next time whatchou let 'er play with."

I saw Danny give his own hands a quick onceover. I gave him the eye and he quick hid his hands behind his back.

"And looka yer hair," my mother went on, clicking her tongue against her teeth, "How'd it git all tangled and I only just brushed it?"

Kate stared at me again and I scrunched up my eyes, meaning for her not to say a word, so when she looked back at my mother she just shrugged her shoulders, staring off into space and looking dumb. But when my mother said, "I'm gonna have to take the brush to that, young lady," I could see Kate stick out her lower lip like she always did whenever the word hairbrush was mentioned. I felt sorry for her she had to get her hair brushed twice in one day, but I caught her eye and gave her another look, looking sorry as I could so she'd know how sorry I was, while at the same time I said again with my eyes, don't tell. And even though the tears were already starting because she knew what was coming, I could see she wasn't going to say anything, nor Danny either, the way he kept holding his hands hid behind him, like he knew already, like me and my older brothers already knew, from that day with red-haired Charley down on the beach, there were some things you couldn't ever tell big people.

That night I heard her saying no again, and my father muttering a curse like he did before, then the bedsprings crashing like he was heaving himself away from her, and everything was still. Except this time after he started snoring, I thought I heard her crying, so quiet it was, though, it was hard at first to tell that's what it was.

The next Sunday at the first holy communion class Sister Joseph Mary told all us boys how to swallow the communion wafer. That when Father Mack came by with the chalice we were to shut our eyes and stick out our tongues, and she warned us not to chew it, not even to let it near our teeth but to shut our mouth and let it melt on our tongue before swallowing it, and be sure and try and get it all down before we left the altar rail. Another thing was we weren't to fold our hands but to keep them pressed together, one palm against the other the whole time, like we were praying, which is what Ronnie been doing all along, acting so holy.

The minute I got in the kitchen door, I told my mother what Sister Joseph Mary said and asked her what would happen if you bit into the wafer by mistake. She was getting the shoulder of pork, that my father managed to get from Gottlieb's on the eye, ready to put in the oven for Sunday dinner but stopped what she was doing long enough to say, "If I took a bite outa you it'd hurt, wouldn't it? Well, oncet the priest has made the bread into the Body of Our Lord if you bite into Him it hurts Him, it's the same thing, that's why you mustn't never bite into it, it's the same thing as biting God."

I warned myself to remember not to chew the wafer, and at the same time I was dying to know if our dancing bare in the woods would d-a-m us all to hell, or would it only d-a-m me and Danny and Kate but not the Snarp brothers because we were Catholic and the Snarp brothers weren't anything. But of course I didn't dare ask her that, or Sister Joseph Mary either.

Not long after we started playing Slaves and Masters me and Earl Jr. were poking around down at the garbage dump one day, looking to see what we could find, hoping mainly to find soda bottles to take back to Gottlieb's for the deposit. Lenny was there with his baby buggy, and Eddie and Cockeye with him, the three of them picking through the mounds of trash. Some of the other men we saw at the dump regular were there too but, like we always did, we kept out of their way.

My eyes getting as sharp as his, I saw them first, itty bits of bright color in the muck. When I nudged Earl Jr. and jerked my head down the way I'd seen him do so not to draw attention, he crouched down and started digging there and in no time pulled a bunch of long bedraggled feathers up out of the mud they were buried in. Pink and purple they were and smelling all mildewy from the damp. "Plumes" Earl Jr. called them and said if we spread them out in his backyard the sun would dry them soon enough, they'd fluff up again and wouldn't smell half as bad. I was staring at them bewildered never seeing nothing like them before down there in the dump, I asked him where had they come from, were they maybe feathers'd fell off of a big bird flying over the swamp that was molting the way our chickens did? I knew right away from the way his eyeballs rolled up in his head I'd gone and said something dumb again. Like he was talking to an idiot, he said, "No, they ain't feathers from no big bird flying over, you moron, my old man said he knows of a couple banjo players in one of the South Philly stringbands lives in Lenape and drinks their beer in Tarkie's every night, these plumes is prolly from some old mummers day costumes they must've chucked in the dump, they look so old they must be from New Years a way, way back." That must've been so because a lot of the feathers had their spines broke and flip-flopped every which way and looked awful moth-eaten besides.

At the thought of Philly my heart still jumped and I asked him did he ever go to the mummers parade? He said, "No, but I seen picstures of it in the *County Seat Weekly*." I said, lying as to the number, "I went lots of times when we lived in South Philly," but didn't tell him it was only down on 2nd Street and not up on Broad. But even so I felt real important because I actually saw the parade and he never did, and told him all about the satin outfits with colored plumes on them like the ones we just dug up in the dump, only lots nicer of course, and the New Years strutters and the string-band music and the men wearing lipstick and dresses and did he know why a man would wear a cherry sewed in his panties?

He gave me that look again like I was the dopiest thing on the face of the earth and my question so dumb it wasn't even fit to answer, saying instead, "No, I ain't never been to no mummers parade and I ain't never seen a man with a cherry in his panties but if I did I wouldn't be such a dumbie but would know what it meant. I may not've been to the mummers parade but I been to the Star movies and the Stanley movies up in Camden and I even been to the Savar movies that costs a whole quarter to get into day or night, and et chop suey oncet in a chink joint on Broadway, and you ain't never been to any of them places, have you? you ain't even been to the Rialto in the county seat yet, so there."

I had to admit to myself I ain't never been any of them places he said and ducked my head and didn't feel as important anymore even though I saw the mummers parade and he never did.

Then looking all high and mighty after he had his say, he handed me the plumes that were so soggy they went all limp like spaghettis in my hands. Then he began scraping his foot around in the mud to see if he could find any more, he scraped and he scraped but that was it. We hadn't gone more'n a couple

steps he all of a sudden squatted down again and this time, his
eye still sharper'n mine, he started pulling frazzled old fringe
out of the mud from some old ripped window shades somebody
must've thrown away so long ago the fringe all had moldy black
stains on it and stunk as bad as the plumes. He tore the fringe
off the bottom of the shades and looping it around his hand and
elbow said he could dry it out in the sun along with the feathers,
and when I asked him what we'd use all of it for all he said was
"Ou'll-yay ee-say," though if I was any quicker I might've known
what he had in mind to use it for.

Taking the feathers and the fringe down to the edge of the
swamp we rinsed it all in the swamp water to get as much of the
mud off as we could before we took it back to spread in Earl Jr.'s
backyard. When we got there, Mrs. Snarp came out on the
backstep hugging her arms under her apron, saying, "Ain't they
pretty plumes—where did you git them?" Then Walter came
running out of the house behind her, yelling, "Whatzat, Earl
Jr.? Whatzat for?" Earl Jr. muttered, "Keep yer pants on, Walter,
you'll find out soon enough," while he at the same time was
scattering the chickens away that came gawking up to take a
look, thinking the feathers might be something to eat—or else
thinking maybe they belonged to some long lost relative as Earl
Jr. said.

What we used them for of course was to decorate ourselves
playing Slaves and Masters in the woods. Once they were dried
out Earl Jr. stuffed them in an old burlap potato bag from relief
and we carried them back to the clearing where we tried them
on. Even though the feathers and fringe been airing and drying
out in the sun for a couple days, they still had a powerful smell
of the dump. But we still took off all of our clothes and despite
the smell tied the curtain fringe around our waists to make a
belt, then stuck the plumes down inside of the belt, front and

rear, Earl Jr. tucking all pink in front and all purple behind, while I tucked in first a pink one then a purple one and so on all around because I thought that looked prettier that way. Tall as I was, though I wasn't nearly as tall as Earl Jr., I still had to pull the quills just about up to my chest so the ends of the feathers wouldn't be dragging on the ground, they were so long. Soon as we were all decked out, Earl Jr. started jumping around making monkey noises and jabbering that African nigger talk like in Tarzan movies. And when he got tired of that he smacked his hand to his mouth and started whooping and hollering and bowing himself up and down and prancing in a circle like a redskin tramping and dancing around a campfire, shaking and shaking his hips so the feathers all shook the way a rooster's tail does after it's done its cock-a-doodle-doo. Then I showed him how the New Years shooters did their strut coming down 2nd Street, and pretending I was strumming a banjo, I started singing, "Oh, Them Golden Slippers," strutting around and strutting around while he sat in the grass in his feathers and fringe, his jaw hanging loose with that grin on his face I was never sure if he was just enjoying himself or mocking me.

But I didn't care, the tips of the feathers were tickling my legs and tickling my hips, they were tickling the tip of my dunkey too, so that Earl Jr. pointed at it and got an even bigger grin on, like he was mocking me and enjoying himself all at the same time, and even though I just knew my face was turning pink as the head of my dunkey peeping out now between the feathers, I didn't care, and kept right on strutting, I loved so much to dance for him.

Kate was too short to wear the feathers and Danny was too, really. But Danny made such a stink when he saw Walter was allowed to wear them and not him we had to tie a couple around his middle just to shut him up, even though the tips of the plumes shot up above his ears making him look like the mummers looked with their headdresses, and the bottoms of them dragged on the ground when he walked or danced. Kate we just draped in the curtain fringe but she wanted in the worst way to wear some of the plumes too, putting on a pout and whining, "If I don't git to wear plumes like Danny I'm gonna tell." So right away what Earl Jr. done was tie more curtain fringe around her head to make an Indian band and stuck some of the plumes in it, saying she looked just like an Indian princess. Then right on the spot he made up a game he called Princess and let Kate sit on a throne he had us heap together with dead weeds and twigs and lined it on top with huckleberry leaves we tore off of the bushes, and she seemed content with that. I breathed a sigh of relief she was. Then Earl Jr. went and picked out one of the cherry switches from the bundle was already cut and we kept stacked off to one side, we been cutting off so many switches from the cherry trees around the clearing it was starting to look bare, so we began saving the ones we used from the times before, those ones, that is, that weren't snapped in half when one of us got too carried away.

The game was Kate would sit on her throne and queen it over us, like Sheena, Queen of the Jungle. Only she was wearing curtain fringe instead of a leopard skin, and clutching in one hand one of her dollbabies and in the other the cherry switch Earl Jr. gave her instead of a dagger. Us boys, all our clothes scattered by now on the blueberry bushes behind us, had to bow down in front of her in nothing but our feathers and the fringe around our middles and between our legs, pretending we were savages from Africa as she ordered us around or took swipes at us with her switch if we didn't move fast enough. She sat with her bare legs spread on the leaves and we all snuck peeps between her legs as we cringed or bowed or danced our way on by, Walter being a smarty, yelling, "Hey, Sheena, who cut off yer peashooter?" Kate stared at him like she didn't know what he meant, but even so, for his being so smart-alecky, she gave him a hard smack with her whip and he jumped away, yowling.

When she got tired of being Princess, Kate showed us how she peed, squatting down like she was doing number two and not standing up like a boy because she didn't have any dunkey. Then Earl Jr. had all of us boys pee together in a circle where she peed, Walter being silly and squatting down like Kate did on the throne, and Kate, seeing him, got the giggles like it was another game. That got us all going, we were all giggling and giggling, so naturally it wasn't long before our dunkeys were poking their heads out between our feathers to see what was going on. Earl Jr., seeing it, got a foxy look and had us stand again in a circle and had us rub our dunkey heads together, that I hadn't ever done before, while poor Kate just had to stand there watching since she didn't have no dunkey to rub against nothing.

It felt so sticky and tickly, Walter tee-hee-hee'd we were f-u-c-k-ing, but Earl Jr. said it wasn't real f-u-c-k-ing, that was different, that was what I knew now was what me and him saw in the Alley Oop and Blondie and Dagwood comic books he stole from his father—It was a word Frank and Buster and the Beezley boys used in secret and that Earl Jr. never used in secret and was the baddest of all the bad words you must never ever say.

The day the package came in the mail Frank and Buster brought it home from Gottlieb's and we all stood leaning on our elbows around the kitchen table terribly excited as my mother cut the string with her best scissors and tore the heavy brown wrapping paper off of the box and unwrapped the tissue careful as she could. When she lifted out the suit Aunt Bridget was lending her for me to wear for my first holy communion, the one Aunt Bridget's Tom, whose room I slept in when Grandmom died, wore at his, my eyes opened up so wide, I'd never seen anything so shivery shiny and white. Seeing it, Slap's eyes lit up too and he hollered in that loud way of his, "Hey, I weared that! I weared that!" My mother said, "That's right, it's the same suit I borrowed for you when it came your turn to make your communion at Sacred Heart and times was just gettin hard, even though they er nothin compared to now. Now let's only hope it fits," she said, looking worried at the suit, then at me, and told me to take off my clothes.

Frank and Buster started snooping and rooting through the box, hoping maybe there was something else in it besides the communion suit. They looked awful disappointed when all they found was a white satin ribbon my mother said was to tie around my arm.

When they saw the short pants were baggy in the seat, they all bust out laughing, my mother muttering about that, but the jacket looked all right, "It'll cover most of the seat anyhow," she said. The smell of mothballs stung my nose, reminding me of the way Aunt Nell's, that used to be Grandmom's, house smelled, and the suit went on smelling that way no matter how much my mother hung it out on the line to air. Except for water, I'd never felt anything so slippery on my skin before, and kept rubbing my fingers up and down the coat sleeve. I could see it was making her nervous.

"Take it off," she ordered, pushing my hand away. "We don't wanna git it dirty."

"Too bad he ain't croaked," Buster sneered. "He looks like he's all dressed up ready to stick in the box."

My mother gave him a dirty look. "That's enough out of you, boy, you watcher mouth." But I knew he just said that because I was getting all the attention and he wasn't, and he oughtn't to of said what he said anyway because Grandmom was in the box and he should've known our mother was still thinking of her.

As she folded the suit and wrapped it up neat again, handling it like it was made of spider webs, I asked her what that cloth was that was so shiny and shivery.

"Silk. Not a red cent to our name and you'll prolly be the only one wearin silk, thanks to yer Aunt Bridget and Uncle Digby. You be sure to remember them in yer prayers tonight."

"He'd look better in a dress," Buster sneered again, like he just couldn't keep his mouth shut.

"Ain't that what his girlfriend nextdoor's gonna wear?" Frank said, and him and Buster har-har-harred over that, while Slap held his hand to his ear going, "Heh? Heh? What's so funny?"

My mother gave both Frank and Buster another look. "Ain't it time for you two to go feed and water the chickens?" Buster made a face but she gave them that look they better get moving before she got her Irish up and the two of them scampered out the back door, their shoulders shaking, they were still snickering over me in a dress to make my first holy communion, them two had the memory of an elephant, never ever forgetting that day I played dressup with Ronnie.

My mother was right, the rest of the boys all had regular cotton suits with regular coats and white satin armbands tied in a bow. Most of them, especially the suits of the boys on relief, were borrowed, like mine, or else were hand-me-downs from older brothers, except for boys like Ronnie and Gerald that had new suits from Hurley's Department Store in Camden. Even Ronnie's brandnew suit was cotton, a double-breasted one just like a grownup's, which some said his mother got him just for show, like her letting him make his first holy communion was all for show, since neither her—"a lapsed Catholic," my mother called her—or Mr. Mahoney ever went to church. And it was true that after he made his communion, Ronnie only went to mass a few Sundays after that before he stopped going too, sleeping late in bed like the Beezley boys did. But before all that he bragged how his mother and father'd driven him up to Camden and had him fitted special for his suit at Hurley's Department Store on Broadway and how his Grandmother and Grandfather O'Shea paid the eight dollars cash for it, not including the new white shoes that cost a whole three dollars extra. But when he saw my silk suit you could see his eyes go green with envy despite he said with a sniff, "How old-fashioned it looks and reeks of mothballs besides." Even so, he kept running his hands down it anyhow, like he was wishing his suit was made of it instead of plain old cotton.

Now sometimes when my father came home at night from the dump truck or working on the road WPA was building through the swamp, he had that bright-eyed look I hadn't seen on his face since Grandmom's funeral and hadn't seen since way before that when we lived on Mifflin Street. When he came in the door with that look, I kept out of his way, scuttling under the dining room table. I could see it put a scare in my mother too, only she never said anything. When he came home looking that way she pretended she didn't see it though you could tell she did, the way her eyes got as dark as his was bright. You could hear it too in the way she talked to him, the way her words came out stiff and like she was talking to him from some other room even though he was right in front of her, the look in her eye saying more of what she wasn't saying than if she'd said it right out. Those times, you could see he was trying hard to pretend like he never had a few, the way he was as careful with his words as with the way he moved. At the supper table he could bury his face behind the *County Seat Weekly* or the Philadelphia *Evening Bulletin* so none of us could see his eyes and he didn't have to see ours. And afterwards too, sitting in his broken down easy chair by the oil lamp in the parlor, he could hide again behind his newspaper.

Sometimes now when the Beezleys came over Mr. Beezley'd bring a quart of Schmidt's with him. From out under the dining room table I could see Mrs. Beezley in the parlor give my mother a look she was so awful sorry as Mr. Beezley poured my father a beer into one of our jelly glasses. My mother gazed back at her with eyes deep as the shadows in the corners of the parlor.

Pretty soon after that when they came over, Mr. Beezley brought two quarts of beer, and then not long after that it was three, and now at night up in bed I could hear my father and him down in the parlor laughing louder'n usual and telling jokes I hardly had to strain my ears leaning over Slap to hear.

Another thing was, he was louder in the bedroom now. When they came up the stairs and he had beer in him, she would be whispering, "Shhh! Shhh! The kids, Stosh!" and he would be hollering, "To hell with the kids!" He'd go stumbling by our door, my brothers stirring in their sleep, Buster sometimes sitting straight up and gaping around like he didn't know where he was, then dropping back down to sleep again. But Slap slept right on through it, I wished sometimes I was deaf as Slap, it might be a blessing.

I'd hear her stop in our doorway to look in and listen a minute, then her steps moving away soft like she was on tiptoe going down the hall, followed by the door of their room shutting, then their voices rumbling behind the door for a long time after, his louder'n hers but hers sounding just as stubborn as his was, like they were both of them being so stubborn neither of them was about to give in, no matter what. And it always finally ended up with my father heaving himself over on the screeching bedsprings, followed a minute later by his snoring, snores so loud you could hear them right through their bedroom door.

The curtain was the same color as the wine Father Mack drank at mass and once I pulled it closed behind me, how deep the dark was surprised me. Inside the confessional box had the same dry dusty smell as the rest of the church. I stumbled a second not being able to see, feeling around for the step to kneel on, and when I found it knelt down hard and clumsy, quick pressing my hands tight together like I was praying, like Sister Joseph Mary told us to. Through the cloth screen I could hear Father Mack mumbling to the boy in the box on the other side, Gerald I knew it was, since he'd been ahead of me in line. I heard Gerald saying something back I couldn't hear, and wondered what sins he would have to confess since Mrs. Feek always said Gerald was just about perfect. Which must of still been true because it wasn't long before I heard the screen on the other side slide shut and the scrape of his shoes as he was getting up out of the box, so he mustn't've had very much to tell. I wished it was me getting out and the whole thing finally over.

Now my eyes were used to the dark I looked up and could just barely make out the body of Jesus Christ like a pale skinny light stretched out on the crucifix over my head. Staring at it, my heart started bumping around my chest like a fly in a bottle.

A second later the inside screen on my side was slid back

with a creak and the deep voice of Father Mack whispered, "Go ahead, my child, make a good confession."

His breath smelled of peppermint Life-Savers like my father's did when he was drinking and didn't want my mother to know.

Now the time'd really come, my heart was going a mile a minute, my mouth felt as dry as the time Earl Jr. said to spit on him and I couldn't spit on him to save my life. I was glad of the dark, though, because it made me feel like I was safe because Father Mack couldn't see me and that made it like it might be a little easier'n I thought—I'd barely slept all night worrying what to say, I knew I lied and was jealous of Gerald and stole sugar and held back my penny from the collection at mass for candy at Gottlieb's—All that I would tell, much as I would rather not, but I worried did I have to tell about our games of Slaves and Masters in the woods? Sister Joseph Mary said anything we kept secret we had to tell and I knew Slaves and Masters was a secret I swore to myself and made Danny and Kate swear never to tell, so I figured it must've been a sin I had to tell, much as I didn't want to. And if it was a sin, whether it was a venial sin or a mortal sin I didn't know, who was there I could've asked except Earl Jr. that would've only laughed in my face, not knowing what I was talking about, him being a heathen.

"Well, my child?..." I could hear him squirming restless on the bench. It was getting close to suppertime and maybe he was in a hurry to get back to the rectory for his dinner. When he had a few, my father said Father Mack didn't look like he ever missed many meals by the size of him, my mother shushed him saying he oughtn't to talk so disrespectful of the priest, especially in front of us kids, but my father said, "Aw gwan, go flap yer ears."

"Yes, yes...." I could hear Father Mack was losing his patience. Glancing up at the crucifix, that all of a sudden sent a bigger chill running through me, I made the sign of the cross like Sister Joseph Mary told us to. At first when I opened my mouth nothing came out but then I licked my lips and tried again, managing to whisper, "Bless me, Father, for I have sinned…"

I hurried real quick through what I figured were my venial sins, lying five times, mainly to my mother, was thoughtless twice, once to Slap and once to Danny, told the sin of pride about the silk communion suit, and my jealousy over Gerald's being at the first table and being teacher's pet—As I went on, the shadow of the priest's head against the screen slumped down slow on his chest like he was dozing off, but when I came to my holding back my penny from the collection basket on Sunday his head shot up and he gave a growl, saying I mustn't never do that any more, not putting my penny in the collection was the same as stealing from God, how was he ever going to get a bell for the church if everybody did what I did, I wouldn't do that any more, would I? And I whispered back I wouldn't, he was so mad, I figured holding your penny back from the collection must be a mortal sin.

When I ran out of little sins to tell I stopped. I could feel the palms of my hands all sweaty. In the silence I saw the dark head of Father Mack outlined against the screen drowse down again, then lift itself, heard another loud creak as he shifted his weight on the bench. He leaned in close to the screen, I was afraid he was going to holler at me again, but instead he said in quiet way, "Is there anything else, my child?" but sounding like he was tired and like he hoped there might not be anything else.

My tongue felt all of a sudden all swollen up. I was hardly breathing, my brain scurrying like a rat in a cage, wondering how much more I should tell. But didn't Sister Joseph Mary say not to hold back, that confessing to the priest was just the same as confessing to God? And didn't she say to receive holy communion with a sin still staining your heart was the worst of mortal sins and God might strike you dead on the spot once the wafer touched your tongue?

I could feel the sweat creeping down my neck. My heart began to really beat, thinking of what the Sister said, that our sins were like bruises in our hearts where Jesus was trying to get in and kiss them and make them all better. And that to make a good confession was to confess all our sins, big and little, and to tell them was to let Jesus in so He could make our hearts as pure as snow and white as our first holy communion clothes.

I saw the silk suit Aunt Bridget sent, hanging all shiny white in the dark closet in my mother's bedroom, it was gleaming in my mind white as Christ on the cross hanging over my head.

"Well, my child..." He was really getting impatient now, tapping his fingers against the panel. I knew I couldn't kneel there much longer and not say anything, there were still more boys waiting in line, and all of the girls to go yet, and it nearly suppertime.

I blurted out, "It's about the games, Father..."

I brought myself up sharp, my heart slamming up in my throat so I couldn't go on. I saw Father Mack's head in shadow turning towards me on the screen.

"What games, my child?"

I took a deep gulp of air. "The games in the woods, Father..." I heard the old wood creak and crack so loud it gave me a start as Father Mack pulled himself closer to the screen.

"Games? Tell me about them, child. What games?"

I glanced up again at the crucified body of Christ hanging over me, and biting my lower lip, made another sign of the cross. Like I was taking a swan dive off of the high bluff over the river, I took an even deeper breath and talking real fast before I lost my nerve, told him everything.

He kept breaking in with, "And then what did you do? And what did it feel like?" and when my tongue got stuck, he would ask, like he was prodding me with a stick, "And did you like it? Did you like it when the branches hit you? And did the others like it? Did you touch each other?" his voice like honey, his voice so smooth and sweet in my ear.

I sank my head against my knuckles, mumbling, "Yes, Father, yes," over and over, even confessing to things we hadn't even done, like once I got started I couldn't shutup, like I was telling him a story in the dark, like I told Slap and Danny in bed in the night, my voice, a whisper to begin with, getting lower and lower so that he kept telling me, "Speak up, my son, speak up," his face a big black shadow pressed against the screen, his breath so soft and raspy like he all of a sudden got a cold.

He seemed so shoved up against me, I felt my whole body straining backwards on the kneeling step, he seemed so dark and big I couldn't hardly breathe. I tried to talk louder but was afraid the boy waiting in the other box to tell his confession, and the other boys, especially Ronnie, that I knew was next in line just a few pews away outside, might hear me through the curtain. I was wishing with all my heart they were real doors like on the confessional boxes at Sacred Heart in South Philly, instead of just curtains that anybody could hear through. My face felt hot like I had a fever, I couldn't think of anything more I wanted to do'n get out of that box as fast as I could. But he kept at me, asking me if there was anything I might've forgot, some little thing, his breath that smelled so sweet of peppermint Life-Savers making me a little sick to my stomach. My bare knees started to hurt from kneeling so long on the hard step, I began to squirm, afraid he was going to ask me my name next, afraid he might even ask me for the names of the others, and hoped, in my being so nervous, I hadn't ratted on anybody by mistake.

I told him about riding on Mr. Mahoney's bare belly in a daydream.

"And what were you thinking?...And how many times?... And did you touch yourself?...."

And finally confessed about seeing the naked man and lady in the woods and how I sometimes dreamed of the man, and thought of him.

"And did you like seeing him?...And did you touch yourself?..." and didn't know what or where he meant, touching myself, but said yes, Father, yes and yes and yes...my voice choking up so I was afraid I was going to bust out crying.

When there wasn't anything left I could think of to tell him, even though he kept asking me was I sure that was all I had to confess, he finally gave me my penance that turned out to be a longer one'n the five Our Fathers and five Hail Marys the Sister said we would all probably be getting, turned out to be twice as many, in fact.

"Stay away from evil companions," he warned, by which I guessed he meant Earl Snarp Jr. "Stay out of the woods," he went on, "Keep your hands off yourself. Don't think so many impure thoughts."

So now I knew what impure thoughts were, they were thinking about what you wanted to touch but mustn't ever.

I saw Father Mack's shadow slump back away from the screen, saw his hand go up to his brow like he was wiping at it. "Now make a good Act of Contrition," he murmured, like he suddenly ran out of steam, like he must be really hungry I thought, it being so close to suppertime, and me keeping him so long.

I bent my head and started to mumble the prayer Sister Joseph Mary taught us, "Oh my God, I am heartily sorry for having offended Thee..." and as I mumbled it I did feel heartily sorry, I did feel heartily ashamed, while Father Mack muttered along in latin, at the end of it his big shadowy hand making the sign of the cross against the cloth of the screen as he gave me absolution.

"God go with you, my child," he whispered, "And remember what I told you," he hissed out in a louder whisper as he slid the screen shut with a snap.

As I got up, my bare knees in my short pants rubbed sore from kneeling so long, I heard the screen on the other side of the confessional shoot open and the mumbly voices begin all over again.

I pushed aside the curtain and stepped out of the box, feeling all wobbly, feeling like I didn't have any blood left in me, but with it all knowing the bruises in my heart had been drained out of me too. I kept my hands together and my head bowed like I was praying, like Sister said to, but that was mainly so I wouldn't have to see the faces of the other boys lined up waiting against the pews on either side. But I'd been kept in the box the longest so far and could feel them staring at me as I went down the aisle towards the altar to do my penance, especially Ronnie with his hands as always when he was in church, pressed together like he was praying so holy. He looked at me worried himself and leaned out just long enough to whisper as I passed, "What took you so long? Did he holler at you?"

That night, instead of waiting my usual turn and having to wash in the same bath water as the two younger ones, my mother, because it was a special occasion, let me go first in the old galvanized wash tub on the kitchen floor. While more water was heating in the big stew pot on the stove for my older brothers' baths, she gave me a good scrubbing, being extra careful around my neck and rubbing inside my ears so hard I winced. When she was through, my skin tingled all over and was as red as the comb on one of the roosters out in the coop. I felt as clean outside now as I felt inside, and when she dried me off, being first at the towel for once, I was surprised and pleased how dry the towel was, it was usually so soggy by the time it got to my turn on bath nights. After she dried me, I felt as white all over as the brandnew cotton underwear she put on me she got from relief just that week. Reminding me that I was fasting and wasn't to have even so much as a crumb of food or a sip of water after midnight and til after communion next day, she gave me a jelly glass of water to drink and sent me up to bed early so I'd stay clean for the morning.

But I couldn't sleep, I was so excited. "Now you be sure'n say yer prayers," she said before she left the bedroom, knowing I was too shy now to say my prayers in front of her, and I said I would. After she was gone and I was about to kneel down at the side of the bed, Slap came hanging in the doorway, watching me.

"You wanna tell me a story?" he asked in that high voice of his. "I'll git undressed and come to bed early if you'll tell me a story."

I shook my head. It didn't seem right to be telling stories the night before my first holy communion. Sister Joseph Mary told us to think only about the coming morning when for the first time we'd be receiving the Body of our Lord into our own body. Just thinking about it made me feel so clean and so dizzy all at once.

Seeing that, Slap put on a long face and leaned against the door jamb for another minute. I was wishing he would go away so I could start my prayers.

"C'mon, Mick," he said and in such a sad, beggy way, and

like always, wanting to please him, I was just about to give in but at the last second shook my head again.

"Sister said. And besides, Mom'll get mad. Anyway, you haven't had your bath yet." I forgot to raise my voice, I was feeling so quiet inside, so he went, "Heh? Heh?" squinting like he always did and sticking his hand behind his ear.

From the foot of the stairs, our mother, that always seemed to know everything that was going on anywhere in the house, hollered up, "Slap, you up there? Don't you be botherin your brother now! You git down her and git ready for yer bath!"

"Aw, jeezoo," Slap muttered, scrunching his lips together, he so hated to get in the washtub he would hide til the very last minute.

"Slap! You comin down here or do I have to come up and drag you down?"

He ran over and quick gave me a kiss then scurried out the door. I felt sorry for him, knowing how much he missed the radio and how much he loved his stories, but I didn't want to do anything would put a bruise back on my heart before morning.

It seemed so strange me being in bed at that hour when I wasn't even sick or been bad or anything. I felt as light as the down in the featherbed that my mother'd shoved to the foot of the bed now the weather was getting warmer. Even the sheets looked whiter'n they ever did.

Just then I heard Sam Beezley come in the front door downstairs, then him and my father yakking and laughing in the parlor, followed by the hiss of a beer bottle being opened. Mr. Beezley called the opener a church key, I wondered why it was called a church key when Sister Joseph Mary said to get drunk, especially on Sunday, was like a slap in God's face. There was the clink of glasses and I felt scared in my belly like I always felt when I knew my father was drinking even though I tried not to be. But I knew now if Jesus was in my heart I could turn Him on, I could turn Him on like the button on our Scott radio when the electric was on, you clicked it and the little people inside came alive and talked to you or sang songs to you, so I didn't have to be scared by myself any more, the Infant of Prague was in my heart, I could turn him on like the radio and listen.

Then I remembered I hadn't said my prayers yet and knelt down by the side of the bed and crossed myself. I prayed for my mother and sister and brothers, even for Buster. I prayed my father wouldn't drink as much as he did before South Philly. I prayed Sam Beezley'd get him a job any day now in the ship-yard. Remembering what Father Mack said to me in confession, I prayed for Earl Jr. I prayed for his foul mouth and his using God's name in vain. I would stop seeing him if I had to. I would stop going into the woods with him to dance. I would stop going into the woods with Danny and Kate and Walter Snarp. I would try not to think impure thoughts of sitting on Mr. Mahoney's bare belly.

My skin still felt tickly from my mother's scrubbing me, like the veils of the Virgin Mother were brushing over me. All of a sudden I felt a gush of excitement that was as silky and nice as the communion suit'd felt against my skin that day when I first tried it on. Then I was baffled when just as quick I felt my new snow-white underwear from relief stretching tight between my legs, it was that same mysterious swelling up as happened dur-ing our games of Slaves and Masters in the woods. And didn't Father Mack say I was to stay out of the woods, by which I guessed he meant even staying out of the woods in my head?

So right away I shut my eyes and said ten Our Fathers and ten Hail Marys one right after the other til the tightness went down and then, not wanting to risk making another bruise on my heart, I squeezed my eyes shut even tighter'n my underwear'd been and tried my hardest to go to sleep.

I woke up so early the window was barely gray from the dawn. Slap lay sleeping beside me, his head thrown back, breathing through his mouth. Danny was on his belly at the foot of the bed, half buried under the feather- bed shoved down there. Across the room, only the noses of my older brothers stuck out from beneath the sheets. I had to pee so bad, like my older brothers always said, my back teeth were floating, all I could think of was getting out to the bucket in the hall as fast I could. But the bucket, as it often was by the morning, especially if my father was drinking beer the night before, was all full up, so I hurried back into the bedroom and got into my pants and sneakers and creeped down the stairs.

Still groggy with sleep, as I passed through the kitchen on my way to the outhouse, I realized how hungry I was when I spotted some broken pretzel sticks in the bottom of a bowl on the kitchen table that must've been leftovers from last night's beer-drinking between my father and Sam Beezley. Without thinking, I snatched one up as I scurried by and popped it in my mouth. It was barely down my throat when I realized to my horror what day it was and what I'd done. Sister Joseph Mary'd warned us it was a sin to receive holy communion with anything in our bellies, not even so much as a drop of water, not even so much as a crumb of food, our bellies were to be tabernacles all nice and clean, ready to receive Our Lord God.

Certain God watched everything I did, even when I picked my nose or was out in the outhouse, I stood like my feet were stuck to the linoleum and, wide awake now, I peeped all around me as if He'd seen me gobble down that pretzel, my shoulders hunched, waiting for the blow. Feeling like all the blood all of a sudden was drained out of me, my heart began to race and I was in such a panic I felt a hard quick shove down in my gut and right away ran out the kitchen door and across the yard fast as I could. For once I didn't hesitate a single second as I yanked open the outhouse door and jumped inside, not even bothering to look under the seat for snakes either, like I still always did, as I tore down my pants and sat myself down on the hole, for the first time since we moved here less afraid of the dark spidery privy than I was of what I might've done, breaking my fast.

As I heard the t-u-r-d's drop away into the dark below, I breathed an awful lot easier, I was so relieved now in thinking my body was all cleaned out again so's to receive the Body of Christ, and tearing off pages of the latest Sears Roebuck catalog Mrs. Beezley'd sent over, I wiped myself extra careful so there wouldn't be any apple butter in my new white underwear for my mother to see when she went to dress me in the silk communion suit.

Later, while she was putting it on me out in the kitchen, and my father, his face gray as death with a hangover, his collar tucked inside his shirt as he shaved with a shaky hand in front of the mirror over the sink, I began to have my doubts and wanted to ask her, in a roundabout way, if you ate even so much as a teensy-eensy bit of a pretzel but did number two right after, had you still broke your fast? But she was so bent on buttoning the jacket and giving it a pull here and a tug there and yanking it down in back to hide the too-big seat, her buck teeth biting down on her lower lip in a worried way, I didn't think she'd hear me anyway, but was afraid my father might and, ever suspicious, start giving me the third degree.

I decided, as she tied and retied the satin bow tighter and tighter on my right arm til she got just the right bow to suit her, that it was probably a whole lot better, and safer, for me to keep my mouth shut.

Once the jacket was buttoned, she crouched down, holding

me at arm's length, and gave me the onceover for the umpteenth time, the look on her face still saying there was something not quite right about the way I looked but she just couldn't put her finger on it.

"It'll jist have to do," she sighed finally, taking another brush at my hair, and standing up called over to my father, "You almost ready?" His face looked fierce as a rooster's as he dabbed his styptic pencil on a couple knicks on his throat. He threw her an annoyed look in the glass, like he'd rather be doing anything else in the whole wide world that morning'n see me making my first holy communion.

My mother pinned on Aunt Maggie's black hat from Grandmom's funeral that was faded in the crown by now from the sun, and just before we left the house to walk to the church, she asked me in a real low voice, "You have to go to the terlet?"

I told her I already had.

As I walked up the road between them, the Mahoney's Chevy went swirling by in a cloud of dust with Mr. and Mrs. Mahoney up front all dressed up like they were going to the movies, and Ronnie sitting up stiff in the back in his brandnew white double-breasted suit from Hurleys, his nose in the air, his hands stuck up in the window already folded in prayer so everybody in Lenape could see how holy he was, roaring by acting like they hadn't seen us. But I didn't care, the silk of my cousin Tom's communion suit felt so slippery and cool rubbing on my arms and on my thighs with every single step I took.

Sister Joseph Mary's wooden clacker was the signal for us boys to leave the communion rail and file back to our seats. But the wafer was stuck like peanut butter to the roof of my mouth. No matter how I worked my tongue to pry it loose and swallow it, it stayed plastered there, drier and stubborner I found out than even the Sister'd said it would be. And she said not to leave the railing til we swallowed it, hadn't she?

I squeezed my eyes shut and worked my tongue, hearing the rustle of cotton as the other boys marched back to the pews, heard Sister Veronica Rose's clacker signaling the girls to rise now and line up in the aisle to march to the altar for their turn at the rail.

Behind me, I also heard faint whisperings out in the church and bowed my head lower, my jaws working harder, careful not to let any of the wafer touch my teeth, imagining the blood that would gush out of my mouth if I did, my palms, still clapped together in prayer, pressing tighter and tighter as I prayed, Please go down, please go down right now....

I jumped as a hand was laid on my shoulder and turning, I was surprised to see my father standing there. He looked embarrassed to be standing up in front of all the people and his adam's apple was going like it always did when he was nervous. I wanted to tell him I couldn't swallow the communion but the wafer was still stuck in my mouth and I knew I mustn't talk in church anyway. He took my hand and led me away from the railing and out the side door by the sacristy. I wondered was he going to holler at me, his face still had that look like ashes.

The morning was cool and no sun, the grass still all wet from the night before. He was all darkness in his Sunday suit that was shiny in the seat and elbows and smelled of tobacco as he leaned down close, closer'n I ever remembered his leaning down to me in a long, long time, and asked me in a voice a lot quieter'n any he used to me since I was little, "Whatsa matter, Mickey, you sick?" His other hand rested easy on my shoulder. I could feel the roughness of it scrape along the silk.

I shook my head, unable to explain right then what the nun

had said, that we weren't to leave the altar rail til we swallowed the wafer, then just at that very moment the last of the wafer slid down.

I must've looked relieved because the next thing he asked was, "You feeling okay now? You feeling okay enough to go back inside?"

His hand for all its roughness was surprisingly warm, the sound of his voice, so close, was also warm in my ear, his breath, like his suit, smelling of cigarettes, his breath like the morning he blew smoke in my ear when I had the earache.

"You wanna go back inside now? Huh? You wanna go back in now, Mick?"

I sensed he was getting impatient but still I waited.

"Huh? Huh? Hey, Mick, look at me. You wanna go back?"

His eyes, still bloodshot from the night before, got that look of a rooster again that was sharp as a Lenilenape arrowhead and never once blinked. But at least his cheeks had some color in them now, his cheeks that smelled of bay rum.

The confusion I had at the altar began to go away. I felt a big calm come over me, feeling my father close, hearing the quiet in his voice that I wasn't used to, knowing now the wafer was down the Son of God was in me, the Son of the Father of all that was white as the wafer, and now He was in me I was all of a whiteness too, inside and out, all the whiter in the shadow of the dark Sunday suit of my father bending over me.

I closed my eyes and nodded I was ready.

There were more arguments between them now, mainly about money and his wanting money for beer out of what little there was, him saying, "I work hard all day and deserve it," and her saying, "There ain't goin to be no beer in the icebox so long as there ain't no food in it." There were picky arguments too over us kids—he'd tell us to do one thing and she'd say to do another so we never knew who to listen to, it was like we were caught in between them and didn't know which way to go.

The worst of it was, the more he drank the more he got an idea in his head she was "running around," as he called it, running around behind his back, and nothing she said could shake it loose. You could hear them arguing about it in their bed at night. At first she just laughed at him, "Gwan with ya, y'old fool," she'd say, half irritated and half humoring him because she knew he was three sheets to the wind and it was the beer talking. But then when he kept it up and kept it up she stopped laughing altogether and next day you could see a dark look in her eye like she was deep downstairs in herself like she was with her mother again and, as if she couldn't wait for Mrs. Beezley to come over in the afternoon, was talking with her mother and was telling her everything, because anybody could see the only running around she ever did was running around the house with a mop or a rag in her hand, cleaning, or running back and forth between the stove and the washboard, cooking and washing for all of us kids, including him, she barely had time to run out to the outhouse.

One night not long after he started accusing her of running around, though who she was running with and where she run to he never would say, he was sitting in the parlor listening while Sam Beezley was talking his shipyard talk, telling my father how he'd been putting in a word for him with this bigshot and with that bigshot, while the two of them were working on their third quart of Schmidts. Hiding crouched as I was in the dark under the dining room table I could see through the tablecloth it was like my father could just taste that job in all the beer he kept gulping down, it was like he had that job in his pocket and was celebrating already.

Now it was late, Kate was already asleep on the old cot my mother'd set up for her in the dining room now she was getting too big for her crib. My brothers, after playing pinochle in the kitchen most of the night—that was the game they played all that summer now they were sick of hearts—had already gone up to bed. When they left, I saw my chance and snuck out from under the dining room table and tiptoed out to the shed where I kept my empty brown bags and boxes I saved up and came back and sat down now at the kitchen table and started drawing pictures of things on the backs of a couple paper bags. Drawing under the oil lamp wasn't as good to draw under as electric light but was better'n nothing. I drew pictures of Mickey Mouse, then drew pictures of Earl Jr., then I erased Earl Jr., remembering what Father Mack said in the confessional, I drew a picture instead of the Infant of Prague that was living in my heart now, drawing it careful as I could with his crown on his head and his bleeding heart that was all on fire.

All the while I kept one ear cocked in the direction of the parlor so I could hear if anybody was coming and at the same time hear Mr. Beezley jawing to my father about his day at the shipyard, that wasn't hard to do he talked so loud and wasn't even deaf like Slap. I liked to hear his shipyard stories even if my mother didn't.

I could see directly through the dining room into the parlor and saw my father's face was as red and his eyes as bleary as Mr. Beezley's was. My mother sat on the day-bed, her crochet needle flashing in the light of the oil lamp at her elbow, her mouth set tight, not having anything to say or to listen to much since Mrs. Beezley'd stayed home that night like she sometimes did when she had something she called "The Curse," she always said it in capital letters even though she said it to my mother in a whisper.

My mother cared as much to hear about the shipyard as she

did to hear them talking about baseball, the only thing I knew she really wanted to hear was did Mr. Beezley get my father a job in the shipyard, and since he hadn't done that up til now, when Mr. Beezley staggered up to go home, I could see she wasn't altogether sorry.

As my father and him stood on the front porch, laughing and slapping each other on the back goodnight, she came out to the kitchen. She was so quiet and quick, like she was sneaking away from my father, by the time I heard her there wasn't enough time to get all my drawings together and beat it up the stairs before she caught me. When she saw me still sitting at the table she raised her eyebrows, saying, "What're you still doin up and wastin good erl?" "I was just drawin," I begged so she wouldn't holler at me, but the look she gave me I knew I better get moving.

She went on out to the shed like she always did at night to get the bucket left out there to air and take it on her way upstairs so we wouldn't have to go out to the outhouse in the dark, she was still so afraid of us younger ones falling down the steps and breaking our necks or falling in the swamp and drowning. I was getting my pictures together quick as I could when she came through again, carrying the bucket in her hand since the handle'd long since broke, and telling me to snap it up and get to bed with the others, "You ain't no privileged character."

She had an exasperated look on her face tonight as she climbed the steps, it was plain to see she was annoyed that my father was drunk again, drunker'n he'd been since Grandmom's funeral. After he came in off the porch and locked the front door, seeing her creeping up the stairs and seeing how irritated she was, he stared at her through the railings while he weaved from side to side and threw her dirty looks as much as to say, I'll have me a few beers if I want, and to h-e-l-l with you.

When she just ignored him and kept going right on up the steps, I could see his jaws starting to work as he ground his teeth while at the same time he clinched his hands into fists, banging them against his thighs, his face flushing a darker red.

"What're you throwin me them looks for?" he snarled, "What're you...?" And when she didn't answer him he went after her, following her up the stairs, shouting at her, his tongue so thick, his eyes all glassy, talking his crazy talk again. "I seen you makin eyes! I know what yer up to! I know yer runnin around! You won't say yes to me so you must be sayin yes to somebody else!"

Even though she was biting her lower lip she still acted like she didn't see him nor hear a word he said. And he all of a sudden got that fierce look in his eye like a rooster about to fight as he lunged up the stairs, going after her with his fists, which I never saw him do before—My mouth flew open, I felt like I was all in an instant froze to the seat of the kitchen chair.

She swung around, her eyes bugging out, looking at him like he really had gone crazy. She hit out at him with the bucket, screaming, "Don'tchou ever lay yer hands on me! Don'tchou ever!" hitting out at him and hitting out at him. He swung his arms up in front of his face so he wouldn't get hit with the bucket and in doing that he swerved against the bannister, his back hitting it so that he stumbled down a few steps.

From the dining room Kate started crying in her sleep and just at that same exact moment Buster came flying down the stairs in his underwear, shouting, *"Mom! Mom!"* The look in my father's eyes when he saw my brother push himself between them and throw his arms around my mother like he wanted to protect her was a look like he'd somehow been cheated, seeing Buster take his mother's side against him. He gave himself a shake, like Buster's shouting made him come to, it seemed like he sobered up for a minute, like he was waking up out of a sleep and didn't know where he was. Dropping his fists, he backed off down the stairs, all of a sudden sheepish, mumbling in defiance like all the fight'd gone out of him, "You go tell yer Father Mack all about it in confession, you go and tell him like you go and tell him everything else behind my back."

But my mother wasn't listening to him, she had an arm around Buster whose legs were shaking like he was cold or scared or so mad he couldn't stop them from shaking. She was stroking his hair, murmuring, "It's all right, it's all right now," and shooed him back up the stairs. Then she turned and again looking past my father's head like he wasn't there, she stood listening til she heard Kate quiet down before she kept on up the stairs herself, clutching the bucket in her hand, her lips pressed so thin, her eyes black with something deeper'n I ever saw in them before, deeper even than the look in her eyes at the Holy Cross cemetery when she saw her mother's casket going down into the ground like a part of herself was going down with it.

My mouth still gaping open, I heard him come stumbling through the unlit dining room. I quick wanted to crawl under the kitchen table but it was like my legs'd gone to sleep, like I was in a dream when you want to run but can't run to save your life. So what I did was I buried my nose in my pictures, pretending to be staring at them and studying them, not knowing what else to do, knowing, drunk as he was, he'd still know I should've been in bed, and seeing I wasn't, I was shivering in my belly he might come after me like he came after my mother, he was still clinching and unclinching his fists like he wanted to smack somebody, smack anything he could.

But when he came and sat down in the kitchen chair by the window, it seemed like, as with my mother with him, I wasn't there at all. Dropping his head, his hair hanging down on either side of his face like it did when he drove the horse and wagon drunk that day with Uncle Jake and Louie at the mummers parade, he just sat there without saying anything, leaning his elbows on his thighs and still squeezing his hands like he was trying to choke something, his leathery hands just twisting and twisting.

Watching him, my heart felt like it was getting tighter, I could hardly breathe, like it was my heart in his hands. I bent closer over my pictures, hoping he was so drunk I really was invisible to him, but still I stared across at him, barely lifting my eyes, afraid he might become aware of my being there and start in on me. All I wanted was to slink out of the room without him seeing me, but I still felt like the seat of my pants was froze to the chair, I wasn't able to do anything but stare at his hair hanging down, stare at the palms of his hands rasping together as he squeezed them...*his hand on my shoulder...the scrape of it over silk...* What I really wanted to do was go to him and push back his hair, what I really wanted to do was put my hand on his shoulder like he did on mine at my first holy communion, he looked so beat down and blue. But I didn't do anything, I just sat there stiff as a dumbie, holding back and holding back like I always did, like I was scared to touch him or go near him, right from that very first time in the kitchen in South Philly when he picked me up off of the floor, grinning at me, I was wondering *who was he?* and staring around for her to tell me who he was.

I tried to keep perfectly still, my face bent over my pencil scratchings of Mickey Mouse and Jesus that were nothing but a blur in my eyes, but still keeping the other eye on him from under my brows. He seemed to be falling asleep in the chair, and seeing my chance I was just sliding off of my own chair to make a run for the stairs when, it being so old, the chair gave a loud squeak that all of a sudden made him look up, gaping at me like he was seeing me for the first time, the expression on his face the same as it'd been on the stairs when he went after my mother, like he was in a daze but was coming out of it, out of some deep black place that while he was in it made his face all dark and twisted so that for a minute he looked like somebody I hadn't ever seen before.

"Whataya doin here?" he mumbled. "Whataya doin up so late?"

My heart was whistling in my ears. I didn't know what to say and started to say I was just going up to bed but the words caught in my throat and all I could do was stare back at him. He lurched up and I cringed back in my chair, but instead of coming after me, he stumbled out through the shed and flung open the backdoor where I heard him vomiting off of the backstep.

I grabbed up my pencil and my pictures and scurried through the dining room. Kate was breathing soft now in her cot, the house was quiet with everybody else in bed. As I quick slipped up the stairs, I heard the backdoor slam, then heard him slide the bolt across the lock, heard him coughing and clearing his throat like he was gagging.

Once up in our bedroom, I threw off my clothes faster'n I ever did before and piled them on the back of the chair along with all my brothers' things as I heard him come crashing up the stairs, cursing to himself as he stumbled in the dark. Buster, like he heard him coming in his sleep, was thrashing around and crying out in the next bed. Fast as I could I stuck my drawings in the very bottom of my drawer in the bureau where I kept all of my pictures in a pile under my underwear, then climbed careful over Slap and slid under the blanket, deciding it'd be safer to say my prayers in bed rather'n kneeling at the side of it with my back exposed where he might see me. The soles of his workboots scraped by on the linoleum out in the hallway and not long after that I heard him still muttering to himself going into their room. I held my breath thinking he might start in on her again but all I heard was the bedsprings creak as he fell onto them with a heavy sigh, followed not long after that by his even heavier snoring.

I let out my breath all in a rush like I'd been holding my breath ever since he went after my mother. I closed my eyes, feeling it was safe enough now to try to go to sleep. But I couldn't, pictures kept racing behind my eyes, I kept seeing him coming after her with his fists, I kept seeing Buster flying down the stairs, then him sitting by the window in the kitchen with his head drooping. I stuck my hand under the mattress and pulled out the piece of brick I kept hidden there from the pavement in front of our old house at 126 Mifflin Street, and held it tight in my hand. I kept thinking maybe if we moved back to Philly then everything'd be all right, that bad as they'd been there things couldn't be any worse'n they were for us now, wondering as I lay there waiting for sleep to come what my mother was thinking right then, having a feeling she was probably still awake too.

Was she thinking what I was thinking, laying with her eyes wide open and staring up at the dark ceiling the way I was, as she listened to his heavy snores lifting and falling in the bed beside her?

The next night when he came in the backdoor from working on the road she gave him the silent treatment, serving him his supper without a word. He looked a little green around the gills, his face all stubbly, him needing a shave. He was quieter'n usual too, and like he was trying to hide, he buried himself behind the sports pages of yesterday's Philadelphia *Bulletin* that

Mrs. Beezley always sent over. Another thing was, he wasn't shoveling in the meat and mashed potatoes and clapping his lips over it like he usually did. He always said, whenever my mother teased him he was making more noise eating'n all of us kids put together, his mother always said that in the old country if you didn't clap your lips over what you ate, it was an insult to the cook, so he told her the louder he ate the more it showed he was enjoying her cooking.

Buster kept sneaking looks at him to see was he sober but you could tell he was, if he'd had a few in him, the newspaper wouldn't be rattling from his hands shaking the way they were.

Us kids were quiet too, not that he ever let us talk at the table while he was reading, but tonight there wasn't the secret looks going around or Frank or Buster making faces at each other and at the rest of us, trying to get us to bust out laughing. Even Kate knew something was up between them, she kept her eye first on one then on the other, like she knew something was different but didn't know what. All except for Slap, that had his face down in his plate and as usual was shoveling it in like there was no tomorrow, we all kept watching them. It was like everybody was eating quick as they could so's to get away from the table, there was such a loud quiet between them it was loud as thunder, making it hard for the rest of us to eat.

It was Frank and Buster's turn to do the dishes and for once, like they knew they better behave themselves since our father was more edgy'n ever, there was no arguing between them over who was going to wash and who was going to dry. After Slap came in from feeding and watering the chickens he shouted, "They's so many skeeters out on the front porch I was gittin et alive, even if we lit a zillion punks, even if we lit a zillion citronella candles, it won't keep em away!" so we all ended up staying inside the parlor. Slap flopped down on his belly on the linoleum and started reading for the umpteenth time an old Superman comic book the Beezley boys gave my brothers so long ago the pages were all smudgy and ripped. I was sitting on the couch between Danny and Kate telling them their favorite story, Shirley Temple in "Poor Little Rich Girl" that was so much their favorite they wanted to hear it over and over, when our father came in and sat down in his old broke chair. He gave me a look before he buried his nose behind the paper as much to say that'll be enough out of you, so I left off where Shirley was eating spaghetti in the poor Italian people's cellar even though I was almost at The End. Kate, though, kept tugging at my elbow, saying, "Then what, Mick? Then what?" even though she knew perfectly well then what. I whispered I'd finish the story another time and for her to go play with her dolls.

Frank and Buster came in now the dishes were done and asked my father like they always did, only tonight asking in a real careful way, was he finished with the sports pages yet. There was a growl in his eye when he fished it out and handed it to them, like even asking to see the sports pages was a bother to him. Even though tonight they tried to keep it down, as usual, the two of them right away started arguing over who was to read what first til my father snarled in a way that told them they better shutup, "I don't want to hear another word out of you two." So they sprawled out beside Slap and Danny, Buster, that read a whole lot faster'n Frank, as usual elbowing Frank to hurry up so he could turn the page.

My mother came in after she saw the kitchen was cleaned up and everything put away, and once she lit the oil lamp, she sat down beside me on the couch with her crocheting. I watched her out of the corner of my eye at the same I tried to draw a picture of Shirley Temple eating a plate of spaghetti out of my memory, my mother was acting so much like nothing was the matter you could see there was.

I tried to concentrate on my drawing and getting Shirley's curls just right, that was harder now in just the flame from the oil lamp, but found my eyes kept glancing on the sneak from one of them to the other. As so often happened when he'd drunk too much the night before and didn't drink the following night— "Givin his gut a rest," my mother always told Mrs. Beezley—he was all agitated and nervous, so that when he went into his cigarette pocket for one of his homemade Buglers his hand shook so bad the cigarettes spilled out of the old crumpled Chesterfield pack he kept them in so you couldn't tell the difference if they were real storebought ones or not. He gave a curse under his breath as he gathered them up out of his lap and stuck them all back in the pack. I watched to see if my mother saw what happened but her eyes were close on her crocheting in a way if she did see anything she pretended she didn't.

When he reached for his matches the matchbook shook in his hand and the newspaper was shaking in the other hand and when he scratched the match across the bottom of the matchbook like he always did without closing the lid even the thumb he scratched it with was shaking. All of a sudden there was a flare-up, the room got a whole lot brighter as the entire pack of matches went up in a ball of flame right in his hand. He groaned, and flinging the newspaper aside, shook his hand fast as he could, trying to shake out the fire, but that only whipped it up all the more. Then he tried blowing on it real hard and finally took his hand and beat it against his trouser leg til it was out, making an awful face as he clenched his fist in his lap, making shushing noises through his teeth the way a kid does as if that will help to quiet the hurt.

Holding up his thumb, he stared amazed at the charred and blistery skin, his eyes as big as Slap's and Danny's were when, distracted by the sudden flare-up, they both glanced up from the comic book they were looking at.

Her, that was so scared of fire she was always getting up in the night to sniff down the stairs for any smoke, she didn't so much as look, pretended not to have noticed any of it, her crochet needle flashing under the lamplight, her mouth tight, her eyes like slits, an expression on her face as much as to say, "Serves you right."

Frank and Buster gaped for a second, tearing themselves away from the sports page to stare at his hand before they turned back to reading about and arguing in hot whispers over who was going to win the pennant.

I turned away too, I couldn't bear seeing his eyes, like the pain in them was all mixed up now with the look of his being cheated all over again as everyone of us ignored him, the very same look he had as when Buster'd jumped in between my mother and him the night before on the stairs. As for me, like I had last night when he came and sat in the kitchen after he'd gone after her, I had another strong feeling I wanted to go to him, not knowing what I'd do if I did. But I felt like I was froze to my seat just like I was last night, only this time it was like I was torn in two between my knowing the pain he caused her because of his drinking, while feeling at the same time just as if the pain in his hand was in my hand too, pain that seemed, from his eyes, as burning as his other look of feeling cheated and being made to feel like a stranger amongst all of us right at that very moment.

Yet I knew that if it had been one of us had burnt ourselves, no matter how mad she may've been at us for something we did, she still would've come running with butter or lard, or Unguentine, if she had it in the medicine chest. I suspected he knew it too and that it only helped spread the bitterness in his eyes, that look that said if it'd been any of us or anybody else, even Charley the cripple or Lenny the Lenilenape, she wouldn't've turned her eyes away, wouldn't've kept jabbing away with her crocheting needle on another one of her doilies like nothing ever happened. /

I kept watching her sideways, watching to see if she would have a change of heart, and seeing she wasn't going to, had it in my own heart to at least ask him did he want me to go get him some butter to put on his hand. But afraid if I did I would be turning against her the way he knew she was turned against him, I sat as stiff and silent as she was, imitating her pretending not to see, imitating her tight-lipped expression that still seemed to say, "Serves him right."

Still and all, I was ashamed in my heart that not one of us asked him how bad it hurt or even offered to run and get butter to put on it or see if there was any Unguentine in the medicine chest.

Finally it was Slap still staring up from Superman, yelled, "Does it hurt, Pop? Does it hurtcha?" Then Kate, hearing him from the corner where she'd been watching bug-eyed, laid down the dollbaby she was playing with and started to cry. But my mother's needle kept flashing like she didn't see any of it and didn't want to hear any of it either, her needle flashing and flashing under the oil lamp.

He had to do it himself finally, got up in that quick way of his like he was a jackknife springing open, his jaw set, that set look on his face. He headed out to the kitchen where you could hear him opening the icebox, followed by his chipping a piece of ice off to rub on it, then his scrabbling with the butter dish. Slap and Danny went back to their comic book while Frank and Buster went on arguing in a louder voice now he was out of the room over the Phillies and the Athaletics and why did Frank have to read every single word and be so slow turning the pages.

That night I was woke up again by their voices coming low and rumbly through the wall like faraway thunder. It made Slap and Danny on either side of me twitch and stir in their sleep. I could sense Buster'd been woke up too and was listening hard in the dark same as me, maybe he was even getting himself ready to jump out of bed to run protect her again, if he had to. One time their voices got so loud it even woke up Slap, then it woke up Danny, Slap jumping and jerking a couple times before he got back to sleep again, Danny rolling over on his belly and riding his dunkey til he went off too.

After that, I heard my mother get up, heard her bare feet padding swift around her side of the bed, her words all muffled but warning him, "You'll wake the kids!" and his spitting out before she shut the door, "To hell with the goddam kids, let 'em all hear! Letcher Father Mack hear me all the way to the rectory! *No more kids!* You hear that, Father Mack? *No more kids!* You tell yer Father Mack that in confession next time!"

She tried to shush him, her whispers begging, then angry when he wouldn't shush, their voices that were lower rumblings now behind the closed door, sounding for a long time after. I could hear Buster lay back down in his bed and not long after hear his breathing coming soft and even as he drifted back to sleep. Me, I slipped my hand under the mattress and slid out the piece of brick from the pavement in front of our old house on Mifflin Street, clinching it tight in my hand. Finally I felt my legs and arms beginning to relax, I thought I might be able to drift asleep now, only to have them all of a sudden jerk me wide awake again when my father lifted his voice one more time, hollering, "C'mon! C'mon!"

Slap and Buster tossed and moaned in their sleep, then a

long quiet followed that was finally broke by the quick shriek of bedsprings from the other room and a smothered groan from my mother like she couldn't breathe.

I lifted my head on the pillow, strained my eyes through the dark door. She was certain, I knew, from all I heard her tell Mrs. Beezley, that she would burn in hell forever and ever if she gave in. I lay my head back, squeezing the piece of brick in my hand, lay watching in the dark between my sleeping brothers as what looked like a tongue of flame out in the hallway flickered then died then flickered up again, listened to the springs sighing in the next room. Then all of a sudden my heart was pounding, hearing the iron squeals of the bed get louder, my brain started running wild seeing pictures of Blondie and Dagwood and Little Orphan Annie and Alley Oop in the comic books Earl Jr. stole from under his father's mattress and showed me in the clearing in the woods...I clapped my eyes shut tight as I could trying to blot them out and like when I used to click on our old Scott radio when the juice was on, I turned on the little Infant of Prague in my heart to drive out those pictures in my head I knew now from Father Mack in confession were impure thoughts....

Then everything stopped. After a minute I heard him getting out of their bed, their door opened and the glow of his cigarette lit up the little hallway, erasing the lick of flame I'd seen, replacing it with his real one. As he peed in the bucket, peeing against the side of it like he always did, like he was trying to soften the sound so nobody'd hear him peeing in the bucket, the smoke from his Bugler drifted into our room, making me so hungry for a cigarette, I breathed in the smell of his smoke, wishing I had me a cigarette right then, even if it was only one of the butts me and my brothers picked up in the gutters on the way to church. He coughed a couple times, then went and got back into bed, leaving their bedroom door open, she always wanted it left open so she could hear any of us if we needed her, and so she could smell the first whiff of smoke in case there was a fire.

When his snoring began there was a sound along with it I thought at first was a breeze at the window or a humming of the wind in the willows back in the swamp. But when I lifted my head up from the pillow and cocked an ear to listen, it was a sound coming from their room, it was a sound like it was her crying that was like a humming and a moaning all to herself for a long time after.

It wasn't long after that Father Mack drove up in his stream-lined Chrysler, making another one of his visits. I was sitting on the front porch minding Danny and Kate when he pulled up. My first thought was to run hide because maybe he did know it was me in my first confession telling him about our games in the woods and he was finally stopping by to tell my mother on me.

But when he came up the steps, fanning his face with his panama hat, he gave us a big smile, bending down and rubbing each of our heads, asking us were we good children? I wondered if it was a trick, Danny and Kate looked like they did too because the both of them gave me a look and I made a yes with my eyes, so they nodded their heads yes along with me, yes, we were good, did he think, him being the priest, we were going to say we were bad? Then he chucked me under the chin, saying what a fine boy I was and what fine children we were, he kept his hand on top of my head and I blushed and didn't know what to say and was so glad just then the screendoor scraped open and my mother came out all flustered like she always was whenever the priest showed up. She had a lopsided grin on her face and had her hand up trying to hide her teeth like always, while the other hand fluttered nervous at the top of her old housedress, her saying in a too-loud voice like she was talking to Slap, "If I knowed you was coming, Father, I'd've changed me dress and washed me face!"

He nodded his head at her saying, "I was just in the neighborhood and thought I'd stop by and see how you all are and give you my blessing."

"Thank you for thinking of us, Father," she said, too loud again, brushing at her dress and at her hair all the while, then staring at us like she hadn't ever seen us before, screeching, "Look at them now—little buggers—Kate look at yer hair! and ain't I jist brushed it this morning?—Danny, let Mickey tie up them sneakers! Oh, look at them now!"

I darted down to tie Danny's sneakers, relieved to get Father Mack's hand off of my head, my mother saying to him in that way she talked in front of teachers and doctors and nurses and priests but never talked that way any other time, "Won't you come in and set a minute, Father?" saying it like she might be eager to get us out of his sight.

He mopped his forehead with his handkerchief and said, "Why thank you, Mrs. Lithwack, I've been running around the parish all morning and don't at all mind taking a load off my feet."

Once they were inside, I put a finger to my lips as a sign to Danny and Kate, then slid off of the porch on my belly and crept down the steps and scooted around the side of the house and in the backdoor. Tiptoeing through the kitchen and into the dining room, I dove under the dining room table that was all dark with the tablecloth hanging all around and squeezed myself into a ball and stuck my hands behind my ears. I just had to hear what was being said in the parlor because in spite of his big smiles and his hand on my head, my heart was pounding for fear he really came to tell my mother what I told him in my first confession.

"...I don't know what to do, Father..." she was saying. "I argue with him and argue with him and tell him what you told me but it don't do no good..."

She started sniffling and fumbled in her apron pocket for her hankie, dabbing at her eyes. Had he told her already about me dancing bare in the clearing and swinging a cherry switch at the others? Father Mack was sitting in my father's old broke down armchair and the look in his eyes behind his rimless glasses was like he was feeling sorry for her, but even so he said, "As a Catholic woman and mother, it's your duty to see that he stops that—There's no greater gift you can give to God than the children you give Him..." saying it quiet and gentle but there was a hardness behind his words like he was mad at her, and my heart fell into my shoes hearing him telling her she had to stop me, figuring she knew everything now about me dancing in the woods without no clothes on, and what was worse was, once her and him started talking again, my father'd know it too.

"I realize that, Father..." she began, her voice breaking like she was afraid to say what she was going to say. "I tried to tell him that...and yet...It don't mean nothing to him...Times is so bad, he says, and him without a job for so long...and one more mouth to feed...no more kids, he says, no more...if it wasn't for relief...."

She really started to cry now, ducking her chin against her chest, like she was trying to hide it and trying to stop it all at once but her shoulders were shaking, giving it away. My ears pricked up even higher, hearing the last thing she said, knowing now they weren't talking about me dancing naked in the woods but what her and my father argued about in bed at night and what he told her to go on tell Father Mack like he said she told him everything. I felt like a big weight dropped off my shoulders, I was so relieved to find out the priest hadn't come to tell on me after all.

Staring at her bowed head, Father Mack's eyes had a look of annoyance in them. On the sneak he pulled back his cuff and gave a quick glance at his watch that was so gold, even the band was all gold, it was like sunbeams dancing in the room, making the stained and faded wallpaper look all the shabbier.

"You must insist—You must pray to God for help—And if there is another mouth to feed, and you mustn't think of it as only another mouth to feed but another blessed visitation from the Lord, God will provide. Trust Him, my child—God always provides."

He pulled himself forward to get up, the chair groaning under him like it never did when my father sat in it, my father was so much skinnier. Seeing he was leaving, I was about to sneak out from under the table and make a beeline out the backdoor and around to the porch again before they got to the front door when, after she blew her nose, apologizing to him for the noise, she asked him, "Will you hear my confession, Father?...It's weighing me down so...."

Her face had a look in it like she had no right to ask him.

He was standing now, looking down at her, his thumb and finger putting a sharper crease in the brim of his hat, a look of impatience in his face like he had to get somewhere in a hurry.

"My child," he said, and it sounded funny him calling her what he called us kids even though she wasn't a child nor wasn't his child either like none of us was, but now she didn't have any mother or any father maybe he thought she was his child. "You must know that I cannot give you absolution so long as you and your husband are disobeying the teachings of the Church—Your soul is in mortal danger, if, God forbid, you should die this day without absolution you know that you will go straight to hell—"—My heart gave a jump hearing that and I right away crossed myself then crossed all my fingers just to make sure it wouldn't happen—"You must say no to him until he stops this wicked thing, which is a mortal sin for you both, but even more of a sin for you because it is your God-given duty to make him stop. When he does, only then can you say yes to him because then saying yes to him is like saying yes to God, saying yes and serving Him in the holiest way a Catholic woman can in blessed propagation of the faith...Until then, you must make him stop...and until you do I cannot hear your confession or give you absolution..." saying it as gentle as he could like he was talking to a child, like he talked to me in the confession box, but even so there was a look in her eyes like he just stuck an icepick in her heart.

"Oh, Father..." she moaned and that was all she could get out, her voice dying away and the look in her eyes like his words just stabbed her.

"I'm sorry, my child," and he went to her and put his hand on her head like he put it on mine out on the porch, "But it's your duty...before I can give you absolution... You understand?"

She nodded, keeping her eyes down.

He cleared his throat, lifted his cuff to sneak another look at his watch. "I can give you my blessing...if you'll kneel down...I can give you that...at least...."

She knelt down in front of him on the linoleum in the middle of the parlor floor and he stood over her humming out latin and making the sign of the cross over her head, then waving his arm he made the sign of the cross all around the room and ended by looking up and making it at the water-stained ceiling over his head which was right exactly where their bedroom was and where their bed stood. When he was done she blessed her-self and me seeing her do it, I blessed myself too, like my hand was her hand, just like the pain in her eyes was my pain. As she struggled to her feet she thanked him and Father Mack, snap-ping on his panama hat that was as bright in the dingy room as his gold watch was, said to her, "I'll be praying for you, Mother," and lifting an eyebrow at her, he said, "And I hope to be seeing you in the confessional very, very soon."

She nodded, hanging her head, and gave a bit of a smile but in her eyes that were still red from her crying there was a look that said she didn't have much hope it would be soon, and maybe never would be.

I quick crawled out quiet as I could from under the table and pretending like I had Lenilenape moccasins on, beat it out the backdoor and around the side of the house and up onto the front porch where Kate was sound asleep by now and Danny was dozing off beside her. I plopped down between them like I never moved an inch the whole time just as the screen door scraped open and Father Mack came out followed by my moth-er, rubbing quick at her eyes with the edge of her apron so none of us'd see she'd been crying.

"Well! Well! Well!" Father Mack let out in that loud voice of his that made Danny give a jump and woke Kate up too, "What have we here, two sleeping beauties?" He reached down with his big hand that made me cringe away, it looked big as one of the shoulders of pork my mother got on the eye sometimes at Gottlieb's for our Sunday dinner. He rubbed all our heads again one more time and turned to my mother, saying with that big grin on his face, "Oh, by the way, now young Mickey here has made his first communion, don't you think it's time he thought of becoming an altar boy, don't you think so, Mother?" calling her mother again when she wasn't his mother, like she wasn't his child either.

My mother, all eager, nodded her head like it would snap off of her neck, but the thought of me standing up in front of all those people in church sent shivers down my spine. When she saw I wasn't saying anything, she said, "Oh, look at the little bugger—Where's your manners, Mickey? Thank the Father."

I felt myself blushing to the roots, but I knew if he was asking me to be an altar boy he mustn't've known it was me after all telling him about Slaves and Masters in the confession box. I mumbled my thank you even though I didn't mean it, but I said thank you because I knew she wanted me to and I would do anything to please her, even to getting up on the altar in front of everybody.

Father Mack boomed out, "Such fine, fine children—Young Mick here looks like he'll make a fine altar boy—Your other brothers have fallen by the wayside, I see," saying it like he was talking to me but was really talking to my mother, like it was somehow her fault they weren't altar boys any more. "There's no greater service a boy can give than serving the priest on the altar of God. Well, Mother, you just send him into the sacristy after mass next Sunday and I'll take care of him."

We all held our breath as he went down the steps, they sagged so under him, but none of the boards broke and I breathed another sigh of relief as we all watched him hurry out to his car, the back of his coat blacker where a big circle of sweat was even though the day wasn't all that hot. He seemed in such a rush he didn't even turn to wave like we all waved to him once he got in behind the wheel and started up the motor and drove off in a cloud of yellow dust like he was going a hundred miles an hour.

The next morning, looking like she hadn't slept all night, she made us our oatmeal and coffee, then right after that she did something she hadn't ever done before so early in the day, she went off saying she had to get something at Gottlieb's and for Frank to keep an eye on the rest of us while she was gone. Slap, once he finally figured out what was going on, hollered out, "I'll go to Gottlieb's fer ya, Ma, I'll gitcha whatever it is ya want!" But she hollered back at him, "No, I got to go do this meself!" then in a quieter voice, "Now the rest of you mind yer big brother, hear? And don't forget to do the dishes and feed and water the chickens and, oh yes, empty the pan under the icebox and put erl in the erlstove." Then, tying Kate's bonnet on that Kate right away tried to tear off til my mother slapped her hand, she put Kate in the wagon and started pulling her off down the road in the direction of the store.

While she was gone, Frank and Buster made Slap empty the pan of melted ice under the icebox and after that made him fill the fuel jug on the oilstove, then had him feed and water the chickens, while they made me and Danny do the dishes, which was just about the same as me doing the dishes all by myself since Danny was about as much help as a baby chick.

All this time, Frank and Buster sprawled on the front porch like we were playing Slaves and Masters, only without taking off our clothes and without any cherry switches, their tongues were their switches tongue-lashing us to do this and do that, since they made themselves the masters, of course, saying since they were the oldest didn't our mother say for us to do as they said? And the way they played it none of the rest of us got a turn to be master like me and Earl Jr. played it in the woods.

The minute she got back from Gottlieb's Slap, seeing her hands were empty, asked her, "Wudja git, Ma? Wudja git?" She looked at him blank for a second, then said, "Nuthin, they was

outa what I wanted," but Kate kept saying, "Telephone, telephone," and Frank cracked the joke he heard from my father that
heard it from Mr. Beezley that went, "Telegram, telephone, tell a
woman!" Buster snickered and my mother gave them a sharp
look, saying, "Never you mind. Here, you, Buster, put the wagon
back under the porch." *"Telephone,"* Kate sang out again, like
she just learned a new word and couldn't get enough of saying
it, so I suspected my mother must've called Aunt Bridget in
South Philly on the Keystone public pay phone at Gottlieb's—I
figured it must've been something real important for her to walk
all the way to Gottlieb's so early in the morning and spend a
whole dime for a phone call all the way to Philadelphia.

Then she did another thing she'd never done before, especially in the middle of the week. She told us all to stay outside
then went in and got into her oldest housedress and scrubbed
and cleaned the whole house from top to bottom, she even
changed all the beds. Frank pestered her at lunchtime when, all
sweaty and red in her cheeks, she took a minute, "What're ya
doin that for, Mom, when it ain't even Saturday?" But she
wouldn't say anything, she told him and Buster to get lunch for
the rest of us, "There's corn mush in the icebox you can slice up
and put Karo on, and be sure to do the dishes afterwards," then
she went on with her cleaning, not even stopping for a cup of
tea, she even ended up scouring the p-i-s-s bucket out in the
backyard that she only ever did on Saturday too. When I saw
her do that, despite she wouldn't tell us anything, an excitement started up in me because I knew now for certain we were
going to get company.

That night when my father came in from working on the
road, you could see he took notice of how extra clean the house
was and you could see him right away get a suspicious look in

his eye, but because the two of them weren't speaking, he didn't say anything.

Early next morning when he went off as usual to the WPA, and after us kids ate our breakfast, my mother, for the first time I could ever remember without them having to beg or sneak down, told Frank and Buster they could go the river and catch some fish for our supper, and to take me and Slap and Danny along but to be sure none of us went in the water. I would just as soon stayed home so I wouldn't miss anything but I knew she was letting us go to the river mainly to keep us out of the house so to keep the house nice and clean. Frank and Buster kept pestering her who was coming even though they suspected all along who it was as much as I did, but all she said was, "Curiosity killt the cat, you'll see soon enough."

All the way to the river Frank and Buster kept betting it was Aunt Nell was coming and they were hoping it was because maybe Sonny'd be coming along with her and they could show him the woods and take him back to the river fishing and swimming. At the river I sat on a rock on the beach the whole time, keeping one eye on Danny and one eye across the water on Philly, anxious to get back to the house soon as I could. But wouldn't you know, in between their fishing my older brothers just have to all jump in the river in their underwear even though they weren't supposed to, so it took all that much longer before we left just so their hair and underwear'd be dry before we got home so my mother wouldn't know they'd been swimming.

As we were coming out of the woods on our way back, Slap dragging the string of catfish in the dust Frank and Buster caught and made him carry because he didn't catch anything, who do we see coming up Lenape Road following behind my mother and Kate from the direction of the busstop on the boulevard but all my aunts from South Philly. They were all dressed in their Sunday dresses and hats and Sunday shoes, each one carrying her best pocketbook in one hand and a shopping bag in the other. We hadn't seen them in so long, we all stopped and stared at them like they were something landed from another planet like in those Flash Gordon serials we saw at the Morris on Saturday afternoons. Slap hollered out, "Look it, Aunt Nell! Look it, Aunt Molly and Aunt Bridget! Look it, Aunt Maggie and Aunt Patty and Aunt Kate!" calling out each and everyone of their names right on down the line before he ran up to them so excited he was still letting the fish drag in the dirt and didn't even know it.

My aunts were so busy complaining about getting sand in their shoes and falling all over each other in the ruts and grabbing onto one another, Aunt Bridget shrilling out, "This is worse'n the Sahara desert!" and Aunt Molly hollering, "Is they any bears around here, Nor'?" they didn't see us at first. But when they finally did spot us, they started shrilling out all the more, Who was these strange-looking brats, they couldn't be my mother's, they couldn't be the kids they used to know from 126 Mifflin Street, we looked like real country hicks, let them just get out of all these here sand driffs so's they could get a better look at us all.

I could see Frank and Buster looking around for Sonny and how disappointed they were he was nowhere in sight. But Slap, fish and all, was hopping up and down grinning like his face would break, yelling, "Oh, it's us all right! Don'tchou know us?" Aunt Bridget said with a tease in her eye because everybody knew Slap was her favorite, "Who is that kid? His face is so dirty I don't know who he is!" Slap went, "Heh? Heh?" because she forgot you have to talk loud to him, it'd been so long since she saw him, and when she shouted it at him again, Slap started squealing and jumping all the harder, he was so excited Aunt

Bridget pretending she didn't know who he was. My mother right away starts in with her usual song-and-dance, "Oh look at them now! Look at yer hands, Slap! And you, Frank, and you, Buster! You'd think we dint have no soap and water!" saying it even though she made us all scrub our hands and faces before we left the house that morning, and made a good check of all our ears. My brothers got an extra bath when they went swimming in the river but she didn't know that, of course.

When the aunts came into the front yard and up the front steps I was so excited to see them I didn't for once hold my breath to see if the steps would break under them like I always did anybody hefty came up them. Aunt Maggie shrank away from the string of catfish Slap was dangling as he kept rushing around them in circles, same as a puppy'll do, her saying, "I ain't never seen anything so ugly, fishes with whiskers."

Everybody was talking all at once but when my mother said, real sharp, "Oh, look at them now, little buggers! Frank, Buster, put them fishpoles under the porch where they belong! Slap, you go wrap them fish in newspaper and stick them in the icebox right this minute! Don't mind this place how dirty it is," she went on, scraping open the screendoor.

Us kids all gave her a look, knowing how hard and long she scrubbed and dusted yesterday, the house never looked so neat and clean before.

"Why, the house ain't all that bad," Aunt Molly was saying, standing at the bottom of the porch steps looking around the outside, and the others all hummed out in a way like they were really saying it wasn't so good either.

When they came into the parlor they all cooed and ahhed and said again it wasn't half bad, Aunt Nell saying it looked so nice and clean.

Even so, my mother ran around straightening things that

were already straightened and saying what a mess the place was, all the while pulling at the hem of her dress like she was trying to hide she didn't have any stockings on, I heard her say to them later on, "It's so hot that's why I don't have no stockings on," but I knew the ones she had were so full of runs and tears she must've been ashamed to wear them in front of her sisters.

When the aunts all sat down and were comfortable, everybody started talking all at once again with nobody listening to anybody else. My mother said she'd pour the water for the tea, then seeing Slap was still dragging the fish on the parlor linoleum and still looking around bug-eyed and grinning foolish at my aunts—if he had a tail I bet it would've been thumping the floor to beat the band—she hollered, "Slap, ain't you put them fish away in the icebox yet?" She rolled her eyes up at her sisters as much as to say, You see what I got to put up with? and grabbing him by the shoulders she steered him out to the kitchen where you could hear water boiling on the stove for the tea she must've put on before she set out for the busstop.

The aunts started reaching down in their shopping bags, bringing out old hand-me-downs mainly for my mother and us to wear. But Aunt Bridget, "Being so rich," they teased her, brought out two dozen cinnamon buns from Heck's bakery on 2nd Street, while Aunt Molly, not to be outdone, brought out two boxes of candy from Whitman's chocolate factory where her two oldest daughters worked—I didn't know which my mouth was watering for more, the Whitman's candy I hadn't had since our last Christmas on Mifflin Street or the cinnamon buns like the ones my father used to bring home from Heck's Sunday mornings after mass.

My mother, coming in with the tea and saying it was awful nice of them to bring all that, sent Frank out for one of her good plates—"Not one of the cracked ones, mind you"—to put the buns on, because my aunts were company. Then she made us kiss each and every aunt before we got a cinnamon bun, like that was what we had to pay before we got a bun, I would've kissed them twice if I had to just to get mine. As we went around kissing their cheeks I saw Aunt Nell and Aunt Molly that was the two oldest had mustaches across their upper lip, the same as was beginning to show, only fainter, on the upper lips of Frank and Buster, and Brother Beezley too. Aunt Nell teased each and every one of us as we kissed her, saying, like Aunt Bridget, "Ain'tcha sorry you moved to the sticks? Don'tcha miss good ole Philly?"

My other brothers just grinned, knowing she was teasing, but I wanted to shout out, *Yes! Yes! I miss it! I wish we were living back there right this very instant!* but I didn't dare.

When the kissing was over with we were each given our cinnamon bun, my eyes bulging greedy at the sight of mine. I sat by the screendoor and ate mine slow as I could, picking out the raisins one by one then peeling the round sticky crust away a teeny bit at a time to get at the thick layer of cinnamon inside, while my brothers wolfed theirs down then looked over at the plate like they were hoping for another one. But my mother ignored them, pouring tea for my aunts from the good china pot and as she did, all the aunts started up again about how we'd all grown like weeds since the last time they saw us and that even though it was the sticks the country air must be doing us all some good.

You could tell my mother was anxious to get us out of the house when she said to the older ones, "Ain't it time now for you all to go out and feed and water the chickens and bring in the eggs? Then when you do that be sure'n stay out and play in the yard so's me and me sisters can talk in peace."

They all grumbled again, wanting to stay, they were as anxious as me to hear all the news from Philly and about Sonny and what he was doing and I wondered did they know what was playing at the Morris and the Lyric? But when she gave them that special look they knew meant business they went out, Danny tagging along behind them to make a pest of himself, he was getting to be their shadow, following my older brothers everywhere they went when they would let him.

I snuck along the edge of the wall trying not to be seen, easing myself down on my belly on the floor quiet as I could next to Kate that was playing by herself in a corner with one of her amputee dolls like she wasn't at all excited by our aunts coming down, it was like she hardly knew who they were and couldn't care less, she was so little when we left the city. When she looked at me I put a finger to my lips not to say nothing and popped another of the raisins thick with honey into my mouth. I settled myself down to listen, sucking the sweetness from the raisin slow as I could, making the flavor of it last as long as possible.

Then wouldn't you know, there was a sudden hush as all the eyes of my aunts turned on me. My mother looked where they were staring and seeing me said, "Gwan you, and bring me in enough potatoes to peel for supper, then bring me a pot of water from the pump to put 'em in," because even though her sisters were visiting, my father would still expect his supper on the table the minute he got in the door whether she was speaking to him or not.

I stuck what was left of my bun in my pocket and dragged myself up, knowing there was no use arguing and hurried out to the shed on the double, hoping by getting what she wanted me to she'd let me stay once I got back. But when I came back with the potatoes, she said to me, "Now you gwan out and help yer brothers and go play with them," staring at me sharp and speaking in that certain tone of voice I knew I better get moving.

I pretended to pull a long face and not saying a word went out of the room like I was heading for the kitchen and the backdoor but slipped instead under the dining room table where I folded my arms around my shins and tucking my head down, scrunched there, listening.

When they were sure I was gone, I heard Aunt Patty say in a knowing way, "Little pitchers have big ears." They all hummed amen to that, Aunt Nell whispering, "He's a strange one, ain't he? always wantin to listen in where the women is even when you lived on Mifflin Street, Nora, he always had his ears open."

There were more hummings from the others and I held my breath as I strained my ears, trying to hear why that was so strange, maybe they would say why it was and I would know once and for all. But my mother broke in with, "Well, he's a big help around the house, specially with takin care of the littler ones, mindin them and pullin them around in the wagon and all."

But then Aunt Nell chimes in with, "Well, just you be careful, you don't wanna go makin a girl outa him," saying it in that bossy way of an older sister, just like my two older brothers talked to us younger ones, saying it in a way like maybe that's already what my mother was doing, using the exact same words Mrs. Beezley used when she warned my mother a couple of times already when she didn't know I was listening out here under the table— "You don't wanna make a sissy outa him," she said, "Like that Ginger Mahoney's makin outa her Ronnie." Hearing Aunt Nell say it, there were more tongue clickings from the other aunts, as if being a girl was just as bad as a boy being like one.

My mother lowered her voice, saying, "Well, he ain't at that age yet, like Frank and Buster is," talking in that tone her and her sisters saved for when they were speaking about incurable diseases, and the rest of them busted out humming in a harmony. Then everything quieted down in the parlor, the tea cups stopped rattling, like the moment'd finally come to hear what they all traveled so far down on the bus from Philly to hear. My mother cleared her throat like she was about to speak, then she cleared it again like she didn't know how to start. I could picture all my aunts leaning forward in their chairs. For a long time the only sound was the scrape of my mother's paring knife, followed by the plop of another potato into the pot. I slid what was left of the cinnamon bun out of my pocket and took only another little nibble to make it last, holding it in my mouth like a communion wafer til the last morsel of flavor was gone before swallowing it. Then I leaned myself in the direction of the parlor, the back of my bare legs coming unstuck from the linoleum that was so sticky in the heat.

My mother started speaking in a voice so low I didn't know at first she was talking, so I missed most of the first words she said. "…And it's gittin no better'n when we was in the city…and the other night he come after me…" Hearing that, there were sharp tongue-clickings from my aunts and I saw my mother and father half way up the stairs again like in a movie and cringed inside.

"…And when he gits into bed after one too many…" She was barely whispering. "…Well, I don't have to tell you how they are…."

Her voice trailed off and a loud drone rose up again from the parlor like a hum of angry bees.

When all the buzzing died down my mother began speaking again, speaking so low, but now my ears pricked up as I heard her say, still in a voice I could hardly hear,

"...and the priest won't give me absolution, no matter how much I beg, he says he won't give it to me til I get him to stop usin..." She hesitated, then whispered in a low, stumbly voice, "...them...*things*," the last words spoke so deep down I almost missed them. After she said it, you could hear her paring knife scraping hard and fast over the skin of another potato, "...He told me to do what I'm supposed to...that what we're doin is a mortal sin..." Her voice caught when she said it, like she couldn't catch her breath. "...And him with no job...and what if there's another mouth to feed?...."

Her voice wandered off again, like it did with Father Mack a few days ago, as her sisters cooed soft to her, all the while me, listening wide-eyed, slow and without thinking, licked the last of the sweetness off of my fingers and another potato dropped in the pot.

"...I don't know what to do. Father says not to say no to him but not to say yes to him either, so long as he's usin them..." There was another catch in her throat like she couldn't bring herself to say it again. "...You know..."

Her words died away in a sigh and then there was the slow scrape of the paring knife over another potato while her sisters sighed along with her, the drone of their sighs like the buzz of the flies around my head as I held my breath beneath the table, afraid to miss a word.

From the sound of her voice I knew she was certain she would burn in hell forever.

Then Aunt Nell spoke up, saying, "Now, now, Nor'," but in a soft, sly way, like the house had ears, saying, "I know of a old priest in a church in South Philly—Saint Lucia's in Little Italy around 7th and Christian," she whispered. There were knowing aha's from a couple of my aunts as Aunt Nell went on, saying, "This ole priest not only hardly speaks any English but he's jist about stone deef to boot, I been to him a couple times myself," she confessed, "when I had things to tell I dint want Father Gallagher or any of our other priests at Sacred Heart to hear," and the same aunts hummed out again like they knew just what she meant.

"You go to him, Nor', you go to him and have him hear yer confession, you tell him everything and you'll be outa that box with yer absolution before you know it!" saying it with a sound in her voice like she just solved everything.

My mother was quiet a minute and Aunt Nell was quiet too like she was letting what she just said sink in, then my mother said, "How am I goin to?... " But Aunt Nell, like she was reading her thoughts, busted in with, "You can tell yer old man yer comin to Philly to see Mom's grave—May her soul rest in peace...." and all the other aunts murmured along with her, "May her soul rest in peace." Then they all hummed along in excited agreement, Aunt Molly saying, "Yes, that's what I'd do, Nora, it ain'tcher fault you can't git eem to stop, God knows I can't git my Jake to stop, I wisht I could git eem to stop with me altogether for all I care for it...." And Aunt Patty saying, "I'd do it if I was in yer shoes," and Aunt Kate putting in, "You ain't been up since Mom passed away, you ain't seen her grave since the funeral." Aunt Bridget shrieked out, "Now don'tchou worry about the money for the bus and the trolley, I'll take care of that!"

My mother said, "I would so want to see Mom's grave now the headstone's up, I dream of her somethin awful..." The scraping of the potato knife came to a halt and with it my aunts all quieted down and in the sudden hush my mother asked in a low trembly voice, "But would that be right? It don't seem right, takin advantage of a deef old priest can't talk no English...Ain't that a sin too?"

There was a long pause followed by plenty of clearings of

the throat and shufflings of feet on the linoleum, then Aunt Nell, being the oldest said, "Well-l-l-l, you'll be goin to confession, won'tcha? You'll be tellin eem everything, won'tcha? It ain'tcher fault he's practically deaf and dumb and don't talk no American, he's a priest, ain't he? If he gives you absolution, where's the harm?" And all her sisters joined in a chorus right off the bat saying Aunt Nell was right, it wasn't a sin, and Aunt Nell, like she saw my mother was weakening, spoke up again real quick, jumping in with, "You jist slide that in when yer tellin eem everything else, that's all, jist slide it in real quick and easy." And there were more hollerings out of "Yezz, yezz, our Nell's right!" Then it was Aunt Molly's turn to confess in a whisper she'd been to the old deaf priest herself once or twice, "What else can you do? You know my Jake's the same when he's had a couple," and the others hummed out, "Yezz, yezz!" Aunt Patty saying, "What else can you do? We all know what men are!"

"Well, I don't know…" my mother began again, but this time in a stronger voice and not as low, like she was thinking maybe she could do it. I was thinking maybe what her sisters was telling her to do wasn't right either, being a trick, but the way they said it sounded like they cared about her in a different way from Father Mack when he said what he said to her, despite he called her my child and called her mother and put his hand on her head and gave her his blessing.

After a minute the rasp of the knife, more agitated this time, picked up again, along with the rattle of cups against saucers and the clatter of spoons, like all my aunts were breathing one big sigh of relief together. Aunt Bridget hooted out which one of them wanted to finish off the last of the buns? Aunt Patty said she was stuffed to the gills, while Aunt Nell said she was getting too fat, but Aunt Kate, the most roly-poly one of the bunch, laughed and said she'd do them all a great big favor by getting rid of it for them, but first she needed something to wash it down, saying, "I'll say one thing, Nora, yer Jersey water's better'n our Philly water, you can't smell or taste a drop of chlorine in the tea, this may be the sticks but you got good water."

But my mother wasn't listening, there was that expression in her eyes that said she was looking inside of herself more'n she was looking out. Her brow was wrinkled up like she was thinking hard about what Aunt Nell just told her, that same faraway look she got when I suspected she was dreaming of Philly or was talking to her mother, and was maybe now thinking of what her mother'd tell her to do.

The parlor got so quiet I could hear the cuckoo clock up on the dining room wall ticking louder'n ever.

Finally she said, "I've talked to our mother so much and when all of you talk it's like she's talkin and if you say it ain't nothin wrong, then it ain't nothin wrong because it's like her talkin through all of you. I'll do it," she said, like it was hard for her to say it, punching the words out like she was short of breath. "The very first chancet I can sneak away I'll do it."

There was the rattle of the teapot against a cup and the slosh of more tea being poured, followed by a babble of excitement from all the others, Aunt Nell saying with a grin in her voice, "That's the best thing, Nor', you'll see," and Aunt Patty agreed, saying, "Don'tchou worry, Nor', yer doin what's right," and a couple of them said amen in a solemn way like they were in church. Then Aunt Bridget, the only one well off enough to have one, shrilled out that when my mother came up to see the old Italian priest she'd let her use her charge plate at Frank & Seder's Department Store on Market Street where she said Uncle Digby always got good bargains on his funeral clothes, saying my mother could use the charge plate when she came to town in case she needed to get anything for the house or for us kids, "Kill two birds with one stone," as she put it, "And if yer Stosh asts any questions you can tell eem that's where you're goin and where you been, you got a good story."

The others agreed that was a good idea, even though my mother complained she could never use Aunt Bridget's Frank & Seder charge plate because she'd never be able to pay her back since it looked like my father was never going to get a job at the shipyard or anywhere else for that matter.... "It looks like we'll be stuck on relief

forever...and now he's drinkin again..." But Aunt Bridget shushed her, saying, "Now don'tchou worry now, Nora—I seen the kids could use some new sneakers now summer's here and I see yer Frank and Buster look like they'll be needin long pants soon enough, and you yerself look like you could use some shoes and stockings..."

I just knew my mother must've been blushing something awful when Aunt Bridget said that, but anybody could see how bad she needed shoes and stockings. She started to protest again but Aunt Bridget shushed her one more time, saying, "Don'tchou worry now, Digby's business is doin fine, people just dyin to see him," she cackled, cracking the same old joke she always cracked so that her sisters groaned. "So don'tchou worry now, you look like you been worryin long enough...." and the others hummed in with yezz, yezz, she did look wore out, it was about time she started thinking a little more about herself— Then all of a sudden the cuckoo jumped four times out of the clock on the dining room wall, making me just about jump out of my skin, and Aunt Maggie hearing it, shouted, "Listen to the time! We better git started for home!" I peeped through the tablecloth into the parlor and at the mention of the word home saw for the fraction of a second a look in my mother's eyes like she was seeing the house on Hoffman Street again that was the only place she ever called home, a look like she was wishing she was leaving now with her sisters to go back home again with them.

When we were trying on the handmedowns out in the kitchen after supper Frank found a dollar bill folded up in an old pair of knickers of cousin Tom's. Then Buster found another dollar folded up just as neat in another pair of knickers belonged to Tom too. I got so excited when I found a dollar pinned inside the pocket of an old yellow shirt used to be our cousin Sonny's and that Aunt Nell'd turned the collar on, I started jumping up and down. My mother's mouth fell open, then she got a suspicious look, then she had us all rooting through all the pockets of all the other handmedowns the aunts brought down in their shopping bags.

It wasn't long before she was the next one found an envelope with a note on it in the pocket of an old gray winter coat I used to see Aunt Bridget wear when we lived in South Philly and even though it was old-fashioned, it was almost as good as new, I was so glad Aunt Bridget gave it to her because I knew she needed a winter coat so bad. She wouldn't read us what was on the envelope no matter how much we begged but I saw there was more money inside of it before she tucked it away in her apron pocket. Right then Danny let out a squeal because he found another dollar bill in a jacket of Cousin Neddy Jr.'s Aunt Maggie gave us was fourteen times too big for Danny, and him and Slap started hopping around like maniacs, hollering did we have to give the money back? could we buy dixie cups? could we buy Pepsi-Colas? But my mother quick put a finger to her lips going, "*Shhh! Shhh!*" jerking her head towards the parlor where my father was sitting reading his paper after supper. With all the shopping bags of handmedowns and the Whitman chocolates, not to mention the house being so extra clean, my father I'm sure must've known her sisters'd been down, but because my mother and him still weren't speaking he didn't say anything, just was scowling in his eyes more'n usual.

When Slap and Danny quieted down she held out her hand for all the money, saying, like she was saying it to herself, "Them sneaks, ain't they somethin—ain't they somethin now."

Frank whispered, "How 'bout buyin a steak, Ma? We ain't had steak in so long." But my mother refolded the money real careful like she never heard him and tucked it with the envelope way deep down in the bottom of her apron pocket so she'd be sure not to lose it, using her apron instead of knotting a stocking to hide the money in like she usually did since she didn't have any stockings to knot. Putting a finger to her mouth again and rolling her eyes towards the parlor, she whispered, "Not a word outa any of you, you hear?" All of us nodded, knowing why we mustn't say a word without having to ask her why it was a secret, because he wasn't drunk tonight and we knew he wasn't drunk because he probably didn't have any money for beer—and if he knew there was money in the house....

I guessed now that they saw first-hand how bad things were for us they felt so sorry for my mother my aunts all got together after their visit and started sending 25¢ each a week, Aunt Nell, since she was the oldest, being the one to collect the quarters and put the money in the mail every Friday.

Since I was always as hungry for something from Philly as I was for something sweet to eat, every Saturday when I saw my chance I snuck upstairs to peek at Aunt Nell's letter in my mother's drawer where she hid it from my father down under her under things. She may of hid the letters from him but he'd have to be blind not to see there was a little extra to eat on the table these days and he must've known where it came from, he'd get such a hard look in his eye like he knew my aunts must be helping out with something every week because he couldn't get a job nowhere but on the WPA that only paid you at relief with rotten potatoes and wormy flour. But he was so proud and since they still weren't speaking yet he kept his mouth shut about it.

Aunt Nell's letter said pretty much what they said every week: "dear nor a little something from all of your loving sisters to help out with the kids i know your stosh will get a job god bless you your loving sister nell" She always wrote like she was absent from school the day they learnt about periods and capitals.

A couple days after my aunts came down we were all in the kitchen eating lunch when Mrs. Beezley came busting in with the *County Seat Weekly*, bringing it over her own self instead of Sister bringing it, she was so excited to show my mother her name in the paper along with all my mother's sisters' names too.

"'Mrs. Stanislaus Lithwack,'" she started reading real loud and with a big grin, "'entertained her sisters at a tea last Tuesday at the Lithwack residence on Lenape Road. The visitors, Nell, Molly, Maggie, Bridget, Patty and last but not least, Kate, are all from Philadelphia. They said they had enjoyed themselves very much exchanging family news over the pastries they had brought with them from the Big City. Mrs. Lithwack, a member of St. Theresa's R.C. church, said she was glad to see her sisters and looked forward to visiting them again soon, perhaps in their own homes next time in the City of Brotherly Love, where this reporter discovered she and all her sisters and brothers were born.' And it's signed, 'Your Lenape Social Notes Reporter, Charley.' Don't he write nice? Ain't that a nice surprise, Nor'? He makes it sound so classy and nice."

Like she hadn't ever seen anything like it before, my mother stared at the newspaper after Mrs. Beezley handed it over so she could see for herself. She was looking a little embarrassed like the first time Charley wrote about us in the paper when we first moved in. Finally she shook her head, saying, "How come this Charley knows all this about me and I ain't never oncet talked to him?"

Mrs. Beezley grinned, winking, "Oh, he's got his ways, Charley does—Charley knows just about everything goes on in this town—But don't he write nice, don't he write classy?"

The following Sunday my mother told me to go in the sacristy after mass to see the priest about learning to be an altar boy.

"All you boys, it's a sin ain't one of you up there servin. You at least got a decent pair of shoes to wear, which is more'n I can say for yer brothers, I don't know what they do with their shoes to be so hard on them."

I must've got a scare in my eyes because she said, "Now don't look so worried, Frank'll go with you." I felt a little better hearing that but still my knees were knocking just thinking of getting up on the altar in front of all the people. But that Frank, all he did after the children's mass was over was take me up to the sacristy door and leave me flat so he could head to Gottlieb's with Buster and Slap to spend their collection pennies on candy. Maybe he took a powder too because he wasn't an altar boy any more and didn't want to face Father Mack, maybe afraid Father Mack'd grab him and try to talk him into being an altar boy again.

I waited quiet by the door shaking in my boots. I could see Father Mack through the curtain that was the same color of wine as the curtain on the confession box, and either because he'd been drinking so much wine all these years saying mass or he was still mad because the bell in the red brick church rang again all during his sermon that morning so he had to shout to the rafters, his heavy face was flushed the same color as the curtain too. He was finishing taking off his vestments, kissing each and every one and saying a prayer over it in latin before he folded it up so neat and put it away in one of the long narrow drawers in the big solid chest of drawers built of dark wood shoved up against the wall.

There was somebody else in the sacristy too. Even though I recognized him from serving mass sometimes, like at the children's mass today, I was still surprised to see the boy they called Rev there, the first time I saw him close up since the day me and Earl Jr.'d been surrounded by him and the other Swamp Rats up on the bluff over the beach. Just thinking about it made me shiver all the more. Rev was still in his surplice and cassock and was standing on tiptoe in the dark closet putting a bottle of wine up on the shelf beside a long row of other wine bottles, while at the same time stealing looks at me over his shoulder as I stood in the doorway.

I was hoping the priest wouldn't notice me so I could sneak away but when he took off the last of his vestments and was down to nothing but his plain black cassock he finally spotted me standing there and raising his eyebrows, grinned and crooked his finger at me to come on in. My heart was thumping to beat the band, I wished Frank was there to tell Father Mack what I came for, I felt so tongue-tied. When he said, "And what can I do for you, my child?" I said all in a rush, saying it so low he had to lean so way down I could hear his belly growling because he hadn't had his breakfast yet, I told him my mother said to come in to be an altar boy like he said I was to do that day at our house. When I was done telling him, he reared back, his eyes squeezed in a big smile behind his glasses as he clamped his hands on my shoulders. His hands were so big I drooped under their weight, I was even more scared'n I already was because like everytime he came near me I was afraid he might recognize my voice from confession and know it was me doing all those things with Earl Jr. and with Danny and Kate and Walter back in the woods.

"Ah yes, you made your first communion a little while back!" he sang out like he was singing in a high mass. "Mrs. Lithwack's little boy—Mickey, is it?—If only more mothers would send me their boys. A fine woman! A wonderful Catholic mother!" Then like he suddenly remembered what my mother told him in our parlor, his brow wrinkled up, his eyes got so dark like they did when the bell in the red brick church was ringing, and he bumbled at his mouth with his fingers. But then just as quick, like it was only a cloud passing in front of the sun, he broke into his grin again, saying, in that deep voice that made me jump like Mr. Beezley's did, "I remember my first pastoral visit to your home, I well remember you and all your brothers!" And again his face got dark as his fingers fluttered to his lips and he muttered, "Too bad none of your older brothers worked out—Well, many are called but few are chosen—" The sun came out on his face again. "Maybe you, Mick, are one of the chosen—Do you think you are?" and his hands big as hams grabbed me by the shoulders again, bending me down.

I bowed my head and whispered, "I don't know, Father." All I knew was I suspected the reason my mother wasn't too worried sending me to be an altar boy was I wasn't as hard on shoes as my older brothers were and was the only one with a decent pair, even though they were from relief and pinched me, but I didn't tell him any of that.

Father Mack kneaded my shoulders like he was making dough for baking, booming out, "Well, we're happy having you, Mick, you're a *mite* on the thin side but maybe your mother can fatten you up, you look like you'll make a good apprentice altar boy!" Then he called out, "Timothy!" And Rev, that'd been eyeing me on the sly all the while, came over, drying his hands from washing the little glass bottles for the water and the wine in a sink in the corner, that he later taught me were called the cruets. Father Mack told me, with his chest swelling up like it was himself he was talking about, that Rev—only he called him Timothy again—been an altar boy for two years now and he taught him his lessons so good there wasn't anything he didn't know about being an altar boy, he knew the latin backwards and forwards and could serve the mass blindfolded if he had to. Rev grinned and ducked his head to one side but you could see it pleased him. Then Father Mack put his arms around the both of us, telling Timothy to teach me the ropes and Timothy was nodding he would, while all the while he kept looking at me with that little grin on his face. I saw again he was like that boy in the movies, that Freddie Bartholomew, but he was even nicer looking'n Freddie Bartholomew ever was.

"Well, now, see if you can find our Mick a surplice and cassock upstairs, Timothy. Show him around. For starters, all you'll have to do the next few weeks, Mick, is stand beside Timothy on the altar and watch everything he does—Timothy can start teaching you the latin responses—You won't find a better teacher than our Timothy—You will learn your latin, won't you?"

I nodded I would, I knew if I learned to say pig latin I could learn to say the other too. Father Mack patted me on the head with his big hand, singing out, "Good! Good! Well then, now that's settled, I leave Mick in your capable hands, my boy." Then as he clapped on his black hat with the rabbit's tail on top Timothy later said was called a biretta, I heard his belly rumbling again, and like he was in a big hurry to get back to the rectory for his breakfast, I was surprised for a man his size he could move so quick out the backdoor and be gone before you knew it.

"I saw you in church a couple times and knew you were a Catholic," Timothy whispered now the priest'd left. "That's why I didn't let the other Swamp Rats bother you that day." He winked, his face breaking into a grin as friendly as it was nice-looking. Then he squeezed my arms, saying, "Father Mack's right, you'll have to put some meat on those bones so you'll be strong enough to carry the missal up and down the altar steps." He put an arm around my shoulder. "Come on, let's go on upstairs and see if we can find a cassock that fits you."

All of a sudden when he said that, I got worried there mightn't be a cassock to fit me and Father Mack wouldn't let me be an altar boy—It was like I did a somersault in my head, because now I wanted to be an altar boy, just like Timothy, more'n anything, I wanted to be one even more'n I was scared of having to learn to say latin and standing up in church in front of all the people.

Near the entrance to the altar he made a turn and led me up a winding staircase that was dark and narrow and was a kind of stairs I only saw in the movies and never climbed up before. I was glad his hand was on my shoulder to show me the way, the stairs were so dark I wondered why there wasn't any light, thinking, as we went around and around up the steps, I was glad Timothy knew that day on the bluff I was a Catholic and he didn't know Earl Jr. was a heathen or the two of us might be drowned now in the middle of the river. But I didn't care about any of that now, I hadn't ever remembered any boy putting their arm around me before the way Timothy did that Sunday morning, not any of my brothers, not even Slap, not Earl Jr. nor Ronnie either, his arm resting so light on my shoulder as the two of us went up the dark winding staircase that was as high as the belltower that didn't have a bell.

When we got to the top of the stairs, the room we came into had white-washed plaster walls like the rest of the church and a big triple window that had the same yellow panes of stained glass in it as the tall skinny windows all around downstairs. One of the windows was open a little and you could see the grass in the churchyard below and some woods, then a corner of a house across the road that was half blue wood shingle and half white clapboard with a closed in porch that I didn't know then was Timothy's house, but it was. The upstairs room was like a hidden away place, so quiet and cool, and there wasn't much in it. Timothy said it was where the cassocks and surplices were kept, and was for the altar boys and choir boys to change in. There was a long table along one wall and in a corner an old broken down armchair like my father's, only this one was made of leather that had a rip up near the headrest where the stuffing was coming out. I gave a little jump because in it sat Padric O'Hara, the husband of the lady that sang and played the organ in the choir, Agnes O'Hara. He was the little man shook so much when he pushed the collection basket around on Sundays, with all the pennies in it it jingled like a tambourine. I saw him working around the church sometimes, sweeping the walks and cutting the grass, and in the winter if the church was smoky, like it often was, Frank and Buster whispered Padric must be in his cups again and forgot to open the damper on the old furnace down in the cellar that was so old Father Mack kept begging for money for a new one, but not, he said, til after he got his bell.

Padric had thin hair combed straight back and was snoring sound asleep.

Tiptoeing into the room and putting a finger to his lips, Timothy whispered, "Don't pay any attention to Padric—" He

stuck his thumb to his mouth like he was drinking out of a bottle and I knew right off what he meant, seeing Padric slumped
in the chair he looked like my father looked when he had a few
too many.

Timothy opened a dark door that was the same color as all
the windows and doors and all the wood everywhere else in the
church. It turned out to be a big closet stuffed with surplices and
cassocks on hangers, not only black cassocks but red ones too
for Christmas.

We went through a whole bunch of cassocks and surplices,
Timothy pulling them out of the closet one after the other and
holding them up against me, before we found a set didn't look
like a tent on me. When I tried it on Timothy said be sure to
watch out I didn't trip over the skirt, maybe I could have my
mother hem it up for me. I was so glad, I was so relieved we
found one that almost fit anyhow, because it meant I was going
to be an altar boy just like Timothy, and thinking it made me
purr in my heart like a cat.

As he helped me unbutton the umpteen buttons down the
front of the cassock and helped me slip out of it, he folded up
the cassock and surplice and handed me the bundle, saying,
"You better have your mother wash and iron them, I don't know
how long they've been in there, they might be a little musty—
And be here seven o'clock sharp tomorrow morning for the early
mass, I'll start showing you what you need to know." Then he
grinned and got a tease in his eyes, saying, "You can get up that
early, can't you?" I nodded I could, if he had of said be there at
dawn I would've said I could.

He reached over and put his hand on my shoulder again.

Ever since her sisters been down my mother started going to
the early mass during the week. And sometimes in the middle

of the day I'd come into the parlor and see her sitting in the armchair by the window staring out and saying her rosary like maybe she was having doubts now about going up to see the deaf old priest in Little Italy and was going to church more and praying extra hard about it.

I was glad she was going to the early mass because that first morning I was to start learning to be an altar boy, walking with her to the church made me feel less nervous. It felt funny me wearing my Sunday shoes on a Monday instead of my sneakers or my maryjanes, my mother made me shine my shoes the night before and I gave them such a spit shine you could just about see your face in them. I had my surplice and cassock folded over my arm that she took time out even though it wasn't a washday to wash and iron special like Timothy said she should. She even hemmed up the cassock a couple inches so I wouldn't be trip-ping over it.

But it turned out it wasn't everybody there like on Sunday, just six or seven ladies kneeling in the front pews with their rosaries in their hands, a couple of them old and dressed in black with black kerchiefs on like they were always at a funeral.

That was all ever showed up morning after morning, except for Charley that showed up sometimes, as always spreading his hankie on the floor in the back just inside the door and kneel-ing on it with one knee. He always slipped out right after mass was over before the ladies came up the aisle, like he didn't like anybody seeing him, like he was back in the woods or down at the beach, he wanted to see you but he didn't want you seeing him.

So when I first came out on the altar with Timothy and Peter Rafferty, the other altar boy, with Father Mack behind us in his biretta and all decked out in his silk vestments and carry-ing the chalice all draped in its silk cover,

I felt a little better, there not being so many people. But I was still shaking even though all I had to do was stand beside Timothy and keep my ears and eyes open, and remember when I knelt down to be sure to hitch the hem of my cassock up over my heels, like Timothy showed me, so I wouldn't trip over backwards on it when I went to stand up.

So just like Father Mack said, I didn't have to do anything while Timothy and Peter Rafferty, that had pimples something awful and giggled and liked to needle a lot and whose older brother got killed in the war later on, it was those two actually did all the work pouring the water and wine into the priest's chalice whenever he held it out and ringing the little bells just before communion time, all the while answering the priest in latin that now being on the altar I could hear it better, sounded a lot harder even than the pig latin Earl Jr. taught me, I wasn't so sure now I could ever catch onto it.

It felt so funny being on the other side of the railing for the first time and being so close to the tabernacle where God lived behind the little door behind the silk curtain, I stared at it and stared at it, wishing I had me Superman's x-ray eyes, so I could see inside of it, see God, it felt like I was close to a fire I felt so hot with excitement every time I looked at it, being so close now.

It felt just as funny being dressed up in the cassock, it was like when I wore one of Mrs. Mahoney's dresses when me and Ronnie played dressup that time. Only here on the altar you were allowed to wear a dress, nobody laughed or made fun, not even my two older brothers, even Father Mack wore one and nobody laughed at him, it would be like laughing at God, Sister Joseph Mary said.

On the way home my mother asked me did I like being an altar boy? I nodded I did, then she gave me a grin that had a little tease in it, saying did I want to be a priest someday like Father Mack? I almost said No, I want to be like Timothy Burnside, but caught myself just in time. When I didn't answer she said, "Well, there's plenty of time to think about that, ain't there?" And even though I didn't do anything but stand and kneel and kneel and stand whenever Timothy did, she told me I did real good my first day on the altar and said how glad she was my shoes at least looked decent from where she sat in the pews.

After that she didn't say another word all the way home, like she was off thinking hard about something else. By the time we got to our house she had a quiet look on her face, like the look on the face of the statue of the Virgin, like she finally made up her mind.

I was on the altar with Timothy and Peter Rafferty every morning, except for Sundays, learning to be an altar boy. Before mass would start Timothy taught me how to fill the wine and water cruets and where to put them in the glass tray on the table at the side of the altar and how to fold the linen hand towel that Anna the housekeeper washed and ironed every day for the priest to dry his fingers on after Timothy or Peter spilled water on them. He showed me where to put the gold platen in its soft velvet bag on the table for communion time, that platen must've cost a pretty penny, what it cost I bet would feed our whole family for a year.

He also kept reminding me I was too skinny, but in a nice way, not like my brothers, and said the easiest way to fatten myself up was to eat like a pig and lay around the house all day doing nothing, otherwise I never would be able to lift the missal, stand and all. I knew both of his ideas would be impossible to do in our house, my mother and father wouldn't stand for my laying around, they always had things for me to do, and in the second place there wasn't ever anything extra to eat in our house to get fat on.

"When you don't have enough meat on your bones, bigger guys tend to pick on you," he said, as if I didn't know it already from Frank and Buster and Ronnie. "You got to fatten yourself up so you can take care of yourself."

But he was bigger and he never picked on me. I felt safe when I was with him in the upstairs room, I felt quiet inside, like I didn't have to be scared any more, despite Padric drunk and snoring away in the corner like my father when he had one too many.

In the upstairs room, once we changed out of our surplices and cassocks every morning after mass, Timothy took special pains to teach me the exact way to say the latin responses, even though neither me nor him nor Peter Rafferty nor any of the other altar boys understood a word of it, while Padric snored away in the old leather chair. Timothy was patient and even encouraged me to say them along with him and Peter during the mass despite I was shy at first and barely spoke them above a whisper. But because I didn't have to know what I was saying or hearing, I learned to say them even quicker it turned out than I learned pig latin from Earl Jr., quicker too because I was so eager to please Timothy, I would do anything to please him. He only had to raise his eyebrows in exasperation when I kept stumbling over words like *laitificat* and *juventutem* for me to be sure to get it right the next time, it was like a knife in my heart if he was impatient or displeased with me.

He did such a good job, when it came time for Father Mack to test me in the sacristy, I went through the responses without a hitch. Father Mack looked amazed behind his glasses and patted me on the head, saying soon as I got strong enough to lift the missal I'd be a full-fledged altar boy in no time. When he heard that, Timothy, standing behind, beamed at me, and I was in seventh heaven.

After that, one morning when it came communion time, he let me, with Father Mack's okay, hold the gold platen under the chins of the ladies receiving holy communion so no crumbs spilled on the floor, which was a wonder none did, my hand was shaking so hard it being the first time I did it. Glancing out into the church I saw my mother was the only one out of all the ladies not at the rail but was kneeling in her pew with her head bowed over her folded hands, it looked like she was either praying hard or else hiding her face. I felt sad in my eyes, seeing how dark she looked in her own.

Timothy was different in so many ways, he didn't go to our school like the rest of us but went to the Catholic school in the county seat because his father worked as an insurance agent there and could pay for it, Timothy driving with him to school in their 1934 Ford. Even though I was terrified of the nuns, I wished I could go there too with him just to be near to wherever he was. He had what my mother called "clean-cut looks" beneath eyebrows that were like dark wings joined together and eyelashes that were just as dark and thick, like Tyrone Power's eyes. His hair was so black it shined blue in the light, and dipped down in that widow's peak over a brow that was smooth and white as the silk in my cousin Tom's communion suit. And his hair was always cut close in a crewcut, winter and summer. The more I knew him the more I wished I had me a widow's peak too, I wished I had me earlobes like his that didn't hang down but cut straight up and across and that nobody in my family had or nobody else I knew had either and that I thought made you special if you had them. I could see under his shirt his chest was strong like Boy's was in the Tarzan movies, he looked stronger and better built'n any of the other Swamp Rats that I later found out were all secretly jealous of him, and more'n a little scared of him too, because he was strong and had nerve and was the first to do the daring things. I never saw him have to raise his fists—like that day the Swamp Rats had me and Earl Jr. surrounded, usually a word or a glance from him was enough to shut any of them up. But you could tell he could take care of himself if he had to. He didn't smoke like me and Earl Jr. or the other Swamp Rats did, he said he didn't want it to cut into his wind when he played baseball and football. So I stopped smoking too, not because I played baseball or football or ever wanted to, but because I wanted to be like him in every way, even though Earl Jr. when he came hanging around trying to get me to go off with him, teased me unmerciful when I gave it up and wouldn't smoke any more with him in the clearing.

Timothy was different from Earl Jr. in every way, he didn't curse and I never heard him tell a lie or brag and his neck and ears were always clean. Another way he was different was you could tell he believed in God an awful lot but he never talked about it and didn't make a big show of it and act holy as all get out when he was in church like that Ronnie did so everybody could see how holy he was.

When I became an altar boy, now if Earl Jr. met me on the road he called me Saint Mickey Mouse and would shake his hips at me and fork his fingers at his lips and give me a wink with that look I couldn't hardly resist, teasing me to come back in the woods with him. But I would quick say me a double prayer to Jesus and Mary so I wouldn't be going off with him and that worked more times'n it didn't.

But Timothy was so different. More'n once I overheard Father Mack tell Timothy's mother, "The boy is definitely priestly material," and Mrs. Burnside smiled behind her glasses in that quiet way of hers like she already knew that, like she already might've known that the minute he was born.

I began to think about him in bed at night, thinking about him as much as I thought about Shirley Temple when I first saw her in the movies, or Earl Jr. a while after he first came into the yard and told me I didn't know my a-s-s from a hole in the ground. I started telling Slap and Danny stories now at night that I made up about me and Timothy that was about two boys being altar boys and wanted to be priests together, not telling them his real name of course. Over the months that followed, I wanted to be like Timothy in the worst way, just like I did when I first started running around with Earl Jr., so that I started imitating him right down to the way he walked and talked, I even tried to talk better'n I did, the way Mrs. Feek always tried to make me do, just because Timothy did, he talked just like his mother and father talked that Mrs. Beezley always said to my mother put on airs like they were better'n anybody else in Lenape because they both graduated from the high school in the county seat and hardly anybody else in Lenape ever did.

In time I began to wonder if I was "priestly material" too, and secretly hoped and prayed I was—hadn't my own mother asked me that first day I was on the altar did I want to be a priest, why would she ask me that if maybe she hadn't seen something in me like Father Mack saw in Timothy?

Another day walking to church in the morning she asked me, "Are you and Timothy gettin to be good boyfriends?" I gave her a look and knew right away from her eyes she was hoping we'd got to be boyfriends so I wouldn't be boyfriends anymore with Earl Jr. that she knew wasn't a Catholic and never washed his ears and never had his mouth washed out either, she bet, and should, she said he had such a bad mouth on him.

I didn't know what to say, I was afraid I'd give myself away if she saw my eyes, so I ran on ahead of her like I sometimes did, I couldn't wait now to get to the church in the mornings. She hollered out, "Whatsa matter, my company ain't good enough for ya?" I stopped and looked back at her, feeling guilty I was so excited about getting to the church, but with a grin and a wave of her hand she said, "Gwan, gwan," and I ran on again.

When I got upstairs to put on my surplice and cassock Padric was there ahead of me as always, snoozing tipsy in the chair in the corner. Timothy said Padric was the sexton that was like a janitor like Mr. Floud at school. Padric told everybody he shook so much because he had what he called the palsy but Timothy said was only the shakes from drinking too much, like I knew from when my father shook some mornings.

When Ronnie found out I was learning to be an altar boy he ran to his mother asking her could he be an altar boy too. But soon as he found out you had to be at the church seven o'clock each and every morning of the week, he soon changed his tune, making a frown, saying, "Well, I'll just have to think about it," and that was the last I heard of his ever wanting to be an altar boy.

It was just as well. I liked it the way it was. Since Peter Rafferty just about broke a leg getting out of his cassock after mass to get out of there and get home, it was just me and Timothy alone together up in the upstairs room, except for Padric which was the same as being by ourselves. It was just me and him with Timothy teaching me my latin or telling me when you rang the little bells and when you took the wine and water up to the priest at the exact right time during the mass, him leaning so close I could smell the Ivory soap he washed himself in. I breathed him in, like if I breathed him in he would be in me, he would be in my heart like when I received holy communion God was in me and I became like Him and if I breathed him in I would become like him....

But I was in a dither now I was an altar boy, wanting to be like Timothy and not wanting to go in the woods anymore with Earl Jr. I tried not to walk like Earl Jr., or talk like him anymore. I was so wrapped up thinking about Timothy, Earl Jr. was fading from me like your brown arms and face do after the summer goes. Still, he'd come around and call for me out in the road, or if nobody was around, he'd call out by the backdoor, his voice and his look still like a powerful horseshoe magnet, pulling me out, "Yo, Mick! Yo, Mickey!" If my mother heard him calling, she'd give me a glance like she wished I wouldn't be running with him, hoping I would take up with Timothy Burnside since he was a Catholic and an altar boy and never cursed nor lied.

Sometimes when Earl Jr. called "Yo, Mick!" out back, I pretended I wasn't home and would squat down below the kitchen window sneaking peeks out at him while my mother glanced at me with a look as if to say, That's right, I'd rather you lied you wasn't home than to be running with him. But other times his calling to me was so strong a pull, I couldn't resist and I ran out of the house before I could see that look come into her eye. The first time that happened I came out and he gave me that look I could never say no to. It made me dying to go off in the woods with him. Even so, I thought of Timothy and started making excuses like I was whining and begging. He looked surprised, it being the first time I hemmed and hawed about going off with him. Then he grinned and gave me that look again, shaking himself a little, shaking his hips in that way I knew what he meant. When I hemmed and hawed some more, he said, "Won'tcher ole lady letcha out?"

Now I was an altar boy, I knew I mustn't lie so I said no, it wasn't that. He said, "Well, what is it then? You gittin so holy now? I see you goin to church every morning witcher ma." I said, "It's just I don't feel like goin into the woods with you right now," which I knew was a lie but only a little white lie. He saw it was, like he always saw right through me, snapping back, "Since you become a altar boy and Saint Mickey Mouse you become so high'n and mighty you ain't no fun no more!" He hacked up a lunger and spit it at my feet, twisting up his face, snarling, "That's what I think of yer creepin Jesus! I spit on eem! I spit on yer God!" And shaking his fist at the sky he shouts, "They ain't no God, if'n they is I double-dare you to strike me down dead this very minute!" saying it more I knew to be mean, knowing how much it shocked the pants off of me.

Even so, I stuck my fingers in my ears and looked back quick at the house to see if my mother or anybody else heard him. Looking so pleased, seeing he was still able to scare me, he gave me a sneery grin.

"I spied you walkin from that church a' yers with that boy they call Rev, that goody-goody thinks he's such a hotshot bossing them scurvy Swamp Rats around—I think he's yer new boyfriend—I think you got a crush on him."

I ducked my head and stared down at his snot in the dirt and didn't say anything, what could I say, it was true.

"You gonna go with me er not?"

I still stared down, not able to look him in the eye, knowing he'd see the lie there in my own eye if I so much as looked at him.

"I got to go in, my mother wants me."

"Me mother wants me! Me mother wants me!" He clapped his hand behind his ear, squinching up his face. "Oh yeah? That's funny, I don't hear yer ole lady callin you."

I kept on staring down. "I got to go in, I got to go in now," saying it like I was begging for him to let me go.

He spit again between my maryjanes and walked away in a huff, cutting around the side of the house and jumping the hedge into the road. I stared after him, torn between wanting to call him back and say, okay, okay, let's go into the woods, then in the same instant Timothy's face passing in front of my eyes once more and not wanting to. I bet Timothy when he was in the woods with the Swamp Rats never took off his clothes and danced for them nor switched their bare behinds with cherry switches, I bet it was something he never did and I better not do anymore either if I wanted to be like him and be a priest with him.

But I wasn't always so strong. Earl Jr. knew it and he knew he had those ways, the way he could give me that look and grin and give his hips a shake. And sometimes out of nowhere I would get to thinking about him and thinking about wanting to follow him to the clearing to dance and sing for him despite my swearing I wouldn't ever again. Those times, even despite what Father Mack said, and despite what my mother said that the Snarps were nothing but pagans and heathens that never went to church, and that Earl Jr. was the worst of the lot, according to Babes Beezley, I felt so wishy-washy, I wanted to make it up to him, and one day not long after he went off in a huff, I worked up the nerve to stick my pride in my pocket, then walked down the road to his house.

"Yo, Earl! Yo, Earl Jr.!" I called and called outside his backdoor. But he didn't answer no matter how long I called, even though I suspected he was inside and probably wasn't doing a darned thing but sneaking looks out at me, paying me back for me doing the same thing to him sometimes, because I saw his brothers and sisters, including that Walter, peeking and grinning out the window at me, while I stood there making a fool of myself, calling and calling. Finally, Mrs. Snarp came out on the backstep, saying, "My Earl Jr. said to tell you he ain't home now." I could see by the way her one tooth wiggled when she grinned and her eyes rolled around she was telling me a fib for him, and like to make up for it she asked me did I want to see the picture of her little Edward again?

After mass, me standing on tiptoe in the closet by the corner, putting the wine and water cruets in their glass tray, up on their shelf. Father Mack standing with his back to me at the chest of drawers across the room, taking off his last vestment, kissing it before tucking it away. When I turned and closed the closet door, he turned too, smiled at me. Kept staring, smiling. He never done that before and I felt funny, feeling my cheeks going rosy, and glanced quick out the window at Timothy's house in the gray morning. As he did most times now, Timothy'd left the sacristy as soon as he'd slipped out of his cassock and'd run across the road to get ready for school, leaving me to tidy up to save him time. I felt important he let me do it, snuffing out the candles on the altar, washing the cruets and putting the wine away; I would've done anything he asked me to do.

When I turned my eyes from the window, I gave a start, seeing's as Father Mack was now standing right over me, his jowly red face still grinning, his eyes crinkling down at me behind his glasses that didn't have no rims. I felt a grab in my belly and my heart began to thump. I wisht Timothy was still there, I wisht I was across the road with him right that very second.

Father Mack inched in closer, smiling. "What lovely eyes you have," he said, his voice as soft as the watered silk of the vestment he'd just slipped out of. I peered up at him, moving back closer into the corner. "What lovely eyes," he breathed again, pushing in closer, so that I could feel his belly pressing against me, feel the buttons of his black cassock pressing against my chest. I heard in my head Mrs. Gottlieb saying near the same thing that first Sunday after mass, and heard again Frank and Buster sneering about it afterwards, and heard Father Mack now say it one more time, his voice coming raspy and quick just like it sounded through the screen in the confessional box when I confessed I danced bare in the woods with Earl Jr.—I thought again it must be bad to have them eyes.

He pressed and pressed until his buttons was hurting me and I turned wild-eyed out the window wishing with all my heart I could see Timothy. And as I wished that, I felt Father Mack easing himself away, and when I looked sideways into his face, he wasn't smiling no more, his face was set and hard. He went quick to the chest of drawers and snatching up his biretta, clapped it down hard on his head and not saying a word, headed down the dark hall past the altar where he didn't even bother to genuflect, like he did every single morning, shoved open the back door and was gone.

I waited a couple minutes after I heard the door slam, then pried myself out of the corner. I looked out the window again, hoping again with all my heart to see Timothy, but he'd probably gone off with his father by now to school in the county seat. As I pulled the surplice over my head and began unbuttoning my cassock, my heart finally slowing down, I began to know something I didn't know before, something with no name, something like that day on the beach when Charley showed up asking us did we have any problems, something that's so deep and dark it didn't have no name yet.

And I knew something else too, I knew why Frank and Buster wasn't altar boys any more, something else I didn't have no words for but understood in that deep, dark place, and would keep there, deep and quiet forever.

Early one Saturday morning not long after that my father left the house with some old buckets with rope tied to the handles to go help Sam Beezley clean out his cesspool and underneath their outhouse—"honeydippin," they called it. The minute he left, my mother shut herself up in the kitchen and washed herself at the pump, then got herself dressed up in her Sunday best dress and hat that even though it was her best, she herself admitted wasn't much to look at. When she was ready she called us all together and told us she was going to catch the next bus to Philly to go with her sisters to visit her mother's grave—"May her soul rest in peace"—and see the new headstone, then on the way home she had some things to get at Frank and Seder's on Market Street on Aunt Bridget's charge plate. Danny got all excited pestering her right away with was she going to get anything for him, and she said, "You'll see." Then Slap started up, hopping around, shrieking he could go pick some wild flowers in the woods for her to put on Grandmom's grave. But she ducked around through the dining room door to take a look at the cuckoo clock and yelled back at him there wasn't time for that, the bus'd be coming down the boulevard any minute, and anyhow the flowers'd probably be all wilted between the bus ride to Philly and the long trolley ride all the way out to Holy Cross cemetery in Yeadon.

"Oh, it won't take but a minute!" Slap hollered. "I'll get-cha some wile roses, they'll keep, and I'll run back so fast!"

Before she was even able to hold up her hand like she didn't want to hear another word, there being a look in her eye like she hadn't slept much all night, Slap raced out the backdoor and was gone. Then when she turned to Frank and Buster and told them they had to stick around the house and mind us younger ones while she was in the city, their faces almost fell on the floor, they both had their hearts so set, once their chores were done, on running over to the Beezleys to watch the honeydipping, as if that was something anybody in their right mind would want to watch just for the fun of it.

Since they still weren't speaking to each other, she left it to us to tell our father where she was if he got back to the house before she did. I was hoping right up to the last minute she might ask me to go with her, but when Slap came tearing in the backdoor with a fistful of wild roses and black-eyed susans, yelling all out of breath, "See, Mom! Dint I tell you I'd be quick! Dint I tell you!" and asked her could he carry them for her to the busstop and she said, "No, you're all to stay here and do your chores," I could see by the set look in her eye that was that, that neither me nor anybody else was going to even get to walk her to the bus let alone go to the city with her. Seeing all the long faces, she said, as she dampened a sheet of old newspaper under the pump and wrapped it around the stems of Slap's flowers, "Now I'll be back before supper," then, like to make us feel better, "And I'll bring you all a surprise from Frank and Seder."

"I want a sailor hat!" Danny piped up, "I want a sailor hat and swimming trunks!" But my mother made like she didn't hear him, like in her eyes she was already gone as she stepped down off the porch clutching the bunch of flowers and crossed the road into the woods, taking the path out to the boulevard to flag down the next bus to Philly, me watching the back of her black hat with its faded crown til I couldn't see her anymore for the trees, then sitting down on the porch steps staring for the longest while at the break in the trees she'd disappeared into.

Around five o'clock my father and Sam Beezley, their overalls spattered and caked with mud and I didn't want to think what all else, came staggering up the road. Mr. Beezley was carrying a bag of beer he must of bought at Tarkie's to treat my father for helping him honeydip, the both of them acting like they'd already got a head of steam up at the saloon, they were so bright-eyed, laughing and joking. I slid over to the far end of the porch as they sat down on the front steps, my father hollering at Slap to go get them jelly glasses to drink out of. Then him and Mr. Beezley got my older brothers giggling so they couldn't stop as they sniffed at each other joking as to which of them smelled the most "fragrant." They were all laughing so hard my brothers never must've thought to tell my father where our mother was, and my father of course didn't ask.

All of a sudden, I heard the gears of the five o'clock bus from Philly grinding through the trees, then heard its brakes squeal to a stop out on the boulevard. I jumped off the porch and ran through the woods to go see was it her coming and when I was halfway along the path, my heart gave a leap, there she was coming through the trees, carrying a brown shopping bag said Frank & Seder on it.

Right off, I tried to read her eyes but couldn't see anything, yes or no, then as I walked backwards in front of her, I started asking her all kinds of questions, what did she buy at Frank and Seder's and did she see Aunt Nell and Sonny and did she see Grandmom's grave with the new headstone, what did the headstone look like, was it nice? But she held up a hand, brushing all my questions aside, and for the first time I saw how worn out she was, even more worn out'n when she left that morning, her saying there was plenty of time to tell us all about that later on, what she wanted to know now was was everything all right at the house? was my father home?

As we came out of the woods, my father eyed her suspicious from the steps, seeing she was dressed in her

Sunday clothes on a Saturday and carrying the shopping bag from Frank and Seder. His eyes narrowed like he was putting two and two together, like he saw right away where she'd been, she'd been seeing her sisters and they'd probably been talking about him. Watching us cross the road, he started plucking nervous at his cigarette pocket like he knew something was up but wasn't sure what it was and likely wouldn't ever know since they weren't speaking, and because of his pride he never would ask her right out what she'd been up to. Then, like he wanted her to be sure'n see it, he guzzled down his beer and, all defiant, held out his glass to Sam Beezley for a refill. But in spite of his big show he dropped his eyes as she came up the steps, glancing away like he couldn't look her in the eye. He didn't say anything either when she spoke to Sam Beezley and not to him, but you could see his lower lip curl up like he wanted to say plenty.

Sam Beezley asked her, his eyes so glassy and merry, "Where you been gallivantin off to?" All she said was, "I been up to Philly seein me sisters," and even though my brothers and Kate crowded after her into the house, pestering her, like I'd done, to know what she got in the Frank and Seder bag, all she did, like with me, was hold up her hand, saying, "Mary Mother of God and all that's holy, give me a chance to catch me breath and git out of this dress to git supper started— You'll hear all about it later after we eat—Frank, you go git the erl stove started." Then staring right at me, she said, "Buster—I mean, Slap—I mean *you, Mick!*" looking exasperated, she was getting us all mixed up like she sometimes did and had to go right down the line til she got the right one, "Mick, you go out and set the table," and without another word she went upstairs to change her clothes.

As I was the last to go in the screendoor I heard Sam

Beezley let out a hoot, then slap my father on the back, getting his needle out, saying, "She been up in Filthydelphia spendin all yer money, Stosh!" My father's eyes got dark like a thundercloud settling in them, he curled up his lower lip again, and giving a sneery laugh, said, "Yeah, what money? C'mon, Sam, you said you'd treat me to as many beers as I dipped buckets of honey for you, so less us have another brew here, we got a lot more to go."

Mr. Beezley busted out har-harring as he tipped the Schmidt's to my father's glass, I could still hear him as I came into the kitchen to set the table for supper.

When my mother came down dressed now in one of her old housedresses, Danny wanted to know right off the bat did she get him a sailor's cap and put on a sour puss when she told him, as she took down her apron behind the kitchen door and tied it on, she couldn't find him no sailor's cap, saying it like you knew she was telling a little white lie because I knew if she bought him something special she'd have to buy the rest of us something special too. But he was all grins when she told him as a special treat from Aunt Nell, that gave her the money to buy it, she brought home a box of fishcakes and a paper tub of spaghetti that had printed on them, when she took them out of her shopping bag, "Less Work For Mother," and that was from the Horn & Hardart's retail shop on Market Street near where she caught the bus, because she knew fishcakes and spaghetti was all our favorite and was the cheapest.

We all sat around the kitchen table watching her heat it up on the stove, me watching her face, waiting for some clue if she'd been to Saint Lucia's, while everybody else started pestering her again with questions about Philly, Slap asking did she put his flowers on Grandmom's grave and was there any other flowers on her grave, what did the new headstone look like? She told him she stuck his roses and daisies right near the new headstone, that looked so nice. Then all of a sudden Slap bust out crying and all us stared at him. My mother came over and petted him on the head, whispering, "Don'tchou cry now, Grandmom's happy in heaven. Here," and she reached in her apron pocket for a wad of the toilet paper she always kept there, if we had it, and shoved it at him for him to blow his nose. Then she told him to go on to the pump and wash his face and be sure to wash his hands too for supper, for all of us to wash our hands, and for Frank to go call our father in to come eat because she still wasn't speaking to him and wouldn't call him in herself. Frank went out but came back without him, saying now Sam Beezley left, our father was asleep in his chair in the parlor still in his muddy overalls with yesterday's *Bulletin* over his face. Buster snorted, like it was funny, but my mother said, not like she was annoyed or mad at him or anything, like you would've expected, "Let eem sleep, it's just as well. Let eem sleep it off," her eyes softening and looking for the first time like she might've found the deaf old priest after all.

After supper, that tasted so good we all said we wished we could have Horn & Hardart fishcakes and spaghetti each and every night of the week, we all gathered around my mother's chair at the kitchen table and watched as she pulled up the shopping bag between her knees. It turned out to be full of pairs of boys' sneakers that relief never handed out and that were called irregulars my mother said were on sale dirt cheap in the bargain basement at Frank and Seder, but you could hardly see the mistakes in them unless you looked real hard. Kate was hopping mad she only got a pair of white anklets for Sunday and a pair of cotton underdrawers but no dress with ribbons. My mother said to her, "Be thankful you got that, me fine miss, and be thankful to yer Aunt Bridget and her charge plate." But you could see Kate wasn't thankful for anything, she still had her heart set on a dress with ribbons like on her Shirley Temple doll, and had a pout on her just as if she was about to get her hair brushed.

I kept an eye on my mother all of that evening, watching for some other hint. After we all had our Saturday night baths in the washtub, all of us boys sat around the parlor in our new sneakers wriggling our toes and staring at them, they smelled so new and rubbery without any raggedy holes like in our old ones. Our mother sat crocheting on the couch, saying hardly a word or giving away any sign. Only her eyes, as I looked up from my drawing on the back of an old paper bag and watched her on the sneak now and again in the light of the oil lamp, seemed calmer for the first time in a long, long while, not pinched or as dark and tired. It was only her mouth got tight everytime she glanced sideways at my father that was still snoring away like a saw in his chair and by now was really smelling as fragrant as him and Sam Beezley'd been joking about, his head, as the newspaper fell down from in front of his face, slipped against the headrest of the chair, making him look just like Padric O'Hara snoozing in his old leather chair in the upstairs room of the church.

By now, Father Mack said I'd been doing so good I could be on the altar on Sundays now with Timothy and Peter. So, at early mass the next morning I saw the same old ladies were there as during the week, their arms hanging over the front pews as they knelt fingering their rosaries, their lips fluttering in silent Hail Marys, my mother among them, wearing the new cotton stockings and new low-heeled black shoes she got for herself from Frank and Seder. The only difference was on this particular morning my mother got up with the rest of them at communion time and came to the railing. I felt a shine for her in my heart bright as the gold paten when it came her turn and

I held the paten under her chin to catch any crumbs, her eyelids shut twitching for the least fraction of a second as Father Mack paused in mumbling his latin to lift his eyebrows in surprise before he stuck the wafer on her tongue. Like he might snatch it back, she flicked it in her mouth, then quick bowed her head over her folded hands, her shoulders shivering a little, and the priest, so you could barely see it, gave her a sidelong smile before he dipped his fingers in the chalice for another wafer, passing on to the next open mouth, and nobody the wiser.

The bell in the red brick church began to ring that Friday afternoon. It kept on ringing like it'd never rung before, the slow clanging of it we could hear all muffled in the distance even as far away as Lenape Road. It being now such a babyish game to me that Frank and Buster only played to keep the younger ones happy, I watched as my brothers and sister played Take A Giant Step out in the road, Frank, being the leader of course, shouting at Slap, "No, you dint say 'May I?' Go back one step," and Slap, shaking his head, stepped back, he was always the furtherest behind in Take A Giant Step, even further behind'n Kate.

When the bell kept on ringing they stopped in their game to listen to it, Slap hollering, "What're we stoppin for? Heh? Heh? What're we stoppin?" Frank said, "That's funny. I ain't never heard the bell in the red brick church ringin on a Friday before." He looked at Buster and Buster shrugged, then they went back to playing their game again.

While I watched I listened to the bell. It sounded like the school bell and got me to thinking about the main thing I'd only been able to think about lately, that we would be going back to school soon, and about how I would be in Miss Riggs' second grade. I was worrying what it would be like having a new teacher, even though Miss Riggs didn't seem as mean as Mrs. Feek could be, I didn't think anybody could be mean as Mrs. Feek, unless it was Miss Jickers that I supposed had to be mean because she was the principal.

The bell was still ringing later that afternoon when my two older brothers, getting sick of playing with the younger ones, moved up onto the porch out of the sun to play one more game of gin rummy, the card game they played all of that summer as much as they played hearts all the summer before. My mother, that'd been out in the kitchen where she'd been wringing out clothes in the washtub, came to the screendoor, pushing the damp hair back from her forehead with her arm. She cocked her ear in the direction of the bell. Slap, seeing her listening, asked her did she know why it was ringing, she said she didn't know why, "Maybe some bigshot in the red brick church died, how do I know? I got me wash to do."

She turned to go, but Frank got all agitated, saying, "Maybe it's somebody bigger'n a proddisin, maybe it's President Roosevelt hisself kicked the bucket, for them to be ringin the bell so long." His eyes got big. "Maybe he got stabbed or shot, and if we only had the juice on we could turn on the old Scott and hear the news, we don't hear nothin no more without no radio—Now our aunts is sendin down a buck-fifty each and every week in the mail, couldn't we get Public Service to turn the 'lectric back on?"

My mother gave him a look like he was accusing her it was her fault the juice was off, saying, "We owe Public Service so much back money they ain't gonna turn the juice on til it gits paid. And as for the money yer aunts send down every week, God bless 'em, that's fer food to eat and to pay off a little of all we owe the Gottliebs, that been so good to us, lettin us put things on the eye all this time. And as fer that bell ringin you'll jist have to wait til yer father gits home, won'tcha? If anything's happened—God forbid if it's President Roosevelt dead!"—She blessed herself real quick because she always said if it wasn't for President Roosevelt we wouldn't even have what little we had— "If that's the end of him, that'd be the end of relief if one of them republicans gits in,"—saying republicans as if they were the same as proddisins— "Then where will we be? So you all better say a prayer it ain't President Roosevelt dead."

I quick said a prayer under my breath it wasn't President Roosevelt was stabbed or shot, but a proddisin at the redbrick church instead.

"If anything's happened, yer father'll prolly hear about it, I'm sure they got a radio over the bar at Tarkie's saloon."

After saying that word saloon her lips disappeared, her mouth got thin as a hair, then she turned without another word and went back to her washtub.

But we didn't have to wait til my father came home. Just as my brothers were begging my mother, that now was out back hanging up the wash, could they go into town and find out why the bell was ringing, Mrs. Beezley, with Sister right behind her, came tearing through the woods faster'n I saw her move since when she came running over to show my mother in the *County Seat Weekly* where Charley wrote about her sisters being down from Philly. She was hollering as she came, "Ja hear the news! Ja hear it! Them stinkin nazis jist invaded Poland! I jist heard it on the radio right in the middle of Our Gal Sunday! I dint think you heard it yet so I come runnin right over to tell you! Them stinkin nazis!"

My mother, her mouth full of clothespins, stared at her like she was talking chinee.

"It means *war!*" Mrs. Beezley shouted at her, like my mother was Slap. "It means we're goin to war and my Sam says if we go to war then they'll need lots a' ships!"

My mother still stared at her, the clothespins hanging out of her mouth looking like long wooden teeth. Mrs. Beezley got all exasperated. "It *means*, Nor'!" she shouted even louder, like you would to a kid to make them understand, "It means yer Stosh'll finally be gittin a job at the yard!"

Now my mother gaped at her like what she was saying was even worse'n chinee. My father getting a job at the yard? It seemed to take a long time for it to sink in but when it did, a look of her finally understanding what Mrs. Beezley'd been saying came into her eyes. She took the clothespins out of her mouth and stared off back over the swamp, her mouth wide open, a look in her eye now like she was seeing something back there she couldn't hardly believe, no more'n she could believe my father might be getting a job at long last.

Sister scooped up Kate and started dancing with her around the yard, then Slap started hopping and dancing along with them, screeching, "No more rotten pertaters! No more wormy mush!" while I watched my mother, I couldn't believe my ears either, and to myself I said a prayer of thanks to the Blessed Mother all her prayers'd been finally answered.

When my father got home that evening from working on the dump truck, my mother was right, from his eyes you could tell he'd made a stop at Tarkie's on the way. But as he came walking up the road his footstep was somehow springier'n usual and when he bounded into the yard and Frank and Buster fell all over him, shouting, "Did you hear the news, Pop? Did you hear it?" he shouted back, "I heard it! I heard it all right, all right!"

When he said it there was a brightness in his eyes even brighter'n the beers he had in him, his cheeks all flushed he was so awful excited. You could hear it in his voice too as he came into the kitchen, telling us it wouldn't be long now, it sure wouldn't, things were looking up, by God, talking in a way you could tell it wasn't just the beer talking.

My mother, mashing the potatoes on the sink, stopped long enough to listen, turning her eyes to give him a sidelong glance, looking at him, quick as it was, like she hadn't looked at him for such a long, long time, before she went back to pounding with the masher again.

My father saw that look. He stumbled for a second in what he was saying about how they was going to need ships, they was sure going to need a lot of ships, his eyes brightening up a notch higher, the darkness he had in them the past couple weeks whenever he looked at her, leaving them for now, his adam's apple jumping up and down.

Tonight, my father ate his meat and mashed potatoes quicker'n ever, keyed up the same way as those nights long ago when the electric was still on and the radio was working and he knew there was going to be a Joe Louis fight.

What I couldn't understand was why my father was getting so excited about Poland, it was so far away, what did he care about Poland? His mother came from Poland, yes, but he hadn't ever seen it.

The bell kept ringing long into the night, ringing in the dark like somebody died, Buster joking Reverend Hoople and Miss Prouty must be taking turns pulling on the rope, and Frank sniggering, "Their arms must be pulled out of their sockets by now they been pullin so long."—The bell clanging far off behind all of the talk on the front porch, as our punks burnt in the shadows and my father and Sam Beezley jabbered away more'n usual over the bottles of beer Sam Beezley brought over like it was a celebration and was going to be a fight night on the radio. Us kids sat around them on the porch floor all ears while my mother and Babes Beezley, on dining room chairs they brought out, sat up against the clapboard, listening for once as the men talked, Babes Beezley smoking one Raleigh after the other.

If we git in it, the yard'll be hoppin, you kin betcher boots on that," Sam Beezley was saying for the umpteenth time. "You mark my words. They already started dredgin the river so's they can launch the USS New Jersey, and they'll be buildin other warships too. You'll see. It won't be long now, Stosh, before you'll be workin right along side of me," he said, clamping my father on the thigh. "I'll see my foreman first thing in the mornin and put in another word fer ya."

My father started rubbing his kneecaps the same way Slap or Danny did when they knew something good was going to happen. And even though they were the same words he'd heard from Sam Beezley's mouth a hundred times before, now Poland been invaded by the nazis it was like they sounded somehow more believable to him than ever. In the gleam of the punks I could see his mouth keen as the blade of the hatchet he chopped off the heads of chickens with for our Sunday dinner.

In the same glow I just barely made out Mrs. Beezley squeeze my mother's knee after she heard what Mr. Beezley said and give my mother a grin and a nod. My mother smiled back but there was still a worried look in her eye like she'd been hearing about my father getting a job at the yard for so long now she'd believe it when she saw it.

The very next morning when Father Mack came bustling into the sacristy he looked so sour-faced and puffy around the eyes like he didn't get much sleep the night before. During mass he was crabby with Timothy and Peter when they weren't fast enough getting the wine and water up to him, or was snapping his fingers because he thought Timothy was too slow getting the missal to the other side of the altar, even though he wasn't. Timothy whispered to me afterwards in the upstairs room Reverend Hoople's bell must of kept Father Mack awake all night even long after it finally stopped ringing, and this morning Father Mack's nose was out of joint because Reverend Hoople showed him up yesterday by letting the whole town know how bad he felt about Poland being invaded by ringing his bell all the livelong day right up until midnight. Father Mack would've too, if he only had a bell.

So, that very next Sunday at the children's mass, Father Mack made another sermon from the altar begging for money to make the bell tower stronger so he could put a bell up in it. He got so red in his face talking about it that for the very first time I put my penny in the collection when Padric O'Hara came jingling around all shaky with the basket, put it in even though my brothers didn't, they gave me a look when I did like I must be crazy.

In second grade I had Miss Riggs that even though she was young, wore her dark brown hair in a bun behind as if she was old. Like Mrs. Feek, but in a nice way, she told me how to say words and not to say "ain't" and to quit saying "me this" and "me that" and to stop picking my nose that was getting to be a terrible habit. And because I wanted to be like Timothy in every way and talk good like him, I tried my hardest to say things right. Every afternoon she read to us, once about an Italian puppet name Pinocchio that came to life and another time about an Indian boy named Wahoo that lived in a teepee. Listening to her read was like listening to the radio that I hadn't heard in so long I could barely wait for the time to come when she'd read to us again.

Another thing was, we sang three times a week like we never sang in Mrs. Feek's class. Miss Riggs would stand up front and blow on a little round pitch pipe and taught us, "Welcome, Sweet Springtime" and "Flow Gently, Sweet Afton." She even let Virginia tapdance once so the whole floor shook, and let the girl named Eleanor that always looked like she had a dirty neck even when she didn't, sing "Mexicali Rose, Stop Cryin."

On top of that, instead of playing the dumb old sticks like in Mrs. Feek's class, we played mouth organs that Miss Riggs went and bought for the whole class out of her own pocketbook at Kresge's five 'n tenny in the county seat—I was sure glad she did because me and a lot of others in the class wouldn't've been able to shell out the 20¢ they cost a piece. I practiced and practiced that mouth organ every spare minute at home, playing "Yankee Doodle" and "Home on the Range," even though, like my practicing with my whistling, it drove everybody nuts, and Frank and Buster teased was I practicing to grow up like Charley? That showed again how much they knew, I never saw Charley ever playing a mouth organ, not even once.

Miss Riggs' dresses weren't as old-fashioned as the dark brown dress with the long skirt down to her ankles Miss Prouty wore every single day in her third grade class, but they were pretty close to it. And she was the only one besides Miss Jickers that drove a car of her own, she drove the other teachers in it to and from school, a Ford V8, dark green, that when she first got it all the boys, including my brothers, crowded around and stared at inside and out and even crawled underneath to take a squint, arguing with each other over was a Ford better'n a Chevy.

I got to the front of the class that year, the very first seat on the boys' side, because I got all A's on my report card. Virginia, that had a head of Shirley Temple curls with more and fatter curls'n any other girl in the second grade and that as the weather got colder wore a Sonja Henie ice skater hood that tied under the chin, was in the front seat on the girl's side. Gerald, that all year sat at the first table in first grade so Mrs. Feek could see his sunny smile all she wanted, was sitting at a desk now somewheres close to the back in Miss Riggs' class, his smile, as Margaret liked to say, brighter'n he was.

It was a puzzle to me because I was still just as tall, if not taller, and wasn't doing anything different from what I did in Mrs. Feek's class, but there I was, up front, what I'd been itching for all last year come true at last. I was feeling glad now, not so much that I was smart, because that would've been the sin of pride as Sister Joseph Mary warned us about, but that I didn't feel so much like I was peculiar.

Margaret moved up too and was in the second seat behind Virginia. She was sweet as pie to her face but behind her back she whispered that if Virginia didn't stop getting so fat she wouldn't be tapdancing much longer, they'd be shipping her off to the Barnum Bailey and Ringling Brothers circus to be one of them dancing elephants.

I was glad I was way over on the other side of the room and not sitting next to Margaret anymore, and not just from being afraid of catching any more of her cooties either, but because of her tongue that could cut sharp as Earl Jr.'s could.

Lots of times when I followed my brothers down the river when they went fishing for catfish for supper, following them at a safe distance since the older Frank and Buster got the less they wanted me hanging around, we saw big rusty freighters with Jap flags docked across at the wharves in the yard. Mr. Beezley said they were taking on scrap iron to ship back over the Pacific Ocean and some of that scrap iron fell off of the cranes as they were loading it in the Jap boats, and it sunk, along with odd pieces of scrap falling overboard as they built the USS New Jersey, to the bottom of the river and ended up getting sucked through the dredge pipe and finally blown out onto our beach in Lenape.

Now the dredge, that sat like a long low barge anchored out in the middle of the river, was going full blast, word got around about all the junk you could find down on the river banks just like it was money laying there waiting to be picked up. So of course my brothers, when they heard it, they started leaving their fishing poles at home to go further upstream fishing for junk instead. I trailed along behind them down to the spot along where the dredge blew in, Buster pulling a wagon he made out of old orange crates he stole from back of Gottlieb's, while Frank and Slap dragged along raggedy old potato sacks from relief, all of them puffing on butts I spotted for them in the gutters along the way. Which I figured was the only reason Frank and Buster let me come tagging behind, since I could still spot a cigarette butt in the gutter at a hundred yards.

We went down early in the mornings before the first blow came, Buster so anxious to get there he couldn't hardly stand it. It was like he was in South Philly again, collecting scrap paper and rags on a Saturday morning to go to the matinee at the Morris, only here it was all scrap metal that brought in more'n just pennies. Once we got there, we took off our sneaks and my brothers rolled up their long pants so my mother wouldn't be screaming bloody murder our dragging mud all through the house. Then we stood around in the hot sun that kept getting hotter and hotter and then poured down over land that kept getting so buried in new layers of mud and clay blown in everyday that not even a weed let alone a tree for some shade grew anywhere. The stink was something terrible.

The same men me and Earl Jr. saw down the dump were

hanging around the dredge too, "junkies," he called them, older men with their beer bellies and their grizzled chins. They had lots of kids to feed, like my father did, and no jobs yet, most of them, like Mr. Snarp, working when they could, along with my father, on the dump truck for relief or for the WPA on the road they were forever building through the swamp, working anyhow they could for whatever they could get. You could tell they resented us kids being there cutting in on their pickings. To get away from their nasty looks I'd stare across at the yard, that in the heat was only a shimmery blur most times of the ships' ways and the black rusty cranes, where you could hear a low roar of machines and metal grinding on metal and a loud chattering noise Mr. Beezley said were the chippers, while over it all came a sound like pile-drivers booming over the water. In one of the biggest ways you could see flashes of orange sparks that Frank said was from the riveters where they were building the USS New Jersey that Mr. Beezley worked on and that scraps of metal blown in by the dredge fell off of. Staring across, I said a quick prayer to both the Blessed Mother and Jesus to get our father a job working on that battleship soon as possible, and also that more junk would fall overboard from it today than did yesterday.

Sometimes I saw Earl Jr. with his father and brother Walter standing off a ways beside their old dilapidated pushcart with its bent out of shape bicycle wheels, all of them standing there staring out at the dredgeboat like the rest of us, waiting for the first blow. But since I was with my older brothers, Earl Jr. acted like he didn't know me. Which was just like him.

Lenny the Lenape and Eddie and Cockeye were there too with their wicker baby buggy, scavaging with the rest of us, Buster said, for their store-bought bottles of rotgut. Sometimes they passed around a bottle, the neck of it all smudged with muddy thumbprints, but they never passed it to any of the other men that, like Mr. Snarp, eyed them through slit eyes, their gullets going, the tips of their tongues licking their upper lips, you could see they were just dying to get a taste of it.

While we all waited, to kill time, I'd sit off a ways on the driest patch of mud making up stories to myself while the sun, climbing the sky, fried my brains. When the whistle out on the dredgeboat started shrilling and black smoke began belching from the stack, I'd jump up. Soon after, the whole length of the big corrugated pipe began to rumble and shake and everybody standing around would tense up and stare at the mouth of it and move in closer, us kids, like chickens in a pecking order, crowding in behind the men. You could hear the roar coming louder and louder through the mouth of the pipe and when the huge gush came, we all had to jump away quick because it was like a geyser turned on its side that blasted out a long distance and blasted for a long time and when the blow was over and the water finally slackened out of the lip, we'd jump in and slurp through the muck along with the rest. At first I didn't like it at all it was so awful sloppy, but I soon got used to it, thinking of all the bottles of Pepsi-Cola and all the dixie cups we got to buy at Gottlieb's from holding back some of the junk money from my mother that was another thing I had to tell in confession every week.

We sank our arms in up to the elbows in the mud, feeling around blind for pieces of scrap metal, me and Slap and any other of the smaller kids, like Walter Snarp, keeping to the fringes, while Frank and Buster and the older boys, including Earl Jr., jumped in closer, and the bigger men got in and claimed the closest places of all. Once, Buster and Eddie grabbed onto a piece of junk under the mud at the same time, I was scared Buster was going to brain Eddie with it if he didn't let go. Eddie must've been ascared too, he saw that look in Buster's eye and he let go his end of it, curling up his lip like he wasn't afraid of Buster but you could tell he was.

Once the blows were over for the day we went down to the river dragging our bags of junk with us, and washed our feet and legs in the water. We washed the junk too, to see what we got and what we saw we got was pigiron mostly, but kept dreaming of copper that was like finding gold, it got the best price from the Italian junkman from Camden that came around once a week in his battered old Ford truck, buying everything and anything, shouting out his truck window in his singsongy way, *"Any rags, any bones, any bottles today?"* He had a bunch of dented old cow bells strung up over the tailgate that clanked with every bump in the road. Buster could hear those bells long before anybody else could and he would race around the back of the house and crawl under the shed where him and Frank'd stored the scrap from the dredge, and he'd start lugging those burlap sacks around to the side of the road long before the truck ever came into view.

Most of what we had the junkman, that Buster kept an eye on like a hawk, only had to weigh up in his brass hand-scale like the Jew junkmen on 3rd Street in South Philly. He never had to sling it up on the big flat scale at the back of his truck like he always had to do with Mr. Snarp's junk, because Earl Jr. told me his father snuck bricks and rocks into the bottom of his burlap bags and even bragged about it afterwards to my father on the dump truck next day.

Most of the money we made went to my mother to help pay off the rent we owed Mrs. Scadder, and went to what we owed on the eye at Gottlieb's, it also went for pennies for church on Sunday that always ended up in the Gottlieb's cash register anyhow for penny candy. But hope and pray as I might there never seemed enough left over to pay off the Public Service electric bill so we could hear the radio again. Sometimes, though, like I said, Frank and Buster kept back a couple nickels for dixie cups and Pepsi-Colas for all of us, Buster warning me he'd slit my throat if I so much as breathed a word. I promised him I wouldn't, why would I tell if it meant getting my throat cut and not being able to enjoy a dixie cup or a bottle of Pepsi-Cola ever again? It didn't make sense, so of course I kept my trap shut.

For weeks excitement'd been building in town as the day got nearer for the launching of the USS New Jersey. Gottlieb's was doing a good business selling little American flags at half price that some said he was finally going to get rid of, they'd been on the shelf so long they only had thirteen stars instead of forty-eight. At school Miss Riggs gave us lectures for days beforehand on how proud we should be to have a battleship named after our state and told us all about "The Vital Statistics," starting from its sixteen-inch guns and the exact number of tons it weighed, to how many thousands of tons of water it would replace once it was in the river.

When the big day came Miss Jickers gave us the morning off from school so we could all go down to the river and see the launching. Even Gottlieb's closed for the morning, which surprised just about everybody because Gottlieb's never closed, except for Christmas and the three hours on Good Friday afternoon that some said, because they were Jews, they wouldn't even close down then if it wouldn't've seemed disrespectful. Most of the workers from the yard were given the morning off, too, including Sam Beezley that, as we gathered down on the beach at the foot of Snake Hill, was standing around explaining everything about the ship for the umpteenth time to my father and anybody else within a hundred yards wanted to listen.

It looked like the whole town turned out on the beach to watch it, it was like a holiday, or the 4th of July, with most of the kids and lots of grownups carrying the little American flags they bought at Gottlieb's. And there was even a Good Humor truck parked on the sand, the man in his suit and cap that was white as vanilla ice cream selling popsicles packed in dry ice from the back of his truck, popsicles that I couldn't take my eyes off of and that only kids with fathers were working could buy—Like that Ronnie Mahoney that stood licking a chocolate popsicle with his mother under her umbrella out of the sun, just the two of them standing a ways off from everybody else, since Mr. Mahoney wasn't with them because he worked at RCA Victor in Camden and not at the yard, so he didn't get the morning off.

The women were all in their summer dresses, some with wide brim hats to keep the sun out of their eyes, or with hankies over their heads like my mother and Mrs. Beezley. And except for those that had to go to work that afternoon at the yard, most of the men were wearing clean shirts and their best caps like it was Sunday. A few were even wearing straw hats and felt hats against the strong sun and getting razzed about it by the men, like Sam Beezley, that were only wearing their work caps.

All of us were standing on the beach that'd been raised up a couple more feet now from all the rocks and mud blown in by the dredge making the channel to the sea for the battleship, as Mr. Beezley was busy explaining to whoever would listen. The yellow sand that Miss Riggs said'd been used in making glass so long ago in Jersey and that stretched for miles and miles along the beach before the dredging began, now was all buried deep underneath it.

Charley was there too, hopping around through the crowd

with his pencil clinched in his crippled fist like a little kid just learning to write. He was scribbling everything down in a nickel copybook like he was getting it all down to write about in the *County Seat Weekly*. There were lots of people talked nasty about him behind his back but were smiling and nodding at him today, hoping, as Mrs. Beezley whispered to my mother, "to git their names in the paper." When Charley came limping by us, she nodded and smiled at him, too.

A number of boys'd climbed high up into the pine trees on the bluff to get a better look. The Swamp Rats were all up in one of the tallest trees off by themselves, Timothy among them. I never could understand why he had to hang around those Swamp Rats. Seeing him, I wished I was with him right then and they weren't, only I wouldn't want to be high up in a tree. I wondered why some boys it didn't bother being up in trees.

I wanted to wave to Timothy in the worst way but because he was with those Swamp Rats, I was afraid they might think I was waving at them instead of Rev, as they called him. Then up in the very top of the tallest pine tree almost at the end of the bluff all by himself, I spied Earl Jr. perched up there so casual just like he would be sitting safe on the ground. I waved to him but he never waved back, I figured he was so high up and so far away maybe he never did see me even though I waved and waved and I knew he had eyes even sharper'n Buster and could of seen me if he wanted. The truth is, I made myself believe he didn't see me because I knew he was still miffed at me on account of him saying I had a crush on Timothy and that Timothy was more my boyfriend now than he was. My mother asked me, "Who you wavin at, you're gonna shake yer arm outa its socket, all that wavin." I right away said I was waving at Timothy Burnside because I knew she wouldn't like it if I said I was waving at Earl Snarp Jr. Mrs. Beezley, seeing it, grinned

over at me real sly and said, "He yer new boyfriend?" I turned
red and looked away like I was pretending to look across the
river to see were they getting ready to launch the USS New
Jersey yet, while Mrs. Beezley looked at my mother and gave her
a wink.

My father and brothers and Mr. Beezley and his boys moved
up closer to the water but I stayed back with my mother and
Kate and Mrs. Beezley where it wasn't so crowded. Everybody
had their eyes trained on the ways over in the shipyard where
all you could see all draped in red white and blue bunting was
the backend of the battleship, that Sam Beezley let everybody
know was the stern, whether they wanted to know it or not. It
was so big you could see it easy all the way from where we were
standing, despite Mr. Beezley insisting on pointing it out to us
like we were all blind. The yard was so quiet today with nobody
working, it might as well of been a Sunday. You couldn't hear
any piledrivers or machinery clanking and banging over the
water, nor any chippers, today all you could hear was a band
playing military marches so far off over the water it sounded all
faint and tinny.

When the music was over, men's voices, that sounded deep
and bossy, started booming across the water from loudspeakers
Sam Beezley was telling everybody was wired high up in the
ship ways. Everybody shoved closer to the shore to hear better
and be sure not to miss anything. My mother didn't like being
shoved so close to the river and she held onto Mrs. Beezley's
arm with one hand and clutched Kate near to her in the other.
The voices booming out from over in the yard were making
what sounded like speeches hardly anybody could understand,
there was such a drone in them and the voices echoed so much,
bouncing back and forth up in the steel girders of the ways.
They had to travel such a long way over the river, even though

most people on the beach put their hands behind their ears, including Slap, and cocked them in the direction of the yard, they kept shaking their heads, exasperated at not being able to hear anything except for maybe a snatch here and there—"… American destiny…destiny…destiny…Naval might…might… might… Strong America… America…America…."

After the speeches were over, everybody started getting restless and began clapping their hands like in the movie- house when the film breaks. Frank and Buster and the Beezley boys got to arguing over who had the bigger guns on their battleships, the Germans or the United States. I wanted to tell them Miss Riggs said the USS New Jersey had sixteen-inch ones and they were the biggest in the world, but I knew they wouldn't listen to me because they thought I was too little to pay any attention to. Then, just at that very minute everybody shaded their eyes and craned forward, it all of a sudden got so quiet there was only the sound of the river slapping on the shore. It was like everybody was holding their breath and every eye was on the battleship as before you knew it, its back end began to shimmy and shake, there were loud ooo's and ahhh's from the crowd as the USS New Jersey, all strung with bunting and bright colored flags, "From stem to stern," as Sam Beezley called it in his shipyard talk, slid down the ways like it was riding on grease. When it hit the river it made such a big explosion of water everybody gasped, and all that had one, lifted their little flags and started waving them like crazy. It was such a big gray hulking thing, it plunged all the way out to the middle of the river as far as to where the dredge boat'd been anchored, before it finally slowed down and sat there a few minutes rocking so mighty like it might tip over before it finally righted itself. Everybody waved their flags even harder and began cheering when they saw a dozen or more tugboats with buffalo hides on their noses come out snorting steam and, like little dogs nipping at her sides, began to nudge the battle-ship back towards the yard, "Gettin her into her moorin for her final fittin out," as Mr. Beezley explained to my father and all us kids and anybody else standing within earshot that cared to listen.

Then all of a sudden the band over the shipyard struck up the National Anthem that always hurt my throat to sing, while Frank and Buster and the Beezley boys, just to be smart, started singing quiet amongst themselves, "Oh, say can you see any bedbugs on me—If you do take a few 'cause I got them off of you," but not so loud my father or Mr. Beezley could hear.

You could see the waves coming like big humped back whales rolling over and over in the water but everybody was so busy with their eyes shut tight trying to sing the Star Spangled Banner they never noticed. But you could see my brothers and the Beezley boys counting to themselves with gleeful, wide-open eyes because they knew it usually took counting up to a hundred for a passing ship's waves to reach the beach, only the USS New Jersey made such a big splash they only had to count up to fifty. They jumped back quick from the shore just as everybody else was trying to hit the high note in "the rockets' red glare" that nobody could hit except for Agnes O'Hara, and when the first wave hit the beach, it was so huge, a lot of the ladies that couldn't jump back out of the way because of the mob pressed in behind them, got their shoes and stockings soaked, and some of the men too that weren't quick enough. The men all laughed at the ladies making faces and squealing, dodging every which way to get back from the water, but most of the boys, some of them having on their best shoes for the occasion, let themselves get sopped on purpose since it was a good excuse to take off their shoes and socks and go wading and jumping in the waves that kept rolling and rolling up on the shore, the highest we ever saw in the river.

My older brothers were right in there with the rest—much to my mother's annoyance. Actually, I suspected she was less afraid they'd ruin or maybe lose their new sneakers from Frank & Seder's than she was that they'd shame her by drowning on her right in front of everybody. Like she was hoping nobody'd hear her, she called to them to come on back in and they right away pulled long pusses and looked embarrassed in front of the other boys, especially the Swamp Rats that'd come down from the trees by now and were splashing each other and everybody else like maniacs. My father, taking it all in, grinned good-natured, like he was pleased at what his boys were doing, and looked like he wouldn't mind jumping in with them himself. He yelled back for my mother to stop her worrying and leave them alone, and she pressed her lips together like she could strangle him, shaming her by going against her in front of all the people.

As the crowd started to break up and head across the beach and climb up Snake Hill back into town, a lot of the men, including my father and Sam Beezley, to their wives' annoyance, ducked into Ye Old Ship Bottom at the foot of the hill, using the day as an excuse for a few quick ones before those that worked in the yard caught the ferry to finish up the rest of their shift, and the others, like my father, went off to their jobs on relief or the WPA. I saw my mother look away like she didn't want to see him going in, like she didn't want to see any of it anymore. Mrs. Beezley gave my mother's shoulder a pat and took her by the arm and marched her up the hill, glaring back at the saloon with an irritated look the same as a lot of the other wives were doing.

As I followed behind them, along with Danny and Kate, I looked up in the tree Earl Jr.'d been sitting in easy as a bird, but he was gone. Then I glanced back a last time over my shoulder and saw the river in the sun that day had a green, dancey brightness and was giving off that sweet milky odor it always had on clear days, the last time from thereon in I ever remembered it smelling so sweet, or looking so clean, so clean you could see your toes right to the bottom and you could see the fish nibbling around them, the fish that all began to die off not long after the war began and the river got black with pollution and the polio.

Miss Prouty was tall as a weed with a pair of little eyeglasses clipped to her nose she said was called pinch-nay that was French meant pinch-your-nose, which it looked like they did, it looked like it sure hurt to wear them. Her hair was coiled around her head and pulled back, like Miss Riggs' and Miss Jickers', into a tight bun at the back. There was a down on her cheeks and chin like what was growing over Frank and Buster's upper lip, and the skin around her mouth was all cobwebby with wrinkles. She had a look like she'd been born old.

Like I said, she wore that same brown dress down to her ankles every day of the year and she said she was the only one left of her family, and from the way she talked and the way she dressed she looked like she was somebody living on from another time, because she was a relative of those bluenoses she called evangelists that she said long ago held tent meetings, singing hymns and praising God all the livelong day, in the camp grove near the fort and in another camp grove back in the woods near where we lived. Earl Jr. told me one of those groves was the very same grove as the clearing way back in the woods where me and him sung and danced bare for each other and where we played our games of Slaves and Masters. If it was, it looked like a good place to have a tent meeting if you wanted to shout and sing and pray and not be bothered by nobody but the birds.

Miss Prouty said she didn't drink any tea or coffee and never, ever even so much as a drop of alcohol. She gave a pretty strong hint none of us should either. I wished with all my heart my father was sitting there in my desk instead of me to hear what she had to say about booze, calling it "the devil's brew."

After she read us the bible first thing in the morning and led us in the Our Father, where all the Catholics in the class stopped short at "For Thine is the kingdom and the power and the glory forever and ever amen" or you'd have to tell it in confession if you said it, and when the salute to the flag was done, Miss Prouty read to us for half an hour. She didn't read stories like Pinocchio or Wahoo the Indian boy like Miss Riggs did, but stories that sounded as old-fashioned as the way she dressed and that always had a lesson to tell you at the end—like never to drink or smoke and to make sure you brush your teeth and wash yourself all over and always wear clean underwear, or "undergarments" as she called them, because as one of her stories went, you never knew when you were going to be in an accident and if you were maimed or killed you wanted to look your best like you were a clean and decent Christian prepared to meet your God and not look like you were heathen trash.

In the morning we had geography and history, and after that we had darn old arithmetic that I just hated. Then after lunch was English where everytime, not just sometimes like with Miss Riggs, when me or anybody said "ain't" or said "me this" or "me that" or said "picsture" instead of *picture*, or talked wrong in any other way, Miss Prouty right away corrected us and was very strict about it, like she was strict in just about every-thing else.

The best part of the day, though, was when after our English was done Miss Prouty'd stand behind her desk, her hands clutched in front of her, the hard lines in her face easing up a little as something came into her eyes like a little flicker of flame that made her pinch-nay shine when she announced it was time for our "nature studies," as she called them.

You could sense the whole class stiffen and lean forward a little in our seats, getting ready, as Miss Prouty cleared her throat and started telling us stories about mainly terrible things she'd seen or read about—or as some, like Margaret, said, made up in her head—enjoying telling us mostly about fires and earthquakes and floods—no calamity was too horrible for her to take on.

When she told her stories about fiery things it was like the hellfire was burning right there in her eyes as bright as it did in Father Mack's eyes when he preached during one of his sermons about the sulphur and the smoke and the thousands of years of scalding heat in purgatory if you committed a mortal sin, his face sweating and red as what I pictured hell itself must look like.

But to me, hearing Miss Prouty tell her stories was almost as good as being at the movies or listening to our old Scott radio when the juice used to be on. Not only me but everybody in the classroom would be leaning over their desks, our mouths hanging open, not a sound in the room but Miss Prouty talking, her voice running on in that low, whispery way of hers, her voice running like a brushfire through the room, making it the most exciting part of the day. Now and again she'd pause to catch her breath and ask, "Am I frightening anybody? If I'm frightening anybody too much I'll stop," and even though she was scaring the daylights out of us we shouted back loud as we could, "Oh no, Miss Prouty!" just to keep her going.

It seemed like the more my father didn't hear any good news from Mr. Beezley about getting him a job at the shipyard the more he drank, drinking not only beer but Dixie Belle gin now when he could get it, because Frank said it was the cheapest. The more he drank the more bad-tempered he got, slapping Frank or Buster for the least little thing. He even smacked Slap once when he told Slap to go clean the chickenhouse and Slap didn't hear him, he hauled off and walloped Slap, hollering, "Dumbie! Dumbie! Jump when I tell you!" so that I could see why the Indians in the movies called it firewater, it lit such a fire in his eyes. Slap looked at him so surprised, because he never hit him so hard before. My mother started to say something but then shut her mouth tight again because she wasn't talking to him and wouldn't speak up for Slap even though you could see she didn't think what my father did was right—It was like she was listening to what Father Mack said to her not to say no to him at night in the bedroom once he stopped using them things, even though I could hear through the wall she wanted to, like no was in her eyes right then too, but it was like she was listening to Father Mack that she wasn't to say no or speak against my father, and so she didn't say anything.

One night not long after that we were all woke up by our mother busting into the room with the flashlight in one hand and an oil lamp in the other. She quick set the oil lamp down on the chest of drawers and rushed around from one bed to the other, waving the flashlight in our eyes, her hair standing out all over her head the way it looked when she first got up in the morning. Only it wasn't morning, the windows were all still dark. And another peculiar thing was, she had on her old winter coat thrown over her nightgown like she was going out somewhere. She was pulling the covers off of us and shouting at us in a voice that was all shrill and choked, "Get up and get dressed fast as you can!"

I sat up in a daze and stared out the window just to make sure—It was still dark outside all right, and I wondered why she was waking us at that hour and what was she so excited about. Her eyes were big as soup plates as she went on shaking each one of us to be sure we were awake, repeating for us to get dressed quick and telling the older ones to help with the youngest. Then she darted out of the room and I could hear her hurrying down the stairs. Now I heard strange voices, not only outside the house but inside as well, with footsteps running back and forth in the rooms below. Far in the distance I could hear the fire siren blowing and blowing. My first thought was to sniff the air and I did, and all of a sudden I was wild with fear, thinking I smelled a faint but bitter smell of smoke. My temples began to pound and I jumped out of bed faster even than when I had to pee in the bucket and began rooting under all our clothes piled on the chair for the knickers I'd taken off the night before. While I was trying to get into them, I shook Slap hard, not only because he didn't hear my mother, but because he could sleep like the dead besides. At the same time, I kept jostling Danny that was already falling asleep again, sitting up.

Frank and Buster were sitting on the edge of their bed by now, yawning and rubbing their eyes in the glare of the oil lamp, looking at each other like they were wondering what was going on too. Slap, finally awake now, had a corner of his mouth pulled up like he was going heh? heh? without making a sound. Dopey from sleep, they all started groping around on the chair for their overalls and feeling under the bed for their sneakers.

Now somebody else was coming up the stairs, a heavy step this time that didn't sound like my mother, and we were all surprised when Babes Beezley came bustling into the room, all out of breath, a cigarette dangling off of her lower lip.

My older brothers, still in their underwear, jumped up with

a yell like she'd caught them in the altogether, which, as I've said before, was something they didn't like anybody to do even if it was another boy.

"How're you all doin in here?" she yelled, her voice screechier'n usual. "C'mon, c'mon, git a move on!" She rushed over and helped Danny button up his shirt that was all buttoned up wrong, and bent over with a grunt to help him tie his sneakers that were all knots, Danny going, "Whuzza? Whuzza?" and Mrs. Beezley screeching, "Never you mind, boy! Jist you git yerself dressed and downstairs on the double! That goes fer all of you!"

I was so nervous with all the hurrying going on around us and not knowing what we were being rushed around for, I put my knickers on backwards. Somehow it seemed very important to take them off and make sure I had them on right even if with the faint smell of smoke and the fire siren still blowing I was scared the house was on fire and if it was, I wondered how come I missed what I'd been laying awake worrying and watching for night after night for such a long time now after hearing Miss Prouty's stories.

Puffing away, an exasperated look on her face, Mrs. Beezley came over and stooping down beside me with another grunt, asked in a peevish way, "Now what's the trouble here?" When I told her I put my pants on backwards, she made a face and said, "It don't matter right now if they is on backwards or frontwards!" And even though I didn't want her to because, like my older brothers, I didn't want her to see me in my underwear either, she shoved me down on the bed, got my knickers off, turned them around right, stuck my legs into them and yanked them up without any fuss—for all her size she could move so quick!—I didn't have time to worry about her seeing anything.

My mother was back in the room by this time, waving the

flashlight, that look of fright still in her eyes. This time she was clutching the worn brown folder tied with brown string she kept our insurance policies and birth certificates and other important papers in, and with her free hand she began shooing us all out of the bedroom and down the stairs, Frank asking, "Where're we goin, Ma?" and her answering, still in that tight voice, "Don'tchou worry about that now, just get goin!" Mrs. Beezley, lumbering down the stairs behind us, puffing on her Raleigh like it was her face on fire, called out in a voice shrill with excitement, "Why, you'll all be comin to our house, of course!" like she was inviting us to a party.

Holding Kate by the hand my mother stood by the front door in the parlor, her lips moving as she counted each one of us as we filed past her out onto the porch. Even scarier was seeing the front yard filled with men in fire helmets and black rubber raincoats and boots, shouting at each other and running back and forth. My father and Mr. Beezley, both in their undershirts, were right in there with them, helping lay down hose that was attached to the pumper on the ancient Lenape Volunteer Fire Company fire engine that was parked practically in our yard. The hose snaked across the yard like a live thing and disappeared back into the swamp, the entire length of it leaking tiny geysers that shot up every so often along its worn out canvas covering. I was surprised to see Charley was there too, since he was only an honorary fireman because he was crippled, but there he was, hobbling over the hoses like a big praying mantis with a fire helmet on. Harry Hawes, that snorted during mass with his asthma and was built like a bull because he was a piano mover and was the boy scout leader of Saint Theresa's Troop 21 that Timothy belonged to, was the fire chief too and was standing on top of the La France fire engine in a white helmet, shouting orders at everybody in a voice louder even than Mr. Beezley's.

I felt my scalp freeze as I stared at the firemen all dark in their rubber raincoats racing back and forth in the headlights of the engine. You could really smell smoke now as we huddled on the porch. I kept wondering, if our house was on fire why didn't we run away instead of standing on the porch like we didn't know which way to go?

Harry Hawes was ordering my father and Mr. Beezley and a couple of the firemen to aim the hose at our roof, and when they did, the water shooting upward sent off sprays of mist in the breeze that when it hit my nose smelled just like the swamp. My mother, getting prodded from behind by Mrs. Beezley, hustled us down the porch steps and when we got down in the yard and I looked back at the house, right then for the first time I saw the showers of sparks and wisps of fire blowing over the roof in the wind. A lot of it was sticking in the split shingles and dancing down the eaves like it was raining fire. All of a sudden, though, I caught my breath, seeing through the trees the Mahoney's house that was one big ball of fire that lit up everything around in a shivering orange light. I stared and I stared, I couldn't believe it, their house was burning just like those pictures I saw in the newsreels at the Morris movies when the Japs dropped bombs on the Chinese people and the little Chinese baby was crying all alone in the middle of the bombed-out street. I stared around and stared around, looking could I see Ronnie and looking could I see his mother and father, and not seeing them anywhere, wondered were they burnt to crisps in their beds like in the nightmares I had, dreaming everybody in my family was burnt alive in our beds, after Miss Prouty told one of her fiery stories in class.

Beyond the trees, some firemen that were all black against the blaze were aiming a piddling stream of water into what looked like a bonfire big as the house itself. Mr. Beezley, stopping in his helping my father and the others to hump the hose up closer to our place, looked over in the direction of what was left of the Mahoney's house and cackled in that way of his so everybody could hear even over all the commotion, "They'd all do better if they jist stood there and pissed on it!" Mrs. Beezley, passing down the dirt walk with my mother that had all of us in tow, gave Mr. Beezley a thump on the shoulder and told him to watch his mouth, then she screeched at him, "Where is our Brother and Sparky?" When he shrugged, rubbing at his shoulder and grinning sheepish at the other firemen, she gave him a dirty look, screaming, "You was s'posed to keep an eye on 'em!" And throwing up her hands, she told my mother to go on ahead, she'd see her back at their place, and headed off through the woods towards the burning house, again moving pretty fast for a lady of her size.

I kept looking for Ronnie and his mother and father. I wanted to ask my mother did she know what happened to them, worrying were they all burnt up, but I could see she was too busy gaping back over her shoulder with that wild look still in her eye. Instead, I thought of all the toys and things up in Ronnie's playroom and watched the clouds of fire and smoke billowing up into the sky—The more I stared the more I thought I saw in the flying sparks the souls of all those dolls and stuffed animals and whole families of paperdolls flying up to heaven, and wondered if Ronnie and his mother and father were rising up with them.

Off to the side of the road were little clumps of people looking on that watched my mother with a sorry look and whispered to one another as we passed. Sadie Gottlieb, that never missed a fire or a drowning, which Babes Beezley said was the only thing would get her out of the store and was her only pleasure in life besides gossiping and eating, was there amongst them. She was looking even fatter in her nightgown and had a shawl thrown over her shoulders.

Then I saw all the Snarps pounding up the road fast as they could so they wouldn't miss anything, Mr. Snarp in his greasy captain's hat and barefeet and Mrs. Snarp with her hair hanging down to her waist and a man's old overcoat thrown over her shoulders. I saw Earl Jr. racing ahead of them, staring bug-eyed at the fire with a grin on his face. He was staring at it so hard he didn't see me as I went on by, even though I waved at him.

Then I spotted Miss Prouty standing a little apart from the others with the Jakes that she boarded with. All of them were dressed like for daytime, Miss Prouty wearing her long brown dress, her hands clutched against her belly, the flames now and again flashing reflected in her pinch-nay, her eyes behind her glasses so bright watching the fire. Like Earl Jr., she didn't see me either when I passed on by, her mouth hanging open in surprise, like she was taking it all in right down to the very last spark so's to be able to tell us all about it in her very next nature study.

"Where we goin, Ma, where we goin?" Little Kate, pressing one of her amputee dolls tight to her chest, kept tugging at my mother's nightgown, but my mother was still too busy gaping back and hurrying us along to pay her any attention. After Kate kept it up for awhile, though, my mother finally lost her temper and told her to stop pestering her. "We'll all be stayin at the Beezley's, dintcha hear? Now quitcher askin."

After a few minutes I thought it might be safe to risk asking, "Where's Ronnie, Mom? Where's his father and his mother?" but she didn't hear me, or at least she pretended she didn't, and kept leading us away down the road towards the woods in the direction of the Beezley's house, still looking back over her shoulder at us, then now and again tossing a glance back at the burning house that lit up the whole sky now in an orange glare. More oftener'n that, though, she peered back with an anxious look at our own house, where you could see in the brightness of the fire the streams of water still being played over the roof by the volunteer firemen, the water pouring off the eaves like rain in a heavy storm.

"Will it go up, Ma? Will our house go up?" Kate went on asking my mother, and my mother shushed her and told her to keep still.

Then I saw him. He was sitting bundled up in a blanket in the backseat of his father's Chevy, that I guessed his father managed to get out of the garage in time and parked under a big tree a safe distance down Lenape Road from the fire, but close enough so they'd still be able to see everything. Ronnie had his head down, his curls all atangle and covered in soot. He looked real mad, his lower lip jutting out like he was about to cry, just the way Kate looked in the mornings when my mother was brushing her hair.

Mrs. Mahoney was sitting on the runningboard wrapped in another blanket and crying her eyes out. She was crying so hard it made the blanket fall open, showing the front of her nightgown that was all white with ribbony bows, the one Ronnie said she got Mr. Mahoney to get her last Christmas because it was just like the one Greta Garbo died of TB in in "Camille." Now it was all singed with holes like cigarette burns down the front. Mr. Mahoney, looking like he didn't know what to do, his skimpy hair sticking up on end, was bending over her, trying to quiet her, while at the same time tearing his eyes away to look up the road at his house burning down, his whole body bending toward it in a way that said he'd rather be up there helping than where he was.

Not that there was much to see of it anymore, or anything that him or anybody could've done, since the glare was dying down now, more from having burnt itself out, as Frank insisted it did, when him and Buster got into an argument about it, than having been put out by the "Smokey Stovers," as Frank sneerily called the Lenape Volunteer Fire Company. But that still didn't stop him and Buster and Slap from gawking around backwards and tripping all over each other in the dark as they watched the last glimmer of the fire die out of the sky.

My mother stopped and went over and said a few words to Mrs. Mahoney. Mrs. Mahoney reached an arm out of her blanket and grabbed my mother's hand and held onto it, her eyes rolling in her head like she was being sucked down in quicksand in the swamp behind what was left of their house, instead of sitting on the runningboard of their car. My mother leaned down and whispered something else to her, which I figured she was asking her if they all wanted to come to the Beezleys with us, but Mrs. Mahoney shook her head. Then my mother patted her on the shoulder and came back to us, Frank asking, "Where they gonna stay, Ma? They gotta place to stay?" My mother said, "They're gonna stay in Camden with her people, they're gonna drive up there tonight, now don't ask me any more questions," and without another word, she started leading us on again down the road and through the woods to the Beezley's house.

At the Beezley's really was like a party, once Mrs. Beezley got back to the house, shoving Brother and Sparky ahead of her through the back door by their elbows. Everybody was too excited to think about sleep and Mrs. Beezley let us all sit, like company, in the parlor, where the furniture was nicer'n ours because Mr. Beezley worked in the shipyard and was bringing home steady money, and because of the things Mrs. Beezley got with her books of yellow stamps from Gottlieb's and from her Raleigh coupons, including the shepherd girl with the clock in her belly that she smoked so many extra packs of cigarettes to get. I was torn between wanting to ask if I could look at the pictures in their new set of World Encyclopedias in a bookshelf in the corner that Sister bragged they got with fourteen books of yellow stamps, and not wanting to miss anything. Even more'n that, I was hoping they would turn on their new Philco radio so we could hear some dance music from the Steel Pier in Atlantic City or from Philadelphia or even from New York City that Mrs. Mahoney said she always listened to late at night. But I guessed it was too late for that because nobody mentioned anything about turning the radio on and I knew my mother wouldn't like it if I asked if I could.

While we waited for my father and Mr. Beezley to get back, Mrs. Beezley had Sister make us all sandwiches from her own homemade grape jelly and homemade bread, while Brother, by now over his sulks about being pulled away from the fire by his mother, showed us how he taught their dog to speak.

My mother, not able to wait for my father to come back, and so on edge she could hardly sit still, sent Frank off to see if our house was still there, and Buster begged so hard to go too, she finally let him. Then wouldn't you know, Brother started whining to his mother could he go along, but she put her foot down, saying no, he'd only get in the way, and Frank and Buster raced out through the back shed, my mother yelling after them, "Right back now, you two! You hear?" Brother kept on whining and pulling such a long puss, Mrs. Beezley said, "Gwan, git outa my sight with that face," and he tore out after my brothers.

When my father and Mr. Beezley, in their undershirts that were more black than white from the soot, came in an hour or so later with Frank and Buster and Brother behind them—my brothers looking sneaky-eyed because they knew they hadn't come back when my mother said to—and told us our house was safe, my mother's hand went to her mouth, her fingers fluttering there, her lips moving, whispering a prayer of thanks. She was so relieved she even forgot to bawl out Frank and Buster for dawdling so long and keeping her on pins and needles. Then my father and Mr. Beezley, both of them looking bright-eyed and merry and smelling of whiskey they said Mr. Tarkie'd passed around at the fire, told us what everybody knew was going to happen right from the start, that the Mahoney place burnt right down to the ground and that they lost everything except the Chevy and the clothes on their backs. "And lucky to have even that!" Mr. Beezley shouted in his loud voice that was louder now he'd had a few snorts. My mother was so glad our house hadn't burnt down she didn't look too bothered right then my father'd had a few too, but it put a scare in my belly as bad as the fire did, seeing his eyes as bright as the Mahoney house burning.

Then they all started guessing about how the fire started, with dark hints from Mr. Beezley that were as dark as his face and hands were sooty, that probably Ginger Mahoney'd fallen asleep with a cigarette, "Reading one of them damn movie magazines."

But it was never decided for certain who or what started the fire. Sam Beezley was the only one kept insisting it was more likely Mrs. Mahoney staying up too late reading her books and movie magazines and falling asleep with a cigarette in her mouth and lying about it, instead of being in bed alongside of her husband where he thought she should've been in the first place, and if she had of been in bed beside her husband, the house wouldn't've never burnt down—And whenever he said it he never failed to give Mrs. Beezley a look. But Mrs. Beezley always said, "Hogwash, it was more likely mice chewing the wires in the wall or stealing kitchen matches started it, an *accident*," she insisted, "like Mrs. O'Leary's cow kickin over the lantern in 'In Old Chicago' with Tyrone Power and Alice Faye," a movie she saw at the Rialto that I heard her tell my mother from the beginning to The End one afternoon while I hid under the dining room table, that was almost as scary as Miss Prouty's version.

But Mr. Beezley was stubborn and kept on insisting it was Mrs. Mahoney smoking and not being in bed with Mr. Mahoney caused it all, and he talked about it like a lot of other people did til long after the dump truck came around and my father and Mr. Snarp and the other workers on relief made a number of trips clearing away what was left of the house, leaving nothing finally but a gaping hole in the ground. I was glad when it was all carted off at last to the dump and I couldn't see the black rubble through the trees anymore or smell the smell of charred wood and ashes at night through our bedroom windows.

Sometimes, after the fire, I would hear my mother get up at night and come across the hall and stand silent at our doorway looking in. She'd sprinkle holy water over our beds from the little bottle with the white cross on the front, the cool drops splashing my face. Then she'd turn and peer down the stairwell for a few moments, listening for Kate and sniffing the air, then I'd hear the rustle of the sleeve of her nightgown as she sprinkled the stairs too before going back to her own bed. For a long time after the fire she would do this several times in a night, sometimes standing restless and uneasy at our door in her long white gown, another watcher in the night.

But there was another fire, not in the stove or only in my head at night, it was in my father's eyes. It flared up higher and higher the more Dixie Belle gin he drank with Mr. Beezley, mainly on Saturday afternoons when whatever work they did together was done. That scared me more'n anything, scared all of us, because it seemed the hotter that look got in his eyes, just his hitting us one wasn't enough. And that's when the beatings began—especially after he'd been drinking and had the shakes and had that look in his eye like one of his roosters out in the run, when they got mad their feathers stood on end, like his nerves seemed to stand on end more and more these days.

They came at any time. Me or my brothers never knew what it was that would set him off. Afterwards, I would try to think and think about what it could've been I'd said or done to make him lose his temper so I could get around doing it in the future, but I could never figure out what it was. Sometimes it'd happen for something so small as me or one of my brothers bothering him while he was trying to read the paper, or one of us not jumping out of his way quick enough, or giving him a look he didn't like—any number of little things you could never know of in advance. It always seemed to happen in the parlor in the evenings, him all of a sudden grabbing one or the other of us after he'd had a few or, like happened on this particular night, when he hadn't had anything to drink and was jumpy and irritable, bothered by the smallest thing rubbing him the wrong way. But I could never figure out in advance what that would be, except for maybe my talking too much sometimes, I seemed to be talking more'n ever lately, I couldn't seem to stop talking. I was so filled at times with a high excitement I didn't understand, or that my father or my brothers didn't understand either, and that they didn't like and had no patience for, that seemed to get on his nerves when he was coming off of a drunk and didn't have any money for any more booze.

Maybe that was it, maybe I talked too much and that got on his nerves. From now on I would try hard not to get so excited and would try to watch my tongue. But the first time it was such a surprise because I didn't know that I was doing anything that evening to make him come after me. What had I been doing? Laying on my belly drawing on the back of empty cracker boxes on the floor under the oil lamp by my mother while she crocheted on the couch. My other brothers were sprawled around on the rest of the parlor floor reading the different parts of the Philadelphia *Bulletin* as soon as my father finished with them. Then I spied Kate playing in the corner with one of her dolls. I couldn't help myself, I crawled over and whispered did her and her doll baby want to hear a story? I thought if I kept my voice down low enough he wouldn't hear. She nodded yes without looking at me, she was so busy changing the bandage on the stump of the latest raggedy old mildewy doll my father'd tossed off of the dump truck, saying yes she would like to hear a story if it was Shirley Temple in "Poor Little Rich Girl." She must've heard that story a thousand times by now! Even so, I hunched down next to her and leaning close to her ear, started telling it to her again, I needed to talk so much, only I changed the story a little here and a little there to make it more interesting to tell. The more I started changing it the more excited I got, and when Kate caught me at it, she stopped me and complained, "That ain't the way it goes, Mick, tell about her sneezin and catchin a cold, tell about her eatin the spizzghettis." And I'd have to stick to the story exactly as she already heard it umpteen thousand times, til I started getting carried away again and the excitement came over me, my whisper getting louder as I began changing this and changing that.

My father gave me a look, that look that should've been a warning to me, because he'd been drinking Dixie Belle gin the night before with Sam Beezley and was in a rotten mood. He stared down at his paper again, rattling it. But that night for some reason, even though I knew I better shutup, I couldn't shutup. It was like I had a part to play, the same way I felt ever after that when he'd come after me, like I had a part to play and there wasn't any way out of it, I had to play it, like we all had a part in it. Even though I saw the danger signs, I kept right on talking, I was so involved in telling the story, my older brothers going *"Shhh!"* once or twice so they could concentrate on the sports page, or maybe it was they were warning me, but I figured I wasn't talking all that loud—And I couldn't stop, even if I wanted, it was like that was what I was supposed to do, that was my part.

I could feel his eyes on me but didn't dare look, only looked when I heard the newspaper slide to the floor and heard the snap of his belt buckle and saw he'd started unbuckling his belt. My words died away then, I shutup finally and stared back at him the way an animal will that's caught in the headlights of a car. Kate, fussing with her doll, was saying, "What then, Mick? What then?" and when I didn't answer, she looked at me and seeing where I was staring, she looked over at my father too with eyes as wide as Danny's that was also staring at him. She started to snivel and moan the same way she did when my mother told her to go get the brush to brush her hair.

He was out of his chair and slithering his belt out of its loops so fast, Kate dropped her doll and shrunk away, while Danny dove under the couch, neither of them knowing who he was coming for. I leapt up, hunching myself small as I could into the corner, gaping around wild, not knowing which way to run, knowing that much as I wanted to, I couldn't run, knowing there wasn't any way out.

My mother looked up puzzled from her crocheting, then seeing him with his belt off, she looked annoyed, then afraid. "What's the matter? What's he done, huh? What?" But my father didn't pay any attention to her, didn't seem to hear anything as he came after me, the belt clamped in his fist, his eyes hard as flint arrows.

Seeing it wasn't going to be either one of them this time, Frank and Buster shoved their faces closer in the sports pages, while

Slap, not hearing anything yet, was giggling to himself over the comics. When my father made a grab for me, I sprung out of the corner and into the middle of the room, almost tripping over Slap that looked up bug-eyed with that heh? heh? look twisting up one side of his face. I ran around the long table in the center, dodging this way and that, knowing that begging him not to beat me was useless once he got that look, as useless as the promises I started shouting out, "I'll be good! I'll be good!" shouting them in spite of me not knowing how it was I'd been bad—Unless it was somebody told him about me and Earl Jr. dancing in the woods or that I played dressup with Ronnie or that I stole sugar from the sugar bowl every chance I got or that I didn't put my penny in the Sunday collection at church.

I figured if I could just get around the table and duck under the couch where Danny was just now peeping out, I'd be all right. But my father lunged a hand at me over the table and caught me by the scruff of the neck, his eyes now as sharp as the hatchet he used to cut off the heads of his chickens, his mouth slit as sharp as the edge of it. He snatched me around to him and lifting the belt high over his head brought it down so hard it whistled in my ears, him shouting, "This'll teach ya!"

I danced around him while he held me by the throat, holding back crying as long as I could, out of pride, but looking back wild at my mother, pleading with my eyes for her to stop him. But she'd already lowered her head again, bent over her crocheting like she didn't want to see. And seeing now she wasn't going to speak up for me like she didn't speak up for Slap either that time, I started crying hard as I could, crying as much from her not saying anything as from the sting of the leather, hurt as much too in my pride I couldn't stop bawling like a baby in front of the others.

But the more I tried to get out of his way, the more furious he got, so that he walloped me all the harder, his face red as Miss Prouty's fires, as red as the fires of Father Mack's hell, his hair all hanging in his face when he bent to me, then sticking up like a rooster's comb when he reared back and raised his arm up again, his breath coming fast the way I sometimes heard it in the night in the dark of their bedroom, the way mine did and the way Earl Jr.'s did, playing Slaves and Masters in the woods.

"You gonna do as I say? You gonna be good?" he shouted, and me yelling back, "Yes! Yes! I'll be good! I'll do anything you want!" promising him anything, not knowing what I was promising, not knowing why he'd come after me, or what I hadn't done that he wanted me to do.

Finally, my mother, low at first, then raising her voice so he would hear her, murmured, "Awright, that's enough now, he's learnt his lesson whatever he done." But it seemed like the very sound of her voice only infuriated him all the more even though her complaining grew fainter and fainter til she fell into a silence like she did when he walloped Slap, as if she knew, like my brothers seemed to know, if he was beating me or any one of us, he wouldn't bother her.

He took a few more licks at me for good measure, his loose hair plastered against his forehead with sweat, the rooster look gone now and a look in his eyes like was in the eyes of the statue of Saint Theresa in church, his eyes rolling like he was in a trance as he shoved me away and I fell to the floor in a heap, rolling myself up in a ball in case he hit out at me again or tried to kick me, you just never knew.

He stood over me mopping the back of his arm over his face, then grabbing the top of his pants he gave them a tug up before he slipped his belt back on. Shoving his hair back, he brushed it back with both his hands, then bent down and snatched up the scattered pages of the newspaper and snapped himself back in his chair, folding himself up into it like he was snapping his jackknife shut. I squinched my eyes tight, listening to his breath coming short and quick, and tried hard to stop my crying, my chest jumping like I had the hiccups, no matter how hard I tried to stop it.

Finally, when I had nerve enough, I uncurled myself on the linoleum and snuck a look around, mainly looking to make sure where he was. I saw he was still sitting in his chair, licking his thumb before snapping over a page of the paper, looking like he was trying hard to read. But his glance was all agitated, darting this way and that over the page, his breathing still coming hard but not as hard as before, his face still flushed, his jaws working. He'd lit one of his Buglers and the curl of smoke rose lazy in the light of the oil lamp despite his hand shaking.

Now that my hollering was over, Frank and Buster went back to reading the comic page now Slap was done with it, and Danny crawled out from under the couch, keeping a close eye on my father the whole time, like he was ready to jump back under the first move my father made. The room went back to the way it was. Only it wasn't really the same, it was like something was cleared away, like the air was after a bad storm, it was clear and calm and quiet. For an instant, my mother's eyes caught mine and I saw there was a look in them of shame as she ducked her head when she saw me looking, and without dropping a stitch said to me in a quiet voice, "Go out and wash yer face now."

The very next day after the beating he seemed calmer and my mother was extra nice to me. At first I thought she was nice because she was sorry for me that I got beat, and that she was feeling bad about her not speaking up. But then I got to see it was more like I somehow did her a favor without my knowing it, that I somehow got her off the hook, and that was our little secret between us. I decided if I did her a favor without even knowing it, then her treating me extra nice and like we had a secret between us was worth any number of beatings.

It wasn't long after that I was laying on my belly after supper on the parlor floor drawing on the back of old brown paper bags and listening to the hum of heat in the coalstove out in the dining room. I didn't hear him coming and didn't get out of his way fast enough, and because I didn't and because he had that fierce look in his eye from being drunk the night before and the two of them'd been rumbling in the night, before I knew what was happening, he came after me again.

I thought if I went away then everything would be all right, I thought if I could only somehow get back to South Philly or if Shirley Temple would only come to pick me up and take me back to Philly with her—or to Hollywood. In one of those movie magazines I saw in Gottlieb's they said, like my mother said long ago, that's where she lived too—If only she'd come and take me away, then things would be better for everybody. If I wasn't there there'd be one less mouth to feed and there'd be a little more money, if I wasn't there maybe there wouldn't be so much trouble between them, and my father wouldn't drink as much, and maybe if someday Mr. Beezley finally got him a job in the shipyard then he wouldn't need to drink at all and I could come back home.

I thought that me and all of my brothers and Kate included were somehow the reason that at night I could hear them arguing through the wall. But it was more like it was something to do with me that I didn't understand, more than that there was too many of us, that if there only wasn't so many of us....

I thought about it a lot at school during the day so that Miss Prouty called me up sharp a few times, asking why was I daydreaming so much and not paying attention to the long division. I thought about it at night too while my brothers snored around me and the voices of the two of them sounded through the wall like a distant storm. I thought if I wasn't there my father maybe wouldn't drink as much, my mother would maybe start singing around the house again and they would sleep more at night instead of arguing, if I wasn't there there'd be one less of us to worry about, one less mouth....

What I finally hit on was this: The very next Sunday I held back the penny my mother gave me for the collection at mass like I always did, pretending to put it in the basket but palming it instead the way Buster showed me. When we got to Gottlieb's I told my brothers to go on inside without me, I must've lost my penny through a hole in my pocket and couldn't buy any candy. Buster said, "Tough tiddy," but Slap felt sorry for me and gave me half of his candy to eat on the way home. I felt awful I was such a liar, the penny was still in my pocket, and I knew I would have to tell it in confession. About lying, I mean—I didn't dare tell Father Mack I was holding back my penny from the collection basket.

The next day after school I waited til everybody was gone, especially my brothers, then I went the long way round through the woods by the river to Gottlieb's so I'd be sure not to bump into Earl Jr. or anybody else. When I got to the store I looked in the door just to be sure Frank'd already been there and got the mail, then I went up to the post office window and reached up under the barred window, put my penny on the counter and asked Mrs. Gottlieb for a postcard.

I must've looked like I just stole candy through the chicken-wire she gave me such a suspicious look, knowing our Frank always bought the stamps and postcards for my mother. Nosy as always, she asked me, "What does a boy with pretty little eye-lashes like you want with a penny postcard?" My heart was in

my throat for fear she wouldn't sell it to me, I said my mother
needed an extra one to write to our Aunt Nell, which I knew
was one more lie I'd have to tell in confession. She said, "Writin to
her sisters in Philly again?" I nodded and she slid the postcard
over the counter and took my penny, saying, "My, she's been
doin a lot of writin to her sisters lately."

I couldn't wait to get away, afraid somebody'd see me and
want to know why I wanted a postcard. I stuck it safe and out of
sight in the middle of my arithmetic book, that Miss Prouty
always gave me extra homework in, I was so dumb in long division, and ran home fast as I could so my mother wouldn't be
wondering where I was.

When I got home she gave me a questioning look but I told
her Miss Prouty asked me to stay clap erasers, another lie to tell
Father Mack I knew, but she believed me and told me to go up
and change out of my school clothes, then go out and see were
there any last-minute eggs laid out in the henhouse.

I was glad when I got up in the bedroom and saw my
brothers'd already changed their clothes and gone off to do
their chores or gone off somewhere with the Beezley boys like
they always did after school. Since we were learning to write in
ink now in Miss Prouty's class, I got my ink bottle and steel-
point pen from off the top of the bureau and listening to make
sure nobody was coming up the steps, sat on the edge of the
bed, took the postcard out of my arithmetic book and, not trusting myself to handwrite because my hand was shaking so
much, I printed in the most careful printing I could: "Dear
Shirley Temple, I need to move out of here, I need to move out
where you are. It will be better if I do. Can you tell me how to be
a movie star? I saw you in Poor Little Rich Girl. You was so
good, I thought a lot about you. I'll do anything you say to do if
only you will tell me how to do it. Sincerely yours," and signed

it "Stanislaus Lithwack, Lenape Rd., Lenape, New Jersey," and made it out to Shirley Temple care of Hollywood, California.

I read it over and checked for mistakes three or four times before blotting it real careful, then, hearing my mother holler up the stairs, "How long's it goin to take you to change them clothes, boy? It'll be pitch dark before you get out to the chicken coop, and besides that the pan of water on the coal stove needs fillin," I quick hid the card in the middle of my arithmetic book again.

The next day after school, once more making sure nobody saw me, I made the long roundabout trip to Gottlieb's, hanging around out front til I saw that nobody was waiting at the post office window and saw Mrs. Gottlieb moving off to sort the last mail of the day at the combination boxes. I crept in the front door, seeing Lenny the Indian dozing on his feet in back by the darkest shelves and Mr. Gottlieb hanging up strings of sausages over the butcher block. Everybody knew Mrs. Gottlieb read all the postcards that came in and went out, even the cards people on vacation sent from Wildwood in the summertime, and blabbed the news in them to whoever would listen, which included Babes Beezley and Charley the stringer for the *County Seat Weekly*, and even though because of that my mother might find out my secret, I fast dropped my card in the slot underneath the barred window before I lost my nerve, deciding I'd worry about that later on as I hightailed it outside, feeling again like I'd been poking my finger through the chickenwire trying to steal candy.

For the next couple of days after that I kept waiting for my mother to pull me aside and tell me she knew about the postcard from Sadie Gottlieb telling Mrs. Beezley. Even my ears'd get to sweating just thinking about it, and what if my father found out? I didn't want to think what he would do to me if he did, and lay awake nights wishing now I hadn't ever sent off that darned postcard. But to my surprise, and relief, nothing happened, it must've been one of the rare times Sadie Gottlieb missed a card, and my being anxious over that changed to waiting on pins and needles everyday to see what mail Frank'd bring home after school. It was hardly anything but the usual bill from Public Service for the electric hadn't been paid yet or ads for things we never had the money to buy, or sometimes— unless it was something personal they didn't want Sadie Gottlieb to read, or they were sending money, then they would send it in a letter sealed in an envelope—sometimes there was a postcard from one of the aunts in South Philly, usually Aunt Nell that always wrote like she was all out of breath and as usual didn't have time for no capitals or punctuation, that I knew Miss Prouty would've hollered at her for if she was in her class.

Then it dawned on me, I'd signed the postcard with my real name like I did in school out of habit, instead of signing my nickname Mickey. And since my father had the same name as me—that I suspected he wasn't too happy about to begin with— maybe if Shirley Temple wrote me a letter he would open it, thinking it was for him. I lost a lot of sleep over that one, I can tell you, and kept asking my mother was there anything I could get for her from Gottlieb's after school so I could pick up the mail at the same time. But she would always say no, Frank'd take care of that, she needed me at home to mind Kate or set the table or whatever. I was asking so many times about saving Frank the trouble of picking up the mail, I could see she was getting suspicious, so I stopped asking.

What I did instead was I started following Frank to Gottlieb's after school, saying I wanted to see the Rialto sign in the window, but what I'd do was stand on tiptoe behind Frank at the post office window, looking over his shoulder, my heart racing, while Mrs. Gottlieb sorted through the "L's" in General Delivery, which was for

people couldn't afford to rent regular mailboxes, like

the Beezleys and the Mahoneys could, what with their fathers working.

Once we were outside, I always asked Frank was there anything good in the mail, hoping to find out if there was something for me. But he always said the same as usual, nothing but bills, or if there was a postcard from Aunt Nell he'd read it outloud. Then I started asking could I carry the mail for him, so I could get a better squint at it on the sly, but he said I might drop and lose something on the way home, and when I asked him again the next time he looked at me as suspicious as my mother, so I quit asking.

Wouldn't you know it would happen on a Saturday when you never knew what time Frank'd go for the mail! I'd just about given up on ever hearing from Shirley Temple when a few weeks after I mailed her the postcard Frank came into the kitchen just before supper with a big envelope yellow as Shirley Temple's curls and handed it to my father. My father'd just finished work for the day fixing the chicken coop roof and was sitting at the table drinking beer out of a jelly glass while my mother stood at the stove cooking supper. He'd been drinking a long time now in front of her, he didn't care anymore and didn't try to hide it from her.

Frank, with a teasing grin, seeing he was still in a pretty jolly mood, asked him, "Who d'ya know in Hollywood, Pop?"

I was setting the table at the time, since it was my turn. I knew right away what it was and wanted to dive right under the table when my father, looking at the envelope like he never saw an envelope before, scrunched up his eyes and reared back, saying, "Hollywood? Who the hell'd be sendin me anything from Hollywood?"

Frank, nervier now, certain our father was still in a good mood, said, "Sadie Gottlieb when she seen where it was from said maybe they want you out there for a screen test, Pop. She said maybe they're lookin for another Clark Gable."

"Sadie Gottlieb!" he snorted. "That blabbermouth—She prolly already steamed it open to snoop inside!"

Kate and my other brothers crowded around him but I kept right on doing what I was doing, trying to act like the envelope didn't matter to me at all, but I was shaking so bad I dropped the forks on the floor.

"Go rinse them off now, clumsy," my mother said quiet from the stove as she stirred her pots, keeping one eye on the envelope in my father's hand.

As I pumped water over the forks at the sink I wished more'n anything now I'd signed my nickname instead of my real name so they'd've known for sure who it was addressed to and I wouldn't have to be going through this agony of waiting for my father to open up the envelope. He got so few letters and what there was of them my mother opened anyhow, she would've opened this one too if he hadn't been sitting right there, which I wished to God now he hadn't been. He treated it all very serious like the envelope was something from the government, first checking the postmark and the address, then inspecting the envelope real careful from top to bottom, then shaking it, then inspecting it from top to bottom one more time, muttering, "From 20th Century Fox Picstures?" so that despite my nervousness as I dried the forks on the dishtowel over the sink, I was beginning to get annoyed at him for dragging out the suspense and all my dreading of what might be inside for him to see.

I was already accepting the fact I was going to get the beating of my life and might get to be more'n just the little bit crippled I prayed for, seeing now you had to be careful what you prayed for.

My mother had a look in her eye like she was thinking, "Oh, gwan and open it!" and gave an impatient stir to her stew.

We all stopped doing what we were doing and stared with our mouths hanging open as my father's brown thumb carefully slit open the flap. He peeked inside like he expected something to jump out at him, then, with a puzzled look, as I held my breath, feeling suddenly cold all over, he stuck in his hand and pulled out what was inside, looking even more baffled as he held it up in front of his face.

What it was was a glossy black and white photograph, like you see in the stills outside the movies, of Shirley Temple taking a bow in her tap shoes and signed in her very own hand.

He stared at it, and stared at it, then he squinted inside of the envelope like there was somebody in there going to tell him what it all meant.

My mother looked over, just as baffled as he was, Buster right away wisecracking, "I dint know you was a member of Shirley Temple's fan club, Pop!"

Frank was the first to laugh, then Slap, rubbing his hands all excited. I saw a gleam in my mother's eye but she didn't let on and kept her grin to herself. I felt her throw me a look, though, over her shoulder and knew she knew.

Since outside of my father I was the only one of my brothers not laughing, busy now setting the supper plates face down to keep any dust off of them the way my mother taught us, when the laughing died away, first my father then all the others stared at me, my brothers staring half afraid, half excited, knowing I was going to get it, so that this time I almost dropped what plates were left in my hands. I knew right off there was no sense trying to lie about it since I was sure my face said everything.

"He seen her in the movies," my mother called out in a wavering way from the stove like she was talking to the air but meaning it for my father even though she was acting like she wasn't. "That's the reason, ain't it?" she asked in my direction. "You sent away for that picsture because you seen her in the movies, dintcha?"

I nodded and went on putting down the plates, afraid to look at my father whose arm I saw reaching for his glass to take a swallow of beer. Kate was pestering and pulling at his pantleg could she have the picture for her Shirley Temple doll to look at, but he brushed her away. "All I want to know," he said, "is how you got the money to send away for a fancy photograph like this?"

When I glanced at him sideways from under my brow, I saw his eyes were sharp with that look of no matter what I said he'd never believe it. I whispered, "It didn't cost me nothin, all I done was send away a penny postcard," not daring to mention to him, of course, what I wrote on it or how I'd got the penny for it in the first place. Even though he looked like he was certain he knew I was lying, I was relieved when he only shoved the photograph at me with a look like he was sorrier'n anything now I had his name, but he didn't do anything more'n that—right then anyhow. Behind his eyes I saw that awful suspicion I'd been seeing so much now lately that made his eyes go a darker blue and that always made me cringe inside. He was looking at me now the way he first looked at the envelope, like I was something that baffled him, he was looking like he would put all that in the back of his mind and save it up for a time when he would come after me when I wasn't expecting it.

I wished in that moment with all my heart that I could go away, that there'd been a letter inside that envelope telling me what to do. But all there was was the signed picture of Shirley Temple grinning out at me.

When I thought about it later in bed I counted myself lucky it was only a picture and not a letter from her saying how to get to Hollywood and be a movie star, since he'd know what I'd been up to and would've gone after me right on the spot. I didn't want to think about what he would've done to me, crippling me worse'n Charley, the cripple, I bet.

All that week Frank and Buster every chance they got started tapdancing around me and singing in little girl voices "On the Good Ship Lollipop." I'd feel the tears scalding my eyes but wouldn't say anything. My mother finally got sick of it and one day called out sharp, "That's enough now, you two!" They stopped their razzing for the time being but teased me unmerciful for the next couple of days whenever my mother wasn't around, they would break into a tapdance every time they saw me coming and call me "Shirley" and "Miz Temple" and ask me did our mother brush out my curls that day after she brushed out our Kate's?

One day I saw Ronnie at recess at school and when I told him about the photograph, he grinned all excited, saying his Grandmother and Grandfather O'Shea'd bought him a whole bunch of new toys, almost as many as he had before the fire, he said he would swap me any one of his new paperdolls from Kresge's five and tenny, including Scarlett O'Hara, for it, he would even throw in his Pinocchio coloring book from Walt Disney that still had a few pages left in it wasn't colored yet. But even though I was sorely tempted, mainly because of the coloring book, I said no, I'd keep the photograph, I wanted it so much and'd gone through so much to get it. Right off the bat, Ronnie started to sulk, saying I was selfish and yelling at me, "Go on back with the babies in third grade, I never want to see your ugly face no more!" and I beat it out of there before he jumped on me and sat on my chest and twisted my arm to get the picture out of me.

I was sorry, though, later I hadn't traded him right then and there because even though I hid the photograph deep down under my underwear in my clothes drawer, somebody—Buster, I strongly suspected—found it and drew a mustache on it, then punched holes in the face with something sharp that must've been the icepick from the kitchen, making Shirley Temple look like she was coming down with the measles, but I didn't care, I kept the photograph anyway.

She called it the LTL that stood for the Loyal Temperance Legion. She belonged to it and the Jakes belonged to it, practically everybody in the red brick church belonged to it, and if my father found out I did too I know he would've killed me.

She must've had a nose for the kids in her class had fathers, and mothers too, that drank, because she came up to each one of us before the bell rang that first Wednesday afternoon and asked us if we wanted to stay. When she asked me if I would stay, I said I would, more to stay on the good side of her than anything else, my long division wasn't getting any better.

Walter Snarp stayed the first time but Earl Jr., saying how Miss Prouty tried to sucker him into it when he was in her class, razzed Walter so much he never came again. Walter, glad to get out of it, sneered he was just as happy not to come anymore, "They ain't nothin but grrr-ulls there anyways." Which wasn't exactly true. I kept my lip buttoned around Earl Jr. about my being in the LTL as much as I kept it buttoned around the house about it for fear it might get back to my father and when he was drunk some night he might take the belt to me again. When my mother asked me why was I late getting home from school on Wednesdays I just told her I was helping Miss Prouty clapping the erasers and washing the blackboards. She always believed me, I was getting to be so good a liar.

What Miss Prouty did was show us big color posters of somebody called John Barleycorn that was like a cartoon in the funnies. He had a dented stovepipe hat and a rag-gedy black coat with tails and a nose as long and thin as Pinocchio's, like he lied all the time. Only John Barleycorn's was red, "Red as the fires of hell!" Miss Prouty shouted as she stood in front of her poster and rapped the tip of her pointer against the tip of John Barleycorn's nose.

He looked familiar to me, not only because my father's nose got just as red when he was drunk, but because of another poster, all old and greasy and curling up at the edges, that I saw hanging on the wall in the backroom of Tarkie's saloon when my mother let me go with Slap one Friday night to pick up a dozen fried oysters that cost a whole twenty-five cents. My mother had the extra quarter because just that day she got a letter from Aunt Bridget with a dollar in it and it being Friday we couldn't eat any meat, my mother said, "My mouth's been waterin for some honest to God fried oysters, I ain't et any in so long." I saw my father give her a funny look that had some worry in it too and wondered why that was.

The man in the poster at Tarkie's looked just like John Barleycorn in Miss Prouty's poster, only his suit was more like the one Reverend Hoople from the red brick church wore, and instead of being red his long thin nose was icy blue with icicles hanging off of it. He was shaking his claw of a finger at a bunch of people that were drinking and dancing all around him and looking like they were at a party having a good time. The words in big red letters across the top of the poster said, "THE PROHIBITIONISTS WILL GET YOU IF YOU DON'T WATCH OUT!"

Now I knew what a bluenose was, that was a person didn't like any drinking or dancing or going to the movies, but I didn't know what a prohibitionist was. I whispered to Slap did he know, as he watched Mrs. Tarkie, that wasn't really Mrs. Tarkie Mrs. Beezley told my mother but something she called Mr. Tarkie's "common-law wife," taking the sizzling oysters she just scooped out of the deepfry and put them in a cardboard box. I had to whisper again to Slap did he know what a prohibitionist was and he went, "Heh? Heh?" never once taking his eyes off of those oysters. Like my mother he said he hadn't eaten fried oysters in so long so that even if he did hear me and knew what a prohibitionist was he couldn't've told me anyhow, all he had eyes for was those oysters. I got to say the delicious smell of them was making my belly gurgle even though at supper I ate only the crust of mine and gave the oyster inside, that I hadn't ever seen or ate before, to Slap, that'd eat anything, it smelled better than it tasted, it looked so green and slimy and wrinkled too like something you would dig up back in the swamp that wasn't even as clean and smooth and white as the inside of a frog's leg.

Most of the girls that stayed after school for the Loyal Temperance Legion all went to the red brick church and were in Miss Prouty's Sunday school class. They were all the smartest in the class and always wore clean dresses and had tight shiny plaits or Shirley temple curls like Margaret and Virginia. Margaret came to the meetings too even though she went to the Baptist Tabernacle on Tabernacle Trail that looked more like a storefront than a for real church. Not a one of them I suspected had a mother or a father touched a drop of anything, so I wondered why they were there. I *knew* why me and Walter Snarp and Eleanor and some of the other kids that were mainly either Catholics or on relief or both were there, because of our fathers, and some of our mothers. And because Miss Prouty said she was afraid we would grow up to be drunkards too if she didn't put a scare into us, which I doubt she could more'n we was scared of it already. So every Wednesday after school she hung those big posters over the blackboard that showed John Barleycorn and the evils of drinking liquor that some of us kids didn't need any poster to tell us about since most of us knew it firsthand.

"It's the drinking and sinning goes on in this town gives it such a blackeye," Miss Prouty'd say practically every meeting. "You'll see the day you go to the high school over in the county seat what I mean—Those of you who do go, that is," she said, throwing her eye at those of us on relief huddling together on one side of the room. "Once they find out you're from Lenape, the other students there will look down on you."

I wondered if she meant if you lived in one of those big houses with the lawns in front I saw in the county seat there wouldn't be any drinking or sinning going on inside, nor any of the kids lived there going into the woods to dance naked for each other, you had to live in Lenape for that, is that what she meant? Then she would go right on, telling us stories about the horrors of drink that, despite all those of us saw it close up at home, bulged our eyes out even so, and as for me made my hair stand on end as much as the stories she told us in nature studies of fires and floods and other natural calamities. She talked on and on about how her and the Jakes and Reverend Hoople and all the other people in the red brick church were trying to pass a law to close up all the saloons in Lenape so's to make it like it used to be in the old days of the camp meetings when only sober, hard-working, God-fearing people lived in the town, not like now—And her eyes cut across the room to where us kids on relief were sitting so that I felt myself slinking down in my seat. Even so, my heart jumped with hope, hearing it. If they closed Tarkie's and Ye Olde Ship Bottom then my father wouldn't have any place to drink any more and maybe him and my mother would be quiet at night and start talking to each other again in the day.

But my father and Mr. Beezley, of course, were dead set against it. I could hear them jawing about it over their beer in the parlor at night while I laid up in bed, leaning over Slap and listening down the stairs, Mr. Beezley, all agitated, shouting, "Them Methodists is tryin to wreck this town not lettin other people enjoy theirselfs with a glass of beer oncet in awhile! Them bluenoses with their faces stiff as cement from never crackin a smile!" My father, his voice louder'n usual like it always was when he had a few, said, "It dint work with the Prohibition"—my ears perked up over that word again—"and it ain't goin to work now." Mrs. Beezley came in sighing with, "They never learn, do they?"

I listened hard to hear if my father was going to say anymore about Prohibition so I could know what it meant. I listened hard too to hear if my mother would say anything but she didn't say a word and I suspected her keeping quiet meant she maybe felt a jump of hope too, if they closed down the saloons in Lenape my father'd have to stop drinking, and if that's what Prohibition meant, then I was all for it, and I suspected she was too but like me she knew she better keep it to herself.

The day they were to vote on it, a whole bunch of people called the wets crowded around the firehouse where everybody was voting, mostly people I saw in our church on Sundays. Some of the men were wearing old army uniforms from World War I that were so tight on them they were pinching in their guts, and some were wearing American Legion outfits while others had on their volunteer firemen's uniforms, like Charley, even though he was too crippled to fight a fire and could only shine the bell and ride along on the engine. Then there were the ladies wearing ladies auxiliary caps and white dresses with capes marching right along behind the men. Some of the men were waving American flags and some with grinning red faces were carrying signs saying KEEP OUR BEER NEAR and all of them were singing God Bless America. Mr. and Mrs. Beezley were there, and my father too, looking bright-eyed, since the three of them just stepped out the front door of Tarkie's up the road that was giving out free beers, all you could drink, Buster said, "Just so's you get to the ballot box and vote wet." They joined right in marching with the crowd, Mr. Beezley carrying a sign Brother said Mr. Beezley made all by himself, saying BLUENOSES GO HOME, while across the street Miss Prouty and the Jakes and Reverend Hoople, along with a smaller bunch of people that went to the red brick church and the Baptist Tabernacle, and were called the drys, were clutching their bibles and praying and beating their tambourines and singing hymns, the whole lot of them never once cracking a smile, like Mr. Beezley said. But if they were like Miss Prouty, that was so filled with worry about all the sinning and evil and fiery disasters there were in the world, I could see why they never had much to smile about.

Me and my brothers and the Beezley boys stood over in the ballfield by the schoolhouse watching it all, while my mother stayed at home with Danny and Kate. She was saying her rosary in the parlor by now I figured because as we went out the door I saw her lips were already moving with praying, because she knew my father would be there with the Beezleys and knew about the free beer and she was so afraid he'd get to drinking and that some of the bluenoses Mr. Beezley said ran the relief might see my father drunk and cut him off the rolls just out of spite. Maybe she was praying at the same time for the same thing I'd been praying for, and that was, much as I didn't like the proddisins, now I was in the LTL I was hoping the bluenoses'd win if it'd mean my father would quit his drinking. I didn't care if it was a sin I'd have to tell in confession, me being on the same side as the proddisins, I was praying for the drys with all my might, as the singing and the shouting in front of the firehouse got louder and louder, like the wets and the drys were trying to outshout and outsing each other.

But when all was said and done, what Miss Prouty said was true, there were more boozers than bluenoses in Lenape because next day when they counted up all the votes in the firehouse the saloons stayed open. My father and Mr. Beezley got more loaded'n usual that night celebrating it, since Mr. Tarkie was giving everybody beer again on the house.

Whenever I looked at the face of John Barleycorn grinning out at me from Miss Prouty's poster, while behind him Death stood in a black hood holding his scythe over John Barleycorn's shoulder, I saw again how John Barleycorn's face was the same color as my father's face when he came home from the saloon at night after working for relief, or when he'd been drinking on the front porch or in the parlor with Sam Beezley. I wondered how long would it be before Death would come with his scythe and cut him down, worrying, when he did, about how we'd eat without my father there working on the dump truck and getting things from relief for us, worrying when he did if we'd still have a roof over our heads.

I was just busting with LTL, so much so I surprised myself as all of a sudden I found myself praying at night that Death would take my father to that "sober Heaven" Miss Prouty promised us would be ours, "through earthly abstinence." Right away I felt awful guilty having such a wish and wondered how I would confess that to Father Mack at my next confession, wishing my own father was dead just to save him. But maybe it was more to save myself, to save all of us, from his beatings, and maybe even more'n anything to save my mother the misery in her eyes, and maybe even more'n that, if he was dead then, oh then, we could all move back to Philadelphia.

My mother sat bundled up in the old coat Aunt Bridget gave her, crocheting another one of her doilies for the arms and backs of the parlor chairs, nuisances that were always getting nudged or elbowed onto the floor by the rest of us even after she tried pinning them in place—"Pick that up," you could hear her say any number of times in a day or evening, like to her keeping the doilies in place would somehow keep everything else in place.

Tonight she had a determined look in her eye, her needle flashing under the oil lamp, as she tried to ignore my little sister, like nothing mattered except to make that doily and then make another and another.

My father buried his face behind the *Bulletin* like the paper was a wall shutting us out, like my mother's crocheting was another kind of wall, like all the doilies she was piling up was a blanket she was knitting to hide herself under.

I had that feeling again like I wanted to go to her, like I'd wanted to go to my father when he burnt his hand that time, I wanted to squeeze beside her on the chair and kiss her face and smooth her hair.

It didn't matter. By now I knew what was the matter with her anyhow and it wasn't any of those things you would've thought. And I also knew that anything I would do or say couldn't change any of it.

Crossing the dining room quiet as I could, like I was in a room where somebody was sick, I went and stood by the window, and stared across the road at the sassafras woods, the last of their branches going dark as night came on, the dark coming quick like it always did over land so flat some evenings seemed like nothing but sky. Overhead the last of the birds were flying to their roosts back in the swamp, fewer of them now that the weather was colder. Now the leaves were all gone I could see the hole in the woods where the Mahoney's house used to be, and wished with all my heart I was up there in the playroom again, warm, and with something sweet to eat and forgetful in playing games with Ronnie again. I hug-ged myself, shivering, as the wind blew in no matter how many old *Bulletins* she stuffed in the cracks.

I knew what was the matter. I knew she was going to have another baby. None of the rest knew yet because she started wearing what she told Mrs. Beezley was a "maternity corset" that Aunt Patty with the identical twins lent her, sending it down through the mail. She'd been pulling it tighter and tighter as each month went by, "So the kids won't see, and for when I go to mass," I heard her whisper to Mrs. Beezley a few days before. Then taking a deep breath she said all in a rush, "And so's he won't know for now and won't drink more'n he's already bin drinkin…" Listening, as I hunched under the dining room table hoping to hear about the latest movie Babes Beezley said she'd seen that Saturday night, knowing from the Rialto sign in Gottlieb's window it was Bette Davis—that was her favorite of all the movie stars—in "All This and Heaven Too."

He walked out on us a week later, stuffed an extra change of workclothes and underwear into a paperbag and went out the door without so much as a goodbye to any of us. He'd been drinking night after night, not only in the parlor after supper with or without Sam Beezley, but at the saloon too. I wondered where he got the money. I was certain my mother did too. Frank whispered to Buster in bed at night he was probably doing odd jobs for Mr. Tarkie or else putting it on the eye like he did at Gottlieb's.

Most evenings after supper he'd go through the woods in the direction of the saloon and he wouldn't come back for hours, sometimes long after we'd been in bed. My mother, as often when she was so mad at him she didn't know what to do, would wash all us younger ones earlier'n usual, scrubbing our ears til we hollered, like she was taking out on our ears what she'd like to take out on him. When that was done and he still wasn't back, she started in on jobs she usually put off as long as she could, like cleaning the oven or cleaning the icebox, or scrubbing down the stairs, she scrubbed them so hard she made them shine like a punishment. One night, before our bedtime, she even went up and cleaned both bedrooms, tearing them apart from top to bottom, before he finally came in. I could hear him staggering up the stairs and hid my head under the covers.

Some nights, though, when he still hadn't come home and there was no more she could think of to do, she'd sit under the oil lamp in the parlor and crochet fast and furious, turning out her endless stream of doilies quicker'n ever, her face fixed with a faraway look like she was over the river and back in South Philly pouring her heart out about him to her sisters. Even though she was wearing the maternity corset and we weren't supposed to know it, she was already beginning to show so much you couldn't miss it if you really looked. Watching her as she crocheted away, you couldn't miss the tight pinch between her eyes either that seemed to be perpetually there lately.

Now when he came home late from the saloon, his face, however hard he tried to rearrange it, would be red as the comb of one of his roosters, his eyes glazed and stupid, his mouth

hanging open like he was about to speak but he never said anything, like his tongue was too thick for him to say anything. That
night was no exception, and when the front door opened and he
came stumbling in, my mother went stiff as a board, keeping
her eyes close on her work and pulling even deeper into herself
like she was folding herself into a silence that spoke louder'n
anything she might've said.

By the color of his face you could tell he'd been downing
shots along with his beer, and since he hadn't ever had the
stomach for whiskey, some nights he barely made it up the
stairs before he passed out, falling on the bed so we could hear
the springs screech from downstairs. Next morning his face was
always the color of ashes but he always got to his work on relief
despite his hangover, he never once missed a day of work
because of one.

When he came in that cold Sunday night from the saloon
the high color of his face was a dead giveaway he'd been drinking boiler-makers. Right away, my brothers squeezed themselves over their homework while my sister crawled over and
pressed her head against my mother's knee. Danny right off the
bat jumped under the nearest armchair while I slunk creeping
across the floor, trying to hide myself behind the couch to get
out of his way and out of his reach, since anyone of us that got
in his way he would just as soon snatch us up by the hair of
the head and beat the living daylights out of us as look at us.

He stood for a long time swaying in the doorway, staring at
her, staring at the top of her bent head, really, since she never once
lifted her gaze from her crocheting to look at him. Because we were
having an early cold snap, he staggered into the dining room to
stoke the stove like he usually did, shoveling the coal in one load
after another like he didn't care we had to watch every shovelful,
then slamming the stove door shut with a bang that rang all

through the house and started Kate whimpering. My mother didn't like him fussing with the heater when he'd been drinking heavy, it made her nervous, and in spite of herself, she shouted out to him, "Leave it alone before you burn the house down!"

He came and stood in the parlor door, the coal shovel in one hand, his face even redder now from the heat of the coals. He asked her, "What did you say?" even though we all knew he heard her the first time. She didn't answer him, just kept on stitching, and that seemed to make him all the madder.

"I'll leave it alone!" he shouted, and swinging around, he heaved the coal shovel over his shoulder hard as he could. It hit the stove with a clang that made us all jump, including my mother, even though she went right on with her crocheting like it never happened.

I pulled myself in tighter behind the couch, peeking out to keep an eye on him, seeing the legs of my brothers draw up and stiffen, all thoughts of their homework forgotten, like we were all afraid he was going to come after one of us for sure now. But instead I heard him climbing the stairs in that quick way of his, despite his load. My brothers all stared at each other with a questioning look til they heard him come down a minute or so later. Peeping out again from under the couch I saw he was clutching a handful of his workclothes and underwear in either fist. He went out to the kitchen where you could hear him rooting in the potato bin where my mother kept the brown paper bags. In a minute, he came back into the parlor, stuffing his clothes into an old paper bag, muttering to himself but muttering loud enough for everybody to hear, "I'll leave it alone, all right—I'll go where I'm wanted..."

My mother, who'd been ignoring him, or trying to, up to now, glared up from her crocheting like she wanted to make sure he really meant to do what he was threatening to do, and when she saw that he was, she shouted, "Go! Go then! I'm sick of you! Sick of you and yer drinkin!"

He stared at her, his jaw dropping, the look of the astonished rooster in his eyes. For the moment he seemed almost sober. I was afraid he was going to go after her and stopped breathing, clenching up my fists, waiting, but instead, without looking at her, he growled, "You won't see me again. I know where to go. I'll go where I'm wanted."

With that he clapped on his greasy work cap, pulled open the door, letting in a rush of cold air, and stepped out into the dark porch, slamming the door so hard after him the loose glass rattled in the frame.

Peeping out from under the couch, I could see my brothers gawking at the front door like they couldn't believe he'd gone. My first feeling wasn't one of relief but a worry that she might call him back, that she might run to the door and call after him she was sorry for what she said. The next thing I felt was a fright starting up in me that we wouldn't be anything without him, that if he left us we wouldn't have anything, wouldn't have even the little we had.

Kate started to bawl worse than when she had her hair brushed. Slap came over and started to pet her, but even as he did he kept gaping around like he didn't know what was going on, like he hadn't heard any of it. I crawled from behind the couch and stared wide-eyed like my brothers at the front door, then back at my mother, her thumb and forefinger bent tighter around the shaft of her crochet needle like she wanted to snap it in two as she poked it in and out with her thread, faster and faster, her face dark and drained. Even so, she looked like she was breathing easier, her eyes seemed less pinched, her mouth more relaxed than I'd seen it for days, it was like she could breathe again.

All of a sudden, the usual low hum of the stove in the dining room became a roar, and the snap in the stove along the chimney pipe became a loud banging. There was a smell of heat. The usually chilly parlor felt warmer now. She was the first to notice, lifting her head all alert like she was sniffing the air, just the way at night she sniffed down the stairs for smoke. Frank caught it too and jumping up ran out in the dining room and came running back twice as fast, his eyes bulging with excitement, yelling, "Mom! Come quick! Look!"

She dropped her crocheting and leapt up and ran out of the room, the rest of us at her heels crowding in at the doorway, seeing there in the darkness the entire flue burning red as John Barleycorn's nose out the back of the overheated stove. The metal was gleaming all molten around through the elbow and was shooting up the entire length of the pipe red as the mercury in a thermometer, rising up closer and closer to where the pipe disappeared through the chimney hole my father'd chopped in the wall, and inching nearer to the peeling wallpaper and dry as tinder slats underneath, fire red as the hell Father Mack and Miss Prouty were always thundering about.

My mother hollered to Frank to quick go pump a bucket of water in the kitchen, and Frank ran out, tearing aside the old blanket hung in the kitchen door, with Buster right on his tail to help him. Then my mother ran to the stove and grabbing the old singed potholder always hanging on the wall there for that purpose, she flipped the metal coil of the flue handle closed. Shielding her face with one arm, she leaned down and swung the draft door shut with a bang, her face and arms tinged bloodred in the glare, her lips trembling, her eyes squinting from the brightness as much as from fear as, all that done, she leapt back swiftly from the heat blasting out from a bed of white-hot coals my father had shoveled on too high.

We stood huddled in the doorway, the squeals of the pump in the kitchen as Frank and Buster worked it rising above the fierce hum of the stove, the ceiling and walls of the dining room glowing pink as wild roses. My mother, without thinking, shielded us with her body, her arms outstretched in front of us, never once taking her eyes off the stove that was gleaming like an inferno. Frank came running in with the water, slopping most of it on the floor in his haste. My mother lifted a hand and told him to put it down, just in case, but said to run get another one and to use the pee bucket if he had to.

Finally, after several long minutes that seemed to take forever, the brightness of the fire, banked now, began to dim real slow. Within moments the tall chimney flue started pinging and crackling as it cooled down, the fiery red bleeding out of it as the pipe gradually went back to its usual color that was blue as the gunbarrel of the pistol hid in my father's drawer. The top and sides of the stove took a little longer cooling down, but when they finally did get back to their rusty iron color, my mother, who stayed watching the stove like a hawk every minute, her arms still stretched out, holding us back, breathed a long deep sigh, allowing her hunched up shoulders to drop at last.

He was gone three days.

For the first time I could ever remember we talked at the supper table that next evening because my father wasn't there to shush us so we wouldn't interfere with his reading the newspaper. We all talked like we were trying not to think of where he was, and Buster even told a joke he heard in school that day, "Why did the moron kill his mother and father? So's he could go on the orphan's picnic!" My mother wrinkled up her nose, saying it was aterrible joke but still and all she grinned along with the rest of us.

After the supper dishes were done, we all sat in the parlor, me laying on my belly on the floor after I did my long division homework, drawing on the backs of empty boxes with the stubs of crayons Ronnie finally let me have when he was still living next door. My sister was cooing to her dolls while she dressed and undressed them behind my father's empty chair, my mother sat on the couch reading the *County Seat Weekly*, and my brothers sat propped up against the long-dead radio, reading the comics and the sports pages of the *Bulletin* that they had first crack at tonight, not having to wait til my father was done with them since my father wasn't there. The fire hummed out in the dining room and Frank kept going to check on it whenever my mother asked him to, she was still so nervous from last night. You could see Frank felt so grown up when he went out to check the stove because he was the one that built the fire that night now our father wasn't here to do it.

The room felt so different somehow from other nights, it was the same room but there was less a feeling of everybody's being on edge. Even my mother's face seemed less distracted as she read all the local doings in Charley's column. In spite of my worriment all day in school, I felt more at ease too, more'n I ever remembered feeling in a long time, my stomach felt less tight and queasy. Even so, every now and then I glanced suddenly over my shoulder, half expecting to see him sitting as always in his chair with its worn, ragged arms, his jelly glass and quart of Schmidt's at his elbow, his face buried behind the *Bulletin*. Despite my fears he might never come back, I still glanced quick over my shoulder just to make sure he really wasn't there, afraid that he might be and, fearing it, felt a twinge of guilt, remembering Father Mack saying, "Above all, honor thy father," something he told us in any number of sermons. "Honoring your mother is the same as honoring the Blessed Mother, but honoring your father is the same as honoring God the Father...."

I stared at my father's empty chair with the unlit oil lamp beside it, then at Kate playing behind it with her dolls. The feeling in the parlor that night was like tomorrow was going to be a day off from school, I sensed the others were feeling that way too. Slap and Danny broke out laughing at something in the comics, and for once, Buster wasn't nagging at Frank to read faster so he could turn to the next sports page. Everything seemed so different I even found I was humming to myself as I gave up on the yellow crayon and started to draw with the remains of a red one that showed up much better in the light, humming as content and warm in my belly as the humming of the stove out in the dining room.

But wouldn't you know, I could've strangled that cuckoo. Like a squealer, it popped out of its doors in the dining room and cuckooed nine times right on schedule. I couldn't believe the time'd gone by so fast! I glanced uneasy at my mother but if she heard it she made no sign and for the first time ever, she didn't say anything about its being bedtime for us younger ones. Since it was a Monday night, I double crossed my fingers, overjoyed I might get the chance to stay up longer. I only wished we had the electric on so I could listen for the first time to Lux Radio Theater right here in the parlor without having to hang half out of bed over Slap with my ear just about on the floor and cocked in the direction of the stairwell, straining to hear it like I always had to when the juice was on.

At first I figured she just forgot the time, maybe because she was so wrapped up in thinking about my father and wondering where he was, just like I'd been doing all that day. As I took another crayon out of the box, I kept glancing at her sideways to see if she'd heard the cuckoo and would remember it was our bedtime. I gave a big sigh of relief as, now she was finishing looking at the paper, she picked up her crocheting and got busy at that, her face less tight than it was this morning, there was even something of a look of contentment in it, just like I was feeling inside. But once or twice I caught her peering up the dark stairway leading to their bedroom and suspected maybe she was putting off going upstairs herself for as long as possible, that she was bending the rules this one time because she was glad to have all our company that night for as long as she could.

The third night he just showed up, stiff-faced, his jaws black from needing a shave, not saying a word to her or any of us. She was standing by the stove cooking supper when he came in through the back and emptied his bag of dirty clothes into the laundry hamper in the shed. Then he came into the kitchen and pumped a basin of water for himself at the sink and went back into the shed and shut the door to wash up, just like he did every night after his work on relief or the WPA, just like nothing'd happened.

My mother acted like she didn't see him come in, but you knew she knew he was there because she set his place for him at the table like she always did, except for the last two nights. By the time he came out of the shed he found the day-old *Evening Bulletin* beside his plate without his having to go through the house looking for it like he usually had to, snatching the sports pages here and the comics there out of our hands, and complaining because we'd gotten the pages all uneven and rumpled. As luck would have it, as a special treat, and maybe to help cheer us up, my mother'd boiled up turnips with the potatoes that night, that next to spaghetti was our favorite, and was always his favorite too. She piled his plate high and drenched the mashed turnips and potatoes in gravy, just the way he liked it.

Without looking at any of us, his face still stiff, his looking like a gangster in the movies with his five o'clock shadow, he unfolded the newspaper slow and solemn and as always, after a quick glance at the headlines, turned to the sports page first thing. We all had to remember to be quiet again, which was hard to do since, as I said, for the past two nights without him there reading his paper we all gabbed back and forth like we never gabbed before at the table, like we were at a party. But as if he'd never been away, he started to eat like he had a tapeworm, clapping his lips louder'n usual. My brothers were watching him from under their brows and my little sister, staring at him like she hadn't ever seen him before, started to ask him where he'd been, but before she could get it out my mother hushed her and told her to eat and keep her eyes on her plate. And she gave a severe look at the rest of us, warning us to do likewise.

That Sunday the most amazing thing happened: the two of them went to early mass together. It was unusual in itself since he always went to the late mass, or the last one, depending on how hungover he was. But for them to go together... Even more unusual was, after mass, as I came out the backdoor of the church, I saw the two of them walking across the field with Father Mack in the direction of the rectory, Father Mack between them with an arm on either of their shoulders, talking to them with his head bowed.

After that, he didn't touch a drop for at least a week.

My father was painting the trim around the parlor that Sunday, using some cheap old paint Mr. Gottlieb couldn't ever sell and threw in when my father did some odd jobs for him around the store, working off some of what he owed him.

These days, my father was a lot quieter and calmer since he

wasn't drinking. When he came back home after being away those three days, he decided to spruce up the place a little in his spare time, like by doing it he was trying to make it up to my mother for walking out on her. He started that particular Sunday morning painting the baseboard and the windows and doorways in the parlor with what was supposed to be glossy white but came out more like a light brown because the paint was so old. Then, too, it looked like it was the first time the trim or anything else'd been painted since the house was built, it just soaked up the paint.

All of a sudden there was a terrific pounding of footsteps out on the porch. We all looked up, surprised to see Sam Beezley galloping up to our front door like we never saw him gallop before, with Brother and Sparky right on his heels. Their dog Blackie was chasing after them barking and wagging his tail like I never saw him so excited before either.

My father stood with his paintbrush hanging in his hand and his mouth gaping open as Sam Beezley came busting in without even knocking or hollering in hello like he usually did. Instead, he was shouting louder'n I ever heard him shout, so that even Slap gave a jump, "The Japs jist bombed Pearl Harbor! It jist come over the radio! The Japs jist bombed Pearl Harbor!"

"A SNEAK ATTACK!" Brother Beezley screamed almost as loud as his father, and jumping up and down like he couldn't hardly stand it. "BY AIR! WHILST EVERYBODY WAS SLEEPIN!"

My father just stood with his mouth flapping like a fish out of water, like he couldn't take in what Sam Beezley or Brother were saying just like none of the rest of us could either. We looked at Mr. Beezley, then at our father, then back again to Mr. Beezley.

I was wondering where Pearl Harbor was.

My mother, hearing all the commotion, came running in from the kitchen and stood in the doorway wiping her hands on her apron, a look on her face like somebody maybe'd been hurt.

"We're in it now!" Sam Beezley grinned, "We're finally in it!" My father grinned back, the high color in both their cheeks and the excitement in their eyes the same as it was the night the bell in the red brick church kept ringing and ringing when the nazis invaded Poland and Sam Beezley told my father he was sure to get a job now. He said it again this time, only louder, so that Kate, peeping out from under the daybed, clapped her hands over her ears. "You'll be sure to get in at the yard now, Stosh! They'll need so many men they won't know what to do! Oh, you'll be sure to get in now, all right, all right!"

Hearing that, my father's eyes went as shiny as the paint he'd been putting on the trim, his face was grinning like it would break in two.

Around noon Earl Jr. hollered for me out the back door. I knew it had to be something awful important for Earl Jr. to come up and yell for me at my house. The very first thing when I came out, he said, "Ja hear?" and when I said I did, he started rubbing the thighs of his overalls, saying all agitated, "We'll show them Japs—we'll show them sneaky sonsabitches!"

Right then my mother shouted out the back for me to come in to dinner and I told Earl Jr. I had to go. He said, "We'll show them sneaky sonsabitches, we'll show 'em!" and kept rubbing himself and giving me the high sign that I knew meant he wanted me to go with him for a walk in the woods, but I said, "I got to go eat." He said, "I'll come by later on," but I didn't say anything and went on back in.

While she was putting dinner on the table, my mother kept asking where Frank was, even once when he was right there under her nose, which got us all laughing. When he said, "Here

I am," and asked her what she wanted, she looked blank and said, "What?" and when he repeated the question, she answered, "Oh, was I calling you?" We all laughed again and she looked miffed at us and went about doing what she was doing, mashing the potatoes, then cutting up the chicken, but you could see there was something on her mind. Today, she dished out the dinner like she wasn't there, and when everybody's plate was filled and she fixed one for herself and sat down, even before she blessed herself before picking up her fork, I caught her sneaking looks at Frank, that expression still in her eyes like she was thinking about something else, something that I didn't understand yet.

That evening after supper Sister Beezley came through the woods to tell us her mother and father said for us to come over and listen to all the latest news about Pearl Har-bor on their radio. I was jumping when I heard it, hoping we would get to hear some of the Sunday night shows we hadn't heard in so long I was forgetting what they sounded like. My mother had all of us wash our faces and comb our hair and because it was cold out, she even made the younger ones get into the leggings from relief that they hated to wear as much as I did when I had to wear them.

My father led us through the woods with the flashlight, warning my mother to be extra careful to watch out for the tree roots sticking up in the path. Once we got to the Beezley's, Blackie came running out barking to meet us, and we all went in through the back and sat in the parlor around the Beezley's new Philco, my father and Sam Beezley looking so serious, each with his head down in front of the speaker as we all listened to the latest news flashes.

"'A day of infamy,' that's what President Roosevelt called it," Mrs. Beezley kept saying to my mother, only she said the President's name like it had a rose in it and not the way we said

it—or the way Earl Jr. said it, "Jewsevelt," he called him, just to
be smart, because he said that's the way Adolf Hitler said it in
the newsreels. Earl Jr. didn't even care if it wasn't for President
Roosevelt, like my mother never tired of saying, the Snarps or
any of us wouldn't have anything to eat or clothes to put on our
back or shoes to wear on our feet, even if the shoes did pinch
something terrible.

"You should of heard it, Nor'," Mrs. Beezley said, "'A day of
infamy,' he called it!"

I didn't know what "infamy" was but the way she said it
sounded pretty awful.

"Five battleships sunk and three more hurt bad!" Mr.
Beezley was shouting at my father, like my father hadn't just
heard it himself. "And ten other warships destroyed or hurt jist
as bad!" Mr. Beezley slapped my father's knee, hollering, "Oh,
they'll need shipyard workers now, jist you see! You'll be takin
the ferry with me acrosst to the yard before you know it, Stosh!"

My father grinned and took a long slug of his ginger ale like
he was wishing it was beer.

Listening to Mr. Beezley, it looked like the rings under Mrs.
Beezley's eyes got darker. She had a highstrung, worried look
like the one my mother had all during our Sunday dinner when
she kept asking where Frank was—only Mrs. Beezley seemed
the more fidgety of the two. She kept on smoking one Raleigh
after another and sneaking worried looks around at her Brother,
like my mother'd been doing all day at our Frank.

When Walter Winchell came on at nine o'clock, Mr. Beezley
told everybody to hush. My father and him hunched their
shoulders and leaned so close to the set this time, it appeared
like they were about to climb into the radio together. Walter
Winchell was spitting his words out like they were machine gun
bullets as he started firing away at "Mr. and Mrs. America and

All the Ships at Sea," even though it didn't sound like there were any ships left in the whole U.S. Navy after what the Japs did. He sounded fit to be tied about the sneak attack by those slant-eyed sneaks that were nothing but dirty cowards and that the United States of America, that was the Land of the Free and the Home of the Brave, would rise up in this dark hour and put down those yellowbellied sons of the Rising Sun. Mr. Beezley himself got so riled up listening that, all sweating and flushed with beer, he jumped up and, lifting his glass high over his head, he cheered so loud everyone of us jumped. Danny and Kate were looking at him like he'd gone crazy as he shouted, "That's right, Walter! We'll git em! We'll git them yella-bellied bastids!"

My father nodded his head quick like a rooster and took another long swig of his ginger ale, the two of them having that same gleeful excitement in their eyes as'd been in their eyes earlier that day, while my mother and Mrs. Beezley just looked at each other, my mother with her arms wrapped around herself and shivering her shoulders with every word Walter Winchell was saying, while Mrs. Beezley lit herself another Raleigh.

As for me, I sat there thinking to myself if there was going to be a war and it meant my father'd get a job at the yard, then I was glad, if it meant a war and him stopping his drinking because he got a job, then I was even more glad, even though I knew it wasn't right and felt ashamed in my heart, I couldn't help it, I'd be glad, glad even though I saw my mother glance again at our Frank that was sprawled on the Beezley's big lumpy couch between Buster and Brother, saw Frank hunch forward with a little frown on his face as he listened to Walter Winchell rat-tat-tatting away, the mustache on his upper lip looking darker tonight, as dark almost as Brother's was, as dark as the circles under Mrs. Beezley's eyes, and my mother glancing at him like she was afraid he might somehow disappear if she didn't keep an eye on him.

When the new baby was born we all spent the night at the Beezley's while Mrs. Beezley stayed with my mother in our house, and when the new baby was christened, Aunt Patty and Uncle Bill came all the way down by bus from Philly and stood for him. They gave him a little white rosary the size for a baby's hands that my mother hung over him in his bassinette, and a blue satin pillow with his name stitched on it, Peter.

After the baby was born, my father, once we were all up in bed and after he'd had a few, would tell Sam Beezley down in the parlor at night it was Father Mack's baby, "Since it was him brung the two of us together again." You could hear my mother pretending to be annoyed as she told him to stop talking so foolish, what he was saying was a sin, but she let it go at that, figuring it was best maybe to let well enough alone, anything so he wouldn't start drinking heavy again.

My mother, of course, wasn't allowed at the baptism, but Sunday a week later, as I watched from the shadows of the doorway leading to the altar after the first mass, she was churched by Father Mack at the side altar of the Blessed Mother. As she knelt at the railing, her head bowed, the eyes of the Virgin, even though they were plaster, seemed to be gazing down in a kindly way at the top of my mother's cheap black hat and the faded shoulders of her best cloth coat, that Aunt Bridget'd given her so long ago. The priest stood over her mumbling in latin while my mother recited in a voice you could hardly hear, "Hail Mary, full of grace, the Lord is with thee. Blessed art thou amongst women, blessed is the fruit of thy womb, Jesus..." bowing her head even lower when she said His name. As I stood, still in my cassock and surplice, watching it all from the entry, Timothy came up from behind and putting his arm around my shoulder began explaining in a whisper, like he was already practicing to be a priest, what everything meant, about the churching, that with the laying on of his hands on her shoulders Father Mack was helping my mother get rid of all the bad blood still in her from after the baby's being born.

"It brings her back into the fold so she can receive communion again," Timothy whispered. "Her womb will be a cleansed tabernacle once more." I didn't know what a womb was, and didn't want to ask because I'd rather die'n let Timothy know how dumb I was, but I figured it must've been another name for belly, where little Peter came from after my mother blew up so big in spite of her wearing the maternity corset, and where Baby Jesus came from, born of the Blessed Mother, and happy in my own heart to have his arm on my shoulder.

In the evenings while my mother was cooking supper my father liked to lift the baby out of his bassinette and carry him into the parlor and sit in his chair with him. Holding the baby between his legs, he cradled his head in his hands, his hands that looked so big and rough compared to the little silky head of the baby that was about the size and shape of a pear and was the color of all the milk he drank. Which was plenty, "We should have a cow stead of chickens," my father said. Like with Kate when she was little, you could see the heart beating on top of the new baby's head, I couldn't get enough of watching it beat.

He'd rock Peter back and forth singing:

"Seesaw knock at the door

Who's there?

Grandpop.

Whaddaya want?

A glass of beer—

Git outa here, ya dirty bum!"

When he sang the last line he'd lean close to the baby and grin at him. The baby'd get all excited and twist itself on his lap and jerk its head away, grinning back even goofier.

"Wheresa bad boy?" my father'd say, his nose touching the baby's nose, the baby staring back at him cross-eyed like he was in a trance, "Wheresa bad boy?" Then the baby would twist away and bust out in its goofy little grin again.

Kate would be watching the two of them from under the daybed like the green-eyed monster, just the way I used to when I saw my mother holding Danny when he was born. She'd crawl out sometimes and come over, hanging onto the arm of the chair, wanting my father to hold her too, but he'd only laugh and rub her curls all up the wrong way, saying with a teasing glint in his eye, "Gwan, yer too big for that now," just like my mother used to say to me when Danny came along. Kate would drag herself away with a face on her a mile long, like she was about to get her hair brushed.

I liked the smell of him so much, I would stick my nose up close and sniff him, he smelled so sweet like milk and Johnson & Johnson baby powder. And like I said, I never tired of watching his heartbeat in the top of his head. But sometimes something came over me, I don't know what, and when nobody was around and I was supposed to be minding him, I started holding the blue satin pillow his godparents gave him over his face as he slept in the bassinette that was borrowed from Mrs. Beezley— "You might jist as well keep it, Nor'," she said when she brought it over, "I ain't plannin to have no more, you can betcher sweet life on that." I would let go of the pillow only when, his hands going, he woke up and started howling and I heard my mother coming.

For a long time after that if I saw a lady on the road all swollen up that way, I ran past her quick as I could because I had an urge to kick her in the belly. But I never ever told anybody that, not even Earl Jr., and certainly never told Father Mack in confessions, not knowing how to, too ashamed and too scared to even if I did.

It was a week after Pearl Harbor when Sam Beezley finally came through and was able to get my father a job at the shipyard. He came running through the woods the minute he got home from work to tell him. He said my father was to start at what was called a linerman that ground rivets on the decks, the lowest job you could start at, "Exceptin," he said, "bein a sweeper or a cleaner of the heads with the niggers. But linerman pays more'n them jobs do and besides that you'll be workin on the boats. It's a start anyhow."

When he told him, my father kept nodding his head like he'd snap his head off and grinning and grinning like he'd split his face open if he grinned any harder. He kept prancing around the kitchen, he just couldn't sit still, I think he would've worked with the niggers if they told him to, he was just so happy to get anything.

Next day after school when me and Earl Jr. were laying back in our clearing in the woods, smoking, Earl Jr., when I told him, said, "It wasn't Sam Beezley got him the job, you dumbie, it's the war startin. My father could get hisself a job any day at the yard too if he wanted and he wouldn't need no Sam Beezley that's full of hot air to do it for him neither."

But I didn't care how my father got the job and if it was Sam Beezley or the war got it for him, I was just so happy he had a job I didn't care who gave it to him.

My mother was happy too, going around the house singing like she hadn't done for such a long time, singing all the old songs I learned from her when we used to live on Mifflin Street, songs like "Pretty Baby" and "Pennies from Heaven." And singing away while she cleaned the house or changed or washed the baby or fed him his Similac, him looking up in her eyes like Danny did, and Kate did, and I must've done too, as he sucked away so greedy at the nipple it was like he was thinking it was the Last Supper, and all the while she would be singing to him, "Small fry, sittin by the river, you ain't the biggest catfish in the deep blue sea..."

And if what was different about my mother was that she was singing again, what was different about my father was that he was walking different ever since Sam Beezley told him the news, he was holding his head and his shoulders higher. Babes Beezley always said he walked like he had springs in his heels but his step was even springier now.

Even more important than any of that was he wasn't drinking as much, like he wanted to keep himself ready for any kind of work they would give him to do at the yard.

Nights, the whole house had a quiet kind of humming going on that made me feel so sleepy and quiet inside, like something'd come to a stop finally. It was like I was getting over something, a fever, or like after awhile when I had my tonsils out and my throat finally didn't feel so raw anymore. I went to sleep a lot quicker most nights too, a lot quicker'n Slap even, which was pretty quick, sometimes right in the middle of a story I was telling, like I knew now I didn't have to worry so much anymore about being a watcher in the night.

Wouldn't you know, my father got caught in the very first air raid drill over in the county seat. It happened the Saturday afternoon him and Sam Beezley drove over there in the old LaSalle to buy workshoes for my father that was to start work that Monday. The ones Gottlieb's had was so old Sam Beezley said Gus Gottlieb must've had them since way before World War

I started, they were so old-fashioned and the leather all cracked and drying up. He said not to buy them, even though they were dirt cheap and my father could've put them on the eye, he would lend my father the money for the shoes til he got his first pay envelope at the yard, and drove him over instead to Perlski's Department Store a block up from the Rialto movie. My father bought a pair of high top safety-toe workshoes there like Sam Beezley told him to and were just like the ones Sam Beezley wore at the yard. And while they were at it, Sam Beezley told him why not buy a pair of Sweet-Orr work pants too—Perlski's ad in the *County Seat Weekly* said SWEET-ORR with the picture of two teams of workhorses trying to pull a pair of Sweet-Orr pants apart and couldn't, they were such strong pants, Sam Beezley said, he himself wouldn't wear anything else. So my father bought them even though he told my mother later on five dollars for the shoes and pants was an awful lot of money to be spending all at once and him not worked a day yet. She said she knew it was but that he needed the shoes, and his old work pants from relief were nothing but patches and rags, so what was done was done, they'd be all right once the money started coming in steady.

What happened about the air raid drill was, as my father later told it as we all hung around the kitchen table, listening, was when him and Mr. Beezley got back to the car from Perlski's Department Store with the workshoes and the Sweet-Orrs. They were just about to get in the LaSalle when the air raid siren went off on the roof of the firehouse back of the courthouse on Quaker Street. My father was telling us all this as he sat lacing up his new workshoes to show my mother, while my mother sat on the other side of the table with her work scissors, snipping off the loose threads and the labels on his work pants that being new was so stiff they could just about stand up by themselves.

"Then all of a sudden," he was saying, bending down as he

looped a lace across the metal catches of one workshoe, "Some air raid warden playin the bigshot in a tin hat come struttin down Quaker Street givin orders for everybody to take cover, even though any fool could see they wasn't no cover to take, 'ceptin in the LaSalle. And when Sam tells him that, he yells, 'You jist git cherself up on that porch, mister, or I'll see yer arrested before you even know what hit you.' But oncet he was outa sight Sam give me a poke in the ribs, we jumped down off of that porch and made a run for it and went back and got in his car and drove off like a bat outa hell, even though the all-clear ain't sounded yet. But Sam stepped on the gas, saying, 'To hell with it, this war's goin to be won by ships not airplanes because no nazi or jap bomber can fly all the way to Jersey.'"

Frank had to get his oar in too, saying, "Them dirty japs flew as far as Pearl Harbor, Pop, that's a long way." My father said, tying a tight bow in each of his new workshoes, "Yeah, but that ain't as far from here as to japan, they can't never do it," even though I knew from Miss Prouty showing us on the map that "heathen japan," as she called it, was quite a distance from Pearl Harbor. But my father said what he said in such a way that as far as he was concerned, that was the end of the conversation.

"How d'ya like 'em?" he said to my mother, standing up and walking around grinning like a kid with new shoes.

She gave a look. "They fit all right?" she asked him, snipping the last of the labels off of the Sweet-Orrs.

"They fit all right," he said. She nodded and I saw her give him a little smile like she was trying to hide it from the rest of us, a smile I hadn't seen her give him for ever so long.

That Sunday night before my father was to start work in the morning I didn't get much sleep. I must've heard him get up umpteen times to light a cigarette. Then he'd come padding out in the hall in his barefeet and take a pee in the bucket, peeing against the side of it like he always did, like, as I said, I did too, copying him, thinking nobody'd hear me peeing that way, me thinking for a split second, like I always did when I heard him at the bucket, of the darkness I saw there in the woods that day when he was changing. Then it seemed no more'n fifteen minutes later after I heard the springs creak with him getting back in the bed, he'd be up and lighting another Bugler and come out to the bucket again. Everytime he got up I could hear my mother say something soft to him like she was trying to quiet him down just by the sound of her voice. But in no time at all he'd be up again and I could see the orange glow of his cigarette flaring in the hallway as he took a drag and stopped by the bucket one more time like as if he'd drunk umpteen quarts of Schmidt's before coming upstairs. But he hadn't touched a drop that night or the night before that, he said to my mother he was so determined not to be hungover or shaky his first day on the job.

He was up and dressed in his new workpants and workshoes and downstairs long before it was light. My mother got up with him to pack his lunch and make his coffee, and just before Sam Beezley came by and knocked at the kitchen door and the two of them went off through the woods and over the fields to catch the ferry, I pressed my hands together under the blankets and said a prayer to the Blessed Mother to not let any bombs drop on the shipyard that day because if they did, then there went his job, and him not having even one full day of work in yet.

When he came home that night his brandnew Sweet-Orrs were all smeared with rust and the top of his new workshoes were too. In spite of how tired he looked he gave my mother a grin when he came into the kitchen where she was stirring her pots and I was rocking the baby in his bassinette to keep him from crying while she cooked. Pinned to my father's work cap was his new CIO union button and his silver shipyard button, number 66293, that he pointed to first thing so my mother would be sure to see them. Even though she had a question in her eyes she saw how tired he was, so all she said was, "You can git to bed good and early tonight." He grinned again and nodded quick, then he went and did something I hadn't ever remembered seeing him doing, he gave her a peck on the cheek. Her eyebrows went up, she looked just as surprised as I was.

He said he didn't have to wash up before supper in our shed like he always did after work on the dump truck for relief, at the yard they had a big washroom with big round sinks for all the men to wash in all at once after the quitting whistle blew, and there was plenty of soap and towels on rollers. When he sat down at the table the day-old *Bulletin* Mrs. Beezley brought over that afternoon—I was thinking how nice it'd be when we could afford to have old Seamus O'Reilly deliver the paper everyday so the news wasn't stale by the time we got it—was folded neat next to his plate, along with the knife he always used to cut up his meat, that used to be his father's knife so long ago and was so old and worn down it was black in spots, and had to always be that knife, he wouldn't use any other.

My mother took his plate and piled it with boiled beef that was his favorite next to pork and that she bought special on the eye at Gottlieb's for his first day on the job. She said she hoped it was the last thing she'd ever have to buy on the eye at Gottlieb's, and slapped on a heap of mashed potatoes that was the last of what we had left in the burlap bag from relief that we all hooted hooray because it meant that was the end of our eating rotten potatoes. She pressed a hollow in his mashed potatoes with the ladle, for the gravy, the way she always did, except when she wasn't speaking to him, because it was the way he liked it, to keep the gravy from running all over his plate.

For the first time I could ever remember, he didn't read the paper while he ate but talked and talked, telling us all about his first day at the yard, while we all listened bug-eyed. What they had him do was grind down rivets on the deck of a cargo ship called the S.S. Sea Challenger that was already launched and was tied up now at one of the docks, "Gettin fitted out for its first voyage." After only one day he was talking like Sam Beezley talked, like he was an old hand at the yard already. He said all his worriment was for nothing because it was the easiest thing running the grinder that was powered by air pressure through a long hose he carried rolled around his shoulder, and the boss never hollered at him once the whole day so he figured he must've done all right. And as luck would have it Sam Beezley was working on the same boat and whenever he could get away from his own job pipe-fitting he came around to see how my father was doing and to teach him the ropes. They ate their lunch together in a little cabin on something he called the poop deck that when he said it Danny and Kate started giggling and wouldn't stop. Even my mother had to laugh, the way he said it, and after supper she said to my father, "Lemme have them work-pants, Stosh, I'll wash em out in the tub and dry em over the stove so's you'll have em clean for tomorrow."

He went to bed right after supper, flinging the Sweet-Orrs down the steps for her to wash. He snored so loud we could hear him all the way down in the parlor that got us kids all laughing louder'n we ever did at Jack Benny or Fibber McGee and Molly. I could see my mother was smiling to herself too, hearing it, when she came back from washing his pants out in the shed, and she kept on smiling as she sat herself on the couch and bent over her crocheting under the oil lamp.

The next morning when we came downstairs she was singing as she stirred the oatmeal, and when I got home from school I could hear her singing wherever she happened to be in the house. I felt like singing myself because everybody and everything seemed lighter, the house seemed lighter, there was a light in it even though the walls were just as peeling and shabby as ever and the lights hadn't been turned on yet.

Speaking of which, with my father's first pay envelope, that we all stood around the kitchen table watching him count out to her, my mother sent Frank up the very next day on the bus to Public Service in Camden with money to pay the light bill that hadn't been paid in so long nobody could remember how long it'd been. Buster was so jealous Frank got the day off from school to go pay the light bill he could hardly see straight. My mother warned Frank umpteen times not to talk to no strangers and to keep his hand on the money in his pocket. Frank kept pulling a face, going, "Aw geezoo, Ma, I know, I know, you don't hafta tell me," like he knew he wasn't a kid any more but my mother didn't know it yet.

That night after supper my father was talking about buying a couple of gallons of that new Kemtone paint to paint the parlor and the dining room with. He said he saw it advertised in the Philadelphia *Bulletin*, the ad said it went on so easy with those new rollers you didn't have to use any paint brush. Wallpaper was getting considered old-fashioned, he said, and he showed my mother samples he got from Gottlieb's and said, "What keller do you like, Nor'?" She picked peach that she said was her favorite color and he said peach it is, he liked that too.

Then he talked about maybe getting a used car, he said he saw a 1934 Essex Terraplane in a lot in the county seat that day him and Sam Beezley went to Perlski's Department Store, fifty bucks it was, five bucks down and five bucks a week. My mother gave a shiver hearing how much it cost and said a car'd just have to wait. Then he even began talking about the possibility of putting in a toilet in the shed off of the kitchen, that really made my mother's eyes light up, and mine along with them. Then he talked too of getting a bucket-a-day second-hand water heater to hook up in the cellar for hot water anytime we wanted it like it used to be in the house on Mifflin Street, and getting Sam Beezley to help him mix up some concrete to cement over the dirt floor in the cellar, and on and on til my mother said hold it, who did he think he was, J.P. Rockafella? What they needed to buy first was a metal lunch kettle for him you could also put a thermos bottle in for his coffee, like Sam Beezley took his lunch in to the yard, and he had to laugh himself, saying, "You're right, Nor'," he knew he was getting carried away.

A couple days later when I came home from school I saw my mother was standing by the sink washing the chimneys from the oil lamps in soap and water like she had to do from time to time, they got so sooty when the wick didn't burn right. Only this time instead of sticking the chimneys back on the lamps, she started wrapping them careful as she could in old pages of the *Bulletin*, then stood up on a chair to put them away on the topmost shelf of the cupboard.

I stared at what she was doing, not daring to hope it was because of what I was hoping so much. She saw me staring and said real casual as she got down off of the chair, like she said it a hundred times a day, "Turn on that lightswitch, will ya, Mick, it's gittin kinda dark in here."

My mouth fell open, I couldn't believe what I heard. She turned and grinned at me as she went over to peep in at the baby sleeping in his bassinette by the stove, saying it again in a coaxing way, "Well gwan, silly, don't stand there with your mouth gapin open catchin flies, push the switch."

I ran to the switch on the wall that hadn't been turned on for so long it felt all stiff and rusty when I pushed it in, and my heart lit up bright as the bare lightbulb up in the kitchen ceiling when it all of a sudden flashed on.

She was lifting the baby by the legs to see if he'd wet himself, but she was really looking over at me, grinning at the look on my face. "My eyes is so wore out from tryin to see," she said, "I'm prayin to the Blessed Mother we don't never have to use them ole erl lamps ever again, 'ceptin only if a storm puts out the lights."

I almost broke a leg getting into the parlor to turn on the old Scott radio. When I got there I was surprised to see not only was it all fresh-dusted but my mother must've gone and polished it with lemon oil, it gleamed so in the last light of day through the windows. When I clicked on the little silver metal clicker on the side that I hadn't turned on in so long I almost forgot where it was, I just knew my eyes must've been as bright as all those colors in the celluloid dial that I hadn't seen light up in so long either, I forgot what the colors were.

I flipped through the dial, twisting between my fingers the worn wood of the knob that hadn't been turned in so long it was as stiff as the lightswitch in the kitchen. And when I heard the hum through the loudspeaker getting louder and louder as the set heated up, then heard all of a sudden through the crackling and static, "...This is KYW in Philadelphia..." Philadelphia! coming through the speaker and into our house again! I almost had a heart attack, I was so excited. I quick twisted the dial again "...WCAU...On the Eastern front the week-long battle still rages..." Kept twisting the dial "...presents Little Orphan Annie...Pepsi-Cola hits the spot!...All over Europe the battles... Pardon me, boy, is that the Chattanooga choo-choo?...WFIL in Phil...All Europe has fallen before the panzer divisions...

President Roosevelt warned Emperor Hirohito…Jack Armstrong, All-American Boy! brought to you by…"

I squatted down close to the loudspeaker, my ear pressed against the familiar brown cloth with the little orange threads running through it that covered the speaker and that smelled of dust and electric and was threadbare and dark with grease stains from all our heads leaning against it through all those years back. I kept twisting the dial til I got all the way back to where I started from "…We return you now to Little Orphan Annie…" and stopped twisting and sat down hugging my knees to listen, my ear pressed so close listening so hard, at first I didn't even see Danny and Kate come up from the cellar where they'd been playing, hearing a sound they probably never remembered hearing in our house before. They plopped themselves down on the floor next to me, listening too.

I shut my eyes. I was in seventh heaven.

That Saturday morning as I was running the dustmop around the parlor, then scrubbing the baseboard and floor as part of my Saturday chores that weren't a chore anymore now I could listen at the same time to "Let's Pretend" and "Grand Central Station" on the radio, my mother sent Frank with money to pay up some more of what we owed at Gottlieb's and had him bring home a bag of turnips and five pounds of potatoes, the first potatoes we ever had to buy at Gottlieb's. Most important, she had him also get a shoulder of pork for our Sunday dinner—"Make sure he puts a pocket in it," she warned him. We hadn't eaten pork for so long I could barely remember what it tasted like, and knew she was getting it special for my father.

Much to my and all my brothers' annoyance, we still had to wear the last of the shoes that were too tight or the shoes that were too big, plus the pillow ticking clothes we got from relief, because the first couple pay envelopes my father got would only stretch so far my mother said. But she promised the first time there was a little extra money, she'd go to the bargain basement again in Frank & Seder's Department Store in Philly and buy us all nice things, but until then.... Frank and Buster made a puss, but Slap that never cared how he looked or what he had on, couldn't've cared less. And me, I was so happy to have the radio and the lights back on and be eating roast pork again on Sunday, much as I hated the clothes from relief, I figured I could wait for store-bought ones.

That same Saturday night, to show his appreciation—though Buster sneered it was just a good excuse for them to get drunk— my father treated Sam Beezley by buying not only a couple of quarts of Schmidt's at Tarkie's but a bottle of Gilbey's gin as well from under the counter, instead of the cheap old Dixie Belle gin he usually bought. As an extra treat he also bought a pint of sloe gin that he knew Mrs. Beezley was fond of, and bought bags of pretzels and potato chips too. The four of them celebrated his new job so much down in the parlor they got pretty merry, even my mother that hardly ever drank a drop, sounded like she was enjoying herself. They were all laughing so, they woke us up, including little Peter, several times during the night, with their shouts and loud laughing, my father and Sam Beezley not even bothering for the first time to keep their voices down when they told their smutty jokes, that my mother for once didn't complain about—Or when Mrs. Beezley told some really juicy gossip she screeched it out instead of whispering like she usually did, so that I hardly got any sleep at all from leaning way over Slap and hanging my ear out the bedroom door so's not to miss a word— Thinking to myself again as I listened, like I did the night the Mahoney house burnt down, if it was a war, I didn't care, if it was war, let it be, if it meant my father got a job at last, if it meant they were all laughing again down in the parlor and her and him would stop their arguing with each other in the night— If it was a war, then I was glad for that and for having the lights on again and the old Scott radio playing and no more rotten potatoes to eat or buggy flour or rancid butter or tight shoes or clothes made out of pillow ticking—They were saying on the radio the lights were going out all over the world but I didn't care, even though I knew it was a sin not to care, the lights were on again in our house and they'd been off so long I was glad they were on again even if they were going off all over the world. I said a prayer thanking the Blessed Mother and said another prayer thanking Jesus, and promised if only my father kept his job I wouldn't go back in the woods with Earl Jr. any more to dance and sing without any clothes on, I would stop smoking cigarette butts from the gutter even, and I would try to stop picking my nose and not lie as much or think unclean thoughts and would stop putting the pillow over the baby's face, I would learn to talk better, like the way Timothy talked, and stop saying ain't and me this and me that, I would try to be like Timothy in every way—Oh! I promised everything and anything to the Blessed Mother and to Jesus if things would only keep going the way they were, and if it was a war...as with my brothers breathing deep and easy all around me I drifted off and off myself into sleep at last...

Michael Rumaker was born March 5, 1932 in Philadelphia, PA, to Michael Joseph and Winifred Marvel Rumaker. He is a graduate of Black Mountain College (1955) and Columbia University (1970). Most of Rumaker's fiction concerns his life as a gay man. His first book, *The Butterfly*, is a fictionalized memoir of his brief affair with a young Yoko Ono, published before Ono became famous. His short stories, *Gringos and other stories*, appeared in 1967. A revised and expanded version appeared in 1991. He began to write directly about his life as a gay man in the volumes *A Day and a Night at the Baths* (1979, 2010) and *My First Satyrnalia* (1981). *Black Mountain Days*, a memoir of his time at Black Mountain College, has a strong autobiographical element. In addition, there are portraits of many students, faculty, and visitors (especially the poets Robert Creeley and Charles Olson) during its last years, 1952-1956.

S P U Y T E N D U Y V I L

Meeting Eyes Bindery
Triton
Lithic Scatter